Tourist Season   KT-104-812

'Fiendish suspense and wicked black humor . . . a rollicking, exciting, exceptional book'
JOHN KATZENBACH

'A remarkable example of what talented writers are doing these days with the mystery novel . . . wonderful'
THE NEW YORK TIMES BOOK REVIEW

'He may well be the funniest writer working in America today'
THE INDEPENDENT

'His books are addictive . . . for entertainment few can match him'
LONDON REVIEW OF BOOKS

'Roars along like a grizzly with a grievance . . . Hiaasen's comic invention
never fails him and his moist malevolence stains every page'
EVENING STANDARD

'Tirelessly inventive screwball thriller in which valiant-for-truth PR man
outfaces sexually deviant dolphin, man-eating pet whale, and sub-moronic
goon addicted to steroids. Aaagh!'
GUARDIAN

Skin Tight

'The action flames, the wit's tinder dry. For snappy prose alone, not to say
neat plot, it's a classic thriller'
MAIL ON SUNDAY

'Taut, fast-paced action. The story jumps. The dialogue is crisp and hot
. . . his style has racing stripes'
NEW YORK TIMES BOOK REVIEW

'Hiaasen brings classic farce to the modern thriller. There is little humour
darker than his, and little funnier'
EVENING STANDARD

'The story is slick, swift and gloriously, if darkly, funny. Whatever
Mr Hiaasen was drinking when he wrote it – I'll have a double'
SUNDAY TELEGRAPH

'A gloriously sleazy and riotously funny tale'
TIME OUT

Double Whammy

'A careful reading of *Double Whammy* will do more to damage the
Florida tourist trade than anything except an actual visit to Florida'
P. J. O'ROURKE

'I went for *Double Whammy* hook, line and sinker, and I think you will too'
WASHINGTON POST

'An outrageously entertaining high-protein experience'
OBSERVER

'A savagely funny crime adventure . . . *Double Whammy* bristles all over'
MIAMI HERALD

Praise for Carl Hiaasen's novels

Strip Tease

'Sharp-eyed, sharp-tongued, wickedly inventive – laughs all the way to the blood bank'
INDEPENDENT ON SUNDAY

'The most devastatingly, scabrously funny book of its kind for years'
OBSERVER

'His eye for the absurd lends his story-telling a hilarious, not to say hysterical, momentum . . . *Strip Tease* unpeels this mouldy apple of corruption right down to its core. The sleazy economy of pay-and-display has not been given a fiercer, or a funnier, come-uppance. Buy yourself a look'
SUNDAY TIMES

'A neat indictment of the US political system, a sly reminder of how pathetic men are, a beautifully timed thriller and – this is the important bit – very funny indeed. If Elmore Leonard, Joe Bob Briggs and Harry Crews sat down together to write a book, it might read something like this'
GQ

'Beside Hiaasen's characters, those of Tom Sharpe (the only comparator that comes to mind) seem models of restraint and good taste. *Strip Tease* is squirmingly funny'
THE TIMES

'[Hiaasen] makes a formidable challenge to Elmore Leonard as the most vibrant chronicler of everyday life in Florida'
DAILY TELEGRAPH

Native Tongue

'Hiaasen is terrific, it is quite a feat to be madly, appallingly, bitingly funny and at the same time thrilling enough to bring one up with a jolt'
OBSERVER

'Endlessly inventive, totally entertaining'
LITERARY REVIEW

'Hiaasen is the funniest writer of crime fiction around . . . the surreal heaps on the farcical to produce the thriller with the highest laugh-out-loud score for many months. Since Hiaasen's last book, to be exact'
TIMES SATURDAY REVIEW

Skin Tight
and *Native Tongue*

Carl Hiaasen is a native of Florida with an outstanding reputation as an investigative journalist exposing local scandals. He now writes a thrice-weekly column for the *Miami Herald* and has been nominated twice for the Pulitzer Prize. He is also the author of *Tourist Season*, *Double Whammy*, *Skin Tight*, *Native Tongue* and *Strip Tease*, and with Bill Montalbano, *Trap Line* and *Powder Burn*.

Also by Carl Hiaasen
in Pan Books

TOURIST SEASON
DOUBLE WHAMMY
STRIP TEASE

By Carl Hiaasen and Bill Montalbano
in Pan Books

POWDER BURN
TRAP LINE

Carl Hiaasen

SKIN TIGHT

AND

NATIVE TONGUE

PAN BOOKS
in association with
MACMILLAN LONDON

Skin Tight first published 1989 by G. P. Putnam's Sons, New York.
First published in Great Britain 1990 by Macmillan London Ltd and
first published by Pan Books Ltd 1991 in association with Macmillan
London Ltd

Native Tongue first published 1991 by Alfred A. Knopf, Inc., New York.
First published in Great Britain 1992 by Macmillan London Ltd and
first published by Pan Books Ltd 1992 in association with Macmillan
London Ltd

This edition published 1994 by Pan Books
a division of Macmillan General Books
Cavaye Place, London SW10 9PG
and Basingstoke
in association with Macmillan London

Associated companies throughout the world

ISBN 0 330 34150 2

Copyright © Carl Hiaasen 1989, 1991, 1994

The right of Carl Hiaasen to be identified as the
author of this work has been asserted by him in accordance
with the Copyright, Designs and Patents Act 1988.

1 3 5 7 9 8 6 4 2

A CIP catalogue record for this book is available from
the British Library

Printed and bound in Great Britain by
Cox & Wyman Ltd, Reading, Berkshire

Skin Tight

Acknowledgement

For his advice, expertise, and good humour, I am grateful to Dr Gerard Grau, and also to his former surgical nurse Connie, who is my wife.

1

On the third of January, a leaden, blustery day, two tourists from Covington, Tennessee, removed their sensible shoes to go strolling on the beach at Key Biscayne.

When they got to the old Cape Florida lighthouse, the young man and his fiancée sat down on the damp sand to watch the ocean crash hard across the brown boulders at the point of the island. There was a salt haze in the air, and it stung the young man's eyes so that when he spotted the thing floating, it took several moments to focus on what is was.

'It's a big dead fish,' his fiancée said. 'Maybe a porpoise.'

'I don't believe so,' said the young man. He stood up, dusted off the seat of his trousers, and walked to the edge of the surf. As the thing floated closer, the young man began to wonder about his legal responsibilities, providing it turned out to be what he thought it was. Oh yes, he had heard about Miami; this sort of stuff happened every day.

'Let's go back now,' he said abruptly to his fiancée.

'No, I want to see what it is. It doesn't look like a fish any more.'

The young man scanned the beach and saw they were all alone, thanks to the lousy weather. He also knew from a brochure back at the hotel that the lighthouse was long ago abandoned, so there would be no one watching from above.

'It's a dead body,' he said grimly to his fiancée.

'Come off it.'

At that instant a big, lisping breaker took the thing on its crest and carried it all the way to the beach, where it stuck—the nose of the dead man grounding as a keel in the sand.

9

The young man's fiancée stared down at the corpse and said, 'Geez, you're right.'

The young man sucked in his breath and took a step back.

'Should we turn it over?' his fiancée asked. 'Maybe he's still alive.'

'Don't touch it. He's dead.'

'How do you know?'

The young man pointed with a bare toe. 'See that hole?'

'That's a hole?'

She bent over and studied a stain on the shirt. The stain was the colour of rust and the size of a sand dollar.

'Well, he didn't just drown,' the young man announced.

His fiancée shivered a little and buttoned her sweater. 'So what do we do now?'

'Now we get out of here.'

'Shouldn't we call the police?'

'It's our vacation, Cheryl. Besides, we're a half-hour's walk to the nearest phone.'

The young man was getting nervous; he thought he heard a boat's engine somewhere around the point of the island, on the bay side.

The woman tourist said, 'Just a second.' She unsnapped the black leather case that held her trusty Canon Sure-Shot.

'What are you doing?'

'I want a picture, Thomas.' She already had the camera up to her eye.

'Are you crazy?'

'Otherwise no one back home will believe us. I mean, we come all the way down to Miami and what happens? Remember how your brother was making murder jokes before we left? It's unreal. Stand to the right a little, Thomas, and pretend to look down at it.'

'Pretend, hell.'

'Come on, one picture.'

'No,' the man said, eyeing the corpse.

'Please? You used up a whole roll on Flipper.'

The woman snapped the picture and said, 'That's good. Now you take one of me.'

'Well, hurry it up,' the young man grumped. The wind was blowing harder from the north-east, moaning through the whippy Australian pines behind them. The sound of the boat engine, wherever it was, had faded away.

The young man's fiancée struck a pose next to the dead body: she pointed at it and made a sour face, crinkling her zinc-coated nose.

'I can't believe this,' the young man said, lining up the photograph.

'Me neither, Thomas. A real live dead body—just like on the TV show. Yuk!'

'Yeah, yuk,' said the young man. 'Fucking yuk is right.'

The day had begun with only a light, cool breeze and a rim of broken raspberry clouds out toward the Bahamas. Stranahan was up early, frying eggs and chasing the gulls off the roof. He lived in an old stilt house on the shallow tidal flats of Biscayne Bay, a mile from the tip of Cape Florida. The house had a small generator powered by a four-bladed windmill, but no air-conditioning. Except for a few days in August and September, there was always a decent breeze. That was one nice thing about living on the water.

There were maybe a dozen other houses in the stretch of Biscayne Bay known as Stiltsville, but none were inhabited; rich owners used them for weekend parties, and their kids got drunk on them in the summer. The rest of the time they served as fancy split-level toilets for seagulls and cormorants.

Stranahan had purchased his house dirt-cheap at a government auction. The previous owner was a Venezuelan cocaine courier who had been shot thirteen times in a serious business dispute, then indicted posthumously. No sooner had the corpse been air-freighted back to Caracas than Customs agents seized the stilt house, along with three condos, two Porsches, a one-eyed scarlet macaw, and a yacht with a hot tub. The hot tub was where the Venezuelan had met his spectacular death, so bidding was feverish. Likewise the macaw—a material witness to its owner's murder—fetched top dollar; before the auction, mischievous Customs agents had taught the bird to say, 'Duck, you shithead!'

By the time the stilt house had come up on the block, nobody was interested. Stranahan had picked it up for forty thousand and change.

He coveted the solitude of the flats, and was delighted to be the only human soul living in Stiltsville. His house, barn-red with brown shutters, sat three hundred yards off the main channel, so most of the weekend boat traffic travelled clear of him. Occasionally a drunk or a total moron would try to clear the banks with a big cabin cruiser, but they did not get far, and they got no sympathy or assistance from the big man in the barn-red house.

January third was a weekday and, with the weather blackening out east, there wouldn't be many boaters out. Stranahan savoured this fact as he sat on the sun deck, eating his eggs and Canadian bacon right out of the frying pan. When a pair of fat, dirty gulls swooped in to nag him for the leftovers, he picked up a BB pistol and opened fire. The birds screeched off in the direction of the Miami skyline, and Stranahan hoped they would not stop until they got there.

After breakfast he pulled on a pair of stringy denim cutoffs and started doing push-ups. He stopped at one hundred and five, and went inside to get some orange juice. From the kitchen he heard a boat coming and checked out the window. It was a yellow bonefish skiff, racing heedlessly across the shallows. Stranahan smiled; he knew all the local guides. Sometimes he'd let them use his house for a bathroom stop, if they had a particularly shy female customer who didn't want to hang it over the side of the boat.

Stranahan poured two cups of hot coffee and went back out on the deck. The yellow skiff was idling up to the dock, which was below the house itself and served as a boat garage. The guide waved up at Stranahan and tied off from the bow. The man's client, an inordinately pale fellow, was preoccupied trying to decide which of four different grades of sunscreen to slather on his milky arms. The guide hopped out of the skiff and climbed up to the sun deck.

'Morning, Captain.' Stranahan handed a mug of coffee to the guide, who accepted it with a friendly grunt. The two men had known each other many years, but this was only the second or third occasion that the captain had gotten out of his boat and come up to the stilt house. Stranahan waited to hear the reason.

When he put down the empty cup, the guide said: 'Mick, you expecting company?'

'No.'

'There was a man this morning.'

'At the marina?'

'No, out here. Asking which house was yours.' The guide glanced over the railing at his client, who now was practising with a fly rod, snapping the line like a horsewhip.

Stranahan laughed and said, 'Looks like a winner.'

'Looks like a long goddamn day,' the captain muttered.

'Tell me about this guy.'

'He flagged me down over by the radio towers. He was in a white Seacraft, a twenty-footer. I thought he was having engine trouble but all he wanted was to know which house was yours. I sent him down toward Elliott Key, so I hope he wasn't a friend. Said he was.'

'Did he give you a name?'

'Tim is what he said.'

Stranahan said the only Tim he knew was an ex-homicide cop named Gavigan.

'That's it,' the fishing guide said. 'Tim Gavigan is what he said.'

'Skinny redhead?'

'Nope.'

13

'Shit,' said Stranahan. Of course it wasn't Timmy Gavigan. Gavigan was busy dying of lung cancer in the VA.

The captain said, 'You want me to hang close today?'

'Hell, no, you got your sport down there, he's raring to go.'

'Fuck it, Mick, he wouldn't know a bonefish from a sperm whale. Anyway, I've got a few choice spots right around here—maybe we'll luck out.'

'Not with this breeze, buddy; the flats are already pea soup. You go on down south, I'll be all right. He's probably just some process-server.'

'Somebody's sure to tell him which house.'

'Yeah, I figure so,' Stranahan said. 'A white Seacraft, you said?'

'Twenty-footer,' the guide repeated. Before he started down the stairs, he said, 'The guy's got some size to him, too.'

'Thanks for the info.'

Stranahan watched the yellow skiff shoot south, across the flats, until all he could see was the long zipper of foam in its wake. The guide would be heading to Sand Key, Stranahan thought, or maybe all the way to Caesar Creek—well out of radio range. As if the damn radio still worked.

By three o'clock in the afternoon, the wind had stiffened, and the sky and the water had acquired the same purple shade of grey. Stranahan slipped into long jeans and a light jacket. He put on his sneakers, too; at the time he didn't think about why he did this, but much later it came to him: splinters. From running on the wooden deck. The raw two-by-fours were hell on bare feet, so Stranahan had put on his sneakers. In case he had to run.

The Seacraft was noisy. Stranahan heard it coming two miles away. He found the white speck through his field glasses and watched it plough through the hard chop. The boat was heading straight for Stranahan's stilt house and staying clean in the channels, too.

14

Figures, Stranahan thought sourly. Probably one of the park rangers down at Elliott Key told the guy which house; just trying to be helpful.

He got up and closed the brown shutters from the outside. Through the field glasses he took one more long look at the man in the Seacraft, who was still a half mile away. Stranahan did not recognize the man, but could tell he was from up North—the guy made a point of shirt-sleeves, on this kind of a day, and the dumbest-looking sunglasses ever made.

Stranahan slipped inside the house and closed the door behind him. There was no way to lock it from the inside; there was no reason, usually. With the shutters down the inside of the house was pitch-black, but Stranahan knew every corner of each room. In this house he had ridden out two hurricanes—baby ones, but nasty just the same. He had spent both storms in total darkness, because the wind knifed through the walls and played hell with the lanterns, and the last thing you wanted was an indoor fire.

So Stranahan knew the house in the dark.

He selected his place and waited.

After a few minutes the pitch of the Seacraft's engines dropped an octave, and Stranahan figured the boat was slowing down. The guy would be eyeing the place closely, trying to figure out the best way up on the flat. There was a narrow cut in the marl, maybe four feet deep at high tide and wide enough for one boat. If the guy saw it and made this his entry, he would certainly spot Stranahan's aluminium skiff tied up under the water tanks. And then he would know.

Stranahan heard the Seacraft's engines chewing up the marly bottom. The guy had missed the deep cut.

Stranahan heard the big boat thud into the pilings at the west end of the house. He could hear the guy clunking around in the bow, grunting as he tried to tie it off against the tide, which was falling fast. Stranahan heard—and felt—the man hoist himself out of the boat and climb to the main deck of the house. He heard the man say: 'Anybody home?'

15

The man did not have a light step; the captain was right—he was a big one. By the vibrations of the plankboards, Stranahan charted the intruder's movements.

Finally the guy knocked on the door and said: 'Hey! Hello there!'

When no one answered, the guy just opened the door.

He stood framed in the afternoon light, such as it was, and Stranahan got a pretty good look. The man had removed his sunglasses. As he peered into the dark house, his right hand went to the waist of his trousers.

'State your business,' Stranahan said from the shadows.

'Oh, hey!' The man stepped backward onto the deck, forfeiting his silhouette for detail. Stranahan did not recognize the face—an odd and lumpy one, skin stretched tightly over squared cheekbones. Also, the nose didn't match the eyes and chin. Stranahan wondered if the guy had ever been in a bad car wreck.

The man said: 'I ran out of gas, and I was wondering if you had a couple gallons to get me back to the marina. I'll be happy to pay.'

'Sorry,' Stranahan said.

The guy looked for the source of the voice, but he couldn't see a damn thing in the shuttered-up house.

'Hey, pal, you OK?'

'Just fine,' Stranahan said.

'Well, then, would you mind stepping out where I can see you?'

With his left hand Stranahan grabbed the leg of a barstool and sent it skidding along the bare floor to no place in particular. He just wanted to see what the asshole would do, and he was not disappointed. The guy took a short-barrelled pistol out of his pants and held it behind his back. Then he took two steps forward until he was completely inside the house. He took another slow step toward the spot where the broken barstool lay, only now he was holding the pistol in front of him.

Stranahan, who had squeezed himself into a spot between

16

the freezer and the pantry, had seen enough of the damn gun.

'Over here,' he said to the stranger.

And when the guy spun around to get a bead on where the voice was coming from, Mick Stranahan lunged out of the shadows and stabbed him straight through with a stuffed marlin head he had gotten off the wall.

It was a fine blue marlin, maybe four hundred pounds, and whoever caught it had decided to mount only the head and shoulders, down to the spike of the dorsal. The trophy fish had come with the Venezuelan's house and hung in the living room, where Stranahan had grown accustomed to its indigo stripes, its raging glass eye and its fearsome black sword. In a way it was a shame to mess it up, but Stranahan knew the BB gun would be useless against a real revolver.

The taxidermied fish was not as heavy as Stranahan anticipated, but it was cumbersome; Stranahan concentrated on his aim as he charged the intruder. It paid off.

The marlin's bill split the man's breastbone, tore his aorta, and severed his spine. He died before Stranahan got a chance to ask him any questions. The final puzzled look on the man's face suggested that he was not expecting to be gored by a giant stuffed fish head.

The intruder carried no identification, no wallet, no wedding ring; just the keys to a rented Thunderbird. Aboard the Seacraft, which was also rented, Stranahan found an Igloo cooler with two six-packs of Corona and a couple of cheap spinning rods that the killer had brought along just for looks.

Stranahan heaved the body into the Seacraft and took the boat out into the Biscayne Channel. There he pushed the dead guy overboard, tossed the pistol into deep water, rinsed down the decks, dove off the stern, and swam back toward the stilt house. In fifteen minutes his knees hit the mud bank, and he waded the last seventy-five yards to the dock.

That night there was no sunset to speak of, because of the dreary skies, but Stranahan sat on the deck anyway. As he stared out to the west, he tried to figure out who wanted him dead, and why. He considered this a priority.

2

On the fourth day of January, the sun came out, and Dr Rudy Graveline smiled. The sun was very good for business. It baked and fried and pitted the facial flesh, and seeded the pores with vile microscopic cancers that would eventually sprout and require excision. Dr Rudy Graveline was a plastic surgeon, and he dearly loved to see the sun.

He was in a fine mood, anyway, because it was January. In Florida, January is the heart of the winter tourist season and a bonanza time for cosmetic surgeons. Thousands of older men and women who flock down for the warm weather also use the occasion to improve their features. Tummy tucks, nose jobs, boob jobs, butt jobs, fat suctions, face lifts, you name it. And they always beg for an appointment in January, so that the scars will be healed by the time they go back North in the spring.

Dr Rudy Graveline could not accommodate all the snowbirds, but he did his damnedest. All four surgical theatres at the Whispering Palms Spa were booked from dawn to dusk in January, February, and half-way into March. Most of the patients asked especially for Dr Graveline, whose reputation greatly exceeded his talents. While Rudy usually farmed the cases out to the eight other plastic surgeons on staff, many patients got the impression that Dr Graveline himself had performed their surgery. This is because Rudy would often come in and pat their wrinkled hands until they nodded off, blissfully, under the nitrous or IV Valium. At that point Rudy would turn them over to one of his younger and more competent protégés.

Dr Graveline saved himself for the richest patients. The regulars got cut on every winter, and Rudy counted on their business. He reassured his surgical hypochondriacs that there was nothing abnormal about having a fifth, sixth, or seventh blepharoplasty in as many years. *Does it make you feel better about yourself?* Rudy would ask them. *Then it's worth it, isn't it? Of course it is.*

Such a patient was Madeleine Margaret Wilhoit, age sixty-nine, of North Palm Beach. In the course of their acquaintance, there was scarcely a square inch of Madeleine's substantial physique that Dr Rudy Graveline had not altered. Whatever he did and whatever he charged, Madeleine was always delighted. And she always came back the next year for more. Though Madeleine's face reminded Dr Graveline in many ways of a camel, he was fond of her. She was the kind of steady patient that offshore trust funds are made of.

On January fourth, buoyed by the warm sunny drive to Whispering Palms, Rudy Graveline set about the task of repairing for the fifth, sixth, or seventh time (he couldn't remember exactly) the upper eyelids of Madeleine Margaret Wilhoit. Given the dromedarian texture of the woman's skin, the mission was doomed and Rudy knew it. Any cosmetic improvement would have to take place exclusively in Madeleine's imagination, but Rudy (knowing she would be ecstatic) pressed on.

Midway through the operation, the telephone on the wall let out two beeps. With a gowned elbow the operating-room nurse deftly punched the intercom box and told the caller that Dr Graveline was in the middle of surgery and not available.

'It's fucking important, tell him,' said a sullen male voice, which Rudy instantly recognized.

He asked the nurse and the anaesthetist to leave the operating room for a few minutes. When they were gone, he said to the phone box: 'Go ahead. This is me.'

The phone call was made from a pay booth in Atlantic City, New Jersey, not that it would have mattered to Rudy. Jersey was all he knew, all he needed to know.

'You want the report?' the man asked.

'Of course.'

'It went lousy.'

Rudy sighed and stared down at the violet vectors he had inked around Madeleine's eyes. 'How lousy?' the surgeon said to the phone box.

'The ultimate fucking lousy.'

Rudy tried to imagine the face on the other end of the line, in New Jersey. In the old days he could guess a face by the voice on the phone. This particular voice sounded fat and lardy, with black curly eyebrows and mean dark eyes.

'So what now?' the doctor asked.

'Keep the other half of your money.'

What a prince, Rudy thought.

'What if I want you to try again?'

'Fine by me.'

'So what'll *that* cost?'

'Same,' said Curly Eyebrows. 'Deal's a deal.'

'Can I think on it?'

'Sure. I'll call back tomorrow.'

Rudy said, 'It's just that I didn't count on any problems.'

'The problem's not yours. Anyway, this shit happens.'

'I understand,' Dr Graveline said.

The man in New Jersey hung up, and Madeleine Margaret Wilhoit started to squirm. It occurred to Rudy that maybe the old bag wasn't asleep after all, and that maybe she'd heard the whole conversation.

'Madeleine?' he whispered in her ear.

'Unngggh.'

'Are you OK?'

'Fine, Papa,' Madeleine drooled. 'When do I get to ride in the sailboat?'

Rudy Graveline smiled, then buzzed for the nurse and anaesthetist to come back and help him finish the job.

During his time at the State Attorney's Office, Mick Stranahan had helped put many people in jail. Most of them were out now, even the murderers, due to a federal court order requiring the state of Florida to seasonally purge its overcrowded prisons. Stranahan accepted the fact that some of these ex-cons harboured bitterness against him, and that more than a few would be delighted to see him dead. For this reason, Stranahan was exceedingly cautious about visitors. He was not a paranoid person, but took a practical view of risk: when someone pulls a gun at your front door, there's really no point to asking what he wants. The answer is obvious, and so is the solution.

The gunman who came to the stilt house was the fifth person that Mick Stranahan had killed in his lifetime.

The first two were North Vietnamese Army regulars who were laying trip wire for land mines near the town of Dak Mat Lop in the Central Highlands. Stranahan surprised the young soldiers by using his sidearm instead of his M-16, and by not missing. It happened during the second week of May 1969, when Stranahan was barely twenty years old.

The third person he killed was a Miami holdup man named Thomas Henry Thomas, who made the mistake of sticking up a fried-chicken joint while Stranahan was standing in line for a nine-piecebox of Extra Double Crispy. To supplement the paltry seventy-eight dollars he had grabbed from the cash register, Thomas Henry Thomas decided to confiscate the wallets and purses of each customer. It went rather smoothly until he came down the line to Mick Stranahan, who calmly took away Thomas Henry Thomas's .38-calibre Charter Arms revolver and shot him twice in the right temporal lobe. In appreciation, the fried-chicken franchise presented Stranahan with three months' worth of discount coupons and offered to put his likeness on every carton of Chicken Chunkettes sold during the month of December 1977. Being broke and savagely divorced, Stranahan took the coupons but declined the celebrity photo.

The shooting of Thomas Henry Thomas (his obvious character flaws aside) was deemed serious enough to dissuade both the Miami and metropolitan Dade County police from hiring Mick Stranahan as an officer. His virulent refusal to take any routine psychological tests also militated against him. However, the State Attorney's

Office was in dire need of a streetwise investigator, and was delighted to hire a highly decorated war veteran, even at the relatively tender age of twenty-nine.

The fourth and most important person that Mick Stranahan killed was a crooked Dade County judge named Raleigh Goomer. Judge Goomer's speciality was shaking down defence lawyers in exchange for ridiculous bond reductions, which allowed dangerous felons to get out of jail and skip town. It was Stranahan who caught Judge Goomer at this game and arrested him taking a payoff at a strip joint near the Miami airport. On the trip to the jail, Judge Goomer apparently panicked, pulled a .22 somewhere out of his black nylon socks, and fired three shots at Mick Stranahan. Hit twice in the right thigh, Stranahan still managed to seize the gun, twist the barrel up the judge's right nostril, and fire.

A special prosecutor sent down from Tampa presented the case to the grand jury, and the grand jury agreed that the killing of Judge Raleigh Goomer was probably self-defence, though a point-blank nostril shot did seem extreme. Even though Stranahan was cleared, he obviously could no longer be employed by the State Attorney's Office. Pressure for his dismissal came most intensely from other crooked judges, several of whom stated that they were afraid to have Mr Stranahan testifying in their court-rooms.

On June 7, 1988, Mick Stranahan resigned from the prosecutor's staff. The press release called it early retirement, and disclosed that Stranahan would be receiving full disability compensation as a result of injuries suffered in the Goomer shooting. Stranahan wasn't disabled at all, but his family connection with a notorious personal-injury lawyer was sufficient to terrify the county into paying him off. When Stranahan said he didn't want the money, the county promptly doubled its offer and threw in a motorized wheelchair. Stranahan gave up.

Not long afterwards, he moved out to Stiltsville and made friends with the fish.

*

A marine patrol boat pulled up to Mick Stranahan's place at half past noon. Stranahan was on the top deck, dropping a line for mangrove snappers down below.

'Got a second?' asked the marine patrol officer, a sharp young Cuban named Luis Córdova. Stranahan liked him all right.

'Come on up,' he said.

Stranahan reeled in his bait and put the fishing rod down. He dumped four dead snappers out of the bucket and gutted them one at a time, tossing their creamy innards in the water.

Córdova was talking about the body that had washed up on Cape Florida.

'Rangers found it yesterday evening,' he said. 'Lemon shark got the left foot.'

'That happens,' Stranahan said, skinning one of the fish fillets.

'The ME says it was one hell of a stab wound.'

'I'm gonna fry these up for sandwiches,' Stranahan said. 'You interested in lunch?'

Córdova shook his head. 'No, Mick, there's some jerks poaching lobster down at Boca Chita so I gotta be on my way. Metro asked me to poke around out here, see if somebody saw anything. And since you're the only one out here . . . '

Stranahan glanced up from the fish-cleaning. 'I don't remember much going on yesterday,' he said. 'Weather was piss-poor, that I know.'

He tossed the fish skeletons, heads still attached, over the rail.

'Well, Metro's not all that excited,' Córdova said.

'How come? Who's the stiff?'

'Name of Tony Traviola, wise guy. Jersey state police got a fat jacket on him. Tony the Eel, loan-collector type. Not a very nice man, from what I understand.'

Stranahan said, 'They think it's a mob hit?'

'I don't know what they think.'

Stranahan carried the fillets into the house and ran them under the tap. He was careful with the water, since the

23

tanks were low. Córdova accepted a glass of iced tea and stood next to Stranahan in the kitchen, watching him roll the fillets in egg yolk and bread crumbs. Normally Stranahan preferred to be left alone when he cooked, but he didn't want Luis Córdova to go just yet.

'They found the guy's boat, too,' the marine patrolman went on. 'It was a rental out of Haulover. White Seacraft.'

Stranahan said he hadn't seen one of those lately.

'Few specks of blood was all they found,' Córdova said. 'Somebody cleaned it pretty good.'

Stranahan laid the snapper fillets in a half-inch of oil in a frying pan. The stove didn't seem to be working, so he got on his knees and checked the pilot light—dead, as usual. He put a match to it and, before long, the fish started to sizzle.

Córdova sat down on one of the wicker barstools.

'So why don't they think it was the mob?' Stranahan asked.

'I didn't say they didn't, Mick.'

Stranahan smiled and opened a bottle of beer.

Córdova shrugged. 'They don't tell me every little thing.'

'First of all, they wouldn't bring him all the way down to Florida to do it, would they, Luis? They got the exact same ocean up in Jersey. So Tony the Eel was already here on business.'

'Makes sense,' Córdova nodded.

'Second, why didn't they just shoot him? Knives are for kids, not pros.'

Córdova took the bait. 'Wasn't a knife,' he said. 'It was too big, the ME said. More like a javelin.'

'That's not like the guineas.'

'No,' Córdova agreed.

Stranahan made three fish sandwiches and gave one to the marine patrolman, who had forgotten about going after the lobster poachers, if there ever were any.

'The other weird thing,' he said through a mouthful of bread, 'is the guy's face.'

24

'What about it?'

'It didn't match the mug shots, not even close. They made him through fingerprints and dentals, but when they got the mugs back from the FBI it looked like a different guy altogether. So Metro calls the Bureau and says you made a mistake, and they say the hell we did, that's Tony Traviola. They go back and forth for about two hours until somebody has the brains to call the ME.' Córdova stopped to gulp some iced tea; the fish was steaming in his cheeks.

Stranahan said, 'And?'

'Plastic surgery.'

'No shit?'

'At least five different operations, from his eyes to his chin. Tony the Eel, he was a regular Michael Jackson. His own mother wouldn't have known him.'

Stranahan opened another beer and sat down. 'Why would a bum like Traviola get his face remade?'

Córdova said, 'Traviola did a nickel for extortion, got out of Rahway about two years ago. Not long afterwards a Purolator truck gets hit, but the robbers turn up dead three days later—without the loot. Classic mob rip. The feds put a warrant out for Traviola, hung his snapshot in every post office along the Eastern seaboard.'

'Good reason to get the old schnoz bobbed,' Stranahan said.

'That's what they figure.' Córdova got up and rinsed his plate in the sink.

Stranahan was impressed. 'You didn't get all this out of Metro, did you?'

Córdova laughed. 'Hey, even the grouper troopers got a computer.'

This was a good kid, Stranahan thought, a good cop. Maybe there was hope for the world after all.

'I see you went out and got the newspaper,' the marine patrolman remarked. 'What's the occasion, you got a pony running at Gulfstream?'

Hell, Stranahan thought, that was a stupid move. On the counter was the *Herald*, open to the page with the

25

story about the dead floater. Miami being what it is, the floater story was only two paragraphs long, wedged under a tiny headline between a one-ton coke bust and a double homicide on the river. Maybe Luis Córdova wouldn't notice.

'You must've got up early to get to the marina and back,' he said.

'Grocery run,' Stranahan lied. 'Besides, it was a nice morning for a boat ride. How was the fish?'

'Delicious, Mick.' Córdova slapped him on the shoulder and said so long.

Stranahan walked out on the deck and watched Córdova untie his patrol boat, a grey Mako outboard with a blue police light mounted on the centre console.

'If anything comes up, I'll give you a call, Luis.'

'No sweat, it's Metro's party,' the marine patrolman said. 'Guy sounds like a dirtbag, anyway.'

'Yeah,' Stranahan said, 'I feel sorry for that shark, the one that ate his foot.'

Córdova chuckled. 'Yeah, he'll be puking for a week.'

Stranahan waved as the police boat pulled away. He was pleased to see Luis Córdova heading south toward Boca Chita, as Luis had said he would. He was also pleased that the young officer had not asked him about the blue marlin head on the living room wall, about why the sword was mended together with fresh hurricane tape.

Timmy Gavigan had looked like death for most of his adult life. Now he had an excuse.

His coppery hair had fallen out in thickets, revealing patches of pale freckled scalp. His face, once round and florid, looked like somebody had let the air out.

From his hospital bed Timmy Gavigan said, 'Mick, can you believe this fucking food?' He picked up a chunk of grey meat off the tray and held it up with two fingers, like an important piece of evidence. 'This is your government in action, Mick. Same fuckers that want to put lasers in outer space can't fry a Salisbury steak.'

Stranahan said, 'I'll go get us some take-out.'

'Forget it.'

'You're not hungry?'

'I got about five gallons of poison in my bloodstream, Mick. Some new formula, experimental super juice. I told 'em to go ahead, why the hell not? If it kills just one of those goddamn cells, then I'm for it.'

Stranahan smiled and sat down.

'A man came out to see me the other day. He was using your name, Tim.'

Gavigan's laugh rattled. 'Not too bright. Didn't he know we was friends?'

'Yeah, that's what I mean. He was telling people he was you, trying to find out where my house was.'

'But he didn't tell *you* he was me?'

'No,' Stranahan said.

Gavigan's blue eyes seemed to light up. 'Did he find your place?'

'Unfortunately.'

'And?'

Stranahan thought about how to handle it.

'Hey, Mick, I haven't got loads of time, OK? I mean, I could check out of this life any second now, so don't make me choke the goddamn story out of you.'

Stranahan said, 'It turns out he was a bad guy from back East. Killer for the mob.'

'*Was?*' Gavigan grinned. 'So that's it. And here I thought you'd come by just to see how your old pal was hanging in.'

'That, too,' Stranahan said.

'But first you want me to help you figure it out, how this pasta-breath tied us together.'

'I don't like the fact he was using your name.'

'How d'you think I feel?' Gavigan handed Stranahan the dinner tray and told him to set it on the floor. He folded his papery hands on his lap, over the thin woollen blanket. 'How would he know we was friends, Mick? You never call, never send candy. Missed my birthday three years in a row.'

27

'That's not true, Timmy. Two years ago I sent a strippergram.'

'You sent that broad? I thought she just showed up lonely at the station and picked out the handsomest cop. Hell, Mick, I took her to Grand Bahama for a week, damn near married her.'

Stranahan was feeling better; Timmy knew something. Stranahan could tell from the eyes. It had come back to him.

Gavigan said, 'Mick, that girl had the finest nipples I ever saw. I meant to thank you.'

'Any time.'

'Like Susan B. Anthony dollars, that's how big they were. Same shape, too. Octagonal.' Gavigan winked. 'You remember the Barletta thing?'

'Sure.' A missing-person's case that had turned into a possible kidnap. The victim was a twenty-two-year-old University of Miami student. Victoria Barletta: brown eyes, black hair, five eight, one hundred and thirty pounds. Disappeared on a rainy March afternoon.

Still unsolved.

'We had our names in the paper,' Gavigan said. 'I still got the clipping.'

Stranahan remembered. There was a press conference. Victoria's parents offered a $10,000 reward. Timmy was there from Homicide, Stranahan from the State Attorney's Office. Both of them were quoted in the story, which ran on the front pages of the *Herald* and the *Miami News*.

Gavigan coughed in a way that startled Mick Stranahan. It sounded like Timmy's lungs had turned to custard.

'Hand me that cup,' Gavigan said. 'Know what? That was the only time we made the papers together.'

'Timmy, we got in the papers all the time.'

'Yeah, but not together.' He slurped down some ginger ale and pointed a bony finger at Stranahan. 'Not together, bucko, trust me. I save all the clippings for my scrapbook. Don't you?'

Stranahan said no.

'You *wouldn't*.' Gavigan hacked out a laugh.

'So you think this Mafia guy got it out of the papers?'

'Not the Mafia guy,' Gavigan said, 'but the guy who hired him. It's a good possibility.'

'The Barletta thing was four years ago, Timmy.'

'Hey, I ain't the only one who keeps scrapbooks.' He yawned. 'Think hard on this, Mick, it's probably important.'

Stranahan stood up and said, 'You get some rest, buddy.'

'I'm glad you took care of that prick who was using my name.'

'Hey, I don't know what you're talking about.'

'Yeah, you do.' Gavigan smiled. 'Anyway, I'm glad you took care of him. He had no business lying like that, using my name.'

Stranahan pulled the blanket up to his friend's neck. 'Good night, Timmy.'

'Be careful, Mick,' the old cop said. 'Hey, and when I croak, you save the newspaper clipping, OK? Glue it on the last page of my scrapbook.'

'It's a promise.'

'Unless it don't make the papers.'

'It'll make the damn papers,' Stranahan said. 'Buried back in the truss ads, where you belong.'

Timmy Gavigan laughed so hard, he had to ring the nurse for oxygen.

3

Four days after the Mafia man came to murder him, Mick Stranahan got up early and took the skiff to the marina. There he jump-started his old Chrysler Imperial and drove down to Gables-by-the-Sea, a ritzy but misnomered neighbourhood where his sister Kate lived with her degenerate lawyer husband and three teenaged daughters from two previous marriages (his, not hers). The subdivision was nowhere near the ocean but fronted a series of man-made canals that emptied into Biscayne Bay. No one complained about this marketing deception, as it was understood by buyers and sellers alike that Gables-by-the-Sea sounded much more toney than Gables-on-the-Canal. The price of the real estate duly reflected this exaggeration.

Stranahan's sister lived in a big split-level house with five bedrooms, a swimming pool, a sauna, and a putting green in the yard. Her lawyer husband even bought a thirty-foot sailboat to go with the dock out back, although he couldn't tell his fore from his aft. The sight of the sparkling white mast poking over the top of the big house made Stranahan shake his head as he pulled into the driveway—Kate's husband was positively born for South Florida.

When Stranahan's sister came to the door, she said, 'Well, look who's here.'

Stranahan kissed her and said, 'Is Jocko home?'

'His name's not Jocko.'

'He's a circus ape, Katie, that's a fact.'

'His name's not Jocko, so lay off.'

'Where's the blue Beemer?'

'We traded it.'

Stranahan followed his sister into the living room, where one of the girls was watching MTV and never looked up.

'Traded for what?'

'A Maserati,' Kate said, adding: 'The sedan, not the sporty one.'

'Perfect,' Stranahan said.

Kate made a sad face, and Stranahan gave her a little hug; it killed him to think his little sister had married a sleazeball ambulance chaser. Kipper Garth's face was on highway billboards up and down the Gold Coast—'If you've had an accident, somebody somewhere owes you money!!! Dial 555-TORT.' Kipper Garth's firm was called The Friendly Solicitors, and it proved to be a marvellously lucrative racket. Kipper Garth culled through thousands of greedy complainants, dumping the losers and farming out the good cases to legitimate personal-injury lawyers, with whom he would split the fees fifty-fifty. In this way Kipper

30

Garth made hundreds of thousands of dollars without ever setting his Bally loafers on a courtroom floor, which (given his general ignorance of the law) was a blessing for his clients.

'He's playing tennis,' Kate said.

'I'm sorry for what I said,' Stranahan told her. 'You know how I feel.'

'I wish you'd give him a chance, Mick. He's got some fine qualities.'

If you like tapeworms, Stranahan thought. He could scarcely hear Kate over the Def Leppard video on the television, so he motioned her to the kitchen.

'I came by to pick up my shot-gun,' he said.

His sister's eyes went from green to grey, like when they were kids and she was onto him.

'I got a seagull problem out at the house,' Stranahan said.

Kate said, 'Oh? What happened to those plastic owls?'

'Didn't work,' Stranahan said. 'Gulls just crapped all over 'em.'

They went into Kipper Garth's study, the square footage of which exceeded that of Stranahan's entire house. His shot-gun, a Remington pump, was locked up with some fancy filigreed bird guns in a maplewood rack. Kate got the key from a drawer in her husband's desk. Stranahan took the Remington down and looked it over.

Kate noticed his expression and said, 'Kip used it once or twice up North. For pheasant.'

'He could've cleaned off the mud, at least.'

'Sorry, Mick.'

'The man is hopeless.'

Kate touched his arm and said, 'He'll be home in an hour. Would you stay?'

'I can't.'

'As a favour, please? I'd like you to straighten out this lawsuit nonsense once and for all.'

'Nothing to straighten out, Katie. The little monkey wants to sue me, fine. I understand.'

The dispute stemmed from a pending disbarment

31

proceeding against Kipper Garth, who stood accused of defrauding an insurance company. One of Kipper Garth's clients had claimed eighty per cent disability after tripping over a rake on the seventeenth hole of a golf course. Three days after the suit had been filed, the man was dumb enough to enter the 26-kilometre Orange Bowl Marathon, dumb enough to finish third, and dumb enough to give interviews to several TV sportscasters.

It was such an egregious scam that even the Florida Bar couldn't ignore it, and with no encouragement Mick Stranahan had stepped forward to testify against his own brother-in-law. Some of what Stranahan had said was fact, and some was opinion; Kipper Garth liked none of it and had threatened to sue for defamation.

'It's getting ridiculous,' Kate said. 'It really is.'

'Don't worry, he won't file,' Stranahan said. 'He couldn't find the goddamn courthouse with a map.'

'Will you ever let up? This is my husband you're talking about.'

Stranahan shrugged. 'He's treating you well?'

'Like a princess. Now will you let up?'

'Sure, Katie.'

At the door, she gave him a worried look and said, 'Be careful with the gun, Mick.'

'No problem,' he said. 'Tell Jocko I was here.'

'Not hello? Or maybe Happy New Year?'

'No, just tell him I was here. That's all.'

Stranahan got back to the marina and wrapped the shot-gun in an oilcloth and slipped it lengthwise under the seats of the skiff. He headed south in a biting wind, taking spray over the port side and bouncing hard in the troughs. It took twenty-five minutes to reach the stilt house; Stranahan idled in on a low tide. As soon as he tied off, he heard voices up above and bare feet on the planks.

He unwrapped the shot-gun and crept up the stairs.

Three naked women were stretched out sunning on the deck. One of them, a slender brunette, looked up

32

and screamed. The others reflexively scrambled for their towels.

Stranahan said, 'What are you doing on my house?'

'Are you going to shoot us?' the brunette asked.

'I doubt it.'

'We didn't know this place was yours,' said another woman, a bleached blonde with substantial breasts.

Stranahan muttered and opened the door, which was padlocked from the outside. This happened occasionally—sunbathers or drunken kids climbing up on the place when he wasn't home. He put the gun away, got a cold beer, and came back out. The women had wrapped themselves up and were gathering their lotions and Sony Walkmans.

'Where's your boat?' Stranahan asked.

'Way out there,' the brunette said, pointing.

Stranahan squinted into the glare. It looked like a big red Formula, towing two skiers. 'Boyfriends?' he said.

The bleached blonde nodded. 'They said this place was deserted. Honest, we didn't know. They'll be back at four.'

'It's all right, you can stay,' he said. 'It's a nice day for the water.' Then he went back inside to clean the shot-gun. Before long the third woman, a true blonde, came in and asked for a glass of water.

'Take a beer,' Stranahan said. 'I'm saving the water.'

She was back to her naked state. Stranahan tried to concentrate on the Remington.

'I'm a model,' she announced, and started talking. Name's Tina, nineteen years old, born in Detroit but moved down here when she was still a baby, likes to model but hates some of the creeps who take the pictures.

'My career is really taking off,' she declared. She sat down on a bar stool, crossed her legs, folded her arms under her breasts.

'So what do you do?' she asked.

'I'm retired.'

'You look awful young to be retired. You must be rich.'

'A billionaire,' Stranahan said, peering through the shiny blue barrel of the shot-gun. 'Maybe even a trillionaire. I'm not sure.'

Tina smiled. 'Right,' she said. 'You ever watch *Miami Vice*? I've been on there twice. Both times I played prostitutes, but at least I had some good lines.'

'I don't have a television,' Stranahan said. 'Sorry I missed it.'

'Know what else? I dated Don Johnson.'

'I bet that looks good on the resumé.'

'He's a really nice guy,' Tina remarked, 'not like they say.'

Stranahan glanced up and said, 'I think your tan's fading.'

Tina the model looked down at herself, seemed to get tangled up in a thought. 'Can I ask you a favour?'

A headache was taking seed in Mick Stranahan's brain. He actually felt it sprouting, like ragweed, out of the base of his skull.

Tina stood up and said: 'I want you to look at my boobs.'

'I have. They're lovely.'

'Please, look again. Closer.'

Stranahan screwed the Remington shut and laid it across his lap. He sat up straight and looked directly at Tina's breasts. They seemed exquisite in all respects.

She said, 'Are they lined up OK?'

'Appear to be.'

'Reason I ask, I had one of those operations. You know, a boob job. For the kind of modelling I do, it was necessary. I mean, I was about a thirty-two A, if you can imagine.'

Stranahan just shook his head. He felt unable to contribute to the conversation.

'Anyway, I paid three grand for this boob job and it's really helped, workwise. Except the other day I did a *Penthouse* tryout and the photog makes some remark about my tits. Says I got a gravity problem on the left side.'

Stranahan studied the two breasts and said, 'Would that be your left or my left?'

'Mine.'

'Well, he's nuts,' Stranahan said. 'They're both perfect.'

'You're not just saying that?'

'I'll prove it,' he said, thinking: I can't believe I'm doing this. He went to the pantry and rummaged noisily until he found what he was searching for, a carpenter's level.

Tina eyed it and said, 'I've seen one of those.'

'Hold still,' Stranahan said.

'What are you going to do?'

'Just watch the bubble.'

The level was a galvanized steel ruler with a clear cylinder of amber liquid fixed in the middle. Inside the cylinder was a bubble of air, which moved in the liquid according to the angle being measured. If the surface was dead level, the bubble sat at the midway point of the cylinder.

Stranahan placed the tool across Tina's chest, so that each end rested lightly on a nipple.

'Now look down slowly, Tina.'

''Kay.'

'Where's the bubble?' he said.

'Smack dab in the centre.'

'Right,' Stranahan said. 'See—they're lined up perfectly.'

He lifted the ruler off her chest and set it on the bar. Tina beamed and gave herself a little squeeze, which caused her to bounce in a truly wonderful way. Stranahan decided to clean the shot-gun one more time.

'Well, back to the sunshine,' Tina laughed, sprinting bare-assed out the door.

'Back to the sunshine,' Mick Stranahan said, thinking that there was no sight in the world like a young lady completely at ease with herself, even if it cost three grand to get that way.

At four-thirty, the red Formula full of husky boyfriends roared up. Stranahan was reading on the sun deck, paying little attention to the naked women. The water was way too shallow for the ski boat, so the boyfriends idled it about fifty yards from the stilt house. After a manly huddle, one of them hopped to the bow and shouted at Mick Stranahan.

'Hey, what the hell are you doing?'

Stranahan glanced up from the newspaper and said nothing. Tina called out to the boat, 'It's OK. He lives here.'

'Put your clothes on!' hollered one of the guys in the boat, probably Tina's boyfriend.

Tina wiggled into a T-shirt. All the boyfriends appeared to be fairly agitated by Stranahan's presence among the nude women. Stranahan stood up and told the girls the water was too low for the ski boat.

'I'll run you out there in the skiff,' he said.

'You better not, Richie's real upset,' Tina said.

'Richie should have more faith in his fellow man.'

The three young women gathered their towels and suntan oils and clambered awkwardly into Stranahan's skiff. He jacked the outboard up a couple notches, so the prop wouldn't hit bottom, and steered out toward the red Formula in the channel. Once alongside the ski boat, he helped the girls climb up one at a time. Tina even gave him a peck on the cheek as she left.

The boyfriends were every bit as dumb and full of themselves as Stranahan figured. Each one wore a gold chain on his chest, which said it all.

'What was that about?' snarled the boyfriend called Richie, after witnessing Tina's goodbye peck.

'Nothing,' Tina said. 'He's an all-right guy.'

Stranahan had already let go, and the skiff had drifted a few yards beyond the ski boat, when Richie slapped Tina for being such a slut. Then he pointed out at Stranahan and yelled something extremely rude.

The boyfriends were quite surprised to see the aluminium skiff coming back at them, fast. They were equally amazed at the nimbleness with which the big stranger hopped onto the bow of their boat.

Richie took an impressive roundhouse swing at the guy, but the next thing the other boyfriends knew, Richie was flat on his back with the ski rope tied around both feet. Suddenly he was in the water, and the boat was moving, and Richie was dragging in the salt spray and yowling at the top of his lungs. The other boyfriends tried to seize the throttle, but the stranger knocked them down quickly and with a minimum of effort.

After about three-quarters of a mile, Tina and the other women asked Stranahan to please stop the speedboat, and he did. He grabbed the ski rope and hauled Richie back in, and they all watched him vomit up sea water for ten minutes straight.

'You're a stupid young man,' Stranahan counselled. 'Don't ever come out here again.'

Then Stranahan got in the skiff and went back to the stilt house, and the Formula sped away. Stranahan fixed himself a drink and stretched out on the sun deck. He was troubled by what was happening to the bay, when boatloads of idiots could spoil the whole afternoon. It was becoming a regular annoyance, and Stranahan could foresee a time when he might have to move away.

By late afternoon most of the other boats had cleared out of Stiltsville, except for a cabin cruiser that anchored on the south side of the radio towers in about four feet of water. A very odd location, Stranahan thought. On this boat he counted three people; one seemed to be pointing something big and black in the direction of Stranahan's house.

Stranahan went inside and came back with the shot-gun, utterly useless at five hundred yards, and the binoculars, which were not. Quickly he got the cabin cruiser into focus and determined that what was being aimed at him was not a big gun, but a portable television camera.

The people in the cabin cruiser were taking his picture.

This was the capper. First the Mafia hit man, then the nude sunbathers and their troglodyte boyfriends, now a bloody TV crew. Stranahan turned his back to the cabin cruiser and kicked off his trousers. This would give them something to think about: moon over Miami. He was in such sour spirits that he didn't even peek over his shoulder to see their reaction when he bent over.

37

Watching the sun slide low, Mick Stranahan perceived the syncopation of these events as providential; things had changed on the water, all was no longer calm. The emotion that accompanied this realization was not fear, or even anxiety, but disappointment. All these days the tranquillity of the bay, its bright and relentless beauty, had lulled him into thinking the world was not so rotten after all.

The minicam on the cabin cruiser reminded him otherwise. Mick Stranahan had no idea what the bastards wanted, but he was sorely tempted to hop in the skiff and go find out. In the end, he simply finished his gin and tonic and went back inside the stilt house. At dusk, when the light was gone, the boat pulled anchor and motored away.

4

After quitting the State Attorney's Office, Stranahan had kept his gold investigator's badge to remind people that he used to work there, in case he needed to get back inside. Like now.

A young assistant state attorney, whose name was Dreeson, took Stranahan to an interview room and handed him the Barletta file, which must have weighed four pounds. In an officious voice, the young prosecutor said: 'You can sit here and make notes, Mr Stranahan. But it's still an open case, so don't take anything out.'

'You mean I can't blow my nose on the affidavits?'

Dreeson made a face and shut the door, hard.

Stranahan opened the jacket, and the first thing to fall out was a photograph of Victoria Barletta. Class picture, clipped from the 1985 University of Miami student year-book. Long dark hair, brushed to a shine; big dark eyes; a long, sharp nose, probably her old man's; gorgeous Italian smile, warm and laughing and honest.

Stranahan set the picture aside. He had never met the girl, never would.

He skimmed the statements taken so long ago by himself and Timmy Gavigan: the parents, the boyfriend, the sorority sisters. The details of the case came back to him quickly in a cold flood.

On March 12, 1986, Victoria Barletta had gotten up early, jogged three miles around the campus, showered, attended a 9 a.m. class in advanced public relations, met her boyfriend at a breakfast shop near Mark Light Field, then bicycled to an 11 a.m. seminar on the history of television news. Afterwards, Vicky went back to the Alpha Chi Omega house, changed into jeans, sneakers, and a sweatshirt, and asked a sorority sister to give her a lift to a doctor's appointment in South Miami, only three miles from the university.

The appointment was scheduled for 1:30 p.m. at a medical building called the Durkos Center. As Vicky got out of the car, she instructed her friend to come back at about 5 p.m. and pick her up. Then she went inside and got a nose job and was never seen again.

According to a doctor and a nurse at the clinic, Vicky Barletta left the office at about 4:50 p.m. to wait on the bus bench out front for her ride back to campus. Her face was splotched, her eyes swollen to slits, and her nose heavily bandaged—not exactly a tempting sight for your average trolling rapist, Timmy Gavigan had pointed out.

Still, they both knew better than to rule it out. One minute the girl was on the bench, the next she was gone.

Three county buses had stopped there between 4:50 and 5:14 p.m., when Vicky's friend finally arrived at the clinic. None of the bus drivers remembered seeing a woman with a busted-up face get on board.

So the cops were left to assume that somebody snatched Victoria Barletta off the bus bench moments after she emerged from the Durkos Center.

The case was treated like a kidnapping, though Gavigan and Stranahan suspected otherwise. The Barlettas had no money and no access to any; Vicky's father was half-owner of a car wash in Evanston, Illinois. Aside from a couple of cranks, there were no ransom calls made to the family, or to the police. The girl was just plain gone, and undoubtedly dead.

Rereading the file four years later, Mick Stranahan began to feel frustrated all over again. It was the damnedest thing: Vicky had told no one—not her parents, her boyfriend, nobody—about the cosmetic surgery; apparently it was meant to be a surprise.

Stranahan and Timmy Gavigan had spent a total of fifteen hours interviewing Vicky's boyfriend and wound up believing him. The kid had cried pathetically; he used to tease Vicky about her shnoz. 'My little anteater,' he used to call her. The boyfriend had been shattered by what happened, and blamed himself: his birthday was March twentieth. Obviously, he sobbed, the new nose was Vicky's present to him.

From a homicide investigator's point of view, the secrecy with which Victoria Barletta planned her doctor's visit meant something else: it limited the suspects to somebody who just happened to be passing by, a random psychopath.

A killer who was never caught.

A victim who was never found.

That was how Mick Stranahan remembered it. He scribbled a few names and numbers on a pad, stuffed everything into the file, then carried it back to a pock-faced clerk.

'Tell me something,' Stranahan said. 'How'd you happen to have this one downtown?'

The clerk said, 'What do you mean?'

'I mean, this place didn't used to be so efficient. Used to take two weeks to dig out an old case like this.'

'You just got lucky,' the clerk said. 'We pulled the file from the warehouse a week ago.'

'This file here?' Stranahan tapped the green folder. 'Same one?'

'Mr Eckert wanted to see it.'

Gerry Eckert was the State Attorney. He hadn't personally gone to court in at least sixteen years, so Stranahan doubted if he even remembered how to read a file.

'So how's old Gerry doing?'

'Just dandy,' said the clerk, as if Eckert were his closest, dearest pal in the world. 'He's doing real good.'

'Don't tell me he's finally gonna pop somebody in this case.'

'I don't think so, Mr Stranahan. He just wanted to refresh his memory before he went on TV. The Reynaldo Flemm show.'

Stranahan whistled. Reynaldo Flemm was a television journalist who specialized in sensational crime cases. He was nationally famous for getting beaten up on camera, usually by the very hoodlums he was trying to interview. No matter what kind of elaborate disguise Reynaldo Flemm would devise, he was always too vain to cover his face. Naturally the crooks would recognize him instantly and bash the living shit out of him. For pure action footage, it was hard to beat; Reynaldo Flemm's specials were among the highest-rated programmes on television.

'So Gerry's hit the big time,' Stranahan said.

'Yep,' the clerk said.

'What did he say about this case?'

'Mr Eckert?'

'Yeah, what did he tell this TV guy?'

The clerk said, 'Well, I wasn't there for the taping. But from what I heard, Mr Eckert said the whole thing is still a mystery.'

'Well, that's true enough.'

'And Mr Eckert told Mr Flemm that he wouldn't be one bit surprised if someday it turns out that Victoria Barletta ran away. Just took one look at her face and ran away. Otherwise, why haven't they found a body?'

Stranahan thought: Eckert hasn't changed a bit, still dumb as a bull gator.

'I can't wait to see the show,' Stranahan remarked.

'It's scheduled to be on March twelfth at 9 p.m.' The

41

clerk held up a piece of paper. 'We got a memo from Mr Eckert today.'

The man from New Jersey did not call Dr Rudy Graveline again for four days. Then, on the afternoon of January eighth, Rudy got a message on his beeper. The beeper went off at a bad moment, when Rudy happened to be screwing the young wife of a Miami Dolphins wide receiver. The woman had come to Whispering Palms for a simple consult—a tiny pink scar along her jawline, could it be fixed?—and the next thing she knew, the doctor had her talking about all kinds of personal things, including how lonely it got at home during the football season when Jake's mind was on the game and nothing else. Well, the next thing she knew, the doctor was taking her to lunch in his black Jaguar sedan with the great Dolby sound system, and the football player's wife found herself thinking how the rich smell of leather upholstery made her hot, really hot, and then—as if he could read her mind—the doctor suddenly pulled off the Julia Tuttle Causeway, parked the Jag in some pepper trees, and started to gnaw her panties off. He even made cute little squirrel noises as he nuzzled between her legs.

Before long the doctor was merrily pounding away while the football player's wife gazed up at him through the spokes of the walnut steering wheel, under which her head had become uncomfortably wedged.

When the beeper went off on Dr Graveline's belt, he scarcely missed a beat. He glanced down at the phone number (glowing in bright green numerals) and snatched the car phone from its cradle in the glove box. With one hand he managed to dial the long-distance number even as he finished with the football player's wife, who by this time was silently counting down, hoping he'd hurry it up. She'd had about all she could take of the smell of new leather.

Dr Graveline pulled away just as the phone started ringing somewhere in New Jersey.

The man answered on the fourth ring. 'Yeah, what?'

'It's me. Rudy.'

42

'You been jogging or what?'

'Something like that.'

'Sounds like you're gonna have a fuckin' heart attack.'

Dr Graveline said: 'Give me a second to catch my breath.'

The football player's wife was squirming back into her slacks. The look on her face suggested disappointment at her partner's performance, but Rudy Graveline did not notice.

'About the deal,' he said. 'I don't think so.'

Curly Eyebrows in New Jersey said: 'Your problem musta gone away.'

'Not really.'

'Then what?'

'I'm going to get somebody local.'

The man in New Jersey started to laugh. He laughed and laughed until he began to wheeze.

'Doc, this is a big mistake. Local is no good.'

'I've got a guy in mind,' Dr Graveline said.

'A Cuban, right? Crazy fuckin' Cuban, I knew it.'

'No, he's not a Cuban.'

'One of my people?'

'No,' Rudy said. 'He's by himself.'

Again Curly Eyebrows laughed. 'Nobody is by himself, Doc. Nobody in this business.'

'This one is different,' Rudy said. Different wasn't the word for it. 'Anyway, I just wanted to let you know, so you wouldn't send anybody else.'

'Suit yourself.'

'And I'm sorry about the other fellow.'

'Don't bring up that shit, hear? You're on one of those cellular phones, I can tell. I hate them things, Doc, they ain't safe. They give off all kinds of fucked-up microwaves, anybody can listen in.'

Dr Graveline said, 'I don't think so.'

'Yeah, well, I read where people can listen on their blenders and hair dryers and shit. Pick up everything you say.'

The football player's wife was brushing on fresh make-up, using the vanity mirror on the back of the sun visor.

The man in Jersey said: 'Your luck, some broad's pickin' us up on her electric dildo. Every word.'

'Talk to you later,' Rudy said.

'One piece of advice,' said Curly Eyebrows. 'This guy you lined up for the job, don't tell him your life story. I mean it, Doc. Give him the name, the address, the dough, and that's it.'

'Oh, I can trust him,' Dr Graveline said.

'Like hell,' laughed the man in New Jersey, and hung up.

The football player's wife flipped the sun visor up, closed her compact, and said, 'Business?'

'Yes, I dabble in real estate.' Rudy zipped up his pants. 'I've decided to go with a Miami broker.'

The woman shrugged. She noticed her pink bikini panties on the floor-mat, and quickly put them in her purse. They were ruined; the doctor had chewed a hole in them.

'Can I drive your car back to the office?' she asked.

'No,' said Rudy Graveline. He got out and walked around to the driver's side. The football player's wife slid across the seat, and Rudy got in.

'I almost forgot,' the woman said, fingering the place on her jaw, 'about my scar.'

'A cinch,' the doctor said. 'We can do it under local anaesthetic, make it smooth as silk.'

The football player's wife smiled. 'Really?'

'Oh sure, it's easy,' Rudy said, steering the Jaguar back on the highway. 'But I was wondering about something else . . . '

'Yes?'

'You won't mind some friendly professional advice?'

'Of course not.' The woman's voice held an edge of concern.

'Well, I couldn't help but notice,' Dr Graveline said, 'when we were making love . . . '

'Yes?'

Without taking his eyes off the road, he reached down and patted her hip. 'You could use a little suction around the saddlebags.'

The football player's wife turned away and blinked.

'Please don't be embarrassed,' the doctor said. 'This is my speciality, after all. Believe me, darling, I've got an eye for perfection, and you're only an inch or two away.'

She took a little breath and said, 'Around the thighs?'

'That's all.'

'How much would it cost?' she asked with a trace of a sniffle.

Rudy Graveline smiled warmly and passed her a monogrammed handkerchief. 'Less than you think,' he said.

The cabin cruiser with the camera crew came back again, anchored in the same place. Stranahan sighed and spat hard into the tide. He was in no mood for this.

He was standing on the dock with a spinning rod in his hands, catching pinfish from around the pilings of the stilt house. Suspended motionless in the gin-clear water below was a dark blue log, or so it would have appeared to the average tourist. The log measured about five feet long and, when properly motivated, could streak through the water at about sixty knots to make a kill. Teeth were the trademark of the Great Barracuda, and the monster specimen that Mick Stranahan called Liza had once left thirteen needle-sharp incisors in a large plastic mullet that some moron had trolled through the Biscayne Channel. Since that episode the barracuda had more or less camped beneath Stranahan's place. Every afternoon he went out and caught for its supper a few dollar-sized pinfish, which he tossed off the dock, and which the barracuda devoured in lightning flashes that churned the water and sent the mangrove snappers diving for cover. Liza's teeth had long since grown back.

Because of his preoccupation with the camera boat, Mick Stranahan allowed the last pinfish to stay on the line longer than he should have. It tugged back and forth, sparkling just below the surface until the barracuda ran out of patience. Before Stranahan could react, the big fish rocketed from under the stilt house and severed the majority of the pinfish as cleanly as a scalpel; a quivering pair of fish lips was all that remained on Stranahan's hook.

'Nice shot,' he mumbled and stored the rod away.

He climbed into the skiff and motored off the flat, toward the cabin cruiser. The photographer immediately put down the video camera; Stranahan could see him conferring with the rest of the crew. There was a brief and clumsy attempt to raise the anchor, followed by the sound of the boat's engine whining impotently in the way that cold outboards do. Finally the crew gave up and just waited for the big man in the skiff, who by now was within hailing distance.

A stocky man with a lacquered helmet of black hair and a stiff bottle-brush moustache stood on the transom of the boat and shouted, 'Ahoy there!'

Stranahan cut the motor and let the skiff coast up to the cabin cruiser. He tied off on a deck cleat, stood up, and said, 'Did I hear you right? Did you actually say *ahoy*?'

The man with the moustache nodded uneasily.

'Where did you learn that, watching pirate movies? Jesus Christ, I can't believe you said that. *Ahoy there! Give me a break.*' Stranahan was really aggravated. He jumped into the bigger boat and said, 'Which one of you assholes is Reynaldo Flemm? Let me guess; it's Captain Blood here.'

The stocky man with the moustache puffed out his chest and said, 'Watch it, pal!'—which took a certain amount of courage, since Mick Stranahan was holding a stainless-steel tarpon gaff in his right hand. Flemm's crew—an overweight cameraman and an athletic young woman in blue jeans—kept one eye on their precious equipment and the other on the stranger with the steel hook.

Stranahan said, 'Why have you been taking my picture?'

'For a story,' Flemm said. 'For television.'

'What's the story?'

'I'm not at liberty to say.'

46

Stranahan frowned. 'What's it got to do with Vicky Barletta?'

Reynaldo Flemm shook his head. 'In due time, Mr Stranahan. When we're ready to do the interview.'

Stranahan said, 'I'm ready to do the interview now.'

Flemm smiled in a superior way. 'Sorry.'

Stranahan slipped the tarpon gaff between Reynaldo Flemm's legs and gave a little jerk. The tip of the blade not only poked through Reynaldo Flemm's Banana Republic trousers, but also through his thirty-dollar bikini underpants (flamenco red), which he had purchased at a boutique in Coconut Grove. The cold point of the gaff came to rest on Reynaldo Flemm's scrotum, and at this frightful instant the air rushed from his intestinal tract with a sharp noise that seemed to punctuate Mick Stranahan's request.

'The interview,' he said again to Flemm, who nodded energetically.

But words escaped the television celebrity. Try as he might, Flemm could only burble in clipped phrases. Fear, and the absence of cue cards, had robbed him of cogent conversation.

The young woman in blue jeans stepped forward from the cabin of the boat and said, 'Please, Mr Stranahan, we didn't mean to intrude.'

'Of course you did.'

'My name is Christina Marks. I'm the producer of this segment.'

'Segment of what?' Stranahan asked.

'Of the Reynaldo Flemm show. *In Your Face.* You must have seen it.'

'Never.'

For Reynaldo, Stranahan knew, this was worse than a gaff in the balls.

'Come on,' Christina Marks said.

'Honest,' Stranahan said. 'You see a TV dish over on my house?'

'Well, no.'

'There you go. Now, what's this all about? And hurry it up, your man here looks like his legs are cramping.'

Indeed, Reynaldo Flemm was shaking on his tiptoes. Stranahan eased the gaff down just a notch or two.

Christina Marks said: 'Do you know a nurse named Maggie Gonzalez?'

'Nope,' Stranahan said.

'Are you sure?'

'Give me a hint.'

'She worked at the Durkos Medical Center.'

'OK, now I remember.' He had taken her statement the day after Victoria Barletta had vanished. Timmy Gavigan had done the doctor, while Stranahan had taken the nurse. He had scanned the affidavits in the State Attorney's file that morning.

'You sure about the last name?' Stranahan asked.

'Sorry—Gonzalez is her married name. Back then it was Orestes.'

'So let's have the rest.'

'About a month ago, in New York, she came to us.'

'To me,' croaked Reynaldo Flemm.

'Shut up,' said Stranahan.

Christina Marks went on: 'She said she had some important information about the Barletta case. She indicated she was willing to talk on camera.'

'To me,' Flemm said, before Stranahan tweaked him once more with the tarpon gaff.

'But first,' Christina Marks said, 'she said she had to speak to you, Mr Stranahan.'

'About what?'

'All she said was that she needed to talk to you first, because you could do something about it. And don't ask me about what, because I don't know. We gave her six hundred bucks, put her on a plane to Florida, and never saw her again. She was supposed to be back two weeks ago last Monday.' Christina Marks put her hands in her pockets. 'That's all there is. We came down here to look for Maggie Gonzalez, and you're the best lead we had.'

Stranahan removed the gaff from Reynaldo Flemm's crotch and tossed it into the bow of his skiff. Almost instantly, Flemm leapt from the stern and bolted for the

48

cabin. 'Get tape of that fucker,' he cried at the cameraman, 'so we can prosecute his fat ass!'

'Ray, knock it off,' said Christina Marks.

Stranahan liked the way she talked down to the big star. 'Tell him,' he said, 'that if he points that goddamn camera at me again, he'll be auditioning for the Elephant Man on Broadway. That's how seriously I'll mess up his face.'

'Ray,' she said, 'did you hear that?'

'Roll tape! Roll tape!' Flemm was all over the cameraman.

Wearily, Stranahan got back into his skiff and said, 'Miss Marks, the interview is over.'

Now it was her turn to be angry. She hopped up on the transom, tennis shoes squeaking on the teak. 'Wait a minute, that's it?'

Stranahan looked up from his little boat. 'I haven't seen Maggie Gonzalez since the day after the Barletta girl disappeared. That's the truth. I don't know whether she took your money and went south or what, but I haven't heard from her.'

'He's lying,' sneered Reynaldo Flemm, and he stormed into the cabin to sulk. A gust of wind had made a comical nest of his hair.

Stranahan hand-cranked the outboard and slipped it into gear.

'I'm at the Sonesta,' Christina Marks said to him, 'if Maggie Gonzalez should call.'

Not likely, Stranahan thought. Not very likely at all.

'How the hell did you find me, anyway?' he called out to the young TV producer.

'Your ex-wife,' Christina Marks called back from the cabin cruiser.

'Which one?'

'Number four.'

That would be Chloe, Stranahan thought. Naturally.

'How much did it cost you?' he shouted.

Sheepishly, Christina Marks held up five fingers.

'You got off light,' Mick Stranahan said, and turned the skiff homeward.

5

Christina Marks was in bed, reading an old *New Yorker*, when somebody rapped on the door of the hotel room. She was hoping it might be Mick Stranahan, but it wasn't.

'Hello, Ray.'

As Reynaldo Flemm breezed in, he patted her on the rump.

'Cute,' Christina said, closing the door. 'I was getting ready to turn in.'

'I brought some wine.'

'No, thanks.'

Reynaldo Flemm turned on the television and made himself at home. He was wearing another pair of khaki Banana Republic trousers and a baggy denim shirt. He smelled like a bucket of Brut. In a single motion he scissored his legs and propped his white high-top Air Jordans on the coffee table.

Christina Marks tightened the sash on her bathrobe and sat down at the other end of the sofa. 'I'm tired, Ray,' she said.

He acted like he didn't hear it. 'This Stranahan guy, he's the key to it,' Flemm said. 'I think we should follow him tomorrow.'

'Oh, please.'

'Rent a van. A van with smoked window panels. We set the camera on a tripod in back. I'll be driving, so Willie gets the angle over my . . . let's see, it'd be my right shoulder. Great shot, through the windshield as we follow this big prick—'

'Willie gets carsick,' Christina Marks said.

Reynaldo Flemm cackled scornfully.

'It's a lousy idea,' Christina said. She wanted him to go away, now.

'What, you trust that Stranahan?'

'No,' she said, but in a way she did trust him. At

least more than she trusted Maggie Gonzalez; there was something squirrelly about the woman's sudden need to fly to Miami. Why had she said she wanted to see Stranahan? Where had she really gone?

Reynaldo Flemm wasn't remotely concerned about Maggie's motives—good video was good video—but Christina Marks wanted to know more about the woman. She had better things to do than sit in a steaming van, tailing a guy who, if he caught them, would probably destroy every piece of electronics in their possession.

'So, what other leads we got?' Reynaldo Flemm demanded. 'Tell me that.'

'Maggie's probably got family here,' Christina said, 'and friends.'

'Dull, dull, dull.'

'Hard work is dull sometimes,' Christina said sharply, 'but how would you know?'

Flemm sat up straight and flared his upper lip like a chihuahua. 'You can't talk to me like that! You just remember who's the star.'

'And you just remember who writes all your lines. And who does all your dull, dull research. Remember who tells you what questions to ask. And who edits these pieces so you don't come off looking like a pompous airhead.' Except that's exactly how Reynaldo came off, most of the time. There was no way around it, no postproduction wizardry that could disguise the man's true personality on tape.

Reynaldo Flemm shrugged. His attention had been stolen by something on the television: Mike Wallace of CBS was a guest on the Letterman show. Flemm punched up the volume and inched to the edge of the sofa.

'You know how old that geezer is?' he said, pointing at Wallace. 'I'm half his age.'

Christina Marks held her tongue.

Reynaldo said, 'I bet *his* producer sleeps with him any time he wants.' He glanced sideways at Christina.

She got up, went to the door, and held it open. 'Go back to your room, Ray.'

51

'Aw, come on, I was kidding.'

'No, you weren't.'

'All right, I wasn't. Come on, Chris, close the door. Let's open the wine.'

'Good night, Ray.'

He got up and turned off the TV. He was sulking.

'I'm sorry,' he said.

'You sure are.'

Christina Marks held all the cards. Reynaldo Flemm needed her far worse than she needed him. Not only was she very talented, but she knew things about Reynaldo Flemm that he did not wish the whole world of television to know. About the time she caught him beating himself up, for example. It happened at a Hyatt House in Atlanta. Flemm was supposed to be out interviewing street-gang members, but Christina found him in the bathroom of his hotel room, thwacking himself in the cheek with a sock full of parking tokens. Reynaldo's idea was to give himself a nasty shiner, then go on camera and breathlessly report that an infamous gang leader named Rapper Otis had assaulted him.

Reynaldo Flemm had begged Christina Marks not to tell the executive producers about the sock incident, and she hadn't; the weeping is what got to her. She couldn't bear it.

For keeping this and other weird secrets, Christina felt secure in her job, certainly secure enough to tell Reynaldo Flemm to go pound salt every time he put the make on her.

On the way out the door, he said, 'I still say we get up early and follow this Stranahan guy.'

'And I still say no.'

'But, Chris, he *knows* something.'

'Yeah, Ray, he knows how to hurt people.'

Christina couldn't be sure, but she thought she saw a hungry spark in the eyes of Reynaldo Flemm.

The next morning Stranahan left the skiff at the marina, got the Chrysler and drove back across the Rickenbacker

Causeway to the mainland. Next to him on the front seat was his yellow notepad, open to the page where he had jotted the names and numbers from the Barletta file. The first place he went was the Durkos Medical Center, except it wasn't there any more. The building was now occupied entirely by dentists: nine of them, according to Stranahan's count from the office directory. He went looking for the building manager.

Every door and hallway reverberated with the nerve-stabbing whine of high-speed dental drills; soon Stranahan's molars started to throb, and he began to feel claustrophobic. He enlisted a friendly janitor to lead him to the superinten-dent, a mammoth olive-coloured woman who introduced herself as Marlee Jones.

Stranahan handed Marlee Jones a card and told her what he wanted. She glanced at the card and shrugged. 'I don't have to tell you nothing,' she said, displaying the kind of public-spirited co-operation that Stranahan had come to appreciate among the Miami citizenry.

'No, you don't have to tell me nothing,' he said to Marlee, 'but I can make it possible for a county code inspector to brighten your morning tomorrow, and the day after that, and every single day until you die of old age.' Stranahan picked up a broom and stabbed the wooden handle into the foam-tile ceiling. 'Looks like pure asbestos to me,' he said. 'Sure hate for the feds to find out.'

Marlee Jones scowled, exhibiting an impressive array of gold teeth: bribes, no doubt, from her tenants. She shuffled to a metal desk and opened a bottom drawer and got out a black ledger. 'All right, smartass, what was that name?'

'Durkos.' Stranahan spelled it. 'A medical group. They were here as of March twelfth, four years ago.'

'Well, as of April first, four years ago, they was gone.' Marlee started to close the ledger, but Stranahan put his hand on the page.

'May I look?'

'It's just numbers, mister.'

'Aw, let me give it a whirl.' Stranahan took the ledger from Marlee Jones and ran down the columns with his forefinger. The Durkos Medical Trust, Inc., had been sole tenant of the building for two years, but had vacated within weeks after Victoria Barletta's disappearance. The ledger showed that the company had paid its lease and security deposits through May. Stranahan thought it was peculiar that, after moving out, the medical group never got a refund.

'Maybe they didn't ask,' Marlee Jones said.

'Doctors are the cheapest human beings alive,' Stranahan said. 'For fifteen grand they don't just ask, they hire lawyers.'

Again Marlee Jones shrugged. 'Some people be in a big damn hurry.'

'What do you remember about it?'

'Who says I was here?'

'This handwriting in the ledger book—it's the same as on these receipts.' Stranahan tapped a finger on a pile of rental coupons. Marlee Jones appeared to be having a spell of high blood pressure.

Stranahan asked again: 'So what do you remember?'

With a groan Marlee Jones heaved her bottom into the chair behind the desk. She said, 'One night they cleared out. Must've backed up a trailer truck, who knows. I came in, the place was empty, except for a bunch of cheapo paintings on the walls. Cats with big eyes, that sorta shit.'

'Were they all surgeons?'

'Seemed like it. But they wasn't partners.'

'Durkos the main man?'

'Was no Durkos that I heard of. Big man was a Dr Graveyard, something like that. The other four guys worked for him. How come I know this is, the day after all the stuff is gone, a couple of the other doctors showed up dressed for work. They couldn't believe their office was emptied.'

Graveline was the name of the surgeon who had operated on Vicky Barletta. There was no point to correcting Marlee Jones on the name. Stranahan said, 'This Dr Graveyard, he didn't even tell the other doctors about the move?'

'This is Miami, lots of people in a big-time hurry.'

'Yeah, but not many pay in advance.'

Marlee Jones finally laughed. 'You right about that.'

'Did anybody leave a forwarding address?'

'Nope.'

Stranahan handed Marlee Jones the ledger book.

'You be through with me?' she asked.

'Yes, ma'am.'

'For good?'

'Most likely.'

'Then can I ask who is it you're workin' for?'

'Myself,' said Mick Stranahan.

Since the day that the Durkos Medical Center had ceased to exist, the life of Nurse Maggie Orestes had gotten complicated. She had gone to work in the emergency room at Jackson Hospital, where one night she had met a man named Ricky Gonzalez. The reason for Ricky Gonzalez's visit to the emergency room was that he had accidentally been run over by a turbocharged Ferrari during the annual running of the Miami Grand Prix. Ricky was a race-car promoter, and he had been posing for pictures with Lorenzo Lamas in pit row, not paying close attention when the Ferrari had roared in and run over both his feet. Ricky broke a total of fourteen bones, while Lorenzo Lamas escaped without a scratch.

Nurse Maggie Orestes attended to Ricky Gonzalez in the emergency room before they put him under for surgery. He was young, dashing, full of promises—and so cheerful, considering what had happened.

A month later they were married at a Catholic church in Hialeah. Ricky persuaded Maggie to quit nursing and be a full-time hostess for the many important social functions that race-car promoters must necessarily conduct. Maggie had hoped she would come to enjoy car racing and the people involved in it, but she didn't. It was noisy and stupid and boring, and the people were worse. Maggie and Ricky had some fierce arguments, and she was on the verge of walking out of the marriage when the second pit-row accident happened.

This time it was a Porsche, and Ricky wasn't so lucky. After the service they cremated him in his complimentary silver Purolator racing jacket, which turned out to be fireproof, so they had to cremate that portion twice. Lorenzo Lamas sent a wreath all the way from Malibu, California. At the wake Ricky's lawyer came up to Maggie Gonzalez and told her the bad news: first, her husband had no life insurance; second, he had emptied their joint bank accounts to pay for his cocaine habit. Maggie had known nothing about the drug problem, but in retrospect it explained her late husband's irrepressible high spirits and also his lack of caution around the race track.

A widowhood of destitution did not appeal to Maggie Gonzalez. She went back to being a nurse with a plan to nail herself a rich doctor or at least his money. In eighteen months she had been through three of them, all disasters—a married pediatrician, a divorced radiologist, and a urologist who wore women's underwear and who wound up giving Maggie a stubborn venereal disease. When she dumped the urologist, he got her fired from the hospital and filed a phoney complaint with the state nursing board.

All this left Maggie Gonzalez with a molten hatred of men and a mind for vengeance.

Money is what pushed her to the brink. With the mortgage payment on her duplex coming due, and only eighty-eight bucks in the checking account, Maggie decided to go ahead and do it. Part of the motive was financial desperation, true, but there was also a delicious hint of excitement—payback, to the sonofabitch who'd started it all.

First Maggie used her Visa card to buy a plane ticket to New York, where she caught a cab to the midtown offices of Reynaldo Flemm, the famous television journalist. There she told producer Christina Marks the story of Victoria Barletta, and cut a deal.

Five thousand dollars to repeat it on camera—that's as high as Reynaldo's people would go. Maggie Gonzalez was disappointed; it was, after all, one hell of a story.

That night Christina Marks got Maggie a room at the

Goreham Hotel, and she lay there watching Robin Leach on TV and worrying about the risks she was taking. She remembered the State Attorney's investigator who had questioned her nearly four years ago, and how she had lied to him. God, what was she thinking of now? Flemm's people would fly straight to Miami and interview the investigator—Stranahan was his name—and he'd tell them she'd never said a word about all this when it happened. Her credibility would be shot, and so would the five grand. Out the window.

Maggie realized she had to do something about Stranahan.

And also about Dr Rudy Graveline.

Graveline was a dangerous creep. To rat on Rudy—well, he had warned her. And rewarded her, in a sense. A decent severance, glowing references for a new job. That was after he closed down the Durkos Center.

Lying there, Maggie got another idea. It was wild, but it just might work. The next morning she went back to Christina Marks and made up a vague story about how she had to go see Investigator Stranahan right away, otherwise no TV show. Reluctantly the producer gave her a place ticket and six hundred in expenses.

Of course, Maggie had no intention of visiting Mick Stranahan. When she got back to Florida, she drove directly to the Whispering Palms Spa and Surgery Center in beautiful Bal Harbour. Dr Rudy Graveline was very surprised to see her. He led her into a private office and closed the door.

'You look frightened,' the surgeon said.

'I am.'

'And a little bouncy in the bottom.'

'I eat when I'm frightened,' Maggie said, keeping her cool.

'So what is it?' Rudy asked.

'Vicky Barletta,' she said. 'Somebody's making a fuss.'

'Oh.' Rudy Graveline appeared calm. 'Who?'

'One of the investigators. A man named Stranahan.'

'I don't remember him,' Rudy said.

57

'I do. He's scary.'

'Did he speak to you?'

Maggie shook her head. 'Worse than that,' she said. 'Some TV people came to my place. They're doing a special on missing persons.'

'Christ, don't tell me.'

'Stranahan's going to talk.'

Rudy said, 'But what does he know?'

Maggie blinked. 'I'm worried, Dr Graveline. It's going to break open all over again.'

'No way.'

Maggie's notion was to get Stranahan out of the way. Whether Dr Graveline bribed him, terrorized him, or worse was immaterial; Rudy could get to anybody. Those who stood in his way either got with the programme or got run over. One time another surgeon had done a corrective rhinoplasty on one of Rudy's botched-up patients, then badmouthed Rudy at a medical society cocktail party. Rudy got so furious that he paid two goons to trash the other doctor's office, but not before stealing his medical files. Soon, the other doctor's surgical patients received personal letters thanking them for being so understanding while he battled that terrible heroin addiction, which now seemed to be under control. Well, almost . . . By the end of the month, the other doctor had closed what was left of his practice and moved to British Columbia.

Maggie Gonzalez was counting on Rudy Graveline to overreact again; she wanted him worried about Stranahan to the exclusion of all others. By the time the doctor turned on the tube and discovered who was the real threat, Maggie would be long gone. And out of reach.

She went on: 'They won't leave me alone, these TV people. They said the case is going to a grand jury. They said Stranahan's going to testify.' She fished in her purse for a tissue. 'I thought you ought to know.'

Rudy Graveline thanked her for coming. He told her not to worry, everything was going to be fine. He suggested she get out of town for a few weeks, and she said that was probably a good idea. He asked if there was anywhere in particular she wanted to go, and she said New York. The doctor said New York is a swell place to visit around Christmas time, and he wrote out a personal cheque for twenty-five hundred dollars. He recommended that Maggie stay gone for at least a month, and said to call if she needed more money. *When*, Maggie said. Not *if* she needed more money, but when.

Later that same afternoon, Dr Rudy Graveline had locked his office door and made a telephone call to a seafood restaurant in New Jersey. He talked to a man who probably had curly eyebrows, a man who promised to send somebody down around the first of the year.

On the day that Tony Traviola, the first hit man, arrived to kill Mick Stranahan, Maggie Gonzalez was in a tenth-floor room at the Essex House hotel. The room had a view of Central Park, where Maggie was taking skating lessons at Donald Trump's ice rink. She planned to lay low for a few more weeks, maybe stop in for a chat at *20/20*. A little competition never hurt. Maybe Reynaldo Flemm would get worried enough to jack up his offer. Five grand sucked, it really did.

Dr Rudy Graveline made an appointment with the second killer for January tenth at three in the afternoon. The man arrived at Whispering Palms a half hour early and sat quietly in the waiting room, scaring the hell out of the other patients.

Rudy knew him only as Chemo, a cruel but descriptive nickname, for he truly did appear to be in the final grim stages of chemotherapy. Black hair sprouted in random wisps from a blue-veined scalp. His lips were thin and papery, the colour of wet cement. Red-rimmed eyes peered back at gawkers with a dull and chilling indifference; the hooded lids blinked slowly, pellucid as a salamander's. And the skin—the skin is what made people gasp, what emptied the waiting room at Whispering Palms. Chemo's skin looked like breakfast cereal, like somebody had glued Rice Krispies to every square centimetre of his face.

This, and the fact that he stood six foot nine, made Chemo a memorable sight.

Dr Graveline was not alarmed, because he knew how Chemo had come to look this way: it was not melanoma, but a freak electrolysis accident in Scranton, many years before. While burning two ingrown hair follicles off the tip of Chemo's nose, an elderly dermatologist had suffered a crippling stroke and lost all hand-eye co-ordination. Valiantly the old doctor had tried to complete the procedure, but in so doing managed to incinerate every normal pore within range of the electrified needle. Since Chemo had eaten five Valiums for breakfast, he was fast asleep on the table when the tragedy occurred. When he awoke to find his whole face blistered up like a lobster, he immediately garrotted the dermatologist and fled the State of Pennsylvania for ever.

Chemo had spent the better part of five years on the lam, seeking medical relief; ointments proved futile, and in fact a faulty prescription had caused the startling Rice Krispie effect. Eventually Chemo came to believe that the only hope was cosmetic surgery, and his quest for a miracle brought him naturally to Florida and naturally into the care of Dr Rudy Graveline.

At three sharp, Rudy motioned Chemo into the consultation room. Chemo ducked as he entered and shut the door behind him. He sat in an overstuffed chair and blinked moistly at Dr Graveline.

Rudy said: 'And how are we doing today?'

Chemo grunted. 'How do you think?'

'When you were here a few weeks ago, we discussed a treatment plan. You remember?'

'Yep,' Chemo said.

'And a payment plan, too.'

'How could I forget?' Chemo said.

Dr Graveline ignored the sarcasm; the man had every right to be bitter.

'Dermabrasion is expensive,' Rudy said.

'I don't know why,' Chemo said. 'You just stick my face in a belt sander, right?'

The doctor smiled patiently. 'It's a bit more sophisticated than that—'

'But the principle's the same.'

Rudy nodded. 'Roughly speaking.'

'So how can it be two hundred bucks a pop?'

'Two hundred and ten,' Rudy corrected. 'Because it requires uncommonly steady hands. You can appreciate that, I'm sure.'

Chemo smiled at the remark. Rudy wished he hadn't; the smile was harrowing, a deadly weapon all by itself. Chemo looked like he'd been teething on cinderblocks.

'I *did* get a job,' he said.

Dr Graveline agreed that was a start.

'At the Gay Bidet,' Chemo said. 'It's a punk club down on South Beach. I'm a greeter.' Again with the smile.

'A greeter,' said Rudy. 'Well, well.'

'I keep out the scum,' Chemo explained.

Rudy asked about the pay. Chemo said he got six bucks an hour, not including tips.

'Not bad,' Rudy said, 'but still . . . ' He scribbled some figures on a pad, then took a calculator out of his desk and punched on it for a while. All very dramatic.

Chemo stretched his neck to look. 'What's the damage?'

'I figure twenty-four visits, that's a minimum,' Rudy said. 'Say we do one square inch every session.'

'Shit, just do it all at once.'

'Can't,' Rudy lied, 'not with dermabrasion. Say twenty-four visits at two ten each, that's—'

'Five thousand and forty dollars,' Chemo muttered. 'Jesus H. Christ.'

Dr Graveline said: 'I don't need it all at once. Give me half to start.'

'Jesus H. Christ.'

Rudy put the calculator away.

'I just started at the club a week ago,' Chemo said. 'I gotta buy groceries.'

Rudy came around the desk and sat down on the edge. In a fatherly tone he asked: 'You have Blue Cross?'

'The fuck, I'm a fugitive, remember?'

'Of course,'

Rudy shook his head and mused. It was all so sad, that a great country like ours couldn't provide minimal health care to all its citizens.

'So I'm screwed,' Chemo said.

'Not necessarily.' Dr Graveline rubbed his chin. 'I've got an idea.'

'Yeah?'

'It's a job I need done.'

If Chemo had had eyebrows, they would have arched.

'If you could do this job,' Rudy went on, 'I think we could work a deal.'

'A discount?'

'I don't see why not.'

Idly, Chemo fingered the scales on his cheeks. 'What's the job?'

'I need you to kill somebody,' Rudy said.

'Who?'

'A man that could cause me some trouble.'

'What kind of trouble?'

'Could shut down Whispering Palms. Take away my medical licence. And that's for starters.'

Chemo ran a bloodless tongue across his lips. 'Who is this man?'

'His name is Mick Stranahan.'

'Where do I find him?'

'I'm not sure,' Rudy said. 'He's here in Miami somewhere.'

Chemo said that wasn't much of a lead. 'I figure a murder is worth at least five grand,' he said.

'Come on, he's not a cop or anything. He's just a regular guy. Three thousand, tops.' Rudy was a bear when it got down to money.

Chemo folded his huge bony hands. 'Twenty treatments, that's my final offer.'

Rudy worked it out in his head. 'That's forty-two hundred dollars!'

'Right.'

'You sure drive a hard bargain,' Rudy said.

Chemo grinned triumphantly. 'So when can you start on my face?'

'Soon as this chore is done.'

Chemo stood up. 'I suppose you'll want proof.'

Rudy Graveline hadn't really thought about it. He said, 'A newspaper clipping would do.'

'Sure you don't want me to bring you something?'

'Like what?'

'A fing..,' Chemo said, 'maybe one of his nuts.'

'That won't be necessary,' said Dr Graveline, 'really it won't.'

6

Stranahan got Maggie Orestes Gonzalez's home address from a friend of his who worked for the state nursing board in Jacksonville. Although Maggie's licence was paid up to date, no current place of employment was listed on the file.

The address was a duplex apartment in a quiet old neighbourhood off Coral Way, in the Little Havana section of Miami. There was a chain-link fence around a sparse brown yard, a ceramic statue of Santa Barbara in the flower bed, and the customary burglar bars on every window. Stranahan propped open the screen door and knocked three times on the heavy pine frame. He wasn't surprised that no one was home.

To break into Maggie Gonzalez's apartment, Stranahan used a three-inch stainless-steel lockpick that he had confiscated from the mouth of an infamous condominium burglar named Wet Willie Jeeter. Wet Willie got his nickname because he only worked on rainy days; on sunny days he was a golf caddy at the Doral Country Club. When they went through Wet Willie's place after the arrest, the cops found seventeen personally autographed photos of Jack Nicklaus, going back to the 1967 Masters. What the cops did not find was any of Wet Willie's burglar tools, due to the fact that Wet Willie kept them well hidden beneath his tongue.

Stranahan found them when he visited Wet Willie in the Dade County Jail, two weeks before the trial. The purpose of the visit was to make Wet Willie realize the wisdom of pleading guilty and saving the taxpayers the expense of trial. Unspoken was the fact that the State Attorney's Office had a miserably weak case and was desperate for a deal. Wet Willie told Stranahan thanks anyway, but he'd just as soon take his chances with a jury. Stranahan said fine and offered Wet Willie a stick of Dentyne, which the burglar popped into his mouth without thinking. The chewing dislodged the steel lockpicks, which immediately stuck fast in the Dentyne; the whole mess eventually lodged itself in Wet Willie's throat. For a few hectic minutes Stranahan thought he might have to perform an amateur tracheotomy, but miraculously the burglar coughed up the tiny tools and also a complete confession. Stranahan kept one of Wet Willie's lockpicks as a souvenir.

The lock on Maggie's door was a breeze.

Stranahan slipped inside and noticed how neat the place looked. Someone, probably a neighbour or a relative, had carefully stacked the unopened mail on a table near the front door. On the kitchen counter was a Princess-model telephone attached to an answering machine. Stranahan pressed the Rewind button, then Play, and listened to Maggie's voice say: 'Hi, I'm not home right now so you're listening to another one of those dumb answering machines. Please leave a brief message and I'll get back to you as soon as possible. Bye now!'

Stranahan played the rest of the tape, which was blank. Either Maggie Gonzalez wasn't getting any calls, or someone was taking them for her, or she was phoning in for her own messages with one of those remote pocket beepers. Whatever the circumstances, it was a sign that she probably wasn't all that dead.

Other clues in the apartment pointed to travel. There was no luggage in the closets, no bras or underwear in the bedroom drawers, no make-up on the bathroom sink. The most interesting thing Stranahan found was crumpled in a waste basket in a corner of the living room: a bank deposit slip for twenty-five hundred dollars, dated the twenty-seventh of December.

Have a nice trip, Stranahan thought.

He let himself out, carefully locking the door behind him. Then he drove three blocks to a pay phone at a 7-Eleven, where he dialled Maggie's phone number and left a very important message on her machine.

At the end of the day, Christina Marks dropped her rented Ford Escort with the hotel valet, bought a copy of the *New York Times* at the shop in the lobby, and took the elevator up to her room. Before she could get the key out of the door, Mick Stranahan opened it from the other side.

'Come on in,' he said.

'Nice of you,' Christina said, 'considering it's my room.'

Stranahan noticed she had one of those trendy leather briefcase satchels that you wear over your shoulder. A couple of legal pads stuck out the top.

'You've been busy.'

'You want a drink?'

'Gin and tonic, thanks,' Stranahan said. After a pause: 'I was afraid the great Reynaldo might see me if I waited in the lobby.'

'So you got a key to my room?'

'Not exactly.'

Christina Marks handed him the drink. Then she poured herself a beer, and sat down in a rattan chair with garish floral pillows that were supposed to look tropical.

'I went to see Maggie's family today,' she said.

'Any luck?'

'No. Unfortunately, they don't speak English.'

Stranahan smiled and shook his head.

'What's so funny?' Christina said. 'Just because I don't speak Spanish?'

Stranahan said, 'Except for probably her grandmother, all Maggie's family speaks perfect English. Perfect.'

'What?'

'Her father teaches physics at Palmetto High School. Her mother is an operator for Southern Bell. Her sister Consuela is a legal secretary, and her brother, what's-his-name . . .'

'Tomàs.'

'Tommy, yeah,' Stranahan said. 'He's a senior account executive at Merrill Lynch.'

Christina Marks put down her beer so decisively that it nearly broke the glass coffee table. 'I sat in the living room, talking to these people, and they just stared at me and said—'

'*No habla* English, *señora*.'

'Exactly.'

'Oldest trick in Miami,' Stranahan said. 'They just didn't want to talk. Don't feel bad, they tried the same thing with me.'

'And I suppose you know Spanish.'

'Enough to make them think I knew more. They're worried about Maggie, actually. Been worried for some time. She's had some personal problems, Maggie has. Money problems, too—that much I found out before her old lady started having chest pains.'

'You're kidding.'

'Second oldest trick,' Stranahan said, smiling, 'but I was done anyway. I honestly don't think they know where she is.'

Christina Marks finished her beer and got another from the small hotel refrigerator. When she sat down again, she kicked off her shoes.

'So,' she said, 'you're ahead of us.'

'You and Reynaldo?'

'The crew,' Christina said, looking stung.

'No, I'm not ahead of you,' Stranahan said. 'Tell me what Maggie Gònzalez knows about Vicky Barletta.'

Christina said, 'I can't do that.'

'How much did you promise to pay?'

66

Again Christina shook her head.

'Know what I think?' Stranahan said. 'I think you and Ray are getting the hum job of your lives.'

'Pardon?'

'I think Maggie is sucking you off, big-time.'

Christina heard herself saying, 'You might be right.'

Stranahan softened his tone. 'Let me give you a hypothetical,' he said. 'This Maggie Gonzalez, whom you've never seen before, shows up in New York one day and offers to tell you a sensational story about a missing college coed. The way she tells it, the girl came to a terrible and ghastly end. And, conveniently, the way she tells it can't ever be proven or disproven. Why? Because it happened a long time ago. And the odds are, Christina, that Victoria Barletta is dead. And the odds are, whoever did it isn't about to come forward to say that Reynaldo Flemm got it all wrong when he told the story on national TV.'

Christina Marks leaned forward. 'Fine. All fine, except for one thing. She names names.'

'Maggie does?'

'Yes. She describes exactly how it happened and who did it.'

'And these people—'

'Person, singular.'

'He? She?'

'He,' Christina said.

'He's still alive?'

'Sure is.'

'Here in town?'

'That's right.'

'Jesus,' Stranahan said. He got up and fixed himself another gin. He dropped a couple of ice cubes, his hands were shaking so much. This was not good. he told himself, getting so excited was definitely not good.

He carried his drink back to the living room and said, 'Is it the doctor?'

'I can't say.' It would violate a confidence, Christina Marks explained. Journalists have to protect their sources.

Stranahan finished half his drink before he spoke again. 'Are you any good?'

Christina looked at him curiously.

'At what you do,' he said irritably, 'are you any damn good?'

'Yes, I think so.'

'Can you keep the great Reynaldo out of my hair?'

'I'll try. Why?'

'Because,' Stranahan said, 'it would be to our mutual benefit to meet once in a while, just you and me.'

'Compare notes?'

'Something like that. I don't know why, but I think I can trust you.'

'Thanks.'

'I'm not saying I do, just that it's possible.'

He put down the glass and stood up.

'What's your stake in this?' Christina Marks asked.

'Truth, justice, whatever.'

'No, it's bigger than that.'

She was pretty sharp, he had to admit. But he wasn't ready to tell her about Tony the Eel and the marlin head.

As she walked Stranahan to the door, Christina said, 'I spent some time at the newspaper today.'

'Reading up, I suppose.'

'You've got quite a clip file,' she said. 'I suppose I ought to be scared of you.'

'You don't believe everything you read?'

'Of course not.' Christina Marks opened the door. 'Just tell me, how much of it was true?'

'All of it,' Mick Stranahan said, 'unfortunately.'

Of Stranahan's five ex-wives, only one had chosen to keep his last name: ex-wife number four, Chloe Simpkins Stranahan. Even after she remarried, Chloe hung on to his name as an act of unalloyed spite. Naturally she was listed in the Miami phone book; Stranahan had begged her to please get a nonpublished number, but Chloe had said that would defeat the whole purpose. 'This way, any girl who wants to call up and check on you, I can tell them the truth. That you're a dangerous lunatic. That's what I'll tell them when they call up, Mick—*honey, he was one dangerous lunatic.*'

Christina Marks had gotten all the Stranahan numbers from directory assistance. When she had called Chloe from New York, Chloe assumed it was just one of Mick's girlfriends, and had given a vitriolic and highly embellished account of their eight-month marriage and nine-month divorce. Finally Christina Marks had cut in and explained who she was and what she wanted, and Chloe Simpkins Stranahan had said: 'That'll cost you a grand.'

'Five hundred,' Christina countered.

'Bitch,' Chloe hissed. But when the cashier's cheque arrived the next afternoon by Federal Express, Chloe faithfully picked up the phone and called Christina Marks (collect) in New York and told her where to locate her dangerous lunatic of an ex-husband.

'Give him a disease for me, will you?' Chloe had said and then had hung up.

The hit man known as Chemo was not nearly as resourceful as Christina Marks, but he did know enough to check the telephone book for Stranahans. There were five, and Chemo wrote them all down.

The day after his meeting with Dr Rudy Graveline, Chemo went for a drive. His car was a royal blue 1980 Bonneville, with tinted windows. The tinted windows were essential to conceal Chemo's face, the mere glimpse of which could cause a high-speed pileup at any intersection.

Louis K. Stranahan was the first on Chemo's list. A Miamian would have recognized the address as being in the middle of Liberty City, but Chemo did not. It occurred to him upon entering the neighbourhood that he should have asked Dr Graveline whether the man he was supposed to kill was black or white, because it might have saved some time.

The address was in the James Scott housing project, a bleak and tragic warren where few outsiders of any colour

69

dared to go. Even on a bright winter day, the project gave off a dark and ominous heat. Chemo was oblivious; he saw no danger here, just work. He parked the Bonneville next to a fenced-in basketball court and got out. Almost instantly the kids on the court stopped playing. The basketball hit the rim and bounced lazily out of bounds, but no one ran to pick it up. They were all staring at Chemo. The only sound was the dental-drill rap of Run-DMC from a distant quadrophonic blaster.

'Hello, there,' Chemo said.

The kids from the project glanced at one another, trying to guess how they should play it; this was one of the tallest white motherfuckers they'd ever seen this side of the Interstate. Also, one of the ugliest.

'Game's full,' the biggest kid declared with a forced authority.

'Oh, I don't want to play,' Chemo said.

A look of relief spread among the players, and one of them jogged after the basketball.

'I'm looking for a man named Louis Stranahan.'

'He ain't here.'

'Where is he?'

'Gone.'

Chemo said, 'Does he have a brother named Mick?'

'He's got six brothers,' one of the basketball players volunteered. 'But no Mick.'

'There's a Dick,' said another teenager.

'And a Lawrence.'

Chemo took the list out of his pocket and frowned. Sure enough, Lawrence Stranahan was the second name from the phone book. The address was close by, too.

As Chemo stood there, cranelike, squinting at the piece of paper, the black kids loosened up a little. They started shooting a few hoops, horsing around. The white guy wasn't so scary after all; shit, there were eight of them and one of him.

'Where could I find Louis?' Chemo tried again.

'Raiford,' said two of the kids, simultaneously.

'Raiford,' Chemo repeated. 'That's a prison, isn't it?'

With this, all the teenagers doubled up, slapping fives, howling hysterically at this gangly freak with the fuzzballs on his head.

'Fuck, yeah, it's a prison,' one of them said finally.

Chemo scratched the top two Stranahans off his list. As he opened the door of the Bonneville, the black kid who was dribbling the basketball hollered, 'Hey, big man, you a movie star?'

'No,' Chemo said.

'I swear you are.'

'I swear I'm not.'

'Then how come I saw you in *Halloween III*?'

The kid bent over in a deep wheeze; he thought this was so damn funny. Chemo reached under the car seat and got a .22-calibre pistol, which was fitted with a cheap mail-order suppressor. Without saying a word, he took aim across the roof of the Bonneville and shot the basketball clean out of the kid's hands. The explosion sounded like the world's biggest fart, but the kids from the project didn't think it was funny. They ran like hell.

As Chemo drove away, he decided he had taught the youngsters a valuable lesson: never make fun of a man's complexion.

It was half past noon when Chemo found the third address, a two-storey Mediterranean-style house in Coral Gables. An ill-tempered Rottweiler was chained to the trunk of an olive tree in the front yard, but Chemo ambled past the big dog without incident; the animal merely cocked its head and watched, perhaps not sure if this odd extenuated creature was the same species he'd been trained to attack.

Chloe Simpkins Stranahan was on the phone to her husband's secretary when the doorbell rang.

'Tell him if he's not home by eight, I sell the Dali. Tell him that right now.' Chloe slammed down the phone and stalked to the door. She looked up at Chemo and said, 'How'd you get past the pooch?'

Chemo shrugged. He was wearing black Raybans, which he hoped would lessen the effect of his facial condition. If

71

necessary, he was prepared to explain what had happened; it wouldn't be the first time.

Yet Chloe Simpkins Stranahan didn't mention it. She said, 'You selling something?'

'I'm looking for a man named Mick Stranahan.'

'He's a dangerous lunatic,' Chloe said. 'Come right in.'

Chemo removed the sunglasses and folded them into the top pocket of his shirt. He sat down in the living room, and put a hand on each of his bony kneecaps. At the wet bar Chloe fixed him a cold ginger ale. She acted like she didn't even notice what was wrong with his appearance.

'Who are you?' she asked.

'Collection agent,' Chemo said. Watching Chloe move around the house, he saw that she was a very beautiful woman: auburn hair, long legs, and a good figure. Listening to her, he could tell she was also hard as nails.

'Mick is my ex,' Chloe said. 'I have nothing good to say about him. Nothing.'

'He owe you money, too?'

She chuckled harshly. 'No, I took him for every god-damn dime. Cleaned his clock.' She drummed her ruby fingernails on the side of the ginger ale glass. 'I'm now married to a CPA,' she said. 'Has his own firm.'

'Nice to hear it,' Chemo said.

'Dull as a dog turd, but at least he's no lunatic.'

Chemo shifted in the chair. 'Lunatic, you keep saying that word. What do you mean? Is Mr Stranahan violent? Did he hit you?'

'Mick? Never. Not me,' Chloe said. 'But he did attack a friend of mine. A male-type friend.'

Chemo figured he ought to learn as much as possible about the man he was supposed to kill. He said to Chloe, 'What exactly did Mick do to this male-type friend?'

'It's hard for me to talk about it.' Chloe got up and dumped a jigger of vodka into her ginger ale. 'He was always on the road, Mick was. Never home. No doubt he was screwing around.'

'You know for a fact?'

72

'I'm sure of it.'

'So you got a . . . boyfriend.'

'You're a smart one,' Chloe said mordantly. 'A god-damn rocket scientist, you are. Yes, I got a *boyfriend*. And he loved me, this guy. He treated me like a queen.'

Chemo said, 'So one night Mr Stranahan gets home early from a trip and catches the two of you—'

'In action,' Chloe said. 'Don't get me wrong, I didn't plan it that way. God knows I didn't want him to walk in on us—you gotta know Mick, it's just not a safe situation.'

'Short fuse?'

'No fuse.'

'So then what?'

Chloe sighed. 'I can't believe I'm telling this to some stranger, a bill collector! Unbelievable.' She polished off her drink and got another. This time when she came back from the bar, she sat down on the divan next to Chemo; close enough that he could smell her perfume.

'I'm a talker,' she said with a soft smile. The smile certainly didn't go with the voice.

'And I'm a listener,' Chemo said.

'And I like you.'

'You do?' This broad is creepy, he thought, a real head case.

'I like you,' Chloe went on, 'and I'd like to help you with your problem.'

'Then just tell me,' Chemo said, 'where I can find your ex-husband.'

'How much are you willing to pay?'

'Ah, so that's it.'

'Everything's got a price,' Chloe said, 'especially good information.'

'Unfortunately, Mrs Stranahan, I don't have any money. Money is the reason I'm looking for Mick.'

Chloe crossed her legs, and Chemo noticed a very fine run in one of her nylon stockings; it seemed to go on for ever, all the way up her thigh. Who knew where it ended? Internally he cautioned himself against such distractions. Any moment now, she was going to say

73

something about his Rice Krispie face—Chemo knew it.

'You're not a bill collector,' Chloe said sharply, 'so cut the shit.'

'All right,' Chemo said. Feverishly he set his limited imagination to work, trying to come up with another story.

'I don't care what you are.'

'You don't?'

'Nope. Long as you're not a friend of Mick's.'

Chemo said, 'I'm not a friend.'

'Then I'll help,' Chloe said, 'maybe.'

'What about the money?' Chemo said. 'The most I can do is a hundred dollars, maybe one-fifty.'

'Fine.'

'Fine?' Christ, he couldn't believe this woman. A hundred bucks.

She said, 'But before I agree to help, you ought to know everything. It would be irresponsible for me not to warn you what you're up against.'

'I can handle myself,' Chemo said with a cold smile. Even that—his fractured, cadaverous leer—didn't seem to bother Chloe Simpkins Stranahan.

She said, 'So you really don't want to know?'

'Go ahead, then, shoot. What did Stranahan do to your precious boyfriend?'

'He put Krazy Glue on his balls.'

'What?'

'A whole tube,' Chloe said. 'He glued the man to the hood of his car. By the balls. Stark naked, glued to the hood of an Eldorado convertible.'

'Jesus H. Christ,' Chemo said.

'Ever seen the hood ornament on a Cadillac?'

Chemo nodded.

'Think about it,' Chloe said grimly.

'And glue burns like hell,' Chemo remarked.

'Indeed it does.'

'So Mick came home, caught you two in the sack—'

'Right here on the divan.'

'Wherever,' Chemo said. 'Anyway, he hauls Mr Studhunk outside and glues him buck naked to the hood of his Caddy.'

'By the testicles.'

'Then what?'

'That's it,' Chloe said. 'Mick packed his suitcase and left. The paramedics came. What more is there?'

'Your male friend—is this the same guy you're married to?'

'No, it isn't,' Chloe said. 'My male-type friend never recovered from his encounter with Mick Stranahan. I mean *never recovered*. You understand what I'm saying?'

'I think so.'

'The doctors insisted there was nothing wrong, medically speaking. I mean, the glue peeled off with acetone, and in a few days the skin healed just like new. But, still, the man was never the same.'

Chemo said, 'It's a major trauma, Mrs Stranahan. It probably takes some time—'

He flinched as Chloe threw her cocktail glass against the wall. 'Time?' she said. 'I gave him plenty of time, mister. And I tried every trick I knew, but he was a dead man after that night with Mick. It was like trying to screw linguini.'

Chemo could imagine the hellish bedroom scene. He felt himself shrivel, just thinking about it.

'I loved that man,' Chloe went on. 'At least, I was getting there. And Mick ruined everything. He couldn't just beat the shit out of him, like other jealous husbands. No, he had to torture the guy.'

In a way, Chemo admired Stranahan's style. Murder is the way Chemo himself would have handled the situation: a bullet in the base of the skull. For both of them.

Chloe Simpkins Stranahan was up and pacing now, arms folded across her chest, heels clicking on the Spanish tiles. 'So you see,' she said, 'this is why I hate my ex-husband so much.'

There had to be more, but who cared? Chemo said, 'You want to get even?'

'Boy, are you a swifty. Yes, I want to get even.'

'Then why should I pay you anything? You should pay *me*.'

Chloe had to smile. 'Good point.' She bent over and picked a chunk of broken glass out of the deep-pile carpet. She looked up at Chemo and asked, 'Who are you, anyway?'

'Doesn't matter, Mrs Stranahan. The question is, how bad do you want revenge on your ex-husband?'

'I guess that is the question,' Chloe said thoughtfully. 'How about another ginger ale?'

7

Of the four plastic surgeons who had worked with Dr Rudy Graveline at the Durkos Center, only one had remained in Miami after the clinic closed. His name was George Ginger, and Stranahan found him on a tennis court at Turnberry Isle in the middle of a weekday afternoon. Mixed doubles, naturally.

Stranahan watched the pudgy little man wheeze back and forth behind the baseline, and marvelled at the atrociousness of his hairpiece. It was one of those synthetic jobs, the kind you're supposed to be able to wear in the shower. In Dr George Ginger's case, the thing on his head looked a lot like a fresh road kill.

Each point in the tennis game became its own little comedy, and Stranahan wondered if this stop was a waste of time, an unconscious stall on his part. By now he knew exactly where to locate Rudy Graveline; the problem was, he didn't know what to ask him that would produce the truth. It was a long way from Vicky Barletta to Tony the Eel, and Stranahan still hadn't found the thread, if there was one. One way or another, Dr Graveline was central to the mystery, and Stranahan didn't want to spook him. For now, he wanted him safe and contented at Whispering Palms.

Stranahan strolled into the dead lane of the tennis court and said, 'Dr Ginger?'

'Yo!' said the doctor, huffing.

Stranahan knew about guys who said yo.

'We need to talk.'

'Do we now?' said Dr Ginger, missing an easy backhand. His doubles partner, a lanky, overtanned woman, shot Stranahan a dirty look.

'Just take a minute,' Stranahan said.

Dr Ginger picked up two of the tennis balls. 'Sorry, but I'm on serve.'

'No, you're not,' Stranahan said. 'And besides, that was the set.' He'd been following the match from a gazebo two courts over.

As Dr Ginger intently bounced one of the balls between his feet, the other players picked up their monogrammed club towels and calfskin racket covers and ambled off the court.

Solemnly George Ginger said, 'The tall fellow was my lawyer.'

'Every doctor should have a lawyer,' said Mick Stranahan. 'Especially surgeons.'

Ginger jammed the tennis balls into the pockets of his damp white shorts. 'What's this all about?'

'Rudy Graveline.'

'I've heard of him.'

This was going to be fun, Stranahan thought. He loved it when they played cool.

'You worked for him at the Durkos Center,' Stranahan said to George Ginger. 'Why don't you be a nice fellow and tell me about it?'

George Ginger motioned Stranahan to follow. He picked a quiet patio table with an umbrella, not far from the pro shop.

'Who are you with?' the doctor enquired in a low voice.

'The board,' Stranahan said. Any board would do; Dr Ginger wouldn't press it.

After wiping his forehead for the umpteenth time, the doctor said, 'There were four of us—Kelly, Greer,

Shulman, and me. Graveline was the managing partner.'

'Business was good?'

'It was getting there.'

'Then why did he close the place?'

'I'm still not certain,' George Ginger said.

'But you heard rumours.'

'Yes, we heard there was a problem with a patient. The sort of problem that might bring in the state.'

'One of Rudy's patients?'

George Ginger nodded. 'A young woman is what we heard.'

'Her name?'

'I don't know.' The doctor was quite a lousy liar.

'How bad a problem?' Stranahan went on.

'I don't know that, either. We assumed it was a major fuck-up, or else why would Graveline pull out so fast?'

'Didn't any of you guys bother to ask?'

'Hell, no. I've been to court before, buddy, and it's no damn fun. None of us wanted to get dragged down that road. Anyway, we show up for work one day and the place is empty. Later we get a certified cheque from Rudy with a note saying he's sorry for the inconvenience, but good luck with our careers. Before you know it, he's back in business at Bal Harbour—of all places—with a frigging assembly-line operation. A dozen boob jobs a day.'

Stranahan said, 'Why didn't you call him?'

'What for? Old times' sake?'

'That certified cheque, it must've been a good one.'

'It was,' Dr Ginger conceded, 'very generous.'

Stranahan picked up the doctor's graphite tennis racket and plucked idly at the strings. George Ginger eyed him worriedly. 'Do you remember the day the police came?' Stranahan asked. 'The day a young female patient disappeared from a bus bench in front of the clinic?'

'I was off that day.'

'That's not what I asked.' Stranahan studied him through the grid of the racket strings.

'I remember hearing about it,' George Ginger said lamely.

'That happened right before Dr Graveline split, didn't it?'

'I think so, yes.'

Stranahan said, 'You consider yourself a bright man, Dr Ginger? Don't look so insulted, it's a serious question.' He put the tennis racket down on the patio table.

'I consider myself to be intelligent, yes.'

'Well, then, didn't you wonder about the timing? A girl gets snatched from in front of your office, and a few weeks later the boss closes up shop. Could that be the fuck-up you guys heard about? What do you think?'

Sourly, George Ginger said, 'I can't imagine a connection.' He picked up his tennis racket and, with a touch of pique, zipped it into its carry case.

Stranahan stood up. 'Well, the important thing is, you still got your medical licence. Now, where can I find the rest of the stooges?'

Dr Ginger wrapped the towel around his neck, a real jock gesture. 'Kelly moved to Michigan. Shulman's up in Atlanta, working for some HMO. Dr Greer is deceased, unfortunately.'

'Do tell.'

'Don't you guys have it in your files? I mean, when a doctor dies?'

'Not in every case,' Stranahan bluffed.

George Ginger said, 'It happened maybe six months after Durkos closed. A hunting accident up around Ocala.'

'Who else was there?'

'I really don't know,' the doctor said with an insipid shrug. 'I'm afraid I'm not clear about all the details.'

'Why,' said Mick Stranahan, 'am I not surprised?'

The Rudy Graveline system was brilliant in its simplicity: sting, persuade, operate, then flatter.

On the wall of each waiting room at Whispering Palms hung a creed: VANITY IS BEAUTIFUL. Similar maxims were posted in the hallways and examining rooms. WHAT'S WRONG WITH PERFECTION? was one of Rudy's favourites. Another: TO IMPROVE ONE'S SELF, IMPROVE ONE'S FACE.

This one was framed in the spa, where post-op patients relaxed in the crucial days following their plastic surgery, when they didn't want to go out in public. Rudy had shrewdly recognized that an after-surgery spa would not only be a tremendous money-maker, it would also provide important positive feedback during recovery. Everyone there had fresh scars and bruises, so no patient was in a position to criticize another's results.

As best as he could, Reynaldo Flemm made mental notes of Whispering Palms during his tour. He was posing as a male exotic dancer who needed a blemish removed from his right buttock. For the purpose of disguise, Flemm had dyed his hair brown and greased it straight back; that was all he could bear to do to alter his appearance. Secretly, he loved it when people stared because they recognized him from television.

As it happened, the nurse who greeted him at Whispering Palms apparently never watched *In Your Face*. She treated Flemm as any other prospective patient. After a quick tour of the facilities, she led him to a consultation room, turned off the lights and showed him a videotape about the wonders of cosmetic surgery. Afterwards she turned the lights back on and asked if he had any questions.

'How much will it cost?' Reynaldo Flemm said.

'That depends on the size of the mole.'

'Oh, it's a big mole,' Reynaldo said. 'Like an olive.' He held up his thumb and forefinger to show her the size of his fictional growth.

The nurse said, 'May I see it?'

'No!'

'Surely you're not shy,' she said. 'Not in your line of work.'

'I'll show it to the doctor,' Flemm said. 'No one else.'

'Very well, I'll arrange for an appointment.'

'With Dr Graveline, please.'

The nurse smiled. 'Really, Mr LeTigre.'

Flemm had come up with the name Johnny LeTigre all by himself. It seemed perfect for a male go-go dancer.

'Dr Graveline doesn't do moles,' the nurse said in a chilly tone. 'One of our other excellent surgeons can take care of it quite easily.'

'It's Dr Graveline or nobody,' Flemm said firmly. 'This is my dancing career, my life we're talking about.'

'I'm sorry, but Dr Graveline is not available.'

'For ten grand I bet he is.'

The nurse tried not to seem surprised. 'I'll be right back,' she said lightly.

When he was alone, Reynaldo Flemm checked himself in the mirror to see how the disguise was holding up. All he needed was a date and time to see the doctor, then he'd come back with Willie and a camera for the showdown—not out on the street, but inside the clinic. And if Graveline ordered them out, Reynaldo and Willie would be sure to leave through the spa exit, tape rolling. It would be dynamite stuff; even Christina would have to admit it.

The nurse returned and said, 'Come with me, Mr LeTigre.'

'Where to?'

'Dr Graveline has agreed to see you.'

'Now?' Flemm squeaked.

'He only has a few minutes.'

A cold prickle of panic accompanied Reynaldo Flemm as he followed the nurse down a long pale-blue hallway. About to meet the target of his investigation and here he was, defenceless—no camera, no tape, no notebooks. He could blow the whole story if he wasn't careful. The only thing in Flemm's favour was the fact that he also had no script. He wouldn't know what to ask even if the opportunity presented itself.

The nurse abandoned him in a spacious office with a grand view of north Biscayne Bay, foamy with whitecaps. Reynaldo Flemm barely had time to snoop the joint over before Dr Rudy Graveline came in and introduced himself. Reynaldo took a good close look, in case he might later have to point him out to Willie from the TV van: lean build, medium height, sandy brown hair.

Had a golfer's tan but not much muscle. Overall, not a bad-looking guy.

Rudy Graveline didn't waste any time. 'Let's see your little problem, Mr LeTigre.'

'Hold on a minute.'

'It's only a mole.'

'To you, maybe,' Reynaldo Flemm said. 'Before we go any further, I'd like to ask you some questions.' He paused, then: 'Questions about your background.'

Dr Graveline settled in behind a gleaming onyx desk and folded his hands. 'Fire away,' he said amiably.

'What medical school did you go to?'

'Harvard,' Rudy replied.

Reynaldo nodded approvingly. He asked, 'How long have you been in practice?'

'Sixteen years,' Dr Graveline said.

'Ah,' said Reynaldo Flemm. He couldn't think of much else to ask, which was fine with Rudy. Sometimes patients wanted to know how high the doctor had placed in his med school class (dead last), or whether he was certified by a national board of plastic and reconstructive surgeons (he was not). In truth, Rudy had barely squeaked through a residency in radiology and had never been trained in plastic surgery. Still, no law prevented him from declaring it to be his speciality; that was the beauty of the medical profession—once you got a degree, you could try whatever you damn well pleased, from brain surgery to gynaecology. Hospitals might do some checking, but never the patients. And failing at one or more specialities (as Rudy had), you could always leave town and try something else.

Still stalling, Reynaldo Flemm said, 'What's involved in an operation like this?'

'First we numb the area with a mild anaesthetic, then we use a small knife to remove the mole. If you need a couple sutures afterward, we do that, too.'

'What about a scar?'

'No scar, I guarantee it,' said Dr Graveline.

'For ten grand, you're damn right.'

The doctor said, 'I didn't realize male strippers made that much money.'

'They don't. It's inheritance.'

If Flemm had been paying attention, he would have noticed a hungry flicker in Dr Graveline's expression.

'Mr LeTigre, you won't mind some friendly professional advice?'

'Of course not.'

'Your nose,' Rudy ventured. 'I mean, as long as you're going to all the trouble of surgery.'

'What the hell is wrong with my nose?'

'It's about two sizes too large for your face. And, to be honest, your tummy could probably come down an inch or three. I can do a liposuction after we excise the mole.'

Reynaldo Flemm said, 'Are you kidding? There's nothing wrong with me.'

'Please don't be embarrassed,' Rudy said. 'This is my speciality. I just thought someone in a job like yours would want to look their very best.'

Flemm was getting furious. 'I *do* look my very best!'

Dr Graveline put his elbows on the desk and leaned forward. Gently he said, 'With all respect, Mr LeTigre, we seldom choose to see ourselves the way others do. It's human nature.'

'I've heard enough,' Reynaldo Flemm snapped.

'If it's the money, look, I'll do the mole and the fat suction as a package. Toss in the rhinoplasty for nothing, OK?'

Flemm said, 'I don't need a goddamn rhinoplasty.'

'Please,' said Dr Graveline, 'go home and think about it. Take a good critical look at yourself in the mirror.'

'Fuck you,' said Reynaldo Flemm, and stormed out of the office.

'It's no sin to have a big honker,' Rudy Graveline called after him. 'Nobody's *born* perfect!'

One hour later, as Rudy was fitting a Mentor Model 7000 Gel-Filled Mammary Prosthesis into the left breast of the future Miss Ecuador, he was summoned from the operating suite to take an urgent phone call from New York.

The semi-hysterical voice on the other end belonged to Maggie Gonzalez.

'Take some deep breaths,' Rudy advised.

'No, you listen. I got a message on my machine,' Maggie said. 'The phone machine at my house.'

'Who was it from?'

'Stranahan. That investigator.'

'Really?' Dr Graveline worked hard at staying calm; he took pride in his composure. He asked, 'What was the message, Maggie?'

'Three words: "*It won't work.*" '

Dr Graveline repeated the message out loud. Maggie sounded like she was bouncing off the walls.

'Don't come back here for a while,' Rudy said. 'I'll wire you some more money.' He couldn't think clearly with Maggie hyperventilating into the phone, and he did need to think. *It won't work.* Damn, he didn't like the sound of that. How much did Stranahan know? Was it a bluff? Rudy Graveline wondered if he should call Chemo and tell him to speed things up.

'What are we going to do?' Maggie demanded.

'It's being done,' the doctor said.

'Good.' Maggie didn't ask specifically what was being done. Specifically, she didn't want to know.

After lunch, Mick Stranahan stopped by the VA hospital, but for the second day in a row the nurses told him that Timmy Gavigan was asleep. They said it had been another poor night, that the new medicine was still giving him fevers.

Stranahan was eager to hear what his friend remembered about Dr Rudy Graveline. Like most good cops, Timmy never forgot an interview; and like most cops, Timmy was the only one who could read his own handwriting. The Barletta file was full of Gavigan-type scribbles.

After leaving the VA, Stranahan drove back to the

marina at Key Biscayne. On the skiff out to Stiltsville, he mentally catalogued everything he knew so far.

Vicky Barletta had disappeared, and was probably dead.

Her doctor had closed up shop a few weeks later and bought out his four partners for fifty thousand dollars apiece.

One of those partners, Dr Kenneth Greer, had never cashed his cheque—this according to microfiche records at the bank.

Approximately seven months after Rudy Graveline closed the Durkos Center, Dr Kenneth Greer was shot to death while hunting deer in the Ocala National Forest. The sheriff's office had ruled it an accident.

The hunter who had somehow mistaken Kenneth Greer for a white-tail buck had given his name as T. B. Luckner of 1333 Carter Boulevard in Decatur, Georgia. If the sheriff in Ocala had troubled himself to check, he would have found that there was no such person and no such address.

The nurse who participated in Victoria Barletta's surgery had recently gone to New York to sell her story to a TV producer.

Shortly afterwards, a paid killer named Tony the Eel showed up to murder Mick Stranahan. Tony, with a brand-new face.

Then the TV producer arrived in Miami to take Stranahan's picture for a prime-time special.

All traced to a four-year-old kidnapping that Mick Stranahan had never solved.

As he steered the boat into the Biscayne Channel, angling out of the messy following chop, he gunned the outboard and made a beeline for his stilt house. The tide was up, making it safe to cross the flats.

On the way, he thought about Rudy Graveline.

Suppose the doctor had killed Vicky. Stranahan checked himself—make that Victoria, not Vicky. Better yet, just plain Barletta. No sense personalizing.

But suppose the doctor had killed her, and suppose Greer knew, or found out. Greer was the only one who didn't cash the buyout cheque—maybe he was holding out for more money, or maybe he was ready to blab to the authorities.

Either way, Dr Graveline would have had plenty of motive to silence him.

And if, for some reason, Dr Graveline had been led to believe that Mick Stranahan posed a similar threat, what would stop him from killing again?

Stranahan couldn't help but marvel at the possibility. Considering all the cons and ex-cons who'd love to see him dead—hoods, dopers, scammers, bikers, and stickup artists—it was ironic that the most likely suspect was some rich quack he'd never even met.

The more Stranahan learned about the case, and the more he thought about what he'd learned, the lousier he felt.

His spirits improved somewhat when he spotted his model friend Tina stretched out on the sun deck of the stilt house. He was especially pleased to notice that she was alone.

8

Stranahan caught four small snappers and fried them up for supper.

'Richie left me,' Tina was explaining. 'I mean, he put me out on your house and left. Can you believe that?'

Stranahan pretended to be listening as he foraged in the refrigerator. 'You want lemon or garlic salt?'

'Both,' Tina said. 'We had a fight and he ordered me to get off the boat. Then he drove away.'

She wore a baggy Jimmy Buffett T-shirt over a cranberry bikini bottom. Her wheat-coloured hair was pulled back in a ponytail, and a charm glinted at her throat; a tiny gold porpoise, it looked like.

'Richie deals a little coke,' Tina went on. 'That's what we were fighting about. Well, part of it.'

Stranahan said, 'Keep an eye on the biscuits so they don't burn.'

'Sure. Anyway, know what else we were fighting about? This is so dumb you won't believe it.'

Stranahan was dicing a pepper on the kitchen countertop. He was barefoot, wearing cutoff jeans and a khaki short-sleeved shirt, open to the chest. His hair was still damp from the shower. Overall, he felt much better about his situation.

Tina said, 'I got this modelling job and Richie, he went crazy. All because I had to do some, you know, nudes. Just beach stuff, nobody out there but me and the photog. Richie says no way, you can't do it. And I said, you can't tell me what to do. Then—then!—he calls me a slut, and I say that's pretty rich coming from a two-bit doper. So then he slugs me in the stomach and tells me to get my butt out of the boat.' Tina paused for a sigh. 'Your house was closest.'

'You can stay for the night,' Stranahan said, sounding downright fatherly.

'What if Richie comes back?'

'Then we teach him some manners.'

Tina said, 'He's still pissed about the last time, when you dragged him through the water.'

'The biscuits,' Stranahan reminded her.

'Oh, yeah, sorry.' Tina pulled the hot tray out of the oven.

For at least thirteen minutes she didn't say anything, because the snapper was excellent and she was hungry. Stranahan found a bottle of white wine and poured two glasses. It was then Tina smiled and said, 'Got any candles?'

Stranahan played along, even though darkness still was an hour away. He lighted two stubby hurricane candles and set them on the oilskin tablecloth.

'This is really nice,' Tina said.

'Yes, it is.'

'I haven't found a single bone,' she said, chewing intently.

'Good.'

'Are you married, Mick?'

'Divorced,' he replied. 'Five times.'

'Wow.'

'My fault, every one,' he added. To some degree, he believed it. Each time the same thing had happened: he'd awakened one morning and felt nothing; not guilt or jealousy or anger, but an implacable numbness, which was worse. Like his blood had turned to novocaine overnight. He'd stared at the woman in his bed and become incredulous at the notion that this was a spouse, that he had married this person. He'd felt trapped and done a poor job of concealing it. By the fifth go-round, divorce had become an eerie out-of-body experience, except for the part with the lawyers.

'Were you fooling around a lot, or what?' Tina asked.

'It wasn't that,' Stranahan said.

'Then what? You're a nice-looking guy, I don't know why a girl would cut and run.'

Stranahan poured more wine for both of them.

'I wasn't much fun to be around.'

'Oh, I disagree,' Tina said with a perkiness that startled him.

Her eyes wandered up to the big mount on the living room wall. 'What happened to Mr Swordfish?'

'That's a marlin,' Stranahan said. 'He fell off the wall and broke his beak.'

'The tape looks pretty tacky, Mick.'

'Yeah, I know.'

After dinner they went out on the deck to watch the sun go down behind Coconut Grove. Stranahan tied a size 12 hook on his fishing line and baited it with a lint-sized shred of frozen shrimp. In fifteen minutes he caught five lively pinfish, which he dropped in a plastic bait bucket. Entranced, Tina sat cross-legged on the deck and watched the little fish swim frenetic circles inside the container.

Stranahan stowed the rod in the stilt house, came out, and picked up the bucket. 'I'll be right back.'

'Where you off to?'

'Downstairs, by the boat.'

'Can I come?'

He shrugged. 'You might not like it.'

'Like what?' Tina asked and followed him tentatively down the wooden stairs toward the water.

Liza hovered formidably in the usual place. Stranahan pointed at the huge barracuda and said, 'See there?'

'Wow, is that a shark?'

'No.'

He reached into the bucket and grabbed one of the pinfish, carefully folding the dorsal so it wouldn't prick his fingers.

Tina said, 'Now I get it.'

'She's like a pet,' Stranahan said. He tossed the pinfish into the water, and the barracuda devoured it in a silent mercury flash, all fangs. When the turbulence subsided, they saw that the big fish had returned to its station; it hung there as if it had never moved.

Impassively Stranahan tossed another pinfish and the barracuda repeated the kill.

Tina stood so close that Stranahan could feel her warm breath on his bare arm. 'Do they eat people?' she asked.

He could have hugged her right then.

'No,' he said, 'they don't eat people.'

'Good!'

'They do strike at shiny objects,' he said, 'so don't wear a bracelet if you're diving.'

'Seriously?'

'It's been known to happen.'

This time he scooped up two pinfish and lobbed them into the water simultaneously; the barracuda got them both in one fierce swipe.

'I call her Liza,' Stranahan said. 'Liza with a z.'

Tina nodded as if she thought it was a perfectly cute name. She asked if she could try a toss.

'You bet.' Stranahan got the last pinfish from the bucket and placed it carefully in the palm of her hand. 'Just throw it anywhere,' he said.

Tina leaned forward and called out, 'Here, Liza! Here you go!'

The little fish landed with a soft splash and spun a dizzy figure eight under the dock. The barracuda didn't move.

Stranahan smiled. In slow motion the addled pinfish corkscrewed its way to the bottom, taking refuge inside an old horse conch.

'What'd I do wrong?' Tina wondered.

'Not a thing,' Stranahan said. 'She wasn't hungry any more, that's all.'

'Maybe it's just me.'

'Maybe it is,' Stranahan said.

He took her by the hand and led her upstairs. He turned on the lights in the house and vented the shutters on both sides to catch the cool night breeze. On the roof, the windmill creaked as it picked up speed.

Tina made a place for herself on a faded lumpy sofa. She said, 'I always wondered what it's like out here in the dark.'

'Not much to do, I'm afraid.'

'No TV?'

'No TV,' Stranahan said.

'You want to make love?'

'There's an idea.'

'You already saw me naked.'

'I haven't forgotten,' Stranahan said. 'The thing is—'

'Don't worry about Richie. Anyway, this is just for fun. We'll keep it casual, OK?'

'I don't do anything casually,' Stranahan said. 'This is my problem.' He was constantly falling in love; how else would you explain five marriages, all to cocktail waitresses?

Tina peeled off the tropical T-shirt and draped it across a barstool. Rockette-style, she kicked her way out of her bikini bottoms and left them in a rumple on the floor.

'How about these tan lines, huh?'

'What tan lines?' he asked.

'Exactly.' Tina pulled the rubber band out of her ponytail and shook her hair free. Then she got back on the sofa and said, 'Watch this.' She stretched out and struck a smoky-eyed modelling pose—a half-turn up on one elbow, legs scissored, one arm shading her nipples.

'That looks great,' Stranahan said, amused but also uneasy.

'It's tough work on a beach,' Tina remarked. 'Sand sticks to places you wouldn't believe. I did a professional job, though.'

'I'm sure.'

'Thanks to you, I got my confidence back. About my boobs, I mean.' She glanced down at herself appraisingly.

'Confidence is everything in the modelling business,' she said. 'Somebody tells you that your ass is sagging or your tits don't match up, it's like an emotional disaster. I was worried sick until you measured them with that carpenter's thing.'

'Glad I could help,' Stranahan said, trying to think of something, anything, more romantic.

She said, 'Anyone ever tell you that you've got Nick Nolte's nose?'

'That's all?' Stranahan said. Nick Nolte was a new one.

'Now the eyes,' Tina said, 'your eyes are more like Sting's. I met him one time at the Strand.'

'Thank you,' Stranahan said. He didn't know who the hell she was talking about. Maybe one of those pro wrestlers from cable television.

Holding her pose, Tina motioned him to join her on the old sofa. When he did, she took his hands, placed them on her staunch new breasts, and held them there. Stranahan assumed a compliment was in order.

'They're perfect,' he said, squeezing politely.

Urgently Tina arched her back and rolled over, Stranahan hanging on like a rock climber.

'While we're on the subject,' he said, 'could I get the name of your surgeon?'

*

Even before the electrolysis accident, Chemo had led a difficult life. His parents had belonged to a religious sect that believed in bigamy, vegetarianism, UFOs, and not paying federal income taxes; his mother, father, and three of their respective spouses were killed by the FBI during a bloody ten-day siege at a post office outside Grand Forks, North Dakota. Chemo, who was only six at the time, went to live with an aunt and uncle in the Amish country of western Pennsylvania. It was a rigorous and demanding period, especially since Chemo's aunt and uncle were not actually Amish themselves, but fair-weather Presbyterians fleeing a mail-fraud indictment out of Bergen County, New Jersey.

Using their hard-won embezzlements, the couple had purchased a modest farm and somehow managed to infiltrate the hermetic social structure of an Amish township. At first it was just another scam, a temporary cover until the heat was off. As the years passed, though, Chemo's aunt and uncle got authentically converted. They grew to love the simple pastoral ways and hearty fellowship of the farm folk; Chemo was devastated by their transformation. Growing up, he had come to resent the family's ruse, and consequently the Amish in general. The plain baggy clothes and strict table manners were bad enough, but it was the facial hair that drove him to fury. Amish men do not shave their chins, and Chemo's uncle insisted that, once attaining puberty, he adhere to custom. Since religious arguments held no sway with Chemo, it was the practical view that his uncle propounded: all fugitives need a disguise, and a good beard was hard to beat.

Chemo sullenly acceded, until the day of his twenty-first birthday when he got in his uncle's pick-up truck, drove down to the local branch of the Chemical Bank, threatened a teller with a pitchfork (the Amish own no pistols), and strolled off with seven thousand dollars and change. The first thing he bought was a Bic disposable safety razor.

The *Philadelphia Inquirer* reported that it was the only bank robbery by an Amish in the entire history of the commonwealth. Chemo himself was never arrested for the crime, but his aunt and uncle were unmasked, extradited back to New Jersey, tried and convicted of mail fraud, then shipped off to a country-club prison in north Florida. Their wheat farm was seized by the US government and sold at auction.

Once Chemo was free of the Amish, the foremost challenge of adulthood was avoiding manual labour, to which he had a chronic aversion. Crime seemed to be the most efficient way of making money without working up a sweat, so Chemo gave it a try. Unfortunately, nature had dealt him a cruel disadvantage: while six foot nine was the perfect height for an NBA forward, for a burglar it was disastrous. Chemo got stuck in the very first window he ever jimmied; he could break, but he could not enter.

Four months in a county jail passed too slowly. He thought often of his aunt and uncle, and upbraided himself for not taking advantage of their vast expertise. They could have taught him many secrets about white-collar crime, yet in his rebellious insolence he had never bothered to ask. Now it was too late—their most recent postcard from the Eglin prison camp had concluded with a religious limerick and the drawing of a happy face. Chemo knew they were lost for ever.

After finishing his stretch for the aborted burglary, he moved to a small town outside of Scranton and went to work for the city parks and recreation department. Before long, he parlayed a phoney but impressive resumé into the post of assistant city manager, a job that entitled him to a secretary and a municipal car. While the salary was only twenty thousand dollars a year, the secondary income derived from bribes and kickbacks was substantial. Chemo prospered as a shakedown artist, and the town prospered, too. He was delighted to discover how often the mutual interests of private enterprise and government seemed to intersect.

The high point of Chemo's municipal career was his savvy trashing of local zoning laws to allow a Mafia-owned-and-operated dog food plant to be built in the suburbs.

Three hundred new jobs were created, and there was talk of running Chemo for mayor.

He greatly liked the idea and immediately began gouging illegal political contributions out of city contractors. Soon a campaign poster was designed, but Chemo recoiled when he saw the finished product: the four-foot photographic blowup of his face magnified the two ingrown hair follicles on the tip of his otherwise normal nose; the blemishes looked, in Chemo's own distraught simile, 'like two ticks fucking'. He ordered the campaign posters shredded, scheduled a second photo session, and drove straight to Scranton for the ill-fated electrolysis treatment.

The grisly mishap and subsequent murder of the offending doctor put an end to Chemo's political career. He swore off public service for ever.

They rented an Aquasport and docked it at Sunday's-on-the-Bay. They chose a table under the awning, near the water. Chemo ordered a ginger ale and Chloe Simpkins Stranahan got a vodka tonic, double.

'We'll wait till dusk,' Chemo said.

'Fine by me.' Chloe slurped her drink like a parched coyote. She was wearing a ridiculous white sailor's suit from Lord and Taylor's; she even had the cap. It was not ideal boatwear.

'I used to work in this joint,' Chloe said, as if to illustrate how far she'd come.

Chemo said, 'This is where you met Mick?'

'Unfortunately.'

The bar was packed for ladies' night. In addition to the standard assembly of slick Latin studs in lizard shoes, there were a dozen blond, husky mates off the charter boats. In contrast to the disco Dannies, the mates wore T-shirts and sandals and deep Gulf Stream tans, and they drank mostly beer. The competition for feminine attention was fierce, but Chemo planned to be long gone before any fights broke out. Besides, he didn't like sitting out in the open, where people could stare.

'Have you got your plan?' Chloe asked.

'The less you know, the better.'

'Oh, pardon me,' she said caustically. 'Pardon me, Mister James Fucking Bond.'

He blinked neutrally. A young pelican was preening itself on a nearby dock piling, and Chemo found this infinitely more fascinating than watching Chloe Simpkins Stranahan in a Shirley Temple sailor cap, sucking down vodkas. It offended him that someone so beautiful could be so repellent and obnoxious; it seemed damned unfair.

On the other hand, she had yet to make the first wisecrack about his face, so maybe she had one redeeming quality.

'This isn't going to get too heavy?' she said.

'Define heavy.'

Chloe stirred her drink pensively. 'Maybe you could just put a good scare in him.'

'Bet on it,' Chemo said.

'But you won't get too tough, right?'

'What is this, all of a sudden you're worried about him?'

'You can hate someone's guts and still worry about him.'

'Jesus H. Christ.'

Chloe said, 'Chill out, OK? I'm not backing down.'

Chemo toyed with one of the infrequent black wisps attached to his scalp. He said: 'Where does your husband think you are?'

'Shopping,' Chloe replied.

'Alone?'

'Sure.'

Chemo licked his lips and scanned the room. 'You see anybody you know?'

Chloe looked around and said, 'No. Why do you ask?'

'Just making sure. I don't want any surprises; neither do you.'

Chemo paid the tab, helped Chloe into the bow of the Aquasport and cast off the ropes. He checked his wristwatch: 5:15. Give it maybe an hour before nightfall.

He handed Chloe a plastic map of Biscayne Bay with the pertinent channel markers circled in red ink. 'Keep that handy,' he shouted over the engine, ''case I get lost.'

She tapped the map with one of her stiletto fingernails. 'You can't miss the goddamn things, they're sticking three storeys out of the water.'

Fifteen minutes later, they were drifting through a Stiltsville channel with the boat's engine off. Chloe Simpkins Stranahan was complaining about her hair getting salty, while Chemo untangled the anchor ropes. The anchor was a big rusty clunker with a bent tongue. He hauled it out of the Aquasport's forward hatch and laid it on the deck.

Then he took some binoculars from a canvas duffel and began scouting the stilt houses. 'Which one is it?' he asked.

'I told you, it's got a windmill.'

'I'm looking at three houses with windmills, so which is it? I'd like to get the anchor out before we float to frigging Nassau.'

Chloe huffed and took the binoculars. After a few moments she said, 'Well, they all look alike.'

'No shit.'

She admitted she had never been on her ex-husband's house before. 'But I've been by there in a boat.'

Chemo said, 'How do you know it was his?'

'Because I saw him. He was outside, fishing.'

'How long ago was this?'

'Three, maybe four months. What's the difference?'

Chemo said, 'Did Mick know it was you in the boat?'

'Sure he did, he dropped his damn pants.' Chloe handed Chemo the binoculars and pointed. 'That's the one, over there.'

'You sure?'

'Yes, Captain Ahab, I am.'

Chemo studied the stilt house through the field glasses. The windmill was turning and a skiff was tied up under the water tanks, but no one was outside.

'So now what?' Chloe asked.

'I'm thinking.'

'Know what I wish you'd do? I wish you'd do to him what he did to my male friend. Krazy Glue the bastard.'

'That would settle things, huh?'

Chloe's tone became grave. 'Mick Stranahan destroyed a man without killing him. Can you think of anything worse?'

'Well,' Chemo said, reaching for the duffel, 'I didn't bring any glue. All I brought was this.' He took out the .22 pistol and screwed on the silencer.

Chloe made a gulping noise and grabbed the bow rail for support. So much for poise, Chemo thought.

'Don't worry, Mrs Stranahan, this is my just-in-case.' He laid the pistol on top of the boat's console. 'All I really need is a little friction.' Smiling, he held up a book of matches from Sunday's bar.

'You're going to burn the house down? That's great!' Chloe's eyes shone with relief. 'Burning the house, that'll freak him out.'

'Big-time,' Chemo agreed.

'Just what that dangerous lunatic deserves.'

'Right.'

Chloe looked at him mischievously. 'You promised to tell me who you really are.'

'No, I didn't.'

'At least tell me why you're doing this.'

'I'm being paid,' Chemo said.

'By who?'

'Nobody you know.'

'Another ex-wife, I'll bet.'

'What did I say?'

'Oh, all right.' Chloe stood up and peered over the gunwale at the slick green water. Chemo figured she was checking out her own reflection.

'Did you bring anything to drink?'

'No,' Chemo replied. 'No drinks.'

She folded her arms to show how peeved she was. 'You mean, I've got to stay out here till dark with nothing to drink.'

'Longer than that,' Chemo said. 'Midnight.'

'But Mick'll be asleep by then.'

'That's the idea, Mrs Stranahan.'

'But how will he know to get out of the house?'

Chemo laughed gruffly. 'Now who's the rocket scientist?'

Chloe's expression darkened. She pursed her lips and said, 'Wait a minute. I don't want you to kill him.'

'Who asked you?'

A change was taking place in Chloe's attitude, the way she regarded Chemo. It was as if she was seeing the man for the first time, and she was staring, which Chemo did not appreciate. Her and her tweezered eyebrows.

'You're a killer,' she said, reproachfully.

Chemo blinked amphibiously and plucked at one of the skin tags on his cheek. His eyes were round and wet and distant.

'You're a killer,' Chloe repeated, 'and you tricked me.'

Chemo said, 'You hate him so much, what do you care if he's dead or not?'

Her eyes flashed. 'I care because I still get a cheque from that son of a bitch as long as he's alive. He's dead, I get zip.'

Chemo was dumbstruck. 'You get alimony? But you're remarried! To a frigging CPA!'

'Let's just say Mick Stranahan didn't have the world's sharpest lawyer.'

'You are one greedy twat,' Chemo said acidly.

'Hey, it's one-fifty a month,' Chloe said. 'Barely covers the lawn service.'

She did not notice the hostility growing in Chemo's expression. 'Killing Mick Stranahan is out of the question,' she declared. 'Burn up the house, fine, but I don't want him dead.'

'Tough titties,' Chemo said.

'Look, I don't know who you are—'

'Sit,' Chemo said. 'And keep your damn voice down.'

The wind was kicking up, and he was afraid the argument might carry across the flats to the house.

Chloe sat down but was not about to shut up. 'You listen to me—'

'I said, keep your damn voice down!'

'Screw you, Velcro-face.'

Chemo's brow crinkled, his cheeks fluttered. He probably even flushed, though this was impossible to discern.

Velcro-face—there it was, finally. The insult. The witch just couldn't resist after all.

'Now what's the matter?' Chloe Simpkins Stranahan said. 'You look seasick.'

'I'm fine,' Chemo said. 'But you shouldn't call people names.'

Then he heaved the thirty-pound anchor into her lap, and watched her pitch over backwards in her silky sailor suit. The staccato trail of bubbles suggested that she was cursing him all the way to the bottom of the bay.

9

Tina woke up alone in bed. She wrapped herself in a sheet and padded groggily around the dark house, looking for Mick Stranahan. She found him outside, balanced on the deck rail with his hands on his hips. He was watching Old Man Chitworth's stilt house light up the sky; a crackling orange torch, visible for miles. The house seemed to sway on its wooden legs, an illusion caused by blasts of raw heat above the water.

Tina thought it was the most breathtaking thing she had ever seen, even better than Old Faithful. In the glow from the blaze she looked up at Stranahan's face and saw concern.

'Somebody living there?' she said.

'No.' Stranahan watched Old Man Chitworth's windmill fall, the flaming blades spinning faster in descent. It hit the water with a sizzle and hiss.

'What started the fire?' Tina asked.

'Arson,' Stranahan said matter-of-factly. 'I heard a boat.'

'Maybe it was an accident,' she suggested. 'Maybe somebody tossed a cigarette.'

'Gasoline,' Stranahan said. 'I smelled it.'

'Wow. Whoever owns that place has some serious enemies, I guess.'

'The man who owns that place just turned eighty-three,' Stranahan said. 'He's on tubes in a nursing home, all flaked out. Thinks he's Eddie Rickenbacker.'

A gust of wind prompted Tina to rearrange her sheet. She got a shiver and edged closer to Mick. She said, 'Some harmless old geezer. Then I don't get it.'

Stranahan said, 'Wrong house, that's all.' He hopped off the rail. 'Somebody fucked up.' So much for paradise, he thought; so much for peace and tranquillity.

Across the bay, from Dinner Key, came the whine of toy-like sirens. Stranahan didn't need binoculars to see the flashing blue dots from the advancing police boats.

Tina clutched his hand. She couldn't take her eyes off the fire. 'Mick, have you got enemies like that?'

'Hell, I've got *friends* like that.'

By midmorning the Chitworth house had burned to the waterline, and the flames died. All that remained sticking out were charred tips of the wood pilings, some still smouldering.

Tina was reading on a deck chair and Stranahan was doing push-ups when the marine patrol boat drove up and stopped. It was Luis Córdova and another man whom Stranahan did not expect.

'Now, there's something you don't see every day,' Stranahan announced, plenty loud. 'Two Cubans in a boat, and no beer.'

Luis Córdova grinned. The other man climbed noisily up on the dock and said, 'And here's something else you don't see every day: an Irishman up before noon, and still sober.'

The man's name was Al García, a homicide detective for

the Metro-Dade police. His J. C. Penney coat jacket was slung over one arm, and his shiny necktie was loosened half-way down his chest. García was not wild about boat rides, so he was in a gruff and unsettled mood. Also, there was the matter of the dead body.

'What dead body?' Mick Stranahan said.

Badger-like, García shuffled up the stairs to the house, with Stranahan and Luis Córdova following single file. García gave the place the once-over and waved courteously to Tina on her lounge chair. The detective half-turned to Stranahan and in a low voice said, 'What, you opened a half-way house for bimbos? Mick, you're a freaking saint, I swear.'

They went inside the stilt house and closed the door. 'Tell me about the dead body,' Stranahan said.

'Sit down. Hey, Luis, I could use some coffee.'

'A minute ago you were seasick,' Luis Córdova said.

'I'm feeling much better, OK?' García scowled theatrically as the young marine patrol officer went to the kitchen. 'Interdepartmental co-operation, that's the buzzword these days. Coffee's a damn good place to start.'

'Easy, man, Luis is a sharp kid.'

'He sure is. I wish he was ours.'

Stranahan said, 'Now about the body . . . '

García waved a meaty brown hand in the air, as if shooing an invisible horsefly. 'Mick, what are you doing way the fuck out here? Somehow I don't see you as Robinson Crusoe, sucking the milk out of raw coconuts.'

'It's real quiet out here.'

Luis Córdova brought three cups of hot coffee.

Al García smacked his lips as he drank. 'Quiet—is that what you said? Jeez, you got dead gangsters floating around, not to mention burning houses—'

'Is this about Tony the Eel?'

'No,' Luis said seriously.

García put down his coffee cup and looked straight at Stranahan. 'When's the last time you saw Chloe?'

Suddenly Mick Stranahan did not feel so well.

'A couple months back,' he said. 'She was on a boat

101

with some guy. I assumed it was her new husband. Why?'

'You mooned her.'

'Can you blame me?'

'We heard about it from the mister this morning.'

Stranahan braced to hear the whole story. Luis Códova opened a spiral notebook but didn't write much. Stranahan listened sombrely and occasionally looked out the window toward the channel where Al García said it had happened.

'A rusty anchor?' Stranahan said in disbelief.

'It got tangled in this silky thing she was wearing,' the detective explained. 'She went down like a sack of cement.' Sensitivity was not García's strong suit.

'The rope is what gave it away,' added Luis Córdova. 'One of the guys coming out to the fire saw the rope drifting up out of the current.'

'Hauled her right in,' García said, 'like a lobster pot.'

'Lord.'

García said, 'Fact is, we really shouldn't be telling you all this.'

'Why not?'

'Because you're the prime suspect.'

'That's very funny.' Stranahan looked at Luis Córdova. 'Is he kidding?'

The young marine patrolman shook his head.

García said, 'Mick, your track record is not so hot. I mean, you already got a few notches on your belt.'

'Not murder.'

'Chloe hated your guts,' Al García said, in the tone of a reminder.

'That's my motive? She hated my guts?'

'Then there's the dough.'

'You think I'd kill her over a crummy one hundred fifty dollars a month?'

'The principle,' Al García said, unwrapping a cigar. 'I think you just might do it over the principle of the thing.'

Stranahan leaned back with a tired sigh. He felt bad

102

about Chloe's death, but mostly he felt curious. What the hell was she doing out here at night?

'I always heard good things about you,' Al García said, 'mainly from Timmy Gavigan.'

'Yeah, he said the same for you.'

'And the way Eckert dumped you from the State Attorney's, that was low.'

Stranahan shrugged. 'They don't forget it when you shoot a judge. It's bound to make people nervous.'

García made a great ceremony of lighting the cigar. Afterwards, he blew two rings of smoke and said, 'For what it's worth, Luis here doesn't think you did it.'

'It's the anchor business,' Luis Córdova explained, 'very strange.' He was trying to sound all business, as if the friendship meant nothing.

Stranahan said, 'The murder's got to be connected to the fire.'

'The fire was an arson,' Luis said. 'Boat gas and a match. These houses are nothing but tinder.' To make his point, he tapped the rubber heel of his shoe on the pine floor.

Stranahan said, 'I think you both ought to know: somebody wants to kill me.'

García's eyebrows shot up and he rolled the cigar from one side of his mouth to the other. 'Who is it, *chico*? Please, make my job easier.'

'I think it's a doctor. His name is Rudy Graveline. Write this down, Luis, please.'

'And why would this doctor want you dead?'

'I'm not sure, Al.'

'But you want me to roust him on a hunch.'

'No, I just want his name in a file somewhere. I want you to know who he is, just in case.'

García turned to Luis Córdova. 'Don't you love the fucking sound of that? *Just in case*. Luis, I think this is where we're supposed to give Mr Stranahan a lecture about taking the law into his own hands.'

Luis said, 'Don't take the law into your own hands, Mick.'

'Thank you, Luis.'

Al García flicked a stubby thumb through his black moustache. 'Just for the record, you didn't invite the lovely Chloe Simpkins Stranahan out here for a romantic reconciliation over fresh fish and wine?'

'No,' Stranahan said. Fish and wine—that fucking García must have scoped out the dirty dinner dishes.

'And the two of you didn't go for a boat ride?'

'No, Al.'

'And you didn't get in a sloppy drunken fight?'

'No.'

'And you didn't hook her to the anchor and drop her overboard?'

'Nope.'

'Luis, you get all that?'

Luis Córdova nodded as he jotted in the notebook. Shorthand, too: Stranahan was impressed.

García got up and went knocking around the house, making Stranahan very nervous. When the detective finally stopped prowling, he stood directly under the stuffed blue marlin. 'Mick, I don't have to tell you there's some guys in Homicide think you aced old Judge Goomer without provocation.'

'I know that, Al. There's some guys in Homicide used to be in business with Judge Goomer.'

'And I know *that*. Point is, they'll be looking at this Chloe thing real hard. Harder than normal.'

Stranahan said, 'There's no chance it was an accident?'

'No,' Luis Córdova interjected. 'No chance.'

'So,' said Al García, 'you see the position I'm in. Until we get another suspect, you're it. The good news is, we've got no physical evidence connecting you. The bad news is, we've got Chloe's manicurist.'

Stranahan groaned. 'Jesus, let's hear it.'

García ambled to a window, stuck his arm out and tapped cigar ash into the water.

'Chloe had her toenails done yesterday morning,' the detective said. 'Told the girl she was coming out here to clean your clock.'

'Lovely,' said Mick Stranahan.

There was a small rap on the door and Tina came in, fiddling with the strap on the top piece of her swimsuit. Al García beamed like he'd just won the lottery; a dreary day suddenly had been brightened.

Stranahan stood up. 'Tina, I want you to meet Sergeant García and Officer Córdova. They're here on police business. Al, Luis, I'd like you to meet my alibi.'

'How do you do,' said Luis Córdova, shaking Tina's hand in a commendably official way.

García gave Stranahan another sideways look. 'I love it,' said the detective. 'I absolutely love this job.'

Christina Marks heard about the death of Chloe Simpkins Stranahan on the six o'clock news. The only thing she could think was that Mick had done it to pay Chloe back for siccing the TV crew on him. It was painful to believe, but the only other possibility was too far-fetched—that Chloe's murder was a coincidence of timing and had nothing to do with Mick or Victoria Barletta. This Christina Marks could not accept; she had to plan for the worst.

If Mick was the killer, that would be a problem.

If Chloe had blabbed about getting five hundred in tipster money from the Reynaldo Flemm show, that would be a problem too. The police would want to know everything, then the papers would get hold of it and the Barletta story would blow up prematurely.

Then there was the substantial problem of Reynaldo himself; Christina could just hear him hyping the hell out of Chloe's murder in the intro: 'The story you are about to see is so explosive that a confidential informant who provided us with key information was brutally murdered only days later . . . ' *Brutally murdered* was one of Reynaldo's favourite on-camera redundancies. Once Christina had drolly asked Reynaldo if he'd ever heard of anyone being *gently* murdered, but he missed the point.

Sometimes, when he got particularly excited about a story, Reynaldo Flemm would actually try to write out the script himself, with comic results. The murder of

Stranahan's ex-wife was just the sort of bombshell to inspire Reynaldo's muse, so Christina decided on a pre-emptive attack. She was reaching across the bed for the telephone when it rang.

It was Maggie Gonzalez, calling collect from somewhere in Manhattan.

'Miss Marks, I got a little problem.'

Christina said: 'We've been looking all over for you. What happened to your trip to Miami?'

'I went, I came back,' Maggie said. 'I told you, there's a problem down there.'

'So what've you been doing the last few weeks,' Christina said, 'besides spending our money?' Christina had just about had it with this ditz; she was beginning to think Mick was right, the girl was ripping them off.

Maggie said, 'Hey, I'm sorry I didn't call sooner. I was scared. Scared out of my mind.'

'We thought you might be dead.'

'No,' said Maggie, barely audible. A long pause suggested that she was fretting over the grim possibility.

'Don't you even want to know how the story is going?' Christina asked warily.

'That's the problem,' Maggie replied. 'That's what I want to talk to you about.'

'Oh?'

Then, almost as an afterthought, Maggie asked, 'Who've you interviewed so far?'

'Nobody,' Christina said. 'We've got a lot of legwork to do first.'

'I can't believe you haven't interviewed anybody!'

Maggie was trolling for something, Christina could tell. 'We're taking it slow,' Christina said. 'This is a sensitive piece.'

'No joke,' Maggie said. 'Real sensitive.'

Christina held the phone in the crook of her shoulder and dug a legal pad and felt-tip pen from her shoulder bag on the bed table.

Maggie went on: 'This whole thing could get me killed, and I think that's worth more than five thousand dollars.'

'But that was our agreement,' Christina said, scribbling along with the conversation.

'That was before I started getting threatening calls on my machine,' said Maggie Gonzalez.

'From who?'

'I don't know who,' Maggie lied. 'It sounded like Dr Graveline.'

'What kind of threats? What did they say?'

'*Threat* threats,' Maggie said impatiently. 'Enough to scare me shitless, OK? You guys tricked me into believing this was safe.'

'We did nothing of the sort.'

'Yeah, well, five thousand dollars isn't going to cut it any more. By the time this is finished, I'll probably have to pack up and move out of Miami. You got any idea what that'll cost?'

Christina Marks said, 'What's the bottom line here, Maggie?'

'The bottom line is, I talked to *20/20*.'

Perfect, Christina thought. The perfect ending to a perfect day.

'I met with an executive producer,' Maggie said.

'Lucky you,' said Christina Marks. 'How much did they offer?'

'Ten.'

'Ten thousand?'

'Right,' Maggie said. 'Plus a month in Mexico after the programme airs . . . you know, to let things cool off.'

'You thought of this all by yourself, or did you get an agent?'

'A what?'

'An agent. Every eyewitness to a murder ought to have his own booking agent, don't you think?'

Maggie sounded confused. 'Ten seemed like a good number,' she said. 'Could be better, of course.'

Christina Marks was dying to find out how much Maggie Gonzalez had told the producer at *20/20*, but instead of asking she said: 'Ten sounds like a winner, Maggie. Besides, I don't think we're interested in the story any more.'

107

During the long silence that followed, Christina tried to imagine the look on Maggie's face.

Finally: 'What do you mean, 'not interested'?'

'It's just too old, too messy, too hard to prove,' Christina said. 'The fact that you waited four years to speak up really kills us in the credibility department . . .'

'Hold on—'

'By the way, are they still polygraphing all their sources over at *20/20*?'

But Maggie was too sharp. 'Getting back to the money,' she said, 'are you saying you won't even consider a counter-offer?'

'Exactly.'

'Have you talked this over with Mr Flemm?'

'Of course,' Christina Marks bluffed, forging blindly ahead.

'That's very weird,' remarked Maggie Gonzalez, 'because I just talked to Mr Flemm myself about ten minutes ago.'

Christina sagged back on the bed and closed her eyes.

'And?'

'And he offered me fifteen grand, plus six weeks in Hawaii.'

'I see,' Christina said thinly.

'Anyway, he said I should call you right away and smooth out the details.'

'Such as?'

'Reservations,' said Maggie Gonzalez. 'Maui would be my first choice.'

10

One of the wondrous things about Florida, Rudy Graveline thought as he chewed on a jumbo shrimp, was the climate of unabashed corruption: there was absolutely no trouble from which money could not extricate you.

Rudy had learned this lesson years earlier when the state medical board had first tried to take away his licence. For the board it had been a long sticky process, reviewing the complaints of disfigured patients, comparing the 'before' and 'after' photographs, sifting through the minutiae of thirteen separate malpractice suits. Since the medical board was made up mostly of other doctors, Rudy Graveline had fully expected exoneration—physicians stick together like shit on a shoe.

But the grossness of Rudy's surgical mistakes was so astounding that even his peers could not ignore it; they recommended that he be suspended from the practice of medicine for ever. Rudy hired a Tallahassee lawyer and pushed the case to a state administrative hearing. The hearing officer acting as judge was not a doctor himself, but some schlump civil servant knocking down twenty-eight thousand a year, tops. At the end of the third day of testimony—some of it so ghastly that Rudy's own attorney became nauseated—Rudy noticed the hearing officer getting into a decrepit old Ford Fairmont to go home to his wife and four kids. This gave Rudy an idea. On the fourth day, he made a phone call. On the fifth day, a brand new Volvo station wagon with cruise control was delivered to the home of the hearing officer. On the sixth day, Dr Rudy Graveline was cleared of all charges against him.

The board immediately reinstated Rudy's licence and sealed all the records from the public and the press—thus honouring the long-held philosophy of Florida's medical establishment that the last persons who need to know about a doctor's incompetence are the patients.

Safe from the sanctions and scrutiny of his own profession, Dr Rudy Graveline viewed all outside threats as problems that could be handled politically; that is, with bribery. Which is why he was having a long lunch with Dade County Commissioner Roberto Pepsical, who was chatting about the next election.

'Shrimp good, no?' said Roberto, who pocketed one in each cheek.

'Excellent,' Rudy agreed. He pushed the cocktail platter

aside and dabbed the corners of his mouth with a napkin. 'Bobby, I'd like to give each of you twenty-five.'

'Grand?' Roberto Pepsical flashed a mouthful of pink-flecked teeth. 'Twenty-five grand, are you serious?'

The man was a hog: a florid, jowly, pug-nosed, rheumy-eyed hog. A cosmetic surgeon's nightmare. Rudy Graveline couldn't bear to watch him eat. 'Not so loud,' he said to the commissioner. 'I know what the campaign law says, but there are ways to duck it.'

'Great!' said Roberto. He had an account in the Caymans; all the commissioners did, except for Lillian Atwater, who was trying out a phoney blind trust in the Dominican Republic.

Rudy said, 'First I've got to ask a favour.'

'Shoot.'

The doctor leaned forward, trying to ignore Roberto's hot gumbo breath. 'The vote on Old Cypress Towers,' Rudy said, 'the rezoning thing.'

Roberto Pepsical lunged for a crab leg and cracked it open with his front teeth. 'Nooooo problem,' he said.

Old Cypress Towers was one of Dr Rudy Graveline's many real estate projects and tax shelters: a thirty-three storey luxury apartment building with a nightclub and health spa planned for the top floor. Only trouble was, the land currently was zoned for low-density public use—parks, schools, ball fields, shit like that. Rudy needed five votes on the county commission to turn it around.

'No sweat,' Roberto reiterated. 'I'll talk to the others.'

The 'others' were the four commissioners who always got pieced out in Roberto Pepsical's crooked deals. The way the system was set up, each of the nine commissioners had his own crooked deals and his own set of locked votes. That way the tally always came out 5–4, but with different players on each side. The idea was to confuse the hell out of the newspaper reporters, who were always trying to figure out who on the commission was honest and who wasn't.

'One more thing,' Dr Rudy Graveline said.

'How about another beer?' asked Roberto Pepsical,

eyeing his empty sweaty glass. 'You don't mind if I get one?'

'Go ahead,' Rudy said, biting back his disgust.

'Crab?' The commissioner brandished another buttery leg.

'No, thanks.' Rudy waited for him to wedge it in his mouth, then said: 'Bobby, I also need you to keep your ears open.'

'For what?'

'Somebody who used to work for me is threatening to go to the cops, trying to bust my balls. They're making up stuff about some old surgical case.'

Roberto nodded and chewed in synchronization, like a mechanical dashboard ornament. Rudy found it very distracting.

He said, 'The whole thing's bullshit, honestly. A disgruntled employee.'

Roberto said, 'Boy, I know how it is.'

'But for a doctor, Bobby, it could be a disaster. My reputation, my livelihood, surely you can understand? That's why I need to know if the cops ever go for it.'

Roberto Pepsical said, 'I'll talk to the chief myself.'

'Only if you hear something.'

Roberto winked. 'I'll poke around.'

'I'd sure appreciate it,' Dr Graveline said. 'I can't afford a scandal, Bobby. Something like that, I'd probably have to leave town.'

The commissioner's brow furrowed as he contemplated his twenty-five large on the wing. 'Don't sweat it,' he said confidently to the doctor. 'Here, have a conch fritter.'

Chemo was in the waiting room when Rudy Graveline got back to Whispering Palms.

'I did it,' he announced.

Rudy quickly led him into the office.

'You got Stranahan?'

'Last night,' Chemo said matter-of-factly. 'So when can we get started on my face?'

Unbelievable, Rudy thought. Very scary, this guy.

'You mean the dermabrasion treatments.'

'Fucking A,' Chemo said. 'We had a deal.'

Rudy buzzed his secretary and asked her to bring him the morning *Herald*. After she went out again, Chemo said, 'It happened so late, probably didn't make the paper.'

'Hmmmm,' said Rudy Graveline, scanning the local news page. 'Maybe that's it—must have happened too late. Tell me about it, please.'

Chemo wet his dead-looking lips. 'I torched his house.' No expression at all. 'He was asleep.'

'You know this for a fact?'

'I watched it go up,' Chemo said. 'Nobody got out.' He crossed his long legs and stared dully at the doctor. The droopy lids made him look like he was about to doze off.

Rudy folded up the newspaper. 'I believe you,' he said to Chemo, 'but I'd like to be sure. By tomorrow it ought to be in the papers.'

Chemo rubbed the palm of one hand along his cheeks, making sandpaper sounds. Rudy Graveline wished he would knock it off.

'What about the TV?' Chemo asked. 'Does that count, if it makes the TV?'

'Of course.'

'Radio, too?'

'Certainly,' Rudy said. 'I told you before, no big deal. I don't need to see the actual corpse, OK, but we do need to be sure. It's very important, because this is a dangerous man.'

'*Was*,' Chemo said pointedly.

'Right. This was a dangerous man.' Rudy didn't mention Stranahan's ominous phone call on Maggie Gonzalez's answering machine. Better to limit the cast of characters, for Chemo's sake. Keep him focused.

'Maybe it's already on the radio,' Chemo said hopefully.

Rudy didn't want to put the guy in a mood. 'Tell you what,' he said in a generous tone, 'we'll go ahead and do the first treatment this afternoon.'

Chemo straightened up excitedly. 'No shit?'

'Why not?' the doctor said, standing. 'We'll try a little patch on your chin.'

'How about the nose?' Chemo said, touching himself there.

Rudy slipped on his glasses and came around the desk to where Chemo was sitting. Because of Chemo's height, even in the chair, the surgeon didn't have to lean over far to get a close-up look at the corrugated, cheesy mass that passed for Chemo's nose.

'Pretty rough terrain,' Rudy Graveline said, peering intently. 'Better to start slow and easy.'

'Fast and rough is fine with me.'

Rudy took off his glasses and struck an avuncular pose, a regular Marcus Welby. 'I want to be very careful,' he told Chemo. 'Yours is an extreme case.'

'You noticed.'

'The machine we use is a Stryker dermabrader—'

'I don't care if it's a fucking Black and Decker, let's just do it.'

'Scar tissue is tricky,' Rudy persisted. 'Some skin reacts better to sanding than others.' He couldn't help remembering what had happened to the last doctor who had screwed up Chemo's face. Getting murdered was even worse than getting sued for malpractice.

'One little step at a time,' Rudy cautioned. 'Trust me.'

'Fine, then start on the chin, whatever,' Chemo said with a wave of a pale hand. 'You're the doctor.'

Those magic words.

How Rudy Graveline loved to hear them.

Compared to other law firms, Kipper Garth's had the overhead problem dicked. He had one central office, no partners, no associates, no 'of counsels'. His major expenses were billboard advertising, cable, telephones (he had twenty lines), and, of course, secretaries (he called them legal aides, and employed fifteen). Kipper Garth's law practice was, in essence, a high-class boiler room.

The phones never stopped ringing. This was because

Kipper Garth had shrewdly put up his billboards at the most dangerous traffic intersections in South Florida, so that the second thing every noncomatose accident victim saw (after the Jaws of Life) was Kipper Garth's phone number in nine-foot red letters: 555-TORT.

Winnowing the incoming cases took most of the time, so Kipper Garth delegated this task to his secretaries, who were undoubtedly more qualified anyway. Kipper Garth saved his own energy for selecting the referrals; some PI lawyers specialized in spinal cord injuries, others in orthopaedics, still others in death-and-dismemberment. Though Kipper Garth was not one to judge a colleague's skill in the courtroom (not having *been* in a courtroom in at least a decade), he knew a fifty-fifty fee split when he saw it, and made his referrals accordingly.

The phone bank at Kipper Garth's firm looked and sounded like the catalogue-order department at Montgomery Ward. By contrast, the interior of Kipper Garth's private office was rich and staid, lit like an old library and just as quiet. This is where Mick Stranahan found his brother-in-law, practising his putting.

'You don't knock any more?' said Kipper Garth, eyeing a ten-footer into a Michelob stein.

'I came to make a little deal,' Stranahan said.

'This I gotta hear.' Kipper Garth wore grey European-cut slacks, a silk paisley necktie and a bone-coloured shirt, the French cuffs rolled up to his elbows. His salt-and-pepper hair had been dyed silver to make him look more trustworthy on billboards.

'Let's forget this disbarment thing,' Stranahan said.

Kipper Garth chuckled. 'It's a little late, Mick. You already testified, remember?'

'How about if I agree not to testify next time?'

Kipper Garth backed away from the next putt and looked up. 'Next time?'

'There's other cases kicking around the grievance committee, am I right?'

'But how do you—'

'Lawyers talk, Jocko.' Stranahan emptied the golf balls

114

out of the beer stein and rolled them back across the carpet toward his brother-in-law. 'I've still got a few friends in town,' he said. 'I'm still plugged in.'

Kipper Garth leaned his putter in the corner behind his desk. 'I'm suing *you*, remember? Defamation, it's called.'

'Don't make me laugh.'

The lawyer's eyes narrowed. 'Mick, I know why you're here. Chloe's been killed and you're afraid you'll take the fall. You need a lawyer, so here you are, looking for a goddamn freebie.'

'I said don't make me laugh.'

'Then what is it?'

'Who's getting your malpractice stuff these days?'

Kipper Garth started flicking through his Rolodex; it was the biggest Rolodex that Stranahan had ever seen, the size of a pot roast. Kipper Garth said, 'I've got a couple main guys, why?'

'These guys you've got, can they get state records?'

'What kind of records?'

Christ, the man was lame. 'Discipline records,' Stranahan explained, 'from the medical board.'

'Gee, I don't know.'

'There's a shocker.'

'What's going on, Mick?'

'This: you help me out, I'll lay off of you. Permanently.'

Kipper Garth snorted. 'I'm supposed to be grateful? Pardon me if I don't give a shit.'

Naturally, thought Stranahan, it would come to this. The pertinent papers were wadded in his back pocket. He got them out, smoothed them with the heel of one hand and laid them out carefully, like solitaire cards, on Kipper Garth's desk.

The lawyer muttered, 'What the hell?'

'Pay attention,' Stranahan said. 'This one here is the bill of sale for your spiffy new Maserati. That's a Xerox of the cheque—fifty-seven thousand, eight something, what a joke. Anyway, the account that cheque was written on is your clients' trust account, Jocko. We're talking deep shit. Forget disbarment, we're talking felony.'

Kipper Garth's upper lip developed an odd tic.

'I'm paying it back,' he said hoarsely.

'Doesn't matter,' Mick Stranahan said. 'Now, some of this other crap—that's a hotel bill from the Grand Bay in Coconut Grove. Same weekend you told Katie you were in Boston with the ABA. Anyway, it's none of my business but you don't look like a man that could drink three bottles of Dom all by your lonesome. See, it's right there on the bill.' Stranahan pointed, but Kipper Garth's eyes were focused someplace else, some place far away. By now his lip was twitching like a porch lizard.

'You,' he said to Stranahan. 'You jerk.'

'Now what's this dinner for two, Jocko? My sister was at grandma's with the kids that night, if memory serves. Dinner for two at Max's Place, what exactly was that? Probably just a client, no?'

Kipper Garth collected himself and said, 'All right, Mick.'

'You understand the situation.'

'Yes.'

'It was easier than you think,' Stranahan said. 'See, once you're plugged in, it's hard to get unplugged. I mean, once you know this stuff is out there, it's real easy to find.' A half dozen phone calls was all it took.

Kipper Garth began folding the papers, creasing each one with a great deal of force.

Stranahan said, 'What scares you more, Jocko: the Florida Bar, the county jail, or an expensive divorce?'

Wearily, Kipper Garth said, 'Did you mean what you said before, about the disbarment and all that?'

'You're asking because you know I don't have to deal, isn't that right? Maybe that's true—maybe you'd do me this favour for nothing. But fair is fair, and you ought to get something in return. So, yeah, I'll lay off. Just like I promised.'

Kipper Garth said, 'Then I'll talk to my guys about getting the damn state files. Give me a name, please.'

'Graveline,' said Stranahan. 'Dr Rudy Graveline.'

Kipper Garth winced. 'Jeez, I've heard that name. I think he's in my yacht club.'

Mick Stranahan clapped his hands. 'Yo ho ho,' he said.

Later, on the way to see her plastic surgeon, Tina asked Mick: 'Why didn't you make love to me last night?'

'I thought you enjoyed yourself.'

'It was sweet, but why'd you stop?'

Stranahan said: 'Because I've got this terrible habit of falling in love.'

Tina rolled her eyes. 'After one night?'

'True story,' Stranahan said. 'All five of the women I married, I proposed to them the first night we went to bed.'

'Before or after?' Tina asked.

'After,' he said. 'It's like a disease. The scary part is, they tend to say yes.'

'Not me.'

'I couldn't take that chance.'

'You're nuts,' Tina said. 'Does this mean we're never gonna do it?'

Stranahan sighed, feeling old and out of it. His ex-wife just gets murdered, some asshole doctor's trying to kill him, a TV crew is lurking around his house—all this, and Tina wants to know about getting laid, wants a time and date. Why didn't she believe him about the others?

He stopped at a self-service Shell station and filled three plastic Farm Stores jugs with regular unleaded. When he went up to pay, nobody said a word. He put the gallon jugs in the trunk of the Imperial and covered them with a bunch of boat rags.

Back in the car, Tina gave him a look. 'You didn't answer my question.'

'You've got a boyfriend,' Stranahan said, wishing he could've come up with something better, more original.

'Richie? Richie's history,' said Tina. *'No problema.'*

117

It always amazed Stranahan how they could make boyfriends disappear, snap, just like that.

'So,' Tina said, 'how about tonight?'

'How about I call you,' he said, 'when things cool off?'

'Yeah,' Tina muttered. 'Sure.'

Stranahan was glad when they got to the doctor's office. It was a two-storey peach stucco building in Coral Gables, a refurbished old house. The plastic surgeon's name was Dicer. Craig E. Dicer; a nice young fellow, too nice to say anything nasty about Rudy Graveline at first. Stranahan badged him and tried again. Dr Dicer took a good hard look at the gold State Attorney's investigator shield before he said: 'Is this off the record?'

'Sure,' said Stranahan, wondering: Where do these guys learn to talk like this?

'Graveline's a butcher,' Dr Dicer said. 'A hacker. Everybody in town's mopped up after him, one time or another. Fortunately, he doesn't do much surgery himself any more. He got wise, hired a bunch of young sharpies, all board certified. It's like a damn factory up there.'

'Whispering Palms?'

'You've seen it?' Dr Dicer asked.

Stranahan said no, but it was his next stop. 'If everybody in Miami knows that Graveline's a butcher, how does he get any patients?'

Dr Dicer laughed caustically. 'Hell, man, the patients don't know. You think some housewife wants her tits poofed goes downtown to the courthouse and looks up the lawsuits? No way. Rudy Graveline's got a big rep because he's socially connected. He did the mayor's niece's chin, this I know for a fact. And old Congressman Carberry? Graveline did his girlfriend's eyelids. Or somebody at Whispering Palms did; Rudy always takes the credit.'

Tina, who hadn't been saying much since the car, finally cut in. 'Talk to models and actresses,' she said. 'Whispering Palms is in. Like tofu.'

'Jesus,' said Stranahan.

Dr Dicer said, 'Can I ask why you're interested?'

'Really, you don't want to know,' Stranahan said.

'I guess not.'

'*I* want to know,' Tina said.

Stranahan pretended not to hear her. He said to Dr Dicer: 'One more question, then we'll let you get back to work. This is hypothetical.'

Dr Dicer nodded, folded his hands, got very studious looking.

Stranahan said: 'Is it possible to kill somebody during a nose job?'

By way of an answer, Dr Dicer took out a pink neoprene replica of a bisected human head, a bronze Crane mallet, and a small Cottle chisel. Then he demonstrated precisely how you could kill somebody during a nose job.

When Chemo got to the Gay Bidet, a punk band called the Chicken Chokers had just finished wringing their sweaty jock straps into a cocktail glass and guzzling it down on stage.

'You're late,' said Chemo's boss, a man named Freddie. 'We already had three fights.'

'Car trouble,' said Chemo. 'Radiator hose.' Not an apology, an explanation.

Freddie pointed at the small bandage and said, 'What happened to your chin?'

'A zit,' Chemo said.

'A zit, that's a good one.'

'What's that supposed to mean?'

'Nothing,' Freddie said. 'Don't mean nothing.' He had to watch the wisecracks around Chemo. The man made him nervous as a gerbil. Freaking seven-foot cadaver, other clubs would kill for a bouncer like that.

Freddie said, 'Here, you got a message.'

Chemo said thank you, went outside to a pay phone on Collins and called Dr Rudy Graveline's beeper. At the tone, Chemo punched in the number of the pay phone, hung up, and waited. All the way out here, he could hear the next band cranking up. The Crotch Rockets, it sounded like. Their big hit was *Lube-Job Lover*. Chemo found it somewhat derivative.

The telephone rang. Chemo waited for the third time before picking up.

'We have got a problem,' said Rudy Graveline, raspy, borderline terrified.

Chemo said, 'Aren't you going to ask about my chin?'

'No!'

'Well, it stings like hell.'

Dr Graveline said, 'I told you it would.'

Chemo said, 'How long've I gotta wear the Band-Aid?'

'Till it starts to heal, for Chrissakes. Look, I've got a major situation here and if you don't fix it, the only person's going to care about your complexion is the goddamn undertaker. One square inch of perfect chin, maybe you're thinking how gorgeous you look. Well, think open casket. How's that for gorgeous?'

Chemo absently touched his new bandage. 'Why're you so upset?'

'Mick Stranahan's alive.'

Chemo thought: The bitch in the sailor suit, she got the wrong house.

'By the way,' Rudy Graveline said angrily, 'I'd like to thank you for not telling me how you drowned the man's wife in the middle of Biscayne Bay. From what was on TV, I'm just assuming it was you. Had your subtle touch.' When Chemo didn't respond for several moments, the doctor said: 'Well?'

Chemo asked, 'Is that a siren at your end?'

'Yes,' Rudy said archly, 'yes, that would be a siren. Now, aren't you going to ask how I know that Stranahan's still alive?'

'All right,' Chemo said, 'how do you know?'

'Because,' the doctor said, 'the bastard just blew up my Jag.'

120

11

Christina Marks knocked twice, and when no one answered she walked in. The man in the hospital bed had a plastic oxygen mask over his mouth. Lying there he looked as small as a child. The covers were pulled up to the folds of his neck. His face was mottled and drawn. When Christina approached the bed, the man's blue eyes opened slowly and he waved. When he lifted the oxygen mask away from his mouth, she saw that he was smiling.

'Detective Gavigan?'

'The one and only.'

'I'm Christina Marks.' She told him why she had come, what she wanted. When she mentioned Vicky Barletta, Timmy Gavigan made a zipper motion across his lips.

'What's the matter?' Christina asked.

'That's an open case, lady. I can't talk about it.' Timmy Gavigan's voice was hollow, like it was coming up a pipe from his dead lungs. 'We got regulations about talking to the media,' he said.

'Do you know Mick Stranahan?' Christina said.

'Sure I know Mick,' Timmy Gavigan said. 'Mick came to see me a while back.'

'About this case?'

'Mick's in my scrapbook,' Timmy Gavigan said, looking away.

Christina said, 'He's in some trouble.'

'He didn't get married again, the dumb bastard?'

Not that kind of trouble, Christina said. This time it was the Barletta case.

'Mick's a big boy,' said Timmy Gavigan. 'My guess is, he can handle it.' He was smiling again. 'Honey, you sure are pretty.'

'Thank you,' said Christina.

'Can you believe, six months ago I'd be trying to charm

121

you right into the sack. Now I can't even get up to take a whizz. Here a gorgeous woman comes to my room and I can't raise my goddamn head, much less anything else.'

She said, 'I'm sorry.'

'I know what you're thinking—a dying man, he's likely to say anything. But I mean it, you're something special. I got high standards, always did. I mean, hell, I might be dead, but I ain't blind.'

Christina laughed softly. Timmy Gavigan reached for the oxygen mask, took a couple of deep breaths, put it down again. 'Give me your hand,' he said to Christina Marks. 'Please, it's all right. What I got, you can't catch.'

Timmy Gavigan's skin was cold and papery. Christina gave a little squeeze and tried to pull away, but he held on. She noticed his eyes had a sparkle.

'You've been to the file?'

She nodded.

'I took a statement from that doctor, Rudy Something.'

Christina said, 'Yes, I read it.'

'Help me out,' said Timmy Gavigan, squinting in concentration. 'What the hell did he say again?'

'He said it was a routine procedure, nothing out of the ordinary.'

'Yeah, I remember now,' Timmy Gavigan said. 'He was a precious thing, too, all business. Said he'd done five thousand nose jobs and this was no different from the others. And I said maybe not, but this time your patient vanished from the face of the earth. And he said she was fine last time he saw her. Walked out of the office all by herself. And I said yeah, walked straight into the fucking twilight zone. Pardon my French.'

Christina Marks said, 'You've got a good memory.'

'Too bad I can't breathe with it.' Timmy Gavigan took another hit of oxygen. 'Fact is, we had no reason to think the doctor was involved. Besides, the nurse backed him up. What the hell was his name again?'

'Graveline.'

Timmy Gavigan nodded. 'Struck me as a little snot. If

122

only you could arrest people for that.' He coughed, or maybe it was a chuckle. 'Did I mention I was dying?'

Christina said yes, she knew.

'Did you say you were on TV?'

'No, I'm just a producer.'

'Well, you're pretty enough to be on TV.'

'Thank you.'

'I'm not being very much help, I know,' said Timmy Gavigan. 'They got me loaded up on morphine. But I'm trying to think if there was something I left out.'

'It's all right, you've been helpful.'

She could tell that each breath was torture.

He said, 'Your idea is that the doctor did it, is that right? See, that's a new angle—let me think here.'

Christina said, 'It's just a theory.'

Timmy Gavigan shifted under the covers and turned slightly to face her. 'He had a brother, was that in the file?'

No, Christina said. Nothing about a brother.

'Probably not,' Timmy Gavigan said. 'It didn't seem important at the time. I mean, the doc wasn't even a suspect.'

'I understand.'

'But he did have a brother, I talked to him maybe ten minutes. Wasn't worth typing it up.' Timmy Gavigan motioned for a cup of water and Christina held it to his lips.

'Jesus, I must be a sight,' he said. 'Anyway, the reason I mention it—let's say the doctor croaked Vicky. Don't know why, but let's say he did. What to do about the body? That's a big problem. Bodies are damn tough to get rid of, Jimmy Hoffa being the exception.'

'What does the doctor's brother do?'

Timmy Gavigan grinned, and colour flashed to his cheeks. 'That's my point, honey. The brother was a tree trimmer.'

Christina tried to look pleased at this new information, but mostly she looked puzzled.

'You don't know much about tree trimming, do you?'

123

Timmy Gavigan said in a teasing tone. Then he gulped more oxygen.

She said, 'Why did you go see the doctor's brother?'

'I didn't. Didn't have to. I met him right outside the clinic—I forget the damn name.'

'The Durkos Medical Center.'

'Sounds right.' Timmy Gavigan paused, and his free hand moved to his throat. When the pain passed, he continued. 'Outside the clinic, I saw this guy hacking on the black olive trees. Asked him if he was there the day Vicky disappeared, if he saw anything unusual. Naturally he says no. After, I ask his name and he tells me George Graveline. So like the genius I am, I say: You related to the doctor? He says yeah, and that's about it.'

'George Graveline.' Christina Marks wrote the name down.

Timmy Gavigan lifted his head and eyed the notebook. 'Tree trimmer,' he said. 'Make sure you put that down.'

'Tell me what it means, please.'

'No, you ask Mick.'

She said, 'What makes you so sure I'll see him?'

'Wild hunch.'

Then Timmy Gavigan said something that Christina Marks couldn't quite hear. She leaned over and asked him, in a whisper, to repeat it.

'I said, you sure are beautiful.' He winked once, then closed his eyes slowly. 'Thanks for holding my hand,' he said.

And then he let go.

Whenever there was a bombing in Dade County, somebody in the Central Office would call Sergeant Al García for help, mainly because García was Cuban and it was automatically assumed that the bombing was in some way related to exile politics. García had left orders that he was not to be bothered about bombings unless somebody actually died, since a dead body was the customary prerequisite of homicide investigation. He also sent detailed memorandums

124

explaining that Cubans were not the only ones who tried to bomb each other in South Florida, and he listed all the mob and labour and otherwise non-Cuban bombings over the last ten years. Nobody at the Central Office paid much attention to García's pleadings, and they still summoned him over the most chickenshit of explosions.

This is what happened when Dr Rudy Graveline's black Jaguar sedan blew up. García was about to tell the dispatcher to piss off, until he heard the name of the complainant. Then, fifteen minutes behind the fire trucks, he drove straight to Whispering Palms.

What had happened was: Rudy had gone to the airport to pick up a potentially important patient, a world-famous actress who had awakened one morning in her Bel Air mansion, glanced at herself naked in the mirror, and burst into tears. She got Dr Graveline's name from a friend of a friend of Parnell Roberts's poolboy, and called to tell the surgeon that she was flying to Miami for an emergency consultation. Because of the actress's fame and wealth (most of it accumulated during a messy divorce from one of the Los Angeles Dodgers), Rudy agreed to meet the woman at the airport and give a personal tour of Whispering Palms. He was double-parked in front of the Pan Am terminal when he first noticed the beat-up old Chrysler pull in behind him, its rear end sticking into traffic. Rudy noticed the car again on his way back to the beach—the actress yammering away about the practical joke she once played on Richard Chamberlain while they were shooting some mini-series; Rudy with a worried eye on the rear-view, because the Imperial was right there, on his bumper.

The other car disappeared somewhere on Alton Road, and Rudy didn't think about it again until he and the actress walked out of Whispering Palms; Rudy with a friendly hand on her elbow, she with a fistful of glossy surgery brochures. The Imperial was parked right across from Rudy's special reserved slot. The same big man was behind the wheel. The actress didn't know anything was wrong until the man got out of the Chrysler and whistled at a yellow cab, which was conveniently parked under a big ficus tree at the north end of the lot. When the taxi pulled up, the man from the Imperial opened the back door and told the actress to get in. He said the cabbie would take her straight to the hotel. She said she wasn't staying in any *hotel*, that she'd rented a villa in Golden Beach where Eric Clapton once lived; the big man said fine, the cabbie knew the way.

Finally the actress got in, the taxi drove off, and it was just the stranger and Rudy Graveline alone in the parking lot. When the man introduced himself, Rudy tried very hard not to act terrified. Mick Stranahan said that he wasn't yet certain why Dr Graveline was trying to have him killed, but that it was a very bad idea, overall. Dr Graveline replied that he didn't know what on earth the man was talking about. Then Mick Stranahan walked across the parking lot, got in his Chrysler, turned on the ignition, placed a coconut on the accelerator, got out of the car, reached through the driver's window and slipped it into Drive. Then he jumped out of the way and watched the Imperial plough directly into the rear of Dr Rudy Graveline's black Jaguar sedan. The impact, plus the three jugs of gasoline that Mick Stranahan had strategically positioned in the Jaguar's trunk, caused the automobile to explode in a most spectacular way.

When Rudy Graveline recounted this story to Detective Sergeant Al García, he left out two details—the name of the man who did it, and the reason.

'He never said why?' said Al García, all eyebrows.

'Not a word,' lied Dr Graveline. 'He just destroyed my car and walked away. The man was obviously deranged.'

García grunted and folded his arms. Smoke was still rising from the Jag, which was covered with foam from the firetrucks. Rudy acted forlorn about the car, but García knew the truth. The only reason the asshole even bothered with the police was for the insurance company.

The detective said, 'You don't know the guy who did this?'

'Never saw him before.'

'That's not what I asked.'

Rudy said, 'Sergeant, I don't know what you mean.'

García was tempted to come out and ask the surgeon if it were true that he was trying to bump off Mick Stranahan, like Stranahan had said. That was a fun question, the kind García loved to ask, but the timing wasn't right. For now, he wanted Rudy Graveline to think of him as a big, dumb cop, not a threat.

'A purely random attack,' García mused.

'It would appear so,' Rudy said.

'And you say the man was short and wiry?'

'Yes,' Rudy said.

'How short?'

'Maybe five one,' Rudy said. 'And he was black.'

'How black?'

'Very black,' the doctor said. 'Black as my tyres.'

Al García dropped to a crouch and shone his flashlight on the front hub of the molten Jag. 'Michelins,' he noted. 'The man was as black as Michelins.'

'Yes, and he spoke no English.'

'Really? What language was it?'

'Creole,' Rudy Graveline said. 'I'm pretty sure.'

García rubbed his chin. 'So what we've got in the way of an arsonist,' he said, 'is a malnourished Haitian midget.'

Rudy frowned. 'No,' he said seriously, 'he was taller than that.'

García said the man apparently had picked the trunk lock in order to put the containers of gasoline inside the doctor's car. 'That shows some thinking,' the detective said.

'Could still be crazy,' Rudy said. 'Crazy people can surprise you.'

One tow truck driver put the hooks on what was left of Rudy's black Jaguar. Another contemplated the remains of the Chrysler Imperial, which García kept referring to as 'that ugly piece of elephant shit'. His hatred for Chryslers went back to his patrol days.

Lennie Goldberg, a detective from Intelligence, came

127

up and said, 'So, what do you think, Al? Think it was Cubans?'

'No, Lennie, I think it was the Shining Path. Or maybe the freaking Red Brigade.' It took Lennie Goldberg a couple of beats to catch on. Irritably García said, 'Would you stop this shit about the Cubans? This was a routine car bomb, OK? No politics, no Castro, no CIA. No fucking Cubans, got it?'

'Jeez, Al, I was just asking.' Lennie thought García was getting very touchy on the subject.

'Use your head, Lennie.' García pointed at the wreck. 'This look like an act of international terrorism? Or does it look like some dirtball in a junker went nuts?'

Lennie said, 'Could be either, Al. With bombings, sometimes you got to look closely for the symbolism. Maybe there's a message in this. Aren't Jaguars manufactured in Britain? Maybe this is the IRA.'

García groaned. A message, for Christ's sake. And symbolism! This is what happens when you put a moron in the intelligence unit: he gets even dumber.

A uniformed cop handed Rudy Graveline a copy of the police report. The doctor folded it carefully with three creases, like a letter, and placed it in the inside pocket of his jacket.

Al García turned his back on Lennie Goldberg and said to Rudy, 'Don't worry, we'll find the guy.'

'You will?'

'No sweat,' said García, noticing how uncomfortable Rudy seemed. 'We'll run the VIN number on the Chrysler and come up with our Haitian dwarf, or whatever.'

'Probably a stolen vehicle,' Rudy remarked.

'Probably not,' said Al García. *Vehicle?* Now the guy was doing Jack Webb. García said: 'No, sir, this definitely was a premeditated act, the act of a violent and unstable perpetrator. We'll do our best to solve it, Doctor, you've got my word.'

'Really, it's not that big a deal.'

'Oh, it is to us,' García said. 'It is indeed a big deal.'

'Well, I know you're awfully busy.'

'Oh, not too busy for something like this,' García said in the heartiest of tones. 'The firebombing of a prominent physician—are you kidding? Starting now, Dr Graveline, your case is a priority one.'

García was having a ball, acting so damn gung ho; the doctor looked wan and dyspeptic.

The detective said, 'You'll be hearing back from me real soon.'

'I will?' said Rudy Graveline.

Reynaldo Flemm had been in a dark funk since his clandestine visit to Whispering Palms. Dr Graveline had lanced his ego; this, without knowing Reynaldo's true identity or the magnitude of his fame. Three days had passed, and Flemm had scarcely been able to peek out the door of his Key Biscayne hotel room. He had virtually stopped eating most solid food, resorting to a diet of protein cereal and lemon Gatorade. Every time Christina Marks knocked, Reynaldo would call out that he was in the bathroom, sick to his stomach, which was almost true. He couldn't tear himself away from the mirror. The surgeon's dire assessment of Reynaldo's nose—'two sizes too large for your face'—was savage by itself, but the casual criticism of his weight was paralysing.

Flemm was examining himself naked in the mirror when Christina came to the door again.

'I'm sick,' he called out.

'Ray, this is stupid,' Christina scolded from the hallway. She didn't know about his trip to the clinic. 'We've got to talk about Maggie,' she said.

There was the sound of drawers being opened and closed, and maybe a closet. For a moment Christina thought he might be getting ready to emerge.

'Ray?'

'What about Maggie?' he said. Now it sounded like he was inches from the door. 'Didn't you straighten out that shit about 20/20?'

Christina said, 'That's what we have to talk about. Fifteen thousand is ludicrous. Let me in, Ray.'

'I'm not well.'

'Open the damn door or I'm calling New York.'

'No, Chris, I'm not at my best.'

'Ray, I've seen you at your best, and it's not all that great. Let me in, or I start kicking.' And she did. Reynaldo Flemm couldn't believe it, the damn door was jumping off its hinges.

'Hey, stop!' he cried, and opened it just a crack.

Christina saw that he wore a towel around his waist, and nothing else. A bright green pair of elastic cycling shorts lay on the floor.

'Hawaii?' Christina said. 'You told that bimbette we'd send her to Hawaii?'

Reynaldo said, 'What choice did I have? You want to lose this story?'

'Yes,' Christina said, 'this story is serious trouble, Ray. I want to pack up and go home.'

'And give it to ABC? Are you nuts?' He opened the door a little more. 'We're getting so close.'

Christina tried to bait him. 'How about we fly up to Spartanburg tomorrow? Do the biker segment, like we planned?'

Reynaldo loved to do motorcycle gangs, since they almost always attacked him while the tape was rolling. The Spartanburg story had a sex-slavery angle as well, but Flemm still didn't bite.

'That'll wait,' he said.

Christina checked both ways to make sure no one was coming down the hall. 'You heard about Chloe Simpkins?'

Reynaldo Flemm shook his head. 'I haven't seen the news,' he admitted, 'in a couple of days.'

'Well, she's dead,' Christina said. 'Murdered.'

'Oh, God.'

'Out by the stilt houses.'

'No shit? What an opener.'

'Forget it, Ray, it's a mess.' She shouldered her way into his room. He sat down on the bed, his knees pressed together under the towel. A tape measure was coiled in his left hand. 'What's that for?' Christina asked, pointing.

'Nothing,' Flemm said. He wasn't about to tell her that he had been measuring his nose in the mirror. In fact he had been taking the precise dimensions of all his facial features, to compare proportions.

He said, 'When is Chloe's funeral? Let's get Willie and shoot the stand-up there.'

'Forget it.' She explained how the cops would probably be looking for them anyway, to ask about the five hundred dollars. In its worst light, somebody might say that they contributed to Chloe's death, put her up to something dangerous.

'But we didn't,' Reynaldo Flemm whined. 'All we got from her was Stranahan's location, and barely that. A house in the bay, she said. A house with a windmill. Easiest five bills that woman ever made.'

Christina said, 'Like I said, it's a big mess. It's time to pull out. Tell Maggie to go fly her kite for Hugh Downs.'

'Let's wait a couple more days.' He couldn't stand the idea of giving up; he hadn't gotten beat up once on this whole assignment.

'Wait for what?' Christina said testily.

'So I can think. I can't think when I'm sick.'

She resisted the temptation to state the obvious. 'What exactly is the matter?'

'Nothing I care to talk about,' Flemm said.

'Ah, one of those male-type problems.'

'Fuck you.'

As she was leaving, Christina asked when he would be coming out of his hotel room to face the real world. 'When I'm good and ready,' Flemm replied defensively.

'Take your time, Ray. Tomorrow's interview is off.'

'You cancelled it—why?'

'It cancelled itself. The man died.'

Flemm gasped. 'Another murder!'

'No, Ray, it wasn't murder.' Christina waved goodbye. 'Sorry to disappoint you.'

131

'That's OK,' he said, sounding like a man on the mend, 'we can always fudge it.'

12

After Timmy Gavigan's funeral, García offered Mick Stranahan a ride back to the marina.

'I noticed you came by cab,' the detective said.

'Al, you got eyes like a hawk.'

'So where's your car?'

Stranahan said, 'I guess somebody stole it.'

It was a nice funeral, although Timmy Gavigan would have made fun of it. The chief stood up and said some good things, and afterwards some cops young enough to be Timmy's grandchildren shot off a twenty-one gun salute and accidentally hit a power transformer, leaving half of Coconut Grove with no electricity. Stranahan had worn a pressed pair of jeans, a charcoal sports jacket, brown loafers and no socks. It was the best outfit he owned; he'd thrown out all his neckties when he moved to the stilt house. Stranahan caught himself sniffling a little toward the end of the service. He made a mental note to clip the obit from the newspaper and glue it in Timmy Gavigan's scrapbook, the way he promised. Then he would mail the scrapbook up to Boston, where Timmy's daughters lived.

Driving back out the Rickenbacker Causeway, García was saying, 'Didn't you have an old Chrysler? Funny thing, we got one of those shitheaps in a fire the other night. Somebody filed off the VIN numbers, so we can't trace the damn thing—maybe it's yours, huh?'

'Maybe,' said Mick Stranahan, 'but you keep it. The block was cracked. I was ready to junk it anyway.'

García drummed his fingers on the steering wheel, which meant he was running out of patience.

'Hey, Mick?'

'What?'

'Did you blow up that asshole's Jag?'

Stranahan stared out at the bay and said, 'Who?'

'The doctor. The one who wants to kill you.'

'Oh.'

Something was not right with this guy, García thought. Maybe the funeral had put him in a mood, maybe it was something else.

'We're getting into an area,' the detective said, 'that makes me very nervous. You listening, *chico*?'

Stranahan pretended to be watching some topless girl on a sailboard.

García said, 'You want to play Charlie Bronson, OK, but let me tell you how serious this is getting. Forget the doctor for a second.'

'Yeah, how? He's trying to kill me.'

'Well, chill on that for a minute and think about this: Murdock and Salazar got assigned to Chloe's murder. Do I have to spell it out, or you want me to stop the car so you can go ahead and puke?'

'Jesus,' said Mick Stranahan.

Detectives John Murdock and Joe Salazar had been tight with the late Judge Raleigh Goomer, the one Stranahan had shot. Murdock and Salazar had been in on the bond fixings, part of the A-team. They were not Mick Stranahan's biggest fans.

'How the hell did they get the case?'

'Luck of the draw,' García said. 'Nothing I could do without making it worse.'

Stranahan slammed a fist on the dashboard. He was damn tired of all this bad news.

García said, 'So they come out here to do a canvass, right? Talk to people at the boat ramp, the restaurant, anyone who might have seen your ex on the night she croaked. They come back with statements from two waitresses and a gas attendant, and guess who they say was with Chloe? You, Blue Eyes.'

'That's a goddamn lie, Al.'

'You're right. I know it's a lie because I drove out here the next day on my lunch hour and talked to these same people myself. On my lunch hour! Show them two mugs, including yours, and strike out. O for ten. So Frick and Frack are lying. I don't know what I can do about it yet—it's a tricky situation, them sticking together on their story.' García took a cigar from his breast pocket. Wrapper and all, he jammed it in the corner of his mouth. 'I'm telling you this so you know how goddamn serious it's getting, and maybe you'll quit this crazy car-bombing shit and give me a chance to do my job. How about it?'

Absently, Stranahan said, 'This is the worst year of my life, and it's only the seventeenth of January.'

García chewed the cellophane off the cigar. 'I don't know why I even bother to tell you anything,' he grumbled. 'You're acting like a damn zombie.'

The detective made the turn into the marina with a screech of the tyres. Stranahan pointed toward the slip where his aluminium skiff was tied up, and García parked right across from it. He kept the engine running. Stranahan tried to open the door, but García had it locked with a button on the driver's side.

The detective punched the lighter knob in the dashboard and said, 'Don't you have anything else you want to ask? Think real hard, Mick.'

Stranahan reached across and earnestly shook García's hand. 'Thanks for everything, Al. I mean it.'

'Hey, are we having the same conversation? What the fuck is the matter with you?'

Stranahan said, 'It's been a depressing week.'

'Don't you even want to know what the waitresses and the pump jockey really said? About the guy with Chloe?'

'What guy?'

García clapped his hands. 'Good, I got your attention. Excellent!' He pulled the lighter from the dash and fired up the cigar.

'What guy?' Stranahan asked again.

Making the most of the moment, García took his note-book from his jacket and read aloud: 'White male, early thirties, approximately seven feet tall, two hundred fifty pounds, freckled, balding—'

134

'Holy shit.'

'—appeared to be wearing fright make-up, or possibly some type of Halloween mask. The waitresses couldn't agree on what, but they all said basically the same thing about the face. Said it looked like somebody dragged it across a cheese grater.'

Mick Stranahan couldn't recall putting anybody in jail who matched that remarkable description. He asked García if he had any leads.

'We're busy calling the circuses to see who's escaped lately,' the detective said sarcastically. 'I swear, I don't know why I tell you anything.'

He pushed the button to unlock the doors. 'We'll be in touch,' he said to Stranahan, waving him out of the police car. 'And stay away from the damn doctor, OK?'

'You bet,' said Mick Stranahan. All he could think of was: *Seven feet tall*. Poor Chloe.

Dr Rudy Graveline now accepted the possibility that his world was imploding, and that he must prepare for the worst. Bitterly he thought of all the crises he had survived, all the professional setbacks, the lawsuits, the peer review hearings, the hospital expulsions, the hasty relocations from one jurisdiction to another. There was the time he augmented the breasts of a two-hundred-pound woman who had wanted a reduction instead; the time he nearly liposuctioned a man's gall bladder right out of his abdomen; the time he mistakenly severed a construction worker's left ear while removing a dime-sized cyst—Rudy Graveline had survived all these. He believed he'd found safe haven in South Florida; having figured out the system, and how to beat it, he was sure he had it made. And suddenly a botched nose job had come back to spoil it all. It didn't seem fair.

Rudy sat at his desk and leafed dispiritedly through the most recent bank statements. The Whispering Palms surgical complex was raking in money, but the overhead was high and the mortgage was a killer. Rudy had not been able to siphon off nearly as much as he had hoped.

Once his secret plan had been to retire in four years with six million put away; it now seemed likely that he would be forced to get out much sooner, and with much less. Having already been banned from practising medicine in California and New York—by far the most lucrative markets for a plastic surgeon—Rudy Graveline's thoughts now turned to the cosmopolitan cities of South America, a new frontier of vanity, sun-baked and ripe with wrinkles; a place where a Harvard medical degree still counted for something. Riffling through his CDs, he wondered if it was too late to weasel out of the Old Cypress Towers project: get liquid and get gone.

He was studying a map of Brazil when Heather Chappell, the famous actress, came into the office. She wore the pink terrycloth robe and bath slippers that Whispering Palms provided to all its VIP guests. Heather's lipstick was candy apple, her skin had a caramel tan, and her frosted blond hair was thick and freshly brushed. She was a perfectly beautiful thirty-year-old woman who, for reasons unfathomable, despised her own body. A dream patient, as far as Rudy Graveline was concerned.

She sat in a low-backed leather chair and said, 'I've had it with the spa. Let's talk about my operation.'

Rudy said, 'I wanted you to unwind for a couple days, that's all.'

'It's been a couple days.'

'But aren't you more relaxed?'

'Not really,' Heather said. 'Your masseur, what's-his-name—'

'Niles?'

'Yeah, Niles. He tried to cornhole me yesterday. Aside from that, I've been bored to tears.'

Rudy smiled with practised politeness. 'But you've had a chance to think about the different procedures.'

'I didn't need to think about anything, Dr Graveline. I was ready the first night off the plane. Have you been dodging me?'

'Of course not.'

'I heard your car got blown up.' She said it in a

schoolgirl's voice, like it was gossip she'd picked up in study hall.

Rudy tried to neutralize his inflection. 'There was an accident,' he said. 'Very minor.'

'The night I came, wasn't it? That hunk in the parking lot, the guy who put me in the taxi. What's going on with him?'

Rudy ignored the question. 'I can schedule the surgery for tomorrow,' he said.

'Fine, but I want you to do it,' Heather said. 'You personally.'

'Of course,' Rudy said. He'd stay in the OR until they put her under, then he'd head for the back nine at Doral. Let one of the young hotshots do the knife work.

'What did you decide?' he asked her.

Heather stood up and stepped out of the slippers. Then she let the robe drop to the carpet. 'You tell me,' she said.

Rudy's mouth went dry at the sight of her.

'Well,' he said. 'Let's see.' The problem was, she didn't need any surgery. Her figure, like her face, was sensational. Her tan breasts were firm and large, not the least bit droopy. Her tummy was tight and flat as an iron. There wasn't an ounce of fat, a trace of a stretch mark, the slenderest serpentine shadow of a spider vein—not on her thighs, her legs, not anywhere. Nothing was out of proportion. Naked, Heather looked like an 'after', not a 'before'.

Rudy was really going to have to scramble on this one. He put on his glasses and said, 'Come over here, Miss Chappell, let me take a closer look.'

She walked over and, to his stupefaction, climbed up on the onyx desk, her bare feet squeaking on the slick black surface. Standing, she vamped a movie pose—one hand on her hip, the other fluffing her hair. As Rudy's eyes travelled up those long legs, he nearly toppled over backwards in his chair.

'The nose, obviously,' Heather said.

137

'Yes,' said Rudy, thinking: She has a great straight nose. What the hell am I going to do?

'And the breasts,' Heather said, taking one in each hand and studying them. Like she was in the produce section, checking out the grapefruits.

Bravely Rudy asked, 'Would you like them larger or smaller?'

Heather glared at him. 'Bigger, of course! And brand-new nipples.'

Jesus, Rudy muttered under his breath. 'Miss Chappell,' he said, 'I wouldn't advise new nipples. There could be serious complications and, really, it isn't necessary.' Little pink rosebuds, that's what her nipples looked like. Why, Rudy wondered, would she ever want new ones?

In a pouty voice, Heather said all right, leave the nipples. Then she pivoted on the desktop and patted her right thigh. 'I want two inches off here.'

'That much?' Rudy was sweating. He didn't see it, plain and simple. Two inches of what?

'Stand up,' Heather told him. 'Look here.'

He did, he looked hard. His chin was about three inches from her pubic bone. 'Two inches,' Heather repeated, turning to show him the other thigh, 'from both sides.'

'As you wish,' the doctor said. What the hell, he'd be on the golf course anyway. Let the whizz-kids figure it out.

Heather dropped to her knees on the desk, so the two of them were nearly face to face. 'And I want my eyelids done,' she said, pointing with a long cranberry fingernail, 'and my neck, too. You said no scars, remember?'

'Don't worry,' Rudy assured her.

'Good,' Heather said. 'Anything else?'

'Not that I can see.'

'How about my butt?' She spun around on the desk, showing it to Rudy; looking over one shoulder, waiting for his professional opinion.

'Well,' said Rudy, running his fingers along the soft round curves.

'Hey,' said Heather, 'easy there.' She squirmed around to face him. 'Are you getting worked up?'

Rudy Graveline said, 'Of course not.' But he was. He couldn't figure it out, either; all the thousands of female bodies he got to see and feel. This was no ordinary lust, this was something fresh and wondrous. Maybe it was the way she bossed him around.

'I saw you in *Fevers of the Heart*,' Rudy said, idiotically. He had rented the cassette for a pool party. 'You were quite good, especially the scene on the horse.'

'Sit down,' Heather told him, and he did. She was bare-assed on the desk, legs swinging mischievously on either side of him. He put a clammy hand on each knee. 'Maybe now's a good time to talk about money,' she said.

For Rudy Graveline, the ultimate test of sobriety. In his entire career he had never traded sex for his surgical services, never even discounted. Money was money, pussy was pussy—a credo he drilled into his sure-handed young assistants. Some things in life you just don't give away.

To Heather Chappell, he said, 'I'm afraid it's going to be expensive.'

'Is it?' She swung one leg up and propped her foot on his right shoulder.

'All these procedures at once, yes, I'm afraid so.'

'How much, Dr Graveline?'

Up came the other leg, and Rudy was scissored.

'Come here a second,' Heather said.

Rudy Graveline was torn between the thing he loved most and the thing he needed most: sex and money. The warm feel of Heather's bare heels on his shoulders was like the weight of the world. And heaven, too.

Her toes tickled his ears. 'I said, come here.'

'Where?' Rudy peeped, reaching out.

'God, are you blind?'

Chemo bought an Ingram sub-machine-gun to go with his .22 pistol. He got it from a man who had come to the club one night with a bunch of Jamaicans. The man himself was not a Jamaican; he was from Colombia. Chemo found this out when he stopped him at the door and told him he couldn't come inside the Gay Bidet with a machine-gun.

'But this is Miami,' the man had said with a Spanish accent.

'I've got my orders,' Chemo said.

The man agreed to let Chemo take the gun while he and his pals went inside, which turned out to be a smart thing. As the band was playing a song called *Suck Till You're Sore*, a local skinhead gang went into a slam-dancing frenzy, and fights broke out all over the place. The Jamaicans took off, but the Colombian stayed behind to do battle. At one point he produced a pocket knife and tried to surgically remove the swastika tattoo off the proud but hairless chest of a teenaged skinhead. The band took a much-needed break while the Beach police rushed in for the arrests. Later, when Chemo spotted the Colombian in the back of the squad car, he tapped on the window and asked about the Ingram. The Colombian said keep it and Chemo said thanks, and slipped a twenty-dollar bill through the crack of the window.

The thing Chemo liked best about the Ingram was the shoulder strap. He put it on and showed it to his boss, Freddie, who said, 'Get the fuck outta here with that thing!'

The next day, January eighteenth, Chemo got up early and drove out to Key Biscayne. He knew it would be unwise to go to the same marina where he had taken Chloe, so he looked around for another boat place. He found one near the Marine Stadium, where they race the big Budweiser speedboats. At first a kid with badly bleached hair tried to rent him a twenty-foot Dusky for a hundred and ten dollars a day, plus a hundred and fifty security deposit. Chemo didn't have that kind of money.

'Got a credit card?' the kid asked.

'No,' said Chemo. 'What about that thing over there?'

'That's a jet ski,' the kid said.

It was designed like a waterbug with handlebars. You drove it like a motorcycle, only standing up. This one was yellow, with the word *Kawasaki* on the front.

'You don't want to try it,' the kid with yellow hair said.

'Why not?'

'Because,' the kid said, laughing, 'you're too tall, man. Hit a wake, it'll snap your spine.'

Chemo figured the guy was just trying to talk him into renting something bigger, something he didn't need.

'How much is the jet ski?' he said.

'Twenty an hour, but you got to sign a waiver.' The kid was thinking that, as tall as this guy is, he doesn't look healthy enough to ride a jet ski; he looks kind of tapped-out and sickly, like he's been hanging from the wall of some dungeon for a couple months. The kid was thinking maybe he ought to ask if the guy knew how to swim, just in case.

Chemo handed him two twenties.

The kid said, 'I'll still need a deposit.'

Chemo said he didn't have any more money. The kid said he'd take Chemo's wristwatch, but Chemo said no, he didn't want to give it up. It was a Heuer diving watch, silver and gold links, made in Switzerlaand. Chemo had swiped it off a young architect who was overdosing in the men's room at the club. While the jerk was lying there in the stall, trying to swallow his tongue, Chemo grabbed his wrist and replaced the Heuer with his own thirty-dollar Seiko with the fake alligator band.

'No jet ski without a deposit,' said the kid with yellow hair.

'How about a gun?' Chemo said.

'What kind?'

Chemo showed him the .22 and the kid said OK, since it was a Beretta he'd hang onto it. He stuck it in the front of his chinos and led Chemo to the jet ski. He showed Chemo how the choke and the throttle worked, and tossed him a bright red life vest.

'You can change in the shed,' the kid said.

'Change?'

'You got a swimsuit, right?' The kid hopped back on

141

the dock and gave Chemo the keys. 'Man, you don't want to ride these things in heavy pants.'

'I guess not,' said Chemo, unbuckling his trousers.

A shrimper named Joey agreed to take Christina Marks anywhere she wanted. When she gave him a hundred-dollar bill, Joey looked at it and said, 'Where you going, Havana?'

'Stiltsville,' Christina said, climbing into the pungent shrimp boat. 'And I need a favour.'

'You bet,' said Joey, tossing off the ropes.

'After you drop me off, I need you to stay close. Just in case.'

Joey aimed the bow down the canal, toward the mouth of Norris Cut. 'In case what?' he asked.

'In case the man I'm going to see doesn't want me to stay.'

Joey grinned and said, 'I can't imagine that. Here, you want a beer?'

He motored down the ocean side of Key Biscayne in amiable silence. Christina stood next to him at the wheel, guardedly watching the swarm of hungry seagulls that wailed and dove behind the stern. When the shrimp boat passed the Cape Florida lighthouse at the tip of the island, Christina saw the stilt houses to the south.

'Which one?' Joey shouted over the engines. When Christina pointed, Joey smiled and gave her a crusty wink.

'What's that mean?'

'Him,' Joey said. 'Why didn't you say so?'

They were maybe two hundred yards off the radio towers and making the wide turn into the channel when Joey nudged Christina Marks and pointed with his chin. Up ahead, something swift and yellow was crossing one of the tidal flats, bouncing severely in the choppy water. It was an odd, gumdrop-shaped craft, and a tall pale figure appeared to be standing in the middle, holding on with both arms.

Joey eased back on the throttle to give way.

'I hate those fool things,' he said. 'Damn tourists don't know where the hell they're going.'

They watched it cross from the starboard side, no more than thirty yards ahead of them. Joey frowned and said, 'I'll be goddamned.' He snatched a rag from his tool box and wiped the salty film from the shrimp boat's windshield.

'Look,' he said to Christina. 'Now you've seen it all.'

The tall pale man driving the jet ski was nude except for his soggy Jockey shorts.

And black sunglasses.

And a gleaming wristwatch.

And an Ingram .45 sub-machine-gun strapped on his bare shoulder.

Christina Marks was astonished. 'What do you suppose he's doing out here with *that*?'

'Whatever the hell he wants,' said Joey the shrimper.

13

Earlier that day, Tina and two of her girlfriends had appeared at the stilt house in a borrowed Bayliner Capri. They saw Mick Stranahan sleeping on the roof beneath the windmill, the Remington shot-gun at his side.

Tina's friends were alarmed. They voted to stay in the boat while Tina went up on the dock and approached the house.

'Richie wants me back,' she called to Stranahan.

He sat up and rubbed his eyes. 'What?'

'I said, Richie wants me back. I wanted you to be the first to know.'

'Why?' Stranahan said, his voice thick.

'So you could change my mind.'

Stranahan noticed that a seagull had crapped all over the shot-gun while he was asleep. 'Damn,' he said under his breath. He took a black bandanna from the pocket of his jeans and wiped the gunstock.

'Well?' came Tina's voice from below. 'You going to change my mind or not?'

'How?'

'Sleep with me.'

'I already did,' Stranahan said.

'You know what I mean.'

'Go back to Richie,' Stranahan advised. 'If he hits you again, file charges.'

'Why are you so afraid?'

Stranahan slid butt-first down the grainy slope of the roof, to a spot from which Tina was visible in her tiny tangerine thong swimsuit.

'We've been over this,' Stranahan said to her.

'But I don't want to marry you,' she said. 'I promise. Even if you ask me afterwards, I'll say no—no matter how great it was. Besides, I'm not a waitress. You said all the others were waitresses.'

He groaned and said, 'Tina, I'm sorry. It just won't work.'

Now she looked angry. One of the other girls in the Bayliner turned on the radio and Tina snapped at her, told her to shut off the damn music. 'How do you know it won't work?' she said to Stranahan.

'I'm too old.'

'Bullshit.'

'And you're too young.'

'Double bullshit.'

'OK,' he said. 'Then name the Beatles.'

'What?' Tina forced a caustic laugh. 'Are you serious?'

'Dead serious,' Stranahan said, addressing her from the edge of the roof. 'If you can name all the Beatles, I'll make love to you right now.'

'I don't believe this,' Tina said. 'The fucking Beatles.'

Stranahan had done the math in his head: she was nineteen, which meant she had been born the same year that the band broke up.

'Well, there's Paul,' Tina said.

'Last name?'

'Come on!'

'Let's hear it.'

'McCartney, OK? I don't believe this.'

Stranahan said, 'Go on, you're doing fine.'

'Ringo,' Tina said. 'Ringo Starr. The drummer with the nose.'

'Good.'

'And then there's the guy who died. Lennon.'

'First name?'

'I know his son is Julian.'

'His son doesn't count.'

Tina said, 'Yeah, well, you're an asshole. It's *John*. John Lennon.'

Stranahan nodded appreciatively. 'Three down, one to go. You're doing great.'

Tina folded her arms and tried to think of the last Beatle. Her lips were pursed in a most appealing way, but Stranahan stayed on the roof. 'I'll give you a hint,' he said to Tina. 'Lead guitar.'

She looked up at him, triumph shining in her grey eyes. 'Harrison,' she declared. 'Keith Harrison!'

Muttering, Stranahan crabbed back up to his vantage beneath the legs of the windmill. Tina said some sharp things, all of which he deserved, and then got on the boat with her friends and headed back across the bay toward Dinner Key and, presumably, Richie.

Joey the shrimper spat over the transom and said, 'Well, there's your boy.'

Christina Marks frowned. Mick Stranahan lay naked in the shape of a T on the roof of the house. His tan legs were straight, and each arm was extended. He had a bandanna pulled down over his eyes to shield them from the white rays of the sun. Christina Marks thought he looked like the victim of a Turkish firing squad.

'He looks like Christ,' said Joey. 'Don't you think he looks like Christ? Christ without a beard, I mean.'

'Take me up to the house,' Christina said. 'Do you have a horn on this thing?'

'Hell, he knows we're here.'

'He's sleeping.'

'No, ma'am,' Joey said. 'You're wrong.' But he sounded the horn anyway. Mick Stranahan didn't stir.

Joey idled the shrimp boat closer. The tide was up plenty high, rushing sibilantly under the pilings of the house. Clutching a brown grocery bag, Christina stepped up on the dock and waved the shrimper away.

'Thanks very much.'

Joey said, 'You be sure to tell him what we saw. About that big freak on the water scooter.'

She nodded.

'Tell him first thing,' Joey said. He pulled back on the throttle and the old diesel moaned into reverse. The engine farted an odious cloud of blue smoke that enveloped Christina Marks. She coughed all the way up the stairs.

When she got to the main deck, Stranahan was sitting on the edge of the roof, legs dangling.

'What's in the bag?'

'Cold cuts, wine, cheese. I thought you might be hungry.'

'This how they do it in New York?'

The sack was heavy, but Christina didn't put it down. She held it like a baby, with both arms, but not too tightly. She didn't want him to think it was a chore. 'What are you talking about?'

'The wine and cheese,' Stranahan said. 'There's a sense of ceremony about it. Maybe it's necessary where you come from, but not here.'

'Fuck you,' said Christina Marks. 'I'm on expense account, hotshot.'

Stranahan smiled. 'I forgot.' He hopped off the roof and landed like a cat. She followed him into the house and watched him slip into blue jean cutoffs, no underwear. She put the bag on the kitchen counter and he went to work, fixing lunch. From the refrigerator he got some pickles and a half pound of big winter shrimp, still in the shell.

146

As he opened the wine, he said, 'Let's get right to it: you've heard something.'

'Yes,' Christina said. 'But first: you won't believe what we just saw. A man with a machine-gun, on one of those water-jet things.'

'Where?'

She motioned with her chin. 'Not even a mile from here.'

'What did he look like?'

Christina described him. Stranahan popped the cork.

'I guess we better eat fast,' he said. He was glad he'd brought the shot-gun down from the roof after Tina and her friends had left, when he went to find a fresh bandanna. Subconsciously he glanced at the Remington, propped barrel-up in the corner of the same wall with the stuffed marlin head.

Christina peeled a shrimp, dipped it tail-first into a plastic thimble of cocktail sauce. 'Are you going to tell me who he is, the man in the underwear?'

'I don't know,' Stranahan said. 'I honestly don't. Now tell me what else.'

This would be the most difficult part. She said, 'I went to see your friend Tim Gavigan at the hospital.'

'Oh.'

'I was there when he died.'

Stranahan cut himself three fat slices of cheddar. 'Extreme unction,' he said. 'Too bad you're not a priest.'

'He wanted me to tell you something. Something he remembered about the Vicky Barletta case.'

With a mouthful of cheese, Stranahan said, 'Tell me you didn't take that asshole up to the VA. Flemm—you didn't let him have a crack at Timmy in that condition, did you?'

'Of course not,' she said sharply. 'Now listen: Tim Gavigan remembered that the plastic surgeon has a brother. George Graveline. He saw him working outside the clinic.'

'Doing what?' Stranahan asked.

'This is what Tim wanted me to tell you. The guy is a tree trimmer. He said you'd know what that means. He was going on about Hoffa and dead bodies.'

147

Stranahan laughed. 'Yeah, he's right. It's perfect.'

Impatiently Christina said, 'You want to fill me in?'

Stranahan chomped on a pickle. 'You know what a wood chipper is? It's like a king-sized sideways Cuisinart, except they use it to shred wood. Tree companies tow them around like a U-Haul. Throw the biggest branches down this steel chute and they come out sawdust and barbecue chips.'

'Now I get it,' Christina said.

'Something can pulverize a mahogany tree, think of what it could do to a human body.'

'I'd rather not.'

'There was a famous murder case up in New Jersey, they had everything but the corpse. The corpse was ground up in a wood chipper so basically all they found was splinters of human bone—not enough for a good forensic ID. Finally somebody found a molar, and the tooth had a gold filling. That's how they made the case.'

Christina was still thinking about bone splinters.

'At any rate,' Stranahan said, 'it's a helluva good lead. Hurry now, finish up.' He wedged the cork into the half-empty wine bottle and started wrapping the leftover cold cuts and cheese in wax paper. Christina was reaching for one last shrimp when he snatched the dish away and put it in the refrigerator.

'Hey!'

'I said hurry.'

She noticed how deliberately he was moving, and it struck her that something was happening. 'What is it, Mick?'

'You mean you don't hear it?'

Christina said no.

'Just listen,' he said, and before she knew it the stilt house was shuttered, and the door closed, and the two of them were alone in the corner of the bedroom, sitting on the wooden floor. At first the only sound Christina Marks heard was the two of them breathing, and then came some scratching noises that Stranahan said were seagulls up on the roof. Finally, when she leaned her head against the plywood wall, she detected a far-away hum. The longer she listened, the more distinct it became. The pitch of the motor was too weak to be an aeroplane and too high to be much of a boat.

'Jesus, it's him,' she said with a tremble.

Stranahan acknowledged the fact with a frown. 'You know,' he said, 'this used to be a pretty good neighbourhood.'

Chemo wondered about the Ingram, about the effects of salt spray on the firing mechanism. He didn't know much about machine-guns, but he suspected that it was best not to get them wet. The ride out to Stiltsville had been wetter than he'd planned.

He parked the jet ski beneath one of the other stilt houses to wait for the shrimp boat to leave Mick Stranahan's place. He saw a good-looking woman in a white cottony top and tan safari shorts hop off the shrimp boat and go upstairs, so Chemo began to work her into the scenario. He didn't know if she was a wife or a girlfriend or what, but it didn't matter. She was there, and she had to die. End of story.

Chemo prised open a toolshed and found a rag for the Ingram. Carefully he wiped off the moisture and salt. The gun looked fine, but there was only one way to be sure. He took an aluminium mop handle from the shed and busted the padlock off the door of the house. Once inside, he quickly found a target: an old convertible sofa, its flowered fabric showing traces of mould and mildew. Chemo shut the door to trap the noise. Then he knelt in front of the sofa, put the Ingram to his shoulder and squeezed off three rounds. Dainty puffs of white fuzz and dust rose with the impact of each bullet. Chemo lowered the gun and carefully examined the .45-calibre holes in the cushions.

Now he was ready. He slung the gun strap over his shoulder and pulled his soggy Jockey shorts up snugly on his waist. He was about to go when he thought of something. Quickly he moved through the house, opening doors until he found a bathroom.

At the sink Chemo took off his sunglasses and put his

face to the mirror. With a forefinger he tested the tiny pink patch of flesh that Dr Rudy Graveline had dermabraded. The patch no longer stung; in fact, it seemed to be coming along nicely. Chemo was extremely pleased, and ventured forth in bright spirits.

Someplace, maybe it was *Reader's Digest*, he had read that salt water actually expedited the healing process.

'Don't move,' Mick Stranahan whispered.

'I wasn't planning on it.'

'Unless I tell you.'

From the hum of the engine, Christina Marks guessed that the jet ski was very close: no more than thirty yards.

Stranahan held the shot-gun across his knees. She looked at his hands and noticed they were steady. Hers were shaking like an old drunk's.

'Do you have a plan?' she asked.

'Basically, my plan is to stay alive.'

'Are you going to shoot him?'

Stranahan looked at her as if she were five years old. 'Now what do you think? *Of course* I'm going to shoot him. I intend to blow the motherfucker's head off, unless you've got some objection.'

'Just asking,' Christina said.

Chemo was thinking: Damn Japanese.

Whoever designed these jet skis must have been a frigging dwarf.

His back was killing him; he had to hunch over like a washerwoman to reach the handlebars. Every time he hit a wave, the gun strap slipped off his bony shoulder. A couple times he thought for sure he'd lost the Ingram, or at least broken it. Damn Japanese.

As he approached Stranahan's stilt house, Chemo started thinking something else. He had already factored the girl into the scenario, figured he'd shoot her first and get it over with. But then he realized he had another problem: surely she had seen him ski past the shrimp boat, probably noticed the machine-gun, probably told Stranahan.

Who had probably put it together.

So Chemo anticipated a fight. Screw the element of surprise; the damn jet scooter was as loud as a Harley. Stranahan could hear him coming two miles away.

But where was he?

Chemo circled the stilt house slowly, eventually riding the curl of his own wake. The windows were down, the door shut. No sign of life, except for a pair of ratty looking gulls on the roof.

A thin smile of understanding came to his lips. Of course—the man was waiting inside. A little ambush action.

Chemo coasted the jet ski up to the dock and stepped off lightly. He took the Ingram off his shoulder and held it in front of him as he went up the stairs, thinking: Where's the logical place for Stranahan to be waiting? In a corner, of course.

He was pleased to find that the wooden deck went around Stranahan's entire house. Walking cautiously on storklike legs, Chemo approached the south-west corner first. Calmly he fired one shot, waist level, through the wall. He repeated the same procedure at each of the other corners, then sat on the rail of the deck and waited. When nothing happened after three minutes, he walked up to the front door and fired twice more.

Then he went in.

Christina Marks was not aware that Stranahan had been hit until she felt something warm on her bare arm. She opened her mouth to scream but Stranahan covered it with his hand and motioned for her to be quiet. She saw that his eyes were watering from the pain of the bullet wound. He removed his hand from her mouth and pointed at his left shoulder. Christina nodded but didn't look.

They heard three more gunshots, each in a different part of the house. Then came a silence that lasted a few agonizing minutes. Finally Stranahan rose to his feet with the shot-gun cradled in his right arm. The left side of his body was numb and wet with blood;

in the twilight of the shuttered house, he looked two-tone.

From the floor Christina watched him move. He pressed his back to the wall and edged toward the front of the house. The next shots made Christina shut her eyes. When she opened them she saw two perfect holes through the front door; twin sunbeams, sharp as lasers, perforated the shadows. Beneath the light shafts, Mick Stranahan lay prone on his belly, elbows braced on the wooden floor. He was aiming at the front door when Chemo opened it.

Stranahan's shot-gun was a Remington 1100, a semi-automatic twelve-gauge, an excellent bird gun that holds up to five shells. Later, when Stranahan measured the distance from the door to where he had lain, he would marvel at how any human being with two good eyes could miss a seven-foot target at a distance of only nineteen feet four inches. The fact that Stranahan was bleeding to death at the time was not, in his view, a mitigating excuse.

In truth, it was the shock of the intruder's appearance that had caused Stranahan to hesitate—the sight of this gaunt, pellucid, frizzle-haired freak with a moonscape face that could stop a freight train.

So Stranahan had stared for a nanosecond when he should have squeezed the trigger. For someone who looked so sickly, Chemo moved deceptively fast. As he dove out of the doorway, the first blast from the Remington sprinkled its rain of birdshot into the bay.

'Shit,' Stranahan said, struggling to his feet. On his way toward the door he slipped on his own blood and went down again, his right cheek slamming hard on the floor; this, just as Chemo craned around the corner and fired a messy burst from the Ingram. Rolling in a sticky mess, Stranahan shot back.

Chemo slammed the door from the outside, plunging the house into darkness once more.

Stranahan heard the man running on the outside deck, following the apron around the house. Stranahan took aim through the walls. He imagined that the man was a rising quail, and he led accordingly. The first blast tore a softball-sized hole in the wall of the living room. The second punched out the shutter in the kitchen. The third and final shot was followed by a grunt and a splash outside.

'Christina!' Stranahan shouted. 'Quick, help me up.'

But when she got there, biting back tears, crawling on bare knees, he had already passed out.

Chemo landed on his back in the water. He kicked his legs just to make sure he wasn't paralysed; other than a few splinters in his scalp, he seemed to be fine. He figured that the birdshot must have missed him, that the concussion so close to his head was what threw him off balance.

Instinctively he held the Ingram high out of the water with his right hand, and paddled furiously with his left. He knew he had to make it under cover of the house before Stranahan came out; otherwise he'd be a sitting duck. Chemo saw that the machine-gun was dripping, so he figured it must have gotten dunked in the fall. Would it still fire? And how many rounds were left? He had lost count.

These were his concerns as he made for the pilings beneath the stilt house. Progress was maddeningly slow; by paddling with only one hand, Chemo tended to move himself in a frothy circle. In frustration he paddled more frenetically, a tactic that decreased the perimeter of his route but brought him no closer to safety. He expected at any second to see Stranahan burst onto the deck with the shot-gun.

Beneath Chemo there appeared in the water a long grey-blue shadow, which hung there as if frozen in glass. It was Stranahan's silent companion, Liza, awakened from its afternoon siesta by the wild commotion.

A barracuda this age is a creature of sublime instinct and flawless precision, an eating machine more calculating and efficient than any shark in the ocean. Over time the great barracuda had come to associate human activity with feeding; its impulses had been tuned by Stranahan's evening pinfish ritual. As Chemo struggled in the shallows, the barracuda was on full alert, its cold eyes trained upward in anticipation. The blue-veined legs that kicked impotently at its head, the spastic thrashing—these posed no threat.

Something else had caught its attention: the familiar rhythmic glint of stunned prey on the water's surface. The barracuda struck with primitive abandon, streaking up from the deep, slashing, then boring back toward the pilings.

There, beneath the house, the great fish flared its crimson gills in a darkening sulk. What it had mistaken for an easy meal of silver pinfish turned out to be no such thing, and the barracuda spat ignominiously through its fangs.

It was a testimony to sturdy Swiss craftsmanship that the Heuer diving watch was still ticking when it came to rest on the bottom. Its stainless silver and gold links glistened against Chemo's pale severed hand, which reached up from the turtle grass like some lost piece of mannequin.

14

On Washington Avenue there was a small shop that sold artificial limbs. Dr Rudy Graveline went there on his lunch hour and purchased four different models of prosthetic hands. He paid cash and made sure to get a receipt.

Later, back at Whispering Palms, he arranged the artificial hands in an attractive row on the top of his onyx desk.

'What about this one?' he asked Chemo.

'It's a beaut,' Chemo said trenchantly, 'except I've already got one on *that* arm.'

'Sorry.' Rudy Graveline picked up another. 'Then look here—state-of-the-art technology. Four weeks of therapy, you can deal blackjack with this baby.'

'Wrong colour,' Chemo remarked.

Rudy glanced at the artificial hand and thought: Of course it's the wrong colour, they're *all* the wrong damn colour. 'It's a tough match,' the doctor said. 'I looked for the palest one they had.'

'I hate them all,' Chemo said. 'Why does it have to be a hand, anyway?'

'You didn't like the mechanical hooks,' Rudy Graveline reminded him. 'Talk about advanced, you could load a gun, even type with those things. But you said no.'

'Damn right I said no.'

Rudy put down the prosthesis and said: 'I wish you wouldn't take that tone with me. I'm doing the best I can.'

'Oh, yeah.'

'Look, didn't I advise you to see a specialist?'

'And didn't I advise you, you're crazy? The cops'll be hunting all over.'

'All right,' Rudy said in a calming voice. 'Let's not argue.'

It had been three weeks since Chemo had shown up behind Whispering Palms on a blood-streaked water scooter—a vision that Dr Rudy Graveline would carry with him for the rest of his life. It had happened during an afternoon consult with Mrs Carla Crumworthy, heiress to the Crumworthy panty-shield fortune. She had come to complain about the collagen injections that Rudy Graveline had administered to give her full, sensual lips, which is just what every rheumatoid seventy-one-year-old woman needs. Mrs Crumworthy had lamented that the results were nothing like she had hoped, that she now resembled one of those Ubangi tribal women from the *National Geographic*, the ones with the ceramic platters in their mouths. And, in truth, Dr Rudy Graveline was concerned about what had happened, because Mrs Crumworthy's lips had indeed grown bulbous and unwieldy and hard as cobblestones. As he examined her (keeping his doubts to himself), Rudy wondered if maybe he had injected too much collagen, or not enough, or if maybe he'd zapped it into the wrong spots. Whatever the cause, the result was undeniable: Mrs Carla Crumworthy looked like a duck wearing mauve lipstick. A malpractice jury could have a ball with this one.

Dr Graveline had been whisking through his trusty Rolodex, searching for a kind-hearted colleague, when Mrs Crumworthy suddenly rose to her feet and shrieked. Pointing out the picture window toward Biscayne Bay, the old woman had blubbered in terror, her huge misshapen lips slapping together in wet percussion. Rudy had no idea what she was trying to say.

He spun around and looked out the window.

The yellow jet ski lay on its side, adrift in the bay. somehow Chemo had dragged himself, soaking wet and stark naked, over the ledge of the seawall behind the clinic. He didn't look well enough to be dead. His grey shoulders shivered violently in the sunshine, and his eyes flickered vaguely through puffy purple slits. Chemo swung the blody stump to show Dr Graveline what had happened to his left hand. He pointed gamely at the elastic wrist tourniquet that he had fashioned from his Jockey shorts, and Rudy would later concede that it had probably saved his life.

Mrs Carla Crumworthy was quickly ushered to a private recovery suite and oversedated, while Rudy and two young assistant surgeons led Chemo to an operating room. The assistants argued that he belonged at a real trauma centre in a real hospital, but Chemo adamantly refused. This left the doctors with no choice but to operate or let him bleed to death.

Gently discouraged from participating in the surgery, Rudy had been content to let the young fellows work unimpeded. He spent the time making idle conversation with the woozy Chemo, who had rejected a general anaesthetic in favour of an old-fashioned intravenous jolt of Demerol.

Since that evening, Chemo's post-op recovery had progressed swiftly and in relative luxury, with the entire staff of Whispering Palms instructed to accommodate his every wish. Rudy Graveline himself was exceedingly attentive, as he needed Chemo's loyalty now more than ever. He had hoped that the killer's spirits would improve at the prospect of reconstructing his abbreviated left arm.

'A new hand,' Rudy said, 'would be a major step back to a normal life.'

'I never had a normal life,' Chemo pointed out. Sure, he would miss the hand, but he was more pissed off about losing the expensive wristwatch.

'What are my other options?' Chemo asked.

'What do you mean?'

'I mean, besides these things.' He waved his stump contemptuously at the artificial hands.

'Well,' Rudy said, 'frankly, I'm out of ideas.' He gathered the prostheses from his desk and put them back in the box. 'I told you, this isn't my field,' he said to Chemo.

'You keep trying to dump me off on some other surgeon, but it won't work. It's you or nobody.'

'I appreciate your confidence,' Rudy said. He leaned forward in his chair and put on his glasses. 'Can I ask, what's that on your face?'

Chemo said, 'It's Wite-Out.'

After a careful pause, Dr Graveline said, 'Can I ask—'

'I thought I might go out to the club later. I wanted to cover up these darn patches.'

Out of pity Rudy had agreed to dermabrade several more one-inch squares along Chemo's chin.

'You covered them with Wite-Out?'

Chemo said, 'Your secretary loaned me a bottle. The colour's just right.'

Rudy cleared his throat. 'It's not so good for your skin. Please, let me prescribe a mild cosmetic ointment.'

'Forget it,' said Chemo. 'This'll do fine. Now what about a new thing for my arm?' With his right hand he gestured at the bandaged limb.

Rudy folded his hands in his lap, a relaxed gesture that damn near exuded professional confidence. 'As I said before, we've gone over most of the conventional options.'

Chemo said, 'I don't like therapy. I want something easy to use, something practical.'

'I see,' said Rudy Graveline.

'And durable, too.'

'Of course.'

'Also, I don't want people to stare.'

Rudy thought: Beautiful. A seven-foot, one-handed geek with Wite-Out painted on his face, and he's worried about people staring.

'So what do you think?' Chemo pressed.

'I think,' said Dr Rudy Graveline, 'we've got to use our imaginations.'

Detective John Murdock bent his squat, porky frame over the rail of the hospital bed and said, 'Wake up, fuckwad.'

Which was pretty much his standard greeting.

Mick Stranahan did not open his eyes.

'Get out of here,' said Christina Marks.

Detective Joe Salazar lit a Camel and said, 'You don't look like a nurse. Since when do nurses wear blue jeans?'

'Good point,' said John Murdock. 'I think you're the one should get out of here.'

'Yeah,' said Joe Salazar. 'We got official business with this man.' Salazar was as short as his partner, only built like a stop sign. Flat, florid face stuck on a pipestem body.

'Now I know who you are,' Christina said. 'You must be Murdock and Salazar, the crooked cops.'

Stranahan nearly busted out laughing, but he pressed his eyes closed, trying to look asleep.

'I see what we got here,' said Murdock. 'What we got here is some kinda Lily Tomlin.'

'Sure,' said Joe Salazar, though he didn't know who his partner was talking about. He assumed it was somebody they'd arrested together. 'Sure,' he chimed in, 'a regular Lily Thomas.'

Christina Marks said, 'The man's asleep, so why don't you come back another time?'

'And why don't you go change your tampon or something?' snapped John Murdock. 'We've got business here.'

'We got questions,' Joe Salazar added. When he took the Camel cigarette out of his mouth, Christina noticed, the end was all soggy and mulched.

She said, 'I was there when it happened, if you want to ask me about it.'

Salazar had brought a Xerox of the marine patrol incident report. He took it out of his jacket, unfolded it, ran a sticky brown finger down the page until he came to the box marked Witnesses. 'So you're Initial C. Marks?'

'Yes,' Christina said.

'We've been looking all over Dade County for you. Two, three weeks we've been looking.'

'I changed hotels,' she said. She had moved from Key Biscayne over to the Grove, to be closer to Mercy Hospital.

John Murdock, the senior of the two detectives, took a chair from the corner, twirled it around, and sat down straddling it.

'Just like in the movies,' Christina said. 'You think better, sitting with your legs like that?'

Murdock glowered. 'What suppose we just throw your tight little ass in the women's annexe for a night or two, would you enjoy that? Just you and all the hookers, maybe a lesbo or two.'

'Teach you some manners,' Joe Salazar said, 'and that's not all.'

Christina smiled coolly. 'And here I thought you boys wanted a friendly chat. Maybe I'll just call hospital security and tell them what's going on up here. After that, maybe I'll call the newspapers.'

Mick Stranahan was thinking: She'd better be careful. These guys aren't nearly as dumb as they look.

Murdock said, 'One time we booked a big lesbo looked just like Kris Kristofferson. I'm not kidding, we're talking major facial hair. And mean as a bobcat.'

'Resisting with violence, two counts,' Salazar recalled. 'On top of the murder.'

'Manslaughter,' John Murdock cut in. 'Actually, womanslaughter, if there is such a thing. Jesus, what a mess. I can't even think about it, so close to lunch.'

'Involved a fire hose,' Salazar said.

'I said enough,' Murdock protested. 'Anyhow, I think she's still in the annexe. The one who looks like Kristofferson. I think she runs the drama group.'

Salazar said, 'You like the theatre, Miss Marks?'

'Sure,' Christina said, 'but mainly I like television. You guys ever been on TV? Maybe you've heard of the Reynaldo Flemm show.'

'Yeah,' Joe Salazar said, excitedly. 'One time I saw him get his ass pounded by a bunch of Teamsters. In slow motion, too.'

'*That* asshole,' Murdock muttered.

'We finally agree,' Christina said. 'Unfortunately, he happens to be my boss. We're in town taping a big story.'

The two detectives glanced at one another, trying to decide on a plan without saying it. Salazar stalled by lighting up another Camel.

Lying in bed listening, Mick Stranahan figured they'd back off now, just to be safe. Neither of these jokers wanted to see his own face on primetime TV.

Murdock said, 'So tell us what happened.' Salazar stood in the empty corner, resting his fat head against the wall.

Christina said, 'You've got photographic memories, or maybe you'd prefer to take some notes?' Murdock motioned to his partner, who angrily stubbed out his cigarette and dug a worn spiral notebook from his jacket.

She began with what she had seen from the wheelhouse of Joey's shrimp boat—the tall man toting a machine-gun on the jet scooter. She told the detectives about how Stranahan had battened down the stilt house, and how the man had started shooting into the corners. She told them how Stranahan had been wounded in the shoulder, and how he had fired back with a shot-gun until he passed out. She told them she had heard a splash outside, then a terrible cry; ten, maybe fifteen minutes later she'd heard somebody rev up the jet ski, but she was too scared to go to a window. Only when the engine was a faint whine in the distance did she peer through the bullet holes in the front door to see if the gunman had gone. She told the detectives how she had half-carried Stranahan down the stairs to where his skiff was docked, and how she had hand-cranked the outboard by herself. She told them how he had groggily pointed across the bay and said there was a big hospital on the mainland, and by the time they got to Mercy there was so much blood in the bottom of the skiff that she was bailing with a coffee mug.

After Christina had finished, Detective John Murdock said, 'That's quite a story. I bet *Argosy* magazine would go for a story like that.'

Joe Salazar leafed through his notebook and said, 'I think I missed something, lady. I think I missed the part where you explained why you're at Stranahan's house in the first place. Maybe you could repeat it.'

Murdock said, 'Yeah, I missed that, too.'

'I'd be happy to tell you why I was there,' Christina said. 'Mr Flemm wanted Mr Stranahan to be interviewed for an upcoming broadcast, but Mr Stranahan declined. I went to his house in the hopes of changing his mind.'

'I'll bet,' Salazar said.

'Joe, be nice,' said his partner. 'Tell me, Miss Marks, why'd you want to interview some dweeb PI? I mean, he's nobody. Hasn't been with the State Attorney for years.'

From his phoney coma Stranahan wondered how far Christina Marks would go. Not too far, he hoped.

'The interview involved a story we were working on, and that's all I can say.'

Murdock said, 'Gee, I hope it didn't concern a murder.'

'I really can't—'

'Because murder is our main concern. Me and Joe.'

Christina Marks said, 'I've co-operated as much as I can.'

'And you've been an absolute peach about it,' said Murdock. 'Fact, I almost forgot why we came in the first place.'

161

'Yeah,' said Detective Joe Salazar, 'the questions we got, you can't really answer. Thanks just the same.'

Murdock slid the chair back to the corner. 'See, we need to talk to Rip Van Rambo here. So I think you'd better go.' He smiled for the first time. 'And I apologize for that wisecrack about the Kotex. Not very professional, I admit.'

'It was tampons,' Joe Salazar said.

'Whatever.'

Christina Marks said, 'I'm not leaving this room. This man is recovering from a serious gunshot wound and you shouldn't disturb him.'

'We spoke to his doctor—'

'You're lying.'

'OK, we put in a call. The guy never called back.'

Salazar walked up to the hospital bed and said, 'He don't look so bad. Anyway, three weeks is plenty of time. Wake him up, Johnny.'

'Have it your way,' Christina said. She got a legal pad from her shoulder bag, uncapped a felt-tip pen, and sat down, poised to write.

'Now what the hell are you doing?' Salazar said.

'Forget about her,' Murdock said. He leaned close to Stranahan's face and sang, 'Mi-ick? Mick, buddy? Rise and shine.'

Stranahan growled sleepily, blowing a mouthful of stale, hot breath directly into Murdock's face.

'Holy Christ,' the detective said, turning away.

Salazar said, 'Johnny, I swear he's awake.' He cupped his hand at Stranahan's ear and shouted: '*Hey, fuckwad, you awake?*'

'Knock it off,' Christina said.

'I know how you can tell,' Salazar went on. 'Grab his dick. If he's asleep, he won't do nothing. If he's awake he'll jump ten feet out of this frigging bed.'

Murdock said, 'Aw, you're crazy.'

'You think he'd let one of us grab his schlong if he was wide awake? I'm telling you, Johnny, it's a sure way to find out.'

'OK, you do it.'

'Nuh-uh, we flip a coin.'

'Screw you, Joe. I ain't touching the man's privates. The county doesn't pay me enough.'

Stranahan was lying there, thinking: Thattaboy, Johnny, stick to the book.

From the corner Christina said, 'Lay a finger on him, I'll see that Mr Stranahan sues the living hell out of both of you. When he wakes up.'

'Not that old line,' Salazar said with a laugh.

She said, 'Beat the shit out of some jerk on the street, that's one thing. Grab a man's sexual organs while he's lying unconscious in a hospital bed—try to get the union worked up about *that*. You guys just kiss your pensions goodbye.'

Murdock shot Christina Marks a bitter look. 'When he wakes up, you be sure to tell him something. Tell him we know he drowned his ex-wife, so don't be surprised if we show up in Stiltsville with a waterproof warrant. Tell him he'd be smart to sell that old house, too, case a storm blows it down while he's off at Raiford.'

With secretarial indifference, Christina jotted every word on the legal pad. Murdock snorted and stalked out the door. Joe Salazar followed two steps behind, pocketing his own notebook, fumbling for a fresh Camel.

'Lady,' he said out the side of his mouth, 'you got to learn some respect for authority.'

That weekend, a notorious punk band called the Fudge Packers was playing the Gay Bidet. Freddie didn't like them at all. There were fights every night; the skinheads, the Latin Kings, the 34th Street Players. This is what Freddie couldn't understand: why the spooks and spics even showed up for a band like this. Usually they had better taste. The Fudge Packers were simply dreadful—four frigging bass guitars, now what the hell kind of music was that? No wonder everybody was fighting: take their minds off the noise.

Since Chemo had disappeared, Freddie had hired a new

head bouncer named Eugene, guy used to play in the World Football League. Eugene was all right, big as a garbage dumpster, but he couldn't seem to get people's attention the way Chemo did. Also, he was slow. Sometimes it took him five minutes to get down off the stage and pound heads in the crowd. By comparison Chemo had moved like a cat.

Freddie also was worried about Eugene's pro-labour leanings. One week at the Gay Bidet and already he was complaining about how loud the music was, could they please turn it down? You're kidding, Freddie had said, turn it down? But Eugene said damn right, his eardrums were fucking killing him. He said if his ears kept hurting he might go deaf and have to file a workman's comp, and Freddie said what's that? Then Eugene started going on about all his football injuries and, later, some shit that had happened to him working construction down in Homestead. He told Freddie about how the unions always took care of him, about how one time he was laid up for six weeks with a serious groin pull and never missed a paycheque. Not one.

Freddie could scarcely believe such a story. To him it sounded like something out of Communist Russia. He was delighted the night Chemo came back to work.

'Eugene, you're fired,' Freddie said. 'Go pull your groin someplace else.'

'What?' said Eugene, cocking his head and leaning closer.

'Don't pull that deaf shit with me,' Freddie warned. 'Now get lost.'

On his way out of Freddie's office, Eugene sized up his towering replacement. 'Man, what happened to you?'

'Gardening accident,' Chemo replied. Eugene grimaced sympathetically and said goodbye.

Freddie turned to Chemo. 'Thank God you're back. I'm afraid to ask.'

'Go ahead. Ask.'

'I don't think so,' Freddie said. 'Just tell me, you OK?'

Chemo nodded. 'Fine. The new band sounds like vomit.'

'Yeah, I know,' Freddie said. 'Geez, you should see the crowd. Be careful in there.'

'I'm ready for them,' Chemo said, hoisting his left arm to show Freddie the new device. He and Dr Rudy Graveline had found it on sale at a True Value hardware store.

'Wow,' said Freddie, staring.

'I got it rigged special for a six-volt battery,' Chemo explained. He patted the bulge under his arm. 'Strap it on with an Ace bandage. Only weighs about nine pounds.'

'Neat,' said Freddie, thinking: Sweet Jesus, this can't be what I think it is.

A short length of anodized aluminium piping protruded from the padding over Chemo's amputation. Bolted to the end of the pipe was a red saucer-sized disc made of hard plastic. Coiled tightly on a stem beneath the disc was a short length of eighty-pound monofilament fishing line.

Freddie said, 'OK, now I'm gonna ask.'

'It's a Weed Whacker,' Chemo said. 'See?'

15

George Graveline was sun-tanned and gnarled and sinewy, with breadloaf arms and wide black Elvis sideburns. The perfect tree trimmer.

George was not at all jealous of his younger brother, the plastic surgeon. Rudy deserved all the fine things in life, George reasoned, because Rudy had gone to college for what seemed like eternity. In George's view, no amount of worldly riches was worth sitting in a stuffy classroom for years at a stretch. Besides, he loved his job as a tree trimmer. He loved the smell of sawdust and fresh sap, and he loved gassing yellow jacket nests; he loved the whole damn outdoors. Even Florida winters could get miserably hot, but a person could adjust. George Graveline had a motto by which he faithfully lived: *Always park in the shade.*

He did not often see his wealthy brother, but that was all right. Dr Rudy was a busy man, and for that matter so was George. In Miami a good tree trimmer always had his hands full: year-round growth, no real seasons, no time for rest. Mainly you had your black olives and your common ficus tree, but the big problem there wasn't the branches so much as the roots. A twenty-year-old ficus had a root system could swallow the New York subway. Digging out a big ficus was a bitch. Then you had your exotics: the Australian pines, the melaleucas, and those God-forsaken Brazilian pepper trees, which most people mistakenly called a holly. Things grew like fungus, but George loved them because the roots weren't so bad and a couple good men could rip one out of the ground, no sweat. His favourite, though, was when people wanted their Brazilian pepper trees trimmed. Invariably these were customers new to Florida, novice suburbanites who didn't have the heart or the brains to actually *kill* a living tree. So they'd ask George Graveline to please just trim it back a little, and George would say sure, no problem, knowing that in three months it'd shoot out even bushier than before and strangle their precious hibiscus as sure as a coathanger. No denying there was damn good money in the pepper-tree racket.

On the morning of February tenth, George Graveline and his crew were chopping a row of Australian pines off Krome Avenue to make room for a new medium-security federal prison. George and his men were not exactly busting their humps, since it was a government contract and nobody ever came by to check. George was parked in the shade, as usual, eating a roast-beef hoagie and drinking a tall Budweiser. The driver's door of the truck was open and the radio was on a country music station, though the only time you could hear the tunes was between the grinding roars of the wood chipper, which was hooked to the bumper of George Graveline's truck. The intermittent screech of the machine didn't disturb George at all; he had grown accustomed to hearing only fragments of Merle Haggard on the radio and to letting his imagination fill in the musical gaps.

Just as he finished the sandwich, George glanced in the rear-view and noticed a big blond man with one arm in a sling. The man wore blue jeans, boots, and a flannel shirt with the left sleeve cut away. He was standing next to the wood chipper, watching George's crew chief toss pine stumps into the steel maw.

George swung out of the truck and said, 'Hey, not so close.'

The man obligingly took a step backward. 'That's some machine.' He gestured at the wood chipper. 'Looks brand new.'

'Had her a couple years,' George Graveline said. 'You looking for work?'

'Naw,' the man said, 'not with this bum wing. Actually I was looking for the boss. George Graveline.'

George wiped the hoagie juice off his hands. 'That's me,' he said.

The crew chief heaved another pine limb into the chipper. The visitor waited for the buzzing to stop, then he said, 'George, my name is Mick Stranahan.'

'Howdy, Mick.' George stuck out his right hand. Stranahan shook it.

'George, we don't know each other, but I feel like I can talk to you. Man to man.'

'Sure.'

'It's about your little brother.'

'Rudolph?' Warily George folded his big arms.

'Yes, George,' Stranahan said. 'See, Rudy's been trying to kill me lately.'

'Huh?'

'Can you believe it? First he hires some mobster to do the hit, now he's got the world's tallest white man with the world's worst case of acne. I don't know what to tell you, but frankly it's got me a little pissed off.' Stranahan looked down at his sling. 'This is from a .45-calibre machine-gun. Honestly, George, wouldn't you be upset, too?'

George Graveline rolled the tip of his tongue around the

167

insides of his cheeks, like he was probing for a lost wad of Red Man. The crew chief automatically kept loading hunks of pine into the wood chipper, which spat them out the chute as splinters and sawdust. Stranahan motioned to George that they should go sit in the truck and talk privately, where it was more quiet.

Stranahan settled in on the passenger side and turned down the country music. George said, 'Look, mister, I don't know who you are but—'

'I told you who I am.'

'Your name is all you said.'

'I'm a private investigator, George, if that helps. A few years back I worked for the State Attorney. On murder cases, mostly.'

George didn't blink, just stared like a toad. Stranahan got a feeling that the man was about to punch him.

'Before you do anything incredibly stupid, George, listen for a second.'

George leaned out the door of the truck and hollered for the crew chief to take lunch. The whine of the wood chipper died, and suddenly the two men were drenched in silence.

'Thank you,' Stranahan said.

'So talk.'

'On March twelfth, 1986, your brother performed an operation on a young woman named Victoria Barletta. Something terrible happened, George, and she died on the operating table.'

'No way.'

'Your brother Rudy panicked. He'd already been in a shitload of trouble over his state medical licence—and killing a patient, well, that's totally unacceptable. Even in Florida. I think Rudy was just plain scared.'

George Graveline said, 'You're full of it.'

'The case came through my office as an abduction-possible-homicide. Everybody assumed the girl was snatched from a bus bench in front of your brother's clinic because that's what he told us. But now, George, new information has come to light.'

'What kind of information?'

'The most damaging kind,' Mick Stranahan said. 'And for some reason, your brother thinks that I am the one who's got it. But I'm not, George.'

'So I'll tell him to leave you alone.'

'That's very considerate, George, but I'm afraid it's not so simple. Things have gotten out of hand. I mean, look at my damn shoulder.'

'Mmmm,' said George Graveline.

Stranahan said, 'Getting back to the young woman. Her body was never found, not a trace. That's highly unusual.'

'It is?'

'Yes, it is.'

'So?'

'So, you wouldn't happen to know anything about what happened, would you?'

George said, 'You got some nerve.'

'Yes, I suppose I do. But how about answering the question?'

'How about this,' said George Graveline, reaching for Mick Stranahan's throat.

With his good arm Stranahan intercepted George's toad-eyed lunge. He seized one of the tree-trimmer's stubby thumbs and twisted it clean out of the socket. It made a faintly audible pop, like a bottle of flat champagne. George merely squeaked as the colour flooded from his face. Stranahan let go of the limp purple thumb, and George pinched it between his knees, trying to squeeze away the pain.

'Boy, I'm really sorry,' Stranahan said.

George grabbed at himself and gasped, 'You get out of here!'

'Don't you want to hear the rest of my theory, the one I'm going to tell the cops? About how you tossed that poor girl's body into the wood chipper just to save your brother's butt?'

'Go on,' George Graveline cried, 'before I shoot you myself.'

Mick Stranahan got out of George's truck, shut the door and leaned in through the open window. 'I think you're overreacting,' he said to the tree trimmer. 'I really do.'

'Eat shit,' George replied, wheezing.

'Fine,' Stranahan said. 'I just hope you're not this rude to the police.'

Christina Marks was dreading her reunion with Reynaldo Flemm. They met at twelve-thirty in the lobby of the Sonesta.

She said, 'You've done something to your hair.'

'I let it grow,' Flemm said self-consciously. 'Where've you been, anyway? What's the big secret?'

Christina couldn't get over the way he looked. She circled him twice, staring.

'Ray, nobody's hair grows that fast.'

'It's been a couple weeks.'

'But it's all the way to your shoulders.'

'So what?'

'And it's so yellow.'

'Blond, goddammit.'

'And so . . . kinky.'

Stiffly, Reynaldo Flemm said, 'It was time for a new look.'

Christina Marks fingered his locks and said, 'It's a bloody wig.'

'Thank you, Agatha Christie.'

'Don't get sore,' she said. 'I kind of like it.'

'Really?'

Despairing of his physical appearance since his visit to Whispering Palms, Reynaldo Flemm had flown back to New York and consulted a famous colorologist, who had advised him that blond hair would make him look ten years younger. Then a make-up man at ABC had told Reynaldo that long hair would make his nose look thinner, while *kinked* long hair would take twenty pounds off his waist on camera.

Armed with this expert advice, Reynaldo had sought out Tina Turner's wig stylist, who was booked solid but happy to recommend a promising young protégé in the SoHo district. The young stylist's name was Leo, and he pretended to recognize Reynaldo Flemm from television, which was all the salesmanship he needed. Reynaldo told Leo the basics of what he wanted, and Leo led him to a seven-hundred-dollar wig that looked freshly hacked off the scalp of Robert Plant, the rock singer. Or possibly Dyan Cannon.

Reynaldo didn't care. It was precisely the look he was after.

'I do kind of like it,' Christina Marks said, 'only we've got to do something about the Puerto Rican moustache.'

Flemm said, 'The moustache stays. I've had it since my first local Emmy.' He put his hands on her shoulders. 'Now, suppose you tell me what the hell's been going on.'

Christina hadn't talked to Reynaldo since the day Mick Stranahan was shot, and then she had told him next to nothing. She had called from the emergency room at Mercy Hospital, and said something serious had happened. Reynaldo had asked if she were hurt, and Christina said no. Then Reynaldo had asked what was so damn serious, and she said it would have to wait for a few weeks, that the police were involved and the whole Barletta story would blow up if they didn't lay low. She had promised to get back to him in a few days, but all she did was leave a message in Reynaldo's box at the hotel. The message had begged him to be patient, and Reynaldo had thought what the hell and gone back to Manhattan to hunt for some new hair.

'So,' he said, to Christina, 'let's hear it.'

'Over here,' she said, and led him to a booth in the hotel coffee shop. She waited until he'd stuffed a biscuit in his mouth before telling him about the shooting.

'Theesus!' Flemm exclaimed, spitting crumbs. He looked as if he were about to cry, and in fact he was. 'You got shot at? Really?'

Christina nodded uneasily.

'With a machine-gun? Honest to God?' Plaintively he added, 'Was it an Uzi?'

'I'm not sure, Ray.'

Christina knew his heart was breaking; Reynaldo had been waiting his entire broadcast career for an experience like that. Once he had drunkenly confided to Christina that his secret dream was to be shot in the thigh—live on national television. Not a life-threatening wound, just enough to make him go down. 'I'm tired of getting beat up,' he had told Christina that night. 'I want to break some new ground.' In Reynaldo's secret dream, the TV camera would jiggle at the sound of gunshots, then pan dramatically to focus on his prone and blood-splattered form sprawled on the street. In the dream, Reynaldo would be clutching his microphone, bravely continuing to broadcast while paramedics worked feverishly to save his life. The last clip, as Reynaldo dreamed it, was a close-up of his famous face: the lantern jaw clenched in agony, a grimace showcasing his luxurious capped teeth. Then the trademark sign-off: *This is Reynaldo Flemm, reporting In Your Face!*—just as the ambulance doors swung shut.

'I can't believe this,' Reynaldo moaned over his breakfast. 'Producers aren't supposed to get shot, the talent is.'

Christina Marks sipped a three-dollar orange juice. 'In the first place, Ray, I wasn't the one who got shot—'

'Yeah, but—'

'In the second place, you would've pissed your pants if you'd been there. This is no longer fun and games, Ray. Somebody is trying to murder Stranahan. Probably the same goon who killed his ex-wife.'

Flemm was still pouting. 'Why didn't you tell me you were going out to Stiltsville?'

'You were locked in your room, remember? Measuring your body parts.' Christina patted his arm. 'Have some more marmalade.'

Worriedly, Reynaldo asked, 'Does this mean you get to do the stand-up? I mean, since you eyewitnessed the shooting and not me.'

'Ray, I have absolutely no interest in doing a stand-up. I don't want to be on camera.'

'You mean it?' His voice dripped with relief. Pathetic, Christina thought; the man is pathetic.

Clearing his throat, Reynaldo Flemm said, 'I've got some bad news of my own, Chris.'

Christina dabbed her lips with the corner of the napkin. 'Does it involve your trip to New York?'

Flemm nodded yes.

'And, perhaps, Maggie Gonzalez?'

'I'm afraid so,' he said.

'She's missing again, isn't she, Ray?'

Flemm said, 'We had a dinner set up at the Palm.'

'And she never showed.'

'Right,' he said.

'Was this before or after you wired her the fifteen thousand?' Christina asked.

'Hey, I'm not stupid. I only sent half.'

'Shit.' Christina drummed her fingernails on the table.

Reynaldo Flemm sighed and turned away. Absently he ran a hand through his new golden tendrils. 'I'm sorry,' he said finally. 'You still want to dump this story?'

'No,' Christina said. 'No, I don't.'

Mick Stranahan looked through mug shots all morning, knowing he would never find the killer's face.

'Look anyway,' said Al García.

Stranahan flipped to another page. 'Is it my imagination,' he said, 'or are these assholes getting uglier every year?'

'I've noticed that, too,' García said.

'Speaking of which, I got a friendly visit from Murdock and Salazar at the hospital.' Stranahan told García what had happened.

'I'll report it to IA, if you want,' García said.

IA was Internal Affairs, where detectives Murdock and Salazar probably had files as thick as the Dade County Yellow Pages.

'Don't push it,' said Stranahan. 'I just wanted you to know what they're up to.'

'Pricks,' García grunted. 'I'll think of something.'

173

'I thought you had clout.'

'Clout? All I got is a ten-cent commendation and a gimp arm, same as you. Only mine came from a sawed-off.'

'I'm impressed,' said Mick Stranahan. He closed the mug book and pushed it across the table. 'He's not in here, Al. You got one for circus freaks?'

'That bad, huh?'

Stranahan said, 'Bad's not the word.' It wasn't.

'Want to try a composite? Let me call one of the artists.'

'No, that's all right,' Stranahan said. 'I wouldn't know where to start. Al, you wouldn't believe this guy.'

The detective gnawed the tip off a cigar. 'He's got to be the same geek who did Chloe. Thing is, I got witnesses saw them out at the marina having a drink, chatting like the best of friends. How do you figure that?'

'She always had great taste in men.' Stranahan stood up, gingerly testing the strap of his sling.

'Where are you going?'

'I'm off to do a B-and-E.'

'Now don't say shit like that.'

'It's true, Al.'

'I'm not believing this. Tell me you're bullshitting, Mick.'

'If it makes you feel better.'

'And call me,' García said in a low voice, 'if you turn up something good.'

At half-past three, Mick Stranahan broke into Maggie Gonzalez's duplex for the second time. The first thing he did was play back the tape on the answering machine. There were messages from numerous relatives, all demanding to know why Maggie had missed her cousin Gloria's baby shower. The only message that Mick Stranahan found interesting was from the Essex House hotel in downtown New York. A nasal female clerk requested that Miss Gonzalez contact them immediately about a forty-three-dollar dry-cleaning bill, which Maggie had forgotten to pay before checking out. The Essex

House clerk had efficiently left the time and date of the phone message: January twenty-eighth at ten o'clock in the morning.

The next thing Mick Stranahan did was to sift through a big stack of Maggie's mail until he found the most recent Visa card bill, which he opened and studied at her kitchen table. That Maggie was spending somebody else's money in Manhattan was obvious: she had used her personal credit card only twice. One entry was $35.50 at Ticketron, probably for a broadway show; the other charge was from a clothing shop for $179.40, more than Maggie was probably carrying in cash at the time. The clothing store was in the Plaza Hotel; the transaction was dated February first.

Mick Stranahan was getting ready to leave the duplex when Maggie's telephone rang twice, then clicked over to the machine. He listened as a man came on the line. Stranahan thought he recognized the voice, but he wasn't certain. He had only spoken with the man once.

The voice on the machine said: 'Maggie, it's me. I tried the Essex but they said you checked out. . . . Look, we've really got to talk. In person. Call me at the office right away, collect. Wherever you are, OK? Thanks.'

As the man gave the number, Stranahan copied it in pencil on the Formica counter. After the caller hung up, Stranahan dialled 411 and asked for the listing of the Whispering Palms Spa and Surgery Center in Bal Harbour. A recording gave the main number as 555-7600. The phone number left by Maggie's male caller was 555-7602.

Rudy Graveline, Stranahan thought, calling on his office line.

The next number Stranahan dialled was 1-212-555-1212. Information for Manhattan. He got the number of the Plaza, dialled the main desk, and asked for Miss Maggie Gonzalez's room. A woman picked up on the fourth ring.

'Is this Miss Gonzalez?' Stranahan asked, trying to mimic a Brooklyn accent.

'Yes, it is.'

'This is the concierge downstairs.' Like there was an *upstairs* concierge. 'We were just wondering if you had any dry cleaning you needed done this evening.'

'What are you talking about? I'm still waiting for those three dresses I sent out Sunday,' Maggie said, not pleasantly.

'Oh, I'm very sorry,' Mick Stranahan said. 'I'll see to it immediately.'

Then he hung up, grabbed the white pages off the kitchen counter, and looked up the number for Delta Airlines.

16

On his way to Miami International, Mick Stranahan stopped at his brother-in-law's law office. Kipper Garth was on the speaker phone, piecing out a slip-and-fall to one of the Brickell Avenue buzzards.

Mick Stranahan walked in and said, 'The files?'

Kipper Garth motioned to a wine-coloured chair and put a finger to his waxy lips. 'So, Chuckie,' he said to the speaker phone, 'what're you thinking?'

'Thinking maybe two hundred if we settle,' said the voice on the other end.

'Two hundred!' Kipper exclaimed. 'Chuckie, you're nuts. The woman tripped over her own damn dachshund.'

'Kip, they'll settle,' the other lawyer said. 'It's the biggest grocery chain in Florida, they always settle. Besides, the dog croaked—that's fifty grand right there for mental anguish.'

'But dogs aren't even allowed in the store, Chuckie. If it was somebody else's dachshund she tripped on, then we'd really have something. But this was her own fault.'

Sardonic laughter crackled over the speaker box. 'Kip,

buddy, you're not thinking like a litigator,' the voice said. 'I went to the supermarket myself and guess what: no signs!'

'What do you mean?'

'I mean no No Dogs Allowed-type signs. Not a one posted in Spanish. So how was our poor Consuela to know?'

'Chuckie, you're beautiful,' said Kipper Garth. 'If that ain't negligence—'

'Two hundred thou,' Chuckie said, 'that's my guess. We'll split sixty-forty.'

'Nope,' Kipper Garth said, staring coldly at the speaker box. 'Half-and-half. Same as always.'

'Excuse me.' It was Mick Stranahan. Kipper Garth frowned and shook his head; not now, not when he was closing the deal.

The voice on the phone said: 'Kip, who's that? You got somebody there?'

'Relax, Chuckie, it's just me,' Stranahan said to the box. 'You know—Kipper's heroin connection? I just dropped by with a briefcase full of Mexican brown. Can I pencil you in for a kilo?'

Frantically Kipper Garth jabbed two fingers at the phone buttons. The line went dead and the speaker box hummed the dial tone. 'You're fucking crazy,' he said to Mick Stranahan.

'I've got a plane to catch, Jocko. Where are the Graveline files?'

'You're crazy,' Kipper Garth said again, trying to stay calm. He buzzed for a secretary, who lugged in three thick brown office folders.

'There's a conference room where you can read this shit in private.'

Mick Stranahan said, 'No, this is fine.' With Kipper Garth stewing, Stranahan skimmed quickly through the files on Rudy Graveline. it was worse than he thought—or better, depending on one's point of view.

'Seventeen complaints to the state board,' Stranahan marvelled.

177

'Yeah, but no action,' Kipper Garth noted. 'Not even a reprimand.'

Stranahan looked up, lifting one of the files. 'Jocko, this is a gold mine.'

'Well, Mick, I'm glad I could help. Now, if you don't mind, it's getting late and I've got a few calls to make.'

Stranahan said, 'You don't understand, I wanted this stuff for you, not me.'

Peevishly Kipper Garth glanced at his wristwatch. 'You're right, Mick, I *don't* understand. What the hell do I want with Graveline's files?'

'Names, Jocko.' Stranahan opened the top folder and riffled the pages dramatically. 'You got seventeen names, seventeen leads on a silver platter. You got Mrs Susan Jacoby and her boobs that don't match. You got Mr Robert Mears with his left eye that won't close and his right eye that won't open. You got, let's see, Julia Kelly with a shnoz that looks like a Phillips screwdriver—Jesus, you see the Polaroid of that thing? What else? Oh, you got Ken Martinez and his lopsided scrotum. . . . '

Kipper Garth waved his arms. 'Mick, that's enough! What would I want with all this crap?'

'I figured you'll need it, Jocko.'

'For what?'

'For suing Doctor Rudy Graveline.'

'Very funny,' Kipper Garth said. 'I told you, the man's in my yacht club. Besides, he's been sued before.'

'Sue him again,' Mick Stranahan said. 'Sue the mother like he's never been sued before.'

'He'd settle out. Doctors always settle.'

'Don't let him. Don't settle for anything. Not for ten million dollars. Sign up one of these poor misfortunate souls and go to the frigging wall.'

Kipper Garth stood up and adjusted his necktie, suddenly on his way to some important meeting. 'I can't help you, Mick. Get yourself another lawyer.'

'You don't do this favour for me,' said Stranahan, 'and I'll go tell Katie about your trip to Steamboat next month with Inga or Olga or whatever the hell her name is, I got it written down here somewhere. And for future reference, Jocko, don't ever put your ski bunny's plane tickets on American Express. I know it's convenient and all, but it's very, very risky. I mean, with the computers they got these days, I can pull out your goddamned seat assignments—5A and 5B, I think it is.'

All Kipper Garth could say was: 'How'd you do that?'

'I told you before, I'm still plugged in.' A travel agent in Coral Gables who owed him one. It was so damn easy Stranahan couldn't bear to tell his brother-in-law.

'What's the point of all this?' Kipper Garth asked.

'Never mind, just do it. Sue the asshole.'

The lawyer lifted his pinstriped coat off the back of the chair and checked it for wrinkles. 'Mick, let me shop this around and get back to you.'

'No, Jocko. No referrals. You do this one all by yourself.'

The lawyer sagged as if struck by a brick.

'You heard me right,' Stranahan said.

'Mick, please.' It was a pitiable peep. 'Mick, I don't do this sort of thing.'

'Sure you do. I see the billboards all over town.'

Kipper Garth nibbled on a thumbnail to mask the spastic twitching of his upper lip. The thought of actually going to court had pitched him into a cold sweat. A fresh droplet made a shiny trail from the furrow of his forehead to the tip of his well-tanned nose.

'I don't know,' he said, 'it's been so long.'

'Aw, it's easy,' Stranahan said. 'One of your paralegals can draw up the complaint. That'll get the ball rolling.' With a thud he stacked the Graveline files on Kipper Garth's desk; the lawyer eyed the pile as if it were nitroglycerine.

'A gold mine,' Stranahan said encouragingly. 'I'll check back in a few days.'

'Mick?'

'Relax. All you've got to do is go down to the courthouse and sue.'

Wanly, Kipper Garth said, 'I don't have to win, do I?'

179

'Of course not,' Stranahan said, patting his arm. 'It'll never get that far.'

Dr Rudy Graveline lived in a palatial three-storey house on northern Biscayne Bay. The house had Doric pillars, two spiral staircases, and more imported marble than the entire downtown art museum. The house had absolutely no business being on Miami Beach, but in fairness it looked no more silly or out of place than any of the other garish mansions. The house was on the same palm-lined avenue where two of the Bee Gees lived, which meant that Rudy had been forced to pay about a hundred thousand more than the property was worth. For the first few years, the women whom Rudy dated were impressed to be in the Bee Gees' neighbourhood, but lately the star value had worn off and Rudy had quit mentioning it.

It was Heather Chappell, the actress, who brought it up first.

'I think Barry lives around here,' she said as they were driving back to Rudy's house after dinner at the Forge.

'Barry who?' Rudy asked, his mind off somewhere.

'Barry Gibb. The singer. *Staying alive, staying alive, ooh, ooh, ooh.*'

As much as he loved Heather, Rudy wished she wouldn't try to sing.

'You know Barry personally?' he asked.

'Oh sure. All the guys.'

'That's Barry's place there,' Rudy Graveline said, pointing. 'And Robin lives right here.'

'Let's stop over,' Heather said, touching his knee. 'It'll be fun.'

Rudy said no, he didn't know the guys all that well. Besides, he never really liked their music, especially that disco shit. Immediately Heather sank into a deep pout, which she heroically maintained all the way back to Rudy's house, up the stairs, all the way to his bedroom. There she peeled off her dress and panties and lay face down on the king-sized bed. Every few minutes she would raise her cheek off the satin pillow and sigh disconsolately, until Rudy couldn't stand it any more.

'Are you mad at me?' he asked. He was in his boxer shorts, standing in the closet where he had hung his suit. 'Heather, are you angry?'

'No.'

'Yes, you are. Did I say something wrong? If I did, I'm sorry.' He was blubbering like a jerk, all because he wanted to get laid in the worst way. The sight of Heather's perfect bare bottom—the one she wanted contoured—was driving him mad.

In a tiny voice she said, 'I love the Bee Gees.'

'I'm sorry,' Rudy said. He sat on the corner of the bed and stroked her peachlike rump. 'I liked their early stuff, I really did.'

Heather said, 'I loved the disco, Rudy. It just about killed me when disco died.'

'I'm sorry I said anything.'

'You ever made love to disco music?'

Rudy thought: What is happening to my life?

'Do you have any Village People tapes?' Heather asked, giving him a quick saucy look over the shoulder. 'There's a song on their first album, I swear, I could fuck all night to it.'

Rudy Graveline was nothing if not resourceful. He found the Village People tape in the discount bin of an all-night record store across from the University of Miami campus in Coral Gables. He sped home, popped the cassette into the modular sound system, cranked up the woofers, and jogged up the spiral staircase to the bedroom.

Heather said, 'Not here.' She took him by the hand and led him downstairs. 'The fireplace,' she whispered.

'It's seventy-eight degrees,' Rudy remarked, kicking off his underwear.

'It's not the fire,' Heather said, 'it's the marble.'

One of the selling points of the big house was an oversized fireplace constructed of polished Italian marble. Fireplaces were considered a cosy novelty in South Florida, but Rudy had never used his, since he was

181

afraid the expensive black marble would blister in the heat.

Heather crawled in and got on her back. She had the most amazing smile on her face. 'Oh, Rudy, it's so cold.' She lifted her buttocks off the marble and slapped them down; the squeak made her giggle.

Rudy stood there, naked and limp, staring like an idiot. 'We could get hurt,' he said. He was thinking of what the marble would do to his elbows and kneecaps.

'Don't be such a geezer,' Heather said, hoisting her hips and wiggling them in his face. She rolled over and pointed to the twin smudges of condensation on the black stone. 'Look,' she said. 'Just like fingerprints.'

'Sort of,' Rudy Graveline mumbled.

She said, 'I must be hot, huh?'

'I guess so,' Rudy said. His skull was ready to split; the voices of the Village People reverberated in the fireplace like mortar fire.

'Oh, God,' Heather moaned.

'What is it?' Rudy asked.

'The song. That's my song.' She squeaked to her knees and seized him ferociously around the waist. 'Come on down here,' she said. 'Let's dance.'

In order to prolong his tumescence, Dr Rudy Graveline had trained himself to think of anything but sex while he was having sex. Most times he concentrated on his unit trusts and tax shelters, which were complicated enough to keep orgasm at bay for a good ten to fifteen minutes. Tonight, though, he concentrated on something different. Rudy Graveline was thinking of his daunting predicament—of Victoria Barletta and the up-coming television documentary about her death; of Mick Stranahan, still alive and menacing; of Maggie Gonzalez, spending his money somewhere in New York.

More often than not, Rudy found he could ruminate with startling clarity during the throes of sexual intercourse. He had arrived at many crucial life decisions in such moments—the clutter of the day and the pressure from his patients seemed to vanish in a crystal vacuum, a mystic physical void that permitted Rudy to concentrate on his problems in a new light and from a new angle.

And so it was that—even with Heather Chappell clawing his shoulders and screaming disco drivel into his ear, even with the flue vent clanging in the chimney above his head, and even with his knees grinding mercilessly on the cold Italian marble—Rudy was able to focus on the most important crisis of his life. Both pain and pleasure dissipated; it was as if he were alone, alert and sensitized, in a cool dark chamber. Rudy thought about everything that had happened so far, and then about what he must do now. It wasn't a bad plan. There was, however, one loose end.

Rudy snapped out of his cognitive trance when Heather cried, 'Enough already!'

'What?'

'I said you can stop now, OK? This isn't a damn rodeo.' She was all out of breath. Her chest was slick with sweat.

Rudy quit moving.

'What were you thinking of?' Heather asked.

'Nothing.'

'Did you come?'

'Sure,' Rudy lied.

'You were thinking of some other girl, weren't you?'

'No, I wasn't.' Another lie.

He had been thinking of Maggie Gonzalez, and how he should have killed her two months ago.

The next day at noon, George Graveline arrived at the Whispering Palms surgery clinic and demanded to see his brother, said it was an emergency. When Rudy heard the story, he agreed.

The two men were talking in hushed, worried tones when Chemo showed up an hour later.

'So what's the big rush?' he said.

'Sit down,' Rudy Graveline told him.

Chemo was dressed in a tan safari outfit, the kind Jim Fowler wore on the *Wild Kingdom* television show.

183

Rudy said, 'George, this is a friend of mine. He's working for me on this matter.'

Chemo raised his eyebrows. 'Happened to your thumb?' he said to George.

'Car door.' Rudy's brother did not wish to share that painful detail of his encounter with Mick Stranahan.

George Graveline had a few questions of his own for the tall stranger, but he held them. Valiantly he tried not to stare at Chemo's complexion, which George assessed as some tragic human strain of Dutch elm disease. What finally drew the tree trimmer's attention away from Chemo's face was the colourful Macy's shopping bag in which Chemo concealed his newly extended left arm.

'Had an accident,' Chemo explained. 'I'm only wearing this until I get a customized cover.' He pulled the shopping bag off the Weed Whacker. George Graveline recognized it immediately—the lightweight household model.

'Hey, that thing work?'

'You bet,' Chemo said. He probed under his arm until he found the toggle switch that jolted the Weed Whacker to life. It sounded like a blender without the top on.

George grinned and clapped his hands.

'That's enough,' Rudy said sharply.

'No, watch,' said Chemo. He ambled to the corner of the office where Rudy kept a beautiful potted rubber plant.

'Oh no,' the doctor said, but it was too late. Gleefully Chemo chopped the rubber plant into slaw.

'Yeah!' said George Graveline.

Rudy leaned over and whispered, 'Don't encourage him. He's a dangerous fellow.'

Basking in the attention, Chemo left the Weed Whacker unsheathed. He sat down next to the two men and said, 'Let's hear the big news.'

'Mick Stranahan visited George yesterday,' Rudy said. 'Apparently the bastard's not giving up.'

'What'd he say?'

'All kinds of crazy shit,' George said.

Rudy had warned his brother not to tell Chemo about

184

Victoria Barletta or the wood chipper or Stranahan's specific accusation about what had happened to the body.

Rudy twirled his eyeglasses and said: 'I don't understand why Stranahan is so damn hard to kill.'

'Least we know he's out of the hospital,' Chemo said brightly. 'I'll get right on it.'

'Not just yet,' Rudy said. He turned to his brother. 'George, could I speak to him alone, please?'

George Graveline nodded amiably at Chemo on his way out the door. 'Listen, you ever need work,' he said, 'I could use you and that, uh . . . '

'Prosthesis,' Chemo said. 'Thanks, but I don't think so.'

When they were alone, Rudy opened the top drawer of his desk and handed Chemo a large brown envelope. Inside the envelope were an eight-by-ten photograph, two thousand dollars in traveller's cheques, and an airline ticket. The person in the picture was a handsome, sharp-featured woman with brown eyes and brown hair; her name was printed in block letters on the back of the photograph. The plane ticket was round-trip, Miami to LaGuardia and back.

Chemo said, 'Is this what I think it is?'

'Another job,' Dr Rudy Graveline said.

'It'll cost you.'

'I'm prepared for that.'

'Same as the Stranahan deal,' Chemo said.

'Twenty treatments? You don't *need* twenty more treatments. Your face'll be done in two months.'

'I'm not talking about dermabrasion,' Chemo said. 'I'm talking about my ears.'

Rudy thought: Dear God, will it never end? 'Your ears,' he said to Chemo, 'are the last things that need surgical attention.'

'The hell is that supposed to mean?'

'Nothing, nothing. All I'm saying is, once we finish the dermabrasions you'll look as good as new. I honestly don't believe you'll want to touch a thing, that's how good your face is going to look.'

Chemo said, 'My ears stick out too far and you know it. You want me to do this hit, you'll fix the damn things.'

'Fine,' Rudy Graveline sighed, 'fine.' There was nothing wrong with the man's ears, only what was between them.

Chemo tucked the envelope into his armpit and bagged up the Weed Whacker. 'Oh yeah, one more thing. I'm out of that stuff for my face.'

'What stuff?'

'You know,' Chemo said, 'the Wite-Out.'

Rudy Graveline found a small bottle in his desk and tossed it to Chemo, who slipped it into the breast pocket of his Jim Fowler safari jacket. 'Call you from New York,' he said.

'Yes,' said Rudy wearily. 'By all means.'

17

Christina Marks slipped out of the first-class cabin while Reynaldo Flemm was autographing a cocktail napkin for a flight attendant. The flight attendant had mistaken the newly bewigged Reynaldo for David Lee Roth, the rock singer. The Puerto Rican moustache looked odd with all that blond hair, but the flight attendant assumed it was meant as a humorous disguise.

Mick Stranahan was sitting in coach, a stack of outdoors magazines on the seat next to him. He saw Christina coming down the aisle and smiled. 'My shadow.'

'I'm not following you,' she said.

'Yes, you are. But that's all right.' He moved the magazines and motioned her to sit down.

'You look very nice.' It was the first time he had seen her in a dress. 'Some coincidence, that you and the anchorman got the same flight as I did.'

Christina said, 'He's not an anchorman. And no, it's not

a coincidence that we're on the same plane. Ray thinks it is, but it's not.'

'Ray thinks it is, huh? So this was your idea, following me.'

'Relax,' Christina said. Ever since the shooting she had stayed close; at first she rationalized it as a journalist's instinct – the Barletta story kept coming back to Stranahan, didn't it? But then she had found herself sleeping some nights at the hospital, where nothing newsworthy was likely to happen; sitting in the corner and watching him in the hospital bed, long after it was obvious he would make a full recovery. Christina couldn't deny she was attracted to him, and worried about him. She also had a feeling he was moderately crazy.

Stranahan said, 'So you guys are going to trail me all around New York. A regular tag team, you and Ray.'

'Ray will be busy,' Christina said, 'on other projects.'

The jetliner dipped slightly, and a shaft of sunlight caught the side of her face, forcing her to look away. For the first time Stranahan noticed a sprinkling of light freckles on her nose and cheeks; cinnamon freckles, the kind that children have.

'Did I ever thank you for saving my life?' he asked.

'Yes, you did.'

'Well, thanks again.' He poured some honey-roasted peanuts into the palm of her hand. 'Why are you following me?'

'I'm not,' she said.

'If it's only to juice up your damn TV show, then I'm going to get angry.'

Christina said, 'It's not that.'

'You want to keep an eye on me.'

'You're an interesting man. You make things happen.'

Stranahan popped a peanut and said, 'That's a good one.'

Christina Marks softened her tone. 'I'll help you find her.'

'Find who?'

'Maggie Gonzalez.'

'Who said she was lost? Besides, you got her on tape, right? The whole sordid story.'

'Not yet,' Christina admitted.

Stranahan laughed caustically. 'Oh brother,' he said.

'Listen, I got a trail of bills she's been sending up to the office. Between the two of us, we could find her in a day. Besides, I think she'll talk to me. The whole sordid story, on tape – like you said.'

Stranahan didn't mention that he already knew where Maggie Gonzalez was staying, and that he was totally confident that he could persuade her to talk.

'You're the most helpful woman I ever met,' he said to Christina Marks. 'So unselfish, too. If I didn't know better, I'd think maybe you were hunting for Maggie because she beat you and the anchorman out of some serious dough.'

Christina said, 'I liked you better unconscious.'

Stranahan chuckled and took her hand. He didn't let go like she thought he would, he just held it. Once, when the plane hit some turbulence, Christina jumped nervously. Without looking up from his *Field & Stream*, Stranahan gave her hand a squeeze. It was more comforting than suggestive, but it made Christina flush.

She retreated to the role of professional interviewer. 'So,' she said, 'tell me about yourself.'

'You first,' Stranahan said; a brief smile, then back to the magazine.

Oddly, she found herself talking – talking so openly that she sounded like one of those video-dating tapes: Let's see, I'm thirty-four years old, divorced, born in Richmond, went to the University of Missouri journalism school, lettered on the swim team, graduated magna, got my first decent news job with the ABC affiliate in St Louis, then three years at WBBM in Chicago until I met Ray at the Gacy trial and he offered me an assistant producer's job, and here I am. Now it's your turn, Mick.

'Pardon?'

'Your turn,' Christina Marks said, 'That's my life story, now let's hear yours.'

Stranahan closed the magazine and centred it on his

lap. He said, 'My life story is this; I've killed five men, and I've been married five times.'

Christina slowly pulled her hand away.

'Which scares you more?' Mick Stranahan said.

When Dade County Commissioner Roberto Pepsical broke the news to The Others (that is, the other crooked commissioners), they all had the same reactions: Nope, sorry, too late.

Dr Rudy Graveline had offered major bucks to rezone prime green space for the Old Cypress Towers project, and the commissioners had gone ahead and done it. They couldn't very well put it back on the agenda and reverse the vote – not without arousing the interest of those goddamned newspaper reporters. Besides, a deal was a deal. Furthermore, The Others wanted to know about the promised twenty-five thousand dollar bribe: specifically, where was it? Was Rudy holding out? One commissioner even suggested that a new vote to rescind the zoning and scrap the project could be obtained only by doubling the original payoff.

Roberto Pepsical was fairly sure that Dr Rudy Graveline would not pay twice for essentially the same act of corruption. In addition, Roberto didn't feel like explaining to the doctor that if Old Cypress Towers were to expire on the drawing board, so would a plethora of other hidden gratuities that would have winged their way into the commissioners' secret accounts. From downtown bankers to the zoning lawyers to the code inspectors, payoffs traditionally trickled upward to the commissioners. The ripple effect of killing a project as large as Rudy's was calamitous, bribery-wise.

Roberto hated being the middleman when the stakes got this high. By nature he was slow, inattentive, and somewhat easily confused. He hadn't taken notes during Rudy's late-night phone call, and maybe he should have. This much he remembered clearly: the doctor had said that he'd changed his mind about Old Cypress Towers, that he'd decided to move his money out of the country instead.

189

When Roberto protested, the doctor told him there'd been all kinds of trouble, serious trouble – specifically, that hinky old surgical case he'd mentioned that day at lunch. The proverbial doo-doo was getting ready to hit the proverbial fan, Rudy had said; somebody was out to ruin him. He told Roberto Pepsical to pass along his most profound apologies to The Others, but there was no other course for the doctor to take. Since his problem wasn't going away, Old Cypress Towers would.

The solution was so obvious that even Roberto grasped it immediately. The apartment project could be rescued, and so could the commissioners' bribes. Once Roberto learned that Dr Rudy Graveline's problem had a name, he began checking with his connections at the Metro-Dade Police Department.

Which led him straight to detectives John Murdock and Joe Salazar.

Roberto considered the mission of such significance that he took the radical step of skipping his normal two-hour lunch to stop by the police station for a personal visit. He found both detectives at their desks. They were eating hot Cuban sandwiches and cleaning their revolvers. It was the first time Roberto had ever seen Gulden's mustard on a .357.

'You're sure,' said the commissioner, 'that this man is a murder suspect?'

'Yep,' said John Murdock.

'Number one suspect,' added Joe Salazar.

Roberto said, 'So you're going to arrest him?'

'Of course,' Salazar said.

'Eventually,' said Murdock.

'The sooner the better,' Roberto said.

John Murdock glanced at Joe Salazar. Then he looked at Roberto and said, 'Commissioner, if you've got any information about this man . . . '

'He's been giving a friend of mine a hard time, that's all. A good friend of mine.' Roberto knew better than to mention Rudy Graveline's name, and John Murdock knew better than to ask.

Joe Salazar said, 'It's a crime to threaten a person. Did Stranahan make a threat?'

'Nothing you could prove,' Roberto said. 'Look, I'd appreciate it if you guys would keep me posted.'

'Absolutely,' John Murdock promised. He wiped the food off his gun and shoved it back in the shoulder holster.

'This is very important,' Roberto Pepsical said. 'Extremely important.'

Murdock said, 'Don't worry, we'll nail the fuckwad.'

'Yeah,' said Joe Salazar. 'It's only a matter of time.'

'Not much time, I hope.'

'We'll do what we can, Commissioner.'

'There might even be a promotion in it.'

'Oh boy, a promotion,' said John Murdock. 'Joey, you hear that? A promotion!' The detective burped at the commissioner and said, 'How about some green instead?'

Roberto Pepsical winced as if a hornet had buzzed into his ear. 'Jesus, are you saying — '

'Money,' said Joe Salazar, chomping a pickle. 'He means money.'

'Let me get this straight: you guys want a bribe for solving a murder?'

'No,' Murdock said, 'just for making the arrest.'

'I can't believe this.'

'Sure you can,' Joe Salazar said. 'Your friend wants Stranahan out of the way, right? The county jail, that's fucking out of the way.'

Roberto buried his rubbery chin in his hands. 'Money,' he murmured.

'I don't know what you guys call it over at Government Center, but around here we call it a bonus.' John Murdock grinned at the county commissioner. 'What *do* you guys call it?'

To Roberto it seemed reckless to be discussing a payoff in the middle of a detective squad room. He felt like passing gas.

In a low voice he said to John Murdock, 'All right, we'll work something out.'

'Good.'

The commissioner stood up. He was about to reach out and shake their hands, but he changed his mind. 'Look, we never had this meeting,' he said to the two detectives.

'Of course not,' John Murdock agreed.

Joe Salazar said, 'Hey, you can trust us.'

About as far as I can spit, thought Robert Pepsical.

Three days before Mick Stranahan, Christina Marks, and Reynaldo Flemm arrived in Manhattan, and four days before the man called Chemo showed up, Maggie Gonzalez walked into a video-rental shop on West 52nd Street and asked to make a tape. She gave the shop clerk seventy-five dollars cash, and he led her to 'the studio', a narrow backroom panelled with cheap brown cork. The studio reeked of Lysol. On the floor was a stained grey mattress and a bright clump of used Kleenex, which, at Maggie's insistence, the clerk removed. A Sony video camera was mounted on an aluminium tripod at one end of the room; behind it, on another stem, was a small bank of lights. The clerk opened a metal folding chair and placed it eight feet in front of the lens.

Maggie sat down, opened her purse and unfolded some notes she had printed on Plaza stationery. While she read them to herself, the clerk was making impatient chewing-gum noises in his cheeks, like he had better things to do. Finally Maggie told him to start the tape, and a tiny red light twinkled over the Sony's cold black eye.

Maggie was all set to begin when she noticed the clerk hovering motionless in the darkest corner, a cockroach trying to blend into the cork. She told the guy to get lost, waited until the door slammed, then took a breath and addressed the camera.

'My name is Maggie Orestes Gonzalez,' she said. 'On the twelfth of March, 1986, I was a witness to the killing of a young woman named Victoria Barletta . . . '

The taping took fourteen minutes. Afterwards Maggie got two extra copies made at twenty dollars each. On the way back to the hotel she stopped at a branch of the

Merchant Bank and rented a safe-deposit box, where she left the two extra videotapes. She took the original up to her room at the Plaza, and placed it in the nightstand, under the room-service menu.

The very next day Maggie Gonzalez took a cab to the office of Dr Leonard Leaper on the corner of 50th Street and Lexington. Dr Leaper was a nationally renowned and internationally published plastic surgeon; Maggie had read up on him in the journals. 'You have a decent reputation,' she told Dr Leaper. 'I hope it's not just hype.' Her experiences in Dr Rudy Graveline's surgical suite had taught her to be exceedingly careful when choosing a physician.

Neutrally Dr Leaper said, 'What can I do for you, young lady?'

'The works,' Maggie replied.

'The works?'

'I want a bleph, a lift, and I want the hump taken out of this nose. Also, I want you to trim the septum so it looks like this.' With a finger she repositioned the tip of her nose at a perky, Sandy Duncan-type angle. 'See?'

Dr Leaper nodded.

'I'm a nurse,' Maggie said. 'I used to work for a plastic surgeon.'

'I figured something like that,' Dr Leaper said. 'Why do you want these operations?'

'None of your business.'

Dr Leaper said, 'Miss Gonzalez, if indeed you worked for a surgeon then you understand I've got to ask some personal questions. There are good reasons for elective cosmetic surgery and bad reasons, good candidates and poor candidates. Some patients believe it will solve all their problems, and of course it won't— '

'Cut the crap,' Maggie said, 'and take my word: surgery will definitely solve my problem.'

'Which is?'

'None of your business.'

Dr Leaper stood up. 'Then I'm afraid I can't help.'

'You guys are all alike,' Maggie complained.

'No, we're not,' Dr Leaper said. 'That's why you're here. You wanted somebody good.'

His composure was maddening. Maggie said, 'All right – will you do the surgery if I tell you the reason?'

'If it's a good one,' the doctor replied.

She said, 'I need a new face.'

'Why?'

'Because I am about to . . . testify against someone.'

Dr Leaper said, 'Can you tell me more?'

'It's a serious matter, and I expect he'll send someone to find me before it's over. I don't want to be found.'

Dr Leaper said, 'But surgery can only do so much— '

'Look, I've seen hundreds of cases, and I know good results from bad results. I also know the limitations of the procedures. You just do the nose, the neck, the eyes, maybe a plastic implant in the chin . . . and let me and Lady Clairol do the rest. I guarantee the bastard won't recognize me.'

Dr Leaper locked his hands. In a grave voice he said, 'Let me understand: you're a witness in a criminal matter?'

'Undoubtedly,' Maggie said. 'A homicide, to be exact.'

'Oh, dear.'

'And I must testify, Doctor.' The word *testify* was a stretch, but it wasn't far from the truth. 'It's the right thing for me to do,' Maggie asserted.

'Yes,' said Dr Leaper, without conviction.

'So, you see why I need your help.'

The surgeon sighed. 'Why should I believe you?'

Maggie said, 'Why should I lie? If it weren't an emergency, don't you think I would have had this done a long time ago, when I could've got a deal on the fees?'

'I suppose so.'

'Please, Doctor. It's not vanity, it's survival. Do my face, you'll be saving a life.'

Dr Leaper opened his schedule book. 'I've got a lipo tomorrow at two, but I'm going to bump him for you. Don't eat or drink anything after midnight— '

'I know the routine,' Maggie Gonzalez said ebulliently. 'Thank you very much.'

'It's all right.'

'One more thing.'

'Yes?' said Dr Leaper, cocking one grey eyebrow.

'I was wondering if there's any chance of a professional discount? I mean, since I *am* a nurse.'

Mick Stranahan stood on the kerb outside LaGuardia Airport and watched Reynaldo Flemm climb into a long black limousine. The limo driver, holding the door, eyed Reynaldo's new hair and looked to Christina Marks for a clue. She said something quietly to the driver, then waved goodbye to Reynaldo in the back seat. Through the smoked grey window Stranahan thought he saw Flemm shoot him a bitter look as the limo pulled away.

'I don't like this place,' Stranahan muttered, his breath frosty.

'What places *do* you like?' Christina asked.

'Old Rhodes Key. That's one place you won't see frozen spit on the sidewalk. Fact, you won't even see a sidewalk.'

'You old curmudgeon.' Christina said it much too sarcastically for Stranahan. 'Come on, let's get a cab.'

Her apartment was off 72nd Street on the Upper East Side. Third floor, one bedroom with a small kitchen and a garden patio scarcely big enough for a Norway rat. The furniture was low and modern: glass, chrome, and sharp angles. One of those sofas you put together like a jigsaw puzzle. Potted plants occupied three of the four corners in the living room. On the main wall hung a vast and frenetic abstract painting.

Stranahan took a step back and studied it. 'Boy, I don't know,' he said.

From the bedroom came Christina's voice. 'You like it?'

'Not really,' Stranahan said.

When Christina walked out, he saw that she had changed to blue jeans and a navy pullover sweater. She stood next to him in front of the painting and said, 'It's supposed to be springtime. Spring in the city.'

'Looks like an Amoco station on fire.'

'Thank you,' Christina said, 'Such a sensitive man.'

Stranahan shrugged. 'Let's go. I gotta check in.'

'Why don't you stay here?' She gave it a beat. 'On the sectional.'

'The sectional? I don't think so.'

'It's safer than a hotel, Mick.'

'I'm not so sure.'

Christina said, 'Don't flatter yourself.'

'It's not me I was thinking of. Believe it or not.'

'Sorry. Please stay.'

'The Great Reynaldo will not be pleased.'

'All the more reason,' Christina said.

They ate a late lunch at a small Italian restaurant three blocks from Christina's apartment. She ordered a pasta salad and Perrier, while Stranahan had spaghetti and meatballs and two beers. Then they took a taxi to the Plaza Hotel.

'She's here?' Christina asked, once in the lobby and again in the elevator.

Stranahan knocked repeatedly on the door to Maggie Gonzalez's room, but no one answered. Maggie was in bed, coasting through a codeine dreamland with a brand new face that she had not yet seen. The sound of Mick Stranahan's knocking was but a muffled drumbeat in her delicious pharamaceutical fog, and Maggie paid it no attention. It would be hours before the drumming returned, and by then she would be conscious enough to stumble toward the door.

Her big mistake had been to call Dr Rudy Graveline four days earlier when she had gotten the message on her machine in Miami. Curiosity had triumphed over common sense; Maggie had been dying for an update on the Stranahan situation. She needed to stay close to Rudy, but not too close. It was a dicey act. She wanted the doctor to believe that they were on the same side, his side. She also wanted to keep the expense money coming.

The phone call, though, had been peculiar. At first Dr

Graveline had seemed relieved to hear her voice. But the more questions Maggie had asked – about Stranahan, the TV people, the money situation – the more remote the doctor had become, his voice getting tighter and colder on the other end. Finally Rudy had said that something had come up in the office, could he call her right back? Certainly, Maggie had said and – stupidly, it turned out – had given Rudy the phone number at the hotel. Days later the doctor still had not called back, and Maggie wondered why in the hell he had tried to reach her in the first place.

The answer was simple.

On the thirteenth of February, the man known as Chemo got off a Pan Am flight from Miami to New York. He wore a dusty broad-brimmed hat pulled down tightly to shadow his igneous face, a calfskin golf-bag cover snapped over his left arm to conceal the prosthesis, a pea-green woollen overcoat to protect against the winter wind, and heavy rubber-soled shoes to combat the famous New York City slush. He also had in his possession a Rapala fishing knife, the phone number of a man in Queens who would sell him a gun, and a slip of prescription paper on which were written these words in Dr Rudy Graveline's spastic scrawl: 'Plaza Hotel, Rm. 966.'

18

When they returned from the Plaza to the apartment, Mick Stranahan said to Christina Marks: 'Sure you want a killer sleeping on the sectional?'

'Do you snore?'

'I'm serious.'

'Me, too.' From a closet she got a flannel sheet, a blanket, and two pillows. 'I've got a space heater that works, sometimes,' she said.

'No, this is fine.' Stranahan pulled off his shoes, turned on Letterman and stretched out on the sofa, which he had rearranged to contain his legs. He heard the shower running in the bathroom. After a few minutes Christina came out in a cloud of steam and sat down at the kitchen table. Her cheeks were flushed from the hot water. She wore a short blue robe, and her hair was wet. Stranahan could tell she'd brushed it out.

'We'll try again first thing in the morning,' he said.

'What?'

'Maggie's room at the hotel.'

'Oh, right.' She looked distracted.

He sat up and said, 'Come sit here.'

'I don't think so,' Christina said.

Stranahan could tell she had the radar up. He said, 'I must've scared you on the plane.'

'No, you didn't.' She wanted to ask about everything, his life; he was trying to make it easier and not doing so well.

'You didn't scare me,' Christina said again. 'If you did, I wouldn't let you stay.' But he had, and she did. That worried her even more.

Stranahan picked up the remote control and turned off the television. He heard sirens passing on the street outside and wished he were home, asleep on the bay.

When Christina spoke again, she didn't sound like a seasoned professional interviewer. She said, 'Five men?'

Stranahan was glad she'd started with the killings. The marriages would be harder to justify.

'Are we off the record?'

She hesitated, then said yes.

'The men I killed,' he began, 'would have killed me first. You'll just have to take my word.' Deep down, he wasn't sure about Thomas Henry Thomas, the fried-chicken robber. That one was a toss-up.

'What was it like?' Christina asked.

'Horrible.'

She waited for the details; often men like Stranahan wanted to tell about it. Or needed to.

But all he said was: 'Horrible, really. No fun at all.'

She said. 'You regret any of them?'

'Nope.'

She had one elbow propped on the table, knuckles pressed to her cheek. The only sound was the hissing of the radiator pipes, warming up. Stranahan peeled off his T-shirt and put it in a neat pile with his other clothes.

'I'll get a hotel room tomorrow.'

'No, you won't,' she said. 'I'm not frightened.'

'You haven't heard about my wives.'

She laughed softly. 'Five already at your age. You must be going for the record.'

Stranahan lay back, hands locked behind his head. 'I fall in love with waitresses. I can't help it.'

'You're kidding.'

'Don't be a snob. They were all smarter than I was. Even Chloe.'

Christina said, 'If you don't mind me saying so, she seemed a very cold woman.'

He groaned at the memory.

'What about the others, what were they like?'

'I loved them all, for a time. Then one day I didn't.'

Christina said, 'Doesn't sound like love.'

'Boy, are you wrong.' He smiled to himself.

'Mick, you regret any of them?'

'Nope.'

The radiator popped. The warmth of it made Stranahan sleepy, and he yawned.

'What about lovers?' Christina asked – a question sure to jolt him awake. 'All waitresses, no exceptions?'

'Oh, I've made some exceptions.' He scratched his head and pretended there were so many he had to add them up. 'Let's see, there was a lady probate lawyer. And an architect . . . make that two architects. Separately, of course. And an engineer for Pratt Whitney up in West Palm. An honest-to-God rocket scientist.'

'Really?'

'Yeah, really. And they were all dumber than I was.'

Stranahan pulled the blanket up to his neck and closed his eyes. 'Good-night, Christina.'

'Good-night, Mick.' She turned off the lights, returned to the kitchen table, and sat in the grey darkness for an hour, watching him sleep.

When Maggie Gonzalez heard the knocking again, she got out of bed and weaved toward the noise. With outstretched arms she staved off menacing walls, doorknobs, and lampshades, but barely. She navigated through a wet gauze, her vision fuzzed by painkillers. When she opened the door, she found herself staring at the breast of a pea-green woollen overcoat. She tilted her throbbing head, one notch at a time, until she found the man's face.

'Uh,' she said.

'Jesus H. Christ,' said Chemo, shoving her back in the room, kicking the door shut behind him, savagely cursing his own rotten luck. The woman was wrapped from forehead to throat in white surgical tape – a fucking mummy! He took the photograph from his overcoat and handed it to Maggie Gonzalez.

'Is that you?' he demanded.

'No.' The answer came from parchment lips, whispering through a slit in the bandages. 'No, it's not me.'

Chemo could tell that the woman was woozy. He told her to sit down before she fell down.

'It's you, isn't it? You're Maggie Gonzalez.'

She said, 'You're making a big mistake.'

'Shut up.' He took off his broad-brimmed hat and threw it on the bed. Through the peepholes in the bandage, Maggie was able to get a good look at the man's remarkable face.

She said, 'My God, what happened to you?'

'Shut the fuck up.'

Chemo unbuttoned his overcoat, heaved it over a chair, and paced. The trip was turning into a débâcle. First the man in Queens had sold him a rusty Colt .38 with only two bullets. Later, on the subway, he had been forced to flee a group of elderly Amish in the fear that they might recognize him from his previous life. And now this – confusion. While Chemo was reasonably sure that the bandaged woman was Maggie Gonzalez, he didn't want to screw up and kill the wrong person. Dr Graveline would never understand.

'Who are you?' Maggie said thickly. 'Who sent you?'

'You ask too many questions.'

'Please, I don't feel very well.'

Chemo took the Colt from the waistband of his pants and pointed it at the bandaged tip of her new nose. 'Your name's Maggie Gonzalez, isn't it?'

At the sight of the pistol, she leaned forward and vomited all over Chemo's rubber-soled winter shoes.

'Jesus H. Christ,' he moaned and bolted for the bathroom.

'I'm sorry,' Maggie called after him. 'You scared me, that's all.'

When Chemo came back, the shoes were off his feet and the gun was back in his pants. He was wiping his mouth with the corner of a towel.

'I'm really sorry,' Maggie said again.

Chemo shook his head disgustedly. He sat down on the corner of the bed. To Maggie his legs seemed as long as circus stilts.

'You're supposed to kill me?'

'Yep,' Chemo said. With the towel he wiped a fleck of puke off her nightgown.

Blearily she studied him and said, 'You've had some dermabrasion.'

'So?'

'So how come just little patches – why not more?'

'My doctor said that would be risky.'

'Your doctor's full of it,' Maggie said.

'And I guess you're an expert or something.'

'I'm a nurse, but you probably know that.'

Chemo said, 'No, I didn't.' Dr Graveline hadn't told him a thing.

Maggie went on, 'I used to work for a plastic surgeon down in Miami. A butcher with a capital B.'

Subconsciously Chemo's fingers felt for the tender spots on his chin. He was almost afraid to ask.

'This surgeon,' he said to Maggie, 'what was his name?'

'Graveline,' she said. 'Rudy Graveline. Personally, I wouldn't let him trim a hangnail.'

Lugubriously Chemo closed his bulbous red eyes. Through the codeine, Maggie thought he resembled a giant nuclear-radiated salamander, straight from a monster movie.

'How about this,' he said. 'I'll tell you what happened to my face if you tell me what happened to yours.'

It was Chemo's idea to have breakfast in Central Park. He figured there'd be so many other freaks that no one would notice them. As it turned out, Maggie's Tut-like facial shell drew more than a few stares. Chemo tugged his hat down tightly and said, 'You should've worn a scarf.'

They were sitting near Columbus Circle on a bench. Chemo had bought a box of raisin bagels with cream cheese. Maggie said her stomach felt much better but, because of the surgical tape, she was able to fit only small pieces of bagel into her mouth. It was a sloppy process, but two fat squirrels showed up to claim the crumbs.

Chemo was saying, 'Your nose, your chin, your eyelids – Christ, no wonder you hurt.' He took out her picture and looked at it appraisingly. 'Too bad,' he said.

'What's that supposed to mean?'

'I mean, you were a pretty lady.'

'Maybe I still am,' Maggie said. 'Maybe prettier.'

Chemo put the photograph back in his coat. 'Maybe,' he said.

'You're going to make me cry and then everything'll sting.'

He said, 'Knock it off.'

'Don't you think I feel bad enough?' Maggie said. 'I get a whole new face – and for what! A month from now and you'd never have recognized me. I could've sat in your lap on the subway and you wouldn't know who I was.'

Chemo thought he heard sniffling behind the bandages. 'Don't fucking cry,' he said. 'Don't be a baby.'

'I don't understand why Rudy sent you,' Maggie whined.

'To kill you, what else?'

'But why now? Nothing's happened yet.'

Chemo frowned and said, 'Keep it down.' The pink patches on his chin tingled in the cold air and made him think about Rudy Graveline. Butcher with a capital B, Maggie had said. Chemo wanted to know more.

A thin young Moonie in worn corduroys came up to the park bench and held out a bundle of red and white carnations. 'Be happy,' the kid said to Maggie. 'Five dollars.'

'Get lost,' Chemo said.

'Four dollars,' said the Moonie. 'Be happy.'

Chemo pulled the calfskin cover off his Weed Whacker and flicked the underarm toggle for the battery pack. The Moonie gaped as Chemo calmly chopped the bright carnations to confetti.

'Be gone, Hop-sing,' Chemo said, and the Moonie ran away. Chemo recloaked the Weed Whacker and turned to Maggie. 'Tell me why the doctor wants you dead.'

It took her several moments to recover from what she had seen. Finally she said, 'Well, it's a long story.'

'I got all day,' Chemo said. 'Unless you got tickets to *Phantom* or something.'

'Can we go for a walk?'

'No,' Chemo said sharply. 'Remember?' He had thrown his vomit-covered shoes and socks out the ninth-floor window of Maggie's room at the Plaza. Now he was sitting in bare feet in Central Park on a forty-degree February morning. He wiggled his long bluish toes and said to Maggie Gonzalez: 'So talk.'

She did. She told Chemo all about the death of Victoria Barletta. It was a slightly shorter recital than she'd put on the videotape, but it was no less shocking.

'You're making this up,' Chemo said.

'I'm not either.'

'He killed this girl with a nose job?'

Maggie nodded. 'I was there.'

'Jesus H. Christ.'

'It was an accident.'

'That's even worse,' Chemo said. He tore off his hat and threw it on the sidewalk, spooking the squirrels. 'This is the same maniac who's working on my face. I can't fucking stand it!'

By way of consolation, Maggie said: 'Dermabrasion is a much simpler procedure.'

'Yeah, tell me about simple procedures.' Chemo couldn't believe the lousy luck he had with doctors. He said, 'So what does all this have to do with him wanting you dead?'

Maggie told Chemo about Reynaldo Flemm's TV investigation (without mentioning that she had been the tipster), told how she had warned Rudy about Mick Stranahan, the investigator. She was careful to make it sound as if Stranahan was the whistle-blower.

'Now it's starting to make sense,' Chemo said. 'Graveline wants me to kill *him*, too.' He held up the arm-mounted Weed Whacker. 'He's the prick that cost me this hand.'

'Rudy can't afford any witnesses,' Maggie explained, 'or any publicity. Not only would they yank his medical licence, he'd go to jail. Now do you understand?'

Do I ever, thought Chemo.

The white mask that was Maggie's face asked: 'Are you still going to kill me?'

'We'll see,' Chemo replied. 'I'm sorting things out.'

'How much is that cheap bastard paying you?'

Chemo plucked his rumpled hat off the sidewalk. 'I'd rather not say,' he muttered, clearly embarrassed. No way would he let that butcher fuck with his ears. Not now.

Christina Marks and Mick Stranahan got to the Plaza Hotel shortly before ten. From the lobby Stranahan called Maggie's room and got no answer. Christina followed him into the elevator and, as they rode to the ninth floor, she watched him remove a small serrated blade from his wallet.

'Master key,' he said.

'Mick, no. I could get fired.'

'Then wait downstairs.'

But she didn't. She watched him pick the lock on Maggie's door, then slipped into the room behind him. She said nothing and scarcely moved while he checked the bathroom and the closets to see if they were alone.

'Mick, come here.'

On the bedstand were two prescription bottles, a plastic bedpan, and a pink-splotched surgical compress. Stranahan glanced at the pills: Tylenol No. 3 and Darvocet. The bottle of Darvocets had not yet been opened. A professional business card lay next to the telephone on Maggie's nightstand. Stranahan chuckled drily when he read what was on the card:

LEONARD R. LEAPER, M.D.
Certified by the American Board of Plastic Surgery
Office: 555-6600 Nights and Emergencies: 555-6677

'How nice,' Christina remarked. 'She took our money and got a facelift.'

Stranahan said, 'Something's not right. She ought to be in bed.'

'Maybe she went for brunch at the Four Seasons.'

He shook his head. 'These scrips are only two days old, so that's when she had the surgery. She's still got to be swollen up like a mango. Would you go out in public looking like that?'

'Depends on how much dope I ate.'

'No,' Stranahan said, scanning the room, 'something's not right. She ought to be here.'

'What do you want to do?'

Stranahan said they should go downstairs and wait in the lobby; in her condition, Maggie shouldn't be hard to spot. 'But first,' he said, 'let's really go through this place.'

Christina went to the dresser. Under a pile of Maggie's bras and panties she found three new flowered bikinis, the price tags from the Plaza Shops still attached. Maggie was definitely getting ready for Maui.

'Oh, Miss Marks,' Stranahan sang out. 'Lookie here.'

It was a video cassette in a brown plastic sleeve. The sleeve was marked with a sticker from Midtown Studio Productions.

Stranahan tossed Christina the tape. She tossed it back.

'We can't take that, it's larceny.'

He said, 'It's not larceny to take something you already own.'

'What do you mean?'

'If this is what I think it is, you've paid for it already. The Barletta story, remember?'

'We don't know that. Could be anything – home movies, maybe.'

Stranahan smiled and stuffed the cassette into his coat. 'Only one way to find out.'

'No,' Christina said.

'Look, you got a VCR at your place. Let's go watch the tape. If I'm wrong, then I'll bring it back myself.'

'Oh, I see. Just sneak in, put it back where you got it, tidy up the place.'

'Yeah, if I'm wrong. If it turns out to be Jane Fonda or something. But I don't think so.'

Christina Marks knew better; it was madness, of course. She could lose her job, blow a perfectly good career if they were caught. But, then again, this hadn't turned out to be the typical Reynaldo Flemm exposé. She had damn near gotten machine-gunned over this one, so what the hell.

Grudgingly she said, 'Is it Beta or VHS?'

Stranahan gave her a hug.

Then they heard the key in the door.

The two couples said nothing for the first few seconds, just stared. Mick Stranahan and Christina Marks had the most to contemplate: a woman wrapped in tape, and a beanpole assassin with one arm down to his knees.

Maggie Gonzalez was the first to speak: 'It's him.'

'Who?' Chemo asked. He had never seen Stranahan up close, not even at the stilt house.

'Him,' Maggie repeated through the bandages. 'What're you doing in my room?'

'Hello, Maggie,' Stranahan said, 'assuming it's you under there. It's sure been a long time.'

'And you!' Maggie grunted, pointing at Christina Marks.

'Hi, again,' said Christina. 'I thought you'd be in Hawaii by now.'

Chemo said, 'I guess everybody's old pals except me.' He pulled the .38 out of his overcoat. 'Nobody move.'

'Another one who watches too much TV,' Stranahan whispered to Christina.

Chemo blinked angrily. 'I don't like you one bit.'

'I assumed as much from the fact you keep trying to kill me.' Stranahan had seen some bizarros in his day, but this one took the cake. He looked like Fred Munster with bulimia. One eye on the gun, Stranahan asked, 'Do you have a name?'

'No,' Chemo said.

'Good. Makes for a cheaper tombstone.'

Chemo told Maggie to close the door, but Maggie didn't move. The sight of the pistol had made her nauseated all over again, and she was desperately trying to keep down her breakfast bagels.

'What's the matter now?' Chemo snapped.

'She doesn't look so hot,' Christina said.

'And who the fuck are you, Florence Nightingale?'

'What happened to your arm?' Christina asked him. A cool customer she was; Stranahan admired her poise.

Chemo got the impression that he was losing control, which made no sense, since he was the one with the pistol, 'Shut up, all of you,' he said, 'while I kill Mr Stranahan here. *Finally.*'

At these words, Maggie Gonzalez upchucked gloriously all over Chemo's gun arm. Given his general translucence, it was impossible to tell if Chemo blanched. He did, however, wobble perceptibly.

Mick Stranahan steeped forward and punched him ferociously in the Adam's apple. The man went down like a seven-foot Tinkertoy, but did not release his grip on the gun. Maggie backed up and screamed, a primal wail that poured from the hole in her bandage and filled the hallway.

Stranahan decided there was no time to finish the job. He pushed Christina Marks through the doorway and told her to go for the elevator. Gagging and spitting blood, Chemo rolled out of his foetal curl and took a wild shot at Christina as she ran down the hall. The bullet twanged impotently off a fire extinguisher and was ultimately stopped by the opulent Plaza wallpaper.

Before Chemo could fire again, Stranahan stomped on his wrist, still slippery from Maggie's used bagels. Chemo would not let go of the gun. With a growl he swung his refurbished left arm like a fungo bat across his body. It caught Stranahan in the soft crease behind the knee and brought him down. The two men wrestled for the pistol while Maggie howled and clawed chimp-like at her swaddled head.

It was a clumsy fight. Tangled in the killer's gangliness, Stranahan could not shield himself from a clubbing by Chemo's oversized left arm. Whatever it was – and it wasn't a human fist – it hurt like hell. His skull chiming, Stranahan tried to break free.

Suddenly he felt the dull barrel of the .38 against his throat. He flinched when he heard the click, but nothing else followed. No flash, no explosion, no smell. The bullet, Chemo's second and only remaining round, was a dud. Chemo couldn't believe it – that asshole in Queens had screwed him royal.

Stranahan squirmed loose, stood up, and saw that they had attracted an audience. All along the corridor, doors were cracked open, some more than others. Under Maggie's keening he could hear excited voices. Somebody was calling the police.

Stranahan groped at his coat to make sure that the videotape was still in his pocket, kicked Chemo once in the groin (or where he estimated that the giant's groin might be), then jogged down the hallway.

Christina Marks was considerate enough to hold the elevator.

19

Dr Rudy Graveline was a fellow who distrusted chance and prided himself on preparation, but he had not planned a love affair with a Hollywood star. Heather Chappell was a distraction – a fragrant, gorgeous, elusive, spoiled, sulky bitch of a distraction. He couldn't get enough of her. Rudy had come to crave the tunnel of clear thinking that enveloped him while making love to Heather; it was like a sharp cool drug. She screwed him absolutely numb, left him aching and drained and utterly in focus with his predicament.

For a while he kept cooking up lame excuses for postponing Heather's elaborate cosmetic surgery – knowing it would put her out of action for weeks. Sex with Heather had become a crucial component of Rudy Graveline's daily regimen; like a long-distance runner, he had fallen into a physical rhythm that he could not afford to break. TV people were after him, his medical career was in jeopardy, a homicide rap was on the horizon – and salvation depended on a crooked halfwit politician and a one-armed, seven-foot hit man. Rudy needed to stay razor-sharp until the crisis was over, and Heather had become vital to his clarity.

He treated her like a queen and it seemed to work. Heather's initial urgency to schedule the surgery had subsided during the day-long shopping sprees, the four-star meals, the midnight yacht cruises up and down the Intracoastal. In recent days, though, she again had begun to press Rudy not only about the date for the operations, but the cost. She was dropping broad hints to the effect that for all her bedroom labours she deserved a special discount, and Rudy found himself weakening on the subject. Finally, one night, she waited until he was inside her to bring up the money again, and Rudy breathlessly agreed to knock forty per cent off the usual fee. Afterwards he was furious at himself, and blamed his moment of weakness on stress and mental fatigue.

Deep down, the doctor knew better: he was trapped. While he dreaded the prospect of Heather Chappell's surgery, he feared that she would leave him if he didn't agree to do it. He probably would have done it for free. He had become addicted to her body – a radiantly perfect body that she now wanted him to *improve*. The task would have posed a career challenge for the most skilful of plastic surgeons; for a hack like Rudy Graveline, it was flat-out impossible. Naturally he planned to let his assistants do it.

Until Heather dropped another surprise.

'My agent says I should tape the operation, love.'

Rudy said, 'You're kidding.'

'Just to be on the safe side.'

'What, you don't trust me?'

'Sure I do,' Heather said. 'It's my damn agent, is all. She says since my looks are everything, my whole career, I should be careful, legal-wise. I guess she wants to make sure nothing goes wrong— '

Rudy sprung out of bed, hands on his hips. 'Look, I told you these operations are not necessary at all.'

'And I told you, I'm sick of doing sitcoms and *Hollywood Squares*. I need to get back in the movies, hon, and that means I need a new look. That's why I came down here.'

Rudy Graveline had never tried to talk anyone out of surgery before, so he was forced to improvise. By and large it was not such a terrible speech. He said, 'God was very good to you, Heather. I have patients who'd give fifty grand to look half as beautiful as you look; teenagers who'd kill for that nose you want me to chisel, housewives who'd trade their first-born child for tits like yours— '

'Rudolph,' Heather said, 'save it.'

He tried to pull up his underwear but the elastic snagged on heavily bandaged kneecaps, the product of the disco tryst in the fireplace.

'I am appalled,' Rudy was huffing, 'at the idea of videotaping in my surgical suite.' In truth he wasn't appalled so much as afraid: a video camera meant he couldn't hand off to the other surgeons and duck out to the golf course. He'd have to perform every procedure himself, just as Heather had demanded. You couldn't drug a damn camera; it wouldn't miss a stitch.

'This just isn't done,' Rudy protested.

'Oh, it is, too,' Heather said. 'I see stuff like that on PBS all the time. Once I saw them put a baboon heart inside a human baby. They showed the whole thing.'

'It isn't done *here*,' Rudy said.

Heather sat up, making sure that the bedsheets slipped off the slope of her breasts. 'Fine, Rudolph,' she said. 'If that's the way you want it, I'll fly back to California tonight. There's only about a dozen first-rate surgeons in Beverly Hills that would give anything to do me.'

The ice in her voice surprised him, though it shouldn't have. 'All right,' he said, pulling on his robe, 'we'll video the surgery. Maybe Robin Leach can use a clip on his show.'

Heather let the wisecrack pass; she was focused on business. She asked Rudy Graveline for a date they could begin.

'A week,' he said. He had to clear his mind a few more times. In another week he also would have heard something definite from Chemo, or maybe Robert Pepsical.

'And we're not doing all this at once,' he added. 'You've got the liposuction, the breast augmentation, the rhinoplasty, the eyelids, and the rhytidectomy – that's a lot of surgery, Heather.'

'Yes, Rudolph.' She had won and she knew it.

'I think we'll start with the nose and see how you do.'

'Or how *you* do,' Heather said.

Rudy had a queasy feeling that she wasn't kidding.

The executive producer of *In Your Face* was a man known to Reynaldo Flemm only as Mr Dover. Mr Dover was in charge of the budget. Upon Reynaldo's return to New

York, he found a message taped to his office door. Mr Dover wanted to see him right away.

Immediately Reynaldo called the apartment of Christina Marks, but hung up when Mick Stranahan answered the phone. Reynaldo was fiercely jealous; beyond that, he didn't think it was fair that he should have to face Mr Dover alone. Christina was the producer, she knew where all the money went. Reynaldo was merely the talent, and the talent never knew anything.

When he arrived at Mr Dover's office, the secretary did not recognize him. 'The music division is on the third floor,' she said, scarcely making eye contact.

Reynaldo riffled his new hair and said, 'It's me.'

'Oh, hi, Ray.'

'What do you think?'

The secretary said, 'It's a dynamite disguise.'

'It's not a disguise.'

'Oh.'

'I wanted a new look,' he explained.

'Why?' asked the secretary.

Reynaldo couldn't tell her the truth – that a rude plastic surgeon told him he had a fat waist and a big honker – so he said: 'Demographics.'

The secretary looked at him blankly.

'Market surveys,' he went on. 'We're going for some younger viewers.'

'Oh, I see,' the secretary said.

'Long hair is making quite a comeback.'

'I didn't know,' she said, trying to be polite. 'Is that real, Ray?'

'Well, no. Not yet.'

'I'll tell Mr Dover you're here.'

Mr Dover was a short man with an accountant's pinched demeanour, a fish-belly complexion, tiny black eyes, and the slick, sloping forehead of a killer whale. Mr Dover wore expensive dark suits and yuppie suspenders that, Reynaldo suspected, needed adjustment.

'Ray, what can you tell me about this Florida project?' Mr Dover never wasted time with small talk.

'It's heavy,' Reynaldo replied.

'Heavy.'

'Very heavy.' Reynaldo noticed his expense vouchers stacked in a neat pile on the corner of Mr Dover's desk. This worried him, so he said, 'My producer was almost murdered.'

'I see.'

'With a machine-gun,' Reynaldo added.

Mr Dover pursed his lips. 'Why?'

'Because we're getting close to cracking this story.'

'You're getting close to cracking my budget, Ray.'

'This is an important project.'

Mr Dover said, 'A network wouldn't blink twice, Ray, but we're not one of the networks. My job is to watch the bottom line.'

Indignantly Reynaldo thought: *I eat twits like you for breakfast.* He was good at thinking tough thoughts.

'Investigations cost money,' he said tersely.

With shiny fingernails Mr Dover leafed through the receipts on his desk until he found the one he wanted. 'Jambala's House of Hair,' he said. 'Seven hundred and seventeen dollars.'

Reynaldo blushed and ground his caps. Christina should be here for this; she'd know how to handle this jerk.

Mr Dover continued: 'I don't intend to interfere, nor do I intend to let these extravagances go on for ever. As I understand it, the programme is due to air next month.'

'All the spots have been sold,' Reynaldo said. 'They've been sold for six months.' He couldn't resist.

'Yes, well I suggest you try not to spend all that advertising revenue before the broadcast date – just in case it doesn't work out.'

'And when hasn't it worked out?'

Reynaldo regretted the words almost instantly, for Mr Dover was only too happy to refresh his memory. There was the time Flemm claimed to have discovered the wreckage of Amelia Earhart's aeroplane (it turned out to be a crop duster in New Zealand); the time he claimed to have an exclusive interview with the second gunman from Dealey Plaza (who, it later turned out, was barely seven years old on the day of the Kennedy assassination); the time he uncovered a Congressional call-girl ring (only to be caught boffing two of the ladies in a mop closet at the Rayburn Building). These fiascos each resulted in a cancelled broadcast, snide blurbs in the press, and great sums of lost revenue, which Mr Dover could recall to the penny.

'Ancient history,' Reynaldo Flemm said defensively.

Unspoken was the fact that no such embarrassments had happened since Christina Marks had been hired. Every show had been finished on time, on budget. Reynaldo did not appreciate the connection, but Mr Dover did.

'You understand my concern,' he said. 'How much longer do you anticipate being down in Miami?'

'Two weeks. We'll be editing.' Sounded good, anyway.

'So, shall we say, one more trip?'

'That ought to do it,' Reynaldo agreed.

'Excellent.' Mr Dover straightened the stack of Reynaldo's expense receipts, lining up all the little corners in perfect angles. 'By the way, Miss Marks wasn't harmed, was she?'

'No, just scared shitless. She's not used to getting shot at.' As if he was.

'Did they catch this person?'

'Nope,' Reynaldo said, hard-bitten, like he wasn't too surprised.

'My,' said Mr Dover. He hoped that Christina Marks was paid up on her medical plan and death benefits.

'I told you it was heavy,' Reynaldo said, rising. 'But it'll be worth it, I promise.'

'Good,' said Mr Dover. 'I can't wait.'

Reynaldo was three steps toward the door when Mr Dover said, 'Ray?'

'Yeah.'

'Forgive me, but I was just noticing.'

'That's all right.' He'd been wondering how long it would take the twerp to mention something about the hair.

But from behind the desk Mr Dover smiled wickedly and

214

patted his midsection. 'You've put on a pound or three, haven't you, Ray?'

In the elevator Reynaldo angrily tore off his seven-hundred-dollar wig and hurled it into a corner, where it lay like a dead Pekinese. He took the limo back to his apartment, stripped off his clothes, and stood naked for a long time in front of the bedroom mirror.

Reynaldo decided that Dr Graveline was right: his nose was too large. And his belly had thickened.

He pivoted to the left, then to the right, then back to the left. He sucked in his breath. He flexed. He locked his knuckles behind his head and tightened his stomach muscles, but his belly did not disappear.

In the mirror Reynaldo saw a body that was neither flabby nor lean: an average body for an average forty-year-old man. He saw a face that was neither dashing nor weak: small darting eyes balanced by a strong, heavy jaw, with a nose to match. He concluded that his instincts about preserving the moustache were sound: when Reynaldo covered his hairy upper lip with a bare finger, his nose assumed even greater prominence.

Of course, something radical had to be done. Confidence was the essence of Reynaldo's camera presence, the core of his masculine appeal. If he were unhappy with himself or insecure about his appearance, it would show up on his face like a bad rash. The whole country would see it.

Standing alone at the mirror, Reynaldo hatched a plan that would solve his personal dilemma and wrap up the Barletta story simultaneously. It was a bold plan because it would not include Christina Marks. Reynaldo Flemm would serve as his own producer and would tell Christina nothing, just as she had told him nothing for two entire weeks after the shooting in Stiltsville.

The shooting. Still it galled him, the sour irony that *she* would be the one to get the glory – after all his years on the streets. To have his producer nearly assassinated while he dozed on the massage table at the Sonesta was the lowest moment in Reynaldo's professional career. He had to atone.

In the past he had always counted on Christina to worry about the actual nuts-and-bolts journalism of the programme. It was Christina who did the reporting, blocked out the interviews, arranged for the climactic confrontations – she even wrote the scripts. Reynaldo Flemm was hopelessly bored by detail, research, and the rigours of fact checking. He was an action guy, and he saved his energy for when the tape was rolling. Whereas Christina had filled three legal pads with notes, ideas, and questions about Victoria Barletta's death, Reynaldo cared about one thing only: who could they get on tape? Rudy Graveline was the big enchilada, and certainly Victoria's still-grieving mother was a solid bet. Mick Stranahan had been another obvious choice – the embarrassed investigator, admitting four years later that he had overlooked the prime suspect, the doctor himself.

But the Stranahan move had backfired, and nearly made a news-industry martyr of Christina Marks. Fine, thought Reynaldo, go ahead and have your fling. Meanwhile Willie and I will be kicking some serious quack ass.

Every time Dr Rudy Graveline got a phone call from New York or New Jersey, he assumed it was the mob. The mob had generously put him through Harvard Medical School, and in return Rudy occasionally extended his professional courtesies to mob guys, their friends or family. It was Rudy himself who had redone the face of Tony (The Eel) Traviola, the hit man who later washed up dead on Cape Florida beach with a marlin hole through his sternum. Fortunately for Rudy, most mob fugitives were squeamish about surgery, so he wound up doing mainly their wives, daughters, and mistresses. Noses, mostly, with the occasional face-lift.

That's the kind of call Rudy expected when his secretary told him that New York was on the line.

'Yes?'

'Hello, Doctor Graveline.'

The voice did not belong to Curly Eyebrows or any of his cousins.

'Who is this?'

'Johnny LeTigre, remember me?'

'Of course.' The hinky male stripper. Rudy said, 'What are you doing in New York?'

'I had a gig in the Village, but I'm on my way back to Miami.' This was Reynaldo Flemm's idea of being fast on his feet. He said, 'Look, I've been thinking about what you said that day at the clinic.'

Rudy Graveline could not remember exactly what he had said. 'Yes?'

'About my nose and my abdomen.'

Then it came back to Rudy. 'Your nose and abdomen, yes, I remember.'

'You were right,' Reynaldo went on. 'We don't always see ourselves the way other people do.'

Rudy was thinking: Get to the damn point.

'I'd like for you to do my nose,' Reynaldo declared.

'All right.'

'And my middle – what's that operation called?'

'Suction-assisted lipectomy,' Rudy said.

'Yeah, that's it. How much'd that set me back?'

Rudy recalled that this was a man who offered ten grand to have a mole removed from his buttocks.

'Fifteen thousand,' Rudy said.

'Geez!' said the voice from New York.

'But that's if I perform the procedures myself,' Rudy explained. 'Keep in mind, I've got several very competent associates who could handle your case for, oh, half as much.'

The way that Rudy backed off on the word *competent* was no accident, but Reynaldo Flemm didn't need a sell job. Quickly he said. 'No, I definitely want you. Fifteen it is. But I need the work done this week.'

'Out of the question.' Rudy would be immersed in preparation for the Heather Chappell marathon.

'Next week at the latest,' Reynaldo pressed.

'Let me see what I can do. By the way, Mr LeTigre, what is the status of your mole?'

Reynaldo had almost forgotten about the ruse that originally had gained his entry to Whispering Palms. Again he had to wing it. 'You won't believe this,' he said to Dr Rudy Graveline, 'but the damn thing fell off.'

'Are you certain?'

'Swear to God, one morning I'm standing in the shower and I turn around and it's gone. Gone! I found it lying there in the bed. Just fell off, like an acorn or something.'

'Hmmm,' Rudy said. The guy was a flake, but who cared.

'I threw it away, is that OK?'

'The mole?'

'Yeah, I thought about saving it in the freezer, maybe having some tests run. But then I figured what the hell and I tossed it in the trash.'

'It was probably quite harmless,' Rudy Graveline said, dying to hang up.

'So I'll call you when I get back to Miami.'

'Fine,' said the doctor. 'Have a safe trip, Mr LeTigre.'

Reynaldo Flemm was beaming when he put down the phone. This would be something. Maybe even better than getting shot on the air.

20

Maggie Gonzalez said: 'Tell me about your hand.'

'Shut up,' Chemo grumbled. He was driving around Queens, trying to find the sonofabitch who had sold him the bad bullets.

'Please,' Maggie said. 'I am a nurse.'

'Too bad you're not a magician, because that's what it's gonna take to make my hand come back. A fish got it.'

At a stop light he rolled down the window and called to a group of black teenagers. He asked where he could locate a man named Donnie Blue, and the teenagers told Chemo to go blow himself. 'Shit,' he said, stomping on the accelerator.

Maggie asked, 'Was it a shark that did it?'

'Do I look like Jacques Cousteau? I don't know what the hell it was – some big fish. The subject is closed.'

By now Maggie was reasonably confident that he wasn't going to kill her. He would have done it already, most conveniently during the scuffle back at the Plaza. Instead he had grabbed her waist and hustled her down the fire exit, taking four steps at a time. Considering the mayhem on the ninth floor, it was a miracle they got out of the place without being stopped. The lobby was full of uniformed cops waiting for elevators, but nobody looked twice at the Fun Couple of the Year.

As Chemo drove, Maggie said, 'What about your face?'

'Look who's talking.'

'Really, what's happened?'

Chemo said, 'You always this shy with strangers? Jesus H. Christ.'

'I'm sorry,' she said. 'Professional curiosity, I guess. Besides, you promised to tell me.'

'Do the words *none of your fucking business* mean anything?'

From behind the bandages a chilly voice said, 'You don't have to be crude. Swearing doesn't impress me.'

Chemo found the street corner where he had purchased the rusty Colt .38 and the dead bullets, but there was no sign of Donnie Blue. Every inquiry was met by open derision, and Chemo's hopes for a refund began to fade.

As he circled the neighbourhood Maggie said, 'You're so quiet.'

'I'm thinking.'

'Me, too.'

'I'm thinking I was seriously gypped by your doctor pal.' Chemo didn't want to admit that he had agreed to murder two people in exchange for a discount on minor plastic surgery.

'If I had known about this dead girl— '

'Vicky Barletta.

'Right,' Chemo said. 'If I had known that, I would have jacked my price. Jacked it way the hell up.'

'And who could blame you,' Maggie said.

'Graveline never told me he killed a girl.'

They were heading out the highway toward LaGuardia. Maggie assumed there were travel plans.

She said, 'Rudy's a very wealthy man.'

'Sure, he's a doctor.'

'I can ruin him. That's why he wanted me dead.'

'Sure, you're a witness,' Chemo said.

Something dismissive in his tone alarmed her once again. She said, 'Killing me won't solve anything now.'

Chemo's forehead crinkled where an eyebrow should have been. 'It won't?'

Maggie shook her head from side to side in dramatic emphasis. 'I made my own tape. A videotape, at a place in Manhattan. Everything's on it, everything I saw that day.'

Chemo wasn't as rattled as she thought he might be, in fact, his mouth curled into a dry smile. His lips looked like two pink snails crawling up a sidewalk.

'A video,' he mused.

Maggie teased it along. 'You have any idea what that bastard would pay for it?'

'Yes,' Chemo said. 'Yes, I think I do.'

At the airport, Maggie told Chemo she had to make a phone call. To eavesdrop he squeezed inside the same booth, his chin digging into the top of her head. She dialled the number of Dr Leonard Leaper and informed the service that she had to leave town for a while, but that the doctor should not be concerned.

'I already told him I was a witness in a murder,' Maggie explained to Chemo. 'If what happened at the hotel turns up in the newspapers, he'll think I was kidnapped.'

'But you were,' Chemo pointed out.

'Oh, not really.'

'Yes, *really*.' Chemo didn't care for her casual attitude; just who did she take him for?

220

Maggie said: 'Know what I think? I think we could be partners.'

They got in line at the Pan Am counter, surrounded by a typical Miami-bound contingent - old geezers with tubas for sinuses; shiny young hustlers in thin gold chains; huge hollow-eyed families that looked like they'd staggered out of a Sally Struthers telethon. Chemo and Maggie fit right in.

He told her, 'I only got one plane ticket.'

She smiled and stroked her handbag, which had not left her arm since their breakfast in Central Park. 'I've got a Visa card,' she said brightly. 'Where we headed?'

'Me, I'm going back to Florida.'

'Not like that, you're not. They've got rules against bare feet, I'm sure.'

'Hell,' Chemo said, and loped off to locate some cheap shoes. He came back wearing fuzzy brown bathroom slippers, size 14, purchased at one of the airport gift shops. Maggie was saving him a spot at the ticket counter. She had already arranged for him to get an aisle seat (because of his long legs), and she would be next to him.

Later, waiting in the boarding area, Maggie asked Chemo if his name was Rogelio Luz Sanchez.

'Oh sure.'

'That's what it says on your ticket.'

'Well, there you are,' Chemo said. He couldn't even *pronounce* Rogelio Luz Sanchez – some alias cooked up by Rudy Graveline, the dumb shit. Chemo looked about as Hispanic as Larry Bird.

After they took their seats on the aeroplane, Maggie leaned close and asked, 'So, can I call you Rogelio? I mean, I've got to call you *something*.'

Chemo's hooded lids blinked twice very slowly. 'The more you talk, the more I want to spackle the holes in that fucking mask.'

Maggie emitted a reedy, birdlike noise.

'I think we can do business,' Chemo said, 'but only on two conditions. One, don't ask any more personal questions, is that clear? Two, don't ever puke on me again.'

'I said I was sorry.'

The plane had started to taxi and Chemo raised his voice to be heard over the engines. 'Once I get some decent bullets I'll be using that gun, and God help you if you toss your cookies when I do.'

Maggie said, 'I'll do better next time.'

One of the flight attendants came by and asked Maggie if she needed a special meal because of her medical condition, and Maggie remarked that she wasn't feeling particularly well. She said the coach section was so crowded and stuffy that she was having trouble breathing. The next thing Chemo knew, they were sitting up in first class and sipping red wine. Having noticed his disability, the friendly flight attendant was carefully cutting Chemo's surf-and-turf into bite-sized pieces. Chemo glanced at Maggie and felt guilt about coming down so hard.

'That was a slick move,' he said, the closest he would come to a compliment. 'I never rode up here before.'

Maggie exhibited no surprise at this bit of news. Her eyes looked sad and moist behind the white husk.

Chemo said, 'You still want to be partners?'

She nodded. Carefully she aimed a forkful of lobster for the damp hole beneath her nostrils in the surgical bandage.

'Graveline's gonna scream when he learns about your videotape,' Chemo said with a chuckle. 'Where is it, anyway?'

When Maggie finished chewing, she said, 'I've got three copies.'

'Good thinking.'

'Two of them are locked up at a bank. The third one, the original tape, that's for Rudy. That's how we get his attention.'

Chemo smiled a yellow smile. 'I like it.'

'You won't like this part,' Maggie said. 'Stranahan swiped the tape from the hotel room. We can't show it to Rudy until we get it back.'

'Hell,' Chemo said. This was terrible – Mick Stranahan and that TV bitch loose with the blackmail goodies. Just

222

terrible. He said, 'I've got to get them before they get to Graveline, otherwise we're blown out of the water. He'll be on the first flight to Panama and we'll be holding our weenies.'

From Maggie came a muffled, disapproving noise.

'It's just an expression,' Chemo said. 'Lighten up, for Chrissakes.'

After the flight attendants removed the meal trays, Chemo lowered the seat back and stretched his endless legs. Almost to himself, he said, 'I don't like this Stranahan guy one bit. When we get to Miami, we hit the ground running.'

'Yes,' Maggie agreed, easing into the partnership, 'we've got to get the tape.'

'That, too,' said Chemo, tugging his hat down over his eyes.

The news of gunshots and a possible kidnapping at the Plaza Hotel rated five paragraphs in the *Daily News*, a page of photos in the *Post* and nothing in the *Times*. That morning New York detectives queried a teletype to the Metro-Dade Police Department stating that the victim of the abduction was believed to be a Miami woman named Margaret Orestes Gonzalez, a guest at the hotel. The police teletype described her assailant as a white male, age unknown, with possible burn scars on his face and a height of either six foot four or eight foot two, depending on which witness you believed. The teletype further noted that a Rapala fishing knife found on the carpet outside the victim's room was traced to a shipment that recently had been sold to a retail establishment known as Bubba's Bait and Cold Beer, on Dixie Highway in South Miami. Most significantly, a partial thumb-print lifted from the blade of the knife was identified as belonging to one Blondell Wayne Tatum, age thirty-eight, six foot nine, one hundred and eighty-one pounds. Mr Tatum, it seemed, was wanted in the state of Pennsylvania for the robbery-at-pitchfork of a Chemical Bank, and for the first-degree murder of Dr Kyle Kloppner, an elderly dermatologist. Tatum was to be considered armed and dangerous. Under AKAs, the police bulletin listed one: Chemo.

'Chemo?' Sergeant Al Garcia read the teletype again, then pulled it off the bulletin board and took it to the Xerox machine. By the time he got back, a new teletype had been posted in its place.

This one was even more interesting, and Garcia's cigar bobbed excitedly as he read it.

The new teletype advised Metro-Dade police to disregard the kidnap query. Miss Margaret Gonzalez had phoned the New York authorities to assure them that she was in no danger, and to explain that the disturbance at the Plaza Hotel was merely a dispute between herself and a male companion she had met in a bar.

Maggie had hung up before detectives could ask if the male companion was Mr Blondell Wayne Tatum.

Commissioner Roberto Pepiscal arranged to meet the two crooked detectives at a strip joint off LeJeune Road, not far from the airport. Roberto got there early and drank three strong vodka tonics to give him the courage to say what he'd been told to say. He figured he was so far over his head that being drunk couldn't make it any worse.

Dutifully the commissioner had carried Detective Murdock's proposal to Dr Rudy Graveline, and now he had returned with the doctor's reply. It occurred to Roberto, even as a naked woman with gold teeth delivered a fourth vodka, that the role of an elected public servant was no longer a distinguished one. He found himself surrounded by ruthless and untrustworthy people – nobody played a straight game any more. In Miami, corruption had become a sport of the masses. Roberto had been doing it for years, of course, but jerks like Salazar and Murdock and even Graveline – they were nothing but dilettantes. Moochers. They didn't know when to back off. The word *enough* was not in their vocabulary. Roberto hated the idea that his future depended on such men.

The crooked cops showed up just as the nude Amazonian mud-wrestling match began on stage. 'Very nice place,'

Detective John Murdock said to the commissioner. 'Is that your daughter up there?'

Joe Salazar said, 'The one on the right, she even looks like you. Except I think you got bigger knockers.'

Roberto Pepsical flushed. He was sensitive about his weight. 'You're really funny,' he said to the detectives. 'Both of you should've been comedians instead of cops. You should've been Lawrence and Hardy.'

Murdock smirked. 'Lawrence and Hardy, huh? I think the commissioner has been drinking.'

Salazar said, 'Maybe we hurt his feelings.'

The vodka was supposed to make Roberto Pepsical cool and brave; instead it was making him hot and dizzy. He started to tell the detectives what Rudy Graveline had said, but he couldn't hear himself speak over the exhortations of the wrestling fans. Finally Murdock seized him by the arm and led him to the restroom. Joe Salazar followed them in and locked the door.

'What's all this for?' Roberto said, belching in woozy fear. He thought the detectives were going to beat him up.

Murdock took him by the shoulders and pinned him to the condom machine. He said, 'Joe and I don't like this joint. It's noisy, it's dirty, it's a shitty fucking joint to hold a serious conversation. We are offended, Commissioner, by what we see taking place on the stage out there – naked young females with wet mud all over their twats. You shouldn't have invited us here.'

Joe Salazar said, 'That's right. Just so you know, I'm a devoted Catholic.'

'I'm sorry,' said Roberto Pepsical. 'It was the darkest place I could think of on short notice. Next time we'll meet at St Mary's.'

Someone knocked on the restroom and Murdock told him to go away if he valued his testicles. Then he said to Roberto: 'What is it you wanted to tell us?'

'It's a message from my friend. The one with the problem I told you about— '

'The problem named Stranahan?'

225

'Yes. He says five thousand each.'

'Fine,' said John Murdock.

'Really?'

'Long as it's cash.'

Salazar added, 'Not in sequence. And not bank-wrapped.'

'Certainly,' Roberto Pepsical said. Now came the part that made his throat go dry.

'There's one part of the plan that my friend wants to change,' he said. 'He says it's no good just arresting this man and putting him in jail. He says this fellow has a big mouth and a vivid imagination.' Those were Rudy's exact words; Roberto was proud of himself for remembering.

Joe Salazar idly tested the knobs on the condom machine and said, 'So you got a better idea, right?'

'Well . . . ' Roberto said.

Murdock loosened his grip on the commissioner and straightened his jacket. 'You're not the idea man, are you? I mean, it was your idea to meet at this pussy parlour.' He walked over to the urinal and unzipped his trousers. 'Joe and I will think of something. We're idea-type guys.'

Salazar said, 'For instance, supposing we get a warrant to arrest the suspect for the murder of his former wife. Supposing we proceed to his residence and duly identify ourselves as sworn police officers. And supposing the suspect attempts to flee.'

'Or resists with violence,' Murdock hypothesized.

'Yeah, the manual is clear,' Salazar said.

Murdock shook himself off and zipped up. 'In a circumstance such as that, we could use deadly force.'

'I imagine you could,' said Roberto Pepsical, sober as a choirboy.

The three of them stood there in the restroom, sweating under the hot bare bulb. Salazar examined a package of flamingo-pink rubbers that he had shaken loose from the vending machine.

Finally Murdock said, 'Tell your friend it sounds fine, except for the price. Make it ten apiece, not five.'

'Ten,' Roberto repeated, though he was not at all surprised. To close the deal, he sighed audibly.

'Come on,' said Joe Salazar, unlocking the door. 'We're missing the fingerpaint contest.'

Over the whine of the outboard Luis Córdova shouted: 'There's no point in stopping.'

Mick Stranahan nodded. Under ceramic skies, Biscayne Bay unfolded in a dozen shifting hues of blue. It was a fine, cloudless morning: seventy degrees, and a northern breeze at their backs. Luis Córdova slowed the patrol boat a few hundred yards from the stilt house. He leaned down and said: 'They tore the place up pretty bad, Mick.'

'You sure it was cops?'

'Yeah, two of them. Not uniformed guys, though. And they had one of the sheriff boats.'

Stranahan knew who it was: Murdock and Salazar.

'Those goons from the hospital,' said Christina Marks. She stood next to Luis Córdova at the steering console, behind the Plexiglas windshield. She wore a red windbreaker, baggy knit pants, and high-top tennis shoes.

From a distance Stranahan could see that the door to his house had been left open, which meant it had probably been looted and vandalized. What the kids didn't wreck, the seagulls would. Stranahan stared for a few moments, then said: 'Let's go, Luis.'

The trip to Old Rhodes Key took thirty-five minutes in a light, nudging sea. Christina got excited when they passed a school of porpoises off Elliott Key, but Stranahan showed no interest. He was thinking about the videotape they had watched at Christina's apartment – Maggie Gonzalez, describing the death of Vicky Barletta. Twice they had watched it. It made him mad but he wasn't sure why. He had heard of worse things, seen worse things. Yet there was something about a doctor doing it, getting away with it, that made Stranahan furious.

When they reached the island, Luis Córdova dropped them at a sagging dock that belonged to an old Bahamian conch fisherman named Cartwright. Cartwright had been told they were coming.

'I got the place ready,' he told Mick Stranahan. 'By the way, it's good to see you, my friend.'

Stranahan gave him a hug. Cartwright was eighty years old. His hair was like cotton fuzz and his skin was the colour of hot tar. He had Old Rhodes Key largely to himself and seldom entertained, but he had happily made an exception for his old friend. Years ago Stranahan had done Cartwright a considerable favour.

'White man tried to burn me out,' he told Christina Marks. 'Mick took care of things.'

Stranahan hoisted the duffel bags over his shoulders and trudged toward the house. He said, 'Some asshole developer wanted Cartwright's land but Cartwright didn't want to sell. Things got sticky.'

The conch fisherman cut in: 'I tell the story better. The man offered me one hunnert towsind dollars to move off the island and when I says no thanks, brother, he had some peoples pour gasoline all on my house. Luckily it rain like hell. Mick got this man arrested and dey put him in the big jail up Miami. That's the God's truth.'

'Good for Mick,' Christina said. Naturally she had assumed that Stranahan had killed the man.

'Asshole got six years and did fifteen months. He's out already.' Stranahan laughed acidly.

'That I didn't know,' Cartwright said thoughtfully.

'Don't worry, he won't ever come back to this place.'

'You don't tink so?'

'No, Cartwright, I promise he won't. I had a long talk with the man. I believe he moved to California.'

'Very fine,' Cartwright said with obvious relief.

House was a charitable description for where the old fisherman lived: bare cinderblock walls on a concrete foundation; no doors in the doorways, no glass in the windows; a roof woven from dried palm fronds.

'Dry as a bone,' Cartwright said to Christina. 'I know it don't look like much, but you be dry inside here.'

Gamely she said, 'I'll be fine.'

Stranahan winked at Cartwright. 'City girl,' he said.

Christina jabbed Stranahan in the ribs. 'And you're Daniel Boone, I suppose. Well, fuck you both. I can handle myself.'

Cartwright's eyes grew wide.

'Sorry,' Christina said.

'Don't be,' Cartwright said with a booming laugh. 'I love it. I love the sound of a womanly voice out here.'

For lunch he fixed fresh lobster in a conch salad. Afterwards he gathered some clothes in a plastic garbage bag, told Mick goodbye and headed slowly down to the dock.

Christina said, 'Where's he going?'

'To the mainland,' Stranahan replied. 'He's got a grandson in Florida City he hasn't seen in a while.'

From where they sat, they could see Cartwright's wooden skiff motoring westward across the bay; the old man had one hand on the stem of the throttle, the other shielding his eyes from the low winter sun.

Christina turned to Stranahan. 'You arranged it this way.'

'He's a nice guy. He doesn't deserve any trouble.'

'You really think they'll find us all the way out here?'

'Yep,' Stranahan said. He was counting on it.

21

The clerical staff of Kipper Garth's law office was abuzz: clients – real live clients – were coming in for a meeting. Most of the secretaries had never seen any of Kipper Garth's clients because he generally did not allow them to visit. Normally all contact took place over the telephone, since Kipper Garth's practice was built exclusively on referrals to other lawyers. The rumour this day (and an incredible one, at that) was that Kipper Garth was going to handle a malpractice case all by himself; one of the senior paralegals had been vaguely instructed to prepare a complaint for civil court. The women who worked Kipper Garth's phone bank figured that it must be a spectacularly egregious case if their boss would tackle it solo, for his fear of going to court was well known. Kipper Garth's staff couldn't wait to get a look at the new clients.

They arrived at eleven sharp, a man and a woman. The clerks, secretaries, and paralegals were startled: it was an unremarkable couple in their mid-thirties. The man was medium-build and ordinary looking, the woman had long ash-blond hair and a nice figure. Neither displayed any obvious scars, mutilations, or crippling deformities. Kipper Garth's staff was baffled – the hushed wagering shifted back and forth between psychiatric aberration and sexual dysfunction.

Both guesses were wrong. The problem of John and Marie Nordstrom was far more peculiar.

Kipper Garth greeted them crisply at the door and led them to two high-backed easy chairs positioned in front of his desk. The lawyer was extremely nervous and hoped it didn't show. He hoped he would ask the right questions.

'Mr Nordstrom,' he began, 'I'd like to review some of the material in the state files.'

Nordstrom looked around the elegant office and said: 'Are we the only ones?'

'What do you mean?'

'Are we the only ones to sue? Over the phone you said a whole bunch of his patients were suing.'

Kipper Garth tugged restlessly at the sleeves of his coat. 'Well, we've been talking to several others with strong cases. I'm sure they'll come around. Meanwhile you and your wife expressed an interest— '

'But not alone,' John Nordstrom said. 'We don't want to be the only ones.' His wife reached across and touched his arm. 'Let's listen to him,' she said. 'It can't hurt.'

Kipper Garth waited for the moment of tension to pass. It didn't. He motioned toward the walnut credenza behind his desk. 'See all those files, Mr Nordstrom? Patients of Dr Rudy Graveline. Most of them have suffered more than you and your wife. Much more.'

Nordstrom said, 'So what's your point?'

'The point is, Mr Nordstrom, a monster is loose.

Graveline is still in business. On a good day his clinic takes in a hundred grand in surgical fees. One hundred grand! And every patient walks in there thinking that Dr Graveline is one brilliant surgeon, and some of them find out the hard way that he's not. He's a putz.'

Mrs Nordstrom said: 'You don't have to tell us.'

Kipper Garth leaned forward and, ministerially, folded his hands. 'For me, this case isn't about money.' He sounded so damn earnest that he almost believed himself. 'It isn't about money, it's about morality. And conscience. And concern for one's fellow man. I don't know about you folks, but my stomach churns when I think how a beast like Rudolph Graveline is allowed to continue to destroy the lives of innocent, trusting people.' Kipper Garth swivelled his chair slowly and gestured again at the stacks of files. 'Look at all these victims – men and women just like yourselves. And to think that the state of Florida has done nothing to stop this beast. It makes me nauseous.'

'Me, too,' said Mrs Nordstrom.

'My mission,' continued Kipper Garth, 'is to find someone with the courage to go after this man. Shut him down. Bring to light his incompetence so that no one else will have to suffer. The place to do that is the courtroom.'

John Nordstrom sniffed. 'Don't tell me the sonofabitch's never been sued before.'

Kipper Garth smiled. 'Oh yes. Yes, indeed, Dr Graveline has been sued before. But he's always escaped the glare of publicity and the scrutiny of his peers. How? By settling the cases out of court. He buys his way out, never goes to trial. This time he won't get off so lightly, Mr Nordstrom. This time, with your permission, I want to take him to the wall. I want to go all the way. I'm talking about a trial.'

It was a damn mellifluous speech for a man accustomed to bellowing at a speaker box. If not moved, the Nordstroms were at least impressed. A self-satisfied Kipper Garth wondered if he could ever be so smooth in front of a jury.

Marie Nordstrom said: 'In person you look much younger than on your billboards.'

231

The lawyer acknowledged the remark with a slight bow.

Mrs Nordstrom nudged her husband. 'Go ahead, tell him what happened.'

'It's all in the file,' John Nordstrom said.

'I'd like to hear it again,' Kipper Garth said, 'in your own words.' He pressed a button on the telephone console, and a stenographer with a portable machine entered the office. She was followed by a sombre-looking paralegal wielding a long yellow pad. Mutely they took positions on either side of Kipper Garth. Nordstrom scanned the trio warily.

His wife said: 'It's a little embarrassing for us, that's all.'

'I understand,' Kipper Garth said. 'We'll take our time.'

Nordstrom shot a narrow look at his wife. 'You start,' he said.

Calmly she straightened in the chair and cleared her throat. 'Two years ago, I went to Dr Graveline for a routine breast augmentation. He came highly recommended.'

'Your manicurist,' John Nordstrom interjected, 'a real expert.'

Kipper Garth raised a tanned hand. 'Please.'

Marie Nordstrom continued: 'I insisted that Dr Graveline himself do the surgery. Looking back on it, I would've been better off with one of the other fellows at the clinic – anyway, the surgery was performed on a Thursday. Within a week it was obvious that something was very wrong.'

Kipper Garth said, 'How did you know?'

'Well, the new breasts were quite . . . hard.'

'Try concrete,' John Nordstrom said.

His wife went on: 'They were extremely round and tight. Too tight. I mean, they didn't even bounce.'

A true professional, Kipper Garth never let his eyes wander below Mrs Nordstrom's neckline.

She said: 'When I saw Dr Graveline again, he assured me that this was normal for cases like mine. He had a name for it and everything.'

'Capsular contracture,' said the paralegal, without looking up from her notes.

'That's it,' Mrs Nordstrom said. 'Dr Graveline told me everything would be fine in a month or two. He said they'd be soft as little pillows.'

'And?'

'And we waited, just like he told us. In the meantime, of course, John kept wanting to try them out.'

'Hey,' Nordstrom said, 'I paid for the damn things.'

'I understand,' said Kipper Garth. 'So you made love to your wife?'

Nordstrom's cheeks reddened. 'You know the rest.'

With his chin Kipper Garth pointed toward the stenographer and the paralegal, both absorbed in transcribing the incident. Nordstrom sighed and said, 'Yeah, I made love to my wife. Or tried to.'

'That's when the accident happened between John and my breasts,' continued Mrs Nordstrom. 'I'm not sure if it was the left one or the right one that got him.'

Nordstrom muttered, 'I'm not sure, either. It was a big hard boob, that's all I knew.'

Kipper Garth said, 'And it actually put your eye out?'

John Nordstrom nodded darkly.

His wife said: 'Technically they called it a detached retina. We didn't know it was so serious right away. John's eye got all swollen and then there was some bleeding. When his vision didn't come back after a few days, we went to a specialist . . . but it was already too late.'

Gently Kipper Garth said, 'I noticed that you told the ophthalmic surgeon a slightly different story. You told him you were poked by a Christmas tree branch.'

Nordstrom glared, with his good eye, at the lawyer. 'What the hell would *you* have told him – that you were blinded by a tit?'

'It must have been difficult,' Kipper Garth said, his voice rich with sympathy. 'And this was your right eye, according to the file.'

'Yeah,' said Nordstrom, pointing.

'They gave him a glass one,' his wife added. 'You can hardly tell.'

'*I* can sure as hell tell,' Nordstrom said.

Kipper Garth asked: 'Did it affect your work?'

'Are you kidding? I lost my job.'

'Really?' The lawyer suppressed a grin of delight, but mentally tacked a couple more zeros to the pain-and-suffering demand.

Mrs Nordstrom said: 'John was an air-traffic controller. You can well imagine the problems.'

'Yeah, and the jokes,' Nordstrom said bitterly.

Kipper Garth leaned back and locked his hands across his vest. 'Folks, how does ten million sound?'

Nordstrom snorted. 'Come off it.'

'We get the right jury, we can probably do twelve.'

'Twelve million dollars – no shit?'

'No shit,' said Kipper Garth. 'Mrs Nordstrom, I need to ask you something. Did this, uh, condition with your breasts ever improve?'

She glanced down at her chest. 'Not much.'

'Not much is right,' said her husband. 'Take my word, they're like goddamn bocci balls.'

The guy would be poison as a witness, Kipper Garth decided; the jury would hate his guts. No wonder other lawyers had balked at taking the case. Kipper Garth thanked the Nordstroms for their time and showed them to the door. He promised to get back to them in a few days with some important papers to review.

After the couple had gone, Kipper Garth ordered the stenographer to transcribe the interview and make a half-dozen copies. Then he told the paralegal to type up a malpractice complaint against Dr Rudy Graveline and the Whispering Palms Spa and Surgery Center.

'Can you handle that?' Kipper Garth asked.

'I think so,' the paralegal said, coolly.

'And afterwards go down to the courthouse and do . . . whatever it is needs to be done.'

'We'll go together,' the paralegal said. 'You might as well learn your way around.'

Kipper Garth agreed pensively. If only his ski bunny knew what their dalliance had cost him. That his black-mailer was his own frigging brother-in-law compounded

234

the humiliation. 'One more question,' Kipper Garth said to his paralegal. 'After we file the lawsuit, then what?'

'We wait,' she replied.

The lawyer giggled with relief. 'That's all?'

'Sure, we wait and see what happens,' the paralegal said. 'It's just like dropping a bomb.'

'I see,' said Kipper Garth. Just what he needed in his life. A bomb.

Freddie was napping in his office at the Gay Bidet when one of the ticket girls stuck her head in the doorway and said there was a man wanted to see him. Right away Freddie didn't like the looks of the guy, and would have taken him for a cop except that cops don't dress so good. The other thing Freddie didn't like about the guy was the way he kept looking around the place with his nose twitching up in the air like a swamp rabbit, like there was something about the place that really stunk. Freddie didn't appreciate that.

'This isn't what I expected,' the man said.

'The fuck you expect, Regine's?' Boldly Freddie took the offensive.

'This isn't a gay bar?' the man asked. 'I assumed from the name . . . '

Freddie said, 'I didn't name the place, pal. All I know is, it rhymes. That doesn't automatically make it no fruit bar. Now state your business or beat it.'

'I need to see one of your bouncers.'

'What for?'

The man said, 'I'm his doctor.'

'He sick?'

'I don't know until I see him,' said Rudy Graveline.

Freddie was sceptical. Maybe the guy was a doctor, maybe not; these days everybody was wearing white silk suits.

'Which of my security personnel you want to see?' asked Freddie.

'He's quite a big man.'

'They're all big, mister I don't hire no munchkins.'

'This one is extremely tall and thin. His face is heavily scarred, and he's missing his left hand.'

'Don't know him,' Freddie said, playing it safe. In case the guy was a clever bail bondsman or an undercover cop with a wardrobe budget.

Rudy said: 'But he told me he works here.'

Freddie shook his head and made sucking sounds through his front teeth. 'I have a large staff, mister, and turnover to match. Not everybody can take the noise.' He jerked a brown thumb toward the fibreboard wall, which was vibrating from the music on the other side.

'Sounds like an excellent band,' Rudy said lamely.

'Cathy and the Catheters,' Freddie reported with a shrug. 'Queen of slut rock, all the way from London.' He pushed himself to his feet and stretched. 'Sorry I can't help you, mister— '

At that instant the ticket girl flung open the door and told Freddie that a terrible fight had broken out and he better come quick. Rudy Graveline was huffing at Freddie's heels by the time a path had been cleared to the front of the stage. There a gang of anorectic Nazi skinheads had taken on a gang of flabby redneck bikers in a dispute over tattoos – specifically, whose was the baddest. The battle had been joined by a cadre of heavy-set bouncers, each sporting a pink Gay Bidet T-shirt with the word *SECURITY* stencilled on the back. The vicious fighting seemed only to inspire more volume from the band and more random slam-dancing from the other punkers.

Towering above the mêlée was Chemo himself, his T-shirt ragged and bloody, and a look of baleful concentration on his face. Even through the blinding strobes, Rudy Graveline could see that the Weed Whacker attached to Chemo's stub was unsheathed and fully operative; the monofilament cutter was spinning so rapidly that it appeared transparent and harmless, like a hologram. In horror Rudy watched Chemo lower the buzzing device into the tangle of humanity – the ensuing screams rose plangently over the music. As if by prearrangement, the other bouncers backed off and let Chemo work, while

Freddie supervised from atop an overturned amplifier.

The fighting subsided quickly. Splints and bandages were handed out to fallen bikers and skinheads alike, while the band took a break. An expression of fatherly admiration in his shoe-button eyes, Freddie patted Chemo on the shoulder, then disappeared backstage. Rudy Graveline worked his way through the sweaty crowd, stepping over the wounded and semiconscious until he reached Chemo's side.

'Well, that was amazing,' Rudy said.

Chemo glanced down at him and scowled. 'Fucking battery died. I hope that's it for the night.'

The surgeon said, 'We really need to talk.'

'Yes,' Chemo agreed. 'We sure do.'

As soon as Chemo and Rudy went backstage, they ran into Freddie, Cathy, and two of the Catheters sharing some hash in a glass pipe. Through a puff of blue smoke Freddie said to Chemo: 'This jerkoff claimed he's your doctor.'

'Was,' Chemo said. 'Can we use the dressing room?'

'Anything you want,' Freddie said.

'Watch out for my python,' Cathy cautioned.

The dressing room was not what Rudy had expected. There was a folding card table, an old-fashioned coat rack, a blue velour sofa, a jagged triangle of broken mirror on the wall and, in one corner, an Igloo cooler full of Heinekens. On the naked floor was a low flat cage made from plywood and chicken wire in which resided a nine-foot Burmese python, the signature of Cathy's big encore.

Rudy Graveline took a chair at the card table while Chemo stretched out on the whorehouse sofa.

Rudy said: 'I was worried when you didn't call from New York. What happened?'

Chemo ran a whitish tongue across his lips. 'Aren't you even going to ask about my face, how it's healing?'

The doctor seemed impatient. 'It looks fine from here. It looks like the dermabrasion is taking nicely.'

'As if you'd know.'

Rudy's mouth twitched. 'Now what is that supposed to mean?'

'It means you're a fucking menace to society. I'm getting myself another doctor – Maggie's picking one out for me.'

Rudy Graveline felt the back of his neck go damp. It wasn't as if he had not expected problems with Chemo – that was the reason for choosing Roberto Pepsical and his crooked cops as a contingency. But it was merely failure, not betrayal, that Rudy had anticipated from his homicidal stork.

'Maggie?' the doctor said. 'Maggie Gonzalez?'

'Yeah, that's the one. We had a long talk, she told me some things.'

'Talking to her wasn't the plan,' Rudy said.

'Yeah, well, the plan has been changed.' Chemo reached into the Igloo cooler and got a beer. He twisted off the cap, tilted the bottle to his lips, and glowered at the doctor the whole time he gulped it down. Then he belched once and said: 'You tried to gyp me.'

Rudy said, 'That's simply not true.'

'You didn't tell me the stakes. You didn't tell me about the Barletta girl.'

The colour washed from Rudy's face. Stonily he stared into his own lap. Suddenly his silk Armani seemed as hot and heavy as an army blanket.

Chemo rolled the empty Heineken bottle across the bare terrazzo floor until it clanked to rest against the snake cage. The sleek green python flicked its tongue once, then went back to sleep.

Chemo said, 'And all this time, I thought you knew what the fuck you were doing. I trusted you with my own face.' He laughed harshly and burped again. 'Jesus H. Christ, I bet your own family won't let you carve the bird on Thanksgiving, am I right?'

In a thin, abraded voice, Rudy Graveline said: 'So Maggie is still alive.'

'Yeah, and she's going to stay that way as long as I say so.' Chemo swung his spidery legs off the sofa and sat up, straight as a lodgepole. 'Because if anything should happen to her, you are going to be instantly famous. I'm talking TV, Dr Frankenstein.'

By now Rudy was having difficulty catching his breath.

Chemo went on. 'Your nurse is a smart girl. She made three videotapes for insurance. Two of them are locked up safe and sound in New York. The other . . . . well, you'd better pray that I find it before it finds you.'

'Go do it.' Rudy's voice was toneless and weak.

'Naturally this will be very expensive.'

'Whatever you need,' the doctor croaked. This was a scenario he had never foreseen, something beyond his worst screaming nightmares.

'I didn't realize plastic surgeons made so much dough,' Chemo remarked. 'Maggie was telling me.'

'The overhead,' Rudy said, fumbling, 'is sky-high.'

'Well, yours just got higher by seven feet.' Chemo produced a small aerosol can of WD-40 and began lubricating the rotor mechanism of the Weed Whacker. Without glancing up from his chore, he said, 'By the way, Frankenstein, you're getting off easy. Last time a doctor screwed me over, I broke his frigging neck.'

In his mental catacomb Rudy clearly heard the snap of the old dermatologist's spine, watched as the electrolysis needle fell from the old man's lifeless hand and clattered on the office floor.

As soon as he regained his composure, Rudy asked, 'Who's got the missing tape?'

'Oh, take a wild guess.' There was amusement in Chemo's dry tone.

'Shit,' said Rudy Graveline.

'My sentiments exactly.'

22

Reynaldo Flemm hadn't even finished explaining the plan before Willie, the cameraman, interrupted. 'What about Christina?' he asked. 'What does she say?'

'Christina is tied up on another project.'

Willie eyed him sceptically. 'What project?'

'That's not important.'

Willie didn't give up; he was accustomed to Reynaldo treating him like hired help. 'She in New York?'

Reynaldo said, 'She could be in New Delhi for all I care. Point is, I'm producing the Barletta segment. Get used to it, buddy.'

Willie settled back to sip his Planter's punch and enjoy the rosy tropical dusk. They had a deck table facing the ocean at an outdoor bar, not far from the Sonesta on Key Biscayne. Reynaldo Flemm was nursing a Perrier, so Willie was confident of having the upper hand. Reynaldo was the only person he knew who blabbed more when he was sober than when he was drunk. Right now Reynaldo was blabbing about his secret plan to force Dr Rudy Graveline to confess in front of the television camera. It was the most ludicrous scheme that Willie had ever heard, the sort of thing he'd love to watch, not shoot.

After a decent interval, Willie put his rum drink on the table and said: 'Who's blocking out the interview?'

'Me.'

'The questions, too?'

Reynaldo Flemm reddened.

Willie said, 'Shouldn't we run this puppy by the lawyers? I think we got serious trespass problems.'

'Ha,' Reynaldo scoffed.

Sure, Willie thought sourly, go ahead and laugh. I'm the one who always gets tossed in the squad car. I'm the one gets blamed when the cops bang up the camera.

Reynaldo Flemm said, 'Let me worry about the legalities, Willie. The question is: can you do it?'

'Sure, I can do it.'

'You won't need extra lights?'

Willie shook his head. 'Plenty of light,' he said. 'Getting the sound is where I see the problem.'

'I was wondering about that, too. I can't very well wear the wireless.'

Willie chuckled in agreement. 'No, not hardly.'

Reynaldo said, 'You'll think of something, you always do. Actually, I prefer the hand-held.'

'I know,' Willie said. Reynaldo disliked the tiny cordless clip-on microphones; he favoured the old baton-style mikes that you held in your hand – the kind you could thrust in some crooked politician's face and make him pee his pants. Christina Marks called it Reynaldo's 'phallic attachment'. She postulated that, in Reynaldo's mind, the microphone had become a substitute for his penis.

As Willie recalled, Reynaldo didn't think much of Christina's theory.

He said to Willie: 'This'll be hairy, but we've done it before. We're a good team.'

'Yeah,' said Willie, half-heartedly draining his glass. Some team. The basic plan never changed: get Reynaldo beat up. *Now remember*, he used to tell Willie, *we got to live up to the name of the show. Stick it right in his motherloving face, really piss him off.* Willie had it down to an art: he'd poke the TV camera directly at the subject's nose, the guy would push the camera away and tear off in a fury after Reynaldo Flemm. *Now remember*, Reynaldo would coach, *when he shoves you, jiggle the camera like you were really shaken up. Make the picture super jerky looking, the way they do on* Sixty Minutes. If by chance the interview subject lunged after Willie instead of Reynaldo, Willie had standing orders to halt taping, shield the camera and defend himself – in that order. Invariably the person doing the pummelling got tired of banging his fists on a bulky, galvanized Sony and redirected his antagonism toward the arrogant puss of Reynaldo Flemm. *It's me they're tuning in to see*, Reynaldo would say, *I'm the talent here.* But if the beating became too severe or if Reynaldo got outnumbered, Willie's job then was to stow the camera (carefully) and start swinging away. Many times he had felt like a rodeo clown, diverting Reynaldo's enraged attackers until Reynaldo could escape, usually by locking himself in the camera van. The van was where, at Reynaldo's insistence, Christina Marks waited during ambush interviews. Reynaldo maintained that this was for her own safety, but in reality he worried that if something happened to her, it might end up on tape and steal his thunder.

Reflecting upon all this, Willie orderd another Planter's punch. This time he asked the waitress for more dark rum on the top. He said to Reynaldo, 'What makes you think this doctor guy'll break?'

'I've met him. He's weak.'

'That's what you said about Larkey McBuffum.'

Larkey McBuffum was a crooked Chicago pharmacist who had been selling steroid pills to junior high school football players. When Reynaldo and Willie had burst into Larkey's drug store to confront him, the old man had maced Willie square in the eyes with an aerosol can of spermicidal birth-control foam.

'I'm telling you, the surgeon's a wimp,' Reynaldo was saying. 'Put a mike in his face and he'll crack like a fucking Triscuit.'

'I'll stay close on him,' Willie said.

'Not too close,' Reynaldo Flemm cautioned. 'You gotta be ready to pull back and get us both in the shot, right before it happens.'

Willie stirred the dark rum with his little finger. 'You mean, when he slugs you?'

'Of course,' Reynaldo said curtly. 'Christ, you ought to know the drill by now. *Of course* when he slugs me.'

'Will that be,' Willie asked playfully, 'before or after the big confession?'

Reynaldo gnawed on this one a few seconds before giving up. 'Just get it, that's all,' he said stiffly. 'Whenever it happens, get every bloody second on tape. Understand?'

Willie nodded. Sometimes he wished he were still free-lancing for the networks. A coup in Haiti was a picnic compared to this.

The Pennsylvania State Police were happy to wire a photograph of Blondell Wayne Tatum to Sergeant Al García at the Metro-Dade Police Department. García was disappointed, for the photograph was practically useless. It had been taken more than twenty years earlier by a feature photographer for a small rural newspaper. At the time, the paper was running a five-part series on how the Amish sect was coping with the social pressures of the twentieth century. Blondell Wayne Tatum was one of several teen-aged Amish youths who were photographed while playing catch with a small pumpkin. Of the group, Blondell Wayne Tatum was the only one wearing a brand-new Rawlings outfielder's mitt.

For purposes of criminal identification, the facsimile of the newspaper picture was insufficient. García knew that the man named Chemo no longer wore a scraggly pubescent beard, and that he since had suffered devastating facial trauma as a result of a freak dermatology accident. Armed with these revisions, García enlisted the help of a police sketch artist named Paula Downs. He tacked the newspaper picture on Paula's easel and said: 'Third one from the left.'

Paula slipped on her eyeglasses, but that wasn't enough. She took a photographer's loupe and peered closely at the picture. 'Stringbean,' she said. 'Sixteen, maybe seventeen years old.'

García said: 'Make him thirty-eight now. Six foot nine, one hundred eighty pounds.'

'No sweat,' Paula said.

'And lose the beard.'

'Let's hope so. Yuk.'

With an unwrapped cigar, García tapped on the photo-graph. 'Here's the hard part, babe. A few years ago this turkey had a bad accident, got his face all fried up.'

'Burns?'

'Yup.'

'What kind – gas or chemical?'

'Electrolysis.'

Paula peered at the detective over the rim of her spectacles and said, 'That's very humorous, Al.'

'I swear. Got it straight from the Pennsylvania cops.'

'Hmmmm.' Paula chewed on the eraser of her pencil as she contemplated the photograph.

Al García described Chemo's face to Paula the way that Mick Stranahan had described it to him. As García spoke, the artist began to draw a freehand composite. She held the pencil at a mild angle and swept it in light clean ovals across the onionskin paper. First came the high forehead, the sharp chin, then the cheekbones and the puffy blowfish eyes and the thin cruel lips. Before long, the gangly young Amish kid with the baseball mitt became a serious-looking felon.

Paula got up and said, 'Be right back.' Moments later she returned with a salt shaker from the cafeteria. She lifted the onionskin and copiously sprinkled salt on the drawing pad. With the heel of her left hand she spread the grains evenly. After replacing the onionskin that bore Chemo's likeness, Paula selected a stubby fat pencil with a soft grey lead. She held it flat to the paper, as if it were a hunk of charcoal, and began a gentle tracing motion across the drawing. Instantly the underlying salt crystals came into relief. García smiled: the effect was perfect. It gave Chemo's portrait a harsh granular complexion, just as Mick Stranahan had described.

'You're a genius,' García told Paula Downs.

She handed him the finished composite. 'You get some winners, Al.'

He went to the Xerox room and made a half-dozen copies of the sketch. He stuck one in John Murdock's mailbox. On the back of Murdock's copy García had printed the name Blondell Wayne Tatum, the AKA, and the date of birth. Then García had written: 'This is your guy for the Simpkins case!!!!'

Murdock, he knew, would not appreciate the help.

García spent the rest of the afternoon on Key Biscayne, showing Chemo's composite to dock boys, bartenders, and cocktail waitresses at Sunday's-on-the-Bay. By four o'clock the detective had three positive IDs saying that the man in the drawing was the same one who had been drinking with Chloe Simpkins Stranahan on the evening she died.

Now Al García was a happy man. When he got back to police headquarters, he called a florist and ordered a dozen long-stemmed roses for Paula Downs. While he was on the phone, he noticed a small UPS parcel on his desk. García tore it open with his free hand.

Inside was a videotape in a plastic sleeve. On the sleeve was a scrap of paper, attached with Scotch tape. A note. 'I told you so. Regards, Mick.'

García took the videotape to the police audio room, where a couple of the vice guys were screening the very latest in bestiality *vérité*. García told them to beat it and plugged Stranahan's tape into a VHS recorder. He watched it twice. The second time, he stubbed out his cigar and took notes.

Then he went searching for Murdock and Salazar.

In the detective room, nobody seemed to know where they were. García didn't like the looks of things.

The copy of Paula's sketch of Blondell Wayne Tatum lay crumpled next to an empty Doritos bag on John Murdock's desk. 'Asshole,' García hissed. He didn't care who heard him. He pawed through the rest of Murdock's debris until he found a pink message slip. The message was from the secretary of Circuit Judge Cassie B. Ireland.

García groaned. Cassie Ireland had been a devoted golfing partner of the late and terminally crooked Judge Raleigh Goomer. Cassie himself was known to have serious problems with drinking and long weekends in Las Vegas. The problems were in the area of chronic inability to afford either vice.

The message to Detective John Murdock from Judge Cassie Ireland's secretary said: 'Warrant's ready.'

Al García used Murdock's desk phone to call the judge's chambers. He told the secretary who he was. Not surprisingly, the judge was gone for the day. Gone straight to the tiki bar at the Airport Hilton, García thought.

To the judge's secretary he said, 'There's been a little mix-up down here. Did Detective Murdock ask Judge Ireland to sign a warrant?'

'Sure did,' chirped the secretary. 'I've still got the paperwork right here. John and his partner came by and picked it up yesterday morning.'

Al García figured he might as well ask, just to make sure. 'Can you tell me the name on the warrant?'

'Mick Stranahan,' the secretary replied. 'First-degree murder.'

Christina Marks found the darkness exciting. As she floated naked on her back, the warm water touched her everyplace. Sometimes she stood up and curled her toes in the cool, rough sand, to see how deep it was. A few yards away, Mick Stranahan broke the surface with a swoosh, a glistening blond sea creature. He sounded like a porpoise when he blew the air from his lungs.

'This is nice,' Christina called to him.

'No hot showers on the key,' he said. 'No shower, period. Cartwright is a no-frills guy.'

'I said it's nice. I mean it.'

Stranahan swam closer and rose to his feet. The water came up to his navel. In the light from a quarter moon Christina could make out the fresh bullet scar on his shoulder; it looked like a smear of pink grease. She found herself staring – he was different out here on the water. Not the same man whom she had seen in the hospital or at her apartment. On the island he seemed larger and more feral, yet also more serene.

'It's so peaceful,' Christina said. They were swimming on a marly bonefish flat, forty yards from Cartwright's dock.

'I'm glad you can relax,' Stranahan said. 'Most women would be jittery, having been shot at twice by a total stranger.'

Christina laughed easily, closed her eyes and let the

wavelets tickle her neck. Mick was right; she ought to be a nervous wreck by now. But she wasn't.

'Maybe I'm losing my mind,' she said to the stars. She heard a soft splash as he went under again. Seconds later something cool brushed against her ankle, and she smiled. 'All right, mister, no funny business.'

From a surprising distance came his voice: 'Sorry to disappoint you, but that wasn't me.'

'Oh no.' Christina rolled over and kicked hard for the deep channel, but she didn't get far. Like a torpedo he came up beneath her and slid one arm under her hips, the other around her chest. As he lifted her briskly out of the water, she let out a small cry.

'Easy,' Stranahan said, laughing. 'It was only a baby bonnet shark – I saw it.'

He was standing waist-deep on the flat, holding her like an armful of firewood. 'Relax,' he said. 'They don't eat bigshot TV producers.'

Christina turned in his arms and held him around the neck. 'Is it gone?' she asked.

'It's gone. Want me to put you down?'

'Not really, no.'

In the moonlight he could see enough of her eyes to know what she was thinking. He kissed her on the mouth.

She thought: This is crazy. I love it.

Stranahan kissed her again, longer than the first time.

'A little salty,' she said, 'but otherwise very nice.' Christina let her hands wander. 'Say there, what happened to your jeans?'

'I guess they came off in the undertow.'

'What undertow?' She started kissing him up and down the neck; giggling, nipping, using the tip of her tongue. She could feel the goose flesh rise on his shoulders.

'There really *was* a shark,' he said.

'I believe you. Now take me back to the island. Immediately.'

Stranahan said, 'Not right this minute.'

'You mean we're going to do it out here?'

'Why not?'

'Standing up?'

'Why not?'

'Because of the sharks. You said so yourself.'

Stranahan said. 'You'll be safe, just put your legs around me.'

'Nice try.'

He kissed her again. This was a good one. Christina wrapped her legs around his naked hips.

Stranahan stopped kissing long enough to catch his breath and say, 'I almost forgot. Can you name the Beatles?'

'Not right this minute.'

'Yes, now. Please.'

'You're a damn lunatic.'

'I know,' he said.

Christina pressed so close and so hard that water sluiced up between her breasts and splashed him on the chin. 'That's what you get,' she said. Then, nose to nose: 'John, Paul, George, and Ringo.'

'You're terrific.'

'And don't forget Pete Best.'

'I think I love you,' Stranahan said.

Later he caught a small grouper from the dock, and fried it for dinner over an open fire. They ate on the ocean side of the island, under a stand of young palms. Stranahan used a pair of old lobster traps for tables. The temperature had dropped into the low seventies with a sturdy breeze. Christina wore a tartan flannel shirt, baggy grey workout trousers, and running shoes. Stranahan wore jeans, sneakers, and a University of Miami sweatshirt. Tucked in the waist of his jeans was a Smith .38 he had borrowed from Luis Córdova. Stranahan was reasonably certain that he would not have to fire it.

Christina was on her second cup of coffee when she said, 'I've been a pretty good sport about all this, don't you agree?'

'Sure.' He had his eyes on the far away lights of a tramp freighter ploughing south in the Gulf Stream.

Christina said, 'I know I've asked before, but I'm going to try again: what the hell are we doing out here?'

'I thought you liked this place.'

'I love it, Mick, but I still don't understand.'

'We can't go back to the stilt house. Not yet, anyway.'

'But why come here?' She was nearly out of patience with the mystery.

'Because I needed a place where something could happen, and no one would see it. Or hear it.'

'Mick— '

'There's no other way.' He stood up and poured out the cold dregs of his coffee, which splattered against the bare serrated coral. He noticed that the tide was slipping out. 'There's no other way to deal with people like this,' he said.

Christina turned to him. 'You don't understand. I can't do this, I can't be a part of this.'

'You wanted to come along.'

'To observe. To report. To get the story.'

Stranahan's laugh carried all the way to Hawk Channel. 'Story?'

She knew how silly it sounded, and was. Willie had the television cameras, and Reynaldo Flemm had Willie. Reynaldo . . . another macho head case. He had sounded so odd when she phoned from the mainland; his voice terse and icy, his laugh thin and ironic. He was cooking up something, although he denied it to Christina. Even when she told him about the wild incident at the Plaza, about how she had almost been shot *again*, Reynaldo's reaction was strangely muted and unreadable. When she had called again two hours later from a pay booth at the marina, the secretary in New York told Christina that Reynaldo had already left for the airport. The secretary went on to report, in a snitchy tone, that Reynaldo had withdrawn fifteen thousand dollars from the emergency weekend travel account – the account normally reserved for commercial airline disasters, killer earthquakes, political assassinations,

249

and other breaking news events. Christina Marks could not imagine what Reynaldo intended to do with fifteen grand, but she assumed it would be a memorable folly.

And there she was in Florida: no camera, no crew, no star. So she had boarded the marine patrol boat with Mick Stranahan and Luis Córdova.

Standing in the moonglow, watching the tide lick the coral under her feet, Christina said again: 'I can't be a part of this.'

Stranahan put an arm around her. It reminded Christina of the hugs her father sometimes gave her when she was a child and something sad had made her cry. A gesture that said he was sorry, but nothing could be done; sometimes the world was not such a good place.

'Mick, let's just go to the police.'

'These *are* the police. Remember?'

She looked at his face, searching the shadows for his expression. 'So that's who you're waiting for.'

'Sure. Who'd you think?'

Christina pretended to slap herself on the forehead. 'Oh, silly me – I thought it might be that huge skinny freak who keeps trying to shoot us.'

Stranahan shook his head. 'Him, we don't wait for.'

'Mick, this still isn't right.'

But the hug was finished, and so was the discussion. 'There's a lantern back at the house,' he told her. 'I want you to take a walk around the island. A long walk, OK?'

23

Joe Salazar said, 'You got to steer yesterday.'

'For Christ's sake,' mumbled Murdock.

'Come on, Johnny, it's my turn.'

They were gassing up the boat at Crandon Marina on Key Biscayne. It was the sheriff's department's boat, a nineteen-foot Aquasport with a forest-green police stripe down the front. It was the same boat that the two detectives had borrowed the day before. The sergeant in charge of the marine division had not wanted to loan the boat to Murdock or Salazar because it was obvious that neither knew how to navigate. The sergeant wondered if they even knew how to swim. Both men were wearing new khaki deck shorts that revealed pale legs, chubby legs that had seldom been touched by salt or sunlight: landlubber's legs. The sergeant had surrendered the Aquasport only when John Murdock flashed the murder warrant and said the suspect had been spotted on a house way out in Stiltsville. The sergeant had asked why they weren't taking any backups along, since there was room on the boat, but Murdock hadn't seemed to hear the question.

When the two detectives had returned to the dock a few hours later, the sergeant had been pleasantly surprised to find no major structural damage to the Aquasport or its drive shaft. But when Murdock and Salazar in their stupid khakis showed up again the following afternoon, the sergeant wondered how long their luck would hold out on the water.

'Go ahead and drive,' Murdock grumped at the gas dock. 'I don't give a shit.'

Joe Salazar took a stance behind the steering console. He tried not to gloat. Then it occurred to him: 'Where do we look now?'

The day before, Stranahan's stilt house had been empty. They had torn the rooms apart for clues to his whereabouts, found none, and departed in frustration. The whole way back, Murdock had complained about how the shoulder holster was chafing through his mesh tank top. Twice they had run the boat aground on bonefish flats, and both times Murdock had forced Salazar to hop out in the mud and push. For this, if for nothing else, Salazar figured that he deserved to be the captain today.

Murdock said: 'I tell you where we look. We look in every goddamn stilt house on the bay.'

'Yeah, like a regular canvass.'

251

'Door to door, except by boat. You know the fuckwad's out there somewhere.'

Joe Salazar felt better now that they had a plan. He paid the dock attendant for the gasoline, cranked up the big Evinrude on the back of the Aquasport, and aimed the bow toward Bear Cut. Or tried. The boat didn't want to move.

The dock attendant snickered. 'Helps to untie it,' he said, pointing with one of his bright white sneakers.

Sheepishly Joe Salazar unhitched the lines off the bow and stern and shoved off. John Murdock said, 'What a wiseass that guy was. Didn't he see we had guns?'

'Sure he did,' Salazar replied, steering tentatively toward the channel.

'This town is gone to shit,' Murdock said, spitting over the gunwale, 'when a guy with a gun has to put up with that kind of bull.'

'Everybody's a wiseass,' Joe Salazar agreed. Nervously he was watching a grey outboard coming in the other direction along the opposite side of the channel. The boat had a blue police light mounted in the centre. A young Latin man in a grey uniform stood behind the windshield. He waved to them: the world-weary wave of one cop to another.

'What do I do?' Salazar asked.

'Try waving back,' said Murdock.

Salazar did. The man in the grey boat changed his course and idled toward them.

'Grouper trooper,' John Murdock whispered. Salazar nodded as if he knew what his partner was talking about. He didn't. He also didn't know how to stop the Aquasport. Every time he pulled down on the throttle, the engine jolted into reverse. When he pushed the lever the other way, the boat would shudder and shoot forward. Backward, forward, backward again. The big Evinrude sounded like it was about to blow up. Joe Salazar could tell that Murdock was seething.

'Try neutral,' the young marine patrolman called. 'Move the throttle sideways till it clicks.'

Salazar did as he was told, and it worked.

'Thanks!' he called back.

Under his breath, Murdock said: 'Yeah, thanks for making us look like a couple of jerkoffs.'

The marine patrol boat coasted up on the port side of the Aquasport. The young officer introduced himself as Luis Córdova. He asked where the two detectives were headed, and if he could help. Joe Salazar told him they were going to Stiltsville to serve a murder warrant.

'Only one guy lives out there that I know of,' Luis Córdova said.

Murdock said: 'That's the guy we want.'

'Mick Stranahan?'

'You know him?'

'I know where he lives,' said Luis Córdova, 'but he's not there now. I saw him only yesterday.'

'Where?' blurted Joe Salazar. 'Was he alone?'

'Yeah, he was alone. Sitting on the conch dock down at Old Rhodes Key.'

Murdock said, 'Where the hell's that?'

'South of Elliott.'

'Where the hell's Elliott?'

The marine patrolman said, 'Why don't you guys just wait a few hours and follow me down? The tide won't be right until dusk. Besides, you might need some extra muscle with this guy.'

'No. Thanks anyway.' John Murdock's tone left no chance for discussion. 'But we could use a map, if you got one.'

Luis Córdova disappeared briefly behind the steering console. When he stood up again, he was smiling. 'Just happened to have an extra,' he said.

A half-hour out of the marina, Joe Salazar said to his partner: 'Maybe we should've asked what he meant about the tides.'

The Aquasport was stuck hard on another mud flat, this one a mile south of Soldier Key. John Murdock cracked open his third can of beer and said: 'You're the one wanted to drive.'

Salazar leaned over the side of the boat and studied the situation. He decided there was no point in getting out to push. 'It's only six inches deep,' he said, a childlike marvel in his voice. 'On the map it sure looked like plenty of water, didn't it?'

Murdock said, 'If you're a starfish, it's plenty of water. If you're a boat, it's a goddamn beach. Another thing: I told you to get three bags of ice. Look how fast this shit is melting.' He kicked angrily at the cooler.

Joe Salazar continued to stare at the shallow gin-clear water. 'I think the tide's coming in,' he said hopefully.

'Swell,' said Murdock. 'That means it's only what? — another four, five hours in the mud. Fanfuckingtastic. By then it'll be good and dark, too.'

Salazar pointed out that the police boat was equipped with excellent lights. 'Once we get off the flat, it's a clean shot down to the island. Deep water the whole trip.'

He had never seen his partner so jumpy and short-tempered. Normally John Murdock was the picture of a cool tough cop, but Salazar had watched a change come over him beginning the night they took the down payment from Commissioner Roberto Pepsical. Five thousand cash, each. Five more when it was done. To persuade the detectives that he was not the booze-swilling letch that he had appeared to be at the nudie joint, the commissioner had arranged the payoff meeting to take place in one of the empty confessionals at St Mary's Catholic Church in Little Havana. The confessional was dimly lit and no bigger than a broom closet; the three conspirators had to stand sidewise to fit. It had been a dozen years since Joe Salazar had stepped inside a confessional and not much had changed. The place reeked of damp linen and guilt, just as he remembered. He and Murdock stuffed the cash in their jackets and bolted out the door together, nearly trampling a quartet of slow-footed nuns. Commissioner Roberto Pepsical stayed alone in the confessional and recited three Hail Marys. He figured it couldn't hurt.

Back in the car, John Murdock had not displayed the crude and cocky ebullience that usually followed the taking of a hefty bribe; rather, his mood had been taciturn and apprehensive. It had stayed that way for two days.

Now with the boat stuck fast on the bonefish flat, Murdock sulked alone in the stern, glaring at the slow crawl of the incoming tide. Joe Salazar lit a Camel and settled in for a long, tense afternoon. He didn't feel so well himself, but at last he knew why. This was the biggest job they'd ever done, and the dirtiest. By a mile.

In fact, the tides would not have mattered if either of the two detectives had known how to read a marine chart. Even at dead low, there was plenty of water from Cape Florida all the way to Old Rhodes Key. All you had to do was follow the channels, which were plainly marked on Luis Córdova's map.

Mick Stranahan knew that Murdock and Salazar would run the boat aground. He also knew that it would be night-time before they could float free, and that they would make the rest of the trip at a snail's pace, fearful of repeating the mishap.

He and Luis Córdova had talked this part out. Together they had calculated that the two detectives would reach the island between nine and midnight, provided they didn't hit the shoal off Boca Chita and shear the prop off the Evinrude. Luis had offered to tail the Aquasport at a discreet distance, but Stranahan told him no. He didn't want the marine patrolman anywhere near Old Rhodes Key when it happened. If Luis was there, he'd want to do it by the book. Wait for the assholes to make their move, then try to arrest them. Stranahan knew it would never work that way – they'd try to kill Luis, too. And even if Luis was as sharp as Stranahan thought, it would be a mess for him afterwards. An automatic suspension, a grand jury, his name all over the newspapers. No way, Stranahan told him, no hero stuff. Just give them the map and get lost.

Besides, Stranahan already had his hands full with Christina Marks on the island.

'I don't want to go for a walk,' she said. 'Grandmothers and widows go for walks. I'm staying here with you.'

'So you can take notes, or what?' He handed her a Coleman lantern. The jumpy white light made their shadows clash on the cinderblock walls. Stranahan said, 'You're not a reporter any more, you're a goddamn witness.'

She said, 'Is this your idea of pillow talk? Half an hour ago we were making love, and now I'm a "goddamn witness". You ever thought of writing poetry, Mick?'

He was down on one knee, pulling items from one of the duffel bags. Without looking up, he said, 'You said you couldn't be a part of this, I'm trying to accommodate you. As for the afterglow, you want to waltz in the moonlight, we'll do that later. Right now there's a pair of bad cops on their way out here to shoot me.'

'You don't know that.'

'Yeah, you're right,' Stranahan said. 'They're probably just collecting Toys for Tots. Now go.'

He stood up. In the lantern light, Christina saw that his arms were full: binoculars, a poplin windbreaker, a pair of corduroys, an Orioles cap, a fishing knife, and a round spool of some kind.

She said, 'It's not for the damn TV show that I want to stay. I'm scared for you. I don't know why – since you're being such a prick – but I'm worried about you, I admit it.'

When Stranahan spoke again, the acid was gone from his voice. 'Look, if you stay . . . if you were to see something, they'd make you testify. Forget reporter's privilege and First Amendment – doesn't count for a damn thing in a situation like this. If you witness a crime, Chris, they put you under oath. You don't want that.'

'Neither do you.'

He smiled drily. She had him on that one. It was true: he didn't want any witnesses. 'You've had enough excitement,' he told her. 'Twice I've nearly gotten you killed. If I were you, I'd take that as a hint.'

Christina said, 'What if you're wrong about them, Mick?

What if they only want to ask more questions? Even if they're coming to arrest you, you can't just— '

'Go,' he said. Later he would explain that these cops were buddies of the late Judge Raleigh Goomer, and that what they wanted from Mick Stranahan was payback. Asking questions was not at all what they had in mind. 'Take the path I showed you. Follow the shoreline about half-way down the island and you'll come to a clearing. You'll see some plastic milk crates, an empty oil drum, an old camp fire hole. Wait there for me.'

Christina gave him a frozen look, but he didn't feel it. His mind was in overdrive, long gone.

'There's some fruit and candy bars in the Tupperware,' he said. 'But don't feed the raccoons, they bite like hell.'

She was twenty yards down the path when she heard him call, 'Hey, Chris, you forgot the bug spray.'

She shook her head and kept walking.

Fifteen minutes later, when Stranahan was sure she was gone, he carried his things down to Cartwright's dock. There he lit another lantern and hung it on a nail in one of the pilings. Then he pulled off his sneakers, kicked out of his jeans, and slid naked into the cool flowing tides.

For Joe Salazar, it was a moment of quiet triumph at the helm. 'By God, we did it.'

John Murdock made a snide chuckle. 'Yeah, we found it,' he said. 'The Atlantic fucking Ocean. A regular needle in a haystack, Joe. And all it took was three hours of dry humping these islands.'

Salazar didn't let the sarcasm dampen his new found confidence. The passage through Sand Cut had been hairy; even at a slow speed, navigating the swift serpentine channel at night was an accomplishment worth savouring. Murdock knew it, too; not once had he tried to take the wheel.

'So this is the famous Elliott Key.' Murdock scratched his sunburned cheeks. The Aquasport idled half a mile off-shore, rocking in a brisk chop. The beer was long gone, the ice melted. In the cool breeze Murdock had slipped into a tan leather jacket, the one he always wore to work; it looked ridiculous over his khaki shorts. Dismally he slapped at his pink shins, where a horsefly was eating supper.

Joe Salazar held the chart on his lap, a flashlight in his right hand. With the other hand he pointed: 'Like I said, Johnny, from here it's a straight nine-mile run to Rhodes. Twelve feet of water the whole way.'

Murdock said, 'So let's go, Señor Columbus. Maybe we can make it before Christmas.' He readjusted his shoulder holster for the umpteenth time.

Salazar hesitated. 'Once we get there, what exactly is the plan?'

'Get that goddamn flashlight out of my face.' Murdock's eyelids were swollen and purple. Too much sun, too much beer. It worried Salazar; he wanted his partner to be sharp.

'The plan is simple,' Murdock said. 'We arrive with bells on – sirens, lights, the works. We yell for Stranahan to come out with his hands up. Go ahead with the whole bit – serve the warrant, do the Miranda, all that shit. Then we shoot him like he was trying to get away.'

'Do we cuff him first?'

'Now, how would that look? No, we don't cuff him first. Jesus Christ.' Murdock spit into the water. He'd been spitting all afternoon. Salazar hoped this wasn't a new habit.

Murdock said, 'See, Joe, we shoot him in the back. That way it looks like he's running away. Then we get on this boat radio, if one of us can figure out how to use the goddamn thing, and call for air rescue.'

'Which'll take for ever to get here.'

'Exactly. But then we're covered, procedure-wise.'

It sounded like a solid plan, with only one serious variable. Joe Salazar decided to put the variable out of his mind. He stowed the flashlight, reclaimed his post at the wheel of the police boat and steered a true course for Old Rhodes Key.

A straight line through open seas. No sweat.

The channel that leads from the ocean to the cut of Old Rhodes Key is called Caesar Creek. It is deep and fairly broad, and well charted with lighted markers. For this Joe Salazar was profoundly thankful. Having mastered the balky throttle, he guided the Aquasport in at half-speed, with John Murdock standing (or trying to) in the bow. Murdock cupped his hands around his eyes to block the peripheral light; he was peering at the island, searching for signs of Mick Stranahan. Two hundred yards from the mouth of the cut, Salazar killed the engine and joined his chubby partner on the front of the boat.

'There he is!' Murdock's breathing was raspy, excited.

Salazar quinted into the night. 'Yeah, Johnny, sitting under that light on the dock.'

They could see the lantern and, in its white penumbra, the figure of a man with his legs hanging over the planks. The figure wore a baseball cap, a tan jacket, and long pants. From the angle of the cap, the man's head appeared to be down, chin resting on his chest.

'Dumb fuckwad's asleep.' Murdock's laugh was high and brittle. He already had his pistol out.

'Then I guess we better do it,' Salazar said.

'By all means.' Murdock dropped to a crouch.

They had tested the blue lights and siren on the way down, so Salazar knew where the switches were. He flipped them simultaneously, then turned the ignition key. As the Evinrude growled to life, Salazar put all his weight to the throttle.

Gun in hand, John Murdock clung awkwardly to the bow rail as the Aquasport planed off and raced toward the narrow inlet. The wind spiked Murdock's hair and flattened his cheeks. His teeth were bared in a wolfish expression that might have passed for a grin.

As the boat got closer, Joe Salazar expected Mick Stranahan to wake up at any moment and look in their direction – but the man didn't move.

A half-mile away, sitting on a milk crate under some trees, Christina Marks heard the police siren. With a shiver she closed her eyes and waited for the sound of gunfire.

They could have come one of several ways. The most likely was the oceanside route, following Caesar Creek into the slender fork between tiny Hurricane Key and Old Rhodes. This was the easiest way to Cartwright's dock.

But a westward approach, out of Biscayne Bay, would leave more options and offer more cover. They could come around Adams Key, or circle the Rubicons and sneak through the grassy flats behind Totten. But that would be a tricky and perilous passage, almost unthinkable for someone who had never made the trip.

Not at night, Stranahan decided, not these guys.

He had gambled that they would come by the ocean.

In the water he had carried only the knife and the spool. Four times he made the swim between Old Rhodes and Hurricane Key; not a long swim, but enervating against a strong outbound current. After pulling himself up on Cartwright's dock for the last time, Stranahan had rubbed the cold ache from his legs and arms. It had taken a long time to catch his breath.

Then he pulled on some dry clothes, got the .38 that Luis Córdova had loaned him, and sat down to wait.

The spool in Stranahan's duffel had contained five hundred yards of a thick plastic monofilament. The line was calibrated to a tensile strength of one hundred and twenty pounds, for it was designed to withstand the deep-water surges of giant marlin and bluefin tuna. It was the strongest fishing line manufactured in the world, tournament quality. For further advantage it was lightly tinted a charcoal grey, which made it practically invisible underwater.

Even out of the water, the line was sometimes impossible to see.

At night, for instance. Stretched across a mangrove creek.

Undoubtedly John Murdock never saw it.

He was squatting toad-like on the front of the boat, training his .357 at the figure on the dock as they made their approach. Under Joe Salazar's hand, the Aquasport was moving at exactly forty-two miles per hour.

Mick Stranahan had strung three taut vectors between the islands. The lines were fastened to the trunks of trees and crossed the water at varying heights. The lowest of the lines was snapped immediately by the bow of the speeding police boat. The other two garrotted John Murdock in the belly and the neck, respectively.

Joe Salazar, in the bewildering final millisecond of his life, watched his partner thrown backwards, bug-eyed and gurgling, smashed to the deck by unseen hands. Then the same spectral claw seized Salazar by the throat, chopped him off his feet, bounced his over-ripe skull off the howling Evinrude and twanged him directly into the creek.

The noise made by the fishing line when it snapped on Joe Salazar's neck was very much like that of a gunshot.

Christina Marks ran all the way back to Cartwright's dock. Along the way she dropped the Coleman lantern, hissing, on some rocks. But she kept running. When she got there, Caesar Creek was black and calm. She saw no boat, no sign of intruders.

On the dock, the familiar figure of a man in a baseball cap slouched beneath another lantern, this one glowing brightly.

'Mick, what happened?'

Then Christina realized that it wasn't a man at all, but a scarecrow wearing Stranahan's poplin jacket and long corduroys. The body of the scarecrow was stuffed with palm leaves and dried seaweed. The head was a green coconut. The baseball cap fit like a charm.

24

The Aquasport wedged itself deep in the mangroves on Totten Key. The engine was dead, but the prop was still twirling when Mick Stranahan got there. Barefoot, he monkeyed through the slick rubbery branches until he could see over the side of the battered boat. In his right hand he held Luis Córdova's .38.

He didn't need it. Detective John Murdock wasn't dead, but he would be soon. He lay motionless on the deck, his knees drawn up in pain. Blackish blood oozed from his nose. Only one eye was open, rhythmically illuminated by the strobing blue police light. Cracked but still flashing, the light dangled from a nest of loose wires on the console. It looked like a fancy electric Christmas ornament.

Stranahan felt his stomach shrink to a knot. He put the pistol in his jeans and swung his legs over the gunwale. 'John?'

Murdock's eye blinked, and he grunted weakly.

Stranahan said, 'Try to take it easy.' Like the guy had a choice. 'One quick question, I've got to ask. You fellows were going to kill me, weren't you?'

'Damn right,' rasped the dying detective.

'Yeah, that's what I thought. I can't believe you're still sore about Judge Goomer.'

Murdock managed a bloody grin and said, 'You dumb fuckwad.'

Stranahan leaned forward and brushed a horsefly off Murdock's forehead. 'But if it wasn't revenge for the judge, then why pull something like this?' Silence gave him the answer. 'Don't tell me somebody paid you.'

Murdock nodded, or tried. His neck wasn't working so well; it looked about twice as long as it was supposed to be.

Stranahan said, 'You took money for this? From who?'

'Eat me,' Murdock replied.

'It was probably the doctor,' Stranahan speculated. 'Or a go-between. That would make more sense.'

Murdock's reply came out as a dank rattle. Mick Stranahan sighed. Queasiness at the sight of Murdock had given way to emotional exhaustion.

'John, it's some kind of city, isn't it? All I wanted out here was some peace and solitude. I was through with all this crap.'

Murdock gave a hateful moan, but Stranahan needed to talk. 'Here I'm minding my own business, feeding the fish, not bothering a soul, when some guy shows up to murder me. At my very own house, John, in the middle of the bay! All because some goddamn doctor thinks I'm going to break open a case that's so old it's mildewed.'

The dying Murdock seemed hypnotized by the flashing blue light. It was ticking much faster than his own heart. One of the detective's hands began to crawl like an addled blue crab, tracking circles on the blood-slickened deck.

Stranahan said, 'I know it hurts, John, but there's nothing I can do.'

In a slack voice Murdock said, 'Fuck you, shithead.' Then his eye closed for the last time.

Mick Stranahan and Christina Marks were waiting when Luis Córdova pulled up to the dock at nine sharp the next morning.

'Where to?' he asked Stranahan.

'I'd like to go back to my house, Luis.'

'Not me,' said Christina Marks. 'Take me to Key Biscayne. The marina is fine.'

Stranahan said, 'I guess that means you still don't want to marry me.'

'Not in a million years,' Christina said. 'Not in your wildest dreams.'

Stranahan turned to Luis Córdova. 'She didn't get much sleep. The accommodations were a bit too . . . rustic.'

'I understand,' said the marine patrolman. 'But, otherwise, a quiet night?'

'Fairly quiet,' Stranahan said.

The morning was sunny and cool. The bay had a light washboard ripple that made the patrol boat seem to fly. As they passed the Ragged Keys, Stranahan nudged Luis Córdova and pointed to the white-blue sky. 'Choppers!' he shouted over the engine noise. Christina Marks saw them, too: three Coast Guard rescue helicopters, chugging south at a thousand feet.

Without glancing from the wheel, Luis Córdova said, 'There's a boat overdue from Crandon. Two cops.'

'No shit?'

'They found a body this morning floating off Broad Creek. Homicide man named Salazar.'

'What happened?'

'Drowned,' yelled Luis Córdova. 'Who knows how.'

Christina Marks listened to the two men going back and forth. She wasn't sure how much Luis Córdova knew, but it was more than Stranahan would ever tell her. She felt angry and insulted and left out.

When they arrived at the stilt house, Stranahan took out the Smith .38 and returned it to Luis. The marine patrolman was relieved to see that it had not been fired.

Stranahan hoisted two of the duffel bags and hopped off the patrol boat.

From the dock he said, 'Take care, Chris.' He wanted to say more, but it was the wrong time. She was still fuming about last night, furious because he wouldn't tell her what had happened. She had kicked the coconut head off the scarecrow, that's how mad she had gotten. It was at that moment he'd asked her to marry him. Her reply had been succinct, to say the least.

Now she turned away coldly and said to Luis Córodva: 'Can we get going, please.'

Stranahan waved them off and trudged up the steps to inspect the looted house. The first thing he saw on the floor was the big marlin head; the tape on the fractured bill had been torn off in the fall. Stranahan stepped over the stuffed fish and went to the bedroom to check for the shot-gun. It was still wedged up in the box spring where he had hidden it.

The whole place was a mess all right, depressing but not irreparable. Stranahan was glad, in a way, to have such a large chore ahead of him. Take his mind off Murdock and Salazar and Old Rhodes Key. And Christina Marks, too.

She was the first woman he had loved who had ever said no to marriage. It was quite a feeling.

Luis Córdova came back to the stilt house as Mick Stranahan was finishing lunch. There was a burly new passenger on the boat: Sergeant Al García.

Stranahan greeted them at the door and said, 'Two Cubans with guns is never good news.'

Luis Córdova said, 'Al is working the dead cops.'

'Cops plural?' Stranahan's eyebrows arched.

García sat down heavily on one of the barstools. 'Yeah, we found Johnny Murdock inside the boat. The boat was up in a frigging tree.'

'Where?' Stranahan asked impassively.

'Not far from where you and your lady friend went camping last night.' García patted his pockets and cursed. He was out of cigars. He took out a pack of Camels and lit one half-heartedly. He glanced up at the beakless marlin hanging from a new nail on the wall.

Luis Córdova said, 'I told Al about how I gave you a lift down to the island after your house got trashed.'

Stranahan wasn't upset. If asked, Luis would tell the truth about what he saw, what he knew for a fact. Most likely he had already told García about loaning the two detectives a map of the bay. Nothing strange about that.

'You hear anything funny last night?' Al García asked. 'By the way, where's the girl?'

'I don't know,' Stranahan said.

'What about last night?'

'A boat went by about eleven. Maybe a little later. Sounded like an outboard. What the hell happened, Al – somebody do these guys?'

García was puffing hard on the cigarette, and blowing circles of smoke, like he did with his stogies. 'Way it looks,' he said, 'they were going wide open. Missed the channel completely.'

'You said the boat was in a tree.'

'That's how fast the bozos were going. Way it looks, Salazar got thrown, hit his head. He drowned right away but the tide took him south.'

'Broad Creek,' Luis Córdova said. 'A mullet man found the body.'

García went on: 'Murdock stayed in the boat, but it didn't save him. We're talking major head trauma. The medical examiner thinks a mangrove branch or something snapped his neck. Same with Salazar. Figures it happened when they hit the trees.'

'Wide open?'

Luis Córdova said, 'The throttle was all the way down. You got to be nuts to run that creek wide open at night.'

'Or amazingly stupid,' Stranahan said. 'Let me guess who they were looking for.'

García nodded. 'You're on some roll, Mick. A regular archangel of death, you are. First your ex, now Murdock and Salazar. I'm noticing that bad things happen to people who fuck with you. Seems to be a pattern going way back.'

Stranahan said, 'I can't help it these jerks don't know how to drive a boat.'

Luis Córdova said, 'It was an accident, that's all.'

'I just find it interesting,' said Al García. 'Maybe the word is ironic, I don't know. Anyway, you're right, Mick. The two boys were coming to pay you a visit. They kept it real quiet around the shop, too. I can only guess why.' He reached in his jacket and took out a soggy white piece of paper. The paper was folded three times, pamphlet sized.

García showed it to Stranahan. 'We found this in Salazar's back pocket.'

Stranahan knew what it was. he'd seen a thousand just like it. The word *warrant* was still legible in the standard judicial calligraphy. As he handed it back to García, Stranahan wondered whether he was about to be arrested.

'What is this?' he asked.

'Garbage,' García replied. He crumped the sodden document in his right hand and lobbed it out a window into the water.

Stranahan smiled. 'You liked the videotape.'

'Obviously,' said the detective.

At the Holiday Inn where they got a room, Maggie Gonzalez was going through the Yellow Pages column by column, telling Chemo which plastic surgeons were good enough to finish the dermabrasion treatments on his face; some of the names were new to her, but others she remembered from her nursing days. Chemo was stooped in front of the bathroom mirror, picking laconically at the patches left on his chin by Dr Rudy Graveline.

Out of the side of his mouth, Chemo said, 'Fucker's not returning my calls.'

'It's early,' Maggie said. 'Rudy sleeps late on his day off.'

'I want to see some cash. Today.'

'Don't worry.'

'The sooner I get the money, the sooner I can take care of this.' Meaning his skin. In the mirror, Chemo could see Maggie's expression – at least, as much of it as the bandages revealed – and something that resembled genuine sympathy in her eyes. Not pity, sympathy.

She was the first woman who had ever looked at him that way. Certainly she seemed sincere about helping him find a new plastic surgeon. Chemo thought: She's either a truly devoted nurse or a sneaky little actress.

Maggie ripped a page of physicians from the phone book and said off-handedly, 'How much are we hitting him for?'

'A million dollars,' Chemo said. His sluglike lips quivered into a smile. 'You said he's loaded.'

'Yeah, he's also cheap.'

'A minute ago you said don't worry.'

'Oh, he'll pay. Rudy's cheap, but he's also a coward. All I'm saying is, he'll try to play coy at first. That's his style.'

'Coy?' Chemo thought: What in the fuck is she talking about? 'I wouldn't know about coy,' he said. 'I got a Weed Whacker strapped to my arm.'

Maggie said, 'Hey, I'm on your side. I'm just telling you, he can be stubborn when he wants.'

'You know what I think? I think you're in this for more than the money. I think you want to see a show.'

Maggie's brown eyes narrowed above the gauze. 'Don't be ridiculous.'

'Yeah,' Chemo said, 'I think you'd enjoy it if the boys got nasty with each other. I think you've got your heart set on blood.'

He was beaming as if he had just discovered the secret of the universe.

Dr Rudy Graveline stared at the vaulted ceiling and contemplated his pitiable existence. Chemo had turned blackmailer. Maggie Gonzalez, the bitch, was still alive. So was Mick Stranahan. And somewhere out there a television crew was lurking, waiting to grill him about Victoria Barletta.

Aside from that, life was peachy.

When the phone rang, Rudy pulled the bedsheet up to his chin. He had a feeling it was more bad news.

'Answer it,' Heather Chappell's muffled command came from beneath a pillow. 'Answer the damn thing.'

Rudy reached out from the covers and seized the receiver fiercely, as if it were the neck of a cobra. The grim gassy voice on the other end of the line belonged to Commissioner Roberto Pepsical.

'You see the news on TV?'

'No,' Rudy said. 'But I got the paper here somewhere.'

'There's a story about two policemen who died.'

'Yeah, so?'

'In a boat accident,' Roberto said.

'Cut to the punch line, Bobby.'

'Those were the guys.'

'What guys?' asked Rudy. Next to him, Heather mumbled irritably and wrapped the pillow tightly around her ears.

'The guys I told you about. *My* guys.'

'Shit,' said Rudy.

Heather looked up raggedly and said: 'Do you mind? I'm trying to sleep.'

Rudy told Roberto that he would call him right back from another phone. He put on a robe and hurried down the hall to his den, where he shut the door. Numbly he dialled Roberto's private number, the one reserved for bagmen and lobbyists.

'Let me make sure I understand,' Rudy said. 'You were using police officers as hit men?'

'They promised it would be a cinch.'

'And now they're dead.' Rudy was well beyond the normal threshold of surprise. He had become conditioned to expect the worst. He said, 'What about the money – can I get it back?'

Roberto Pepsical couldn't believe the nerve of this cheapskate. 'No, you can't get it back. I paid them. They're dead. You want the money back, go ask their widows.'

The commissioner's tone had become impatient and firm. It made Rudy nervous; the fat pig should have been apologizing all over himself.

Rudy said, 'All right, then, can you get somebody else to do it?'

'Do what?'

'Do Stranahan. The offer's still open.'

Roberto laughed scornfully on the other end; Rudy was baffled by this change of attitude.

'Listen to me,' the commissioner said. 'The deal's off, for ever. Two dead cops is major trouble, Doctor, and you just better hope nobody finds out what they were up to.'

Rudy Graveline wanted to drop the subject and crawl back to bed. 'Fine, Bobby,' he said. 'From now on, we never even met. Goodbye.'

'Not so fast.'

Oh brother, Rudy thought, here we go.

Roberto said, 'I talked to The Others. They still want the original twenty-five.'

'That's absurd. Cypress Towers is history, Bobby. I'm through with it. Tell your pals they get zippo.'

'But you got your zoning.'

'I don't need the damn zoning,' Rudy protested. 'They can have it back, understand? Peddle it to some other dupe.'

Roberto's voice carried no trace of understanding, no patience for a compromise. 'Twenty-five was the price of each vote. You agreed. Now The Others want their money.'

'Don't you ever get sick of being an errand boy?'

'It's my money, too,' Roberto said soberly. 'But yeah, I do get sick of being an errand boy. I get sick of dealing with cheap scuzzbuckets like you. When it comes to paying up, doctors are the fucking worst.'

'Hey,' Rudy said, 'it doesn't grow on trees.'

'A deal is a deal.'

In a way, Roberto was glad that Dr Graveline was being such a prick. It felt good to be the one to drop the hammer for a change. He said, 'You got two business days to cover me and The Others.'

'What?' Rudy bleated.

'Two days, I'm calling my banker in the Caymans and having him read me the balance of my account. If it's not heavier by twenty-five, you're toast.'

Rudy thought: This can't be the same man, not the way he's talking to me.

Roberto Pepsical went on, detached, businesslike: 'Me and The Others got this idea that we – meaning the county – should start certifying all private surgical clinics. Have your own testing, licence hearings, bi-monthly inspections, that sort of thing. It's our feeling that the general public needs to be protected.'

'Protected?' Rudy said feebly.

'From quacks and such. Don't you agree?'

Rudy thought: The whole world has turned upside down.

'Most clinics won't have anything to worry about,' Robert said brightly, 'once they're brought up to county standards.'

'Bobby, you're a bastard.'

After Rudy Graveline slammed down the phone, his hand was shaking. It wouldn't stop.

At the breakfast table, Heather stared at Rudy's trembling fingers and said, 'I sure don't like the looks of that.'

'Muscle spasms,' he said. 'It'll go away.'

'My surgery is tomorrow,' Heather said.

'I'm aware of that, darling.'

They had spent the better part of the morning discussing breast implants. Heather had collected testimonials from all her Hollywood actress friends who ever had boob jobs. Some of them favoured the Porex line of soft silicone implants, others liked the McGhan Biocell 100, and still others swore by the Replicon. Heather herself was leaning toward the Silastic II Teardrop model, because they came with a five-year written warranty.

'Maybe I better check with my agent,' she said.

'Why?' Rudy asked peevishly.

'This is my body we're talking about. My career.'

'All right,' Rudy said. 'Call your agent. What do I know? I'm just the surgeon.' He took the newspaper to the bathroom and sat down on the john. Ten minutes later, Heather knocked lightly on the door.

'It's too early on the coast,' she said. 'Melody's not in the office.'

'Thanks for the bulletin.'

'But a man called for you.'

Rudy folded the newspaper across his lap and braced his chin in his hands. 'Who was it, Heather?'

'He didn't give his name. Just said he was a patient.'

'That certainly narrows it down.'

'He said he came up with a number. I think he was talking about money.'

Crazy Chemo. It had to be. 'What did you tell him?' Rudy asked through the door.

'I told him you were unavailable at the moment. He didn't sound like he believed me.'

'Gee, I can't imagine,' said Rudy.

'He said he'll come by the clinic later.'

'Splendid.' He could hear her breathing at the door. 'Heather, is there something else?'

'Yes, there was a man out front. A process server from the courthouse.'

Rudy felt himself pucker at both ends.

Heather said, 'He rang the bell about a dozen times, but I wouldn't open the door. Finally, he went away.'

'Good girl,' Rudy said. He sprang off the toilet, elated. He flung open the bathroom door, carried Heather into the shower, and turned on the water, steamy hot. Then he got down on his bare knees and began kissing her silky, perfect thighs.

'This is our last day,' she said in a whisper, 'before the operation.'

Rudy stopped kissing and looked up, the shower stream hitting him squarely in the nostrils. Through the droplets he could see the woman of his dreams squeezing her perfect breasts in her perfect hands. With a playful laugh, she said, 'Say so long to these little guys.'

God, Rudy thought, what am I doing? The irony was wicked. All the rich geezers and chunky bimbos he had conned into plastic surgery, patients with no chance of transforming their looks or improving their lives – now he finds one with a body and face that are absolutely flawless, perfect, classic, and she's begging for the knife.

A crime against nature, Rudy thought; and he, the instrument of that crime.

He stood up and made reckless love to Heather right there in the shower. She braced one foot on the bath faucet, the other on the soap dish, but Rudy was too lost in his own locomotions to appreciate the artistry of her balance.

The faster he went, the easier it was to concentrate. His mind emptied of Chemo and Roberto and Stranahan and

Maggie. Before long Rudy Graveline was able to focus without distraction on his immediate crisis: the blond angel under the shower, and what she had planned for the next day.

Before long, an idea came to Rudy. It came to him with such brilliant ferocity that he mistook it for an orgasm.

Heather Chappell didn't particularly care what it was, as long as it was over. The hot water had run out, and she was freezing the orbs of her perfect bottom against the clammy bathroom tiles.

25

Mick Stranahan asked Al García to wait in the car while he went to see Kipper Garth. The law office was a chorus of beeping telephones as Stranahan made his way through the labyrinth of modular desks. The secretaries didn't bother to try to stop him. They could tell he wasn't a client.

Inside his personal sanctum, Kipper Garth sat in a familiar pose, waiting for an important call. He was tapping a Number 2 pencil and scowling at the speaker box. 'I did exactly what you wanted,' he said to Stranahan. 'See for yourself.'

The Nordstroms' malpractice complaint was clipped in a thin brown file on the corner of Kipper Garth's desk. He had been waiting all day for the moment to show his brother-in-law how well he had done. He handed Stranahan the file and said, 'Go ahead, it's all there.'

Stranahan remained standing while he read the lawsuit. 'This is very impressive,' he said, half-way down the second page. 'Maybe Katie's right, maybe you do have some genuine talent.'

Kipper Garth accepted the compliment with a cocky no-sweat shrug. Stranahan resisted the impulse to enquire which bright young paralegal had composed the document, since the author could not possibly be his brother-in-law.

'This really happened?' Stranahan asked. 'The man lost an eye to a . . . '

'Hooter,' Kipper Garth said. 'His wife's hooter, fortunately. Means we can automatically double the pain-and-suffering.'

Stranahan was trying to imagine a jury's reaction to such a mishap. The case would never get that far, but it was still fun to think about.

'Has Dr Graveline been served?'

'Not yet,' Kipper Garth reported. 'He's ducked us so far, but that's fine. We've got a guy staking out the medical clinic, he'll grab him on the way in or out. The lawsuit's bad enough, but your man will go ape when he finds out we've got a depo scheduled already.'

'Excellent,' Stranahan said.

'He'll get it postponed, of course.'

'It doesn't matter. The whole idea is to keep the heat on. That's why I brought this,' Stranahan handed Kipper Garth a page of nine names, neatly typed.

'The witness list,' Stranahan explained. 'I want you to file it with the court as soon as possible.'

Skimming it, Kipper Garth said, 'This is highly unusual.'

'How would you know?'

'Is is, dammit. Nobody gives up their witnesses so early in the case.'

'You do,' said Mick Stranahan. 'As of now.'

'I don't get it.'

'Heat, Jocko, remember? Send one of the clerks down to the courthouse and put this list in the Nordstrom file. You might even courier a copy over to Graveline's place, just for laughs.'

Kipper Garth noticed that all but one of the names on the witness list belonged to other doctors – specifically, plastic and reconstructive surgeons: experts who would presumably testify to Rudy Graveline's shocking incompetence in the post-op treatment of Mrs Nordstrom's encapsulated breast implants.

274

'Not bad,' said Kipper Garth, 'but who's this one?' With a glossy fingernail he tapped the last name on the list.

'That's a former nurse,' Stranahan said.

'Disgruntled?'

'You might say that.'

'And about what,' said Kipper Garth, 'is she prepared to testify?'

'The defendant's competence,' Stranahan replied, 'or lack thereof.'

Kipper Garth stroked a chromium sideburn. 'Witness-wise, I think we're better off sticking with these hotshot surgeons.'

'Graveline won't give a shit about them. The nurse's name is what will get his attention. Trust me.'

With feigned authority, the lawyer remarked that testimony from an embittered ex-employee wouldn't carry much weight in court.

'We're not going to court,' Stranahan reminded him. 'Not for malpractice, anyway. Maybe for a murder.'

'You're losing me again,' Kipper Garth admitted.

'Stay lost,' said Stranahan.

George Graveline's tree-trimming truck was parked off Crandon Boulevard in a lush tropical hammock. Button-woods, gumbo limbo, and mahogany trees – plenty of shade for George Graveline's truck. The county had hired him to rip out the old trees to make space for some tennis courts. Before long a restaurant would spring up next to the tennis courts and, after that, a major resort hotel. The people who would run the restaurant and the hotel would receive the use of the public property for practically nothing, thanks to their pals on the county commission. In return, the commissioners would receive a certain secret percentage of the refreshment concessions. And the voters would have brand-new tennis courts, whether they wanted them or not.

George Graveline's role in this civic endeavour was small, but he went at it with uncharacteristic zest. In the first two hours he and his men cleared two full acres of virgin woods.

Afterwards George Graveline sat down in the truck cab to rest, while his workers tossed the uprooted trees one at a time into the automatic wood chipper.

All at once the noise died away. George Graveline opened his eyes. He could hear his foreman talking to an unfamiliar voice behind the truck. George stuck his head out the window and saw a stocky Cuban guy in a brown suit. The Cuban guy had a thick moustache and a fat unlit cigar in one corner of his mouth.

'What can I do for you?' George Graveline asked.

The Cuban guy reached in his coat and pulled out a gold police badge. As he walked up to the truck, he could see George Graveline's Adam's apple sliding up and down.

Al García introduced himself and said he wanted to ask a few questions.

George Graveline said, 'You got a warrant?'

The detective smiled. 'I don't need a warrant, *chico*.'

'You don't?'

García shook his head. 'Nope. Here, take a look at this.' He showed George Graveline the police composite of Blondell Wayne Tatum, the man known as Chemo. 'Ever see this bird before?'

'No, sir,' said the tree trimmer, but his expression gave it away. He looked away too quickly from the drawing; anyone else would have stared.

García said, 'This is a friend of your brother's.'

'I don't think so.'

'No?' García shifted the cigar to the other side of his mouth. 'Well, that's good to know. Because this man's a killer, and I can't think of one good reason why he'd be hanging out with a famous plastic surgeon.'

George Graveline said, 'Me neither.' He turned on the radio and twirled the tuner knob back and forth, pretending to look for his favourite country station. García could sense the guy was about to wet his pants.

The detective said, 'I'm not the first homicide man you ever met, am I?'

'Sure. What do you mean?'

'Hell, it was four years ago,' García said. 'You probably don't even remember. It was outside your brother's office, the place he had before he moved over to the beach.'

With a fat brown finger George Graveline scratched his neck. He scrunched his eyebrows, as if trying to recall.

García said: 'Detective's name was Timmy Gavigan. Skinny Irish guy, red hair, about so big. He stopped to chat with you for a couple minutes.'

'No, I surely don't remember,' George said, guardedly.

'I'll tell you exactly when it was – it was right after that college girl disappeared,' García said. 'Victoria Barletta was her name. Surely you remember. There must've been cops all over the place.'

'Oh yeah.' Slowly it was coming back to George; that's what he wanted the cop to think.

'She was one of your brother's patients, the Barletta girl.'

'Right,' said George Graveline, nodding. 'I remember how upset Rudolph was.'

'But you don't remember talking to Detective Gavigan?'

'I talked to lots of people.'

García said, 'The reason I mention it, Timmy remembered you.'

'Yeah, so?'

'You know, he never solved that damn case. The Barletta girl, after all these years. And now he's dead, Timmy is.' García stepped to the rear of the truck. Casually he put one foot on the bumper, near the hitch of the wood chipper. George Graveline opened the door of the truck and leaned out to keep an eye on the Cuban detective.

The two men were alone. George's workers had wandered off to find a cool place to eat lunch and smoke some weed; it was hard to unwind with a cop hanging around.

Curiously Al García bent over the wood chipper and peered at a decal on the engine mount. The decal was in the cartoon likeness of a friendly raccoon. 'Brush Bandit – is that the name of this mother?'

'That's right,' said George Graveline.

277

'How does it work exactly?'

George motioned sullenly. 'You throw the wood into that hole and it comes out here, in the back of the truck. All grinded up.'

García whistled over his cigar. 'Must be some nasty blade.'

'It's a big one, yessir.'

García took his foot off the truck bumper. He held up the drawing of Chemo one more time. 'You see this guy, I want you to call us right away.'

'Surely,' said George Graveline. The detective gave him a business card. The tree trimmer glanced at it, decided it was authentic, slipped it into the back pocket of his jeans.

'And warn your brother,' García said. 'Just in case the guy shows up.'

'You betcha,' said George Graveline.

Back in the unmarked county car, parked a half-mile down the boulevard at the Key Biscayne fire station, Mick Stranahan said: 'So how'd it go?'

'Just like we figured,' García replied. '*Nada*.'

'What do you think of Timmy's theory? About how they got rid of the body?'

'If the doctor really killed her then, yeah, it's possible. That's quite a machine brother George has got himself.'

Stranahan said, 'Too bad brother George won't flip.'

García rolled up the windows and turned on the air-conditioning to cool off. He knew what Stranahan was thinking and he was right: brother George could blow the whole thing wide open. If Maggie were dead or gone, the videotape alone would not be enough for an indictment. They would definitely need George Graveline to talk about Vicky Barletta.

'I'm going for some fresh air,' Stranahan said. 'Why don't you meet me back here in about an hour?'

García said, 'Where the hell you off to?'

Stranahan got out of the car. 'For a walk, do you mind? Go get some coffee or flan or something.'

'Mick, don't do anything stupid. It's too nice a day for being stupid.'

'Hey, it's a lovely day.' Stranahan slammed the car door and crossed the boulevard at a trot.

'Shit,' García muttered. *Mierda*!

He drove down to the Oasis restaurant and ordered a cup of over-powering Cuban coffee. Then he ordered another.

George Graveline was still alone when Mick Stranahan got there. He was leaning against the truck fender, staring at his logger boots. He looked up at Stranahan, straightened, and said, 'You put that damn cop on my ass.'

'Good morning, George,' said Stranahan. 'It's certainly nice to see you again.'

'Fuck you, you hear?'

'Are we having a bad day? What is it – cramps?'

George Graveline was one of those big, slow guys who squint when they get angry. He was squinting now. Methodically he clenched and unclenched his fists, as if he were practising isometrics.

Stranahan said, 'George, I've still got that problem I told you about last time. Your brother's still got some goon trying to murder me. I'm really at the end of my rope.'

'You got that right.'

'My guess,' continued Stranahan, 'is that you and Rudy had a brotherly talk after last time. My guess is that you know exactly where I can locate this goony hit man.'

'Screw you,' said George Graveline. He kicked the switch on the wood chipper and the motor growled to life.

Stranahan said, 'Aw, what'd you do that for? How'm I supposed to hear you over all that damn racket?'

George Graveline lunged with both arms raised stiff in fury, a Frankenstein monster with Elvis jowls. He was clawing for Stranahan's neck. Stranahan ducked the grab and punched George Graveline hard under the heart. When the tree trimmer didn't fall, Stranahan punched him twice in the testicles. This time George went down.

279

Stranahan placed his right foot on the husky man's neck and applied the pressure slowly, shifting his weight from heel to toe. By reflex George's hands were riveted to his swollen scrotum. He was helpless to fight back. He made a noise like a tractor tyre going flat.

'I can't believe you did that,' Stranahan muttered. 'Isn't it possible to have a civilized conversation in this town without somebody trying to kill you?'

It was a rhetorical question but George Graveline couldn't hear it over the wood chipper, anyway. Stranahan leaned over and shouted: 'Where's the goon?'

George did not answer promptly, so Stranahan added more weight on the Adam's apple. George was not squinting any more; both eyes were quite large.

'Where is he?' Stranahan repeated.

When George's lips started moving, Stranahan let up. The voice that came out of the tree trimmer's mouth had a fuzzy electronic quality. Stranahan knelt to hear it.

'Works on the beach,' said George Graveline.

'Can we be more specific?'

'At a club.'

'What club, George? There's lots of nightclubs on Miami Beach.'

George blinked and said, 'Gay Bidet.' Now it was done, he thought. His brother Rudy was a goner.

'Thank you, George,' said Stranahan. He removed his shoe from the tree trimmer's throat. 'This is a good start. I'm very encouraged. Now let's talk about Vicky Barletta.'

George Graveline lay there with his head in the moist dirt, his groin throbbing. He lay there worrying about his brother the doctor, about what horrible things would happen to him all because of George's big mouth. Rudy had confided in him, trusted him, and now George had let his brother down. Lying there dejectedly, he decided that no matter how much pain was inflicted upon him, he wasn't going to tell Mick Stranahan what had happened to that college girl. Rudy had made a mistake, everybody makes mistakes. Why, one time George himself got a work order mixed up and cut down a whole row of fifty-foot royal palms, when it was mangy old Brazilians he was supposed to chop. Still, they didn't put him in jail or anything, just made him pay a fine. Hundred bucks a tree, something like that. Why should a doctor be treated any different? As he reflected upon Rudy's turbulent medical career, George Graveline removed one of his hands from his swollen scrotum. The free hand happened to settle on a hunk of fresh-cut mahogany concealed by his left leg. The wood was heavy, the bark coarse and dry. George closed his fingers around it. It felt pretty good.

Still kneeling, Mick Stranahan nudged George Graveline's shoulder and said, 'Penny for your thoughts.'

And George hit him square on the back of the skull.

Stranahan didn't see the blow, and at first he thought he'd been shot. He heard a man shouting and what sounded like an ambulance. The rescue scene played vividly in his imagination. He waited to feel the paramedics' hands ripping open his shirt. He waited for the cold clap of the stethoscope on his chest, for the sting of the IV needle in his arm. He waited for the childlike sensation of being lifted onto the stretcher.

None of this came, yet the sound of the ambulance siren would not go away. In his crashing sleep, Stranahan grew angry. Where were the goddamn EMTs? A man's been shot here!

Then, blessedly, he felt someone lifting him. Lifting him under the arms, someone strong. It hurt, oh, God, how it hurt, but that was all right – at least they had come. But then he was falling again, falling or dying, he couldn't be sure. And in his crashing sleep he heard the moan of the siren rise to such a pitch that he wanted to cover his ears and scream for it to stop, please God.

And it did stop.

Somebody shut off the wood chipper.

Stranahan awoke to the odd hollow silence that follows a sharp echo. His eardrums fluttered. The air smelled pungently of cordite. He found himself on his knees, weaving, a drunk waiting for communication. His shirt was damp, his pulse rabbity. He checked himself and

281

saw he was mistaken, he hadn't been shot. There was no ambulance, either, just the tree truck.

Al García sat on the bumper. His gun was in his right hand, which hung heavily at his side. He was as pale as a flounder.

There was no sign of George Graveline anywhere.

'You all right?' Stranahan asked.

'No,' said the detective.

'Where's the tree man?'

With the gun García pointed toward the bin of the tree truck, where the wood chipper had spit what bone and jelly was left of George Graveline.

After he had tried to feed Mick Stranahan into the maw.

And Al García had shot him twice in the back.

And the impact of the bullets had slammed him face-forward down the throat of the tree-eating machine.

26

Chemo got the Bonneville out of the garage and drove out to Whispering Palms, but the receptionist said that Dr Graveline wasn't there. Noticing the dramatic topography of Chemo's face, the receptionist told him she could try the doctor at home for an emergency. Chemo said thanks, anyway.

After leaving the clinic, he walked around to the side of the building where the employees parked. Dr Graveline's spiffy new Jaguar XJ-6 was parked in its space. This was the Jaguar that the doctor had purchased immediately after Mick Stranahan had blown up his other one. The sedan was a rich shade of red; candy apple, Chemo guessed, though the Jaguar people probably had a fancier name for it. The windows of the car were tinted grey so that you couldn't see inside. Chemo assumed that Dr Graveline had a burglar alarm wired on the thing, so he was careful not to touch the doors or the hood.

He ambled to the rear of the clinic, by the water, and peeked through the bay window into Rudy's private office. There was the doctor, yakking on the phone. Chemo was annoyed; it was rude of Graveline to be ducking him this way. Rude, hell. It was just plain stupid.

When Chemo turned the corner of the building, he saw a short man in an ill-fitting grey suit standing next to Rudy's car. The man wore dull brown shoes and black-rimmed eyeglasses. He looked to be in his mid-fifties. Chemo walked up to him and said, 'Are you looking for Graveline?'

The man in the black-rimmed glasses appraised Chemo skittishly and said, 'Are you him?'

'Fuck no. But this is his car.'

'They told me he wasn't here.'

'They lied,' Chemo said. 'Hard to believe, isn't it?'

The man opened a brown billfold to reveal a cheap-looking badge. 'I work for the county,' he said. 'I'm trying to serve some papers on the doctor. I been trying two, three days.'

Chemo said, 'See that side door? You wait there, he'll be out soon. It's almost five o'clock.'

'Thanks,' said the process server. He went over and stood, idiotically, by the side entrance to the clinic. He clutched the court papers rolled up in one hand, as if he were going to sat the doctor when he came out.

Chemo slipped the calfskin sheath off the Weed Whacker and turned his attention to Rudy's new Jaguar. He chose as his starting place the left front fender.

Initially it was slow going – those British sure knew how to paint an automobile. At first the Weed Whacker inflicted only pale stripes on the deep red enamel. Chemo tried lowering the device closer to the fender and bracing it in position with his good arm. It took fifteen minutes for the powerful lawn cutter to work its way down to the base steel of the sedan. Chemo moved its buzzing head back and forth in a sweeping motion to enlarge the scar.

From his waiting post outside the clinic door, the process server watched the odd ceremony with rapt fascination. Finally he could stand it no longer, and shouted at Chemo.

Chemo turned away from the Jaguar and looked at the man in the black-rimmed glasses. He flicked the toggle switch to turn off the Weed Whacker, then cupped his right hand to his ear.

The man said, 'What are you doing with that thing?'

'Therapy,' Chemo answered. 'Doctor's orders.'

Like many surgeons, Dr Rudy Graveline was a compulsive man, supremely organized but hopelessly anal retentive. The day after the disturbing phone call from Commissioner Roberto Pepsical, Rudy meticulously wrote out a list of all his career-threatening problems. By virtue of the scope of his extortion, Roberto Pepsical was promoted to the number three spot, behind Mick Stranahan and Chemo. Rudy studied the list closely. In the larger context of a possible murder indictment, Roberto Pepsical was chickenshit. Expensive chickenshit, but chickenshit just the same.

Rudy Graveline dialled the number in New Jersey and waited for Curly Eyebrows to come on the line.

'Jeez, I told you not to call me here. Let me get to a better phone.' The man hung up, and Rudy waited. Ten minutes later the man called back.

'Lemme guess, your problem's got worse.'

'Yes,' said Rudy.

'That local talent you hired, he wasn't by himself after all.'

'He was,' Rudy said, 'but not now.'

'That's pretty funny.' Curly Eyebrows laughed flatulently. Somewhere in the background a car blasted its horn. The man said, 'You rich guys are something else. Always trying to do it on the cheap.'

'Well, I need another favour,' Rudy said.

'Such as what?'

'Remember the hunting accident a few years ago?'

Curly Eyebrows said, 'Sure. That doctor. The one was giving you a hard time.'

The man in New Jersey didn't remember the name of the dead doctor, but Rudy Graveline certainly did. It was Kenneth Greer, one of his former partners at the Durkos Center. The one who figured out what had happened to Victoria Barletta. The one who was trying to blackmail him.

'That was a cinch,' said Curly Eyebrows. 'I wish they all could be hunters. Every deer season we could clean up the Gambinos that way. Hunting accidents.'

The man in New Jersey had an itch – on the line Rudy Graveline heard the disgusting sound of fat fingers scratching hairy flesh. He tried not to think about it.

'Somebody new is giving me a hard time,' the doctor said. 'I don't know if you can help, but I thought I'd give it a shot.'

'I'm listening.'

'It's the Dade County Commission,' Rudy said. 'I need somebody to kill them. Can you arrange it?'

'Wait a minute— '

'All of them,' Rudy said, evenly.

'Excuse me, Doc, but you're fucking crazy. Don't call me no more.'

'Please,' Rudy said. 'Five of them are shaking me down for twenty-five grand each. The trouble is, I don't know which five. So my idea is to kill all nine.'

Curly Eyebrows grunted. 'You got me confused.'

Patiently Rudy explained how the bribe system worked, how each commissioner arranged for four crooked colleagues to go along on each controversial vote. Rudy told the man in New Jersey about the Old Cypress Towers project, about how the commissioners were trying to pinch him for the zoning decision he no longer needed.

'Hey, a deal is a deal,' Curly Eyebrows said unsympathetically. 'Seems to me you got yourself in a tight situation.' Now it sounded like he was picking his teeth with a comb.

285

Rudy said, 'You won't help?'

'Won't. Can't. Wouldn't.' The man coughed violently, then spit. 'Much as the idea appeals to me personally – killing off an entire county commission – it'd be bad for business.'

'It was just an idea,' Rudy said. 'I'm sorry I bothered you.'

'Want some free advice?'

'Why not.'

Curly Eyebrows said, 'Who's the point man in this deal? You gotta know his name, at least.'

'I do.'

'Good. I suggest something happens to the bastard. Something awful bad. This could be a lesson to the other eight pricks, you understand?'

Rudy Graveline said yes, he understood.

'Trust me,' said the man in New Jersey. 'I been in this end of it for a long time. Sort of thing makes an impression, especially dealing with your mayors and aldermen and those types. These are not exactly tough guys.'

'I suppose not.' Rudy cleared his throat. 'Listen, that's a very good idea. Just do one of them.'

'That's my advice,' said the man in New Jersey.

'Could you arrange it?'

'Shit, I ain't risking my boys on some lowlife county pol. No way. Talent's too hard to come by these days – you found that out yourself.'

Rudy recalled the newspaper story about Tony the Eel, washed up dead on the Cape Florida beach. 'I still feel bad about that fellow last month,' the doctor said.

'Hey, it happens.'

'But still,' said Rudy morosely.

'You ought to get out of Florida,' advised Curly Eyebrows. 'I been telling all my friends, it's not like the old days. Fuck the pretty beaches, Doc, them Cubans are crazy. They're not like you and me. And then there's the Jews and the Haitians, Christ!'

'Times change,' said Rudy.

'I was reading up on it, some article about stress. Florida

286

is like the worst fucking place in America for stressing out, besides Vegas. I'm not making this up.'

Dispiritedly, Rudy Graveline said, 'It seems like everybody wants a piece of my hide.'

'Ain't it the fucking truth.'

'I swear, I'm not a violent person by nature.'

'Costa Rica,' said the man in New Jersey. 'Think about it.'

Commissioner Roberto Pepsical got to the church fifteen minutes early and scouted the aisles: a bag lady snoozing on the third pew, but that was it. To kill time Roberto lit a whole row of devotional candles. Afterwards he fished through his pocket change and dropped a Canadian dime in the coin box.

When the doctor arrived, Roberto waddled briskly to the back of the church. Rudy Graveline was wearing a tan sports jacket and dark, loose-fitting pants and a brown striped necktie. He looked about as calm as a rat in a snake hole. In his right hand was a black Samsonite suitcase. Wordlessly Roberto brushed past him and entered one of the dark confessionals. Rudy waited about three minutes, checked over both shoulders, opened the door, and went in.

'God,' he exclaimed.

'He's here somewhere.' The commissioner chuckled at his own joke.

Rudy had never been inside a confession booth before. It was smaller and gloomier than he had imagined; the only light was a tiny amber bulb plugged into a wall socket.

Roberto had planted his fat ass on the kneeling cushion with his back to the screen. Rudy checked to make sure there wasn't a priest on the other side, listening. Priests could be awful quiet when they wanted.

'Remember,' the commissioner said, raising a finger. 'Whisper.'

Right, Rudy thought, like I was going to belt out a Gershwin tune. 'Of all the screwy places to do this,' he said.

'It's quiet,' Roberto Pepsical said. 'And very safe.'

'And very small,' Rudy added. 'You had anchovies for dinner, didn't you?'

'There are no secrets here,' said Roberto.

With difficulty, Rudy wedged himself and the Samsonite next to the commissioner on the kneeling bench. Roberto's body heat bathed both of them in a warm acrid fog, and Rudy wondered how long the oxygen would hold out. He had never heard of anyone suffocating in confession; on the other hand, that was exactly the sort of incident the Catholics would cover up.

'You ready?' Roberto asked with a wink. 'What's that in your pocket?'

'Unfortunately, that's a subpoena. Some creep got me on the way out of the clinic tonight.' Rudy had been in such a hurry that he hadn't even looked at the court papers; he was somewhat accustomed to getting sued.

Roberto said, 'No wonder you're in such a lousy mood.'

'It's not that so much as what happened to my new car. It got vandalized – actually, scoured is the word for it.'

'The Jag? That's terrible.'

'Oh, it's been a splendid day,' Rudy said. 'Absolutely splendid.'

'Getting back to the money . . . '

'I've got it right here.' The doctor opened the suitcase across both their laps, and the confessional was filled with the sharp scent of new money. Rudy Graveline was overwhelmed – it really did *smell*. Roberto picked up a brick of hundred-dollar bills. 'I thought I said twenties.'

'Yeah, and I would've needed a bloody U-Haul.'

Roberto Pepsical snapped off the bank wrapper and counted out ten thousand dollars on the floor between his feet. Then he added up the other bundles in the suitcase to make sure the total came to one twenty-five.

Grinning, he held up one of the loose hundreds. 'I don't see many of these. Whose picture is that – Eisenhower's?'

'No,' said Rudy, stonily.

'What'd the bank say? About you taking all these big bills.'

'Nothing,' Rudy said. 'This is Miami, Bobby.'

'Yeah, I guess.' Ebulliently the commissioner restacked the cash bundles and packed them in the Samsonite. He scooped up the loose ten thousand dollars and shoved the thick wad into the pockets of his suit. 'This was a smart thing you did.'

Rudy said, 'I'm not so sure.'

'You know that plan I told you about . . . about licensing the medical clinics and all that? Me and The Others, we decided to drop the whole thing. We figure that doctors like you got enough rules and regulations as it is.'

'Glad to hear it,' said Rudy Graveline. He wished he had brought some Certs. Roberto could use a whole roll.

'How about a drink?' the commissioner asked. 'We could stop at the Versailles, get a couple pitchers a *sangria*.'

'Yum.'

'Hey, it's my treat.'

'Thanks,' said the doctor, 'but first you know what I'd like to do? I'd like to say a prayer. I'd like to thank the Lord that this problem with Cypress Towers is finally over.'

Roberto shrugged. 'Go ahead.'

'Is it all right, Bobby? I mean, since I'm not Catholic.'

'No problem.' The commissioner grunted to his feet, turned around in the booth and got to his knees. The cushion squeaked under his weight. 'Do like this,' he said.

Rudy Graveline, who was slimmer, had an easier time with the turnaround manoeuvre. With the suitcase propped between them, the two men knelt side by side, facing the grated screen through which confessions were heard.

'So pray,' Roberto Pepsical said. 'I'll wait til! you're done. Fact, I might even do a couple Hail Marys myself, long as I'm here.'

Rudy shut his eyes, bowed his head, and pretended to say a prayer.

Roberto nudged him. 'I don't mean to tell you what to do,' he said, 'but in here it's not proper to pray with your hands in your pockets.'

'Of course,' said Rudy, 'I'm sorry.'

He took his right hand from his pants and placed it on Roberto's doughy shoulder. It was too dark for the commissioner to see the hypodermic syringe.

'Hail Mary,' Roberto said, 'full of grace, the Lord is with thee. Blessed ar-ow!'

The commissioner pawed helplessly at the needle sticking from his jacket at the crook of the elbow. Considering Rudy's general clumsiness with injections, it was a minor miracle that he hit the commissioner's antecubital vein on the first try. Roberto Pepsical hugged the doctor desperately, a panting bear, but already the deadly potassium was streaming toward the valves of his fat clotty heart.

Within a minute the seizure killed him, mimicking the symptoms of a routine infarction so perfectly that the commissioner's relatives would never challenge the autopsy.

Rudy removed the spent syringe, retrieved the loose cash from Roberto's pocket, picked up the black suitcase, and slipped out of the stuffy confessional. The air in the church seemed positively alpine, and he paused to breathe it deeply.

In the back row, an elderly Cuban couple turned at the sound of his footsteps on the terrazzo. Rudy nodded solemnly. He hoped they didn't notice how badly his legs were shaking. He faced the altar and tried to smile like a man whose soul had been cleansed of all sin.

The old Cuban woman raised a bent finger to her forehead and made the sign of the cross. Rudy worried about Catholic protocol and wondered if he was expected to reply. He didn't know how to make the sign of the cross, but he put down the suitcase and gave it a gallant try. With a forefinger he touched his brow, his breast, his right shoulder, his left shoulder, his navel, then his brow again.

'Live long and prosper,' he said to the old woman and walked out the doors of the church.

*

When he got home, Rudy Graveline went upstairs to see Heather Chappell. He sat next to the bed and took her hand. She blinked moistly over the edge of the bandages.

Rudy kissed her knuckles and said, 'How are you feeling?'

'I don't know about you,' Heather said, 'but I'm feeling a hundred years old.'

'That's to be expected. You had quite a day.'

'You sure it went OK?'

'Beautifully,' Rudy said.

'The nose, too?'

'A masterpiece.'

'But I don't remember a thing.'

The reason Heather couldn't remember the surgery was because there had been no surgery. Rudy had drugged her copiously the night before and kept her drugged the whole day. Heather had lain unconscious for seven hours, whacked out on world-class pharmaceutical narcotics. By the time she awoke, she felt like she'd been sleeping for a month. Her hips, her breasts, her neck, and her nose were all snugly and expertly bandaged, but no scalpel had touched her fine California flesh. Rudy hoped to persuade Heather that the surgery was a glowing success; the absence of scars, a testament to his wizardry. Obviously he had weeks of bogus post-operative counselling ahead of him.

'Can I see the video?' she asked from the bed.

'Later,' Rudy promises. 'When you're up to snuff.'

He had ordered (by FedEx) a series of surgical training cassettes from a medical school in California. Now it was simply a matter of editing the tapes into a plausible sequence. Gowned, masked, and anaesthetized on the operating table, all patients looked pretty much alike to a camera. Meanwhile, all you ever saw of the surgeon was his gloved hands; Heather would never know that the doctor on the videotape was not her lover.

She said, 'It's incredible, Rudolph, but I don't feel any pain.'

'It's the medication,' he said. 'The first few days, we keep you pretty high.'

Heather giggled. 'Eight miles high?'

'Nine,' said Rudy Graveline, 'at least.'

He tucked her hand beneath the sheets and picked up something from the bedstand. 'Look what I've got.'

She squinted through the fuzz of the drugs. 'Red and blue and white,' she said dreamily.

'Plane tickets,' Rudy said. 'I'm taking you on a trip.'

'Really?'

'To Costa Rica. The climate is ideal for your recovery.'

'For how long?'

Rudy said, 'A month or two, maybe longer. As long as it takes, darling.'

'But I'm supposed to do a *Password* with Jack Klugman.'

'Out of the question,' said Rudy. 'You're in no condition for that type of stress. Now get some sleep.'

'What's that noise?' she asked, lifting her head.

'The doorbell, sweetheart. Lie still now.'

'Costa Rica,' Heather murmured. 'Where's that, anyhow?'

Rudy kissed her on the forehead and told her he loved her.

'Yeah,' she said. 'I know.'

Whoever was at the door was punching the button like it was a jukebox. Rudy hurried down the stairs and checked through the glass peephole.

Chemo signalled mirthlessly back at him.

'Shit.' Rudy sighed, thought of his Jaguar, and opened the door.

'Why did you destroy my car?'

'Teach you some manners,' Chemo said. Another bandaged woman stood at his side.

'Maggie?' Rudy Graveline said. 'Is that you?'

Chemo led her by the hand into the big house. He found the living room and made himself comfortable in an antique rocking chair. Maggie Gonzalez sat on a white leather sofa. Her eyes, which were Rudy's only clue to her mood, seemed cold and hostile.

Chemo said, 'Getting jerked around is not my favourite thing. I ought to just kill you.'

'What good would that do?' Rudy said. He stepped closer to Maggie and asked, 'Who did your face?'

'Leaper,' she said.

'Leonard Leaper? Up in New York? I heard he's good – mind if I look?'

'Yes,' she said, recoiling. 'Rogelio, make him get away!'

'Rogelio?' Rudy looked quizzically at Chemo.

'It's your fucking fault,' he said. 'That's the name you put on the tickets. Now leave her alone.' Chemo stopped rocking. He eyed Rudy Graveline as if he were a palmetto bug.

The surgeon sat near Maggie on the white leather sofa and said to Chemo, 'So how're the dermabrasions healing?'

Self-consciously the killer's hand went to his chin. 'All of a sudden you're concerned about my face. Now that you're afraid.'

'Well, you look good,' Rudy persisted. 'Really, it's a thousand per cent improvement.'

'Jesus H. Christ.'

Irritably Maggie said, 'Let's get to the point, OK? I want to get out of here.'

'The money,' Chemo said to the doctor. 'We decided on one million, even.'

'For what!' Rudy was trying to stay cool, but his tone was trenchant.

Chemo started rocking again. 'For everything,' he said. 'For Maggie's videotape. For Stranahan. For stopping that TV show about the dead girl. That's worth a million dollars. In fact, the more I think about it, I'd say it's worth two.'

Rudy folded his arms and said, 'You do everything you just said, and I'll gladly give you a million dollars. As of now, you get nothing but expenses because you haven't done a damn thing but stir up trouble.'

'That's not true,' Maggie snapped.

'We've been busy,' Chemo added. 'We got a big surprise.'

Rudy said, 'I've got a big surprise, too. A malpractice suit. And guess whose name is on the witness list?'

He jerked an accusing thumb at Maggie, who said, 'That's news to me.'

Rudy went on. 'Some fellow named Nordstrom. Lost his eye in some freak accident and now it's all my fault.'

Maggie said, 'I never heard of a Nordstrom.'

'Well, your name is right there in the file. Witness for the plaintiff. Why should I pay you people a dime?'

'All the more reason,' Chemo said. 'I believe it's called hush money.'

'No,' said the doctor, 'that's not the way it goes.'

Chemo stood up from the rocker. He took two large steps across the living room and punched Rudy Graveline solidly in the gut. The doctor collapsed in a gagging heap on the Persian carpet. Chemo turned him over with one foot. Then he cranked up the Weed Whacker.

'Oh God,' cried Rudy, raising his hands to shield his eyes. Quickly Maggie moved out of the way, her facial bandages crinkled in trepidation.

'I got a new battery,' Chemo said. 'A Die-Hard. Watch this.'

He started weed-whacking Rudy's fine clothes. First he shredded the shirt and tie, then he tried trimming the curly brown hair on Rudy's chest. The doctor yelped pitiably as nasty pink striations appeared beneath his nipples.

Chemo was working the machine toward Rudy's pubic zone when he spied something inside the tattered lining of the surgeon's tan coat. He turned off the Weed Whacker and leaned down for a closer look.

With his good hand Chemo reached into the silky entrails of Rudy's jacket and retrieved the severed corner of a one-hundred-dollar bill. Excitedly he probed around until he found more: handfuls, blessedly unshredded.

Chemo spread the money on the coffee table, beneath which Rudy thrashed and moaned impotently. The stricken surgeon observed the accounting firsthand, gazing up through the frosted glass. As the cash grew to cover the table, Rudy's face hardened into a mask of abject disbelief. On his way back from the church he had meant to stop at the clinic and return the money to the drop safe. Now it was too late.

'Count it,' Chemo said to Maggie.

Excitedly she riffled through the bills. 'Nine thousand two hundred,' she reported. 'The rest is all chopped up.'

Chemo dragged Dr Graveline from under the coffee table. 'Why you carrying this much cash?' he said. 'Don't tell me the Jag dealer won't take credit cards.' His moist salamander eyes settled on the black Samsonite, which Rudy had stupidly left in the middle of the hallway.

Rudy sniffed miserably as he watched Chemo kick open the suitcase and crouch down to count the rest of the money. 'Well, well,' said the killer.

'What are you going to do with it?' the doctor asked.

'Gee, I think we'll give it to the United Way. Or maybe Jerry's kids.' Chemo walked over to Rudy and poked his bare belly with the warm head of the Weed Whacker. 'What the hell you think we're going to do with it? We're gonna spend it, and then we're gonna come back for more.'

After they had gone, Dr Rudy Graveline sprawled on the rumpled Persian carpet for a long time, thinking: This is what a Harvard education has gotten me – extorted, beaten, stripped, scandalized, and chopped up like an artichoke. The doctor's fingers gingerly explored the tumescent stripes that crisscrossed his chest and abdomen. If it didn't sting so much, the sight would be almost comical.

It occurred to Rudy Graveline that Chemo and Maggie had forgotten to tell him their big secret, whatever it was they had done, whatever spectacular felony they had committed to earn this first garnishment.

And it occurred to Rudy that he wasn't all that curious. In fact, he was somewhat relieved not to know.

The man from the medical examiner's office took one look in the back of the tree truck and said: 'Mmmm, lasagna.'

'That's very funny,' said Al García. 'You oughta go on the Carson show. Do a whole routine on stiffs.'

The man from the medical examiner's office said, 'Al, you gotta admit— '

'I told you what happened.'

' —but you gotta admit, there's a humorous aspect.'

Coroners made Al García jumpy; they always got so cheery when somebody came up with a fresh way to die.

The detective said, 'If you think it's funny, fine. You're the one's gotta do the autopsy.'

'First I'll need a casserole dish.'

'Hilarious,' said García. 'Absolutely hilarious.'

The man from the medical examiner's office told him to lighten up, said everybody needs a break in the monotony, no matter what line of work. 'I get tired of gunshot wounds,' the coroner said. 'It's like a damn assembly line down there. GSW head, GSW thorax, GSW neck – it gets old, Al.'

García said, 'Listen, go ahead, make your jokes. But I need you to keep this one outta the papers.'

'Good luck.'

The detectives knew it wouldn't be easy to keep the lid on George Graveline's death. Seven squad cars, an ambulance, and a body wagon – even in Miami, that'll draw a crowd. The gawkers were being held behind yellow police ribbons strung along Crandon Boulevard. Soon the minicams would arrive, and the minicams could zoom in for close-ups.

'I need a day or two,' García said. 'No press, and no next of kin.'

The man from the medical examiner shrugged. 'It'll take

at least that long to make the ID considering what's left. I figure we'll have to go dental.'

'Whatever.'

'I'll need to impound the truck,' the coroner said. 'And this fancy toothpick machine.'

García said he would have them both towed downtown.

The coroner stuck his head into the maw of the wood chipper and examined the blood-smeared blades. 'There ought to be bullet fragments,' he said, 'somewhere in this mess.'

García said, 'Hey, Sherlock, I told you what happened. I shot the asshole, OK? My gun, my bullets.'

'Al, don't take all the fun out of it.' The man from the medical examiner reached into the blades of the wood chipper and carefully plucked out an item that the untrained eye would have misidentified as a common black woolly-bear caterpillar.

The coroner held it up for Al García to see.

The detective frowned. 'What, do I get a prize or something? It's a sideburn, for Chrissakes.'

'Very good,' said the coroner.

García flicked the soggy nub of his cigar into the bushes and went looking for George Graveline's crew of tree trimmers. There were three of them sitting sombrely in the back seat of a county patrol car. Al García got in front, on the passenger side. He turned around and spoke to them through the cage. The men's clothes smelled like pot. García asked if any of them had seen what had happened, and to a one they answered no, they'd been on their lunch break. The officers from Internal Review had asked the same thing.

'If you didn't see anything,' García said, 'then you don't have much to tell the reporters, right?'

In unison the tree trimmers shook their heads.

'Including the name of the alleged victim, right?'

The tree trimmers agreed.

'This is damned serious,' said García. 'I don't believe you boys would purposely obstruct a homicide investigation, would you?'

297

The tree trimmers promised not to say a word to the media. Al García asked a uniformed cop to give the men a lift home, so they wouldn't have to walk past the minicams on their way to the bus stop.

By this time, the ambulance was backing out, empty. García knocked on the driver's window. 'Where's the guy you were working on?'

'Blunt head wound?'

'Right. Big blond guy.'

'Took off,' said the ambulance driver. 'Gobbled three Darvocets and said so long. Wouldn't even let us wrap him.'

García cursed and bearishly swatted at a fresh-cut buttonwood branch.

The ambulance driver said, 'You see him, be sure and tell him he oughta go get a skull X-ray.'

'You know what you'd find?' García said. 'Shit for brains, that's what.'

Reynaldo Flemm picked up an attractive young woman at a nightclub called Biscayne Baby in Coconut Grove. He took her to his room at the Grand Bay Hotel and asked her to wait while he ran the water in the Roman tub. Still insecure about his impugned physique, Reynaldo didn't want the young woman to see him naked in the bright light. He lowered himself into the bath, covered the vital areas with suds, double-checked himself in the mirrors, then called for the young woman to join him. She came in the bathroom, stripped, and climbed casually into the deep tub. When Reynaldo tickled her armpits with his toes, the young woman politely pushed his legs away.

'So, what do you do?' he asked.

'I told you, I'm a legal secretary.'

'Oh, yeah.' When Reynaldo got semi-blitzed on screwdrivers, his short-term memory tended to vapour-lock. 'You probably recognize me,' he said to the young woman.

'I told you already – no.'

Reynaldo said, 'Normally my hair's black. I coloured it this way for a reason.'

He had revived the Johnny LeTigre go-go dancer disguise for his confrontation with Dr Rudy Graveline. He had dyed his hair brown and slicked it straight back with a wet comb. He looked like a Mediterranean sponge diver.

'Imagine me with black hair,' he said to the legal secretary, who flicked a soap bubble off her nose and said no, she still wouldn't recognize him.

He said, 'You get TV, right? I'm Reynaldo Flemm.'

'Yeah?'

'From *In Your Face*.'

'Oh, sure.'

'Ever seen it?'

'No,' said the secretary, 'but I don't watch all that much television.' She was trying to be nice. 'I think I've seen your commercials,' she said.

Flemm shrunk lower in the tub.

'Is it, like, a game show?' the woman asked.

'No, it's a news show. I'm an investigative reporter.'

'Like that guy on *Sixty Minutes*?'

Reynaldo bowed his head. Feeling guilty, the secretary slid across the tub and climbed on his lap. She said, 'Hey, I believe you.'

'Thanks a bunch.'

She felt a little sorry for him; he seemed so small and wounded among the bubbles. She said, 'You certainly look like you could be on television.'

'I *am* on fucking television. I've got my own show.'

The woman said, 'OK, whatever.'

'I could loan you a tape – you got a VCR?'

The secretary told him to hush. She put her lips to his ear and said, 'Why don't we try it right here?'

Reynaldo half-heartedly slipped one arm around her waist and began kissing her breasts. They were perfectly lovely breasts, but Reynaldo's heart wasn't in it. After a few moments the woman said, 'You're not really in the mood, huh?'

'I *was*.'

'I'm sorry. Here, let me do your back.'

Reynaldo's buttocks squeaked as he turned around in

the tub so the secretary could scrub him. He watched her in the mirror; her hands felt wondrously soothing. Eventually he closed his eyes.

'There you go,' she said, kneading his shoulder blades. 'My great big TV star.'

Reynaldo found he was getting excited again. He touched himself, underwater, just to make sure. He was smiling until he opened his eyes and saw something new in the mirror.

A man standing in the doorway. The man with the tarpon gaff.

'Sorry to interrupt,' said Mick Stranahan.

The woman squealed and dove for a towel. Reynaldo Flemmm groped for floating suds to cover his withering erection.

'I was looking for Christina,' Stranahan said. He walked up to the Roman tub with the gaff held under one arm, like a riding crop. 'She's not in her hotel room.'

'How'd you find me?' Reynaldo's voice was reedy and taut, definitely not an anchorman's voice.

'Miami is not one of the world's all-time great hotel towns,' Stranahan said. 'Hotshot celebrities like you always end up in the Grove. But tell me: why's Christina still registered out at Key Biscayne?'

Nervously the secretary said, 'Who's Christina?'

Stranahan said: 'Ray, I asked you a question.' He poked the fish gaff under the suds and scraped the point across the bottom of the tub. The steel screeched ominously against the ceramic. Reynaldo Flemm drew up his knees and sloshed protectively into a corner.

'Chris doesn't know I'm here,' he said. 'I ditched her.'

Stranahan told the legal secretary to get dressed and go home. He waited until she was gone from the bathroom before he spoke again.

'I checked Christina's room at the Sonesta. She hasn't been there for two days.'

Reynaldo said, 'What're you going to do to me?' He couldn't take his eyes off the tarpon gaff. Wrapping his arms around his knees, he said, 'Don't hurt me.'

'For Christ's sake.'

'I mean it!'

'Are you crying?' Stranahan couldn't believe it – another dumb twit overreacting. 'Just tell me about Christina. Her notebooks were still in the room, and so was her purse. Any ideas?'

'Uuunnngggh.' The pink of Flemm's tongue showed between his front teeth. It was a cowering, poodle-like expression, amplified by trembling lips and liquid eyes.

'Settle down,' said Stranahan. His head felt like it was full of wet cement. The Darvocets had barely put a ripple in the pain. What a shitty day.

He said, 'You haven't seen her?'

Violently Reynaldo shook his head no.

They heard a door slam – the secretary, making tracks. Stranahan used the gaff to pull the plug in the Roman tub. Wordlessly he watched the soapy water drain, leaving Reynaldo bare and shrivelled and flecked with suds.

'What's with the hairdo?' Stranahan asked.

Reynaldo composed himself and said, 'For a show.'

Stranahan tossed him a towel. He said, 'I know what you're doing. You're acting Christina out of the Barletta story. I saw your notes on the table.'

Flemm reddened. It had taken him three hours to come up with ten questions for Dr Rudy Graveline. Carefully he had printed the questions on a fresh legal pad, the way Christina Marks always did. He had spent the better part of the afternoon trying to memorize them before calling it quits and heading over to Biscayne Baby for some action.

'I don't care about your show,' Stranahan said, 'but I care about Christina.'

'Me, too.'

'It looked like somebody pushed his way into her hotel room. There was a handprint on the door.'

Reynaldo said, 'Well, it wasn't mine.'

'Stand up,' Stranahan told him.

Flemm wrapped himself into the towel as he stood up in the tub. Stranahan measured him with his eyes. 'I believe you,' he said. He went back to the living room to wait for Reynaldo to dry off and get dressed.

When Flemm came out, wearing an absurd muscle shirt and tight jeans, Stranahan said, 'When are you going to see the doctor?'

'Soon,' Reynaldo replied. Then, blustery: 'None of your business.' He felt so much tougher with a shirt on.

Stranahan said, 'If you wait, you'll have a better story.'

Reynaldo rolled his eyes – how many times had he heard that one! 'No way,' he said. The snide pomposity had returned to his voice.

'Ray, I'm only going to warn you once. If something's happened to Christina because of you, or if you do something that brings her any harm, you're done. And I'm not talking about your precious TV career.'

Flemm said, 'You sound pretty tough, long as you've got that hook.'

Stranahan tossed the tarpon gaff at Reynaldo and said, 'There – see if it works for you, too.'

Reynaldo quickly dropped it on the carpet. As a rule he didn't fight with crazy people unless cameras were rolling. Otherwise, what was the point?

'I hope you find her,' Reynaldo said.

Stranahan stood to leave. 'You better pray that I do.'

At the Gay Bidet, Freddie didn't even bother to get up from the desk to introduce himself. 'I'm gonna tell you the same as I told that Cuban cop, which is nothing. I got a policy not to talk about employees, past or present.'

Stranahan said, 'But you know the man I'm asking about.'

'Maybe, maybe not.'

'Is he here?'

'Ditto,' said Freddie. 'Now get the fuck gone.'

'Actually, I'm going to look around.'

'Oh, you are?' Freddie said. 'Like hell.' He punched a black buzzer under the desk. The door opened and Stranahan momentarily was drowned by the vocal stylings of the Fabulous Foreskins, performing their opening set.

The man who entered Freddie's office was a short muscular Oriental. He wore a pink Gay Bidet security T-shirt, stretched to the limit.

Freddie said, 'Wong, please get this dog turd out of my sight.'

Stranahan waved the tarpon gaff and its sinister glint caused Wong to hesitate. Disdainfully Freddie glowered at the bouncer and said, 'What happened to all that kung fu shit?'

Wong's chest began to swell.

Stranahan said, 'I've had a lousy day, and I'm really in no mood. You like having a liquor licence?'

Freddie said, 'What're you talkin' about, do I like it?'

'Because you oughta enjoy it tonight, while you can. If you don't answer my questions, here's what happens to you and this toilet bowl of a nightclub: first thing tomorrow, six nasty bastards from Alcohol and Beverage come by and shut your ass down. Why? Because you lied when you got your liquor licence, Freddie. You got a felony record in Illinois and Georgia, and you lied about that. Also, you've been serving to minors, big time. Also, your bartender just tried to sell me two grammes of Peruvian. You want, I can keep going.'

Freddie said, 'Don't bother.' He instructed Wong to get lost. When they were alone again, he said to Stranahan, 'That rap in Atlanta was no good.'

'So you're not a pimp. Excellent. The beverage guys will be very impressed, Freddie. Be sure to tell them you're not a pimp, no matter what the FBI computer says.'

'What the fuck is it you want?'

'Just tell me where I can find my tall, cool friend. The one with the face.'

Freddie said, 'Truth is, I don't know. He took off a couple days ago. Picked up his paycheque and quit. Tried to give me back the T-shirt, the dumb fuck – like somebody else would wear the damn thing. I told him to keep it for a souvenir.'

'Did he say where he was going?' Stranahan asked.

'Nope. He had two broads with him, you figure it

out.' Freddie flashed a mouthful of nubby yellow teeth. 'Creature from the Black Lagoon, and still he gets more poon than me.'

'What did the women look like?' Stranahan asked.

'One, I couldn't tell. Her face was all busted up, cuts and bruises and Band-Aids. He must've beat the hell out of her for something. The other was a brunette, good-looking, on the thin side. Not humungous titties but nice pointy ones.'

Stranhan couldn't decide whether it was Freddie or the music that was aggravating his headache. 'The thin one – was she wearing blue jeans?'

Freddie said he didn't remember.

'Did they say anything?'

'Nope, not a word.'

'Did he have a gun?'

Freddie laughed again. 'Man, he doesn't need a gun. He has that whirly thing on his arm.' Freddie told Stranahan what the thing was and how the man known as Chemo would use it.

'You're kidding.'

'Like hell,' said Freddie. 'Guy was the best goddamn bouncer I ever had.'

Stranahan handed the club owner a fifty-dollar bill and the phone number of the bait shop at the marina. 'This is in case he comes back. You call me before you call the cops.'

Freddie pocketed the money. Reflectively he said: 'Freak like that with two broads, man, it just proves there's no God.'

'We'll see,' said Stranahan.

28

Chemo's first instinct was to haul ass with the doctor's cash, which was more than he would see in a couple of Amish lifetimes. Forget about the Stranahan hit, just blow town. Maggie Gonzalez told him, don't be such a small-timer, remember what we've got here: a surgeon on the hook. A money machine, for God's sake. Maggie assured him that a million, even two million, was do-able. There wasn't anything that Rudy Graveline wouldn't give to save his medical licence.

Goosing the Bonneville along Biscayne Boulevard, Chemo said, 'What I've got now, I could get my face patched and still have enough for a year in Barbados. Maybe even get some real hair – those plug deals they stick in your scalp. I read where that's what they did to Elton John.'

'Sure,' Maggie said. 'I know some doctors who do hair.'

She was trying to play Chemo the way she had played all her men, but it wasn't easy. Beyond his desire for a clear complexion, she had yet to discover what motivated him. While Chemo appreciated money, he hardly displayed the proper lust for it. As for sex, he expressed no interest whatsoever. Maggie chose to believe that he was deterred by her bruises and bandages; once the facelift had healed, her powers of seduction would return. Then the only obstacle would be a logistical one: what would you do with the Weed Whacker under the sheets?

As Chemo pulled up on the Holiday Inn at 125th Street, Maggie said, 'If it would make you feel better, we could move to a nicer hotel.'

'What would make me feel better,' Chemo said, 'is for you to give me the keys to the suitcase.' He turned off the ignition and held out his right hand.

Maggie said, 'You think I'm dumb enough to try and rip you off?'

'Yes,' said Chemo, reaching for her purse. 'Plenty dumb enough.'

Christina Marks heard the door open and prayed it was the maid. It wasn't.

The lights came on and Chemo loomed incuriously over the bed. He checked the knots at Christina's wrists and ankles, while Maggie stalked into the bathroom and slammed the door.

After Chemo removed the towel from her mouth, Christina said, 'What's the matter with her?'

'She thinks I don't trust her. She's right.'

'For what it's worth,' Christina said, 'she already conned my boss out of a bundle.'

'I'll keep that in mind.' Chemo sat on the corner of the bed, counting the cash that he had taken from Dr Rudy Graveline's pockets. Counting wasn't easy with only one hand. Christina watched inquisitively. After he was finished, Chemo put five thousand in the suitcase with the rest of the haul; forty-two hundred went down the heels of his boots. He slid the suitcase under the bed.

'How original,' Christina said.

'Shut up.'

'Could you untie me, please? I have to pee.'

'Jesus H. Christ.'

'You want me to wet the bed?' she said. 'Ruin all your cash?'

Chemo got Maggie out of the bathroom and made her help undo the knots. They had bound Christina to the bed frame with nylon clothesline. Once freed, she rubbed her wrists and sat up stiffly.

'Go do your business,' Chemo said. Then, to Maggie: 'Stay with her.'

Christina said, 'I can't pee with somebody watching.'

'What?'

'She's right,' Maggie said. 'I'm the same way. I'll just wait outside the door.'

'No, do what I told you,' Chemo said.

'There's no window in there,' Christina said. 'What'm I going to do, escape down the toilet?'

When she came out of the bathroom, Chemo was standing by the door. He led her back to the bed, made her lie down, then tied her again – another tedious chore, one-handed.

'No gag this time,' Christina requested. 'I promise not to scream.'

'But you'll talk,' said Chemo. 'That's even worse.'

Since the morning he had kidnapped her from the hotel on Key Biscayne, Chemo had said practically nothing to Christina Marks. Nor had he menaced or abused her in any sense – it was as if he knew that the mere sight of him, close up, was daunting enough. Christina had spied the butt of a revolver in Chemo's baggy pants pocket, but he had never pulled it; this was a big improvement over the two previous encounters, when he had nearly shot her.

She said, 'I just want to know why you're doing this, what exactly you want.'

He acted as if he never heard her. Maggie handed Christina a small cup of Pepsi.

'Don't let her drink too much,' Chemo cautioned. 'She'll be going to the head all night.'

He turned on the television set and grimaced: pro basketball – the Lakers and the Pistons. Chemo hated basketball. At six foot nine, he had spent his entire adulthood explaining to rude strangers that no, he didn't play pro basketball. Once a myopic Celtics fan had mistaken him for Kevin McHale and demanded an autograph; Chemo had savagely bitten the man on the shoulder, like a horse.

He began switching channels until he found an old *Miami Vice*. He turned up the volume and scooted his chair closer to the tube. He envied Don Johnson's three-day stubble; it looked rugged and manly. Chemo himself had not shaved, for obvious reasons, since the electrolysis accident.

He turned to Maggie and asked, 'Can they do hair plugs on your chin, too?'

'Oh, I'm sure,' she said, though in fact she had never heard of such a procedure.

Pinned to the bed like a butterfly, Christina said, 'Before long, somebody's going to be looking for me.'

Chemo snorted. 'That's the general idea.' Didn't these women ever shut up? Didn't they appreciate his potential for violence?

Maggie sat next to Christina and said, 'We need to get a message to your boyfriend.'

307

'Who – Stranahan? He's not my boyfriend.'

'Still, I doubt if he wants to see you get hurt.'

Christina appraised herself – strapped to a bed, squirming in her underwear – and imagined what Reynaldo Flemm would say if he came crashing through the door. For once she'd be happy to see the stupid sonofabitch, but she knew there was no possibility of such a rescue. If Mick couldn't find her, Ray didn't have a prayer.

'If it's that videotape you're after, I don't know where it is—'

'But surely your boyfriend does,' said Maggie.

Chemo pointed at the television. 'Hey, lookie there!' On the screen, Detective Sonny Crockett was chasing a drug smuggler through Stiltsville in a speedboat. This was the first time Christina had seen Chemo smile. It was a harrowing experience.

Maggie said, 'So how do you get in touch with him?'

'Mick? I don't know. There's no phone out there. Any time I wanted to see him, I rented a boat.'

A commercial came on the television, and Chemo turned to the women. 'Jesus, I don't want to go back to that house – enough of that shit. I want him to come see me. And he will, soon as he knows I've got you.'

In her most lovelorn voice, Christina said to Maggie, 'I really don't think Mick cares one way or the other.'

'You better hope he does,' said Chemo. He pressed the towel firmly into Christina's mouth and turned back to watch the rest of the show.

On the morning of February eighteenth, the last day of Kipper Garth's law career, he filed a motion with the Circuit Court of Dade County in the cause of Nordstrom v. Graveline, Whispering Palms, *et al*.

The motion requested an emergency court order freezing all the assets of Dr Rudy Graveline, including bank accounts, certificates of deposit, stock portfolios, municipal bonds, Keogh funds, Individual Retirement Accounts, and real estate holdings. Submitted to the judge with Kipper Garth's motion was an affidavit from the Beachcomber

Travel Agency stating that, on the previous day, one Rudolph Graveline had purchased two first-class aeroplane tickets to San José, Costa Rica. In the plea (composed entirely by Mick Stranahan and one of the paralegals), Kipper Garth asserted that it was Dr Graveline's intention to flee the United States permanently.

Normally, a request involving a defendant's assets would have resulted in a full-blown hearing and, most likely, a denial of the motion. But Kipper Garth's position (and thus the Nordstroms') was buttressed by a discreet phone call from Mick Stranahan to the judge, whom Stranahan had known since his days as a young prosecutor in the DUI division. After a brief reminiscence, Stranahan told the judge the true reason for his call; that Dr Rudy Graveline was a prime suspect in an unsolved four-year-old abduction case that might or might not be a homicide. Stranahan assured his friend that, rather than face the court, the surgeon would take his dough and make a run for it.

The judge granted the emergency order shortly after nine o'clock in the morning. Kipper Garth was astonished at his own success; he never dreamed litigation could be so damn easy. He fantasized a day when he could get out of the referral racket altogether, when he would be known and revered throughout Miami as a master trial attorney. Kipper Garth liked the billboards, though. However high he might soar among the eagles of Brickell Avenue, the billboards definitely had to stay . . .

At ten forty-five, Rudy Graveline arrived at his bank in Bal Harbour and asked to make a wire transfer of $250,000 from his personal account to a new account in Panama. He also requested $60,000 in US currency and traveller's cheques. The young bank officer who was assisting Rudy Graveline left his office for several minutes. When he returned, one of the bank's vice presidents stood solemnly at his side.

Rudy took the news badly.

First he wept, which was merely embarrassing. Then he became enraged and hysterical and, finally, incoherent. He staggered, keening, into the bank lobby, at which point two enormous security guards were summoned to escort the surgeon from the premises.

By the time they deposited Rudy in the parking lot, he had settled himself and stopped crying.

Until one of the bank guards had pointed at the fender of the car and said, 'The hell happened to your Jag, brother?'

Perhaps it was the euphoria of a legal triumph, or perhaps it was simple prurient curiosity that impelled Kipper Garth to drop by the Nordstrom household during his lunch hour. The address was in Morningside, a pleasant old neighbourhood of bleached stucco houses located a few blocks off the seediest stretch of Biscayne Boulevard.

Marie Nordstrom was surprised to see Kipper Garth, but she welcomed him warmly at the door, led him to the Florida room, and offered him a cup of coffee. She wore electric-blue Lycra body tights, and her ash-blond hair was pulled back in a girlish ponytail. Kipper couldn't take his eyes off the subject of litigation, her breasts. The exercise outfit left nothing to the imagination; these were the merriest-looking breasts that Kipper Garth had ever seen. It was difficult to think of them as weapons.

'John's not here,' Mrs Nordstrom said. 'He got a job interview over at the jai-alai fronton. You take cream?'

Kipper Garth took cream. Mrs Nordstrom placed the coffee pot on a glass tray. Kipper Garth made space for her on the sofa, but she moved to a love seat, facing him from across the coffee table.

Kipper Garth said, 'I just wanted to bring you up to date on the malpractice case.' Matter-of-factly he told Mrs Nordstrom about the emergency court order to freeze Dr Graveline's assets.

'What exactly does that mean?'

'It means his money won't be going anywhere, even if he does.'

Mrs Nordstrom was not receiving the news as exuberantly as Kipper Garth had hoped; apparently she could not appreciate the difficulty of what he had done.

310

'John and I were talking just last night,' she said. 'The idea of going to trial . . . I don't know, Mr Garth. This has been so embarrassing for both of us.'

'We're in it now, Mrs Nordstrom. There's no turning back.' Kipper Garth tried to suppress the exasperation in his voice: here Rudy Graveline was on the ropes and suddenly the plaintiffs want to back out.

'Maybe the doctor would be willing to settle the case,' ventured Mrs Nordstrom.

Kipper Garth put down the coffee cup with a clack and folded his arms. 'Oh, I'm sure he would. I'm sure he'd be delighted to settle. That's exactly why we won't hear of it. Not yet.'

'But John says— '

'Trust me,' the lawyer said. He paused and lowered his eyes. 'Forgive me for saying so, Mrs Nordstrom, but settling this case would be very selfish on your part.'

She looked startled at the word.

Kipper Garth went on: 'Think of all the patients this man has harmed. This *alleged* surgeon. If we don't stop him, nobody will. If you settle the case, Mrs Nordstrom, the butchery will continue. You and your husband will be wealthy, yes, but Rudy Graveline's butchery will continue. At his instruction, the court file will be sealed and his reputation preserved. Again. Is that really what you want?'

Kipper Garth had listened intently to his own words, and was impressed by what he had heard; he was getting damn good at oratory.

A few awkward moments passed and Mrs Nordstrom said, 'They've got an opening for a coach over at the jai-alai. John used to play in college, he was terrific. He even went to Spain one summer and trained with the Basques.'

Kipper Garth had never heard of a Scandinavian jai-alai coach, but his knowledge of the sport was limited. Oozing sincerity, he told Mrs Nordstrom that he hoped her husband got the job.

She said, 'Thing is, he can't tell anybody about his eye. They'd never hire him.'

'Why not?'

'Too dangerous,' Mrs Nordstrom said. 'The ball they use is like a rock. A *pelota* it's called. John says it goes like a hundred sixty miles an hour off those walls.'

Kipper Garth finished his coffee. 'I've never been to a jai-alai game.' He hoped she would take the hint and change the conversation.

'If you're playing, it helps to have two good eyes,' Mrs Nordstrom explained. 'For depth perception.'

'I think I understand.'

'John says they won't let him coach if they find out about the accident.'

Now Kipper Garth got the picture. 'That's why you want to settle the lawsuit, isn't it?'

Mrs Nordstrom said yes, they were worried about publicity. 'John says the papers and the TV will go crazy with a story like this.'

Kipper thought: John is absolutely right.

'But you're a victim, Mrs Nordstrom. You have the right to be compensated for this terrible event in your life. It says so in the Constitution.'

'John says they let cameras in the courtrooms. Is that true?'

'Yes, but let's not get carried away— '

'If it were your wife, would you want the whole world to see her tits on the six o'clock news?' Her tone was prideful and indignant.

'I'll speak to the judge, Mrs Nordstrom. Please don't be upset. I know you've been through hell already.' But Kipper Garth was excited by the idea of TV cameras in the courtroom – it would be better than billboards!

Marie Nordstrom was trying not to cry and doing stolidly. She said, 'I blame that damn Reagan. He hadn't busted up the union, John'd still have his job in the flight tower.'

Kipper Garth said, 'Leave it to me and the two of you will be set for life. John won't need a job.

Mrs Nordstrom wistfully gazed at the two sturdy, silicon-enhanced, Lycra-covered cones on her chest. 'They say contractures are easy to fix, but I don't know.'

Kipper Garth circled the coffee table and joined her on the love seat. He put an unpractised arm around her shoulders. 'For what it's worth,' he said, 'they *look* spectacular.'

'Thank you,' she whispered, 'but you just don't know – how could you?'

Kipper Garth removed the silk handkerchief from his breast pocket and gave it to Mrs Nordstrom, who sounded like the SS *Norway* when she blew her nose.

'Know what I think?' said Kipper Garth. 'I think you should let me feel them.'

Mrs Nordstrom straightened and gave a stern sniffle.

The lawyer said: 'The only way I can begin to understand, the only way I can convey the magnitude of this tragedy to a jury, is if I can experience it myself.'

'Wait a minute – you want to feel my boobs?'

'I'm your lawyer, Mrs Nordstrom.'

She eyed him doubtfully.

'If it were a burn case, I'd have to see the scar. Dismemberment, paraplegia, same goes.'

'Looking is one thing, Mr Garth. Touching is something else.'

'With all respect, Mrs Nordstrom, your husband is going to make a lousy witness in this case. He's going to come across as a selfish prick. Remember what he said that day in my office? Bocci balls, Mrs Nordstrom. He said your breasts were hard as bocci balls. This is not the testimony of a sensitive, caring spouse.'

She said, 'You'd be bitter, too, if it was your eye that got poked out.'

'Granted. But let me try to come up with a more gentle description of your condition. Please, Mrs Nordstrom.'

'All right, but I won't take my clothes off.'

'Of course not!'

She slid a little closer on the love seat. 'Give me your hands,' she said. 'There you go.'

313

'Wow,' said Kipper Garth.

'What'd I tell you?'

'I had no idea.'

'You can let go now,' Mrs Nordstrom said.

'Just a second.'

But one second turned into ten seconds, and ten seconds turned into thirty, which was plenty of time for John Nordstrom to enter the house and size up the scene. Without a word he loaded up the wicker *cesta* and hurled a goatskin jai-alai ball at the slimy lawyer who was feeling up his wife. The first shot sailed wide to the left and shattered a jalousie window. The second shot dimpled the arm of the love seat with a flat *thunk*. It was then that Kipper Garth released his grip on Marie Nordstrom's astoundingly stalwart breasts and made a vain break for the back door. Whether the lawyer fully comprehended his ethical crisis or fled on sheer animal instinct would never be known. John Nordstrom's third and final jai-alai shot struck the occipital seam of Kipper Garth's skull. He was unconscious by the time his silvery head smacked the floor.

'Ha!' Nordstrom exclaimed.

'I take it you got the job,' said his wife.

Willie the cameraman said they had two ways to go; they could crash the place or sneak one in.

Reynaldo Flemm said: 'Crash it.'

'Think of the timing,' Willie said. 'The timing's got to be flawless. We've never tried anything like this.' Willie was leaning toward trying a hidden camera.

Reynaldo said: 'Crash it. There's no security, it's a goddamn medical clinic. Who's gonna stop you, the nurse?'

Willie said he didn't like the plan; too many holes. 'What if the guy makes a run for it? What if he calls the police?'

Reynaldo said: 'Where's he gonna go, Willie? That's the beauty of this thing. The sonofabitch can't run away, and he knows it. Not with the tape rolling. They got laws.'

'Jesus,' Willie said, 'I don't like it. We've got to have a signal, you and me.'

'Don't worry,' Reynaldo said, 'we'll have a signal.'

'But what about the interview?' Willie asked. It was another way of bringing up Christina Marks.

'I wrote my own questions,' Reynaldo said sharply. 'Ball busters, too. You just wait.'

'OK,' Willie said. 'I'll be ready.'

'Seven sharp,' Reynaldo said. 'I can't believe you're so nervous – this isn't the Crips and Bloods, man, it's a candyass doctor. He'll go to pieces, I guarantee it. True confessions, you just wait.'

'Seven sharp,' Willie said. 'See you then.'

After the cameraman had gone, Reynaldo Flemm called the Whispering Palms Spa and Surgery Center to confirm the appointment for Johnny LeTigre. To his surprise, the secretary put him through directly to Dr Graveline.

'We still on for tomorrow morning?'

'Certainly,' the surgeon said. He sounded distracted, subdued. 'Remember: nothing to eat or drink after midnight.'

'Right.'

'I thought we'd start with the rhinoplasty and go on to the liposuction.'

'Fine by me,' said Reynaldo Flemm. That's exactly how he had planned it, the nose job first.

'Mr LeTigre, I had a question regarding the fee . . . '

'Fifteen thousand is what we agreed on.'

'Correct,' said Rudy Graveline, 'but I just wanted to make sure – you said something about cash?'

'Yeah, that's right. I got cash.'

'And you'll have it with you tomorrow?'

'You bet.' Reynaldo couldn't believe this jerk. Probably grosses two million a year, and here he is drooling over a lousy fifteen grand. It was true what they said about doctors being such cheap bastards.

'Anything else I need to remember?'

'Just take plenty of fluids,' Rudy said mechanically, 'but nothing after midnight.'

'I'll be a good boy,' Reynaldo Flemm promised. 'See you tomorrow.'

29

The wind kicked up overnight, whistled through the planks of the house, slapped the shutters against the walls. Mick Stranahan climbed naked to the roof and lay down with the shotgun at his right side. The bay was noisy and black, hissing through the pilings beneath the house. Above, the clouds rolled past in churning grey clots, celestial dust devils tumbling across a low sky. As always, Stranahan lay facing away from the city, where the halogen crime lights stained an otherwise lovely horizon. On nights such as this, Stranahan regarded the city as a malignancy and its sickly orange aura as a vast misty bubble of pustular gas. The downtown skyline, which had seemed to sprout overnight in a burst of civic priapism, struck Stranahan as a crass but impressive prop, an elaborate movie set. Half the new Miami skyscrapers had been built with coke money and existed largely as an inside joke, a mirage to please the banks and the Internal Revenue Service and the chamber of commerce. Everyone liked to say that the skyline was a monument to local prosperity, but Stranahan recognized it as a tribute to the anonymous genius of Latin American money launderers. In any case, it was nothing he wished to contemplate from the top of his stilt house. Nor was the view south of downtown any kinder, a throbbing congealment from Coconut Grove to the Gables to South Miami and beyond. Looking westward on a clearer evening, Stranahan would have fixed on the newest coastal landmark: a sheer ten-storey cliff of refuse known as Mount Trashmore. Having run out of rural locations in which to conceal its waste, Dade County had erected a towering fetid landfill along the shore of Biscayne Bay. Stranahan could not decide which sight was more offensive, the city skyline or the mountain of garbage. The turkey buzzards, equally ambivalent, commuted regularly from one site to the other.

Stranahan was always grateful for a clean ocean breeze. He sprawled on the eastern slope of the roof, facing the Atlantic. A DC-10 took off from Miami International and passed over Stiltsville, rattling the windmill on Stranahan's house. He wondered what it would be like to wake up and find the city vaporized, the skies clear and silent, the shoreline lush and virginal! He would have loved to live here at the turn of the century, when nature owned the upper hand.

The cool wind tickled the hair on his chest and legs. Stranahan tasted salt on his lips and closed his eyes. One of his ex-wives, he couldn't remember which, had told him he ought to move to Alaska and become a hermit. You're such an old grump, she had said, not even the grizzly bears'd put up with you. Now Stranahan recalled which wife had said this: Donna, his second. She had eventually grown tired of all his negativity. Every big city has crime, she had said. Every big city has corruption. Look at New York, she had said. Look at Chicago. Those are great goddamn cities, Mick, you gotta admit. Like so many cocktail waitresses, Donna steadfastly refused to give up on humanity. She believed that the good people of the world outnumbered the bad, and she got the tips to prove it. After the divorce, she had enrolled in night school and earned her Florida real estate licence; Stranahan had heard she'd moved to Jacksonville and was going great guns in the waterfront condo market. Bleakly it occurred to him that all his former wives (even Chloe, who had nailed a CPA for a husband) had gone on to greater achievements after the divorce. It was if being married to Stranahan had made each of them realize how much of the real world they were missing.

He thought of Christina Marks. How did he get mixed up with such a serious woman? Unlike the others he had loved and married, Christina avidly pursued that which was evil and squalid and polluted. Her job was to expose it. There

317

was not a wisp of true innocence about her, not a trace of cheery waitress-type optimism . . . yet something powerful attracted him. Maybe because she slogged through the same moral swamps. Crooked cops, crooked layers, crooked doctors, crooked ex-wives, even crooked tree trimmers – these were the spawn of the city bog.

Stranahan's fingers found the stock of the shot-gun, and he moved it closer. Soon he fell asleep, and he dreamed that Victoria Barletta was alive. He dreamed that he met her one night in the Rathskellar on the University of Miami campus. She was working behind the bar, wearing a pink butterfly bandage across the bridge of her nose. Stranahan ordered a beer and a cheeseburger medium, and asked her if she wanted to get married. She said sure.

The boat woke him up. It was a familiar yellow skiff with a big outboard. Stranahan saw it a mile away, trimmed up, running the flats. He smiled – the bonefish guide, his friend. With all the low dirty clouds it was difficult to estimate the time, but Stranahan figured the sun had been up no more than two hours. He dropped from the roof, stowed the Remington inside the house, and pulled on a pair of jeans so as not to startle the guide's customers, who were quite a pair. The man was sixty-five, maybe older, obese and grey, with skin like rice parchment; the woman was twenty-five tops, tall, dark blond, wearing bright coral lip gloss and a gold choker necklace.

The guide climbed up to the stilt house and said, 'Mick, take a good look. Fucking lipstick on a day like this.'

From the skiff, tied up below, Stranahan could hear the couple arguing about the weather. The woman wanted to go back, since there wasn't any sun for a decent tan. The old man said no, he'd paid his money and by God they would fish.

Stranahan said to his friend, 'You've got the patience of Job.'

The guide shook his head. 'A killer mortgage is what I've got. Here, this is for you.'

It was an envelope with Stranahan's name printed in block letters on the outside. 'Woman with two black eyes told me to give it to you,' the guide said. 'Cuban girl, not bad looking, either. She offered me a hundred bucks.'

'Hope you took it.'

'I held out for two,' the guide said.

Stranahan folded the envelope in half and tucked it in the back pocket of his jeans.

The guide said, 'You in some trouble?'

'Just business.'

'Mick, you don't have a business.'

Stranahan grinned darkly. 'True enough.' He knew what his friend was thinking: single guy, cosy house on the water, a good boat for fishing, a monthly disability cheque from the state – how could anybody fuck up a sweet deal like that?

'I heard some asshole shot hell out of the place.'

'Yeah.' Stranahan pointed to a sheet of fresh plywood on the door. The plywood covered two of Chemo's bullet holes. 'I've got to get some red paint,' Stranahan said.

The guide said, 'Forget the house, what about your shoulder?'

'It's fine,' Stranahan said.

'Don't worry, it was Luis who told me.'

'No problem. You want some coffee?'

'Naw.' The bonefish guide jerked a thumb in the direction of his skiff. 'This old fart, he's on the board of some steel company up north. That's his secretary.'

'God bless him.'

The guide said, 'Last time they went fishing, I swear, she strips off the bottom of her bathing suit. Not the top, Mick, the bottom part. All day long, flashing her bush in my face. Said she was trying to bleach out her hair. Here I'm poling like a maniac after these goddamn fish, and she's turning somersaults in front of the boat, trying to keep her bush in the sun.'

Stranahan said, 'I don't know how you put up with it.'

'So today there's no sunshine and of course she's throwin' a fit. Meanwhile the old fart says all he wants is a world-record bonefish on fly. That's all. Mick, I'm too old for this shit.' The guide pulled on his cap so tightly that it crimped the tops of his ears. Lugubriously he descended the stairs to the dock.

'Good luck,' Stranahan said. Under the circumstances, it sounded ridiculous.

The guide untied the yellow skiff and hopped in. Before starting the engine, he looked up at Stranahan and said, 'I'll be out here tomorrow, even if the weather's bad. The next day, too.'

Stranahan nodded; it was good to know. 'Thanks, Captain,' he said.

After the skiff was gone, Stranahan returned to the top of the house and took the envelope out of his pocket. He opened it calmly because he knew what it was and who it was from. He'd been waiting for it.

The message said: 'We've got your girlfriend. No cops!' And it gave a telephone number.

Mick Stranahan memorized the number, crumpled the paper, and tossed it off the roof into the milky waves. 'Somebody's been watching too much television,' he said.

That afternoon, Mick Stranahan received another disturbing message. It was delivered by Luis Córdova, the young marine patrol officer. He gave Stranahan a lift by boat from Stiltsville to the Crandon Marina, where Stranahan got a cab to his sister Kate's house in Gables-by-the-Sea.

Sergeant Al García was fidgeting on the front terrace. Over his J. C. Penney suit he was wearing what appeared to be an authentic London Fog trenchcoat. Stranahan knew that García was upset because he was smoking those damn Camels again. Even before Stranahan could finish paying the cabbie, García was charging down the driveway, blue smoke streaming from his nostrils like one of those cartoon bulls.

'So,' the detective said, 'Luis fill you in?'

Stranahan said yes, he knew that Kipper Garth had been gravely injured in a domestic dispute.

García blocked his path up the drive. 'By a client, Mick. Imagine that.'

'I didn't know the client, Al.'

'Name of Nordstrom, John Nordstrom.' García was working the sodden nub of the Camel the same way he worked the cigars, from one side of his mouth to the other. Stranahan found it extremely distracting.

'According to the wife,' García said, 'the assailant returned home unexpectedly and found your brother-in-law, the almost deceased— '

'Thank you, Al.'

' —found the almost deceased fondling his wife. Whereupon the assailant attempted to strike the almost deceased at least three times with *pelotas*. That's a jai-alai ball, Mick. The third shot struck your brother-in-law at the base of the skull, rendering him unconscious.'

'The dumb shit. How's Kate?'

'Puzzled,' García said. 'But then, aren't we all?'

'I want to see her.' Stranahan sidestepped the detective and made for the front door. His sister was standing by the bay window of the Florida room and staring out at Kipper Garth's sailboat, the *Pain-and-Suffering*, which was rocking placidly at the dock behind the house. Stranahan gave Kate a hug and kissed her on the forehead.

She sniffed and said, 'Did they tell you?'

'Yes, Kate.'

'That he was groping a client – did they tell you?'

Stranahan said, 'That's the woman's story.'

Kate gave a bitter chuckle. 'And you don't believe it? Come on, Mick, *I* believe it. Kipper was a pig, let's face it. You were right, I was wrong.'

Stranahan didn't know what to say. 'He had some good qualities.' Jesus, how stupid. '*Has* some good qualities, I mean.'

'The doctors say it's fifty-fifty, but I'm ready for the worst. Kipper's not a fighter.'

'He might surprise you,' Stranahan said without conviction.

'Mick, just so you know – I was aware of what he was up to. Some of the excuses, God, you should have heard them. Late nights, weekends, trips to God knows where. I pretended to believe him because . . . because I like this life, Mick. The house . . . this great yard. I mean, it sounds selfish, but it felt *good* here. Safe. This is a wonderful neighbourhood.'

'Katie, I'm sorry.'

'Neighbourhoods like this are hard to find, Mick. You know, we've only been burglarized twice in four years. That's not bad for Miami.'

'Not at all,' Stranahan said.

'See, I had to weigh these things every time I thought about leaving.' Kate put a hand on his arm and said, 'You know about all his fooling around.'

'Not everything.'

'Thanks for not mentioning it.' She was sincere.

Stranahan felt like a complete shit, which he was. 'This is my fault,' he said. 'I told Kipper to take this case. I *made* him take it.'

'How?' she asked. 'And why?'

'Whatever you're thinking, it's even worse. I can't tell you the details, Kate, because there's going to be trouble and I want you clear of it. But you ought to know that I'm the one who got Kipper involved.'

'But you're not the one who played grab-the-tittie with your client. *He* did.' She turned back to the big window and folded her arms. 'It's so . . . tacky.'

'Yes,' Stranahan agreed. 'Tacky's the word.'

When he came out of the house, García was waiting.

'Wasn't that courteous of me, not barging in and making a big Cuban scene in front of your sister?'

'Al, you're a fucking prince among men.'

'Know why I'm wearing this trenchcoat? It's brand new,

by the way. I hadda go to another funeral: Bobby Pepsical, the county commissioner. Dropped dead in confession.'

'Good place for it. He was a stone crook.'

'Course he was, Mick. But I got a feeling he didn't get his penance.'

'Why not?'

'Because there wasn't a priest in there. Bobby's confessing to an empty closet – that's pretty weird, huh? Anyway, they make a bunch of us go to the fucking funeral, because of who he was. That's why I've got the new coat. It was raining.'

Stranahan said, 'How was it? Did they screw him into the ground? That's about how crooked he was.'

'I know, but Christ, have some respect for the dead.' García rubbed his temples like he was massaging a cramp. 'See, this is what's got me so agitated, Mick. Ever since I got into this thing with you and the doctor, so many people are dying. Dying weird, too. There's your ex, and Murdock and Salazar – another funeral! Then the business with that goddamn homicidal tree man. So after all that, here I am standing in the rain, watching them plant some scuzzbucket politician who croaks on his knees in an empty confessional, and my frigging beeper goes off. Lieutenant says some big-shot lawyer got beaned by a jai-alai ball and could be a homicide any second. A jai-alai ball! On top of which the big-shot lawyer turns out to be *your* brother-in-law. It's like a nightmare of weirdness!'

'It's been a bad month,' Stranahan conceded.

'Yeah, it sure has. So what about these Nordstroms?'

'I didn't know them, I told you.'

García lit up another cigarette and Stranahan made a face. 'Know why I'm smoking these things? Because I'm agitated. I get agitated whenever I get jerked around, and I hate to waste a good cigar on agitation.'

Stranahan said, 'Can you please not blow it in my face? That's all I ask.'

The detective took the cigarette out of his mouth and held it behind his back. 'There, you happy? Now help me out, Mick. The assailant's wife, she says Kipper Garth phones her out of the blue and asks if she wants to sue – guess who – Rùdy Graveline! Since he's the quack who gave her the encapsulated whatchamacallits.'

'If that's what she says, fine.'

'But lawyers aren't supposed to solicit.'

'Al, this is Miami.'

García took a quick drag and hid the Camel again. 'My theory is you somehow got your sleazy, almost-deceased brother-in-law to sue Graveline, just to bust his balls. Shake things up. Maybe flush the giant Mr Blondell Tatum out of his fugitive gutter. I don't expect you to open up your heart, Mick, but just tell me this: did it work? Because if it did, you're a fucking genius and I apologize for all the shitty things I've been saying about you in my sleep.'

'Did what work?'

García grinned venomously. 'I thought we were buddies.'

'Al, I'm not going to shut you out,' Stranahan said. 'For God's sake, you saved my life.'

'Aw, shucks, you remembered.'

Stranahan said: 'Which one do you want, Al? The freaky hit man or the doctor?'

'Both.'

'No, I'm sorry.'

'Hey, I could arrest your ass right now. Obstruction, tampering, I'd think of something.'

'And I'd be out in an hour.'

García's jaw tightened for a moment and he turned away, stewing. When he turned back, he seemed more amused than angry.

'The problem is, Mick, you're too smart. You know the system too damn well. You know there's only so much I can get away with.'

'Believe me, we're on the same side.'

'I know, *chico*, that's what scares me.'

'So, which of these bastards do you want for yourself – the surgeon or the geek?'

'Don't rush me, Mick.'

30

Early on the morning of February nineteenth, Reynaldo Flemm, the famous Shock Television journalist, arrived at the Whispering Palms Spa and Surgery Center for the most sensational interview of his sensational career. A sleepy receptionist collected the $15,000 cash and counted it twice; if she was surprised by the size of the surgeon's fee, she didn't show it. The receptionist handed Reynaldo Flemm two photocopied consent forms, one for a phinoplasty and one for a suction-assisted lipectomy. Reynaldo skimmed the paperwork and extravagantly signed as 'Johnny LeTigre'.

Then he sat down to wait for his moment. On a buff-coloured wall hung a laminated carving of one of Rudy Graveline's pet sayings: TO IMPROVE ONE'S SELF, IMPROVE ONE'S FACE. That wasn't Reynaldo's favourite Rudyism. His favourite was framed in quilted Norman Rockwell-style letters above the water fountain: VANITY IS BEAUTIFUL. That's the one Reynaldo had told Willie about. Be sure to get a quick shot on your way in, he had told him. What for? Willie had asked. For the irony, Reynaldo Flemm had exclaimed. For the irony! Reynaldo was proud of himself for thinking up that camera shot; usually Christina Marks was in charge of finding irony.

Soon an indifferent young nurse summoned Reynaldo to a chilly examining room and instructed him to empty his bladder, a tedious endeavour that took fifteen minutes and produced scarcely an ounce. Reynaldo Flemm was a very nervous man. In his professional life he had been beaten by Teamsters, goosed by white supremacists, clubbed by Mafia torpedoes, pistol-whipped by Bandito bikers, and kicked in the groin by the Pro-Life Posse. But he had never undergone surgery. Not even a wart removal.

Flemm stiffly removed his clothes and pulled off his high

325

top Air Jordans. He changed into a baby-blue paper gown that hung to his knees. The nurse gave him a silly paper cap to cover his silly dyed hair, and paper shoe covers for his bare feet.

A nurse anaesthetist came out of nowhere, brusquely flipped up the tail of Reynaldo's gown and stuck a needle in his hip. The hypodermic contained a drug called Robinul, which dries up the mouth by inhibiting oral secretions. Next the nurse seized Reynaldo's left arm, swabbed it, and stuck it cleanly with an IV needle that dripped into his veins a lactated solution of five per cent dextrose and, later, assorted powerful sedatives.

The anaesthetist then led Reynaldo Flemm and his IV apparatus into Suite F, one of four ultramodern surgical theatres at Whispering Palms. She asked him to lie on his back and, as he stretched out on the icy steel, Reynaldo frantically tried to remember the ten searing questions he had prepared for the ambush of Dr Rudy Graveline.

One, did you kill Victoria Barletta on March 12, 1986?

Two, why would one of your former nurses say that you did?

Three, isn't it true that you've repeatedly gotten into trouble for careless and incompetent surgery?

Four, how do you explain . . .

Explain?

Explain this strap on my fucking legs!

'Please quiet down, Mr LeTigre.'

And my arms! What've you done to my arms? I can't move my goddamn arms!

'Try to relax. Think pleasant thoughts.'

Wait, wait, wait, wait, wait!

'You ought to be feeling a little drowsy.'

This is wrong. This is not right. I read up on this. I got a fucking pamphlet. You're supposed to tape my eyes, not my arms. What are you smiling at, you dumb twat? Lemme talk to the doctor! Where's the doctor? Jesus Christ, that's cold. What are you *doing* down there!

'Good morning, Mr LeTigre.'

Doctor, thank God you're here! Listen good now: these

326

Nazi nurse bitches are making a terrible mistake. I don't wanna general, I wanna local. Just pull the IV, OK? I'll be fine, just pull the tubes before I pass out.

'John, we're having a little trouble understanding you.'

No shit, Sherlock, my tongue's so dry you could light a match on it. Please yank the needles, I can't think with these damn needles. And make 'em quit fooling around with me down there. Christ, it's cold! What're they doing!

'I assumed they told you – there's been a change of plans. I've decided to do the lipectomy first, then the rhinoplasty. It'll be easier that way.'

No no no, you gotta do the nose first. Do the fucking nose.

'You should try to relax, John. Here, hold still, we're going to give you another injection.'

No no no no no no no.

'That didn't hurt a bit, did it?'

I wanna ask I gotta ask right now . . .

'Go ahead, push the Sublimaze.'

Did you kill . . . ?

'What did he say?'

Is it true you killed . . . ?

'This guy looks sort of familiar.'

Did you . . . kill Victoria . . . Principal?

'Victoria Principal! Boy, is he whacked out.'

Well did you?

'Where's the mask? Start the Forane. Give him the mask.'

Willie hadn't slept much, fretting about Reynaldo's big plan. He had tried to call Christina Marks in New York, but the office said she was in Miami. But where? Reynaldo's plan was the craziest thing Willie had ever heard, starting with the signal. Willie needed a signal to know when to come crashing into the operating room with the camera. The best that Reynaldo could come up with was a scream. Willie would be in the waiting room. Reynaldo would scream.

'What exactly will you scream?' Willie had asked.

'I'll scream: WILLIE!'

Willie thought Reynaldo was joking. He wasn't.

'What about the other patients in the waiting room? I mean, here I am with a TV camera and a sound pack – what do I tell these people?'

'Tell 'em you're from PBS,' Reynaldo had said. 'Nobody hassles PBS.'

The shot that Reynaldo Flemm most fervently wanted was this: himself prone, prepped, cloaked in blue, preferably in the early stages of rhinoplasty and preferably bloody. That was the good thing about a nose job, you could ask for a local. Most plastic surgeons want their rhinoplasty patients to be all the way zonked, but you could get it done with a local and a mild IV if you could stand a little pain. Reynaldo Flemm had no doubt he could stand it.

Willie would burst like a fullback into the operating room, tape rolling, toss the baton mike to Reynaldo on the table, Reynaldo would poke it in Rudy Graveline's face and pop the questions. Bam bam bam. The nurses and scrub techs would drop whatever they were doing and run, leaving the hapless surgeon to dissolve, alone, before the camera's eye.

Wait'll he realizes who I am, Reynaldo had chortled. Be sure you go extra tight on his face.

Willie had said he needed a soundman, but Reynaldo said no, out of the question; this was to be a streamlined attack.

Willie had said all right, then we need a better signal. Just screaming isn't good enough, he had said. What if somebody else starts screaming first, some other patient?

'Who else would scream your name?' Reynaldo had asked in a caustic tone. 'Listen to what I'm saying.'

The plan was bold and outrageous, Willie had to admit. No doubt it would cause a national sensation, stir up all the TV critics, not to mention Johnny Carson's gag writers. There would be a large amount of cynical speculation among Ray's colleagues that what he really wanted out of this caper was a free nose job – a theory that occurred even to Willie as he listened to Reynaldo map out the big ambush. The possibility of coast-to-coast media ridicule was no deterrent; the man seemed to relish being maligned as a hack and a clown and a shameless egomaniac. He said they were jealous, that's what they were. What other broadcast journalist in America had the guts to go under the knife just to get an interview? Mike Wallace? Not in a million years, the arrogant old prune. Bill Moyers? That liberal pussy would faint if he got a hangnail!

Yeah, Willie had said, it's quite a plan.

Brilliant, Reynaldo had crowed. Try brilliant.

However inspired, the plan's success depended on several crucial factors, not the least of which was the premise that Reynaldo Flemm would be conscious for the interview.

Although the surgical procedure known as liposuction, or fat sucking, was developed in France, it has achieved its greatest mass-market popularity in the United States. It is now the most common cosmetic procedure performed by plastic surgeons in the country, with more than a hundred thousand operations every year. The mortality rate for suction-assisted lipectomy is relatively low, about one death for every ten thousand patients. The odds of complications – which include blood clots, fat embolisms, chronic numbness, and severe bruising – increase considerably if the surgeon performing the liposuction has had little or no training in the procedure. Rudy Graveline fell decisively into this category – a doctor who had taken up liposuction for the simple reason that it was exceedingly lucrative. No state law or licensing board or medical review committee required Rudy to study liposuction first, or become proficient, or even be tested on his surgical competence before trying it. The same libertarian standards applied to rhinoplastics or haemorrhoidectomies or even brain surgery: Rudy Graveline was a licensed physician, and legally that meant he could try any damn thing he wanted.

He did not give two hoots about certification by the

American Board of Plastic Surgery, or the American Academy of Facial Plastic and Reconstructive Surgery, or the American Society of Plastic and Reconstructive Surgeons. What were a couple more snotty plaques on the wall? His patients could care less. They were rich and vain and impatient. In some exclusive South Florida circles, Rudy's name carried the glossy imprimatur of a Gucci or de La Renta. The lacquered old crones at La Gorce or the Biltmore would point at each other's shiny chins and taut necks and sculpted eyelids and ask, not in a whisper but a haughty bray, 'Is that a Graveline?'

Rudy was a designer surgeon. To have *him* suck your fat was an honour, a social plum, a mark (literally) of status. Only a boor, white trash or worse, would ever question the man's techniques or complain about the results.

Ironically, most of the surgeons who worked for Rudy Graveline at Whispering Palms were completely qualified to do suction lipectomies; they had actually trained for it – studied, observed, practised. While Rudy admired their dedication, he thought they were overdoing things – after all, how difficult could such an operation really be? The fat itself was abundantly easy to find. Suck it out, close 'em up, next case! Big deal.

To be on the safe side, Rudy read two journal articles about liposuction and ordered an instructional video cassette for $26.95 from a medical supply firm in Chicago. The journal articles turned out to be dense and fairly boring, but the video was an inspiration. Rudy came away convinced that any fool doctor with half a brain could vacuum fat with no problem.

The typical lipectomy patient was not a grotesque hypertensive blimp, but – like Johnny LeTigre – a healthy person of relatively normal stature and weight. The object of their complaint was medically mundane – bumper-car hips, droopy buttocks, gelantinous thighs, or old-fashioned 'love handles' at the waist. Properly performed, liposuction would remove contour. Improperly performed, the surgery would leave a patient lumpy and lopsided and looking for a lawyer.

On the morning of Reynaldo Flemm's undercover mission, nothing as sinister as a premonition caused Rudy Graveline to change his mind about doing the nose job first. What changed the doctor's mind, as usual, was money. Because a lipectomy usually required general anaesthesia, it was more labour-intensive (and costly) than a simple rhinoplasty. Rudy figured the sooner he could get done with the heavy stuff, the sooner he could get the anaesthetist and her gas machine off the clock. He could do the rhino later with intravenous sedation, which was much cheaper.

That Rudy Graveline could still worry about overhead at this point, with his career crumbling, was a tribute both to his power of concentration and his ingrained devotion to profit.

He grabbed a gloveful of Reynaldo Flemm's belly roll and gave a little squeeze. Paydirt. Fat city.

Rudy selected a Number 15 blade and made a one-quarter inch incision in Reynaldo's navel. Through this convenient aperture Rudy inserted the cannula, a long tubular instrument that resembled in structure the nose of an anteater. Rudy rammed the blunt snout of the cannula into the soft meat of Reynaldo's abdomen, then scraped the instrument back and forth to break up the tissue. With his right foot the surgeon tapped a floor pedal that activated a suction machine, which vacuumed the fat particles through small holes in the tip of the cannula, down a long clear plastic tube to a glass bottle.

Within moments, the first yellow glops appeared.

Johnny LeTigre's spare tyre!

Soon he would be a new man.

In the waiting room, Willie got to talking with some of the other patients. There was a charter-boat captain with a skin cancer the size of a toad on his forehead. There was a dancer from the Miami ballet who was getting her buttocks suctioned for the second time in as many years. There was a silver-haired Nicaraguan man whom Willie had often seen on television – one of the Contra leaders – who was getting his eyelids done for eighteen hundred dollars. He said the CIA was picking up the tab.

The one Willie liked best was a red-haired stripper from the Solid Gold club up in Lauderdale. She was getting new boobs, of course, but she was also having a tattoo removed from her left thigh. When the stripper heard that Willie was from PBS, she asked if she could be in his documentary and hiked up her corduroy miniskirt to show off the tattoo. The tattoo depicted a green reticulated snake eating itself. Willie said, in a complimentary way, that he had never seen anything like it. He made sure to get the stripper's phone number so that he could call her about the imaginary programme.

The hour passed without a peep from Reynaldo Flemm, and Willie began to get jittery. Reynaldo had said give it to nine o'clock before you freak, and now it was nine o'clock. The halls of Whispering Palms were quiet enough that Willie was certain he would have heard a scream. He asked the ballet dancer, who had been here before, how far it was from the waiting area to the operating room.

'Which operating room?' she replied. 'They've got four.'

'Shit,' said Willie. 'Four?'

This was shocking news. Reynaldo Flemm had made it sound like there was only one operating room, and that he would be easy to find. More worried than ever, Willie decided to make his move. He hoisted the Betacam to his shoulder, checked the mike and the cables and the belt pack and the battery levels, turned on the Frezzi light (which caused the other patients to mutter and shield their eyes), and went prowling through the corridors in search of Reynaldo Flemm.

When the telephone on the wall started tweeting, Dr Rudy Graveline glanced up from Johnny LeTigre's gut and said: 'Whoever it is, I'm not here.'

The circulating nurse picked up the phone, listened for several moments, then turned to the doctor. 'It's Ginny at the front desk. There's a man with a minicam running all over the place.'

Rudy's surgical mask puckered. 'Tell her to call the police . . . No! Wait— ' Oh Jesus. Stay calm. Stay extremely calm.

'He just crashed in on Dr Kloppner in Suite D.'

Rudy grunted unhappily. 'What does he want? Did he say what he wants?'

'He's looking for you. Should I tell Ginny to call the cops or what?'

The nurse-anaesthetist interrupted: 'Let's not do anything until we finish up here. Let's close up this patient and get him off the table.'

'She's right,' Rudy said. 'She's absolutely right. We're almost done here.'

'Take your time,' the anaesthetist said with an edge of concern. Under optimum conditions, Rudy Graveline scared the daylights out of her. Under stress, there was no telling how dangerous he could be.

He said, 'What're we looking at here?'

'One more pocket, maybe two hundred ccs.'

'Let's do it, OK?'

The wall phone started tweeting again.

'Screw it,' said Rudy. 'Let it go.'

He gripped the cannula like a carving knife, scraping frenetically at the last stubborn colony of fat inside Reynaldo's midriff. The suction machine hummed contentedly as it filled the glass jar with gobs of unwanted pudge.

'One more minute and we're done,' Rudy said.

Then the doors opened and an awesome white light bathed the operating room. The beam was brighter and hotter than the surgical lights, and it shone from the top of a camera, which sat like a second head on the shoulder of a man. A man who had no business in Rudy Graveline's operating room.

The man with the camera cried out: 'Ray!'

Rudy said, 'Get out of here this minute.'

'Are you Dr Graveline?'

Rudy's hand continued to work on Reynaldo Flemm's belly. 'Yes, I'm Dr Graveline. But there's nobody named Ray here. Now get out before I phone the police.'

But the man with the camera on his shoulder shuffled closer, scorching the operating team with his fierce, hot light. The anaesthetist, the scrub nurse, the circulating nurse, even Rudy flinched from the glare. The camera-headed man approached the table and zoomed in on the sleeping patient's face, which was partially concealed by a plastic oxygen mask. The voice behind the camera said, 'Yeah, that's him!'

'Who?' Rudy said, rattled. 'That's Ray?'

'Reynaldo Flemm!'

The scrub nurse said: 'I told you he looked familiar.'

Again Rudy asked: 'Who? Reynaldo who?'

'That guy from the TV.'

'This has gone far enough,' Rudy declared, fighting panic. 'You better . . . just get the hell out of my operating room.'

Willie pushed forward. 'Ray, wake up! It's me!'

'He can't wake up, you asshole. He's gassed to the gills. Now turn off that spotlight and get lost.'

The scope of the journalistic emergency struck Willie at once. Reynaldo was unconscious. Christina was gone. The tape was rolling. The batteries were running out.

Willie thought: It's up to me now.

The baton microphone, Ray's favourite, the one Willie was supposed to toss to him at the moment of ambush, was tucked in Willie's left armpit. Grunting, contorting, shifting the weight of the Betacam on his shoulder, Willie was able to retrieve the mike with his right hand. In an uncanny imitation of Reynaldo Flemm, Willie thrust it toward the face of the surgeon.

Above the surgical mask, Rudy Graveline's eyes grew wide and fearful. He stared at the microphone as if it were the barrel of a Mauser. From behind the metallic hulk of the minicam, the voice asked: 'Did you kill Victoria Barletta?'

A bullet could not have struck Rudy Graveline as savagely as those words.

His spine became rigid.

The pupils of his eyes shrunk to pinpricks.

His muscles cramped, one by one, starting in the toes. His right hand, the one that the held the cannula, the one buried deep in the livid folds of Reynaldo Flemm's freshly vacuumed tummy – his right hand twisted into a spastic nerveless talon.

With panic welling in her voice, the anaesthetist said: 'All right, that's it!'

'Almost done,' the surgeon said hoarsely.

'No, that's enough!'

But Dr Rudy Graveline was determined to finish the operation. To quit would be an admission of . . . *something*. Composure – that's what they taught you at Harvard. Above all, a physician must be composed. In times of crisis, patients and staff relied on a surgeon to be cool, calm, and composed. Even if the man lying on the operating table turned out to be . . . Reynaldo Flemm, the notorious undercover TV reporter! That would explain the woozy babbling while he was going under – the jerkoff wasn't talking about Victoria Principal, the actress. He was talking about Victoria Barletta, she of the fateful nose job.

The pain of the muscle cramps was so fierce that it brought viscous tears to Rudy Graveline's eyes. He forced himself to continue. He lowered his right shoulder into the rhythm of the liposuction, back and forth in a lumberjack motion, harder and harder.

Again, the faceless voice from behind the TV camera: 'Did you kill that girl?'

The black eye of the beast peered closer, revolving clockwise in its socket – Willie, remembering Ray's instructions to zoom tight on Rudy's face. The surgeon stomped on the suction pedal as if he were squashing a centipede. The motor thrummed. The tube twitched. The glass jar filled.

Time to stop.

Time to stop.

But Dr Rudy Graveline did not stop.

He kept on poking and sucking . . . the long hungry snout of the mechanical anteater slurping through the pit of Reynaldo's abdomen . . . down, down, down through the fascia and the muscle . . . snorkelling past the intestines, nipping at the transverse colon . . . down, down, down the magic anteater burrowed.

Until it glomped the aorta.

And the plastic tube coming out of Reynaldo's navel suddenly turned bright red.

The jar at the other end turned red.

Even the doctor's arm turned red.

Willie watched it all through the camera's eye. The whole place, turning red.

31

The first thing Chemo bought with Rudy's money was a portable phone for the Bonneville. No sooner was it out of the box than Maggie Gonzalez remarked, 'This stupid toy is worth more than the car.'

Chemo said, 'I need a private line. You'll see.'

They were driving back to the Holiday Inn after spending the morning at the office of Dr George Ginger, the plastic surgeon. Maggie knew Dr Ginger from his early days as one of Rudy's more competent underlings at the Durkos Center. She trusted George's skill and his discretion. He could be maddeningly slow, and he had terrible breath, but technically he was about as good as cosmetic surgeons come.

Chemo had prefaced the visit to Dr Ginger with this warning to Maggie: 'If he messes up my face, I'll kill him on the spot. And then I'll kill you.'

The second thing that Chemo had bought with Rudy's money was a box of bullets for the rusty Colt .38. Brand new rounds, Federals. The good stuff.

Maggie had said, 'You're going into this with the wrong attitude.'

Chemo frowned. 'I've had rotten luck with doctors.'

'I know, I know.'

'I don't even like this guy's name, George Ginger.

Sounds like a fag name to me.' Then he had checked the chambers on the Colt and slipped it into his pants.

'You're hopeless,' Maggie had said. 'I don't know why I even bother.'

'Because otherwise I'll shoot you.'

Fortunately the dermabrasion went smoothly. Dr George Ginger had never seen a burn case quite like Chemo's, but he wisely refrained from enquiry. Once, when Chemo wasn't looking, the surgeon snuck a peek at the cumbersome prosthesis attached to the patient's left arm. An avid gardener, Dr Ginger recognized the Weed Whacker instantly, but resisted the impulse to pry.

The sanding procedure took about two hours, and Chemo endured stoically, without so much as a whimper. When it was over, he no longer looked as if someone had glued Rice Krispies all over his face. Rather, he looked as if he had been dragged for five miles behind a speeding dump truck.

His forehead, his cheeks, his nose, his chin all glowed with a raw, pink, oozing sheen. The spackled damage of the errant electrolysis needle had been scraped away for ever, but now it was up to Chemo to grow a new skin. While he might never enjoy the radiant peachy complexion of, say, a Christie Brinkley, at least he would be able to stroll through an airport or a supermarket or a public park without causing small children to cringe behind their mothers' skirts. Chemo conceded that this alone would be a vast improvement, socially.

Before leaving the office, Maggie Gonzalez had asked Dr George Ginger to remove her sutures and inspect the progress of her New York facelift. He reported – with toxic breath – that everything was healing nicely, and gave Maggie a make-up mirror to look for herself. She was pleased by what she saw: the angry purple bruises were fading shadows under the eyes, and the incision scars had shrunk to tender rosy lines. She was especially delighted with her perky new nose.

Dr Ginger studied the still-swollen promontory from several angles and nodded knowingly. 'The Sandy Duncan.'

Maggie smiled. 'Exactly!'

Popping a codeine Tylenol, Chemo said, 'Who the fuck is Sandy Duncan?'

In the Bonneville, on the way back to the motel, Chemo remarked, 'Three grand seems like a lot for what he did.'

'All he did was make you look human again,' Maggie said. 'Three grand was a bargain, if you ask me. Besides, he even gave a professional discount – fifteen per cent off because I'm a nurse.'

As he steered, Chemo kept leaning toward the middle of the seat to check himself in the rear-view. It was difficult to judge the result of the dermabrasion, since his face was slathered in a glue-coloured ointment. 'I don't know,' he said. 'It's still pretty broken out.'

Maggie thought: Broken out? It's seeping, for God's sake. 'You heard what the doctor said. Give it a couple weeks to heal.' With that she leaned over and commandeered the rear-view to examine her own refurbished features.

A beep-beep noise came chirping out of the dashboard; the car phone. With a simian arm Chemo reached into the glove compartment and snatched it on the second ring.

With well-acted nonchalance, he wedged the receiver between his ear and his left shoulder. Maggie thought it looked ridiculous to be riding in a junker like this and talking on a fancy car phone. Embarrassed, she scooted lower in the seat.

'Hullo,' Chemo said into the phone.

'Hello, Funny Face.' It was Mick Stranahan. 'I got your message.'

'Yeah?'

'Yeah.'

'And?'

'And you said to call, so I am.'

Chemo was puzzled at Stranahan's insulting tone of voice. The man ought to be scared. Desperate. Begging. At least polite.

Chemo said, 'I got your lady friend.'

'Yeah, yeah, I read the note.'

'So, you're waiting to hear my demands.'

'No,' said Stranahan. 'I'm waiting to hear you sing the fucking aria from *Madame Butterfly* . . . *Of course* I want to hear your demands.'

'Christ, you're in a shitty mood.'

'I can barely hear you,' Stranahan complained. 'Don't tell me you got one of those yuppie Mattel car phones.'

'It's a Panasonic,' Chemo said, sharply.

Maggie looked over at him with an impatient expression, as if to say: Get on with it.

As he braked for a stop light, the phone slipped from Chemo's ear. He took his good hand off the wheel to grab for it.

'Hell!' The receiver was gooey with the antibiotic ointment from his cheeks.

Stranahan's voice cracked through the static. 'Now what's the matter?'

'Nothing. Not a damn thing.' Chemo carefully propped the receiver on his shoulder. 'Look, here's the deal. You want to see your lady friend alive, meet me at the marina at midnight tonight.'

'Fuck you.'

'Huh?'

'That means no, Funny Face. No marina. I know what you want and you can have it. Me for her, right?'

'Right.' Chemo figured there was no sense trying to bullshit this guy.

'It's a deal,' Stranahan said, 'but I'm not going anywhere. You come to me.'

'Where are you now?'

'I'm at a pay phone on Bayshore Drive, but I won't be here long.'

Impatiently Chemo said, 'So where's the meet?'

'My place.'

'That house? No fucking way.'

'Fraid so.'

The car phone started sliding again. Chemo groped frantically for it, and the Bonneville began to weave off the road. Maggie reached over and steadied the wheel.

Chemo got a grip on the receiver and snarled into it: 'You hear what I said? No way am I going back to that damn stilt house.'

'Yes, you are. You'll be getting another call with more information.'

'Tell me now!'

'I can't,' Stranahan said.

'I'll kill the Marks girl, I swear.'

'You're not quite that stupid, are you?'

The hot flush of anger made Chemo's face sting even worse. He said, 'We'll talk about this later. What time you gonna call?'

'Oh, not me,' Mick Stranahan said. 'I won't be the one calling back.'

'Then who?' Chemo demanded.

But the line had gone dead.

Willie played the videotape for his friend at WTVJ, the NBC affiliate in Miami. Willie's friend was sufficiently impressed by the blood on his shirt to let him use one of the editing rooms. 'You gotta see this,' Willie said.

He punched the tape into the machine and sat back to chew on his knuckles. He felt like an orphan. No Christina, no Reynaldo. He knew he should call New York, but he didn't know what to say or who to tell.

Willie's friend, who was a local news producer, pointed to the monitor. 'Where's that?' he asked.

'Surgery clinic over in Bal Harbour. That's the waiting room.'

The friend said. 'You were portable?'

'Right. Solo the whole way.'

'So where's Flemm? That doesn't look like him.'

'No, that's somebody else.' The monitor showed an operating room where a tall bald doctor was hunched over a chubby female patient. The bald doctor was gesticulating angrily at the camera and barking for a nurse to call the authorities. 'I don't know who that was,' Willie said. 'Wrong room.'

'Now you're back in the hallway, walking. People are yelling, covering their faces.'

'Yeah, but here it comes,' Willie said, leaning forwards. 'Bingo. That's Ray on the table.'

'Jeez, what're they doing?'

'I don't know.'

'It looks like a goddamn Caesarean.'

Willie said, 'Yeah, but it was supposed to be a nose job.'

'Go on!'

The audio portion of the tape grew louder.

'*Yeah, that's him!*'

'*Who? That's Ray?*'

'*Reynaldo Flemm.*'

'*I told you he looked familiar.*'

'*Who? Reynaldo who?*'

'*That guy from from the TV.*'

'*This has gone far enough . . .* '

When the frame filled with Reynaldo Flemm's gaping muzzled face, Willie's friend hit the Pause button and said, 'Fucker never looked better.'

'You know him?'

'I knew him back from Philadelphia. Back when he was still Ray Fleming.'

'You're kidding,' Willie said.

'No, man, that's his real name. Raymond Fleming. Then he got on this bi-ethnic kick . . . "Reynaldo Flemm" – half Latin, half Eastern bloc. Told everybody in the business that his mother was a Cuban refugee and his father was with the Yugoslavian Resistance. Shit, I laugh about it but that's when his career really took off.'

Willie said, 'Romania. What he told me, his old man was with the Romanian Underground.'

'His old man sold Whirlpools in Larchmont, I know for a fact. Let's see the rest.'

Willie pressed the Fast Forward and squeaked the tape past the part when he confronted Dr Rudy Graveline about Victoria Barletta; he didn't want his producer friend to hear the dead woman's name, on the off-chance that the story could salvaged. Willie slowed the tape to normal speed just as he zoomed in on the doctor's quavering eyes.

'Boris Karloff,' said Willie's friend.

'Watch.'

The camera angle widened to show Rudy Graveline feverishly toiling over Reynaldo's belly. Then came a mist of blood, and one of the nurses began shouting for the surgeon to stop.

'Geez,' said Willie's friend, looking slightly queasy. 'What's happening?'

The doctor abruptly wheeled from the operating table to confront the camera directly. In his bloody right hand was a wicked-looking instrument connected to a long plastic tube. The device was making an audible slurp-slurp noise.

'*Your turn, fat boy!*'

Willie's friend gestured at the monitor and said: 'He called you fat boy?'

'Watch!'

On the screen, the surgeon lunged forward with the pointy slurp-slurping device. There was a cry, a dull clunk. Then the picture got jerky and went grey.

Willie pressed the Stop button. 'I hauled ass,' he explained to his friend. 'He came at me with that sucking . . . *thing*, so I took off.'

'Don't blame you, man. But what about Ray?'

Willie took the videotape out of the editing console. 'That's what got me scared. I get in the van and take off, right? Stop at the nearest phone booth and call this clinic. Whispering Palms is the name.'

'Yeah, I've heard of it.'

'So I call. Don't say who I am. I ask about Reynaldo Flemm. I say he's my brother. I'm s'posed to pick him up after the operation. Ask can I come by and get him. Nurse gets on the line and wants to know what's going on. She wants to know how come Ray was using a phoney name when he checks in at the place. Johnny Tiger, some shit like that. I tell her I haven't got the faintest – maybe he was embarrassed, didn't want his nose job to turn up

342

in the gossip columns. Then she says, well, he's not here. She says the doctor, this Rudy Graveline, the nurse says he drove Ray to Mount Sinai. She says she's not allowed to say anything more on the phone. So I haul ass over to Emergency at Sinai and guess what? No Ray anywhere. Fact there's nothing but strokes and heart attacks. No Reynaldo Flemm!'

Willie's friend said, 'This is too fucking weird. Even for Miami.'

'Best part is, now I gotta call New York and break the news.'

'Oh, man.'

Willie said, 'Maybe I'll ship the tape first.'

'Might as well,' agreed the producer. 'What about Ray? Think he's all right?'

'No,' said Willie. 'You want the truth, I'd be fucking amazed if he was all right.'

The nurses had wanted to call 911, but Rudy Graveline had said no, there wasn't time. I'll take him myself, Rudy had said. He had run to the parking lot (stopping only at the front desk to pick up Reynaldo's $15,000), got the Jag and pulled up at the staff entrance.

Back in the operating suite, the anaesthetist had said: 'Everything's going flat.'

'Then hurry, goddammit!'

They had gotten Reynaldo on a gurney and wheeled him to Rudy's car and bundled him in the passenger seat. The scrub nurse even tried to hook up the safety belt.

'Oh, forget it,' Rudy had said.

'But it's a law.'

'Go back to work!' Rudy had commanded. The Jaguar had peeled rubber on its way out.

Naturally he had no intention of driving to Mount Sinai Hospital. What was the point? Rudy glanced at the man in the passenger seat and still did not recognize him from television. True, Reynaldo Flemm was not at his telegenic best. His eyes were half-closed, his mouth was half-open, and his skin was the colour of bad veal.

343

He was also exsanguinating all over Rudy's fine leather seats and burled walnut door panels. 'Great,' Rudy muttered. 'What else.' As the surgeon sped south on Alton Road, he took out the portable telephone and called his brother's tree company.

'George Graveline, please. It's an emergency.'

'Uh, he's not here.'

'This is his brother. Where's he working today?'

The line clicked. Rudy thought he had been cut off. Then a lady from an answering service came on and asked him to leave his number. Rudy hollered, but she wouldn't budge. Finally he surrendered the number and hung up.

He thought: I must find George and his wood-chipping machine. This is very dicey, driving around Miami Beach in a $47,000 sedan with a dead TV star in the front seat. *Bleeding* on the front seat.

The car phone beeped and Rudy grabbed at it in frantic optimism. 'George!'

'No, Dr Graveline.'

'Who's this?'

'Sergeant García, Metro Homicide. You probably don't remember, but we met that night the mysterious midget Haitian blew up your car.'

Rudy's heart was pounding. Should he hang up? Did the cops know about Flemm already? But how – the nurses? Maybe that moron with the minicam!

Al García said: 'I got some bad news about your brother George.'

Rudy's mind was racing. The detective's words didn't register. 'What – could you give me that again?'

'I said I got bad news about George. He's dead.'

Rudy's foot came off the accelerator. He was coasting now, trying to think. Which way? Where?

García went on: 'He tried to kill a man and I had to shoot him. Internal Review has the full report, so I suggest you talk to them.'

Nothing.

'Doctor? You there?'

'Yuh.'

344

No questions, nothing.

'The way it went down, I had no choice.'

Rudy said dully, 'I understand.' He was thinking: It's awful about George, yes, but what am I going to do with this dead person in my Jaguar?

García could sense that something strange was going on at the end of the line. He said, 'Look, I know it's a bad time, but we've got to talk about a homicide. A homicide that may involve you and your brother. I'd like to come over to the clinic as soon as possible.'

'Make it tomorrow,' Rudy said.

'It's about Victoria Barletta.'

'I'm eager to help in any way I can. Come see me tomorrow.' The surgeon sounded like a zombie. A heavily sedated zombie. If there was a realm beyond sheer panic, Rudy Graveline had entered it.

'Doctor, it really can't wait— '

'For heaven's sake, Sergeant, give me some time. I just found out my brother's dead, I need to make the arrangements.'

'To be blunt,' García said, 'as far as George goes, there's not a whole lot left to arrange.'

'Call me tomorrow,' Rudy Graveline said curtly. Then he threw the car phone out the window.

When the phone rang again in the Bonneville, Chemo gloated at Maggie Gonzalez. 'I told you this would come in handy.'

'Quit picking at your face.'

'It itches like hell.'

'Leave it be!' Maggie scolded. 'You want it to get infected? Do you?'

On the other end of the phone was Rudy Graveline. He sounded worse than suicidal.

Chemo said, 'Hey, Doc, you in your car? I'm in mine.' He felt like the king of the universe.

'No, I'm home,' Rudy said. 'We have a major problem.'

'What's this *we* stuff? I don't have a problem. I got a

345

hundred-twenty odd grand, a brand new face, a brand new car phone. Life's looking better every day.'

Rudy said, 'I'm delighted for you, I really am.'

'You don't sound too damn delighted.'

'He got Heather.' The doctor choked out the words.

'Who's Heather?' Chemo said.

'My . . . I can't believe . . . when I got home, she was gone. He took her away.'

Maggie asked who was on the line and Chemo whispered the doctor's name. 'All right,' he said to Rudy, 'you better tell me what's up.'

Suddenly Rudy Graveline remembered what Curly Eyebrows had warned him about cellular phones, about how private conversations sometimes could be picked up on outside frequencies. In his quickening state of emotional deterioration, Rudy clearly envisioned – as if it were real – some nosy Coral Gables housewife overhearing his felonious litany on her Anna toaster oven.

'Come to my house,' he instructed Chemo.

'I can't, I'm waiting on a call.'

'This is it.'

'What? You mean this is the phone call he— '

'Yes,' Rudy said. 'Get out here as fast as you can. We're going on a boat ride.'

'Jesus H. Christ.'

32

Maggie and Chemo left Christina Marks tied up in the trunk of the Bonneville, which was parked in Rudy Graveline's flagstone driveway. Miserable as she was, Christina didn't worry about suffocating inside the car; there were so many rust holes, she could actually feel a breeze.

For an hour Maggie and Chemo sat on the white leather sofa in Rudy's living room and listened to the doleful story of how he had come home to find his lover, his baby doll, his sweetie pie, his Venus, his sugar bunny, his punkin, his blond California sunbeam missing from the bedroom.

They took turns studying the kidnap note, which said: 'Ahoy! You're invited to a Party!'

On the front of the note was a cartoon pelican in a sailor's cap. On the inside was a hand-drawn chart of Stiltsville. Chemo and Rudy grimly agreed that something had to be done permanently about Mick Stranahan.

Chemo asked about the fresh dark drops on the foyer, and Rudy said that it wasn't Heather's blood but someone else's. In chokes and sighs he told them about the mishap at the clinic with Reynaldo Flemm. Maggie Gonzalez listened to the gruesome account with amazement; she had never dreamed her modest extortion scheme would come to this.

'So where is he?' she asked.

'In there,' Rudy replied. 'The Sub-Zero.'

Chemo said, 'The what? What're you talking about?'

Rudy led them to the kitchen and pointed at the cabinet-sized refrigerator. 'The Sub-Zero,' he said.

Maggie noticed that the aluminium freezer trays had been stacked on the counter, along with a half-dozen Lean Cuisines and three pints of chocolate Häagaen-Dazs.

Chemo said, 'That's a big fridge, all right.' He opened the door and there was Reynaldo Flemm, upright and frosty as a Jell-O pop.

'It was the only way he could fit,' explained Rudy. 'See, I had to tear out the damn ice maker.'

Chemo said, 'He sure looks different on TV.' Chemo propped open the refrigerator door with one knee; the cold air made his face feel better.

Maggie said nothing. This wasn't part of the plan. She was trying to think of a way to sneak out of Rudy's house and run. Go back to the motel room, grab the black Samsonite, and disappear for about five years.

Chemo closed the freezer door. He pointed to more brownish spots on the bone-coloured tile and said, 'If you got a mop, she can clean that up.'

347

'Wait a second,' Maggie said. 'Do I look like a maid?'

'You're gonna look like a cabbage if you don't do what I say.' Balefully Chemo brandished the Weed Whacker.

Maggie recalled the savage thrashing of Rudy Graveline and said, 'All right, put that stupid thing away.'

While Maggie mopped, Rudy moped. He seemed shattered, listless, inconsolable. He needed to think; he needed the soothing rhythm of athletic copulation, the sweet crystal tunnel of clarity that only Heather's loins could give him.

The day had begun with such promise!

Up before dawn to pack their bags. And the airline tickets – he had placed them in Heather's purse while she slept. He would drive to the clinic, perform the operation on the male go-go dancer, collect the fifteen grand, and come home for Heather. Then it was off to the airport! Fifteen thousand was plenty for starters – a month or two in Costa Rica in a nice apartment. Time enough for Rudy's Panamanian lawyer to liquidate the offshore trusts. After that, Rudy and Heather could breathe again. Get themselves some land up in the mountains. Split-level ranch house on the side of a hill. A stable, too; she loved to ride. Rudy envisioned himself opening a new surgery clinic; he had even packed his laminated Harvard diploma, pillowing it tenderly in the suitcase among his silk socks and designer underwear. San José was crawling with wealthy expatriates and aspiring international jet-setters. An American plastic surgeon would be welcomed vivaciously.

Now, disaster. Heather – fair, nubile, perfectly apportioned Heather – had been snatched from her sick bed.

'We need a boat,' Rudy Graveline croaked. 'For tonight.'

Chemo said, 'Yeah, a big one. If I'm going back to that damn house I want to stay dry. See if you can find us a Scarab thirty-eight.'

'Are you nuts?'

'Just like they had on *Miami Vice*.'

'You *are* nuts. Who's going to drive it?' Rudy stared pointedly at the unwieldy garden tool attached to Chemo's left arm. 'You?'

'Yeah, me. Just get on the phone, see what you can do. We've gotta move before the cops show up.'

Rudy looked stricken by the mention of police.

'Well, Jesus,' Chemo said, 'you got a dead man in your fridge. This is a problem.'

Maggie was rinsing the mop in the kitchen sink. She said, 'I've got an idea about that. You might not like it, but it's worth a try.'

Rudy shrugged wearily. 'Let's hear it.'

'I used to work for a surgeon who knew this guy . . . this guy who would buy certain things.'

'Surely you're not suggesting— '

'It's up to you,' Maggie said. 'I mean, Dr Graveline, you've got yourself a situation here.'

'Yeah,' said Chemo. 'Your ice cream is melting.'

The man's name was Kimbler, and his office was in Miami's hospital district; a storefront operation on 12th Street, a purse-snatcher's jog from Jackson Hospital or the Medical Examiner's Office. The magnetic sign on the door of the office said: 'International Bio-Medical Exports, Inc.' The storefront window was tinted dark blue and was obscured by galvanized burglar mesh.

Kimbler was waiting for them when they arrived – Rudy, Chemo, Maggie, and Christina. Chemo had the Colt .38 in his pants pocket, pointed at Christina the whole time. He had wanted to leave her in the trunk of the Pontiac, but there was not enough room.

Kimbler was a rangy thin-haired man with tortoiseshell glasses and a buzzard's-beak nose. The office was lighted like a stockroom, with cheap egg-carton overheads. Rows of grey steel shelves covered both walls. The shelves were lined with old-fashioned Mason jars, and preserved in the Mason jars were assorted human body parts: ears, eyeballs, feet, hands, fingers, toes, small organs, large organs.

Chemo looked around and, under his breath, said, 'What the fuck.'

Kimbler gazed with equal wonderment at Chemo, who was truly a sight – his freshly sanded face glistening with

Neosporin ointment, his extenuated left arm cloaked with its calfskin golf-bag cover, his radish-patch scalp, his handsome Jim Fowler safari jacket. Kimbler examined Chemo as if he were a prized future specimen.

'This is some hobby you got,' Chemo said, picking up a jar of gall bladders. 'This is better than baseball cards.'

Kimbler said, 'I've got the proper permits, I assure you.'

Maggie explained that Kimbler sold human tissue to foreign medical schools. She said it was perfectly legal.

'The items come from legitimate sources,' Kimbler added. 'Hospitals. Pathology labs.'

Items. Christina was nauseated at the concept. Or maybe it was just the sweet dead smell of the place.

Kimbler said, 'It may sound ghoulish, but I provide a much-needed service. These items, discarded organs and such, they would otherwise go to waste. Be thrown away. Flushed. Incinerated. Overseas medical schools are in great need of clinical teaching aids – the students are extremely grateful. You should see some of the letters.'

'No thanks,' Chemo said. 'What's a schlong go for these days?'

'Pardon me?'

Maggie cut in: 'Mr Kimbler, we appreciate you seeing us on short notice. We have an unusual problem.'

Kimbler peered theatrically over the tops of his glasses. A slight smile came to his lips. 'I assumed as much.'

Maggie went on, 'What we have is an entire . . . *item.*'

'I see.'

'It's a pauper-type situation. Very sad – no family, no funds for a decent burial. We're not even sure who he is.'

Christina could scarcely contain herself. She had gotten a quick glimpse of a body as they angled it into the trunk of the Bonneville. A young man; that much she could tell.

Kimbler said to Maggie: 'What can you tell me of the circumstances? The manner of death, for instance.'

She said, 'An indigent case, like I told you. Emergency

350

surgery for appendicitis.' She pointed at Rudy. 'Ask him, he's the doctor.'

Rudy Graveline was stupefied. He scrambled to catch up with Maggie's yarn. 'I was doing . . . he had a chronic heart condition. Bad arrhythmia. He should've said something before the operation, but he didn't.'

Kimbler pursed his lips. 'You're a surgeon?'

'Yes.' Rudy wasn't dressed like a surgeon. He was wearing Topsiders, tan cotton pants, and a Bean crewneck pullover. He was dressed for a boat ride. 'Here, wait.' He took out his wallet and showed Kimbler an ID card from the Dade County Medical Society. Kimbler seemed satisfied.

'I realize this is out of the ordinary,' Maggie said.

'Yes, well, let's have a look.'

Chemo pinched Christina by the elbow and said, 'We'll wait here.' He handed Maggie the keys to the Bonneville. She and Rudy led the man named Kimbler to the car, which was parked in a city lot two blocks away.

When Maggie opened the trunk, Rudy turned away. Kimbler adjusted his glasses and craned over the corpse as if he were studying the brush strokes on a fine painting. 'Hmmmmm,' he said. 'Hmmmmmm.'

Rudy edged closer to block the view of the trunk, in case any pedestrians got curious. His concern was groundless, for no one gave the trio a second look; half the people in Miami did their business out of car trunks.

Kimbler seemed impressed by what he saw. 'I don't get many whole cadavers,' he remarked. 'Certainly not of this quality.'

'We tried to locate a next of kin,' Rudy said, 'but for some reason the patient had given us a phoney name.'

Kimbler chuckled. 'Probably had a very good reason. Probably a criminal of some type.'

'Every place we called was a dead end,' Rudy said, lamely embellishing the lie.

Maggie stepped in to help. 'We were going to turn him over to the county, but it seemed like such a waste.'

'Oh, yes,' said Kimbler. 'The shortage of good cadavers . . . by good, I mean white and well-nourished. Most

of the schools I deal with – for instance, one place in
Dominica, they had only two cadavers for a class of sixty
medical students. Tell me how those kids are ever going
to learn gross anatomy.'

Rudy started to say something but thought better of it.
The whole deal was illegal as hell, no doubt about it.
But what choice did he have? For the first time in his
anal-retentive, hyper-compulsive professional life he had
lost control of events. He had surrendered himself to the
squalid street instincts of Chemo and Maggie Gonzalez.

Kimbler was saying, 'Two measly cadavers, both
dysenteries. Weighed about ninety pounds each. For
sixty students! And this is not so unusual in some of
these poor countries. There's a med school on Guadeloupe,
the best they could do was monkey skeletons. To help out
I shipped down two hearts and maybe a half-dozen lungs,
but it's not the same as having whole human bodies.'

Shrewd haggler that she was, Maggie had heard enough.
Slowly she closed, but did not lock, the rusty trunk of the
Bonneville; Reynaldo Flemm had begun to thaw.

'So,' she said, 'you're obviously interested.'

'Yes,' said Kimbler. 'How does eight hundred sound?'

'Make it nine,' said Maggie.

Kimbler frowned irritably. 'Eight-fifty is pushing it.'

'Eight seventy-five. Cash.'

Kimbler still wore a frown, but he was nodding. 'All
right. Eight seventy-five it is.'

Rudy Graveline was confused. 'You're paying *us*?'

'Of course,' Kimbler replied. He studied Rudy doubtfully. 'Just so there's no question later, you *are* a medical
doctor? I mean, your state licence is current. Not that you
need to sign anything, but it's good to know.'

'Yes,' Rudy sighed. 'Yes, I'm a doctor. My licence is
up to date.' As if it mattered. If all went as planned,
he'd be gone from the country by this time tomorrow.
He and Heather, together on a mountaintop in Costa
Rica.

The man named Kimbler tapped cheerfully on the trunk
of the Bonneville. 'All right, then. Why don't you pull

around back of the office. Let's get this item on ice straightaway.'

Mick Stranahan brought Heather Chappell a mug of hot chocolate. She pulled the blanket snugly around her shoulders and said, 'Thanks, I'm so damn cold.'

He asked how she was feeling.

'Beat up,' she replied. 'Especially after that boat ride.'

'Sorry,' Stranahan said. 'I know it's rough as hell – there's a front moving through so we got a big westerly tonight.'

Heather sipped tentatively at the chocolate. The kidnapper, whoever he was, watched her impassively from a wicker barstool. He wore blue jeans, deck shoes, a pale yellow cotton shirt and a poplin windbreaker. To Heather the man looked strong, but not particularly mean.

In the middle of the living room was a card table, covered by an oilskin cloth. On the table was a red Sears Craftsman toolbox. The kidnapper had been carrying it when he broke into Dr Graveline's house.

Heather nodded toward the toolbox and said, 'What's in there?'

'Just some stuff I borrowed from Rudy.'

The furniture looked like it came from the Salvation Army, but still there was a spartan cosiness about the place, especially with the soft sounds of moving water. Heather said, 'I like your house.'

'The neighbourhood's not what it used to be.'

'What kind of fish is that on the wall?'

'It's a blue marlin. The bill broke off, I've got to get it fixed.'

Heather said, 'Did you catch it yourself?'

'No.' Stranahan smiled. 'I'm no Hemingway.'

'I read for *Islands in the Stream*. With George C. Scott – did you see it?'

Stranahan said no, he hadn't.

'I didn't get the part, anyway,' said Heather. 'I forget now who played the wife. George C. Scott was Hemingway, and there was lots of fishing.'

353

The beakless marlin stared down from the wall. Stranahan said, 'It used to be paradise out here.'

Heather nodded; she could picture it. 'What're you going to do with me?'

'Not much,' said Stranahan.

'I remember you,' she said. 'From the surgery clinic. That night in the parking lot, you put me in the cab. The night Rudolph's car caught fire.'

'My name is Mick.'

Being a famous actress, Heather didn't customarily introduce herself. This time she felt like she had to.

Stranahan said, 'The reason I asked how you're feeling is this.' He held up three pill bottles and gave them a rattle. 'These were on the nightstand by your bed. Young Dr Rudy was keeping you loaded.'

'Painkillers, probably. See, I just had surgery.'

'Not painkillers,' Stranahan said. 'Seconal 100s. Industrial strength, enough to put down an elephant.'

'What . . . why would he do that?'

Stranahan got off the barstool and walked over to Heather Chappell. In his right hand was a small pair of scissors. He knelt down in front of her and told her not to move.

'Oh, God,' she said.

'Be still.'

Carefully he clipped the bandages off her face. Heather expected the salty cool air to sting the incisions, but she felt nothing but an itchy sensation.

Stranahan said, 'I want to show you something.' He went to the bathroom and came back with a hand mirror. Heather studied herself for several moments.

In a puzzled voice she said, 'There's no marks.'

'Nope. No scars, no bruises, no swelling.'

'Rudolph said . . . See, he mentioned something about microsurgery. Lasers, I think he said. He said the scars would be so small— '

'Bullshit.' Stranahan handed her the scissors. She gripped them in her right hand like a pistol.

'I'm going in the other room for a little while,' he

said. 'Call me when you're done and I'll explain as much as I can.'

Ten minutes later Heather was pounding on the bedroom door. She had cut off the remaining bandages and phoney surgical dressings. She was standing there naked, striped with gummy adhesive, and crying softly. Stranahan bundled her in the blanket and sat her on the bed.

'He was s'posed to do my boobs,' she said. 'And my hips. My nose, eyelids . . . everything.'

'Well, he lied,' said Stranahan.

'Please, I wanna go back to LA.'

'Maybe tomorrow.'

'What's going on?' Heather cried. 'Can I use your phone, I've got to call my manager. Please?'

'Sorry,' said Stranahan. 'No telephone. No ship-to-shore. No fax. The weather's turned to shit, so we're stuck for the night.'

'But I'm s'posed to do a *Password* with Jack Klugman. God, what day is it?'

Stranahan said: 'Can I ask you something? You're a beautiful girl – you get points for that, OK – but how could you be so fucking dumb?'

Heather stopped crying instantly, gulped down her sobs. No man had ever talked to her this way. Well, wait; Patrick Duffy had, once. She was playing a debutante on *Dallas* and she forgot one lousy line. One out of seventeen! But later at least Patrick Duffy had said he was sorry for blowing his stack.

Mick Stranahan said, 'To trust yourself to a hack like Graveline, Jesus, it's pathetic. And for what? Half an inch off your hips. A polyurethane dimple in your chin. Plastic bags inside your breasts. Think about it: a hundred years from now, your coffin cracks open and there's nothing inside but two little bags of silicone. No flesh, no bones, everything's turned to ashes except for your boobs. They're bionic. Eternal!'

In a small voice Heather said, 'But everybody does it.'

Stranahan tore off the blanket, and for the first time Heather was truly afraid. He told her to stand up.

'Look at yourself.'

Diffidently she lowered her eyes.

'There's not a thing wrong with you,' Stranahan said. 'Tell me what's wrong with you.'

The wind shook the shutters, and shafts of cold air sliced the room. Heather shivered, sat down, and put her hands over her nipples. Stranahan folded his arms as if he were awaiting something: an explanation.

'You're a man, I don't expect you to understand.' She wondered if he would try to touch her in some way.

'Vanity I understand,' Stranahan said. 'Men are experts on the subject.' He picked the blanket off the floor. Indifferently he draped it across her lap. 'I think there's some warm clothes in one of the drawers.'

He found a grey sweatsuit with a hood and a pair of men's woollen socks. Hurriedly Heather got dressed. 'Just tell me,' she said, still trembling, 'why did Rudolph lie about this? I can't get over it – why didn't he do the operation?'

'I guess he was scared. In case you didn't notice, he's crazy about you. He probably couldn't bear the thought of something going wrong in surgery. It's been known to happen.'

'But I paid him,' Heather said. 'I wrote the bastard a personal cheque.'

'Stop it, you're breaking my heart.'

Heather glared at him.

'Look,' said Stranahan, 'I've seen his Visa bill. Swanky restaurants, designer clothes, a diamond here and there – you made out pretty well. Did he mention he was going to fly you away on a tropical vacation?'

'I remember him saying something about Costa Rica, of all places.'

'Yeah, well, don't worry. The trip's off. Rudy's had a minor setback.'

Heather said, 'So tell me what's going on.'

'Just consider yourself damn lucky.'

'Why? What are you talking about?'

'Rudy killed a young woman just like you. No, I take

that back – she wasn't just like you, she was innocent. And he killed her with a nose job.'

Heather Chappell cringed. Unconsciously her hand went to her face.

'That's what this is about,' Stranahan said. 'You don't believe me, ask him yourself. He's on his way.'

'Here?'

'That's right. To save you and to kill me.'

'Rudolph? No way.'

'You don't know him like I do, Heather.'

Stranahan went from room to room, turning off the lights. Heather followed, saying nothing. She didn't want to be left alone, even by him. Carrying a Coleman lantern, Stranahan led her out of the stilt house and helped her climb to the roof. The windmill whistled and thrummed over their heads.

Heather said, 'God, this wind is really getting nasty.'

'Sure is.'

'What kind of gun is that?'

'A shot-gun, Heather.'

'I can't believe Rudolph is coming all the way out here on a night like this.'

'Yep.'

'What's the shot-gun for?'

'For looks,' said Stranahan. 'Mostly.'

33

Al García was feeling slightly guilty about lying to Mick Stranahan until Luis Córdova's patrol boat conked out. Now Luis was hanging over the transom, poking around the lower unit; García stood next to him, aiming a big waterproof spotlight and cursing into the salt spray.

García thought: I hate boats. Car breaks down, you just walk away from it. With a damn boat, you're stuck.

They were adrift about half a mile west of the

Seaquarium. It was pitch black and ferociously choppy. A chilly north-westerly wind cut through García's plastic windbreaker and made him wish he had waited until dawn, as he had promised Stranahan.

It did not take Luis Córdova long to discover the problem with the engine. 'It's the prop,' he said.

'What about it?'

'It's gone,' said Luis Córdova.

'We hit something?'

'No, it just fell off. Somebody monkeyed with the pin.'

García considered this for a moment. 'Does he know where you keep the boat?'

'Sure,' said Luis Córdova.

'Shit.'

'I better get on the radio and see if we can get help.'

Al García stowed the spotlight, sat down at the console and lit a cigarette. He said, 'That bastard. He didn't trust us.'

Luis Córdova said, 'We need a new prop or a different boat. Either way, it's going to take a couple hours.'

'Do what you can.' To the south García heard the sound of another boat on the bay; Luis Córdova heard it, too – the hull slapping heavily on the waves. The hum of the engine receded as the craft moved further away. They knew exactly where it was going.

'Goddamn,' said García.

'You really think he did this?'

'I got no doubt. The bastard didn't trust us.'

'I can't imagine why,' said Luis Córdova, reaching for the radio.

Driving across the causeway to the marina, Chemo kept thinking about the stilt house and the monster fish that had eaten off his hand. As hard as he tried, he could not conceal his trepidation about going back.

When he saw the boat that Rudy Graveline had rented, Chemo nearly called off the expedition. 'What a piece of shit,' he said.

It was a twenty-one-foot outboard, tubby and slow, with an old sixty-horse Merc. A cheap hotel rental, designed for abuse by tourists.

Chemo said, 'I'm not believing this.'

'At this hour I was lucky to find anything,' said Rudy.

Maggie Gonzalez said, 'Let's just get it over with.' She got in the boat first, followed by Rudy, then Christina Marks.

Chemo stood on the pier, peering across the bay toward the amber glow of the city. 'It's blowing like a fucking typhoon,' he said. He really did not want to go.

'Come on,' Rudy said. He was frantic about Heather; more precisely, he was frantic about what he would have to do to get her back. He had a feeling that Chemo didn't give a damn one way or another, as long as Mick Stranahan got killed.

As Chemo was unhitching the bow rope, Christina Marks said, 'This is really a bad idea.'

'Shut up,' said Chemo.

'I mean it. You three ought to get away while you can.'

'I said shut up.'

Maggie said, 'She might be right. This guy, he's not exactly a stable person.'

Chemo clumped awkwardly into the boat and started the engine. 'What, you want to spend the rest of your life in jail? You think he's gonna forget about everything and let us ride off into the sunset?'

Rudy Graveline shivered. 'All I want is Heather.'

Christina said, 'Don't worry, Mick won't hurt her.'

'Who gives a shit,' said Chemo, gunning the throttle with his good hand.

By the time they made it to Stiltsville, Chemo felt like his face was aflame. The rental boat rode like a washtub, each wave slopping over the gunwale and splashing spray against the raw flesh of his cheeks. The salt stung like cold acid. Chemo soon ran out of profanities. Rudy Graveline was no help, nor were the women; they were all soaking wet, queasy, and glum.

As he made a wide weekend-sailor's turn into the Biscayne Channel, Chemo slowed down and pointed with the Weed Whacker. 'What the fuck?' he said. 'Look at that.'

Across the bonefish flats, Stranahan's stilt house was lit up like a used-car lot. Lanterns hung off every piling, and swung eerily in the wind. The brown shutters were propped open and there was music, too, fading in and out with each gust.

Christina Marks laughed to herself. 'The Beatles,' she said. He was playing 'Happiness Is a Warm Gun'.

Chemo snorted. 'What, he's trying to be cute?'

'No,' Christina said. 'Not him.'

Maggie Gonzalez swept a whip of wet hair out of her face. 'He's nuts, obviously.'

'And we're not?' Rudy said. He got the binoculars and tried to spot Heather Chappell on the stilt house. He could see no sign of life, human or otherwise. He counted a dozen camp lanterns aglow.

The sight of the place brought back dreadful memories for Chemo. Too clearly he could see the broken rail where he had fallen to the water that day of the ill-fated jet ski assault. He wondered about the fierce fish, whatever it was, dwelling beneath the stilt house. Inwardly he speculated about its nocturnal feeding habits.

Maggie said, 'How are we going to handle this?'

Rudy looked at her sternly. 'We don't do anything until Heather's safe in this boat.'

Chemo grabbed Christina's arm and pulled her to the console. 'Stand here, next to me,' he said. 'Real close, in case your jerkoff boyfriend gets any ideas.' He pressed the barrel of the Colt .38 to her right breast. With the stem of the Weed Whacker he steadied the wheel.

As the boat bucked and struggled across the shallow bank toward Mick Stranahan's house, Christina Marks accepted the probability that she would not live through the next few moments. 'For the record,' she said, 'he's *not* my boyfriend.'

Maggie nudged her with an elbow and whispered. 'You could've done worse.'

Chemo stopped the boat ten yards from the dock.

The stereo had died. The only sound was the thrum of the windmill and the chalkboard squeak of the Colemans, swinging in the gusts. The house scorched the sky with its watery brightness; a white torch in the blackest middle of nowhere. Christina wondered: Where did he get so many bloody lanterns?

Chemo looked down at Rudy Graveline. 'Well? You're the one who got the invitation.'

Rudy nodded grimly. On rubbery legs he made his way to the bow of the boat; the rough, wet ride had drubbed all the nattiness out of his L. L. Bean wardrobe. The doctor cupped both hands to his mouth and called out Stranahan's name.

Nothing.

He glanced back at Chemo, who shrugged. The .38 was still aimed at Christina Marks.

Next Rudy called Heather's name and was surprised to get a reply.

'Up here!' Her voice came from the roof, where it was darker.

'Come on down,' Rudy said excitedly.

'No, I don't think so.'

'Are you all right?'

'I'm fine,' said Heather. 'No thanks to you.'

Chemo made a sour face at Rudy. 'Now what?'

'Don't look at me,' the doctor said.

Chemo called out to Heather: 'We're here to save you. What's your fucking problem?'

Suddenly Heather appeared on the roof. For balance she held onto the base of the windmill. She was wearing a grey sweatsuit with a hood. 'My problem? Ask him.' She pulled the hood off her head, and Rudy Graveline saw that the bandages were gone.

'Damn,' he said.

'Let's hear it,' Chemo muttered.

'I was supposed to do some surgery, but I didn't. She thought – see, I told her I did it.'

Maggie Gonzalez said, 'You're right. Everybody out here is crazy.'

'I paid you, you bastard!' Heather shouted.

'Please, I can explain,' Rudy pleaded.

Chemo was disgusted. 'This is some beautiful moment. She doesn't want to be rescued, she hates your damn guts.'

Heather disappeared from the roof. A few moments later she emerged, still alone, on the deck of the stilt house. Rudy Graveline tossed her the bow rope and she wrapped it around one of the dock cleats. The surgeon stepped out of the boat and tried to give her a hug, but Heather backed up and said, 'Don't you touch me.'

'Where's Stranahan?' Chemo demanded.

'He's around here somewhere,' Heather said.

'Can he hear us?'

'I'm sure.'

Chemo's eyes swept back and forth across the house, the deck, the roof. Every time he glanced at the water he thought of the terrible fish and how swiftly it had happened before. His knuckles were blue on the grip of the pistol.

A voice said: 'Look here.'

Chemo spun around. The voice had come from beneath the stilt house, somewhere in the pilings, where the tide hissed.

Mick Stranahan said: 'Drop the gun.'

'Or what?' Chemo snarled.

'Or I'll blow your new face off.'

Chemo saw an orange flash, and instantly the lantern nearest his hand exploded. Maggie shrieked and Christina squirmed from Chemo's one-armed clasp. On the deck of the house, Rudy Graveline dropped to his belly and covered his head.

Chemo stood alone with his lousy pistol. His ears were roaring. Shards of hot glass stuck to his scalp. He thought: That damn shot-gun again.

When the echo from the gunfire faded, Stranahan's

voice said: 'That's buckshot, Mr Tatum. In case you were wondering.'

Chemo's face was killing him. He contemplated the damage that a point-blank shot-gun blast would do to his complexion, then tossed the Colt .38 into the bay. Perhaps a deal could be struck; even after splurging on the car phone, there was still plenty of money to go around.

Stranahan ordered Chemo to get out of the boat. 'Carefully.'

'No shit.'

'Remember what happened last time with the 'cuda.'

'So that's what it was.' Chemo remembered seeing pictures of barracudas in sports magazines. What he remembered most were the incredible teeth. 'Jesus H. Christ,' he said.

Stranahan didn't mention that the big barracuda was long gone – off to deeper water to wait out the cold. Probably laid up in Fowey Rocks.

Chemo moved with crab-like deliberation, one gangly limb at a time. Between the rocking of the boat and the lopsided weight of his prosthesis, he found it difficult to balance on the slippery gunwale. Maggie Gonzalez came up from behind and helped boost him to the dock. Chemo looked surprised.

'Thanks,' he said.

From under the house, Stranahan's voice: 'All right, Heather, get in the boat.'

'Wait a second,' said Rudy.

'Don't worry, she'll be all right.'

'Heather, don't!' Rudy was thinking about that night in the fireplace, and that morning in the shower. And about Costa Rica.

'Hands off,' said Heather, stepping into the boat.

By now Christina Marks had figured out the plan. She said, 'Mick, I want to stay.'

'Ah, you changed your mind.'

'What— '

'You want to get married after all?'

The words hung in the night like the mischievous cry of

363

a gull. Then, from under the stilt house, laughter. 'Everything's just a story to you,' Stranahan said. 'Even me.'

Christina said, 'That's not true.' No one seemed particularly moved by her sincerity.

'Don't worry about it,' Stranahan said. 'I'll still love you, no matter what.'

Rudy cautiously got to his feet and stood next to Chemo. In the flickering lantern glow, Chemo looked more waxen than ever. He seemed hypnotized, his puffy blowfish eyes fixed on the surging murky waves.

Heather said, 'Should I untie the boat now?'

'Not just yet,' Stranahan called back. 'Check Maggie's jacket, would you?'

Maggie Gonzalez was wearing a man's navy pea jacket. When Heather reached for the pockets, Maggie pushed her arm away.

There was a metallic clunking noise under the house: Stranahan, emerging from his sniper hole. Quickly he clambered out of the aluminium skiff, over the top of the water tank, pulling himself one-handed to the deck of the house. His visitors got a good long look at the Remington.

'Maggie, be a good girl,' Stranahan said, 'Let's see what you've got.'

Christina took one side of the coat and Heather took the other. 'Keys,' Christina announced, holding them up for Stranahan to see. One was a tiny silver luggage key, the other was from a room at the Holiday Inn.

Chemo blinked sullenly and patted at his pants. 'Jesus H. Christ,' he said. 'The bitch picked my pockets.'

He couldn't believe it: Maggie had lifted the keys while helping him out of the boat! She planned to sneak back to the motel and steal all the money.

'I know how you feel,' Stranahan said to Chemo. He reached into the boat and plucked the keys from Christina's hand. He put them in the front pocket of his jeans.

'What now?' Rudy whined, to anyone who might have a clue.

Chemo's right hand crept to his left armpit and found

364

the toggle switch for the battery pack. The Weed Whacker buzzed, stalled once, then came to life.

Stranahan said, 'I'm impressed, I admit it.' He aimed the Remington at Chemo's head and told him not to move.

Chemo paid no attention. He took two giraffe-like steps across the dock and, with a vengeful groan, dove into the stern of the boat after Maggie. They all went down in a noisy tangle – Chemo, Maggie, Heather and Christina – the boat listing precariously against the pilings.

Mick Stranahan and Rudy Graveline watched the mêlée from the lower deck of the stilt house. One woman's scream, piercing and feline, rose above the uproar.

'Do something!' the doctor cried.

'All right,' said Stranahan.

Later, Stranahan gathered all the lanterns and brought them inside. Rudy Graveline lay in his undershorts on the bed; he was handcuffed spread-eagle to the bedposts. Chemo was unconscious on the bare floor, folded into a corner. With the shutters latched, the lanterns made the bedroom as bright as a television studio.

Rudy said, 'Are they gone?'

'They'll be fine. The tide's running out.'

'I'm not sure if Heather can swim.'

'The boat won't sink. They'll all be fine.'

Rudy noticed fresh blood on Stranahan's forehead, where he had been grazed by the Weed Whacker. 'You want me to look at that?'

'No,' Stranahan said acidly. 'No, I don't.' He left the bedroom and returned with the red Sears Craftsman toolbox. 'Look what I've got,' he said to Rudy.

Rudy craned to see. Stranahan opened the toolbox and began to unpack. 'Recognize any of this stuff?'

'Yes, of course . . . what're you doing?'

'Before we get started, there's something I ought to tell you. The cops have Maggie's videotape, so they know about what you did to Vicky Barletta. Whether they can convict you is another matter. I mean, Maggie is not exactly a prize

365

witness. In fact, she'd probably change her story again for about twenty-five cents.'

Rudy Graveline swallowed his panic. He was trying to figure out what Stranahan wanted and how to give it to him. Rudy could only assume that, deep down, Stranahan must be no different than the others: Maggie, Bobby Pepsical, or even Chemo. Surely Stranahan had a scam, an angle. Surely it involved money.

Stranahan went out again and returned with the folding card table. He placed it in the centre of the room, covered with the oilskin cloth.

'What is it?' the doctor said. 'What do you want?'

'I want you to show me what happened.'

'I don't understand.'

'To Vicky Barletta. Show me what went wrong.' He began placing items from the toolbox on the card table.

'You're insane,' said Rudy Graveline. It seemed the obvious conclusion.

'Well, if you don't help,' Stranahan said, 'I'll just have to wing it.' He tore open a package of sterile gloves and put them on. Cheerily he flexed the latex fingers in front of Rudy's face.

The surgeon stared back, aghast.

Stranahan said, 'Don't worry, I did some reading up on this. Look here, I got the Marcaine, plenty of cotton, skin hooks, a whole set of new blades.'

From the toolbox he selected a pair of doll-sized surgical scissors and began trimming the hairs in Rudy Graveline's nose.

'Aw, no!' Rudy said, thrashing against the bedposts.

'Hold still.'

Next Stranahan scrubbed the surgeon's face thoroughly with Hibiclens soap.

Rudy's eyes began to water. 'What about some anaesthesia?' he bleated.

'Oh yeah,' said Stranahan. 'I almost forgot.'

Chemo awoke and rolled over with a thonk, the Weed Whacker bouncing on the floor planks. He sat up slowly, groping under his shirt. The battery sling was gone; the Weed Whacker was dead.

'Ah!' said Mick Stranahan. 'The lovely Nurse Tatum.'

A knot burned on the back of Chemo's head, where Stranahan had clubbed him with the butt of the Remington. Teetering to his feet, the first thing Chemo focused upon was Dr Rudy Graveline – cuffed half-naked to the bed. His eyes were taped shut and a frayed old beach towel had been tucked around his neck. A menacing tong-like contraption lay poised near the surgeon's face: a speculum, designed for spreading the nostrils. It sounded like something Moe would have used on Curly.

Stranahan stood at a small table cluttered with tubes and gauze and rows of sharp stainless-steel instruments. In one corner of the table was a heavy grey textbook, opened to the middle.

'What the fuck?' said Chemo. His voice was foggy and asthmatic.

Stranahan handed him a sterile glove. 'I need your help,' he said.

'No, not him,' objected Rudy, from the bed.

'This is where we are,' Stranahan said to Chemo. 'We've got his nose numb and packed. Got the eyes taped to keep out the blood. Got plenty of sponges – I'm sorry, you look confused.'

'Yeah, you could say that.' Scraggles of hair rose on the nape of Chemo's scalp. His stomach heaved against his ribs. He wanted out – but where was the goddamn shot-gun?

'Put the glove on,' Stranahan told him.

'What for?'

'The doctor doesn't want to talk about what happened to Victoria Barletta – she died during an operation exactly like this. I know it's been four years, and Dr Graveline's had hundreds of patients since then. But my idea was that we might be able to refresh his memory by re-enacting the Barletta case. Right here.'

Rudy fidgeted against the handcuffs.

Chemo said, 'For Christ's sake, just tell him what he wants to hear.'

'There's nothing to tell,' said Rudy. By now he was fairly certain that Stranahan was bluffing. Already Stranahan had skipped several fundamental steps in the rhinoplasty. He had not attempted to file the bony dorsum, for example. Nor had he tried to make any incisions inside of Rudy's nostrils. This led Rudy to believe that Stranahan wasn't serious about doing a homemade nose job, that he was merely trying to frighten the doctor into a cheap confession.

To Chemo, of course, the makeshift surgical suite was a gulag of horrors. One glimpse of Rudy, blindfolded and splayed like a pullet on a bed, convinced Chemo that Mick Stranahan was monstrously deranged.

Stranahan was running a forefinger down a page of the surgical text. 'Apparently this is the most critical part of the operation – fracturing the nasal bones on both sides of the septum. This is very, very delicate.' He handed Chemo a small steel mallet and said, 'Don't worry, I've been reading up on this.'

Chemo tested the weight of the mallet in his hand. 'This isn't funny,' he said.

'Is it supposed to be? We're talking about a young woman's death.'

'Probably it was an accident,' Chemo said. He gestured derisively at Rudy Graveline. 'The guy's a putz, he probably just fucked up.'

'But you weren't there. You don't know.'

Chemo turned to Rudy. 'Tell him, you asshole.'

Rudy shook his head. 'I'm an excellent surgeon,' he insisted.

Stranahan foraged through the toolbox until he found the proper instrument.

'What's that, a chisel?' Chemo said.

'Very good,' Stranahan said. 'Actually, it's called an osteotome. A Storz number four. But basically, yeah, it's just a chisel. Look here.'

He leaned over the bed and pinched the bridge of Rudy Graveline's nose. With the other hand he gingerly slipped the osteotome into the surgeon's right nostril, aligning the instrument lengthwise along the septum.

'Now, Mr Tatum, I'll hold this steady while you give it a slight tap— '

'Nuggghhh,' Rudy protested. The dull pressure of the chisel reawakened the fear that Stranahan was really going to do it.

'Did you say something?' Stranahan asked.

'You were right,' the surgeon said. His voice came out in a wheeze. 'About the Barletta girl.'

'You killed her?'

'I didn't mean to, I swear to God.' Between the pinch of Stranahan's fingers and the poke of the osteotome, Rudy Graveline talked like he had a terrible cold.

He said, 'What happened was, I let go of her nose. It was . . . terrible luck. I let go just when the nurse hit the chisel, so— '

'So it went all the way up.'

'Yes. The radio was on, I lost my concentration. The Lakers and the Sonics. I didn't do it on purpose.'

Stranahan said, 'And afterwards you got your brother to destroy the body.'

'Uh-huh.' Rudy couldn't nod very well with the Number 4 osteotome up his nostril.

'And what about my assistant?' Stranahan glanced over at Chemo. 'You hired him to kill me, right?'

Rudy's Adam's apple hopped up and down like a scalded toad. Sightless, he imagined the scene by what he could hear: the plink of the instruments, the two men breathing, the wind and the waves shaking the house, or so it seemed.

Stranahan said, 'Look, I know it's true. I'd just like to hear the terms of the deal.'

Rudy felt the chisel nudge the bony plate between the eye sockets, deep in his face. He was, understandably, reluctant to give Mick Stranahan the full truth – that the price on his head was to be paid in discount dermatological treatments.

Rudy said, 'It was sort of a trade.'

'This I gotta hear.'

'Tell him,' Rudy said blindly to Chemo. 'Tell him the arrangement with the dermabrasion, tell— '

Chemo reacted partly out of fear of incrimination and partly out of embarrassment. He let out a feral grunt and swung the mallet with all his strength. It was a clean blow to the butt of the osteotome, precisely the right spot.

Only much too hard. So hard that it knocked the chisel out of Stranahan's hand.

So hard that the instrument disappeared entirely, as if inhaled by Rudy Graveline's nose.

So hard that the point of the chisel punched through the brittle plate of the ethmoid bone and penetrated Rudy Graveline's brain.

The hapless surgeon shuddered, kicked his left leg, and went limp. 'Damn,' said Stranahan, jerking his hand away from the blood.

This he hadn't planned. Stranahan had anticipated having to kill Chemo, at some point, because of the man's stubborn disposition to violence. He had figured that Chemo would grab for the shot-gun or maybe a kitchen knife, something dumb and obvious; then it would be over. But the doctor, alive and indictable, Stranahan had promised to Al García.

He looked up from the body and glared at Chemo. 'You happy now?'

Chemo was already moving for the door, wielding the mallet and neutered Weed Whacker as twin bludgeons, warning Stranahan not to follow. Stranahan could hear the seven-foot killer clomping through the darkened house, then out on the wooden deck, then down the stairs toward the water.

When Stranahan heard the man coming back, he retrieved the Remington from under the bed and waited.

Chemo was panting as he ducked through the doorway. 'The fuck did you do to your boat?'

'I shot a hole in it,' Stranahan said.

'Then how do we get off this goddamn place?'

'Swim.'

Chemo's lips curled. He glowered at the bulky lawn appliance strapped to the stump of his arm. He could unfasten it, certainly, but how far would he get? Paddling

370

with one arm at night, in these treacherous waters! And what about his face – it would be excruciating, the stringent salt water scouring his fresh abrasions. Yet there was no other way out. It would be lunacy to stay.

Stranahan lowered the gun and said, 'Here, I think this belongs to you.'

He took something out of his jacket and held it up, so the gold and silver links caught the flush of the lantern lights. Chemo's knees went to rubber when he saw what it was.

The Swiss diving watch. The one he lost to the barracuda.

'Still ticking,' said Mick Stranahan.

34

At dawn the cold front arrived under a foggy purple brow, and the wind swung dramatically to the north. The waves off the Atlantic turned swollen and foamy, nudging the boat even further from the shore of Cape Florida. The tide was still creeping out.

The women were weary of shouting and waving for help, but they tried once more when a red needlenose speedboat rounded the point of the island. The driver of the speedboat noticed the commotion and cautiously slowed to approach the other craft. A young woman in a lemon cotton pullover sat beside him.

She stood up and called out: 'What's the matter?'

Christina Marks waved back. 'Engine trouble! We need a tow to the marina.'

The driver, a young muscular Latin, edged the speedboat closer. He offered to come aboard and take a look at the motor.

'Don't bother,' said Christina. 'The gas line is cut.'

'How'd that happen?' The young man couldn't imagine.

It was a strange scene so early on a cold morning:

three women alone on rough water. The one, a slender brunette, looked pissed off about something. The blonde in a sweatsuit was unsteady, maybe seasick. Then there was a Cuban woman, attractive except for an angry-looking bald patch on the crown of her head.

'You all right?' the young man asked.

The Cuban woman nodded brusquely. 'How about giving us a lift?'

The young man in the speedboat turned to his companion and quietly said, 'Tina, I don't know. Something's fucked up here.'

'We've got to help,' the young woman said. 'I mean, we can't just leave them.'

'There'll be other boats.'

Christina Marks said, 'At least can we borrow your radio? Something happened out here.' She motioned toward the distant stilt houses.

'What was it?' said Tina, alarmed.

Maggie Gonzalez, who had prison to consider, said firmly: 'Nothing happened. She's drunk out of her mind.'

And Heather Chappell, who had her career to consider, said: 'We were s'posed to meet some guys for a party. The boat broke down, that's all.'

Christina's eyes went from Heather to Maggie. She felt like crying, and then she felt like laughing. She was as helpless and amused as she could be. So much for sisterhood.

'I know how that goes,' Tina was saying, 'with parties.'

Heather said, 'Please, I don't feel so hot. We've been drifting for hours.' Her face looked familiar, but Tina wasn't sure.

The Cuban woman with the bald patch said, 'Do you have an extra soda?'

'Sure,' said Tina. 'Ritchie, throw them a rope.'

Sergeant Al García bent over the rail and got rid of his breakfast muffins.

'I thought you were a big fisherman,' needled Luis

Córdova. 'Who was it told me you won some fishing tournament.'

'That was different.' García wiped his moustache with the sleeve of the windbreaker. 'That was on a goddamn lake.'

The journey out to Stiltsville had been murderously rough. That was García's excuse for getting sick – the boat ride, not what they had found inside the house.

Luis Córdova chucked him on the arm. 'Anyway, you feel better now.'

The detective nodded. He was still smouldering about the patrol boat, about how it had taken three hours to get a new pin for the prop. Three crucial hours, it turned out.

'Where's Wilt?' García asked.

'Inside. Pouting.'

The man known as Chemo was standing up, his right arm suspended over his head. Luis Córdova had handcuffed him to the overhead water pipes in the kitchen. As a security precaution, the Weed Whacker had been unstrapped from the stump of Chemo's left arm. Trailing black and red cables, the yard clipper lay on the kitchen bar.

Luis Córdova pointed at the monofilament coil on the rotor. 'See that – human hair,' he said to Al García. 'Long hair, too; a brunette. Probably a woman's.'

García turned to the killer. 'Hey, Wilt, you a barber?'

'Fuck you.' Chemo blinked neutrally.

'He says that a lot,' said Luis Córdova. 'It's one of his favourite things. All during the Miranda, he kept saying it.'

Al García walked over to Chemo and said, 'You're aware that there's a dead doctor in the bedroom?'

'Fuck you.'

'See,' said Luis Córdova. 'That's all he knows.'

'Well, at least he knows *something*.' García groped in his pocket and came out with a wrinkled handkerchief. He put the handkerchief to his face and returned to the scene in the bedroom. He came out a few minutes later and said, 'That's very unpleasant.'

'Sure is,' agreed Luis Córdova.

'Mr Tatum, since you're not talking, you might as well listen.' García arranged himself on one of the wicker barstools and stuck a cigar in his mouth. He didn't light it.

He said, 'Here's what's happened. You and the doctor have a serious business disagreement. You lure the dumb bastard out here and try to torture some dough out of him. But somehow you screw it up – you kill him.'

Chemo reddened. 'Horse shit,' he said.

Luis Córdova looked pleased. 'Progress,' he said to García. 'We're making progress.'

Chemo clenched his fist, causing the handcuff to rattle against the rusty pipe. He said, 'You know damn well who it was.'

'Who?' García raised the palms of his hands. 'Where is the mystery man?'

'Fuck you,' Chemo said.

'What I can't figure out,' said the detective, 'is why you didn't take off. After all this mess, why'd you stay on the house? Hell, *chico*, all you had to do was jump.'

Chemo lowered his head. His cheeks felt hot and prickly; a sign of healing, he hoped.

'Maybe he can't swim,' suggested Luis Córdova.

'Maybe he's scared,' García said.

Chemo said nothing. He closed his eyes and concentrated on the soothing sounds of freedom; the wind and the waves and the gulls, and the ticking of his waterproof wristwatch.

Al García waited until he was outside to light up the cigar. He turned a shoulder to the wind and cupped the match in his hand.

'I called for the chopper,' said Luis Córdova. 'And a guy from the ME.'

'Gives us what, maybe half an hour?'

'Maybe,' said the young marine patrolman. 'We got time to check the other houses. Wilt's not going anywhere.'

García tried to blow a smoke ring, but the wind sucked it away. The cusp of the front had pushed through, and

374

the sky over Biscayne Bay was clearing. the first sunlight broke out of the haze in slanted golden shafts that fastened to the water like quartz, lighting up the flats.

'I see why you love it out here,' García said.

Luis Córdova smiled. 'Some days it's like a painting.'

'Where do you think he went?'

'Mick? He might be dead. Guy that size could probably take him. Dump the body off the house.'

García gnawed sceptically at the end of the cigar. 'It's possible. Or he could've got away. Don't forget, he had that pump gun.'

'His skiff's sunk,' Luis Córdova noted. 'Somebody blasted a hole in the bottom.'

'Weird,' said Al García. 'But if I had to guess, I'd say he probably wasn't around when all this happened. I'd say he got off the house.'

'Maybe.'

'Whatever happened out here, it was between Tatum and the doctor. Maybe it was money, maybe it was something to do with surgery. Christ, you notice that guy's arm?'

'His face, too,' said Luis Córdova. 'What you're saying makes sense. Just looking at him, he's not the type to file a lawsuit.'

'But doing it with a hammer, that's cold.' García puffed his cheeks as if to whistle. 'On the other hand, your victim ain't exactly Marcus Welby . . . whatever. It all fits.'

That was the main thing.

A small boat, a sleek yellow outboard, came speeding across the bonefish flats. It was headed south on a line toward Soldier Key. García watched the boat intently, walked around the house to keep it in view.

'Don't worry, I know him,' said Luis Córdova. 'He's a fishing guide.'

'Wonder why he's out here alone.'

'Maybe his clients didn't show. That happens when it blows hard – these rubes'll chicken out at the dock. Meanwhile it turns into a nice day.'

Just south of Stiltsville, the yellow skiff angled off the flats and stopped in a deep blue channel. The guide took out a rod and casted a bait over the side. Then he sat down to wait.

'See?' said Luis Córdova. 'He's just snapper fishing.'

García was squinting against the sun. 'Luis, you see something else out there?'

'Whereabouts?'

The detective pointed. 'I'd say a quarter mile. Something in the water, between us and that island.'

Luis Córdova raised one hand to block the glare. With the other hand he adjusted his sunglasses. 'Yeah, now I see it,' he said. 'Swimming on top. Looks like a big turtle.'

'Yeah?'

'Grandpa loggerhead. Or maybe it's a porpoise. You want me to get the binoculars?'

'No, that's OK.' García turned around and leaned his back against the wooden rail. He was grinning broadly, the stogie bobbing under his moustache. 'I've never seen a porpoise before, except for the Seaquarium.'

'Well, there's still a few wild ones out here,' Luis Córdova said. 'If that's what it was.'

'That's what it was,' said Al García. 'I'm sure of it.'

He tapped the ashes off the cigar and watched them swirl and scatter in the sea breeze. 'Come on,' he said, 'let's go see if Wilt's learned any new words.'

Epilogue

BLONDELL WAYNE TATUM, also known as Chemo, pleaded guilty in Dade Circuit Court to the murders of Dr Rudy Graveline and Chloe Simpkins Stranahan. He later was extradited to Pennsylvania, where he confessed to the unsolved slaying of Dr Gunther MacLeish, a semi-retired dermatologist and pioneer in the use of electrolysis to remove unwanted facial hair. Because of his physical handicap, and because of favourable testimony from sympathetic Amish elders, Tatum received a relatively lenient sentence of three seventeen-year terms, to be served concurrently. He is now a trusty in charge of the winter vegetable garden at the Union Correctional Institution at Raiford, Florida.

MAGGIE ORESTES GONZALEZ pleaded no contest to one count of obstruction for lying to investigators after Victoria Barletta's death. She received a six-month suspended sentence, but was ordered to serve one hundred hours of community service as a volunteer nurse at the Dade County Stockade, where she was taken hostage and killed during a food-related riot.

HEATHER CHAPPELL continued to appear in numerous television shows, including *Matlock*, *L.A. Law* and *Murder, She Wrote*. Barely five months after Dr Rudy Graveline's death, Heather quietly entered an exclusive West Hollywood surgical clinic and underwent a breast augmentation, a blepharoplasty, a rhinoplasty, a complete rhytidectomy, a chin implant, and suction lipectomies of the thighs, abdomen, and buttocks. Soon afterward, Heather's movie career was revived when she was offered – and accepted – the role of Triana, a Klingon prostitute, in *Star Trek VII: The Betrayal of Spock*.

KIPPER GARTH never fully recovered from his *pelota* injuries and retired from the law. His lucrative personal injury practice was purchased by a prominent Miami Beach firm, which sought – and received – permission to retain the use of Kipper Garth's name and likeness in all future advertising and promotion.

The Dade County Grand Jury refused to indict JOHN NORDSTROM for assaulting his lawyer. Nordstrom and his wife pursued their malpractice claim against the Whispering Palms Spa and Surgery Center and eventually settled out of court for $315,000, forty per cent of which went straight to their new attorney.

MARIE NORDSTROM'S contractured breast implants were repaired in a simple out-patient procedure performed by Dr George Ginger. The operation took only ninety minutes and was a complete success.

The seat held on the County Commission by ROBERTO PEPSICAL was filled by his younger brother, Charlie. The zoning rights to the Old Cypress Towers project were eventually picked up by a group of wealthy South American investors. Ignoring protests from environmentalists and local home owners, the developers paved over the ballpark and playground to construct a thirty-three-storey luxury condominium tower, with a chic roof-top night-club called Freddie's. Nine weeks after it opened, the entire building was seized by the Drug Enforcement Administration in a money-laundering probe that was code-named 'Operation Piranha'.

The popular television show *In Your Face* was cancelled after the disappearance and presumed death of its star, REYNALDO FLEMM. The programme's executive producers soon announced that a $25,000 scholarship in Reynaldo's name would be awarded to the Columbia University School of Journalism, from which, ironically, he had been twice expelled.

Exporter J. W. KIMBLER received a personal letter from the vice-chancellor of the Leeward Islands Medical University in Guadeloupe. the note said: 'Thank you for your most recent shipment, which has become the highlight of our spring semester. On behalf of the faculty and of the future surgeons who study here, accept my deepest gratitude for a superior product.'

For his dramatic videotaped footage of Reynaldo Flemm's cosmetic surgery, cameraman WILLIE VELASQUEZ was offered – and accepted – his own news-documentary programme on the Fox Television Network. *Eyewitness Undercover!* premiered in the 8 p.m. time slot on Thursdays, and in four major markets decisively beat out *The Cosby Show* in both the Nielsens and Arbitrons.

CHRISTINA MARKS declined an offer to become a producer for Willie's new programme. Instead, she left television and took a job as an assistant city editor at the *Miami Herald*, and with it a pay cut of approximately $135,000. Soon after moving to Miami, she purchased a second-hand Boston Whaler and a nautical chart of South Biscayne Bay.

The parents of Victoria Barletta were puzzled to receive, via UPS, a black Samsonite suitcase containing approximately $118,400 in cash. A letter accompanying the money described it as a gift from the estate of Dr Rudy Graveline. The letter was signed by a retired investigator named MICK STRANAHAN and bore no return address.

NATIVE TONGUE

FOR MY BROTHER ROB

This is a work of fiction. The events described are imaginary. However, the depiction of aberrant sexual behaviour by bottle-nosed dolphins is based on true cases on file with the Florida state marine laboratory in St. Petersburg.

1

On July 16, in the aching torpid heat of the South Florida summer, Terry Whelper stood at the Avis counter at Miami International Airport and rented a bright red Chrysler LeBaron convertible. He had originally signed up for a Dodge Colt, a sensible low-mileage compact, but his wife had told him go on, be sporty for once in your life. So Terry Whelper got the red LeBaron plus the extra collision coverage, in anticipation of Miami drivers. Into the convertible he inserted the family—his wife Gerri, his son Jason, his daughter Jennifer—and bravely set out for the turnpike.

The children, who liked to play car games, began counting all the other LeBarons on the highway. By the time the Whelpers got to Snapper Creek, the total was up to seventeen. "And they're all rentals," Terry muttered. He felt like a fool; every tourist in Miami was driving a red LeBaron convertible.

"But look at all this legroom," said his wife.

From the back seat came Jennifer's voice: "Like, what if it rains?"

"Like, we put up the top," Terry said.

His wife scolded him for being sarcastic with their daughter. "She's only eleven, for heaven's sake."

"Sorry," said Terry Whelper. Then louder, over his shoulder: "Jenny, I'm sorry."

"For what?"

Terry shook his head. "Nothing, hon."

It started raining near Florida City, and of course the convertible top wouldn't go up; something was stuck, or maybe Terry wasn't pushing the right button on the dash. The Whelpers sought shelter at an Amoco station, parked near the full-service pumps and waited for the cloudburst to stop. Terry was dying to tell his wife I-told-you-so, sporty my ass, but she wouldn't look up from the paperback that she was pretending to read.

Jennifer asked, "Like, what if it rains all day and all night?"

"It won't," said Terry, trying hard to be civil. .

The shower stopped in less than an hour, and the Whelpers were off again. While the kids used beach towels to dry off the interior of the convertible, Gerri passed around cans of Pepsi-Cola and snacks from the gas station vending machine. In vain Terry fiddled with the buttons on the car radio, trying to find a station that played soft rock.

The Whelpers were halfway down Card Sound Road when a blue pickup truck passed them the other way doing at least eighty. Without warning, something flew out of the truck driver's window and landed in the back seat of the LeBaron. Terry heard Jason yell; then Jennifer started to wail.

"Pull over!" Gerri cried.

"Easy does it," said her husband.

The convertible skidded to a halt in a spray of grass and gravel. The Whelpers scrambled from the car, checked themselves for injuries and reassembled by the side of the road.

"It was two guys," Jason declared, pointing down the road. "White guys, too."

"Are you sure?" asked his mother. The family had been on guard for possible trouble from blacks and Hispanics; a neighbor in Dearborn had given them the scoop on South Florida.

"They looked white to me," Jason said of the assailants.

Terry Whelper frowned. "I don't care if they were purple. Just tell me, what did they throw?"

Jennifer stopped crying long enough to say: "I dunno, but it's alive."

Terry said, "For Christ's sake." He walked over to the convertible and leaned inside for a look. "I don't see anything."

Jennifer cried even harder, a grating subhuman bray. "You . . . don't . . . believe . . . me!" she said, sobbing emphatically with each word.

"Of course we believe you," said her mother.

"I saw it, too," said Jason, who rarely took his sister's side on anything. "Try down on the floor, Dad."

Terry Whelper got into the back of the LeBaron, squeezed down to his knees and peered beneath the seat. The children heard him say, "Holy shit," then he leapt out of the car.

"What is it?" asked his wife.

"It's a rat," said Terry Whelper. "The ugliest goddamn rat I ever saw."

"They threw a rat in our car?"

"Apparently."

Jason said, "Too bad we didn't bring Grandpa's gun."

Gerri Whelper looked shaken and confused. "Why would they throw a rat in our car? Is it alive?"

"Very much so," Terry reported. "It's eating from a bag of Raisinets."

"Those are mine!" Jennifer cried.

The Whelpers stood there discussing the situation for fifteen minutes before a highway patrol car pulled up, and a young state trooper asked what was the matter. He listened sympathetically to the story about the rat in the rented LeBaron.

"You want me to call the Avis people?" he asked. "Maybe they'll send another car."

"Actually, we're on a pretty tight schedule," explained Gerri Whelper. "We've got reservations at a motor lodge in Key Largo. They said we had to be there by five or else we lose the rooms."

Jennifer, who had almost stopped crying, said: "I don't care about the motel, I want a different car."

Terry Whelper said to the trooper, "If you could just help me get rid of it."

"The rat?"

"It's a big one," Terry said.

"Well, I can probably shoot it."

"Could you?" Gerri said. "Please?"

The trooper said, "Technically, it's against regulations. But since you're from out of town . . ."

He stepped out of the patrol car and unsnapped the holster strap on his .357.

"Wow!" said Jason.

Jennifer put her arms around her mother's waist. Terry Whelper manfully directed his brood to move safely out of the line of fire. The state trooper approached the LeBaron with the calm air of a seasoned lawman.

"He's under the seat," Terry advised.

"Yeah, I see him."

The trooper fired three times. Then he holstered the gun, reached into the convertible and picked up what remained of the creature by what remained of its tail. He tossed the misshapen brown lump into some holly bushes.

"Thank you so much," said Gerri Whelper.

"You say it was a blue pickup. You didn't happen to see the license plate?"

"No," said Terry. He was wondering what to tell Avis about the bullet holes in the floorboard. When the kids climbed back in the rental car, their mother said, "Don't touch any of those raisins! We'll get more candy when we get to the Amazing Kingdom."

"Good, I want a Petey Possum Popsicle," Jennifer said, nearly recovered from the trauma. Jason asked if he could keep one of the empty shell casings out of the state trooper's revolver, and the trooper said sure.

Terry Whelper grimly contemplated the upcoming journey in the red, rat-befouled LeBaron. He felt fog-headed and emotionally drained. To think, just that morning he'd been safe and sound in his bed back in Michigan.

"Don't forget to buckle up," said the trooper, holding the door open.

Terry said, "This ever happen before?"

"What do you mean?"

"This rat business."

"I'm sure it has. We don't hear about everything." The trooper smiled as he closed Terry Whelper's door. "Now, you all have a nice vacation."

▼ ▼ ▼

In the blue pickup truck, still heading north, Danny Pogue said, "That was the damnedest thing I ever saw."

Bud Schwartz, who was driving, said, "Yeah, that was some shot. If I do say so."

"There was kids in that car."

"It was just a mouse, for Chrissakes."

"It wasn't a mouse, it was a rat." Danny Pogue poked his partner in the shoulder. "What if those was your kids? You like it, somebody throws a fucking rat in their laps?"

Bud Schwartz glanced at the place on his shoulder where Danny Pogue had touched him. Then he looked back at the highway. His bare bony arms got rigid on the steering wheel. "I wasn't exactly aiming for the kids."

"Were too."

After a few strained moments, Bud Schwartz said, "You don't see that many convertibles anymore."

"So when you finally see one, you throw a rat in it? Is that the deal?" Danny Pogue picked at a pair of ripe pimples on the peak of his Adam's apple.

"Let's just drop it," said Bud Schwartz.

But Danny Pogue remained agitated all the way to Florida City. He told Bud Schwartz to let him off in front of the Long John Silver's.

"No way," said Bud Schwartz.

"Then I'll jump outta the goddamn truck."

Danny Pogue would damn sure try it, too, Bud thought. Jump out of the damn truck purely on principles.

Bud Schwartz said, "Hey, you don't want to do that. We've gotta go get your money."

"I'll find my own ride."

"It'll look hinky, we don't show up together."

Danny Pogue said, "I'm not riding nowhere with a guy that throws rats on little kids. Understand?"

"What if I said I was sorry," Bud Schwartz said. "I'm sorry, all right? It was a shitty thing to do. I feel terrible, Danny, honest to God. I feel like a shit."

Danny Pogue gave him a sideways look.

"I mean it," said Bud Schwartz. "You got me feeling so bad I got half a mind to cry. Swear to God, look here—my eyes are all watered up. For a second I was thinking of Bud, Jr., about what I'd do, some asshole threw a rat or any other damn animal at my boy. Probably kill him, that's what I'd do."

As he spun through this routine, Bud Schwartz was thinking: The things I do to keep him steady.

And it seemed to work. In no time Danny Pogue said, "It's all right, Bud. Least nobody got hurt."

"That's true."

"But don't scare no more little kids, understand?"

Bud Schwartz said, "I won't, Danny. That's a promise."

Ten minutes later, stopped at a traffic light in Cutler Ridge, Danny Pogue turned in the passenger seat and said, "Hey, it just hit me."

He·was grinning so wide that you could count all the spaces where teeth used to be.

"What?" said Bud Schwartz.

"I remember you told me that Bud Schwartz wasn't your real name. You said your real name was Mickey Reilly."

"Mike. Mike Reilly," said Bud Schwartz, thinking, Here we go.

"Okay, then how could you have a kid named Bud, Jr.?"

"Well—"

"If your name's Mike."

"Simple. I changed the boy's name when I changed mine."

Danny Pogue looked skeptical. Bud Schwartz said, "A boy oughta have the same name as his daddy, don't you agree?"

"So his real name was—"

"Mike, Jr. Now it's Bud, Jr."

"You say so," said Danny Pogue, grinning again, a jack-o'-lantern with volcanic acne.

"What, you don't believe me?"

"No, I don't believe you," said Danny Pogue, "but it was a damn good story. Whatever your fucking name is."

"Bud is just fine. Bud Schwartz. And let's not fight no more, we're gonna be rich."

Danny Pogue got two beers out of the Styrofoam cooler in the back of the cab. He popped one of the cans for his partner and handed it to him. "I still can't believe they're payin' us ten grand apiece to steal a boxful of rats."

"This is Miami," said Bud Schwartz. "Maybe they're voodoo rats. Or maybe they're fulla dope. I heard where they smuggle coke in French rubbers, so why not rats."

Danny Pogue lifted the box from behind the front seat and placed it carefully on his lap. He leaned down and put his ear to the lid. "Wonder how many's in there," he said.

Bud Schwartz shrugged. "Didn't ask."

The den box was eighteen inches deep, and twice the size of a briefcase. It was made of plywood, painted dark green, with small hinged doors on each end. Air holes had been drilled through the side panels; the holes were no bigger than a dime, but somehow one of the animals had managed to squeeze out. Then it had scaled the front seat and perched on Danny Pogue's headrest, where it had balanced on its hind legs and wiggled its velvety snout in the air. Laughing, Bud Schwartz had deftly snatched it by the tail and dangled it in his partner's face. Over Danny Pogue's objections, Bud Schwartz had toyed with the rodent for six or seven miles, until he'd spotted the red convertible coming the other way down the road. Then he had said, "Watch this," and had tossed the animal out the window, into the passing car.

Now Danny Pogue lifted the green box off his lap and said, "Sure don't weigh much."

Bud Schwartz chuckled. "You want a turn, is that it? Well, go ahead then, grab one."

"But I don't wanna get bit."

"You got to do it real fast, way I did. Hurry now, here comes one of them Winnebagos. I'll slow down when we go by."

Danny Pogue said, "The top of this box ain't even locked."

"So what're you waiting for?" said his partner. "Pop goes the weasel."

▼ ▼ ▼

After the rat attack, the Whelper family rode in edgy silence until they arrived at the Amazing Kingdom of Thrills. They parked the red

LeBaron in the Mr. Bump-a-Rump lot, Section Jellybean, and took the tram to the main gate. There they came upon a chaotic scene: police cars, an ambulance, TV trucks, news photographers. The ticket turnstiles were all blocked.

"Swell," said Terry Whelper. "Beautiful."

"Maybe they're filming a movie," his wife suggested. "Maybe it's not real."

But it was. The center of attention was a supremely tanned young man in a blue oxford shirt with a dark red club tie, loosened fashionably at the throat. Once all the TV lights were on, the man started to read from a typed sheet of paper. He said he was a spokesperson for the company.

"This is a message for all our friends and visitors to the Amazing Kingdom of Thrills," the man began. "We deeply regret the incident that disturbed today's Summerfest celebration. We are proud of our security arrangements here at the park, and proud of our safety record. Up until today, there had been—and I say this unequivocally—no serious crimes committed within our friendly gates."

In the swell of the crowd, Terry Whelper felt his wife's chin digging into his shoulder blade. "What do you suppose he's talking about?" she said.

The man in the oxford shirt continued: "We believe there was no way to anticipate, much less prevent, what happened this afternoon in the Rare Animal Pavilion."

Terry Whelper said, "This oughta be good." A large woman wearing a damp cotton blouse and a Nikkormat around her neck turned and shot him a dirty look.

The man at the TV microphones was saying, "At approximately 2:15 p.m., two men entered the compound and attacked one of the wildlife exhibits with a sledgehammer, breaking the glass. One of our park employees courageously tried to stop the intruders, but was overpowered and beaten. The two men then grabbed a box of specimens from the exhibit arena and ran. In the confusion, the suspects managed to escape from the park, apparently by mingling with ordinary tourists aboard the Jungle Jerry Amazon Boat Cruise."

Jason Whelper said, "Specimens? What kinda specimens?"

Jennifer announced, "I don't want to go on the Jungle Jerry anymore."

Terry Whelper told the children to be quiet and listen. The tanned man in the blue shirt was saying that the park employee who had so bravely tried to stop the crime was being rushed to the hospital for X-rays.

"Hey, look!" said Jason, pointing.

Somebody in an oversized polyester animal outfit was being loaded into the ambulance.

"That's Robbie Raccoon!" cried Jennifer Whelper. "He must be the one who got hurt."

All around them in the crowd, other tourist children began to whimper and sniffle at the sight of Robbie Raccoon on the stretcher. Jason swore he saw some blood on Robbie Raccoon's nose.

"No, he's going to be fine," said Gerri Whelper. "See there, he's waving at us!"

And, indeed, whoever was inside the Robbie Raccoon costume managed a weak salute to the crowd before the ambulance doors swung closed.

"It's gotta be ninety-eight degrees out here," marveled Terry Whelper. "You'd think they'd get the poor guy out of that raccoon getup."

Terry Whelper's wife whispered urgently to the nape of his neck, "Not in front of Jennifer. She thinks he's real."

"Oh, you're kidding," Terry said.

Under the TV lights, the tan young spokesperson finally was revealing what had been stolen in the daring robbery.

"As many of you know," he said, "the Amazing Kingdom of Thrills is home to several endangered varieties of wildlife. Unfortunately, the animals that were stolen this afternoon are among the rarest, and most treasured, in our live-animal collection. In fact, they were believed to be the last two surviving specimens of the blue-tongued mango vole." Here the handsome spokesman paused dramatically. Then: "The animals were being kept here in a specially climatized habitat, in the hope that they might breed and keep the species alive. Tragically, that dream came to an end this afternoon."

"Mango voles!" exclaimed Jason Whelper. "Dad, did you hear? Maybe that's what landed in our car. Maybe those guys in the pickup truck were the crooks!"

Terry Whelper took his son by the arm and led him back toward the tram, away from the tourist crowd. Gerri and Jennifer followed steadfastly.

Gerri whispered to her husband: "What do you think? Maybe Jason is right."

"I don't know what to think. You were the one who wanted to come to Florida."

Jason cut in: "Dad, there was only two of those mangos left in the whole wide world. And we shot one!"

"No, we didn't. The policeman did."

"But we told him to!"

Terry Whelper said, "Be quiet, son. We didn't know."

"Your father's right," added Gerri. "How were we to know?"

Jennifer hugged her mother fiercely around the waist. "I'm so scared—can we drive to Epcot instead?"

"Excellent idea," said Terry Whelper. Like a cavalry commander, he raised his right arm and cocked two fingers toward the parking lot. "Everybody back to the car."

2

As soon as Charles Chelsea got back to the Publicity Department, he took a poll of the secretaries. "How was I?" he asked. "How'd I do? What about the necktie?"

The secretaries told Chelsea that he looked terrific on television, that loosening the necktie was a nifty touch, that overall it was quite a solid performance. Chelsea asked if Mr. Kingsbury had called, but the secretaries said he hadn't.

"Wonder why not," said Chelsea.

"He's playing golf up at Ocean Reef."

"Yeah, but he's got a cellular. He could've called." Chelsea told one of the secretaries to get Joe Winder, and then went into his private office and closed the door.

Ten minutes later, when Joe Winder got there, Charles Chelsea was watching himself on the VCR, reliving the press conference.

"Whadja think?" he asked, motioning at the television screen in the cabinet.

"I missed it," said Joe Winder.

"You missed it? It was your bloody speech—how'd you miss it?"

"I heard you were dynamite."

Charles Chelsea broke into a grin. "Yeah? Who said?"

"Everybody," lied Joe Winder. "They said you're another Mario Cuomo."

"Well, your speech had something to do with it."

It wasn't a speech, Winder thought; it was a *statement*. Forty lines, big deal.

"It was a great speech, Joe," Chelsea went on, "except for one part.

Specially climatized habitat. That's a mouthful. Maybe we should've tried something else." With pursed lips he repeated the culprit phrase: "Climatized habitat—when I was trying to say it, I accidentally spit on that girl from Channel 10. The cute one. Next time be more careful, okay? Don't sneak in any zingers without me knowing."

Joe Winder said, "I was in a hurry." The backs of his eyeballs were starting to throb. Sinus headache: Chelsea always gave him one. But Winder had to admit, the guy looked like a million bucks in an oxford shirt. He looked like a vice president in charge of public relations, which he was.

Chelsea was saying, "I don't even know what it means, climatized habitat."

"That's the beauty of it," Winder said.

"Now, now." Chelsea wagged a well-tanned finger. "None of that, Joey. There's no place for cynics here at the Amazing Kingdom. You know what Kingsbury says."

"Yeah. We're all little kids." Winder kneaded his skull with both hands, trying to squeeze out the pain.

"Children," Charles Chelsea said. He turned off the VCR and spun his chair to face Joe Winder. "The moment we walk through that gate, we're all children. We see the world through children's eyes; we cry children's tears, we laugh children's laughter. We're all innocent again, Joe, and where there's innocence there can't be cynicism. Not here in the Amazing Kingdom."

Joe Winder said, "You're giving me a fucking headache. I hope you're happy."

Charles Chelsea's blue eyes narrowed and darkened. "Look, we hired you because you're good and you're fast. But this isn't a big-city newsroom. you can't use that type of coarse language. Children don't talk like that, Joe. That's gutter language."

"Sorry," said Winder, concealing his amusement. Gutter language, that was a good one.

"When's the last time you heard a child say that word?"

"Which word, Charlie?"

"You know. The 'F' word."

"I've heard children say it. Plenty of times."

"Not here, you haven't." Charles Chelsea sat up straight, trying to radiate authority. "This is a major event for us, Joey. We've had a robbery on the premises. Felons invaded the theme park. Somebody could've been hurt."

"Rat-nappers," Winder remarked. "Not exactly Ted Bundy."

"Hey," Chelsea said, tapping a lacquered fingernail on the desk.

"Hey, this is serious. Mr. X is watching very closely to see how we do. All of us, Joe, all of us in Publicity are on red alert until this thing blows over. We mishandle it, and it blows up into a story about crime at the Amazing Kingdom. If we can spin it around, it's a story about a crime against Nature. Nature with a capital 'N.' The annihilation of an entire species. Where's your notebook?"

"Downstairs, on my desk."

"Listen, you're my ace in the hole. Whatever gets dumped in my lap gets dumped in yours."

Joe Winder's sinuses hurt so much he thought his eyeballs must be leaking from the inside. He didn't want to be Chelsea's ace in the hole.

Chelsea said, "And, Joe, while we're at it, what'd I tell you about the hair? No braids."

"But it's all the rage," Winder said.

"Get it cut before Kingsbury sees you. Please, Joe, you look like a Navajo nightmare."

"Nice talk, Charlie."

"Sit down," said Chelsea, "and put on your writing cap."

"I'd love to look as spiffy as you, but you bought up all the oxford shirts in Miami. Either that or you wear the same one every day."

Chelsea wasn't listening. "Before we begin, there's some stuff you need to know."

"Like what?"

"Like their names."

"Whose names?"

"The voles," Charles Chelsea said. "Vance and Violet—two helpless, adorable, fuzzy little furballs. Mated for life. The last of their species, Joey."

With a straight face, Winder repeated the names of the missing creatures. "Vance and Violet Vole. That's lovely." He glanced at his wristwatch, and saw that it was half past five. "Charlie," he said, "you don't happen to have any Darvons?"

Chelsea said, "I wish you were writing this stuff down."

"What the hell for?"

"For the story. The story of how Francis X. Kingsbury tried everything in his power to save the blue-tongued mango voles from extinction."

"Only to be thwarted by robbers?"

"You got it," said Charles Chelsea. "Stay late if necessary and take a comp day next week—I need a thousand words by tomorrow morning. I promised Corporate a press kit." He stood up and waited for Joe Winder to do the same. "Get with Koocher for more background on the missing animals. He's got reams of pictures, too, in case you need inspiration. By the way, did you ever get to see them?"

Winder felt oddly detached. "The voles? No, not in person," he said. "I wasn't even aware they had names."

"They do now."

At the door, Charles Chelsea winked and shook Joe Winder's hand. "You know, Joe, some people in the organization weren't too thrilled when we brought you aboard. I mean, after what happened up at Disney."

Winder nodded politely. Chelsea's hand felt moist and lifeless, like a slab of cold grouper.

"But, by God, I knew you'd be fine. That speech today was masterful, Joey, a classic."

"A classic."

"I need you on this one. The other kids are fine, they can turn a phrase. But they're right out of school, most of them, and they're not ready for something so big. For this I need somebody with scars. Combat experience."

With effort, Joe Winder said, "Guess I'm your man."

Charles Chelsea chucked him on the arm and opened the door.

"What about a reward?" Winder asked. "In the press release, should I say we're offering a reward?"

Thinking about it, Chelsea nearly rubbed the tan off his chin. "I guess it couldn't hurt," he said finally. "What do you think?"

"For two rats? Ten grand is good."

"Voles, Joe. Don't ever say rats. And five grand is plenty."

Winder shrugged. "The park netted forty-two million dollars last year. I know a few reporters who'd be happy to remind us."

"All right, go for ten," said Charles Chelsea. "But don't overplay it. Otherwise every geek in Miami is going to show up at the gate with shoe boxes full of God knows what."

The thought of it made Joe Winder smile for the first time all day.

▼ ▼ ▼

One of the few things Winder liked about his new job was the golf cart he got to drive around the Amazing Kingdom of Thrills. It was a souped-up Cushman with an extra set of twelve-volts, and headlights scavenged off a real Jeep. It was the closest thing to a company car that Joe Winder ever had, and sometimes (especially on that long downhill stretch between Magic Mansion and the Wet Willy) he could stomp on the tiny accelerator and forget what exactly he did for a living.

At night Joe Winder tried to drive more carefully, because it was harder to watch out for the tourists. The tourists at the Amazing Kingdom seldom paid attention to where they were going; they wandered and weaved, peered and pointed. And who could blame them? There were so many colorful and entertaining distractions. Before Charles Chelsea had given Joe Winder the keys to the Cushman, he had warned him to be wary when driving near the tourists. "Whatever you do, don't hit one," Chelsea had said. "If you're going to crash, aim for a building," he had advised, "or even a park employee. Anything but a paying customer."

So Joe Winder drove with extra caution in the golf cart at night. He arrived at the Rare Animal Pavilion shortly after eight, and parked in the back. Dr. Will Koocher, the vole man, was waiting inside with handouts and glossy photographs. Winder sat on a lab stool and skimmed the material.

Koocher said, "We kept the information fairly general. They tell me the pictures usually go over big."

As Winder studied the photographs, he said, "Cute little buggers."

"They're just rodents," the doctor noted, without malice.

"You don't understand," Winder said, "Cuteness is vital for a story like this." He explained how newspapers and television stations got much more excited about animal stories when the animal came across as cuddly and lovable. "I'm not saying it's good or bad, but that's the way it is."

Will Koocher nodded. "Like with the manatees—everybody wants to save the manatees, but nobody gives a hoot about the poor crocodiles."

"Because they're not particularly cute," Winder said. "Who wants to hug a reptile?"

"I see your point." Will Koocher was a gaunt young man with the longest neck that Joe Winder had ever seen. He seemed painfully earnest and shy, and Winder liked him immediately.

"I'll tell you what I can," Koocher said, "but I've only been here a month."

Like everything else at the Amazing Kingdom, the Vole Project had begun as a scheme to compete with Walt Disney World. Years earlier, Disney had tried to save the dusky seaside sparrow, a small marsh bird whose habitat was being wiped out by overdevelopment along Florida's coastline. With much fanfare, Disney had unveiled a captive-breeding program for the last two surviving specimens of the dusky. Unfortunately, the last two surviving specimens were both males, and even the wizards of Disney could not induce the scientific miracle of homosexual procreation. Eventually the sparrow fell to extinction, but the Disney organization won gobs of fawning publicity for its conservation efforts.

Not to be outdone (although he invariably was), Francis X. Kingsbury had selected another endangered species and commanded his staff save it, ASAP. And so the Vole Project was born.

Koocher had gotten the phone call while finishing his thesis at Cornell. "I'd published two field studies on the genus *Microtus*, so I suppose that's where they got my name. Anyway, this guy Chelsea calls and asks if I'd heard of *Microtus mango*, and I said no, all my work was on the northern species. He sent me a scientific paper that had been published, and offered me a job. Forty grand a year."

"That's good money right out of school."

"Tell me about it. I burned up the interstate getting down here."

"And that's when you met Violet and Vance."

"Who's that?"

"The voles," Winder said. "They've got names now."

"Really?" Will Koocher looked doubtful. "I always called them Male One and Female One."

"Not anymore. Kingsbury's got big plans, PR-wise. The little mango cuties are going to be famous—don't be surprised if the networks show up tomorrow."

"Is that so," Koocher said, with not the wildest enthusiasm. Winder sensed that the scientist disapproved of anthropomorphizing rodents, so he decided to lay off the Vance-and-Violet routine. Instead he asked about the tongue

"Well, it really is blue," Koocher said stiffly. "Remarkably blue."

"Could I say indigo?" Joe Winder was taking notes.

"Yeah," said Koocher, "that's about right." He started to say something more, but caught himself.

Joe Winder asked: "So what killed off the rest of them? Was it disease?"

"No, same old story. The encroachment of mankind." Koocher unfolded a map that illustrated how the mango vole had once ranged from the Middle Keys up to Palm Beach. As the coastline surrendered to hotels, subdivisions and condominiums, the voles' territory shrank. "They tell me the last known colony was here, on North Key Largo. One of Kingsbury's foremen found it in 1988, but so did a hungry barn owl. They were lucky to save the two that they did."

"And they mated for life?" said Winder.

Koocher seemed amused. "Who told you that?"

"Chelsea."

"That figures. Voles don't mate for life. They mate for fun, and they mate with just about anything that resembles another vole."

Winder said, "Then here's another dumb question: Why were there only two in our exhibit? They'd been together, what, a year? So where're all the bouncing baby voles?"

Edgily, Koocher said, "That's been our biggest disappointment."

"I did some reading up on it," Winder said. "With your typical *Microtus*, the female gives birth every two months. Each litter's got eight or nine babies—at that rate, you could replenish the whole species in a year."

Will Koocher shifted uncomfortably. "Female One was not receptive," he said. "Do you understand what that means?"

"Do I ever."

"This was an extreme case. The female nearly killed the male on several occasions. We had to hire a Wackenhut to watch the cage."

"A guard?" said Joe Winder.

"To make sure she didn't hurt him."

Winder swallowed a laugh. Apparently, Koocher saw no humor in the story. He said, "I felt sorry for the little guy. The female was much larger, and extremely hostile. Every time the male would attempt to mount her, she would attack."

Joe Winder put his notebook away. He'd think of a way to write around the reproduction question.

Koocher said: "The female vole wasn't quite right."

"In what way?"

But Koocher was staring past him. Winder turned and saw Charles Chelsea on the other side of the glass door. Chelsea gave a chipper, three-fingered salute and disappeared.

The doctor said, "Now's not a terrific time to get into all this. Can we talk later?"

"You bet. I'll be in the publicity office."

"No, not here. Can I call you at home in a day or two?"

Winder said sure. "But I've got to write the press release tonight. If there's something I ought to know, please tell me before I make an ass of myself."

Koocher stood up and smoothed the breast of his lab coat. "That business about the networks coming—were you serious?"

"Cute sells," Winder said. "You take an offbeat animal story on a slow news day, we're talking front page."

"Christ." Koocher sighed.

"Hey, I'm sorry," Winder said. He hadn't meant to come off as such a coldhearted prick. "I know what these little critters meant to you."

Will Koocher smiled ruefully. He folded the habitat map and put it away. He looked tired and sad, and Winder felt bad for him. "It's all right," the young scientist said. "They were doomed, no matter what."

"We're all doomed," said Joe Winder, "if you really think about it." Which he tried not to.

▼ ▼ ▼

Bud Schwartz parked the pickup truck under an immense ficus tree. He told Danny Pogue not to open the doors right away, because of all the mosquitoes. The insects had descended in a sibilant cloud, bouncing off the windows and the hood and the headlights.

"I bet we don't have no bug spray," said Danny Pogue.

Bud Schwartz pointed at the house. "On the count of three, make a run for it."

Danny Pogue remarked that the old place was dark. "She saving on the electricity, or what? I bet she's not even home. I bet she was hoping we got caught, so she wouldn't have to pay us."

"You got no faith," said Bud Schwartz. "You're the most negative fucking person I ever met. That's why your skin's broke out all the time —all those negative thoughts is like a poison in your bloodstream."

"Wait a minute, now. Everybody gets pimples."

Bud Schwartz said, "You're thirty-one years old. Tell me that's normal."

"Do we got bug spray or not?"

"No." Bud Schwartz unlocked his door. "Now let's go—one, two, three!"

They burst out of the pickup and bolted for the house, flailing at mosquitoes as they ran. When they got inside the screened porch, the two men took turns swatting the insects off each other. A light came on, and Molly McNamara poked out of the door. Her white hair was up in curlers, her cheeks were slathered in oily yellow cream and her broad, pointy-shouldered frame was draped in a blue terry-cloth bath-robe.

"Get inside," she said to the two men.

Immediately Bud Schwartz noticed how grim the woman looked. The curlers, cream and bathrobe didn't help.

The house was all mustiness and shadows, made darker and damper by the ubiquitous wood paneling. The living room smelled of jasmine, or some other old-woman scent. It reminded Bud Schwartz of his grandmother's sewing room.

Molly McNamara sat down in a rocker. Bud Schwartz and Danny Pogue just stood there like the hired help they were.

"Where are they?" Molly demanded. "Where's the box?"

Danny Pogue looked at Bud Schwartz, who said, "They got away."

Molly folded her hands across her lap. She said, "You're lying to me."

"No, ma'am."

"Then tell me what happened."

Before Bud Schwartz could stop him, Danny Pogue said, "There was holes in the box. That's how they got out."

Molly McNamara's right hand slipped beneath her bathrobe and came out holding a small black pistol. Without saying a word she shot Danny Pogue twice in the left foot. He fell down, screaming, on the smooth pine floor. Bud Schwartz couldn't believe it; he tried to speak, but there was no air in his lungs.

"You boys are lying," Molly said. She got up from the rocker and left the room. She came back with a towel, chipped ice, bandages and a roll of medical adhesive tape. She told Bud Schwartz to patch up his partner before the blood got all over everything. Bud Schwartz knelt on the floor next to Danny Pogue and tried to calm him. Molly sat down and started rocking.

"The towel is for his mouth," she said, "so I don't have to listen to all that yammering."

And it was true, Danny Pogue's wailing was unbearable, even allowing for the pain. It reminded Bud Schwartz of the way his first wife had sounded during the thrashings of childbirth.

Molly said, "It's been all over the news, so at least I know that you went ahead and did it. I suppose I'm obliged to pay up."

Bud Schwartz was greatly relieved; she wouldn't pay somebody she was about to kill. The thought of being murdered by a seventy-year-old woman in pink curlers was harrowing on many levels.

"Tell me if I'm wrong," Molly said. "Curiosity got the best of you, right? You opened the box, the animals escaped."

"That's about the size of it," said Bud Schwartz, wrapping a bandage around Danny Pogue's foot. He had removed the sneaker and the sock, and examined the wounds. Miraculously (or maybe by design) both bullets had missed the bones, so Danny Pogue was able to wiggle all his toes. When he stopped whimpering, Bud Schwartz removed the towel from his mouth.

"So you think they're still alive," Molly said.

"Why not? Who'd be mean enough to hurt 'em?"

"This is important," said Molly. The pistol lay loose on her lap, looking as harmless as a macramé.

Danny Pogue said, "We didn't kill them things, I swear to God. They just scooted out of the damn truck."

"They're awful fast," added Bud Schwartz.

"Oh, please," said Molly McNamara, shaking her head. Even Danny Pogue picked up on the sarcasm.

"We didn't know there was only two," he said. "We thought there must be a whole bunch in a box that size. That's how come we wasn't so worried when they got away—see, we thought there was more."

Molly started rocking a little faster. The rocking chair didn't squeak a bit on the varnished pine. She said, "I'm very disappointed in the both of you."

Bud Schwartz helped his partner limp to an ottoman. All he wanted was to get the money and get the hell out of this spooky old house, away from this crazy witch.

"Here's the really bad news," said Molly McNamara. "It's your truck—only about a thousand people saw you drive away. Now, I don't know if they got the license tag, but they sure as hell got a good description. It's all over the TV."

"Shit," said Bud Schwartz.

"So you're going to have to keep a low profile for a while."

Still breathing heavily, Danny Pogue said, "What's that mean?"

Molly stopped rocking and sat forward. "For starters, say good-bye to the pickup truck. Also, you can forget about going home. If the police got your tag, they'll be waiting."

"I'll take my chances," said Bud Schwartz.

"No, you won't," said Molly. "I'll give you a thousand dollars each. You'll get the rest in two weeks, if things die down. Meanwhile, I've arranged a place for you boys to stay."

"Here?" asked Danny Pogue in a fretful, pain-racked voice.

"No, not here," Molly said. "Not on your life."

She stood up from the rocker. The pistol disappeared again into a fuzzy pocket of the blue robe. "Your foot's going to be fine," she announced to Danny Pogue. "I hope I made my point."

The bafflement on the two men's faces suggested otherwise.

Molly McNamara said, "I chose you for a reason."

"Come on," said Bud Schwartz, "we're just burglars."

"And don't you ever forget it," Molly said.

Danny Pogue couldn't believe she was talking to them this way. He couldn't believe he was being terrorized by an old lady in a rocking chair.

"There's something else you should know," said Molly McNamara. "There are others."

Momentarily Bud Schwartz's mind had stuck on that thousand dollars she'd mentioned. He had been thinking: Screw the other nine, just grab the grand and get lost. Now she was saying something about others—what others?

"Anything happens to me," Molly said, "there's others that know who you are. Where you live. Where you hang out. Everything."

"I don't get it," muttered Danny Pogue.

"Burglars get shot sometimes," Molly McNamara said. "Nobody says boo about it, either. Nobody gets arrested or investigated or anything else. In this country, you kill a burglar and the Kiwanis gives you a plaque. That's the point I was trying to make."

Danny Pogue turned to Bud Schwartz, who was staring down at his partner's swollen foot and wondering if it was too late to make a run for it. Finally he said, "Lady, we're very sorry about your animals."

"They're not my animals," said Molly, "any more than you are."

3

At half past ten Joe Winder went down to The Catacombs, the underground network of service roads that ran beneath the Amazing Kingdom of Thrills. It was along these winding cart paths, discreetly out of view from visitors, that the food, merchandise, money and garbage were moved throughout the sprawling amusement park. It was also along these secret subterranean passageways that the kiddie characters traveled, popping up suddenly at strategic locations throughout the Amazing Kingdom and imploring tourists to snap their picture. No customers ("guests" was the designated term) ever were allowed to venture into The Catacombs, lest they catch a glimpse of something that might tarnish their image of the Amazing Kingdom—a dog rooting through a dumpster, for example. Or one of Uncle Ely's Elves smoking a joint.

Which is what Joe Winder saw when he got to the bottom of the stairs.

"I'm looking for Robbie Raccoon," he said to the elf, who wasn't particularly jolly or gnomelike.

The elf belched blue smoke and asked which Robbie Raccoon he was looking for, since there were three.

"The one who was on duty this afternoon," Winder said. "The one who fought with the rat robbers."

The big elf pointed with the smoldering end of the joint. "Okay, there's a locker room on the west side. Just follow the orange signs." He took another drag. "I'd offer you a hit, but I got this nasty chest virus. Hate to pass it along."

"Sure," said Joe Winder. "No problem."

The lockers were at the end of a damp concrete tunnel that smelled of stale laundry and ammonia. Robbie Raccoon was straddling the bench, trying to unzip his head. Winder introduced himself, and explained that he was from the Publicity Department.

"I'm writing a press release about what happened earlier today," he said. "A few quick questions is all."

"Fire away," said Robbie Raccoon. The words came out muffled, from a small opening in the neck of the costume.

Winder said, "I can barely hear you."

With a grunt Robbie Raccoon removed his head, which was as large as a beach ball. Joe Winder was startled by what he saw beneath it: long shimmering blond hair, green eyes and mascara. Robbie Raccoon was a woman.

She said, "If you're going to make a joke, get it over with."

"No, I wasn't."

"Don't think this is my life ambition or anything."

"Of course not," said Joe Winder.

The woman said her name was Carrie Lanier. "And I got my SAG card," she said, still somewhat defensive. "That's the only reason I took this stupid job. I'm going to be an actress."

Mindlessly Winder said, "You've got to start somewhere."

"Darn right."

He waited for Carrie Lanier to remove the rest of the raccoon outfit, but she didn't. He took out his notebook and asked her to describe what had happened at the Rare Animal Pavilion.

Carrie shrugged in an exaggerated way, as if she were still in character. "It was two men, we're talking white trash. One of them has a sledgehammer, and they're both walking real fast. I start to follow, don't ask me why—I just had a hunch. All of a sudden the one with the hammer smashes out the glass in one of the exhibits."

"And you tried to stop him?"

"Yeah, I jumped the guy. Climbed on his back. He turned around and clobbered me pretty solid. Thank God for this." Carrie knocked on the crown of the raccoon head, which was propped face-up on the bench. Her fist made a sharp hollow sound. "Chicken wire, plaster and Kevlar," she explained. "They say it's bulletproof."

Joe Winder wrote this down, even though Charles Chelsea would never let him use it in the press release. At the Amazing Kingdom, each publicity announcement was carefully purged of all intriguing details. Winder was having a tough time kicking the habit of taking good notes.

Carrie Lanier said, "He knocked me down pretty hard, but that's about it. There was a tour group from Taiwan, Korea, someplace like that. They helped me off the ground, but by then the two dirtbags were long gone. I could've done without the ambulance ride, but Risk Management said I had to."

"Can I say you suffered a slight head injury?" Joe Winder asked, pen poised.

"No," said Carrie Lanier. "As soon as the X-rays came out negative, they hauled me back to work. I'm fine."

That wouldn't go over well with Charles Chelsea; the vole story was infinitely more dramatic if a park employee had been wounded in the rescue attempt.

"Not even a headache?" Winder persisted.

"Yeah, I've got a headache," Carrie said. "I've always got a headache. Take a whiff of this place." She stood up and yanked on the fluffy striped raccoon tail, which was attached to the rump of the costume by a Velcro patch. The tail made a ripping sound when Carrie took it off. She tossed it in her locker and said, "Why would anyone steal rats?"

"Voles," said Joe Winder.

"The guys who did it, boy, what a pair. Scum of the earth."

Again Winder didn't bother to write this down.

"It's crazy," said Carrie Lanier. She reached beneath her left armpit and found, deep in the fur, another zipper. Carefully she unzipped the costume lengthwise down to her ankle. She did the same on the other side. As she stepped out of the animal outfit, Winder saw that she was wearing only a bra and panties. He tried not to stare.

Carrie hung the costume on a pair of hooks in the locker. She said, "This damn thing weighs a ton, I wish you'd write that down. It's about a hundred twenty degrees inside, too. OSHA made them put in air conditioners, but they're always broken."

Winder stepped closer to examine the raccoon costume, not Carrie Lanier in her bra (which was the type that unhooked in the front; pink with lacy cups). Winder held up the animal suit and said, "Where's the AC?"

"In the back. Here, look." Carrie showed him. "The batteries last about two hours max, then forget about it. We tried to call the feds and complain—what a joke. They haven't been out here since the day Petey Possum died."

"Do I want to hear this story?"

"Heart attack," Carrie Lanier went on. "This was Sessums. Billy Sessums. The very first Petey Possum. He'd been twenty-two years with Disneyland—Goofy, Pluto, you name it. Billy was a pro. He taught me plenty."

"So what happened?"

"One of those days. Ninety-two in the shade, one twelve inside the possum suit. The AC went out, and so did Billy." Carrie Lanier paused reflectively. "He was an older fella but still . . ."

"I'm sorry," said Joe Winder. He put his notebook away. He was starting to feel prickly and claustrophobic.

Carrie said, "You're gonna put my name in the press release?"

"I'm afraid not. It's company policy not to identify the actors who portray the animal characters. Mr. Kingsbury says it would spoil the illusion for the children."

Carrie laughed. "Some illusion. I've had kids grab my boobs, right through the costume. One time there was a Shriner, tried to goose me in the Magic Mansion."

Winder said, "How'd they know you were a woman?"

"That's the scary part." Her eyes flashed mischievously. "What if they didn't know I was a woman? What if they thought I was a real raccoon? What would Mr. Francis X. Kingsbury say about that?" She took a pair of blue jeans out of the locker and squirmed into them. "Anyhow, I don't want my name in any stupid press release," she said. "Not for this place."

"Maybe not, but you did a brave thing," said Winder.

As Carrie buttoned her blouse, she said, "I don't want my folks knowing what I do. You blame me?"

"You make lots of little children happy. What's wrong with that?"

She looked at him evenly. "You're new here, aren't you?"

"Yeah," Joe Winder said.

"My job's crummy, but you know what? I think your job is worse."

▼ ▼ ▼

Joe Winder wrote the press release in forty minutes. "Theft of Rare Animals Stuns Amazing Kingdom." Ten paragraphs on the crime itself, with a nod to the heroics of Robbie Raccoon ("who barely escaped serious injury"). Three paragraphs of official reaction ("a sad and shocking event") from Francis X. Kingsbury, chairman and president of the park. Three grafs more of scientific background on the blue-tongued mango vole, with a suitable quote from Dr. Will Koocher.

A hundred words about the $10,000 reward, and a hundred more announcing new beefed-up security precautions at the park.

Winder put the press release on Charles Chelsea's desk and went home. By the time he called Nina, it was nearly one in the morning. He dialed the number and hoped she would be the one to answer.

"Hello, sugar," Nina said.

"It's me."

"God, I need to talk to a real man," she said. "I had a fantasy that got me so hot. We were on the bow of a sailboat. Making love in the sun. I was on top. Suddenly a terrible storm came—"

"Nina, it's me!"

"—but instead of hiding in the cabin, we lashed each other to the deck and kept on doing it in the lightning and thunder. Afterwards the warm rain washed the salt off our bodies. . . ."

"For Christ's sake."

"Joe?"

"Yeah, it's me. Why don't you ever listen?"

"Because they don't pay me to listen," Nina said. "They pay me to talk."

"I wish you'd get a normal job."

"Joe, don't start."

Nina was a voice for one of those live dial-a-fantasy telephone services. She worked nights, which put a strain on her personal relationships. Also, every time Joe Winder called, it cost him four bucks. At least the number was easy to remember: 976-COME.

Nina said, "What do you think about the lightning-and-thunder business? I added it to the script myself."

"What was it before—something about whales, right?"

"Porpoises, Joe. *A school of friendly porpoises leaped and frolicked in the water while we made love. Our animal cries only seemed to arouse them.*"

Nina had a wonderful voice, Winder had to admit. "I like the new stuff better," he agreed. "The storm idea is good—you wrote that yourself?"

"Don't sound so surprised." She asked him how his day had gone, and he told her about the stolen voles.

Nina said, "See? And you thought you were going to be bored."

"I am bored. Most of the time."

"Joe, it's never going to be like the old days."

He wasn't in the mood to hear it. He said, "How's it going with you?"

"Slow," Nina said. "Beverly went home early. It's just me and Miriam."

"Any creeps call in?" Of course creeps had called—who else would bother?

"The usual jack-off artists," Nina reported. "They're harmless, Joe, don't worry. I just give a straight read, no moans or groans, and still they get off in about thirty seconds. I had one guy fall asleep afterwards. Snoring like a baby."

Sometimes she talked about her job as if it were a social service, like UNICEF or Meals on Wheels.

"When will you be home?" Winder asked.

The usual, Nina said, meaning four in the morning. "Want me to wake you up?"

"Sure." She had loads of energy, this girl. Winder needed somebody with energy, to help him use up his own. One of the drawbacks of his high-paying bullshit PR job was that it took absolutely nothing out of him, except his pride.

Hurriedly Nina said, "Joe, I got another call waiting."

"Make it short and sweet."

"I'll deal with you later, sailor boy."

And then she hung up.

▼ ▼ ▼

Winder couldn't sleep, so he put a Warren Zevon tape in the stereo and made himself a runny cheese omelet. He ate in the living room, near the speakers, and sat on a box because there were no chairs in the apartment. The box was filled with old newspaper clippings, his own, as well as plaques and certificates from various journalism awards that he had received over the years. The only important journalism award that wasn't in the box was the single one that impressed anybody—the Pulitzer Prize, which Joe Winder had never won.

When he was first interviewed for the publicity-writing job at the Amazing Kingdom of Thrills, Joe Winder had been asked if he'd ever gotten a Pulitzer. When he answered no, Charles Chelsea had threatened to put him on the polygraph machine.

"I never won," Winder insisted. "You can look it up."

And Charles Chelsea did. A Pulitzer on the wall would have disqualified Joe Winder from the PR job just as surely as flunking a urinalysis for drugs.

"We're not in the market for aggressive, hard-bitten newshounds," Chelsea had warned him. "We're looking for writers with a pleasing, easygoing style. We're looking for a certain attitude."

"I'm flexible," Joe Winder had said. "Especially my attitude."

Chelsea had grilled him about the other journalism awards, then about the length of his hair, then about the thin pink scar along his jawline.

Eyeing Winder's face at close range, the publicity man had said, "You look like a bar fighter Did you get that scar in a fight?"

"Car accident," Joe Winder had lied, figuring what the hell, Chelsea must've known the truth. One phone call to the newspaper, and any number of people would've been happy to drop the dime.

But Chelsea never said another word about the scar, never gave a hint that he'd even picked up the rumor. It was Joe Winder's journalism achievements that seemed to disturb the publicity man, although these concerns were ultimately outweighed by the discovery that Winder had been born and raised in Florida. The Publicity Department at the Amazing Kingdom was desperate for native talent, somebody who understood the mentality of tourists and crackers alike.

The Disney stint hadn't hurt Joe Winder's chances, either; he had worked among the enemy, and learned many of their professional secrets. So Charles Chelsea had set aside his doubts and hired him.

That was two weeks ago. It was still too early for Winder to compare the new job with the one at Disney World. Certainly Disney was slicker and more efficient than the Amazing Kingdom, but it was also more regimented and impersonal. The Disney bureaucracy, and its reach, was awesome. In retrospect Joe Winder wasn't sure how he had lasted as long as he did, six months, before he was caught having sex on Mr. Toad's Wild Ride and fired for not wearing his ID card. Winder felt especially bad that the young woman with whom he'd been dallying, a promising understudy to Cinderella, had also been dismissed over the incident; she for leaving Main Street during Mickey's Birthday Parade.

During the job interview at the Amazing Kingdom, Charles Chelsea had told him: "You work for us, you'd better keep it in your pants, understand?"

"I've got a girlfriend now," Joe Winder had said.

"Don't think you won't be tempted around here."

Winder hadn't been tempted once, until today. Now he was thinking about Carrie Lanier, the fearless beauty inside a seven-foot racoon suit.

This is what happens when you turn thirty-seven, Winder thought; the libido goes blind with fever. What else could explain his attraction to Nina? Or her attraction to him?

Being a newspaper reporter had left Joe Winder no time for such reckless attachments. Being a flack left him all the time in the world.

Now that he was forbidden to write about trouble, he seemed determined to experience it.

He finished his omelet and opened a beer and slumped down on the floor, between the stereo speakers. Something had been nagging at him all afternoon, ever since the insufferable Chelsea had drafted him to help with the robbery crisis. In the push toward his deadline, it was clear to Joe Winder that none of his writing skills had eroded—his speed at the keyboard, his facile vocabulary, his smooth sense of pacing and transition. Yet something from the old days was missing.

Curiosity. The most essential and feral of reporters' instincts, the urge to pursue. It was dead. Or dying.

Two strangers had invaded a family theme park in broad daylight and kidnapped a couple of obscure rodents from an animal exhibit. Winder had thoroughly and competently reported the incident, but had made no effort to explore the fascinating possibilities. Having established the *what*, he had simply ignored the *why*.

Even by South Florida standards the crime was perverse, and the old Joe Winder would have reveled energetically in its mysteries. The new Joe Winder had merely typed up his thousand words, and gone home.

Just as he was supposed to do.

So this is how it feels, he thought. This is how it feels to sell out. On the stereo, Warren Zevon was singing about going to the Louvre museum and throwing himself against the wall. To Joe Winder it sounded like a pretty good idea.

He closed his eyes tightly and thought: Don't tell me I'm getting used to this goddamn zombie job. Then he thought: Don't tell me I'm getting drunk on one lousy beer.

He crawled across the carpet to the phone, and tried to call Nina at the service. The woman named Miriam answered instead, and launched into a complicated fantasy involving trampolines and silver ankle bracelets. Miriam was struggling so valiantly in broken English ("Ooooh, bebee, chew make me comb so many time!") that Joe Winder didn't have the heart to interrupt.

What the hell, it was only four bucks. He could certainly afford it.

4

On the morning of July 17, Danny Pogue awoke in a cold sweat, his T-shirt soaked from neck to navel. He kicked the covers off the bed and saw the lump of gauze around his foot. It wasn't a dream. He limped to the window and from there he could see everything: the Olympic-sized swimming pool, the freshly painted tennis courts, the shady shuffleboard gazebo. Everywhere he looked there were old people with snowy heads and pale legs and fruit-colored Bermuda shorts. All the men wore socks with their sandals, and all the women wore golf visors and oversized sunglasses.

"Mother of Christ," said Danny Pogue. He hollered for his partner to come quick.

Bud Schwartz ambled in, looking settled and well rested. He was spooning out half a grapefruit, cupped in the palm of one hand. "Do you believe this fucking place?" he said to Danny Pogue. "What a gas."

"We gotta get out."

"How come?"

"Just look." Danny Pogue pointed out the window.

"So now you got a problem with senior citizens? What—they don't have the right to have fun? Besides, there's some young people that live here, too. I saw a couple a hot ones out by the swimming pool. Major titties."

"I don't care," mumbled Danny Pogue.

"Hey," Bud Schwartz said. "She shot your foot, not your weenie."

"Where is she?"

"Long gone. You want some lunch? She loaded up at the Publix, you should see. Steaks, chops, beer—we're set for a couple a weeks, easy."

Danny Pogue hopped back to the bed and peeled off the damp shirt. He spotted a brand-new pair of crutches propped in the corner. He said, "Bud, I'm gonna split. Seriously, I'm taking off."

"I can give you ten thousand reasons not to."

"Speaking of which."

"She's bringing a grand for each of us, just like she promised," said Bud Schwartz. "Good faith money is what she called it."

"Invisible is what I call it."

"Hey, lighten the fuck up. She's an old lady, Danny. Old ladies never lie." Bud Schwartz lobbed the grapefruit skin into some kind of designer wastebasket. "What's wrong with you, man? This is like a vacation, all expenses paid. Look at this freaking condo—two bedrooms, two bathrooms. Microwave in the kitchen, Cinemax on the cable. Say what you will, the old geezer knows how to live."

"Who is she?" Danny Pogue asked.

"Who cares?"

"I care. She shot me."

Bud Schwartz said, "Just some crazy, rich old broad. Don't worry about it."

"It's not you that got shot."

"She won't do it again, Danny. She got it out of her system." Bud Schwartz wiped his hands on the butt of his jeans to get the grapefruit juice off. He said, "She was pissed, that's all. On account of us losing the rats."

Danny Pogue said, "Well, screw that deal. I'm leaving." He made a move for the crutches but faltered, hot and dizzy. Molly McNamara had fed him some pain pills late last night; that much he remembered.

"I don't know where you think you're going," said Bud Schwartz. "The truck's history."

"I'll hitch," said Danny Pogue woozily.

"Look in the mirror. Your own mother wouldn't pick you up. The Hell's Fucking Angels wouldn't pick you up."

"Somebody'll stop," Danny Pogue said. "Especially with me on them crutches."

"Oh, sure."

"Maybe even some girls." Danny Pogue eased himself back on the pillow. He took deep breaths and tried to blink away the haze in his brain.

"Have another codeine," said Bud Schwartz. "Here, she got a whole bottle." He went to the kitchen and came back with a cold Busch.

Danny Pogue swallowed two more pills and slurped at the beer can noisily. He closed his eyes and said, "She ain't never gonna pay us, Bud."

"Sure she is," said his partner. "She's loaded, just look at this place. You should see the size of the TV."

"We better get away while we can."

"Go back to sleep," said Bud Schwartz. "I'll be down at the pool."

▼ ▼ ▼

The Mothers of Wilderness met every other Tuesday at a public library in Cutler Ridge. This week the main item on the agenda was the proposed bulldozing of seventy-three acres of mangroves to make room for the back nine of a championship golf course on the shore of North Key Largo. The Mothers of Wilderness strenuously opposed the project, and had begun to map a political strategy to obstruct it. They pursued such crusades with unflagging optimism, despite the fact that they had never succeeded in stopping a single development. Not one. The builders ignored them. Zoning boards ignored them. County commissioners listened politely, nodded intently, then ignored them, too. Of all the environmental groups fighting to preserve what little remained of Florida, the Mothers of Wilderness was regarded as the most radical and shrill and intractable. It was also, unfortunately, the smallest of the groups and thus the easiest to brush off.

Still, the members were nothing if not committed. Molly Mc-Namara steadfastly had refused all offers to merge her organization with the Audubon Society or the Sierra Club or the Friends of the Everglades. She wanted no part of coalitions because coalitions compromised. She enjoyed being alone on the fringe, enjoyed being the loose cannon that establishment environmentalists feared. The fact that the Mothers of Wilderness was politically impotent did not diminish Molly McNamara's passion, though occasionally it ate at her pride.

She ran the meetings with brusque efficiency, presiding over a membership that tended to be retired and liberal and well-to-do. For its size, the Mothers of Wilderness was exceedingly well financed; Molly knew this was why the other environmental groups wooed her, in hopes of a merger. The Mothers had bucks.

They had hired a hotshot Miami land-use lawyer to fight the golf course project, which was called Falcon Trace. The lawyer, whose name was Spacci, stood up at the meeting to update the Mothers on the progress of the lawsuit, which, typically, was about to be thrown out of court. The case was being heard in Monroe County—specifically, Key West—where many of the judges were linked by conspiracy or simple inbreeding to the crookedest politicians. Moreover, the zoning lawyer admitted he was having a terrible time ascertaining the true owners of the Falcon Trace property; he had gotten as far as a blind trust in Dallas, then stalled.

Molly McNamara thanked Spacci for his report and made a motion to authorize another twenty thousand dollars for legal fees and investigative expenses. It passed unanimously.

After the meeting, Molly took the lawyer aside and said, "Next time I want to see some results. I want the names of these bastards."

"What about the lawsuit?"

"File a new one," Molly said. "You ever considered going federal?"

"How?" asked Spacci. "On what grounds?"

Pinching his elbow, Molly led him to an easel behind the rostrum. Propped on the easel was an aerial map of North Key Largo. Molly pointed and said, "See? There's where they want the golf course. And right here is a national wildlife refuge. That's your federal jurisdiction, Counselor."

The lawyer plucked a gold pen from his breast pocket and did some pointing of his own. "And right here, Ms. McNamara, is a two-thousand-acre amusement park that draws three million tourists every year. We'd be hard pressed to argue that one lousy golf course would be more disruptive to the habitat than what's already there—a major vacation resort."

Molly snapped, "You're the damn attorney. Think of something."

Bitterly she remembered the years she had fought the Kingsbury project; the Mothers of Wilderness had been the only group that had never given up. Audubon and the others had realized immediately that protest was futile; the prospect of a major theme park to compete with Disney World carried an orgasmic musk to local chambers of commerce. The most powerful of powerful civic leaders clung to the myth that Mickey Mouse was responsible for killing the family tourist trade in South Florida, strangling the peninsula so that all southbound station wagons stopped in Orlando. What did Miami have to offer as competition? Porpoises that could pitch a baseball with their blowholes? Wisecracking parrots on unicycles? Enjoyable diversions, but scarcely in the same high-tech league with Disney. The Mouse's sprawling self-contained empire sucked tourists' pockets inside out; they came, they spent until there was nothing left to spend; then they went home *happy*. To lifelong Floridians it was a dream concept: fleecing a snowbird in such a way that he came back for more. Astounding! So when Francis X. Kingsbury unveiled his impressive miniature replica of the Amazing Kingdom of Thrills—the Wet Willy water flume, the Magic Mansion, Orky the Killer Whale, Jungle Jerry, and so on—roars of exultation were heard from Palm Beach to Big Pine. The only cry of dismay came from the Mothers of Wilderness, who were (as usual) ignored.

"No golf course," Molly told Spacci the lawyer, "and no more chickenshit excuses from you." She sent him away with the wave of a blue-veined hand.

After the rank and file had gone home, Molly gathered the board of directors in the back of the library. Five women and two men, all nearly as gray as Molly, they sat in molded plastic chairs and sipped herbal tea while Molly told them what had happened.

It was a bizarre and impossible scheme, but no one asked Molly why she had done it. They knew why. In a fussy tone, one of the Mothers said: "This time you went too far."

"It's under control," Molly insisted.

"Except for the voles. They're not under control."

Another Mother asked: "Any chance of finding them?"

"You never know," said Molly.

"Horseshit," said the first Mother. "They're gone for good. Dead, alive, it doesn't matter if we can't locate the damn things."

Molly said, "Please. Keep your voice down."

The second Mother: "What about these two men? Where are they now?"

"My condo," Molly replied. "Up at Eagle Ridge."

"Lord have mercy."

"That's enough," said Molly sharply. "I said it's under control, and it's under control."

A silence fell over the small group. No one wished to challenge her authority, but this time things had really gotten out of hand. This time there was a chance they could all go to jail. "I'll have some more tea," the first Mother said finally, "and then I'd love to hear your new plan. You do have one?"

"Of course I do," said Molly McNamara. "For heaven's sake."

▼ ▼ ▼

When Joe Winder got to work, Charles Chelsea was waiting in yet another blue oxford shirt. He was sitting on the edge of Winder's desk in a pose of casual superiority. A newspaper was freshly folded under one arm. "Fine job on the press release," Chelsea said. "I changed a word or two, but otherwise it went out just like you wrote it."

Calmly Joe Winder said, "Which word or two did you change?"

"Oh, I improved Mr. Kingsbury's comments. Couple of adverbs here and there."

"Fine." Winder wasn't so surprised. It was well known that Chelsea invented all of Francis X. Kingsbury's quotes. Kingsbury was one of those men who rarely spoke in complete sentences. Didn't have to. For publicity purposes this made him perfectly useless and unquotable.

Chelsea said, "I also updated the info on Robbie Raccoon. Turns out he got a mild concussion from that blow to the head."

Winder forced a smile and set his briefcase on the desk. "It's a she, Charlie. And she was fine when I spoke to her last night. Not even a bruise."

Chelsea's voice took on a scolding tone. "Joey, you know the gender rule. If it's a male character, we always refer to it with masculine pronouns—regardless of who's inside the costume. I explained all this the day you were hired. It comes straight from Mr. X. Speaking of which, weren't you supposed to get a haircut?"

"Don't be a dork, Charlie."

"What's a dork?"

"You're not serious."

Charles Chelsea said, "Really, tell me. You called me a dork, I'd like to know what exactly that is."

"It's a Disney character," said Joe Winder. "Daffy Dork." He opened the briefcase and fumbled urgently for his sinus medicine. "Anyway, Charlie, the lady in the coon suit didn't have a concussion. That's a lie, and it's a stupid lie because it's so easy to check. Some newspaper reporter is going to make a few calls and we're going to look sleazy and dishonest, all because you had to exaggerate."

"No exaggeration," Charles Chelsea said, stiffening. "I spoke with Robbie Raccoon myself, first thing this morning. He said he got dizzy and sick overnight. Doctor said it's probably a concussion."

Winder popped two pills into his mouth and said, "You're amazing."

"We'll have a neurologist's report this afternoon, in case anybody wants to see. Notarized, too." Chelsea looked pleased with himself. "Mild concussion, Joe. Don't believe me, just ask Robbie."

"What'd you do, threaten to fire her? Bust her down to the elf patrol?"

Charles Chelsea stood up, shot his cuffs, gave Joe Winder his coldest, hardest look. "I came down here to thank you for doing such outstanding work, and look what I get. More of your cynicism. Just because you had a rotten night, Joey, it's no reason to rain on everyone else's parade."

Did the man really say that? Winder wondered. Did he really accuse me of raining on his parade? "That's the only reason you're here?" Winder said. "To thank me?"

"Well, not entirely." Charles Chelsea removed the newspaper from under his arm, unfolded it and handed it to Joe Winder. "Check the last three paragraphs."

It was the story about the theft of the blue-tongued mango voles. The *Herald* had stripped it across the top of the Local News page, a feature play. "Hey," Winder said brightly, "they even used one of our pictures."

"Never mind that, just read the last three grafs."

The newspaper story ended like this:

> An anonymous caller identifying himself as an animal-rights activist telephoned the Miami office of the Associated Press late Monday and took credit for the incident at the popular theme park. The caller claimed to be a member of the radical Wildlife Rescue Corps.
>
> "We freed the voles because they were being exploited," he said. "Francis Kingsbury doesn't care about saving the species, he just wanted another stupid tourist attraction."
>
> Officials at the Amazing Kingdom of Thrills were unavailable for comment late Monday night.

Joe Winder gave the newspaper back to Charles Chelsea and said, "What a kick in the nuts. I'll bet the boss man is going batshit."

"You find this amusing?"

"Don't you?" Winder asked. "I guess not."

"No," said Chelsea. He refolded the newspaper and returned it to his armpit. "What do you suggest in the way of a response?"

"I suggest we forget the fucking voles and get on with our lives."

"This is serious."

Winder said, "So I was right, Kingsbury's on a tear. Then I would suggest you tell him that we're waiting to see if there's any truth to this claim. Tell him that if we say anything now, it might turn around and bite us in the rat hole."

Chelsea started rubbing his chin, a sign of possible cognition. "Go on," he told Winder. "I'm listening."

"For instance, suppose the real Wildlife Rescue Corps calls up and denies any involvement. Hell, Charlie, there's a good chance the caller was a crank. Had nothing to do with the group. To play it safe, we don't respond for now. We say absolutely nothing."

"But if it turns out to be true?"

"Then," said Joe Winder, "we express outrage that any organization, no matter how worthy its cause, would commit a violent felony and endanger the lives of innocent bystanders."

Chelsea nodded enthusiastically; he liked what he was hearing. "Not just any bystanders," he said. "Tourists."

Winder went on: "We would also recount Mr. Kingsbury's many philanthropic gifts to the ASPCA, the World Wildlife Fund, Save the Beavers, whatever. And we would supply plenty of testimonial quotes from eminent naturalists supporting our efforts on behalf of the endangered mango vole."

"Excellent," Charles Chelsea said. "Joe, that's perfect."

"Pure unalloyed genius," Winder said.

"Let's hope it doesn't come to that," Chelsea said. "You don't want to spend the rest of the week writing about rodents. Too much like covering City Hall, right?"

Joe Winder chuckled politely. He could tell Chelsea was worried about pitching it to Kingsbury.

In a hopeful voice, Chelsea said, "You think the guy was really just a nut? This guy who called the AP?"

"Who knows," Winder said. "We've certainly got our share."

Charles Chelsea nodded hopefully. A simple nut would be fine with him, PR-wise; it's the zealots you had to worry about.

"The only thing to do is wait," said Joe Winder. Already he could feel his sinuses drying up. He felt suddenly clearheaded, chipper, even optimistic. Maybe it was the medicine flushing his head, or maybe it was something else.

Like having a real honest-to-God story, for a change. A story getting good and hot.

Just like the old days.

5

Chelsea had a stark, irrational fear of Francis X. Kingsbury. It was not Kingsbury's physical appearance (for he was gnomish and flabby) but his volcanically profane temper that caused Chelsea so much anxiety. Kingsbury long ago had practically ceased speaking in complete sentences, but his broken exclamations could be daunting and acerbic.

The words struck venomously at Charles Chelsea's insecurities, and made him tremble.

On the afternoon of July 17, Chelsea finished his lunch, threw up, flossed his teeth and walked briskly to Kingsbury's office. Kingsbury was leaning over the desk; the great man's sleeves were rolled up to reveal the famous lewd tattoo on his doughy left forearm. The other arm sparkled with a gold Robbie Raccoon wristwatch, with emerald insets. Today's surfer-blond hairpiece was longish and curly.

Kingsbury grunted at Charles Chelsea and said: "Wildlife Rescue Corps?" He raised his hands. "Well?"

Chelsea said, "The group exists, but the phone call could be a crank. We're checking it out."

"What's this exploitation—shit, we're talking about, what, some kind of rodent or such goddamn thing."

Not even close to a quotable sentence, Chelsea thought. It was astounding—the man spoke in overtorqued, expletive-laden fragments that somehow made perfect sense. At all times, Charles Chelsea knew exactly what Francis X. Kingsbury was talking about.

The publicity man said, "Don't worry, sir, the situation is being contained. We're ready for any contingency."

Kingsbury made a small fist. "Damage control," he said.

"Our top gun," Chelsea said. "His name is Joe Winder, and he's a real pro. Offering the reward money was his idea, sir. The AP led with it this morning, too."

Kingsbury sat down. He fingered the florid tip of his bulbous nose. "These animals, there's still a chance maybe?"

Chelsea could feel a chilly dampness spreading in deadly crescents from his armpits. "It's unlikely, sir. One of them is dead for sure. Shot by the highway patrol. Some tourists apparently mistook it for a rat."

"Terrific," said Kingsbury.

"The other one, likewise. The bandits threw it in the window of a Winnebago camper."

Kingsbury peered from beneath dromedary lids. "Don't," he said, exhaling noisily. "This is like . . . no, don't bother."

"You might as well know," said Chelsea. "It was a church group from Boca Raton in the Winnebago. They beat the poor thing to death with a golf umbrella. Then they threw it off the Card Sound Bridge."

There, Chelsea thought. He had done it. Stood up and delivered the bad news. Stood up like a man.

Francis X. Kingsbury entwined his hands and said: "Who knows about this? Knows that *we* know? Anybody?"

"You mean anybody on the outside? No." Charles Chelsea paused.

"Well, except the highway patrol. And I took care of them with some free passes to the Kingdom."

"But civilians?"

"No, sir. Nobody knows that we know the voles are dead."

"Fine," said Francis X. Kingsbury. "Good time to up the reward."

"Sir?"

"Make it a million bucks. Six zeros, if I'm not mistaken."

Chelsea took out a notebook and a Cross pen, and began to write. "That's one million dollars for the safe return of the missing voles."

"Which are dead."

"Yes, sir."

"Simple, hell. Very simple."

"It's a most generous offer," said Charles Chelsea.

"Bullshit," Kingsbury said. "It's PR, whatever. Stuff for the fucking AP."

"But your heart's in the right place."

Impatiently Kingsbury pointed toward the door. "Fast," he said. "Before I get sick."

Chelsea was startled. Backing away from Kingsbury's desk, he said, "I'm sorry, sir. Is it something I said?"

"No, something you are." Kingsbury spoke flatly, with just a trace of disgust.

On the way back to his office, Charles Chelsea stopped in the executive washroom and threw up again.

▼ ▼ ▼

Like many wildly successful Floridians, Francis X. Kingsbury was a transplant. He had moved to the Sunshine State in balding middle age, alone and uprooted, never expecting that he would become a multi-millionaire.

And, like so many new Floridians, Kingsbury was a felon on the run. Before arriving in Miami, he was known by his real name of Frankie King. Not Frank, but Frankie; his mother had named him after the singer Frankie Laine. All his life Frankie King had yearned to change his name to something more distinguished, something with weight and social bearing. A racketeering indictment (twenty-seven counts) out of Brooklyn was as good an excuse as any.

Once he was arrested, Frankie King exuberantly began ratting on his co-conspirators, which included numerous high-ranking members of the John Gotti crime organization. Frankie's testimony conveniently glossed the fact that it was he, not the surly Zuboni brothers, who had personally flown to San Juan and picked up the twenty-seven crate-loads of bootleg "educational" videotapes that were eventually sold to the New York City school system for $119.95 apiece. Under oath, Frankie King indignantly blamed the Zubonis and, indirectly, John Gotti himself for failing to inspect the shipment once it had arrived at JFK. On the witness stand, Frankie expressed tearful remorse that, in TV classrooms from Queens to Staten Island, students expecting to see "Kermit's Wild West Adventure" were instead exposed to a mattress-level montage of Latin porn star Pina Kolada deepthroating a semi-pro soccer team.

The Zuboni brothers and a cluster of dull-eyed kneecappers were swiftly convicted by a horrified jury. The reward for Frankie King's cooperation was a suspended sentence, ten years' probation and a new identity of his choosing: Francis X. Kingsbury. Frankie felt the "X" was a classy touch; he decided it should stand for Xavier.

When the man from the Witness Relocation Program told him that Miami would be his new home, Frankie King thought he had died and gone to heaven. *Miami!* Frankie couldn't believe his good fortune; he had no idea the U.S. government could be so generous. What Frankie did not know was that Miami was the prime relocation site for scores of scuzzy federal snitches (on the theory that South Florida was a place where just about any dirtbag would blend in smoothly with the existing riffraff). Frankie King continued to entertain the false notion that he was somebody special in the witness program, a regular Joe Valachi, until he saw the accommodations provided by his government benefactors: a one-bedroom apartment near the railroad tracks in beautiful downtown Naranja.

When Frankie complained about the place, FBI agents reminded him that the alternative was to return to New York and take his chances that John Gotti was a compassionate and forgiving fellow. With this on his mind, Francis X. Kingsbury began a new life.

Like all Floridians with time on their hands, he went to night school and got his real-estate license. It was an entirely new racket, and Frankie worked at it tirelessly; first he specialized in small commercial properties, then citrus groves and farmlands. Doggedly he worked his way east toward the good stuff—oceanfront, the Big O. He went from condos to prime residential estates in no time flat.

Francis X. Kingsbury had found a new niche. He was, undeniably, a whiz at selling Florida real estate. In five short years he had accumulated more money than in an entire lifetime of mob bunko, jukebox skimming and mail fraud. He had a home down on Old Cutler, a beautiful young wife and a closetful of mustard blazers. But he wanted more.

One day he walked into the boardroom of Kingsbury Realty and announced that he was selling the business. "I'm ready to move up in the world," he told his startled partners. "I'm ready to become a developer."

Six months later, Kingsbury stood before a luncheon meeting of the Greater Miami Chamber of Commerce and unveiled his model of the Amazing Kingdom of Thrills. It was the first time in his life that Frankie had gotten a standing ovation. He blushed and said: "Florida is truly the land of opportunity."

His probation officer, standing near the salad bar, had to bite back tears.

▼ ▼ ▼

"This is a very bad idea, Charlie." Joe Winder was talking about the phony million-dollar reward. "A very bad idea. And cynical, I might add."

Over the phone, Chelsea said: "Don't give me any lectures. I need five hundred words by tomorrow morning."

"This is nuts."

"And don't overdo it."

"This is not just dumb," continued Joe Winder, "it's dishonest. The blue-tongued mango voles are dead, Charlie. Everybody at the park is talking about it."

Chelsea said, "Mr. X is adamant. He considers the money a symbolic gesture of his commitment to preserving the environment."

"Did you write that yourself?" Winder asked. "That's fucking awful, Charlie. *Symbolic gesture!* You ought to be shot."

"Joey, don't talk to me that way. This thing was your idea, offering a reward."

"I was wrong," Winder said. "It was a big mistake."

"No, it was genius. The AP had it all over the wires."

"Look, I'm trying to save your ass," Winder said. "And mine, too. Listen to me. This morning, a man with a cardboard box showed up at the front gate of the Amazing Kingdom. Said he'd found the missing voles. Said he'd come to collect his ten-thousand-dollar reward. Listen to me, Charlie. Know what was in the box? Rabbits. Two baby rabbits."

"So what? They don't look anything like a vole."

"They do when you cut their ears off, Charlie. That's what the sonofabitch had done. Cut the ears off a couple of little tiny bunny rabbits."

Charles Chelsea gasped.

"I know, I know," Winder said, "Think about what's going to happen we dangle a million bucks out there. Think of the freaks and sadists and degenerates stampeding this place."

"Holy Christ," said Chelsea.

"Now," said Joe Winder, "think of the headlines."

"I'll talk to Kingsbury."

"Good."

"Maybe I'll bring you along."

"No thank you."

"You owe me," said Chelsea. "Please. I've been good to you, Joe. Remember who hired you in the first place." .

Thanks for reminding me, Winder thought, for the two-thousandth time. "I'm not the right man to deal with Mr. X," he said. "I make a lousy first impression."

"You're right," said Chelsea, rethinking his plan. "Tell me one thing—that sicko with the bunny rabbits . . . what happened?"

"Don't worry," said Winder. "We paid him to go away."

"How much? Not the whole ten grand?"

"No, not ten grand." Winder sighed. "Try fifty bucks. And he was delighted, Charlie. Positively thrilled."

"Thank God for that." There was a brittle pause on Chelsea's end. "Joe?"

"What?"

"This is turning into something real bad, isn't it?"

▼ ▼ ▼

Late in the afternoon, Joe Winder decided to drive down to the Rare Animal Pavilion and find out more about the voles. He needed someone to take his mind off the rabbit episode, which made him heartsick. He should've seen it coming—naturally some greedy psychopath would mutilate helpless bunny rabbits for ten lousy thousand fucking dollars. It's South Florida, isn't it? Winder should've anticipated the worst. That's why Chelsea had hired him, for his native instinct.

The door to the vole lab was locked but the lights were on. Winder knocked twice and got no answer. He could a hear a telephone ringing on the other side of the door. It stopped briefly, then began ringing again. He used his car keys to rap sharply on the glass, but there was no sign of Koocher. Winder figured the doctor was taking a late lunch.

He strolled out to the pavilion, where he found a group of tourists milling around the empty mango-vole exhibit. A tarpaulin had been hung to cover the mess, but somebody had lifted a corner to peek inside the enclosure, which was littered with glass and smudged with fingerprint dust. A yellow police ribbon lay crumpled like a dead snake on the porch of the vole hutch. Some of the tourists were snapping pictures of the scene of the crime.

A voice behind Joe Winder said, "You work here?"

It was an old woman wearing a floppy pink Easter hat and a purse the size of a saddlebag. She eyed Joe Winder's ID badge, which was clipped to his belt.

"You a security man?" the woman asked.

Winder tried to remember what Chelsea had told him about speaking to park visitors; some gooey greeting that all employees were supposed to say. *Welcome to the Amazing Kingdom. How can I help you?* Or was it: *How may I help you?* No, that wasn't it. *How can we help you?*

Eventually Joe Winder said, "I work in Publicity. Is something wrong?"

The old lady made a clucking noise and foraged in her enormous purse. "I've got a little something for you."

In a helpful tone Winder said, "The Lost and Found is down by the killer-whale tank."

"This isn't lost and it isn't found." The old lady produced an envelope. "Here," she said, pressing it into Joe Winder's midsection. "And don't try to follow me."

She turned and scuttled off, one hand atop her head, holding the Easter hat in place. Winder stuffed the envelope into his pocket and started after her. "Hey! Wait a second."

He had taken only three steps when a fist came out of somewhere and smashed him behind the right ear. He pitched forward on the walkway, skidding briefly on his face. When he awoke, Joe Winder was staring at shoes: Reeboks, loafers, sandals, Keds, orthopedics, Hush Puppies, flip-flops. The tourists had gathered in a murmuring semicircle around him. A young man knelt at his side, asking questions in German.

Winder sat up. "Did anybody see who hit me?" His cheek stung, and he tasted blood on his lower lip.

"Beeg orange!" sputtered a woman wearing two cameras around her neck. "Beeg orange man!"

"Swell," Winder said. "Did he have a cape? A ray gun?"

The young German tourist patted him on the shoulder and said: "You okay, *ja?*"

"Yah," Winder muttered. "Fall down go boom."

He picked himself up, waved idiotically at his audience and retreated to the men's room. There he tore open the old lady's envelope and studied the message, which was typed double-spaced on ordinary notebook paper. It said: "WE DID IT. WE'RE GLAD. LONG LIVE THE VOLES."

It was signed by the Wildlife Rescue Corps.

With copies, Joe Winder noted glumly, to every major news organization on the planet.

▼ ▼ ▼

Bud Schwartz shook Danny Pogue awake and said, "Look who's here. I told you not to worry."

Molly McNamara was in the kitchen, fussing around. Danny Pogue was on the sofa in the living room. He had fallen asleep watching *Lady Chatterley IV* on Cinemax.

Bud Schwartz sat down, grinning. "She brought the money, too," he said.

"All of it?"

"No, just the grand. Like she said before."

"You mean the two grand," Danny Pogue said. "One for each of us." He didn't entirely trust his partner.

Bud Schwartz said, "Yeah, that's what I meant. A thousand bucks each."

"Then let's see it."

Molly came in, drying her hands on a flowered towel. She looked at Danny Pogue as if he were a dog that was supposed to stay off the good furniture. She said, "How's that foot?"

"Hurts." Danny Pogue frowned. "Hurts like a bitch."

"He's all out of them pills," added Bud Schwartz.

"Already?" Molly sounded concerned. "You finished the whole bottle?"

"Danny's got what you call a high resistance to pharmaceuticals," Bud Schwartz said. "We had to double the dose."

"Bull," said Danny Pogue. "Bud here just helped hisself."

"Is that true?" asked Molly McNamara. "Did you take some of your friend's pills?"

"Aw, come on," said Bud Schwartz. "Jesus Christ, there's nothing else to do around here. I was bored stiff."

"That was prescription medicine," Molly said sternly.

She went back to the kitchen and got her handbag. It was the largest handbag that Bud Schwartz or Danny Pogue had ever seen. Molly took out another plastic bottle of codeine pills and handed them to Danny Pogue. Then she took out her gun and shot Bud Schwartz once in the left hand.

He fell down, shaking his arm as if it were on fire.

In a whisper Danny Pogue said, "Oh Lord Jesus." He felt the blood floo ling out of his brain, and saw the corners of the room get fuzzy.

Molly said, "Am I getting through to you fellows?" She returned the gun to her purse. "There will be no illegal drug activity in this condominium, is that clear? The owners' association has very strict rules. Here, take this." She handed Danny Pogue two packets of cash. Each packet was held together with a fresh bank wrapper.

"That's one thousand each, just like I promised," she said. Then, turning to Bud Schwartz: "Does it hurt?"

"The fuck do you think?" He was squeezing the wounded purple hand between his knees. "Damn right it hurts!"

"In that case, you may borrow your friend's pills. But only as needed." Then Molly McNamara put on her floppy pink Easter hat and said good night.

▼ ▼ ▼

Nina was naked, kneeling on Joe Winder's back and rubbing his shoulders. "See, isn't this better than sex?"

"No," he said, into the pillow. "Good, but not better."

"It's my night off," Nina said. "All week long, all I do is talk about it."

"We don't have to talk," Joe Winder mumbled. "Let's just do."

"Joe, I need a break from it." She kneaded his neck so ferociously that he let out a cry. "You understand, don't you?"

"Sure," he said. It was the second time in a week that they'd had this conversation. Winder had a feeling that Nina was burning out on her job; practically nothing aroused her lately. All she wanted to do was sleep, and of course she talked in her sleep, said the most tantalizing things.

It was driving Joe Winder crazy. "I had a particularly lousy day," he said. "I was counting on you to wear me out."

Nina climbed off his back. "I love you," she said, slipping her long legs under the sheets, "but at this moment I don't have a single muscle that's the least bit interested."

This, from the same wonderful woman who once left fingernail grooves in the blades of a ceiling fan. Winder groaned in self-pity.

From the other side of the bed came Nina's delicious voice: "Tell me the weirdest thing that happened to you today."

It was a bedtime ritual, exchanging anecdotes about work. Joe Winder said: "Some creep claimed he found the missing voles, except they weren't voles. They were baby rabbits. He was trying to con us." Winder left out the grisly details.

"That's a tough one to beat," Nina remarked.

"Also, I got slugged in the head."

"Really?" she said. "Last night I had a caller jerk himself off in eleven seconds flat. Miriam said it might be a new world's record."

"You timed it?"

"Sort of." Playfully she reached between his legs and tweaked him. "Miriam has an official Olympic stopwatch."

"Nina, I want you to get another job. I'm serious."

She said, "That reminds me—some strange guy phoned for you this afternoon. A doctor from the park. He called twice."

"Koocher?"

"Yeah," said Nina. "Interesting name. Anyway, he made it sound important. I told him to try you at the office, but he said no. He wouldn't leave a message, either, just said he'd call back. The second time he said to tell you a man from Security was in the lab."

Joe Winder lifted his head off the pillow. "A man from Security."

"That's what he said."

"Anything else?" Winder was thinking about the empty laboratory: lights on, phone ringing. Maybe he should've tried the back door.

"I told him you'd be home soon, but he said he couldn't call back. He said he was leaving with the guy from Security." Nina propped herself on one elbow. "Joe, what's going on over there?"

"I thought I knew," said Winder, "but obviously I don't."

With a fingertip she traced a feathery line down his cheek. "Do me a favor," she said.

"I know what you're going to say."

She scooted closer, under the covers, and pressed against him. "But things are going so great."

Winder kissed her on the tip of the nose, and started to roll out of bed.

"Joe, don't go crazy on me," Nina said. "Please."

He rolled back, into her arms. "All right," he said. "Not just yet."

6

The next morning, in the hallway by the water fountain, Charles Chelsea seized Joe Winder by the sleeve and tugged him into the office. Two men shared opposite ends of Chelsea's leather sofa—one was the immense Pedro Luz, chief of Security for the Amazing Kingdom, and the other was a serious-looking fellow with a square haircut and a charcoal suit.

"Joe," Chelsea said, "this gentleman is from the FBI."

"I can see that."

Chelsea cleared his throat. "This is Agent Hawkins."

Joe Winder stuck out his hand. "Billy, isn't it? You worked a Coral Gables Savings job about four years back."

The agent smiled cautiously. "And you were with the *Herald*."

"Right."

"Dated one of the tellers."

"Right again."

Charles Chelsea was trying to set some sort of record for clearing his throat. "What a coincidence that you two guys know each other."

Joe Winder sat down and stretched his legs. "Bank robbery. Billy here was the lead agent. Funny story, too—it was the Groucho guy."

"Yeah," said Hawkins, loosening up. "Wore the big nose and the eyebrows, even carried a cigar. We finally caught up with him in Clearwater."

"No kidding?" Winder said, knowing that it was driving Chelsea crazy, all this friendly conversation with a real FBI man. "All the way up in Clearwater?"

"Gentlemen," Chelsea cut in, "if you don't mind."

"What is it, Charlie?"

"Agent Hawkins is here at Mr. Kingsbury's personal request." Chelsea lowered his voice. "Joe, there were three notes delivered to employees in the park. Each was signed by this Wildlife Rescue Corps."

Winder reached in his pocket. "You mean like this?" He handed his copy to Billy Hawkins. He told him what had happened at the Rare Animal Pavilion—the old lady in the Easter bonnet, the phantom punch. Hawkins took it all down in a notebook.

Chelsea tried to contain his irritation. "Why didn't you report this to Security?" he asked Joe Winder.

"Because I didn't want to interrupt Pedro's nap."

Pedro Luz darkened. Every now and then he dozed off in the security office. "All you had to do was ring the buzzer," he snapped at Winder. He glanced at the FBI man, whose expression remained impassive and nonjudgmental. "I've had a touch of the flu," Pedro Luz added defensively. "The medicine makes me sleepy." For a large man he had a high tinny voice.

"Never mind," said Charles Chelsea. "The point is, everybody's calling up for comment. The networks. The wires. We're under siege, Joe."

Winder felt his headache coming back. Agent Billy Hawkins admitted that the federal government didn't know much about the Wildlife Rescue Corps.

"Most of these groups seem to specialize in rodents," the agent said. "Laboratory rats, mostly. Universities, pharmaceutical houses—those are the common targets. What usually happens, they break in at night and free the animals."

"But we weren't doing experiments." Chelsea was exasperated. "We treated Vance and Violet as royalty."

"Who?" the agent said.

"The voles," Joe Winder explained cheerfully.

Charles Chelsea continued to whine. "Why have they singled out the Amazing Kingdom? We didn't abuse these creatures. Quite the opposite."

"You do any vivisections here?" asked Agent Hawkins. "These groups are quite vocal against vivisection."

Chelsea paled. "Vivisection? Christ, we gave the little bastards fresh corn on the cob every morning. Sometimes even citrus!"

"Well, this is what we've got." Hawkins flipped backwards in his notebook. "Two white males ages twenty-five to thirty-five, fleeing the scene in a 1979 blue Ford pickup, license GPP-B06. The registration comes back to a convicted burglar whose current alias is Buddy Michael Schwartz. I might add that Mr. Schwartz's rap sheet shows no history of a social conscience with regard to animal rights, or any other."

"Somebody hired him," Joe Winder said.

"Most likely," agreed the FBI man. "Anyway, they dragged the truck out of a rock pit this morning. No bodies."

"Any sign of the voles?"

Billy Hawkins allowed himself a slight frown. "We believe the animals are dead." He handed Winder copies of the highway patrol reports, which described the incident with the tourist family in the red LeBaron, as well as the subsequent Winnebago attack. As Winder scanned the reports, Charles Chelsea reminded him to keep the news under his hat.

Agent Hawkins said, "I heard something on the radio about a million-dollar reward."

"Right!" Winder said.

"How can you do that," the FBI man said, "when you know these animals are dead?"

Joe Winder was having a wonderful time. "Go ahead," he said to Charles Chelsea. "Explain to the gentleman."

"Where's Koocher?" Chelsea grumbled. "I left about a dozen messages."

"Let's ask Pedro," said Joe Winder. "He sent one of his boys over to the lab yesterday. Must've had a reason."

Charles Chelsea folded his hands on the desk, waiting. Agent Billy Hawkins turned slightly on the couch to get a better angle on the security chief. Joe Winder arched his eyebrows and said, "How about it, Pedro? Something else happen at the Rare Animal Pavilion?"

Pedro Luz scowled, his tiny black eyes receding under the ledge of his forehead. "I don't know what you're talking about," he said. "Nothing happened nowhere." He fumbled with his clipboard. "See? There is no report."

▼ ▼ ▼

The Security Department at the Amazing Kingdom of Thrills was staffed exclusively by corrupt ex-policemen, of which there was a steady supply in South Florida. The chief of Security, Pedro Luz, was a black-haired pinheaded giant of a young man who had been fired from the Miami Police for stealing cash and cocaine from drug dealers, then pushing them out of a Beechcraft high over the Everglades. Pedro Luz's conviction had been overturned by an appeals court, and the charges ultimately dropped when the government's key witness failed to appear for the new trial. The witness's absence was later explained when bits and pieces of his body were found in a shrimper's net off Key West, although there was no evidence linking this sad turn of events to Pedro Luz himself.

Once the corruption and murder charges had been dismissed, Pedro Luz promptly sued the police department to reclaim his old job, plus back wages and vacation time. Meanwhile, to keep his hand in law enforcement, Pedro Luz went to work at Francis X. Kingsbury's vacation theme park. The pay was only $8.50 an hour, but as a perk Pedro was given free access to the executive gym, where he spent hours of company time lifting weights and taking anabolic steroids. This leisurely regimen was interrupted by the embarrassing daylight theft of the prized voles—and a personal communication of urgency from Francis X. Kingsbury himself. Chief Pedro Luz immediately put the security staff on double shifts, and rented a cot for himself in the office.

Which is where he snoozed at one-thirty in the afternoon when he heard a knock on the bulletproof glass.

Pedro Luz sat up slowly and swung his thick legs off the bed. He stood up, strapped on his gun, straightened the shoulders of his uniform shirt. The knocking continued.

Through the glass, Pedro Luz saw a wiry brown man in a sweaty tank top. The man battled a spastic tic on one side of his face; it looked as if a wasp were loose in one cheek.

Pedro Luz opened the door and said, "What do you want?"

"I'm here for the money," the man said, twitching. He clutched a grocery bag to his chest. "The million dollars."

"Go away," said Pedro Luz.

"Don't you even want to see?"

"The voles are dead."

The wiry man said, "But I heard on the news—"

"Go away," said Pedro Luz, "before I break your fucking legs."

"But I found the mango voles. I want my money."

Pedro Luz stepped out of the office and closed the door. He stood a full foot taller than the man with the grocery bag, and outweighed him by a hundred pounds.

"You don't listen so hot," Pedro Luz said.

The man's face twitched uncontrollably as he tried to open the bag. "Just one look," he said, "please."

Pedro Luz seized the man by the throat and shook him like a doll. The grocery bag fell to the ground and tore open. Pedro Luz was so involved in assaulting the derelict that he didn't notice what came out of the bag: two half-starved, swaybacked ferrets, eyes glazed and bluish, lips flecked with foam. Instantly they settled in chewing on Pedro Luz's right ankle, and did not stop until he tore them off, bare-handed, and threw them with all his might against the nearest wall.

▼ ▼ ▼

One hour later, the Publicity Department of the Amazing Kingdom of Thrills faxed the following statement to all media, under the caption "Rare Voles Now Believed Dead":

> Police authorities reported today that the blue-tongued mango voles stolen this week from the Amazing Kingdom of Thrills are probably dead. According to the Florida Highway Patrol and the Federal Bureau of Investigation, the rare mammals—believed to be the last of the species—were killed while crossing a highway after being abandoned by the robbers who took them.
>
> Francis X. Kingsbury, founder and chairman of the Amazing Kingdom, expressed shock and sorrow at the news. "This is a tragedy for all of us at the park," he said Wednesday. "We had come to love and admire Vance and Violet. They were as much a part of our family as Robbie Raccoon or Petey Possum."
>
> Mr. Kingsbury, who had offered $1 million for the safe return of the missing animals, said he will use part of the money as a reward for information leading to the arrest and conviction of those responsible for the crime.
>
> A radical outlaw group calling itself the Wildlife Rescue Corps has claimed responsibility for the robbery at the popular amusement resort. Mr. Kingsbury said he was "shocked and dismayed that anyone claiming to support such a cause would commit crimes of violence—crimes that ultimately led not only to the animals' deaths, but to the extinction of an entire species."
>
> Charles Chelsea, vice president in charge of public relations, said that the blue-tongued mango voles were provided with the best possible care while in captivity at the Amazing Kingdom. Only last year, the Florida Audubon Society praised the Vole Project as "a shining example of private enterprise using its vast financial resources to save a small but precious resource of nature."
>
> Next week, the Amazing Kingdom of Thrills will present a multi-media retrospective featuring slides and videotapes of the voles during their time at the park. Entitled "Vance and Violet: The Final Days,"

the presentation will be shown three times daily at the Rare Animal Pavilion.

Tickets will be $4 for adults, $2.75 for children and senior citizens.

▼ ▼ ▼

In the cafeteria, Charles Chelsea handed Joe Winder the fax and said, "Nice job, big guy."

Winder stopped on the last sentence. "You're charging money? For a goddamn slide show?"

"Joey, we're running a business here. We're not the *National Geographic*, okay? We're not a charity."

"A rodent slide show." Joe Winder wadded up the press release. "The amazing thing is not that you'd do it, because I'd think you'd charge tourists twenty bucks to watch the pelicans fuck, if they'd let you. The amazing thing is, people will actually come and pay." He clapped his hands once, loudly. "I love this business, Charlie. Every day I learn something new."

Chelsea tightened his necktie. "Christ, here we go again. I try to pay you a compliment, and you twist it into some sort of cynical . . . *commentary*." ·

"Sorry," said Winder. He could feel his sinuses filling up like a bathtub.

"For your information," said Chelsea, "I got people calling all the way from Alaska, wanting to buy Vance-and-Violet T-shirts." Chelsea sighed, to show how disappointed he was in Joe Winder's attitude. Then he said, with an edge of reluctance, "You did some nice writing on this piece, Joe. Got us all off the hook."

"Thanks, boss. And you're right—it was a piece."

Chelsea sat down, eyeing the fast-food debris on Joe Winder's tray. One of Uncle Ely's Elves, sitting at the other end of the table, belched sonorously. Charles Chelsea pretended not to notice. He said, "Not to brag, Joey, but I think I did a pretty fair job with this ditty myself. Mr. X loved his quotes. He said I made him sound like a real human being."

With the tips of his fingers, Joe Winder began to rub both his temples in a ferocious circular motion.

Chelsea asked, "Now what's the matter?"

"Headache." Winder squinted as tightly as he could, to wring the pain out of his eyeballs. "Listen, I called Dr. Koocher's house. He didn't go home last night. His wife is scared out of her mind."

"Maybe he just got depressed and tied one on. Or maybe he's got a girlfriend."

Joe Winder decided not to tell Chelsea that Koocher had tried to reach him. "His wife's eight months pregnant, Charlie. She says he usually calls about nineteen times an hour, but she hasn't heard a word since yesterday."

"What would you like me to do?"

"Worry like hell," said Winder. He stood up. "Also, I'd like your permission to talk to Pedro Luz. I think he's hiding something."

Charles Chelsea said, "You can't talk to him, Joe. He's in the hospital." He paused wearily and shook his head. "Don't ask."

"Come on, Charlie."

"For rabies shots."

"I should've guessed," Winder said. "My condolences to the dog."

"It wasn't a dog," Chelsea said. "Can't this wait till tomorrow? Pedro's in a lot of pain."

"No," said Joe Winder, "that's perfect."

▼ ▼ ▼

Pedro Luz had been taken to the closest emergency room, which was Mariners' Hospital down on Plantation Key. The nurse on duty remembered Pedro Luz very well, and directed Joe Winder to a private room on the second floor.

He didn't bother to knock, just eased the door open. The impressive bulk of Pedro Luz was propped up in bed, watching a Spanish-language soap opera on Channel 23. He was sucking on one end of the plastic IV tube, which he had yanked out of his arm.

"That doesn't go in your mouth," Winder told him.

"Yeah, well, I'm thirsty."

"You're bleeding all over the place."

"What do you care?" said Pedro Luz. With a corner of the sheet he swabbed the blood from his arm. "You better get out of here. I mean right now."

Joe Winder pulled a chair close to the bed and sat down. Pedro Luz smelled like a fifty-five-gallon drum of rubbing alcohol. His luxuriant hair stood in oily black spikes, and his massive neck was covered with angry purple acne, a side effect of the fruit-and-steroid body-building diet.

"You like your job?" Winder asked him.

"What do you mean—at the Kingdom? Sure, I guess." The security man pulled the covers off his legs, so Joe Winder could see the bandages on his ferret-gnawed ankle. "Except for shit like this," said Pedro Luz. "Otherwise, it's an okay job most of the time."

Winder said, "So you really wouldn't want to get fired."

"The hell are you talking about?"

"For lying. I think you're lying."

"What about?"

Joe Winder said, "Don't play dumb with me." As if the guy had a choice. "Tell me why you sent a man to Koocher's lab yesterday. I know you did, because he called me about it."

Pedro Luz got red in the cheeks. The cords in his neck stood out like a rutting bull's. "I already told you," he said. "I don't have no report on that guy."

"He's missing from the park."

"Then I'll do up a report," Pedro Luz said. He breathed deeply, as if trying to calm himself. "Soon as I get outta here, I'll make a report." He took the IV tube out of his mouth. "This stuff's not so bad," he said thoughtfully. "Tastes like sugar syrup." He replaced the tube between his lips and sucked on it loudly.

Joe Winder said, "You're a moron."

"What did you say?"

"Make that a submoron."

Pedro Luz shrugged. "I'd beat the piss out of you, if I didn't feel so bad. They gave me about a million shots." He leered woozily and opened his gown. "See, they broke two needles on my stomach."

Joe Winder couldn't help but admire Pedro Luz's physique. He could see the bright crimson spots where the hypodermics had bent against the muscle.

"Least I won't get the rabies," said Pedro Luz, drawing merrily on the tube. "You oughta take off, before I start feeling better."

Winder stood up and slid the chair back to its corner. "Last chance, Hercules. Tell me why you sent a man to the lab yesterday."

"Or else what?"

"Or we play 'This Is Your Life, Pedro Dipshit.' I tell Kingsbury's people all about your sterling employment record with the Miami Police Department. I might even give them a copy of the indictment. A spine-chilling saga, Pedro. Not for the meek and mild."

Pedro Luz removed the tube and wiped his lips on the sleeve of his gown. He looked genuinely puzzled. "But they know," he said. "They know all about it."

"And they hired you anyway?"

" 'Course," said Pedro Luz. "It was Kingsbury himself. He said every man deserves a second chance."

"I admire that philosophy," Joe Winder said, "most of the time."

"Yeah, well, Mr. X took a personal liking to me. That's why I'm not too worried about all your bullshit."

"Yes," said Joe Winder. "I'm beginning to understand."

"Because you couldn't get me fired no matter what," said Pedro Luz. "And you know what else? Don't never call me a moron again, if you know what's good for you."

"I guess I don't," said Joe Winder. "Obviously."

7

The ticket taker at the Wet Willy attraction was trying to control his temper. *Firm, but friendly.* That's how you deal with difficult customers; that's what they taught in ticket-taker training.

The young man, who was new to the job, said, "I'm sorry, sir, but you can't cut to the front of the line. These other people have been waiting for a long time."

"These other people," the man said; "tell me, do they own this fucking joint?"

The ticket taker did not recognize Francis X. Kingsbury, who wore thong sandals, baggy pastel swim trunks and no shirt. He also had a stopwatch hanging from a red lanyard around his neck.

"Now, you don't want me to call Security," the ticket taker said.

"Nothing but idiots," Kingsbury muttered, pushing his pallid belly through the turnstile. He shuffled up two flights of stairs to the launching ramp, and dropped to all fours.

The Wet Willy ride was one of the Amazing Kingdom's most popular thrill attractions, and one of the cheapest to operate. A marvel of engineering simplicity, it was nothing but a long translucent latex tube. The inside was painted in outrageous psychedelic hues, and kept slippery with drain water diverted at no cost from nearby drinking fountains. The narrow tube descended from a height of approximately six stories, with riders plunging downhill at an average angle of twenty-seven exhilarating degrees.

Francis X. Kingsbury was exceptionally proud of the Wet Willy because the whole contraption had been his idea, his concept. The design engineers at the Amazing Kingdom had wanted something to compete with Disney's hugely successful Space Mountain ride. Kingsbury had collected all the press clippings about Space Mountain and used a bright yellow marker to emphasize his contempt for the project, particularly the development cost. "Seventeen million bucks," he had scoffed, "for a frigging roller ride in the dark."

The engineers had earnestly presented several options for the Amazing Kingdom—Jungle Coaster, Moon Coaster, Alpine Death Coaster—but Kingsbury rejected each for the obvious reason that roller-coaster cars and roller-coaster tracks cost money. So did the electricity needed to run them.

"Gravity!" Kingsbury had grumped. "The most underused energy source on the planet."

"So you're suggesting a slide," ventured one of the engineers. "Maybe a water slide."

Kingsbury had shaken his head disdainfully. Slides *look* cheap, he'd complained, we're not running a goddamn State Fair. A tube would be better, a sleek space-age tube.

"Think condom," he had advised the engineers. "A three-hundred-foot condom."

And so the Wet Willy was erected. Instantly it had become a sensation among tourists at the park, a fact that edified Kingsbury's belief that the illusion of quality is more valuable than quality itself.

Lately, though, ridership figures for the Wet Willy had shown a slight but troubling decline. Francis X. Kingsbury decided to investigate personally, without notifying the engineers, the ticket takers, the Security Department or anyone else at the park. He wanted to test his theory that the ride had become less popular because it had gotten slower. The stopwatch would tell the story.

The way the Wet Willy was designed, a 110-pound teenager would be able to slide headlong from the ramp to the gelatin-filled landing sac in exactly 22.7 seconds. Marketing specialists had calibrated the time down to the decimal point—the ride needed to be long enough to make customers think they were getting their money's worth, yet fast enough to seem dangerous and exciting.

Francis X. Kingsbury weighed considerably more than 110 pounds as he crawled into the slippery chute. Ahead of him, he saw the wrinkled bare soles of a child disappear swiftly into the tube, as if flushed down a rubber commode. Kingsbury pressed the button on the stopwatch, eased to his belly and pushed off. He held his arms at his sides, like an otter going down a riverbank. In this case, an overweight otter in a ridiculous Jack Kemp hairpiece.

Kingsbury grimaced as he swooshed downward, skimming on a thin plane of clammy water. He thought: This is supposed to be fun? The stopwatch felt cold and hard against his breastbone. The bright colors on the walls of the tube did little to lift his spirits; he noticed that some of the reds had faded to pink, and the blues were runny. Not only that, sections of the chute seemed irregular and saggy, as if the latex were giving way.

He took his eyes off the fabric long enough to notice, with alarm, that he was gaining on the youngster who had entered the Wet Willy ahead of him. Being so much heavier, Francis X. Kingsbury was plummeting earthbound at a much faster speed. Suddenly he was close enough to hear the child laughing, oblivious to the danger—no! Close enough to make out the grinning, bewhiskered visage of Petey Possum waving from the rump of the youngster's swimming trunks.

"Shit," said Kingsbury. Feverishly he tried to brake, digging into the rubber with his toes and fingernails. It was no use: gravity ruled the Wet Willy.

Kingsbury overtook the surprised child and they became one, hurtling down the slick pipe in a clumsy union of tangled torsos.

"Hey!" the kid cried. "You're smushing me!" It was a boy, maybe nine or ten, with bright red hair and freckles all over his neck. Francis X. Kingsbury now steered the kid as if he were a toboggan.

They hit the gelatin sac at full speed and disengaged. The boy came out of the goo bawling, followed by Kingsbury, who was studying the dial of the stopwatch and frowning. He seemed not to notice the solemn group waiting outside the exit: the earnest young ticket taker, plus three uniformed security men. All were breathing heavily, as if they had run the whole way.

The ticket taker pointed at Kingsbury and said, "That's him. Except he wasn't bald before."

The security men, all former crooked cops recruited by Pedro Luz, didn't move. They recognized Mr. X right away.

The ticket taker said, "Get him, why don't you!"

"Yeah," said the red-haired tourist kid. "He hurt me."

"Mildew," said Francis X. Kingsbury, still preoccupied. "Fucking mildew under my fingernails." He looked up and, to no one in particular, said: "Call Maintenance and have them Lysol the Willy, A-S-A-P."

The tourist kid raised the pitch of his whining so that it was impossible to ignore. "That's the man who tried to smush me. On my bottom!"

"Give the little turd a free pass to the Wild Bill Hiccup," said Francis X. Kingsbury. "And *him*," pointing at the ticket taker, "throw his ass, I mean it, off the property."

The boy with the Petey Possum swimsuit ran off, sniffling melodramatically. As the security men surrounded the ticket taker, Kingsbury said, "What, like it takes three of you monkeys?"

The men hesitated. All were reluctant to speak.

"You," Kingsbury said, nodding at the smallest of the guards. "Go back up and slide this goddamn tube. Yeah, you heard me. See if you can beat twenty-seven-point-two."

The security man nodded doubtfully. "All right, sir."

"Yeah, and my hair," said Kingsbury, "its up there somewhere. Grab it on the way down."

▼ ▼ ▼

Bud Schwartz paused at the door and looked back. "It don't seem right," he said. "Maybe just the VCR."

"Forget it." Danny Pogue was rocking on his crutches down by the elevator. "Where we gonna hide anything? Come on, Bud, let's just go."

The elevator came and Danny Pogue clumped in. With one crutch he held the elevator door and waited for his partner. Bud Schwartz was trying to tear himself away from Molly McNamara's fancy condo. "Look at all this shit we're leaving behind," he said longingly. "We could probably get five hundred easy for the Dolbys."

Danny Pogue leaned out of the elevator. "And how the fuck we supposed to carry 'em? Me with these toothpicks and you with one good arm. Would you get your ass moving, please, before the bitch comes back?"

As they rode to the first floor, Danny Pogue said, "Besides, we got no car."

Bud Schwartz grunted sourly, wondering what became of the blue pickup. "I feel like she owes us."

"She does owe us. She owes us nine grand, to be exact. But we agreed it wasn't worth waiting, right?"

"I mean, owes us for this." Bud Schwartz brandished a gauze-wrapped hand. "Shooting us, for no good reason."

"She's a nut case. She don't need a reason." They got off the elevator and for once Danny Pogue led the way, swinging on his crutches.

They could see the gatehouse at the main entrance, on the other side of the condominium complex. Rather than follow the sidewalks, they decided to shorten the trip by cutting across the grounds, which were sparsely landscaped and dimly lit. In the still of the evening, the high-rise community of Eagle Ridge was at rest, except for a noisy bridge tournament being held in the rec room. On the screened porches of ground-floor apartments, couples could be seen watering their plants or feeding their cats.

As the two outsiders made their way across the darkened shuffleboard courts, Danny Pogue's left crutch gave out and he went down with a cry.

"Goddamn," he said, splayed on the concrete. "Look here, somebody left a puck on the court."

Bud Schwartz said, "It's not a puck. Pucks are for hockey."

Danny Pogue held the plastic disk like a Danish. "Then what do you call it?"

"I don't know what you call it," said Bud Schwartz, "but people are staring, so why don't you get up before some fucking Good Samaritan calls 911."

"I ought to sue the assholes for leaving this damn thing lying around."

"Good idea, Danny. We'll go see a lawyer first thing in the morning. We'll sue the bastards for a jillion trillion dollars. Then we'll retire down to Club Med." With great effort, Bud Schwartz helped Danny Pogue off the cement and steadied him on the crutches.

"So who's watching us?"

"There." Bud Schwartz raised his eyes toward a third-floor balcony, where three women stood and peered, arms on their hips, like cranky old cormorants drying their wings.

"Hey!" Danny Pogue yelled. "Get a life!"

The women retreated into the apartment, and Danny Pogue laughed. Bud Schwartz didn't think it was all that funny; he'd been in a rotten frame of mind ever since Molly McNamara had shot him in the hand.

As they approached the gatehouse, Danny Pogue said, "So where's the taxi?"

"First things first," said Bud Schwartz. Then, in a whisper: "Remember what we talked about. The girl's name is Annie. Annie Lefkowitz."

He had met her that afternoon by the swimming pool and gotten nowhere—but that's who they were visiting, if anybody asked. No way would they mention Molly McNamara; never heard of her.

A rent-a-cop came out of the gatehouse and nodded neutrally at the two men. He was a young muscular black with a freshly pressed uniform and shiny shoes. Over his left breast pocket was a patch that said, in navy-blue stitching: "Eagle Ridge Security." Danny Pogue and Bud Schwartz were surprised to see what appeared to be a real Smith & Wesson on his hip.

The rent-a-cop said: "Looks like you guys had a rough night."

"Barbecue blew up," said Bud Schwartz. "Ribs all over the place."

Danny Pogue extended his wounded foot, as if offering it for examination. "Burns is all," he said. "We'll be okay."

The rent-a-cop didn't seem in a hurry to move out of the way. He asked for their names, and Bud Schwartz made up a couple of beauts. Ron Smith and Dick Jones.

"Where are you staying?" the rent-a-cop said. "Which building?"

"With Amy Leibowitz," answered Danny Pogue.

"Lefkowitz," said Bud Schwartz, grinding his molars. "Annie *Lefkowitz*. Building K."

"Which unit?" asked the rent-a-cop.

"We're visiting from up North," said Bud Schwartz. "We're not related or anything. She's just a friend, if you know what I mean."

"But which unit?"

Bud Schwartz made a sheepish face. "You know, I don't even remember. But her last name's Lefkowitz, you can look it up."

The rent-a-cop said: "There are four different Lefkowitzes that live here. Hold tight, I'll be right back."

The guard went back inside, and Danny Pogue leaned closer to his partner. The gatehouse cast just enough light to reveal a change in Bud Schwartz's expression.

"So help me God," said Danny Pogue, "if you leave me here, I'll go to the cops."

"What're you talking about?"

"You're gonna run, goddamn you."

"No, I'm not," said Bud Schwartz, although that was precisely what he was considering. He had spotted the yellow taxi, parked near a mailbox across the street.

"Don't even think about it," said Danny Pogue. "You're still on probation."

"And you're on parole," Bud Schwartz snapped. Then he thought: Hell, what are we worried about? We're not even arrested. And this jerk-off's not even a real cop.

"This guy, he can't stop us from leaving," said Bud Schwartz. "He can stop us from trying to get in, but he can't stop us from getting out."

Danny Pogue thought about this. "You're right," he said. "Why don't we just take off?"

"Taking off is not how I'd describe it, considering the shape we're in. Limping off is more like it."

"I wonder if that gun's loaded," said Danny Pogue. "Or if he's allowed to use it."

Bud Schwartz told him not to worry, they could still talk their way out of it. When the rent-a-cop came out of the gatehouse, he held a clipboard in one hand and a big ugly Maglite in the other.

"Miss Lefkowitz says she's had no visitors."

Bud Schwartz looked stunned. "Annie? Are you sure you got the right one?" He stuck with it, digging them in even deeper. "She's probably just pissed off 'cause we're leaving, that's all. Got a good taste and doesn't want to let go."

The rent-a-cop pointed the white beam of the Maglite at Bud Schwartz's face and said, "Why don't you fuckheads come with me."

Danny Pogue retreated a couple of steps. "We didn't do nothin' wrong."

"You lied," said the rent-a-cop. "That's wrong."

Half-blind from the flashlight, Bud Schwartz shielded his eyes and said, "Look, I can explain about Annie." He was ummming and awwwwing, trying to come up with something, when he heard a shuffling noise off to his left. The rent-a-cop aimed the flashlight toward Danny Pogue, but Danny Pogue was gone.

Bud Schwartz said, "I'm not believing this."

The rent-a-cop seemed mildly annoyed. They could hear the frantic thwuck-thwuck of the crutches, heading down the unlit road.

"Bastard," said Bud Schwartz. He felt sharp fingers—impressively strong—seize the loose span of flesh where his neck met his shoulder.

"Before I go get the gimper," said the rent-a-cop, pinching harder, "how about you telling me some portion of the truth."

"Really I can't," said Bud Schwartz. "I'd like to, but it's just not possible."

Then the Maglite came down against the top of his forehead, and the shutters of his brain slammed all at once, leaving the interior of his skull very cool, black, empty.

▼ ▼ ▼

Joe Winder parked at the end of the gravel road and changed out of his work clothes. The necktie was the first thing to come off. He put on a pair of cutoffs, slipped into some toeless sneakers, slathered on some Cutter's and grabbed his spinning rod out of the car. He found the path through the mangroves—his path, to the water's edge. He came here almost every day after work, depending on how badly the wind was blowing. Sometimes he fished, sometimes he sat and watched.

Today he made his way quickly, worried about missing the best of the tide. When he got to the shoreline, he put on the Polaroids and swept the shallow flats with his eyes. He spotted a school of small bonefish working against the current, puffing mud about forty yards out. He grinned and waded out purposefully, sliding his feet silently across the marly bottom. A small plane flew over and the rumble of the engine flushed the fish. Joe Winder cursed, but kept his gaze on the nervous wake, just in case. Sure enough, the bonefish settled down and started feeding again. As he edged closer, he counted five in all, small black torpedoes.

As Joe Winder lifted his arm to cast, he heard a woman call out his name. The distraction was sufficient to ruin his aim; the small pink jig landed smack in the middle of the school, causing the fish to depart at breakneck speed for Andros Island and beyond. An absolutely terrible cast.

He turned and saw Nina waving from the shore. She was climbing out of her blue-jeans, which was no easy task.

"I'm coming out," she called.

"I can see that."

And out she came, in an aqua T-shirt, an orange Dolphins cap, black panties and white Keds. Under these circumstances, it was impossible for Joe Winder to stay angry about the bonefish.

Nina was laughing like a child when she reached him. "The water's so warm," she said. "Makes me want to dive in."

He gave her a left-handed hug. "Did you put on some bug spray?" he asked.

"Designer goo," said Nina. "Some sort of weird enzyme. The bugs gag on it."

Joe Winder pointed with the tip of the fishing rod. "See that? They're mocking me." Another school of bonefish cavorted, tails flashing, far out of human casting range.

"I'll take your word for it," said Nina, squinting. "Joe, what'd you do to your hair?"

"Cut it."

"With what?"

"A steak knife. I couldn't find the scissors."

Nina reached up and touched what was left. "For God's sake, why?"

"Chelsea said I looked like one of the Manson family."

Nina frowned. "Since when do you give a hoot what Charlie Chelsea thinks."

"It's part of the damn dress code. Kingsbury's cracking down, or so

Charlie says. I was trying to be a team player, like you wanted." Joe Winder spotted a small bonnet shark cruising the shallows, and cast the jig for the hell of it. The shark took one look and swam away arrogantly.

Joe Winder said, "So now I look like a Nazi."

"No," said Nina, "the Nazis had combs."

"How's the new routine coming? I assume that's why you're here." It was the time of the week when the girls on the sex-phone line had to update their shtick.

"Tell me what you think." Nina reached into the breast pocket of the T-shirt and pulled out a folded piece of notebook paper. Carefully she unfolded it. "Now, be honest," she said to Winder.

"Always."

" 'Kay, here goes." She cleared her throat. "You say 'Hello.' "

"Hello!" Joe Winder sang out.

"*Hi, there,*" said Nina, reading. "*I was just thinking about you. I was thinking it would be so nice to go on a train, just you and me. A long, romantic train ride. I love the way trains rock back and forth. At first they start out so slow and hard, but then*"—here Nina had scripted a pause—"*but then they get faster and stronger. I love the motion of a big locomotive, it gets me so hot.*"

"Gets me going," suggested Joe Winder. "Hot is a cliché."

Nina nodded in agreement. "That's better, yeah. *I love the motion of a big locomotive, it really gets me going.*"

Joe Winder noticed that the tide was slowing. These fish would be gone soon.

But there was Nina in her black panties. Knee deep in the Atlantic. Blond hair tied back under her cap with a pink ribbon. Reading some damn nonsense about sex on the Amtrak, in that killer voice of hers. The words didn't matter, it was all music to Joe Winder; he was stirred by the sight of her in the water with the sun dropping behind the Keys. At times like this he sure loved Florida.

Nina told him to quit staring at her all sappy and listen, so he did.

"*Sometimes, late at night, I dream that you're a locomotive. And I'm riding you on top, stretched out with my legs around your middle. First we go uphill, real slow and hard and rough. Then all of a sudden I'm riding the engine down, faster and harder and hotter until . . .*"

"Until what?" Joe Winder said.

"Until whatever," said Nina with a shrug. "I figure I'd just leave the rest to their imagination."

"No," said Winder. "A metaphor like that, you need a big ending." He slapped a mosquito that had penetrated the sheen of Cutter's on his neck. "How about: *We're going downhill, out of control, faster and hotter. I scream for you to stop but you keep pumping and pumping until I explode, melting against you.*"

From someplace—her bra?—Nina produced a ballpoint pen and began to scribble. "The pumping business is a bit much," she said, "but I like the melting part. That's good imagery, Joe, thanks."

"Any time."

"Miriam's writing up another hot-tub blowjob."

"Not again," said Joe Winder.

"She says it's going to be a series." Nina folded up the notebook paper and slipped it back in the pocket of her shirt. "I'm going to be late to work if I don't get a move on. You coming in?"

"No, there's another school working that deep edge. I'm gonna try not to brain 'em with this feather."

Nina said good luck and sloshed back toward shore. Halfway there, she turned and said, "My God, I almost forgot. I got one of those phone calls at home."

Winder stopped tracking the fish. He closed the bail on his spinning reel, and tucked the rod in the crook of an elbow. "Was it Koocher?" he asked, across the flat.

Nina shook her head. "It was a different voice from last time." She took a half-dozen splashy steps toward him, so she wouldn't have to yell so far. "But that's what I wanted to tell you. The guy today said he was Dr. Koocher, only he wasn't. It was the wrong voice from before."

Joe Winder said, "You're sure?"

"It's my business, Joe. It's what I do all night, listen to grown men lie."

"What exactly did he say, Nina? The guy who called. Besides that he was Koocher."

"He said all hell was breaking loose at the park."

"All hell," repeated Winder.

"And he said he wanted to meet you tonight at the Card Sound Bridge."

"When?"

"Midnight sharp." Nina shifted her weight from one leg to the other, rippling the water. "You're not going," she said. "Please?"

Joe Winder looked back across the flats, lifeless in the empty auburn dusk. "No sign of those fish," he said. "I believe this tide is officially dead."

Bud Schwartz didn't have to open his eyes to know where he was; the scent of jasmine room freshener assailed his nostrils. He was in Molly McNamara's place, lying on the living-room sofa. He could feel her stare, unblinking, like a stuffed owl.

"I know you're awake," she said.

He elected not to open his eyes right away.

"Son, I know you're there."

It was the same tone she had used the first time they met, at one of the low points in Bud Schwartz's burglary career; he had been arrested after his 1979 Chrysler Cordoba stalled in the middle of 163rd Street, less than a block from the duplex apartment he had just burglarized with his new partner, Danny Pogue. The victim of the crime had been driving home when he saw the stalled car, stopped to help and immediately recognized the Sony television, Panasonic clock radio, Amana microwave and Tandy laptop computer stacked neatly in the Cordoba's back seat. The reason the stuff was lying in the back seat was because the trunk was full of stolen Neil Diamond cassettes that the burglars could not, literally, give away.

Bud Schwartz had been smoking in a holding cell of the Dade County Jail when Molly McNamara arrived. At the time, she was a volunteer worker for Jackson Memorial Hospital and the University of Miami Medical School; her job was recruiting jail inmates as subjects for medical testing, a task that suited her talent for maternal prodding. She had entered the holding cell wearing white rubber-soled shoes, a polyester nurse's uniform and latex gloves.

"I'm insulted," Bud Schwartz had said.

Molly McNamara had eyed him over the top of her glasses and said, "I understand you're looking at eighteen months."

"Twelve, tops," Bud Schwartz had said.

"Well, I'm here to offer you a splendid opportunity."

"And I'm here to listen."

Molly had asked if Bud Schwartz was interested in testing a new ulcer drug for the medical school.

"I don't have no ulcers."

"It doesn't matter," Molly had said. "You'd be in the control group." A pill a day for three months, she had explained. Sign up now, the prosecutor asks the judge to chop your time in half.

"Your friend's already agreed to it."

"That figures," Bud Schwartz had said. "I end up with ulcers, he'll be the cause of it."

When he'd asked about possible side effects, Molly read from a printed page: headaches, high blood pressure, urinary-tract infections.

"Run that last one by me again."

"It's unlikely you'll experience any problems," Molly had assured him. "They've been testing this medication for almost two years."

"Thanks, just the same."

"I know you're smarter than this," Molly had told him in a chiding tone.

"If I was really smart," Bud Schwartz had said, "I'd put new plugs in the car."

A week later she had returned, this time without the rubber gloves. Pulled his rap sheet out of her purse, held it up like the Dead Sea Scrolls.

"I've been looking for a burglar," she had said.

"What for?"

"Ten thousand dollars."

"Very funny," Bud Schwartz had said.

"Call me when you get out. You and your friend."

"You serious?"

"It's not what you think," Molly had said.

"I can't think of anything. Except maybe you're some kinda snitch for the cops."

"Be serious, young man." Again with the needle in her voice, worse than his mother. "Don't mention this to anyone."

"Who the hell would believe it? Ten grand, I swear."

"Call me when you get out."

"Be a while," he said. "Hey, is it too late to get me in on that ulcer deal?"

That was six months ago.

▼ ▼ ▼

Bud Schwartz touched the place on his brow where the rent-a-cop's flashlight had clobbered him. He could feel a scabby eruption the size of a golf ball. "Damn," he said, opening his eyes slowly.

Molly McNamara moved closer and stood over him. She was wearing her reading glasses with the pink roses on the frames. She said, "Your friend is in the bedroom."

"Danny's back?"

"I was on my way here when I spotted him at the Farm Stores. He tried to get away, but—"

"You didn't shoot him again?" Bud Schwartz was asking more out of curiosity than concern.

"No need to," said Molly. "I had the Cadillac. I think your friend realized there's no point in getting run over."

With a wheeze, Bud Schwartz sat up. His ears pounded and stomach juices bubbled up sourly in his throat. As always, Molly was prompt with the first aid. She handed him a towel filled with chipped ice and told him to pack it against his wound.

Danny Pogue clumped into the living room and sat on the other end of the sofa. "You look like shit," he said to Bud Schwartz.

"Thank you, Tom Selleck." From under the towel Bud Schwartz glared with one crimson eye.

Molly McNamara said, "That's enough, the both of you. I can't begin to tell you how much trouble you've caused."

"We was trying to get out of your hair is all," said Danny Pogue. "Why're you keeping us prisoners?"

Molly said, "Aren't we being a bit melodramatic? You are not prisoners. You're simply two young men in my employ until I decide otherwise."

"In case you didn't hear," said Bud Schwartz, "Lincoln freed the slaves a long time ago."

Molly McNamara ignored the remark. "At the gatehouse I had to tell Officer Andrews a lie. I told him you were my nephews visiting from Georgia. I told him we'd had a fight and that's why you were trying to sneak out of Eagle Ridge. I told him your parents died in a plane crash when you were little, and I was left responsible for taking care of you."

"Pitiful," said Bud Schwartz.

"I told him you both had emotional problems."

"We're heading that direction," Bud Schwartz said.

"I don't like to lie," Molly added sternly. "Normally I don't believe in it."

"But shooting people is okay?" Danny Pogue cackled bitterly. "Lady, pardon me for saying, but I think you're goddamn fucking nutso."

Molly's eyes flickered. In a frozen voice she said, "Please don't use that word in my presence."

Danny Pogue mumbled that he was sorry. He wasn't sure which word she meant.

"I'm not certain Officer Andrews believed any of it," Molly went on. "I wouldn't be surprised if he reported the entire episode to the condominium association. You think you've got problems now! Oh, brother, just wait."

Bud Schwartz removed the towel from his forehead and examined it for bloodstains. Molly said, "Are you listening to me?"

"Hanging on every word."

"Because I've got some very bad news. For all of us."

Bud Schwartz grunted wearily. What now? What the hell now?

"It was on the television tonight," Molly McNamara said. "The mango voles are dead. Killed on the highway."

Nervously Danny Pogue glanced at his partner, whose eyes were fixed hard on the old woman. Waiting, no doubt, to see if she pulled that damn pistol from her sweater.

Molly said, "I don't know all the details, but I suppose it's not important. I feel absolutely sick about this."

Good, thought Bud Schwartz, maybe she's not blaming us.

But she was. "If only I'd known how careless and irresponsible you were, I would never have recruited you for this job." Molly took off her rose-framed glasses and folded them meticulously. Her gray eyes were misting.

"The blue-tongued mango voles are extinct because of me," she said, blinking, "and because of you."

Bud Schwartz said, "We're real sorry."

"Yeah," agreed Danny Pogue. "It's too bad they died."

Molly was downcast. "This is an unspeakable sin against Nature. The death of these dear animals, I can't tell you—it goes against everything I've worked for, everything I believe in. I was so stupid to entrust this project to a couple of reckless, clumsy criminals."

"That's us," said Bud Schwartz.

Danny Pogue didn't like his partner's casual tone. He said to Molly, "We didn't know they was so important. They looked like regular old rats."

The old woman absently fondled the buttons of her sweater. "There's no point belaboring it. The damage is done. Now we've got to atone."

"Atone," said Bud Schwartz suspiciously.

"What does that mean?" asked Danny Pogue. "I don't know that word."

Molly said, "Tell him, Bud."

"It means we gotta do something to make up for all this."

Molly nodded. "That's right. Somehow we must redeem ourselves."

Bud Schwartz sighed. He wondered what crazy lie she'd told the rent-a-cop about their gunshot wounds. And this condo association—what's she so worried about?

"Have you ever heard of the Mothers of Wilderness?" asked Molly McNamara.

"No," said Bud Schwartz, "can't say that I have." Danny Pogue said he'd never heard of them, either.

"No matter," said Molly, brightening, "because as of tonight, you're our newest members. Congratulations, gentlemen!"

Restlessly Danny Pogue squeezed a pimple on his neck. "Is it like a nature club?" he said. "Do we get T-shirts and stuff?"

"Oh, you'll enjoy it," said Molly. "I've got some pamphlets in my briefcase."

Bud Schwartz clutched at the damp towel. This time he pressed it against his face. "Cut to the chase," he muttered irritably. "What the hell is it you want us to do?"

"I'm coming to that," said Molly McNamara. "By the way, did I mention that Mr. Kingsbury is offering a reward to anyone who turns in the vole robbers?"

"Oh, no," said Danny Pogue.

"Quite an enormous reward, according to the papers."

"How nice," said Bud Schwartz, his voice cold.

"Oh, don't worry," Molly said. "I wouldn't dream of saying anything to the authorities."

"How could you?" Danny Pogue exclaimed. "You're the one asked us to rob the place!"

Molly's face crinkled in thought. "That'd be awfully hard to swallow, that an old retired woman like myself would get involved in such a distasteful crime. I suppose the FBI would have to decide whom to believe—two young fellows with your extensive criminal pasts, or an older woman like myself who's never even had a parking ticket."

Danny Pogue angrily pounded the floor with one of his crutches. "For someone who don't like to lie, you sure do make a sport of it."

Bud Schwartz stretched out on the sofa, closed his eyes and smiled in resignation. "You're a piece a work," he said to Molly McNamara. "I gotta admit."

▼ ▼ ▼

The Card Sound Bridge is a steep two-lane span that connects the northern tip of Key Largo with the South Florida mainland. Joe Winder got there two hours early, at ten o'clock. He parked half a mile down the road and walked the rest of the way. He staked out a spot on some limestone boulders, which formed a jetty under the eastern incline of the bridge. From there Winder could watch for the car that would bring the mystery caller to this meeting.

He knew it wouldn't be Dr. Will Koocher; Nina was never wrong about phone voices. Joe Winder had no intention of confronting the impostor, but at least he wanted to get a good look, maybe even a tag number.

Not much was biting under the bridge. Effortlessly Winder cast the same pink wiggle-jig he'd been using on the bonefish flats. He let it sink into the fringe of the sea grass, then reeled in slowly, bouncing the lure with the tip of his rod. In this fashion he picked up a couple of blue runners and a large spiny pinfish, which he tossed back. The other fishermen were using dead shrimp with similar unexciting results. By eleven most of them had packed up their buckets and rods and gone home, leaving the jetty deserted except for Joe Winder and two other diehards.

The other men stood side by side, conversing quietly in Spanish. As Joe Winder watched them more closely, it seemed that the men were doing more serious talking than fishing. They were using Cuban yo-yo rigs, twirling the lines overhead and launching the baits with a loud plop into the water. Once in a while they'd pull in the lines and cast out again, usually without even checking the hooks.

One of the men was a husky no-neck in long canvas pants. The other was short and wiry, and as dark as coffee. Both wore baseball caps and light jackets, which was odd, considering the heat. Every few minutes a pair of headlights would appear down Card Sound Road, and Joe Winder would check to see if the car stopped at the foot of the bridge. After a while, he noticed that the two other fishermen were doing the same. This was not a good sign.

As midnight approached, the other men stopped pretending to fish and concentrated on the road. Joe Winder realized that he was stranded on the jetty with two goons who probably were waiting to ambush him. Worse, they stood squarely between Winder and the relative safety of the island. The most obvious means of escape would be jumping into Card Sound; while exceptionally dramatic, such a dive would prove both stupid and futile. The bay was shallow and provided no cover; if the goons had guns, they could simply shoot him like a turtle.

Joe Winder's only hope was that they wouldn't recognize him in the dark with his hair hacked off. It was a gray overcast night, and he was doing a creditable impersonation of a preoccupied angler. Most likely the goons would be expecting him at twelve sharp, some dumb shmuck hollering Koocher's name under the bridge.

The strategy of staying invisible might have worked if only a powerful fish had not seized Joe Winder's lure. The strike jolted his arms, and reflexively he yanked back hard to set the hook. The fish streaked toward the rocks, then back out again toward open water. The buzz of Winder's reel cut like a saw through the stillness of the bay. The two goons stopped talking and looked up to see what was happening.

Joe Winder knew. It was a snook, a damn big one. Any other night he would have been thrilled to hook such a fish, but not now. From the corner of his eye he could see the goons rock-hopping down the jetty so they could better view the battle. Near a piling the fish broke to the surface, shaking its gills furiously before diving in a frothy silver gash. The goons pointed excitedly at the commotion, and Winder couldn't blame them; it was a grand fish.

Joe Winder knew what to do, but he couldn't bring himself to do it. Palm the spool. Break the damn thing off, before the two guys got any closer. Instead Joe Winder was playing the fish like a pro, horsing it away from the rocks and pilings, letting it spend itself in short hard bursts. What am I, crazy? Winder thought. From up here I could never land this fish alone. The goons would want to help, sure they would, and then they'd see who I was and that would be it. One dead snook and one dead flack.

Again the fish thrust its underslung snout from the water and splashed. Even in the tea-colored water the black lateral stripe was visible along its side. Twelve pounds easy, thought Winder. A fine one.

One of the goons clapped his hands and Joe Winder looked up. "Nize goying," the man said. "Dat's some fugging fish." It was the short wiry one.

"Thanks," said Winder. Maybe he was wrong. Maybe these weren't the bad guys, after all. Or maybe they hadn't come to hurt him; maybe they just wanted to talk. Maybe they had Koocher and were scheming for a ransom.

After five minutes of back-and-forth, the snook was tiring. Twenty yards from the jetty it glided to the surface and flopped its tail once, twice. Not yet, Winder thought; don't give up yet, you marvelous bastard.

He heard their heavy footsteps on the rocks. Now they were behind him. He heard their breathing. One of them was chewing gum. Joe Winder smelled hot spearmint and beer.

"What're you waiting for?" asked the big one.

"He's not ready," Winder said, afraid to turn and give them a look at his face. "He's still got some gas."

"No, look at the fugging thin," said the little one. "He juice about dead, mang."

The snook was dogging it on top, barely putting a bend in Joe Winder's fishing rod.

"That's some good eating," the big no-neck goon remarked.

Winder swallowed dryly and said, "Too bad they're out of season."

He heard both of the men laugh. "Hey, you don't want him, we'll take it off your hands. Fry his ass up in a minute. Right, Angel?"

The little one, Angel, said, "Yeah, I go down and grab hole the fugging thin." He took off his baseball cap and scrabbled noisily down the rocks.

Joe Winder got a mental picture of these two submorons in yellowed undershirts—swilling beer, watching "Wheel" on the tube—cooking up the snook on a cheap gas stove in some rathole Hialeah duplex. The thought of it was more than he could stand. He placed his hand on the spool of the reel and pulled once, savagely.

The snook had one good powerful surge left in its heart, and the fishing line snapped like a rifle shot. Joe Winder fell back, then steadied himself. "Goddammit," he said, trying to sound disappointed.

"That was really stupid," said the big goon. "You don't know shit about fighting a fish."

"I guess not."

The wiry one had been waiting by the water when the fish got off. Cursing in Spanish, he monkeyed back up the rocks. To guide himself, he held a small flashlight in one hand. The beam caught Joe Winder flush in the face; there was nothing he could do.

Instantly the big goon grabbed him by the shoulder. "Hey! You work at the park."

"What park?"

The wiry one said, "Doan tell me he's the guy."

"Yup," said the big one, tightening his grip.

The men edged closer. Joe Winder could sense they were angry about not recognizing him sooner.

"Mr. Fisherman," said the big one acidly.

"That's me," said Winder. "You must be the one who wanted to talk about Dr. Koocher."

The goon named Angel turned off the flashlight and buried it in his jacket. "Two hours with these damn mosquitoes and you standing right here, the whole fugging tine!" He punched Joe Winder ferociously in the kidney.

As Winder fell, he thought: So they're not here to chat.

His head bounced against limestone and he began to lose consciousness. Then he felt himself being lifted by the armpits, which hurt like hell. They were carrying him somewhere in a hurry.

The husky one, Spearmint Breath, was talking in Joe Winder's ear. "What'd he say on the phone?"

"Who?"

"The rat doctor."

"Nothing." Winder was panting.

"Aw, bullshit."

"I swear. He left a message, that's all." Winder tried to walk but felt his legs pedaling air, being swept along. "Just a message was all," he said again. "He wanted to see me but he didn't say why."

In his other ear, Joe Winder heard the wiry one call him a stinken fugging liar.

"No, I swear."

They had him up against the side of a truck. Bronco. White. Rusty as hell. Ford Bronco, Winder thought. In case I live through this.

In case anybody might be interested.

The big goon spun Joe Winder around and pinned his arms while the one named Angel slugged him on the point of the jaw. Then he hit him once in each eye. Winder felt his face start to bloat and soften, like a melon going bad. With any luck, total numbness would soon follow.

Angel was working up a sweat. Every time he threw a punch, he let out a sharp yip, like a poodle. It would have been hilarious except for the pain that went with it.

Finally, Spearmint Breath said, "I don't think he knows jack shit." Then he said something in Spanish.

Angel said, "Chur he does, the cokesucker." This time he hit Joe Winder in the gut.

Perfect. Can't breathe. Can't see. Can't talk.

The big goon let go, and Winder fell limp across the hood of the truck.

The man named Angel said, "Hey, what the fug." There was something new in his voice; he sounded very confused. Even in a fog, Joe Winder could tell that the little creep wasn't talking to him—or to Spearmint Breath, either.

Suddenly a great turmoil erupted around the truck, and the man named Angel gave out a scream that didn't sound anything like a little dog. The scream made Joe Winder raise his head off the fender and open what was left of his eyelids.

Through misty slits he saw the husky no-neck goon running toward the bridge. Running away as fast as he could.

Where was Angel?

Something lifted Joe Winder off the truck and laid him on the gravel. He struggled to focus on the face. Face? Naw, had to be a mask. A silvery beard of biblical proportions. Mismatched eyes: one as green as mountain pines, the other brown and dead. Above that, a halo of pink flowers. Weird. The mask leaned closer and whispered in Joe Winder's ear.

The words tumbled around like dice in his brainpan. Made no damn sense. The stranger bent down and said it again.

"I'll get the other one later."

Joe Winder tried to speak but all that came out was a gulping noise. He heard a car coming down the old road and turned his head to see. Soon he became mesmerized by the twin beams of yellow light, growing larger and larger; lasers shooting out of the mangroves. Or was it a spaceship?

When Winder turned back, he was alone. The man who had saved his life was gone.

The car went by in a rush of noise. Joe Winder watched the taillights vanish over the crest of the bridge. It was an hour before he could get to his feet, another twenty minutes before he could make them move in any sensible way.

As he staggered along the pavement, he counted the cars to keep his mind off the pain. Seven sped past without stopping to help. Winder was thinking, Maybe I feel worse than I look. Maybe the blood doesn't show up so well in the dark. Two or three drivers actually touched the brakes. One honked and hurled a Heineken bottle at him.

The eighth car went by doing seventy at least, heading eastbound to the island. Joe Winder saw the brake lights wink and heard the tires squeal. Slowly the car backed up. The door on the passenger side swung open.

A voice said: "My God, are you all right?"

"Not really," said Joe Winder. Half-blind, he was trying to fit himself into the car when he encountered something large and fuzzy on the upholstery.

It was an animal head. He hoped it was not real.

Carrie Lanier picked it up by the snout and tossed it into the back seat. She took Joe Winder's elbow and helped him sit down. Reaching across his lap, she slammed the car door and locked it. "I can't believe this," she said, and stepped on the accelerator.

To Joe Winder it felt as if they were going five hundred miles an hour, straight for the ocean.

Carrie Lanier kept glancing over at him, probably to make sure he was still breathing. After a while she said, "I'm sorry, what was your name again?"

"Joe. Joe Winder."

"Joe, I can't believe they did this to you."

Winder raised his head. "Who?" he said. "Who did this to me?"

9

Carrie Lanier pulled off Joe Winder's shoes and said, "You want me to call your girlfriend?"

Winder said no, don't bother. "She'll be home in a couple hours."

"What does she do? What kind of work?"

"She talks dirty," said Joe Winder, "on the phone."

Carrie sat on the edge of the bed. She put a hand on his forehead and felt for fever.

He said, "Thanks for cleaning me up."

"It's all right. You want more ginger ale?"

"No, but there's some Darvocets in the medicine cabinet."

"I think Advils will do just fine."

Winder grunted unhappily. "Look at me. You ever see a face like this on an Advil commercial?"

She brought him one lousy Darvocet and he swallowed it dry. He felt worse than he could remember ever feeling, and it wasn't only the pain. It was anger, too.

"So who beat me up?" he said.

"I don't know," said Carrie Lanier. "I imagine it was somebody from the park. I imagine you stuck your nose where it doesn't belong."

"I didn't," Joe Winder said, "not yet."

He felt her rise from the bed, and soon heard her moving around the apartment. He called her name and she came back to the bedroom, sitting in the same indentation on the mattress.

"I was looking for something to bandage those ribs."

"That's okay," said Winder. "It only hurts when I breathe."

Carrie said, "Maybe I don't need to tell you this, but the Amazing

Kingdom is not what it seems. It's not fun and games, there's a ton of money at stake."

"You mean it's a scam?"

"Hey, everything's a scam when you get down to it." Her voice softened. "All I'm saying is, stick to your job. I know it's boring as hell, but stick to it anyway. You shouldn't go poking around."

Joe Winder said, "My poking days are over."

"Then what were you doing out there tonight?"

"Meeting someone at the bridge. What about you?"

"I had a free-lance gig," Carrie said. "A birthday party up in South Miami. Mummy and Daddy wanted Junior to meet Robbie Raccoon in person. What the heck, it was an easy five hundred. And you should've seen the house. Or should I say mansion."

Floating, Joe Winder said: "What do you have to do at these parties?"

"Dance with the kiddies. Waggle my coon tail. Juggle marshmallows, whatever. And pose for pictures, of course. Everybody wants a picture."

She touched his brow again. "You're still hot. Maybe I ought to call your girlfriend at work."

"Don't do that," said Joe Winder, "please." He didn't want Carrie to hook up with Miriam by accident. Miriam and her hot-tub "blowyobs."

"This is important," he said. "Did you see anyone else on the road out there? Like maybe a circus-type person."

"You're not well," said Carrie Lanier.

"No, I mean it. Big guy with a beard. Flowers on his head." It sounded so ridiculous, maybe he'd hallucinated the whole thing.

"That's not a circus person you're describing. That's Jesus. Or maybe Jerry García."

"Whatever," Joe Winder said. "Did you see anybody on the road? That's all I'm asking."

"Nope," Carrie said. "I really ought to be on my way. What'd you decide about calling the cops?"

"Not a good idea," said Winder. "Especially with Dr. Koocher still missing. Maybe the bad guys'll call back."

"The creeps who did this to you?" Carrie sounded incredulous. "I don't think so, Joe."

She didn't say anything for several moments. Joe Winder tried to read her expression but she had turned away.

"How much does she make, your girlfriend, talking sexy on the phone?"

"Not much. Two hundred a week, sometimes two fifty. They get a bonus for selling videos. And panties, too. Twenty bucks a pair. They buy 'em wholesale from Zayre's."

"Two fifty, that stinks," said Carrie Lanier. "But, hey, I've been there. You do what you have to."

"Nina's got no complaints," said Joe Winder. "She says there's a creative component to every job; the trick is finding it."

Carrie turned around, glowing. "She's absolutely right, your girlfriend is. You know what I did before I got my SAG card? I worked in a cough-drop factory. Wrapping the lozenges in foil, one at a time. The only way I kept from going crazy—each cough drop, I'd make a point to wrap it differently from the others. One I'd do in squares, the next I'd do in a triangle, the one after that I'd fold into a rhombus or something. Believe me, it got to be a challenge, especially at thirty lozenges per minute. That was our quota, or else we got docked."

Joe Winder said the first dumb thing that popped into his brain. "I wonder if Nina has a quota."

"She sounds like she's doing just fine," Carrie said. "Listen, Joe, I think you ought to know. There's a rumor going around about the rat doctor. Supposedly they found a note."

"Yeah?"

"You know what kind of note I mean. The bad kind. Good-bye, cruel world, and all that. Supposedly they found it in his desk at the lab."

Joe Winder said, "What exactly did it say, this supposed note?"

"I don't know all the details." Carrie Lanier stood up to go. "Get some rest. It's just a rumor."

"Give me another pill, and sit down for a second."

"Nope, I can't."

"Get me another goddamn pill!"

"Go to sleep, Joe."

▼ ▼ ▼

By eight the next morning, a crowd had gathered beneath the Card Sound Bridge to see the dead man hanging from the center span. From a distance it looked like a wax dummy with an elongated neck. Up close it looked much different.

The crowd was made up mostly of tourist families on their way down to the Florida Keys. They parked haphazardly on the shoulder of the road and clambered down to where the police cars and marine patrols were positioned, blue lights flashing in that insistent syncopation of emergency. A few of the tourist husbands took out portable video cameras to record the excitement, but the best vantage was from the decks of the yachts and sleek sailboats that had dropped anchor in the channel near the bridge. The mast of one of the sloops had snagged on the hanging dead man and torn off his trousers as the vessel had passed through the bridge at dawn. By now everyone had noticed that the corpse wore no underwear.

A man from the Dade County Medical Examiner's Office stood on the jetty and looked up at the dead body swinging in the breeze, forty feet over the water. Standing next to the man from the medical examiner's was FBI Agent Billy Hawkins, who was asking lots of questions that the man from the medical examiner's didn't answer. He was keenly aware that the FBI held absolutely no authority in this matter.

"I was on my way to the park," Agent Hawkins was saying, "and I couldn't help but notice."

With cool politeness, the man from the medical examiner's office said: "Not much we can tell you at the moment. Except he's definitely dead, that much is obvious." The coroner knew that most FBI agents went their whole careers without ever setting eyes on an actual corpse. The way Billy Hawkins was staring, he hadn't seen many.

"The poor bastard has no pants," the agent observed. "What do you make of that?"

"Sunburned testicles is what I make of that. If we don't haul him down soon."

Agent Hawkins nodded seriously. He gave the coroner a card. The feds, they loved to hand out cards.

The man from the medical examiner's played along. "I'll call if anything turns up," he lied. The FBI man said thanks and headed back toward his car; he was easy to track—a blocky gray suit moving through a bright sea of Hawaiian prints and Day-Glo surfer shorts. A dog in a flower bed.

The amused coroner soon was joined by an equally amused trooper from the Florida Highway Patrol.

"Nice day for a hangin'," drawled the trooper. His name was Jim Tile. He wore the standard mirrored sunglasses with gold wire frames.

"I don't see a rope," said the coroner, gesturing at the dead man high above them. "What the hell's he hanging with?"

"That would be fishing line," Jim Tile said.

The coroner thought about it for several moments. Then he said, "All right, Jim, what do you think?"

"I think it's a pretty poor excuse for a suicide," said the trooper.

A tanned young man in a crisp blue shirt and a red necktie worked his way out of the crowd. The man walked up to the coroner and somberly extended his right hand. He wore some kind of plastic ID badge clipped to his belt. The coroner knew that the tanned young man wasn't a cop, because his ID badge was in the shape of an animal head, possibly a raccoon or a small bear.

Charles Chelsea gestured toward the dead man without looking. In a voice dripping with disgust, he said, "Can't you guys do something about that?"

"We're working on it," replied the coroner.

"Well, work a little faster."

The man from the medical examiner's looked down at Charles Chelsea's animal-head ID and smiled. "These things can't be hurried," he said.

A jurisdictional dispute had delayed the removal of the offending body for most of the morning. It was a tricky geographic dilemma. The middle of the Card Sound Bridge marked the boundary line between Dade and Monroe counties. The Monroe County medical examiner's man had arrived first on the scene, and decided that the dead man was hanging in Dade County airspace and therefore was not his responsibility. The Dade County medical examiner's man had argued vigorously that the victim had most certainly plummeted from the Monroe County side of the bridge. Besides which the Dade County morgue was already packed to the rafters with homicides, and it wouldn't kill Monroe County to take just one. Neither coroner would budge, so the dead body just hung there for four hours until the Monroe County medical examiner announced that he was needed at a fatal traffic accident in Marathon, and scurried away, leaving his colleague stuck with the corpse—and now some whiny pain-in-the-ass PR man.

The coroner said to Charles Chelsea: "We've got to get some pictures. Take some measurements. Preserve the scene, just in case."

"In case of what? The poor jerk killed himself." Chelsea sounded annoyed. Preserving the scene was the opposite of what he wanted.

Trooper Jim Tile removed his sunglasses and folded them into a breast pocket. "I guess I can go home. Now that we got an expert on the case."

Charles Chelsea started to rebuke this impertinent flatfoot, but changed his mind when he took a good look. The trooper was very tall and very muscular and very black, all of which made Chelsea edgy. He sensed that Jim Tile was not the sort to be impressed by titles, but nonetheless he introduced himself as a vice president at the Amazing Kingdom of Thrills.

"How nifty," said the trooper.

"Yes, it is," Chelsea said pleasantly. Then, lowering his voice: "But, to be frank, we could do without this kind of spectacle." His golden chin pointed up at the hapless corpse. Then he jerked a thumb over his shoulder at the chattering throng of onlookers.

"All these people," Chelsea said urgently, "were on their way to our theme park."

"How do you know?" asked Jim Tile.

"Look around here—where else would they be going? What else is there to see?"

"In other words, you would like us to remove the deceased as quickly as possible."

"Yes, exactly," said Charles Chelsea.

"Because it's competition."

The publicity man's eyes narrowed. Frostily he said, "That's not at all what I meant." Giving up on the black policeman, he appealed to the coroner's sense of propriety: "All the young children hanging around—they shouldn't be witness to something like this. Vacations are for fun and fantasy, not for looking at dead bodies."

Jim Tile said, "They seem to be enjoying it."

"We didn't ask for an audience," the coroner added. He was accustomed to gawkers in Miami. Shopping malls were the worst; drug dealers were always leaving murdered rivals in the trunks of luxury automobiles at shopping malls. The crowds were unbelievable, pushing and shoving, everybody wanting a peek at the stiff.

The coroner told Charles Chelsea: "This always happens. It's just a sick fact of human nature."

"Well, can't you hurry up and get him—it—down? The longer it stays up there, the more people will stop." Chelsea paused to survey the size of the crowd. "This is horrible," he said, "right in the middle of Summerfest. It's giving all these folks the wrong idea."

Jim Tile couldn't wait to hear more. "The wrong idea about what?"

"About Florida," said Charles Chelsea. The indignation in his tone was authentic. "This is not the image we're trying to promote. Surely you can understand."

Grimly he turned and disappeared into the gallery of onlookers.

The coroner once again fixed his attention on what was hanging from the Card Sound Bridge. He asked Jim Tile, "So what do you think about getting him down from there?"

"Easy," said the trooper. "I'll go up and cut the line."

"You really think that's safe?"

Jim Tile looked at him curiously.

"With all these people milling around," said the coroner. "What if he hits somebody? Look at all these damn boats." He frowned and shook his head. "I think we've got a serious liability risk here. Somebody could be injured or killed."

"By a falling corpse," said Jim Tile thoughtfully.

"You betcha. Look at all these damn tourists."

Jim Tile took out a bullhorn and ordered the boats to weigh anchor. He also instructed the bystanders to get off the jetty under threat of arrest. Then he went to the top of the bridge and quickly found what he was looking for: a nest of heavy monofilament fishing line tangled around the base of a concrete column. One end of the monofilament was attached to the type of flat plastic spool used by Cuban handline fishermen. The other end of the line led over the side of the bridge, and was attached to the dead man's neck.

The trooper got a 35-millimeter camera out of the patrol car and took pictures of the column and the knot. Then he got down on his belly and extended his head over the side of the bridge and snapped several aerial-type photographs of the hanging corpse.

After Jim Tile put the camera away, he waved twice at the coroner, still standing on the rocks below. Then, when the coroner gave the signal, the trooper unfolded his pocketknife and cut through the monofilament fishing line.

He heard the crowd go *oooooohhhh* before he heard the splash. A marine patrol boat idled up to the dead man and fished him out of the water with a short-handled gaff.

They were loading the body into the van when the coroner told his theory to Jim Tile. "I don't think it's a suicide," he said.

"What, somebody was using him for bait?"

"No, this is what I think happened," said the coroner, demonstrating with his arms. "You know how these Cuban guys twirl the fishlines over their heads real fast to make a long cast? It looks to me like he messed up and wrapped the damn thing tight around his neck, like a bolo. That's what I think." He picked up a clipboard and began to write. "What was the color of his eyes? Brown, I think."

"I didn't look," said Jim Tile. He wasn't crazy about dead bodies.

The man from the medical examiner's reached into the van and tugged at the woolen blanket, revealing the dead man's features.

"I was right," said the coroner, scribbling again. "Brown they are."

Jim Tile stared at the rictus face and said, "Damn, I know that guy." He wasn't a fisherman.

"A name would be nice," the coroner said. "He lost his wallet when he lost his pants."

Angel, the trooper said. Angel Gaviria. "Don't ask me how to spell it."

"Where do you know him from?"

"He used to be a cop." Jim Tile yanked the blanket up to cover the dead man's face. "Before he got convicted."

"Convicted of what?"

"Everything short of first-degree murder."

"Jesus Christ. And here he is, out of the slammer already."

"Yeah," said Jim Tile. "Modeling neckwear."

▼ ▼ ▼

Bud Schwartz had been a two-bit burglar since he was seventeen years old. He was neither proud of it nor ashamed. It was what he did, period. It suited his talents. Whenever his mother gave him a hard time about getting an honest job, Bud Schwartz reminded her that he was the only one of her three children who was not in psychoanalysis. His sister was a lawyer and his brother was a stockbroker, and both of them were miserably fucked up. Bud Schwartz was a crook, sure, but at least he was at peace with himself.

He considered himself a competent burglar who was swift, thorough and usually cautious. The times he'd been caught—five in all— these were flukes. A Rottweiler that wasn't in the yard the night before. A nosy neighbor, watering her begonias at three in the goddamn morning. A getaway car with bad plugs. That sort of thing. Occupational hazards, in Bud Schwartz's opinion—plain old lousy luck.

Normally he was a conservative guy who played the odds and didn't like unnecessary risks. Why he ever accepted the rat-napping job from Molly McNamara, he couldn't figure. Broad daylight, thousands of people, the middle of a fucking theme park. Jesus! Maybe he did it just to break the monotony. Or maybe because ten grand was ten grand.

Definitely a score. In his entire professional burgling career, Bud Schwartz had never stolen anything worth ten thousand dollars. The one time he'd pinched a Rolex Oyster, it turned out to be fake. Another time he got three diamond rings from a hotel room on Key Biscayne— a big-time movie actress, too—and the fence informed him it was all zircon. Fucking paste. Or so said the fence.

Who could blame him for saying yes to Molly McNamara, or at least checking it out? So when he gets out of jail, he rounds up Danny Pogue—Danny, who's really nothing but a pair of hands; somebody you drag along to help carry the shit to the car. But reliable, as far as that goes. Not really smart enough to pull anything.

So together they meet the old lady once, twice. Get directions, instructions. Go over the whole damn thing until they're bored to tears, except for the part about what to do with the voles. Bud Schwartz had assumed the whole point was to free the damn things, the way Molly talked. "Liberate" was the word she'd used. Of course, if he'd known then what he knew now, he wouldn't have chucked that one little rat into the red convertible. If he'd known there were only two of the damn things left on the whole entire planet, he wouldn't ever have let Danny take a throw at the Winnebago.

Now the voles were gone, and Bud Schwartz and Danny Pogue were nursing their respective gunshot wounds in the old lady's apartment.

Watching a slide show about endangered species.

"This formidable fellow," Molly McNamara was saying, "is the North American crocodile."

Danny Pogue said, "Looks like a gator."

"No, it's a different animal entirely," said Molly. "There's only a few dozen left in the wild."

"So what?" said Danny Pogue. "You got tons of gators. So many they went and opened a hunting season. I can't see gettin' all worked up about crocodiles dyin' off, not when they got a season on gators. It don't make sense."

Molly said, "You're missing the point."

"He can't help it," said Bud Schwartz. "Just go on to the next slide."

Molly clicked the remote. "This is the Schaus' swallowtail butterfly."

"Now that's pretty," said Danny Pogue. "I can see wanting to save somethin' like that. Isn't that a pretty butterfly, Bud?"

"Beautiful," said Bud Schwartz. "Really gorgeous. Next?"

Molly asked why he was in such a hurry.

"No reason," he replied.

Danny Pogue snickered. "Maybe 'cause there's a movie he wants to see on cable."

"Really?" Molly said. "Bud, you should've told me. We can always continue the orientation tomorrow."

"That's okay," Bud Schwartz said. "Go on with the program."

"*Amazon Cheerleaders*," said Danny Pogue. "We seen the ending the other night."

Molly said, "I don't believe I've heard of that one."

"Get on with the slides," said Bud Schwartz gloomily. Of all the partners he'd ever had, Danny Pogue was turning out to be the dumbest by a mile.

A picture of something called a Key Largo wood rat appeared on the slide screen, and Danny exclaimed: "Hey, it looks just like one a them voles!"

"Not really," said Molly McNamara patiently. "This hardy little fellow is one of five endangered species native to the North Key Largo habitat." She went on to explain the uniqueness of the island—hardwood hammocks, brackish lakes and acres of precious mangroves. And, only a few miles offshore, the only living coral reef in North America. "Truly a tropical paradise," said Molly McNamara, "which is why it's worth fighting for."

As she clicked through the rest of the slides, Bud Schwartz was thinking: How hard would it be to overpower the old bat and escape? Two grown men with six functional limbs, come on. Just grab the frigging purse, take the gun—what could she do?

The trouble was, Bud Schwartz wasn't fond of guns. He didn't mind stealing them, but he'd never pointed one at anybody, never fired one, even at a tin can. Getting shot by Molly McNamara had only reinforced his view that guns were a tool for the deranged. He knew the law, and the law smiled on harmless unarmed house burglars. A burglar with a gun wasn't a burglar anymore, he was a robber. Not only did robbers get harder time, but the accommodations were markedly inferior. Bud Schwartz had never been up to Raiford but he had a feeling he wouldn't like it. He also had a hunch that if push came to shove, Danny Pogue would roll over like a big dumb puppy. Do whatever the cops wanted, including testify.

Bud Schwartz decided he needed more time to think.

A new slide came up on the screen and he told Molly McNamara to wait a second. "Is that an endangered species, too?" he asked.

"Unfortunately not," Molly said. "That's Francis X. Kingsbury, the man who's destroying the island."

Danny Pogue lifted his chin out of his hands and said, "Yeah? How?"

Mr. Kingsbury is the founder and chief executive officer of the Amazing Kingdom of Thrills—the so-called amusement park you boys raided the other day. It's a tourist trap, plain and simple. It brings traffic, garbage, litter, air pollution, effluent—Kingsbury cares nothing about preserving the habitat. He's a developer."

The word came out as an epithet.

Bud Schwartz studied the jowly middle-aged face on the screen. Kingsbury was smiling, and you could tell it was killing him. His nose was so large that it seemed three-dimensional, a huge mottled tuber of some kind, looming out of the wall.

"Public enemy number one," said Molly. She glared at the picture on the screen. "Yes, indeed. The park is only a smokescreen. We've got reason to believe that Mr. Kingsbury holds the majority interest in a new golfing resort called Falcon Trace, which abuts the Amazing

Kingdom. We have reason to believe that Kingsbury's intention is to eventually bulldoze every square inch of ocean waterfront. You know what that means?"

Danny Pogue pursed his lips. Bud Schwartz said nothing; he was trying to guess where the old coot was heading with this.

Molly said, "It means no more crocodiles, no more wood rats, no more swallowtail butterflies."

"No more butterflies?" Danny Pogue looked at her with genuine alarm. "What kinda bastard would do something like that?"

"This kind," said Molly, aiming a stern papery finger at the screen.

"But we can stop him, right?" Bud Schwartz was smiling.

"You can help, yes."

"How?" Danny Pogue demanded. "What do we do?"

Molly said, "I need to know the full extent of Mr. Kingsbury's financial involvement—you see, there are legal avenues we could pursue, if only we knew." She flicked off the slide projector and turned on a pair of brass table lamps. "Unfortunately," she said, "Mr. Kingsbury is a very secretive man. Every document we've gotten, we've had to sue for. He is extremely wealthy and hires only the finest attorneys."

From his expression it was clear that Danny Pogue was struggling to keep up. "Go on," he said.

Bud Schwartz inhaled audibly, a reverse sigh. "Danny, we're burglars, remember? What do burglars do?"

Danny Pogue glanced at Molly McNamara, who said, "Your partner's got the right idea."

"Wait a second," said Danny Pogue. "More voles?"

"Jesus Christ, no," Bud Schwartz said. "No more voles."

By now he was planning ahead again, feeling better about his prospects. He was wondering about Francis X. Kingsbury's money, and thinking what a shame that a bunch of greedy lawyers should get so much of it, all for themselves.

10

Nina didn't believe him, not for a second.

"You were drinking. You opened your big fat mouth and somebody smacked you."

"No," Joe Winder said. "That's not what happened."

Well, the truth would only frighten her. He sat up and squinted brutally at the sunlight.

"I'm so disappointed in you," Nina said. She studied the bruises on his face, and not out of concern; she was looking for clues.

"I wasn't drinking," said Joe Winder. That much he had to assert, out of pride. "They were muggers, that's all."

Nina pointed to his wallet, which was on the dresser. "Muggers, Joe? Some muggers."

"A car scared them off."

She rolled her eyes. "You're only making it worse."

"What happened to trust?" Winder said. "What happened to true goddamn love?" He got out of bed and tested his legs. Nina watched reproachfully.

"I smell perfume," she said. "Did you bring a woman home last night?"

"No, a woman brought *me*. She saw me on Card Sound Road and wanted to go to the police. I told her to bring me here so I could be with the love of my life."

"Did you screw her?"

"Only six or seven times." He went to the bathroom and stuck his face under the shower and screamed at the top of his lungs, it hurt so bad. He screamed until his ears reverberated. Then he came out, dripping, and said: "Nina, be reasonable. Who'd make love with me, looking like this?"

"Not me."

"Not anybody. Besides, I was half blind. I probably would've stuck it in her ear by mistake."

Nina smiled. Finally.

Winder asked her who'd called so damn early. The phone is what woke him up.

"Your employer, Mr. Charles Chelsea. He wanted you to know there was a dead person hanging from the bridge this morning."

Joe Winder shuffled back to the shower. This time he stepped all the way in and braced his forehead against the tile. He made the water as hot as he could bear. Maybe the dead man was Angel, he thought, or maybe it was the big guy who'd saved him from Angel.

When Winder got out, Nina stood poised with a towel in her hand. She wore a white halter top and no panties. Winder took the towel and draped it over his head.

"Why do you do this to me," he mumbled.

"Did you hear what I said? About the dead man?" She peeled off the halter and climbed in the shower. "Did you save me some hot water? I've got to shave my legs." She turned the faucet handles and cursed the cold.

"Sorry," said Joe Winder. Raising his voice over the beating of the water: "So why is Chelsea calling me, just because there's some dead guy? The bridge is five miles from the Kingdom."

Nina didn't answer; just filed the question away and kept on shaving. Joe Winder sat down on the toilet and watched the fixtures fog up. Plenty of hot water, he thought; no problem.

When she came out, he remarked how beautiful she looked. "Like a sleek arctic seal."

"Oh stop it."

"Don't dry off, please. Don't ever dry off."

"Get your hand away from there." Nina slapped him sharply. "Put your clothes on. Chelsea's waiting at the office."

Joe Winder said, "I'm phoning in sick."

"No, you're not. You can't." She wrapped the towel around her hair and left the rest bare. "He wasn't calling about the dead person on the bridge, he was calling about the whale."

"Orky?"

Nina opened the bathroom door to let out the steamy humidity. Joe Winder impulsively clutched her around the waist. He pressed his cheek against her damp thigh, and began to hum the tune of "Poor Pitiful Me." Nina pried him loose and said, "I'm glad you don't get beat up every day."

Something was out of alignment in Winder's brain. He blinked three or four times, slowly, but even as the steam cleared it didn't go away. Double vision! The bastards had pounded him that badly. Nina's bare bottom appeared to him as four gleaming porcelain orbs.

Distractedly, he said, "Go on. Something about the whale?"

"Yes," said Nina. She stood before the mirror, checking her armpits for stubble. "Chelsea said the whale is dead."

"Hmmm," said Joe Winder. Orky the Killer Whale.

"And?" he said.

"And, I don't know." Nina stepped into her panties. "He said for you to come right away. He said it was an emergency."

"First let's go to bed." Winder came up behind her. In the mirror he saw two pairs of hands cupping two pairs of nipples. He saw two faces that looked just like his—lumpy, lacerated, empurpled—nuzzling the tan silky slopes of two feminine necks.

"All right, Joe," Nina said, turning around. "But I've got to be honest: I'm very disappointed in you—"

"It wasn't what you think."

"—and I'm only doing this because you're in pain." Mechanically Nina took his hand and led him toward the bed. She kicked off her underwear and unwrapped the towel from her hair. Winder was grinning like an idiot.

"I'm warning you," Nina said, "this isn't an act of passion, it's an act of pity."

"I'll take it," said Joe Winder. "But, please, no more talking for a while."

"All right," she said. "No more talking."

▼ ▼ ▼

Orky the Killer Whale had come to the Amazing Kingdom of Thrills under clouded circumstances. His true name (or the name bestowed by his human captors off the coast of British Columbia) was Samson. Delivered in a drugged stupor to a north California marine park, he was measured at twenty-nine feet and seven inches, a robust male example of the species *orca*. Samson was larger than the other tame killer whales in the tank, and proved considerably more recalcitrant and unpredictable. In his first six months of captivity he mauled two trained porpoises and chomped the tail off a popular sea lion named Mr. Mugsy. Trainers worked overtime trying to teach their new star the most rudimentary of whale tricks—leaping through a plastic hoop, or snatching a dead mackerel from the fingers of a pretty model—with minimal success. One day he would perform like a champ, the next he would sink to the bottom of the tank and fart belligerently, launching balloon-sized bubbles of fishy gas to the surface. The audience seldom found this entertaining. Eventually most of the seasoned whale trainers refused to enter the water with Samson. Those who tried to ride his immense black dorsal were either whiplashed or pretzeled or corkscrewed into semiconsciousness.

Quite by accident, it was discovered that Samson was enraged by the color green. This became evident on the day that the human trainers switched to vivid Kelly-green tank suits without telling the other performing mammals. Samson was supposed to open the first show by fetching an inflatable topless mermaid and gaily delivering it to a young man on a ladder, in exchange for a fistful of smelts. On this particular morning, Samson retrieved the toy, carried it across the water on his snout, flipped it into the bleachers, snatched the green-clad trainer off the ladder, flipped *him* into the bleachers, then dived to the bottom of the tank and began to pass gas relentlessly. Each time somebody tried to lure him up, Samson shot from the depths with his mouth open, the great black-and-white jaws clacking like a truck door. The crowd loved it. They thought it was part of the act.

Reluctantly the curators of the California marine park concluded that this whale was one dangerous rogue. They attempted to peddle him to another marine park, far away on the western coast of Florida, but first they changed his name to Ramu. The transaction took place at a time when ocean-theme parks around the country were reporting various troubles with trained killer whales, and animal-rights groups were seeking legislation to prevent capturing them for exhibit. Word of Samson's behavioral quirks had spread throughout the marine-park industry, which is why it was necessary to change his name before trying to sell him.

The day the deal was done, Samson was tranquilized, lashed to a canvas litter and placed aboard a chartered Sikorsky helicopter. There workers took turns sponging him with salt water during the arduous cross-country flight, which lasted seventeen hours, including stops for refueling. By the time Samson arrived in Sarasota, he was in a vile and vindictive mood. During his first fifteen minutes in the new tank, he savagely foreshortened a pectoral fin on another male orca and destroyed the floating basket through which he was supposed to slam-dunk beach balls. Weeks passed with little improvement in the new whale's temperament. One fateful Sunday, the animal abruptly awakened from its funk, tail-walked across the tank and did a dazzling double somersault before hundreds of delighted tourists. When a stubby woman in a green plaid sundress leaned too close with her Nikon, the whale seized her in his teeth, dragged her once around the tank, then spit her out like an olive pit.

It was then that Samson's new owners realized that they had been duped; they'd bought themselves a bum whale. Ramu was in fact the infamous and incorrigible Samson. Immediately the beast was quarantined as a repeat offender, while the Sarasota theme park made plans to resell him under the misleadingly gentle name of Orky.

Francis X. Kingsbury was the ideal chump. The soon-to-be-opened Amazing Kingdom of Thrills was shopping for a major ocean attraction to compete with Disney World's "living reef." Kingsbury saw the Orky offer as a bargain of a lifetime—a trained killer whale for only nine hundred bucks, plus freight! Kingsbury snapped at it.

Orky was more than a disappointment, he was a dud. No one at the Amazing Kingdom could train the whale to do a single trick on cue; capable of wondrous gymnastic feats, the animal remained oblivious of regimen and performed only when he damn well felt like it. Often he did his best work in the middle of the night, when the stadium was empty. But on those nocturnal occasions, when the park was closed and there was no one to reward him with buckets of dead mullet, Orky furiously would ram the sides of the whale tank until the Plexiglas cracked and the plaster buckled.

Because it was impossible to predict his moods, Orky's shows were not posted in a regular schedule. Tourists paid their money, took their seats and hoped for the best. Once in a great while, the killer whale would explode in exuberant ballet, but more often he just sulked or blew water aimlessly.

One time Francis X. Kingsbury had suggested punishing the mammoth creature by withholding supper. Orky retaliated by breaking into the pelican pool and wolfing down nine of the slow-moving birds. After that, Kingsbury said to hell with the goddamn whale and gave up on training the beast. He knew he'd been scammed but was too proud to admit it. Kingsbury's corporate underlings sensed that Orky was a sore spot with the boss, and avoided mentioning the whale exhibit in his presence.

Until today.

With Orky unexpectedly dead, the subject was bound to come up. Charles Chelsea decided on a pre-emptive strike. He broke the news as Francis Kingsbury was munching his regular breakfast bagel. "Good," Kingsbury said, spraying crumbs. "Hated that fucking load."

"Sir, it's not good," said Charles Chelsea, "publicity-wise."

"How do you figure," Kingsbury said. "I mean, shit, what's a lousy whale to these people. You know who I mean—the media."

Charles Chelsea said he would try to explain it on the way to the autopsy.

▼ ▼ ▼

Joe Winder's vision returned to normal after making love to Nina; he regarded this as providential. He took a cab to Card Sound Road and retrieved his car. When he got back to the apartment, he changed to a long-sleeved shirt, charcoal trousers and a navy necktie, in the hope that high fashion would divert attention from his pulverized face. When he got to the Amazing Kingdom, he saw he had nothing to worry about. Everybody was staring at the dead killer whale.

They had hauled the remains to one of the parking lots, and roped a perimeter to keep out nosy customers. To conceal Orky's corpse, which was as large as a boxcar, Charles Chelsea had rented an immense tent from an auto dealership in Homestead. The tent was brilliantly striped and decorated with the legend "SOUTH FLORIDA TOYOTA-THON." A dozen or so electric fans had been requisitioned to circulate the air, which had grown heavy with the tang of dead whale. The staff veterinarian, a man named Kukor, was up to his knees in Orky's abdomen when Joe Winder arrived.

"Joe, thank God," said Chelsea, with an air of grave urgency. He led Winder to a corner and said, "Mr. X is here, to give you some idea."

"Some idea of what?"

"Of how serious this is."

Joe Winder said, "Charlie, I don't mean to be disrespectful but I'm not sure why I'm needed." Over his shoulder, he heard somebody crank up a chain saw.

"Joey, think! First the damn mango voles and now Orky. It's gonna look like we're neglecting the wildlife. And this whole killer-whale thing, it's gotten very controversial. There was a piece in *Newsweek* three weeks ago." Charles Chelsea was sweating extravagantly, and Winder assumed it had something to do with the presence of Francis X. Kingsbury.

Chelsea went on, "I know it's unpleasant, Joe, but you can leave as soon as Doc Kukor gives us a cause of death."

Joe Winder nodded. "How many words?"

"Three hundred. And I need it for the early news."

"Fine, Charlie. Later you and I need to talk."

Chelsea was peering through the flaps in the tent, making sure that no gawkers had sneaked past the security men.

"Listen to me," Joe Winder said. "There's some big trouble in this park. I got the shit kicked out of me last night because of it."

For the first time Chelsea noticed the battered condition of Joe Winder's face. He said, "What the hell happened? No, wait, not now. Not with Mr. X around. We'll chat later, I promise."

Winder grabbed his elbow. "I need to know everything about the dead man at the bridge."

Chelsea shook free and said, "Later, Joe, for heaven's sake. Let's tackle the crisis at hand, shall we?"

Together they returned to the autopsy. Instead of concentrating on Orky's entrails, Joe Winder scanned the small group of official observers: a state wildlife officer, taking notes; the tow-truck drivers who had hauled the whale corpse to the tent; three of Uncle Ely's Elves, apparently recruited as extra manpower; and Francis X. Kingsbury himself, mouthing obscenities over the gruesome ceremony.

Nervously Chelsea directed Joe Winder to Kingsbury's side and introduced him. "This is the fellow I told you about," said the PR man. "Our ace in the hole."

Kingsbury chuckled darkly. "Blame us for this? Some fucking fish croaks, how can they blame us?"

Joe Winder shrugged. "Why not?" he said.

Cutting in quickly, Chelsea said: "Don't worry, sir, it'll die down. It's just the crazy pro-animal types, that's all." He planted a moist hand on Winder's shoulder. "Joe's got the perfect touch for this."

"Hope so," said Francis X. Kingsbury. "Meanwhile, the stink, holy Christ! Don't we have some Glade. I mean, this is fucking rank."

"Right away," said Chelsea, dashing off in search of air freshener.

Kingsbury gestured at the billowing tent, the murmuring onlookers, the husk of deceased behemoth. "You believe this shit?" he said to Joe Winder. "I'm a goddamn real-estate man is all. I don't know from animals."

"It's a tricky business," Winder agreed.

"Who'd believe it, I mean, looking at this thing."

It was quite a strange scene, Joe Winder had to admit. "I'm sure they can find a new whale for the show."

"This time mechanical," Kingsbury said, jabbing a finger at Orky's lifeless form. "No more real ones. Computerized, that'd be the way to go. That's how Disney would handle it, eh?"

"Either that or a hologram," said Joe Winder with a wink. "Think of all the money you'd save on whale food."

Just then Dr. Kukor, the veterinarian, tripped on something and fell down inside Orky's closet-sized stomach cavity. Two of Uncle Ely's Elves bravely charged forward to help, hoisting the doctor to his feet.

"Oh my," Kukor said, pointing. The elves ran away frantically, their huge curly-toed shoes slapping noisily on the blood-slickened asphalt.

"What?" barked Francis X. Kingsbury. "What is it?"

"I don't believe this," said the veterinarian.

Kingsbury stepped forward to see for himself and Joe Winder followed, though he was sorry he did.

"Call somebody," wheezed Dr. Kukor.

"Looks like a human," Kingsbury remarked. He turned to stare at Winder because Winder was clinging to his arm. "Don't puke on me or you're fired," said Kingsbury.

Joe Winder was trying not to pass out. The corpse wasn't in perfect condition, but you could tell who it was.

A wan and shaky Dr. Kukor stepped out of Orky's excavated

carcass. "Asphyxiation," he declared numbly. "The whale choked to death."

"Well, damn," said Francis X. Kingsbury.

Joe Winder thought: Choked to death on Will Koocher. Koocher, in a mint-green golf shirt.

"Somebody call somebody," Kukor said. "This is way out of my field."

Winder reeled away from the scene. In a croaky voice he said, "That's the worst thing I ever saw."

"You?" Kingsbury laughed harshly. "Three fucking tons of whale meat, talk about a nightmare."

"Yes," Joe Winder said, gasping for fresh air.

"I'm thinking South Korea or maybe the Sudan," Kingsbury was saying. "Stamp it 'Tuna,' who the hell would ever know? Those little fuckers are starving."

"What?" said Winder. "What did you say?"

"Providing I can get some goddamn ice, pronto."

Charles Chelsea decreed that there should be no mention of Dr. Will Koocher in the press release. "Stick to Orky," he advised Joe Winder. "Three hundred words max."

"You're asking me to lie."

"No, I'm asking you to omit a few superfluous details. The whale died suddenly overnight, scientists are investigating, blah, blah, blah. Oh, and be sure to include a line that Mr. Francis X. Kingsbury is shocked and saddened." Chelsea paused, put a finger to his chin. "Scratch the 'shocked,'" he said. "'Saddened' is plenty. 'Shocked' makes it sound like something, I don't know, something—"

"Out of the ordinary?" said Joe Winder.

"Right. Exactly."

"Charlie, you are one sorry bucket of puss."

Chelsea steepled his hands on his chest. Then he unfolded them. Then he folded them once more and said, "Joe, this is a question of privacy, not censorship. Until Dr. Koocher's wife is officially notified, the least we can do is spare her the agony of hearing about it on the evening news."

For a moment, Winder saw two Charles Chelseas instead of one. Somewhere in the cacophonous gearbox of his brain, he heard the hiss of a petcock, blowing off steam. "Charlie," he said blankly, "the man was eaten by a fucking thirty-foot leviathan. This isn't going to remain our little secret very long."

Chelsea's brow wrinkled. "Eventually, yes, I suppose we'll have to make some sort of public statement. Seeing as it was our whale."

Joe Winder leaned forward on one elbow. "Charlie, I'm going to be honest."

"I appreciate that."

"Very soon I intend to kick the living shit out of you."

Chelsea stiffened. He shifted in his chair. "I don't know what to make of a remark like that."

Joe Winder imagined his eyeballs pulsating in the sockets, as if jolted by a hot wire.

Charles Chelsea said, "You mean, punch me? Actually punch me?"

"Repeatedly," said Winder, "until you are no longer conscious."

The publicity man's voice was plaintive, but it held no fear. "Do you know what kind of day I've had? I've dealt with two dead bodies—first the man on the bridge, and now the vole doctor. Plus I've been up to my knees in whale guts. I'm drained, Joe, physically and emotionally drained. But if it makes you feel better to beat me up, go ahead."

Joe Winder said he was a reasonable man. He said he would reconsider the beating if Charles Chelsea would show him the suicide note allegedly written by Dr. Will Koocher.

Chelsea unlocked a file drawer and took out a sheet of paper with block printing on it. "It's only a Xerox," he said, handing it to Winder, "but still it breaks your heart."

It was one of the lamest suicide notes that Joe Winder had ever seen. In large letters it said: "TO MY FRIENDS AND FAMILY, I SORRY BUT I CAN'T GO ON. NOW THAT MY WORK IS OVER, SO AM I."

The name signed at the bottom was "*William Bennett Koocher, PhD.*"

Winder stuffed the Xerox copy in his pocket and said, "This is a fake."

"I know what you're thinking, Joey, but it wasn't only the voles that got him down. There were problems at home, if you know what I mean."

"My goodness." Winder whistled. "Problems at home. I had no idea."

Chelsea continued: "And I know what else you're thinking. Why would anybody kill himself in this . . . *extreme* fashion? Jumping in a whale tank and all."

"It struck me as a bit unorthodox, yes."

"Well, me too," said Chelsea, regaining some of his starch, "until I remembered that Koocher couldn't swim a lick. More to the point, he was deathly afraid of sharks. It's not so surprising that he chose to drown himself here, indoors, rather than the ocean."

"And the green shirt?"

"Obviously he wasn't aware of Orky's, ah, problem."

Joe Winder blinked vigorously in an effort to clear his vision. He said, "The man's spine was snapped like a twig."

"I am told," said Charles Chelsea, "that it's not as bad as it appears. Very quick, and nearly painless." He took out a handkerchief and discreetly dried the palms of his hands. "Not everyone has the stomach for using a gun," he said. "Myself, I'd swallow a bottle of roach dust before I'd resort to violence. But, anyway, I was thinking: Maybe this was Koocher's way of joining the lost voles. A symbolic surrender to Nature, if you will. Sacrificing himself to the whale."

Chelsea squared the corners of the handkerchief and tucked it into a pants pocket. He looked pleased with his theory. Sagely he added, "In a sense, what happened that night in Orky's tank was a purely natural event: Dr. Koocher became part of the food chain. Who's to say he didn't plan it that way?"

Joe Winder stood up, clutching the corners of Charles Chelsea's desk. "It wasn't a suicide," he said, "and it wasn't an accident."

"Then what, Joe?"

"I believe Koocher was murdered."

"Oh, for God's sake. At the Amazing Kingdom?"

Again Winder felt the sibilant whisper from a valve letting off pressure somewhere deep inside his skull. He reached across the desk and got two crisp fistfuls of Chelsea's blue oxford shirt. "*I sorry but I can't go on?*"

Perplexed, Chelsea shook his head.

Joe Winder said, "The man was a PhD, Charlie. *I sorry but I can't go on?* Tonto might write a suicide note like that, but not Dr. Koocher."

Chelsea pulled himself free of Winder's grip and said: "It was probably just a typo, Joe. Hell, the man was terribly depressed and upset. Who proofreads their own damn suicide note?"

Pressing his knuckles to his forehead, Winder said, "A typo? With a Magic Marker, Charlie? *I sorry* is not a bummed-out scientist making a mistake; it's an illiterate moron trying to fake a suicide note."

"I've heard just about enough." Chelsea circled the desk and made for the door. He stepped around Winder as if he were a rattlesnake.

Chelsea didn't leave the office. He held the door open for Joe Winder, and waited.

"I see," said Winder. On his way out, he stopped to smooth the shoulders of Chelsea's shirt, where he had grabbed him.

"No more talk of murder," Charles Chelsea said. "I want you to promise me."

"All right, but on the more acceptable subject of suicide—who was the dead guy hanging from the Card Sound Bridge?"

"I've no idea, Joe. It doesn't concern us."

"It concerns me."

"Look, I'm starting to worry. First you threaten me with physical harm, now you're blabbing all these crazy theories. It's alarming, Joe. I hope I didn't misjudge your stability."

"I suspect you did."

Warily, Chelsea put a hand on Winder's arm. "We've got a tough week ahead. I'd like to be able to count on you."

"I'm a pro, Charlie."

"That's my boy. So you'll give me Orky by four o'clock?"

"No sweat," Winder said. "Three hundred words."

"Max," reminded Charles Chelsea, "and keep it low key."

"My middle name," said Joe Winder.

▼ ▼ ▼

In the first draft of the press release, he wrote: *Orky the killer whale, a popular but unpredictable performer at the Amazing Kingdom of Thrills, died suddenly last night after asphyxiating on a foreign object.*

Chelsea sent the press release back, marked energetically in red ink.

In the second draft, Joe Winder wrote: *Orky the whale, one of the most colorful animal stars at the Amazing Kingdom of Thrills, passed away last night of sudden respiratory complications.*

Chelsea returned it with a few editing suggestions in blue ink.

In the third draft, Winder began: *Lovable Orky the whale, one of the most colorful and free-spirited animal stars at the Amazing Kingdom of Thrills, was found dead in his tank this morning.*

While pathologists conducted tests to determine the cause of death, Francis X. Kingsbury, founder of the popular family theme park, expressed deep sorrow over the sudden loss of this majestic creature.

"We had come to love and admire Orky," Kingsbury said. "He was as much a part of our family as Robbie Raccoon or Petey Possum."

Joe Winder sent the press release up to Charles Chelsea's office and decided not to wait for more revisions. He announced that he was going home early to have his testicles reattached.

Before leaving the park, Winder stopped at a pay phone near the Magic Mansion and made a few calls. One of the calls was to an old newspaper source who worked at the Dade County Medical Examiner's Office. Another call was to the home of Mrs. Will Koocher, where a friend said she'd already gone back to Ithaca to await her husband's coffin. A third phone call went to Nina at home, who listened to Joe Winder's sad story of the dead vole doctor, and said: "So the new job isn't working out, is that what you're saying?"

"In a nutshell, yes."

"If you ask me, your attitude is contributing to the problem."

Joe Winder spotted the acne-spackled face of Pedro Luz, peering suspiciously from behind a Snappy-the-Troll photo gazebo, where tourists were lined up to buy Japanese film and cameras. Pedro Luz was again sucking on the business end of an intravenous tube; the tube snaked up to a bottle that hung from a movable metal sling. Whenever Pedro Luz took a step, the IV rig would roll after him. The liquid dripping from the bottle was the color of weak chicken soup.

Joe Winder said to Nina: "My attitude is not a factor."

"Joe, you sound . . ."

"Yes?"

"Different. You sound different."

"Charlie made me lie in the press release."

"And this comes as a shock? Joe, it's a whole different business from before. We talked about this at length when you took the job."

"I can fudge the attendance figures and not lose a minute of sleep. Covering up a murder is something else."

On Nina's end he heard the rustling of paper. "I want to read you something," she said.

"Not now, please."

"Joe, it's the best thing I've ever done."

Winder glanced over toward the Snappy photo gazebo, but Pedro Luz had slipped out of sight.

Nina began to read: *Last night I dreamed I fell asleep on a diving board; the highest one, fifty meters. It was a hot steamy day, so I took my top off and lay down. I was so high up that no one but the sea gulls could see me. The sun felt wonderful. I closed my eyes and drifted off to sleep—*

"Not '*meters*,' " Winder cut in. " '*Meters*' is not a sexy word."

Nina kept going: *When I awoke, you were standing over me, naked*

*and brown from the sun. I tried to move but I couldn't—you had used
the top of my bikini to tie my hands to the board. I was helpless, yet
afraid to struggle . . . we were up so high. But then you knelt between
my legs and told me not to worry. Before long, I forgot where we
were. . . .*

"Not bad." Joe Winder tried to sound encouraging, but the thought
of trying to have sex on a high-diving board made his stomach pitch.

Nina said: "I want to leave something to the imagination. Not like
Miriam, she's unbelievable. *I took chew in my mouth and sock like a
typhoon.*"

Winder conceded that this was truly dreadful.

"I've got to listen to that pulp all night long," Nina said. "While
she's clipping her toenails!"

"And I thought I had problems."

She said, "Was that sarcasm? Because if it was—"

The telephone receiver was getting heavy in Joe Winder's hand. He
wedged it in the crook of his shoulder and said, "Can I tell you what I
was thinking just now? I was thinking about the gastric secretions inside
a killer whale's stomach. I was thinking how unbelievably powerful the
digestive juices must be in order for a whale to be able to eat swordfish
beaks and seal bones and giant squid gizzards and the like."

In a flat voice, Nina said, "I have to go now, Joe. You're getting
morbid again."

"I guess I am."

The click on the other end seemed an appropriate punctuation.

▼ ▼ ▼

On the way home he decided to stop and try some bonefishing at
his secret spot. He turned off County Road 905 and came to the familiar gravel path that led through the hardwoods to the mangrove shore.

Except the woods were gone. The buttonwoods, the mahogany, the
gumbo-limbos—all obliterated. So were the mangroves.

Joe Winder got out of his car and stared. The hammock had been
flattened; he could see all the way to the water. It looked as if a twenty-
megaton bomb had gone off. Bulldozers had piled the dead trees in
mountainous tangles at each corner of the property.

Several hundred yards from Joe Winder's car, in the center of what
was now a vast tundra of scrabbled dirt, a plywood stage had been
erected. The stage was filled with men and women, all dressed up in
the dead of summer. A small crowd sat in folding chairs laid out in
rows in front of the stage. Joe Winder could hear the brassy strains of

"America the Beautiful" being played by a high-school band, its lone tuba glinting in the afternoon sun. The song was followed by uneven applause. Then a man stood up at a microphone and began to speak, but Joe Winder was too far away to hear what was being said.

In a daze, Winder kicked out of his trousers and changed into his cutoffs. He got his fly rod out of the trunk of the car and assembled it. To the end of the monofilament leader he attached a small brown epoxy fly that was intended to resemble a crustacean. The tail of the fly was made from deer hair; Winder examined it to make sure it was bushy enough to attract fish.

Then he tucked the fly rod under his left arm, put on his Polaroid sunglasses and marched across the freshly flattened field toward the stage. Absolutely nothing of logic went through his mind.

The man at the microphone turned out to be the mayor of Monroe County, Florida. It was largely a ceremonial title that was passed in odd-numbered years from one county commissioner to another, a tradition interrupted only by death or indictment. The current mayor was a compact fellow with silvery hair, olive skin and the lean fissured face of a chain-smoker.

"This is a grand day for the Florida Keys," the mayor was saying. "Nine months from today, this will be a gorgeous fairway." A burst of masculine clapping. "The sixteenth fairway, if I'm not mistaken. A four-hundred-and-twenty-yard par-four dogleg toward the ocean. Is that about right, Jake?"

A heavyset man sitting behind the mayor grinned enormously in acknowledgment. He had squinty eyes and a face as brown as burned walnut. He waved at the audience; the hearty and well-practiced wave of a sports celebrity. Joe Winder recognized the squinty-eyed man as Jake Harp, the famous professional golfer. He looked indefensibly ridiculous in a bright lemon blazer, brown beltless slacks, shiny white loafers and no socks.

At the microphone, the mayor was going on about the championship golf course, the lighted tennis courts, the his-and-her spas, the posh clubhouse with its ocean view and, of course, the exclusive luxury waterfront homesites. The mayor was effervescent in his presentation, and the small overdressed audience seemed to share his enthusiasm. The new development was to be called Falcon Trace.

"And the first phase," said the mayor, "is already sold out. We're talking two hundred and two units!"

Joe Winder found an empty chair and sat down. He propped the fly rod in his lap so that it rose like a nine-foot CB antenna out of his crotch. He wondered why he hadn't heard about this project, considering that the property abutted the southern boundary of the Amazing Kingdom of Thrills. He didn't remember seeing anything in the newspapers about a new country club. He felt a homicidal churning in his belly.

Not again, he thought. Not again, not again, not again.

The mayor introduced Jake Harp—"one of the greatest crosshanded putters of all time"—and the audience actually rose to its feet and cheered.

Jake Harp stood at the podium and waved ebulliently. Waved and waved, as if he were the bloody pope.

"Welcome to Falcon Trace," he began, reading off an index card. "Welcome to my new home."

More clapping as everyone settled back in their chairs.

"You know, I've won the PGA three times," said Jake Harp, "and finished third in the Masters twice. But I can honestly say that I was never so honored as when y'all selected me as the touring pro for beautiful Falcon Trace."

A voice piped up near the stage: "You rot in hell!"

A strong empassioned voice—a woman. The crowd murmured uncomfortably. Jake Harp nervously cleared his throat, a tubercular grunt into the microphone.

Again the woman's voice rose: "We don't need another damn golf course. Why don't you go back to Palm Springs with the rest of the gangsters!"

Now she was standing. Joe Winder craned to get a good look.

The famous golfer tried to make a joke. Painfully he said, "I guess we got ourselves a golf widow in the audience."

"No," the woman called back, "a real widow."

On stage, Jake Harp bent over and whispered something to the mayor, who was smoking fiercely. Someone signaled to the conductor of the high-school band, which adroitly struck up a Michael Jackson dance number. Meanwhile three uniformed sheriff's deputies materialized and edged toward the rude protester. The woman stood up, shook a fist above the silvery puff that was her head and said something that Joe Winder couldn't quite hear, except for the word "bastard."

Then she put on a floppy pink Easter bonnet and permitted herself to be arrested.

Well, hello, thought Winder. The lady from the Wildlife Rescue Corps, the one who'd slipped him the note at the Amazing Kingdom.

Joe Winder watched the deputies lead the old woman away. He wanted to follow and ask what in the hell was going on, but she was quickly deposited in the back of a squad car, which sped off toward

Key Largo. As Jake Harp resumed his speech, Winder got up and walked past the stage toward the ocean. In a few minutes he found the familiar stretch of shoreline where he usually searched for bonefish, but the water was too milky to see over the tops of his own sneakers. As he waded into the flats, he could hear the high-school band begin to play "The Star Spangled Banner," signaling the climax of the groundbreaking ceremony.

As he slid his feet across the rocks and sea grass, Joe Winder started false-casting his fly, stripping out the line as he moved forward. The water was murky, roiled, just a mess. There would be no fish here, Winder knew, but still he drove the meat of the line seventy feet hard into the wind, and watched the tiny plop of the fly when it landed.

Joe Winder fished in manic motion because he knew time was running out. Before long, this fine little bay would be a stagnant ruin and the only fish worth catching would be gone, spooked by jet skis, sailboarders, motorboats and plumes of rank sewage blossoming from submerged drainage pipes.

Welcome to Falcon Trace.

He took another step and felt something seize his right ankle. When he tried to pull free, he lost his balance and fell down noisily in the water. He landed on his ass but quickly rolled to his knees, careful to hold the expensive Seamaster fly reel high and dry. Irritably Winder groped beneath the surface for the thing that had tripped him.

His fingers closed around the slick branch of a freshly cut tree. He lifted it out of the water, examined it, then let it drop again. A red mangrove, bulldozed, ripped out by the roots and dumped on the flats. Illegal as hell, but who besides the fish would ever know?

Joe Winder knelt in the shallows and thought about what to do next. Back on the soon-to-be-sixteenth hole, the band played on. After a while, the music stopped and voices could be heard, collegial chamber-of-commerce good-old-boy voices, dissipating in the afternoon breeze. Not long afterward came the sounds of luxury cars being started.

Eventually the place got quiet, and Joe Winder knew he was alone again in his favorite fishing spot. He stayed on his knees in the water until the sun went down.

▼ ▼ ▼

In the evening he drove out to the Card Sound Bridge and parked. He got a flashlight from the trunk and began to walk along the road, keeping close to the fringe of the trees and playing the light along the ground. Soon he found the place where he had been beaten by the two goons, Angel and Spearmint Breath. Here Joe Winder slowed his pace and forced himself to concentrate.

He knew what he was looking for: a trail.

He'd spent most of his childhood outdoors, cutting paths to secret hideaways in the hammocks, glades and swamps. At a young age he had become an expert woodsman, a master of disappearing into impenetrable pockets where no one else wanted to go. Every time his father bought a new piece of property, Joe Winder set out to explore each acre. If there was a big pine, he would climb it; if there was a lake or a creek, he'd fish it. If there was a bobcat, he'd track it; a snake, he'd catch it.

He would pursue these solitary adventures relentlessly until the inevitable day when the heavy machinery appeared, and the guys in the hard hats would tell him to beat it, not knowing he was the boss's kid.

On those nights, lying in his bed at home, he would wait for his mother to come in and console him. Often she would suggest a new place for his expeditions, a mossy parcel off Old Cutler Road, or twenty acres in the Gables, right on the bay. Pieces his father's company had bought, or was buying, or was considering.

Raw, tangled, hushed, pungent with animals, buzzing with insects, glistening with extravagant webs, pulsing, rustling and doomed. And always the portal to these mysterious places was a trail.

Which is what Winder needed on this night.

Soon he found it: an ancient path of scavengers, flattened by raccoons and opossums but widened recently by something much larger. As Winder slipped into the woods, he felt ten years old again. He followed the trail methodically but not too fast, though his heart was pounding absurdly in his ears. He tried to travel quietly, meticulously ducking boughs and stepping over rotted branches. Every thirty or so steps, he would turn off the flashlight, hold his breath and wait. Before long, he could no longer hear the cars passing on Card Sound Road. He was so deep in the wetlands that a shout or a scream would be swallowed at once, eternally.

He walked for fifteen minutes before he came upon the remains of a small campfire. Joe Winder knelt and sniffed at the half-burned wood; somebody had doused it with coffee. He poked at the acrid remains of something wild that had been cooked in a small rusty pan. He swung the flashlight in a semicircle and spotted a dirty cooler, some lobster traps and a large cardboard box with the letters "EDTIAR" stamped on the side. On the ground, crumpled into a bright pile, was a florescent-orange rainsuit. Winder unfolded it, held it up to gauge the size. Then he put it back the way he found it.

Behind him, a branch snapped and a voice said, "How do you like the new pants?"

Winder wheeled around and pointed the flashlight as if it were a pistol.

The man was eating—and there was no mistaking it—a fried snake on a stick.

"Cottonmouth," he said, crunching off a piece. "Want some?"

"No thanks."

"Then we've got nothing to talk about."

Joe Winder politely took a bite of snake. "Like chicken," he said.

The man was cleaning his teeth with a fishhook. He looked almost exactly as Joe Winder remembered, except that the beard was now braided into numerous silvery sprouts that drooped here and there from the man's jaw. He was probably in his early fifties, although it was impossible to tell. The mismatched eyes unbalanced his face and made his expression difficult to read; the snarled eyebrows sat at an angle of permanent scowl. He wore a flowered pink shower cap, sunglasses on a lanyard, a heavy red plastic collar and no shirt. At first Joe Winder thought that the man's chest was grossly freckled, but in the flashlight's trembling beam the freckles began to hover and dance: mosquitoes, hundreds of them, feasting on his blood.

In a strained voice Joe Winder said, "I can't help but notice that thing on your neck."

"Radio collar." The man lifted his chin so Winder could see it. "Made by Telonics. A hundred fifty megahertz. I got it off a dead panther."

"Does it work?" Winder asked.

"Like a charm." The man snorted. "Why else would I be wearing it?"

Joe Winder decided this was something they could chat about later. He said, "I didn't mean to bother you. I just wanted to thank you for what you did the other night."

The stranger nodded. "No problem. Like I said, I got a pair of pants out of the deal." He slapped himself on the thigh. "Canvas, too."

"Listen, that little guy—Angel Gaviria was his name. They found him hanging under the bridge." Winder's friend at the medical examiner's office had confirmed the identity.

"What do you know," the stranger said absently.

"I was wondering about the other one, too," said Winder, "since they were trying to kill me."

"Don't blame you for being curious. By the way, they call me Skink. And I already know who you are. And your daddy, too, goddamn his soul."

He motioned for Joe Winder to follow, and crashed down a trail that led away from the campfire. "I went through your wallet the other night," Skink was saying, "to make sure you were worth saving."

"These days I'm not so sure."

"Shit," said Skink. "Don't start with that."

After five minutes they broke out of the hardwoods into a substantial clearing. A dump, Joe Winder noticed.

"Yeah, it's lovely," muttered Skink. He led Winder to the oxidized husk of an abandoned Cadillac, and lifted the trunk hatch off its hinges. The nude body of Spearmint Breath had been fitted inside, folded as neatly as a beach chair.

"Left over from the other night," Skink explained. "He ran out of steam halfway up the big bridge. Then we had ourselves a talk."

"Oh Jesus."

"A bad person," Skink said. "He would've brought more trouble."

An invisible cloud of foul air rose from the trunk. Joe Winder attempted to breath through his mouth.

Skink played the beam of the flashlight along the dead goon's swollen limbs. "Notice the skeeters don't go near him," he said, "so in one sense, he's better off."

Joe Winder backed away, speechless. Skink handed him the light and said, "Don't worry, this is only temporary." Winder hoped he wasn't talking to the corpse.

Skink replaced the trunk hatch on the junked Cadillac. "Asshole used to work Security at the Kingdom. He and Angel baby. But I suppose you already knew that."

"All I know," said Winder, "is that everything's going bad and I'm not sure what to do."

"Tell me about it. I still can't believe they shot John Lennon and it's been—what, ten years?" He sat down heavily on the trunk of the car. "You ever been to the Dakota?"

"Once," Joe Winder said.

"What's it like?"

"Sad."

Skink twirled the fishhook in his mouth, bit off the barb, and spit it out savagely. "Some crazy shithead with a .38—it's the story of America, isn't it?"

"We live in violent times. That's what they say."

"Guys like that, they give violence a bad name." Skink stretched out on the trunk, and stared at the stars. "Sometimes I think about that bastard in jail, how he loves all the publicity. Went from being nobody to The Man Who Shot John Lennon. I think some pretty ugly thoughts about that."

"It was a bad day," Joe Winder agreed. He couldn't tell if the man was about to sleep or explode.

Suddenly Skink sat up. With a blackened fingernail he tapped the radio collar on his neck. "See, it's best to keep moving. If you don't move every so often, a special signal goes out. Then they think the panther's dead and they all come searching."

"Who's they?"

"Rangers," Skink replied. "Game and Fish."

"But the panther *is* dead."

"You're missing the whole damn point."

As usual, Joe Winder wondered which way to take it, and decided he had nothing to lose. "What exactly are you doing out here?" he asked.

Skink grinned, a stunning, luminous movie-star grin.

"Waiting," he said.

12

On the morning of July 21, a Saturday, Molly McNamara drove Bud Schwartz and Danny Pogue to the Amazing Kingdom of Thrills for the purpose of burglarizing the office of Francis X. Kingsbury.

"All you want is files?" asked Bud Schwartz.

"As many as you can fit in the camera bag," Molly said. "Anything to do with Falcon Trace."

Danny Pogue, who was sitting in the back seat of the El Dorado, leaned forward and said, "Suppose there's some other good stuff. A tape deck or a VCR, maybe some crystal. Is it okay we grab it?"

"No, it is not," Molly replied. "Not on my time."

She parked in the Cindy-the-Sun Queen lot and left the engine running. The radio was tuned to the classical station, and Bud Schwartz asked if Molly could turn it down a notch or two. She went searching through her immense handbag and came out with a Polaroid camera. Without saying a word, she snapped a photograph of Bud Schwartz, turned halfway in the seat and snapped one of Danny Pogue. The flashbulb caused him to flinch and make a face. Molly plucked the moist negatives from the slot in the bottom of the camera and slipped them into the handbag.

"What's that all about?" said Danny Pogue.

"In case you get the itch to run away," Molly McNamara said, "I'd feel compelled to send your photographs to the authorities. They are still, I understand, quite actively investigating the theft of the mango voles."

"Pictures," said Bud Schwartz. "That's cute."

Molly smiled pleasantly and told both men to listen closely. "I rented you a blue Cutlass. It's parked over by the tram station. Here are the keys."

Bud Schwartz put them in his pocket. "Something tells me we won't be cruising down to Key West."

"Not if you know what's good for you," Molly said.

Danny Pogue began to whine again. "Ma'am, I don't know nothin' about stealing files," he said. "Now I'm a regular bear for tape decks and Camcorders and shit like that, but frankly I don't do much in the way of, like, *reading*. It's just not my area."

Molly said, "You'll do fine. Get in, grab what you can and get out."

"And hope that nobody recognizes us from before." Bud Schwartz arched his eyebrows. "What happens then? Or didn't you think of that."

Molly chuckled lightly. "Don't be silly. No one will recognize you dressed the way you are."

She had bought them complete golfing outfits, polyester down to the matching socks. Danny Pogue's ensemble was raspberry red and Bud Schwartz's was baby blue. The pants were thin and baggy; the shirts had short sleeves and loud horizontal stripes and a tiny fox stitched on the left breast.

Bud Schwartz said, "You realize we look like total dipshits."

"No, you look like tourists."

"It's not that bad," agreed Danny Pogue.

"Listen," Molly said again. "When you're done with the job, get in the Cutlass and come straight back to my place. The phone will ring at one sharp. If you're not there, I'm going directly to the post office and mail these snapshots to the police, along with your names. Do you believe me?"

"Yeah, sure," said Bud Schwartz.

She got out of the Cadillac and opened the doors for the burglars.

"How is your hand?" she asked Bud Schwartz. "Better let your friend carry the camera bag."

She held Danny Pogue's crutch (mending quickly, he was down to one) while he slipped the camera bag over his right shoulder. "The tram's coming," she announced. "Better get moving."

As the men hobbled away, Molly called out cheerfully and waved good-bye, as if she were their mother, or a loving old aunt.

With a trace of fondness, Danny Pogue said, "Look at her."

"Look at *us*," said Bud Schwartz. "Real fucking pros."

"Well, at least it's for a good cause. You know, saving them butter-flies."

Bud Schwartz eyed his partner in a clinical way. "Danny, you ever had a CAT scan?"

"A what?"

"Nothing."

The burglars were huffing pretty heavily by the time they made it to the tram. They climbed on the last car, along with a family of nine from Minneapolis. Every one of them had sandy hair and Nordic-blue eyes and eyebrows so blond they looked white in the sunlight.

A little girl of about seven turned to Danny Pogue and asked what had happened to his foot.

"I got shot," he said candidly.

The little girl flashed a glance at her mother, whose eyes widened.

"A tetanus shot," said Bud Schwartz. "He stepped on a rusty nail."

The mother's eyes softened with relief. "Where are you from?" she asked the men.

"Portugal," said Danny Pogue, trying to live up to the tourist act.

"Portugal, Ohio," Bud Schwartz said, thinking: There is no hope for this guy; he simply can't be allowed to speak.

The tiny blond girl piped up: "We heard on the radio that the whale died yesterday. Orky the whale."

"Oh no," said Danny Pogue. "You sure?"

The tram rolled to a stop in front of the main gate, where the burglars got off. Nodding good-bye to the blond Minneapolitans, Bud Schwartz and Danny Pogue slipped into the throng and located the shortest line at the ticket turnstiles.

In a gruff tone, Bud Schwartz said, "*Portugal?* What kind of fuck-head answer is that?"

"I don't know, Bud. I don't know a damn thing about tourists or where they come from."

"Then don't say anything, you understand?" Bud Schwartz got out the money that Molly had given them to buy the admission tickets. He counted out thirty-six dollars and handed the cash to his partner.

"Just hold up one finger, that's all you gotta do," said Bud Schwartz. "One finger means one ticket. Don't say a goddamn thing."

"All right," Danny Pogue said. "Man, I can't believe the whale croaked, can you?"

"Shut up," said Bud Schwartz. "I'm not kidding."

▼ ▼ ▼

Danny Pogue didn't seem the least bit nervous about returning to the scene of their crime. To him the Amazing Kingdom of Thrills was a terrific place, and he strutted around with a permanent grin. Bud Schwartz thought: He's worse than these damn kids.

Outside the Magic Mansion, Danny Pogue stopped to shake hands with Petey Possum. A tourist lady from Atlanta took a photograph, and Danny Pogue begged her to send him a copy. At this point Bud Schwartz considered ditching the dumb shit altogether and pulling the job alone.

Golf duds and all, Bud Schwartz was antsy about being back on the premises so soon after the rat-napping; it went against his long-standing aversion to dumb risk. He wanted to hurry up and get the hell out.

It wasn't easy locating Francis X. Kingsbury's office because it didn't appear on any of the colorful maps or diagrams posted throughout the amusement park. Bud Schwartz and Danny Pogue checked closely; there was the Cimarron Trail Ride, Orky's Undersea Paradise, the Wet Willy, the Jungle Jerry Amazon Boat Cruise, Bigfoot Mountain, Excitement Boulevard, and so on, with no mention of the administration building. Bud Schwartz decided Kingsbury's headquarters must be somewhere in the geographic center of the Amazing Kingdom of Thrills, and for security reasons probably wasn't marked.

"Why don't we ask somebody?" Danny Pogue suggested.

"Very smart," said Bud Schwartz. "I got a better idea. Why don't we just paint the word 'thief' in big red letters on our goddamn foreheads?"

Danny Pogue wasn't sure why his partner was in such a lousy mood. The Kingdom was awesome, fantastic, sensational. Everywhere they went, elves and fairy princesses and happy animal characters waved or shook hands or gave a hug.

"I never seen so much friendliness," he remarked.

"It's the crutch," said Bud Schwartz.

"No way."

"It's the damn crutch, I'm tellin' you. They're only being nice because they got to, Danny. Anytime there's a customer on crutches, they make a special point. You know, in case he's dying a some fatal disease."

Danny Pogue said, "You go to hell."

"Ten bucks says it's right in the training manual."

"Bud, I swear to God."

"Gimme the crutch and I'll prove it."

Danny Pogue said, "You're the one's always on my ass about attitude. And now just listen to yourself—all because people're actin' nice to me and not to you."

"That's not it," said Bud Schwartz, but when he turned around his partner was gone. He found him on line at the Wild Bill Hiccup rodeo ride; Danny Pogue had stashed his crutch in the men's room and was determined to give Wild Bill Hiccup a go. Bud Schwartz was tired of bickering.

The ride was set up in an indoor corral that had been laboriously fabricated, from the brown-dyed dirt to the balsa fence posts to the polyethylene cowshit that lay in neat regular mounds, free of flies. Twenty-five mechanical bulls (only the horns were real) jumped and bucked on hidden tracks while a phony rodeo announcer described the action through a realistically tinny megaphone.

During this particular session, the twenty-five bulls were mounted by twenty-three tourists and two professional crooks. Before the ride began, Bud Schwartz leaned over to Danny Pogue and told him to be sure and fall off.

"What?"

"You heard me. And make it look good."

When the bell rang, Bud Schwartz hung on with his good hand and bounced back and forth for maybe a minute without feeling anything close to excitement. Danny Pogue, however, was launched almost instantly from the sponge hump of his motorized Brahma—a tumble so spectacular that it brought three Company Cowpokes out of the bronco chute at a dead run. They surrounded Danny Pogue, measured his blood pressure, palpated his ribs and abdomen, listened to his heart, shined a light in his eyeballs and finally shoved a piece of paper under his nose.

"Why don't you put your name on this, li'l pardner?" said one of the Cowpokes.

Danny Pogue examined the document, shook his head and handed it to Bud Schwartz for interpretation.

"Release of liability," Bud Schwartz said. He looked up with a dry smile. "This means we can't sue, right?"

"Naw," said the solicitous Cowpoke. "All it means is your buddy's not hurt."

"Says who?" said Bud Schwartz. "Bunch a dumb cowboy shit-kickers. Thanks, but I think we'll try our luck with an actual doctor."

The Cowpokes didn't look so amiable anymore, or so Western. In fact, they were starting to look like pissed-off Miami insurance men. Danny Pogue got to his feet, dusted off his butt and said, "Hell, Bud, it's my fault anyhow—"

"Not another word." Bud Schwartz seized his partner by the elbow, as if to prop him up. Then he announced to the Cowpokes: "We'd like to file a complaint about this ride. Where exactly is the administration office?"

The Cowpoke in charge of the blood-pressure cuff said, "It's closed today."

"Then we'll come back Monday," said Bud Schwartz. "Where is the office, please?"

"Over Sally's Saloon," the Cowpoke answered. "Upstairs, ask for Mr. Dexter in Risk Management."

"And he'll be in Monday?"

"Nine sharp," muttered the Cowpoke.

The other tourists watched curiously as Bud Schwartz led Danny Pogue haltingly out of the corral. By this time the Wild Bill Hiccup attraction had come to a complete and embarrassing stop (a man with a sprocket wrench had beheaded Danny Pogue's bull), and Bud Schwartz wanted to depart the arena before his partner spoiled the plan by saying something irretrievably stupid.

Into Danny Pogue's ear he said, "You're doing fine."

"It wasn't on purpose."

"Yeah, I had a feeling."

As they watched Danny Pogue's genuine hobble, the three Cow-pokes from Risk Management began to worry that they might have missed something during their quickie medical exam.

One of them called out: "Hey, how about a wheelchair?"

Without turning around, Bud Schwartz declined the offer with the wave of an arm.

"No thanks, li'l pardner," he called back.

▼ ▼ ▼

The same tool that picked the lock on Francis X. Kingsbury's office did the job on the rosewood file cabinet.

"So now what?" Danny Pogue said.

"We read." Bud Schwartz divided the files into two stacks. He showed his partner how to save time by checking the index labels.

"Anything to do with banks and property, put it in the bag. Also, anything that looks personal."

"What about Falcon Trace?" asked Danny Pogue. "That's what Mrs. McNamara said to get."

"That, too."

They used pocket flashlights to examine the files because Bud Schwartz didn't want to turn on the lights in Kingsbury's office. They were on the third floor of the administration building, above Sally's Cimarron Saloon. Through the curtains Bud Schwartz could watch the Wild West show on the dusty street below. Tourists shrieked as two scruffy bank robbers suddenly opened fire on the sheriff; bloodied, the sheriff managed to shoot both bandits off their horses as they tried to escape. The tourists cheered wildly. Bud Schwartz grunted and said, "Now there's a job for you. Fallin' off horses."

Sitting on the floor amid Kingsbury's files, Danny Pogue looked orphaned. He said, "I know lawyers that couldn't make sense a this shit." He couldn't take his eyes off a portable Canon photocopier: seventy-five bucks, staring him in the face.

"We'll give it an hour," said Bud Schwartz, but it didn't take him that long to realize that his partner was right. The files were impenetrable, stuffed with graphs and pie charts and computer printouts that meant nothing to your average break-in artist. The index tabs were marked with hopelessly stilted titles like "Bermuda Intercontinental Services, Inc.," and "Ramex Global Trust, N.A.," and "Jersey Premium Market Research."

Bud Schwartz arbitrarily selected the three thickest files and stuffed them in the camera bag. This would keep the old bat busy for a while.

"Look here," said Danny Pogue, holding up a thin file. "Credit cards."

The index tab was marked "Personal Miscellany." Inside was a folder from the American Express Company that listed all the activity on Francis X. Kingsbury's Platinum Card for the previous twelve months. Bud Schwartz's expression warmed as he skimmed the entries.

Reading over his shoulder, Danny Pogue said. "The guy sure knows how to eat."

"He knows how to buy jewelry, too." Bud Schwartz pointed at some large numbers. "Look here."

"Yeah," said Danny Pogue, catching on. "I wonder where he keeps it, all that jewelry."

Bud Schwartz slipped Kingsbury's American Express folder into the camera bag. "This one's for us," he told his partner. "Don't show the old lady unless I say so."

Danny Pogue said, "I heard a that place in New York. Cartier's." He pronounced it "Car-teer's." "That's some expensive shit they sell."

"You bet," said Bud Schwartz. Another thin file had caught his attention. He opened it on his lap, using his good hand to hold the flashlight while he read. The file contained Xeroxed copies of numerous old newspaper clippings, and three or four letters from somebody at the U.S. Department of Justice. The letterhead was embossed, and it felt important.

"Jesus," said Bud Schwartz, sizing things up.

"What is it?"

He thrust the file at Danny Pogue. "Put this in the damn bag, and let's get going."

"Danny Pogue peered at the index tab and said, "So what does it mean?"

"It means we're gonna be rich, li'l pardner."

Danny Pogue contemplated the name on the file folder. "So how do you pronounce it anyway?"

"Gotti," said Bud Schwartz. "Rhymes with body."

13

Rummaging through a dead man's belongings at midnight was not Joe Winder's idea of fun. The lab was as cold and quiet as a morgue. Intimate traces of the late Will Koocher were everywhere: a wrinkled lab coat hung on the back of a door; a wedding picture in a brass frame on a corner of his desk; a half-eaten roll of cherry-flavored Tums in the drawer; Koocher's final paycheck, endorsed but never cashed.

Winder shivered and went to work. Methodically he pored through the vole files, and quickly learned to decipher Koocher's daily charts: size, weight, feeding patterns, sleeping patterns, stool patterns. Some days there was blood work, some days there were urine samples. The doctor's notes were clinical, brief and altogether unenlightening. Whatever had bothered Koocher about the mango-vole program, he hadn't put it in the charts.

It was an hour before Joe Winder found something that caught his eye: a series of color photographs of the voles. These were different from the glossy publicity pictures—these were extreme close-ups taken from various angles to highlight anatomical characteristics. Typed labels identified the animals as either "Male One" or "Female One." Several pictures of the female had been marked up in red wax pencil, presumably by Will Koocher. In one photograph, an arrow had been drawn to the rump of the mango vole, accompanied by the notation "CK. TAIL LENGTH." On another, Koocher had written: "CK. MICROTUS FUR COLOR—IS THERE BLOND PHASE?" In a third photograph, the animals' mouth had carefully been propped open with a Popsicle stick, which allowed a splendid frontal view of two large yellow incisors and a tiny indigo tongue.

Obviously the female vole had troubled Koocher, but why? Winder slipped the photos into his briefcase, and turned to the next file. It contained a muddy Xerox of a research paper titled, "Habitat Loss and the Decline of *Microtus mango* in Southeastern Florida." The author of the article was listed as Dr. Sarah Hunt, PhD, of Rollins College. In red ink Koocher had circled the woman's name, and put a question mark next to it. The research paper was only five pages long, but the margins were full of Koocher's scribbles. Winder was trying to make sense of them when he heard a squeaking noise behind him.

In the doorway stood Pedro Luz—pocked, bloated, puffy-eyed Pedro. "The fuck are you doing?" he said.

Joe Winder explained that a janitor had been kind enough to loan him a key to the lab.

"What for?" Pedro Luz demanded.

"I need some more information on the voles."

"Haw," said Pedro Luz, and stepped inside the lab. The squeaking came from the wheels of his mobile steroid dispenser, the IV rig he had swiped from the hospital. A clear tube curled from a hanging plastic bag to a scabby junction in the crook of Pedro Luz's left arm; the needle was held in place by several cross-wraps of cellophane tape.

The idea had come to him while he was hospitalized with the ferret bites. He had been so impressed with the wonders of intravenous refueling that he'd decided to try it with his anabolic steroids. Whether this method was effective, or even safe, were questions that Pedro Luz hadn't considered because the basic theory seemed unassailable: straight from bottle to vein, just like a gasoline pump. No sooner had he hung the first bag than he had felt the surge, the heat, the tingling glory of muscles in rapture. Even at ease, his prodigious biceps twitched and rippled as if prodded by invisible electrodes.

Joe Winder wondered why Pedro Luz kept staring down at himself, smiling as he admired the dimensions of his own broad chest and log-sized arms.

"Are you feeling all right?" Winder asked.

Pedro Luz looked up from his reverie and blinked toadlike.

Affably, Winder remarked, "You're working mighty late tonight."

Pedro Luz grunted: "I feel fine." He walked up to the desk and grabbed the briefcase. "You got no authorization to be here after hours."

"Mr. Chelsea won't mind."

Invoking Charlie's name made no impression on Pedro Luz, who plucked a leaf out of Joe Winder's hair. "Look at this shit on your head!"

"I spent some time in the mangroves," Winder said. "Ate snake-on-a-stick."

Pedro Luz announced: "I'm keeping your damn briefcase." He tucked it under his right arm. "Until I see some fucking authorization."

"What's in the IV bag?" Joe Winder asked.

"Vitamins," said Pedro Luz. "Now get the hell out."

"You know what I think? I think Will Koocher was murdered."

Pedro Luz scrunched his face as if something toxic were burning his eyes. His jaw was set so rigidly that Joe Winder expected to hear the teeth start exploding one by one, like popcorn.

Winder said, "Well, I guess I'll be going."

Pedro Luz followed him out the door, the IV rig squeaking behind them. To the back of Winder's neck, he growled, "You dumb little shit, now I gotta do a whole report."

"Pedro, you need some rest."

"The doctor wasn't murdered. He killed hisself."

"I don't think so."

"Man, I used to be a cop. I know the difference between murder and suicide."

Pedro Luz turned around to lock the laboratory door. Joe Winder thought it would be an excellent moment to snatch his briefcase from the security man and make a run for it. He figured Pedro Luz could never catch him as long as he was attached to the cumbersome IV rig.

Winder pondered the daring maneuver too long. Pedro Luz glanced over his shoulder and caught him staring at the briefcase.

"Go ahead," the big man taunted. "Just go ahead and try."

▼ ▼ ▼

Francis X. Kingsbury and Jake Harp had an early starting time at the Ocean Reef Club, up the road a few miles from the Amazing Kingdom of Thrills. Kingsbury played golf two or three times a week at Ocean Reef, even though he was not a member and would never be a member. A most exclusive outfit, the Ocean Reef board had voted consistently to blackball Kingsbury because it could not verify several important details of his biography, beginning with his name. Infuriated by the rejection, Kingsbury made himself an unwelcome presence by wheedling regular golf invitations from all acquaintances who happened to be members, including the famous Jake Harp.

Reluctantly Jake Harp had agreed to play nine holes. He didn't like golf with rich duffers but it was part of the deal; playing with Francis X. Kingsbury, though, was a special form of torture. All he talked about was Disney this and Disney that. If the stock had dropped a point or two, Kingsbury was euphoric; if the stock was up, he was bellicose and depressed. He referred to the Disney mascot as Mickey Ratface, or sometimes simply The Rat. "The Rat's updating his pathetic excuse for a jungle cruise," Kingsbury would report with a sneer. "The fake hippos must be rusting out." Another time, while Jake Harp was lining up a long putt for an eagle, Kingsbury began to cackle. "The Rat's got a major problem at the Hall of the Presidents! Heard they had to yank the Nixon robot because his jowls were molting!"

Jake Harp, a lifelong Republican, had suppressed the urge to take a Ping putter and clobber Francis X. Kingsbury into a deep coma. Jake Harp had to remain civil because of the Falcon Trace gig. It was his second chance at designing a golf course and he didn't want to screw up again; over on Sanibel they were still searching for that mysterious fourteenth tee, the one Jake Harp's architects had mistakenly located in the middle of San Carlos Bay.

As for his title of Falcon Trace "touring pro," it was spending money, that's all—tape a couple of television spots, get your face on a billboard, play a couple of charity tournaments in the winter. Hell, no one seriously expected you to actually show up and give golf lessons. Not the great Jake Harp.

In the coffee shop Francis X. Kingsbury announced that he was in a hurry because he was leaving town later in the day. The sooner the better, thought Jake Harp.

Standing on the first tee, Kingsbury spotted two of the Ocean Reef board members waiting in a foursome behind them. The men smiled thinly and nodded at him. Kingsbury placidly flipped them the finger. Jake Harp grimaced and reached for his driver.

"Love it," said Kingsbury. "Think they're such hot snots."

Jake Harp knocked the ball two hundred and sixty yards down the left side of the fairway. Kingsbury hit it about half as far and shrugged as if he didn't care. Once he got in the golf cart, he drove like a maniac and cursed bitterly.

"Our club'll make this place look like a buffalo latrine." The cart jounced heedlessly along the asphalt path. "Like fucking Goony Golf —I can't wait."

Jake Harp, who was badly hung over, said: "Let's take it easy, Frank."

"They're dying to know how I did it," Kingsbury went on, full tilt. "This island, it's practically a goddamn nature preserve. I mean, you can't mow your lawn without a permit from the fucking EPA."

He stomped the brake, got out and lined up his second shot. Jake Harp asked: "You gonna use the driver again?"

Kingsbury swung like a canecutter, topping the ball noisily. It skidded maybe eighty yards, cutting a bluish vector through the dew-covered grass.

"Keep your head down," advised Jake Harp.

Kingsbury hopped back in the cart and said: "Grandfathering, that's how I did it. The guy I bought from, he'd had his permits since '74. I'm talking Army Corps, Fish and Wildlife, even Interior. The state—well, yeah, that was a problem. For that I had to spread a little here and there. And Monroe County, forget it."

He shut up long enough to get out and hit again. This time he switched to a four-wood, which he skied into a liver-shaped bunker. "Fuck me," muttered Francis Kingsbury. He remained silent as Jake Harp casually knocked his second shot thirty feet from the pin.

"What was that, a five-iron? A six?"

"A six," replied Jake Harp, pinching the bridge of his nose. He figured if he could just cut off circulation, it would starve the pain behind his eyeballs and make his hangover go away.

Kingsbury punched the accelerator and they were off again. "You know how I got the county boys? The ones giving me a bad time, I promised 'em units. Not raw lots, no fucking way—town houses is all, the one-bedrooms with no garage."

"Oh," said Jake Harp, feeling privileged. He'd been given a double lot, oceanfront, plus first option on one of the spec homes.

"Townhouses," Kingsbury repeated with a laugh. "And they were happy as clams. All I got to do, it's easy, is sit on the titles until Phase One is built. You know, keep it off the tax rolls for a few months. 'Case some damn reporter shows up at the courthouse and starts looking up names."

Jake Harp didn't understand the nuances of Francis Kingsbury's scheme. The man was proud of himself, that much was obvious.

When they pulled up to the sand trap, they saw that Kingsbury's golf ball was practically buried under the lip. It appeared to have landed at the approximate speed and trajectory of a mortar round.

Kingsbury stood over the ball for a long time, as if waiting for it to make a move. Finally he said to Jake Harp: "You're the pro. What the hell now, a wedge? A nine, maybe?"

"Your only prayer," said Jake Harp, forcing a rheumy chuckle, "is a stick of dynamite." Miraculously, Kingsbury needed only three swings to blast out of the bunker, and two putts to get down.

While waiting on the next tee, Jake Harp said he thought it would be better if he didn't do any more speaking engagements on behalf of Falcon Trace.

Kingsbury scowled. "Yeah, I heard what happened, some broad."

"I'm not comfortable in those situations, Frank."

"Well, who the hell is? We got her name, the old bitch." Kingsbury took out a wood and started whisking the air with violent practice swings. Jake Harp could scarcely stand to look.

"One of those damn bunny huggers," Kingsbury was saying. "Anti this and anti that. Got some group, the Mothers of some fucking thing."

"It doesn't really matter," said Jake Harp.

"The hell is doesn't." Francis X. Kingsbury stopped swinging and pointed the polished head of the driver at Jake Harp's chest. "Now that we know who she is, don't you worry. This shit'll stop—it's been taken care of. You'll be fine from now on."

"I'm a golfer is all. I don't do speeches."

Kingsbury wasn't listening. "Maybe these assholes'll let us play through." He hollered down the fairway toward the other golfers, but they seemed not to hear. Kingsbury teed up a ball. He said, "Fine, they want to be snots."

"Don't," pleaded Jake Harp. The slow-playing foursome was well within the limited range of Kingsbury's driver. "Frank, what's the hurry?"

Kingsbury had already coiled into his backswing. "Yuppie snots," he said, following through with a ferocious grunt. The ball took off like a missile, low and true.

Terrific, thought Jake Harp. The one time he keeps his left arm straight.

The other golfers scattered and watched the ball streak past. They reassembled in the middle of the fairway, shook their fists at Kingsbury and began a swift march back toward the tee.

"Shit," said Jake Harp. He didn't have the energy for a fistfight; he didn't even have the energy to watch.

Francis X. Kingsbury put the wood in his bag, and sat down behind the steering wheel of the golf cart. The angry players were advancing in an infantry line that was the color of lollipops. Where Kingsbury came from, it would be hard to regard such men as dangerous.

"Aw, let's go," said Jake Harp.

Kingsbury nodded and turned the golf cart around. "Trying to make a point is all," he said. "Etiquette, am I right? Have some fucking common courtesy for other players."

Jake Harp said, "I think they got the message." He could hear the golfers shouting and cursing as they drove away. He hoped none of them had recognized him.

On the drive back to the clubhouse, Francis Kingsbury asked Jake Harp for the name of the restaurant manager at Ocean Reef.

"I've got no idea," Jake Harp said.

"But you're a member here."

"Frank, I'm a member of seventy-four country clubs all over the damn country. Some I've never even played."

Kingsbury went on: "The reason I asked, I got a line on a big shipment of fish. Maybe they'd want to buy some."

"I'll ask around. What kind of fish?"

"Tuna, I think. Maybe king mackerel."

"You don't know?"

"Hell, Jake, I'm a real-estate man, not a goddamn chef. It's a trailer full of fish is all I know. Maybe six thousand pounds."

Jake Harp said, "Holy Jesus."

Francis Kingsbury wasn't about to get into the whole messy story. He'd been having a devil of a time penetrating the Sudanese bureaucracy; UNICEF was no better. *Yes, of course we'd welcome any famine relief, but first you'll have to fill out some forms and answer some questions. . . .* Meanwhile, no one at the Amazing Kingdom seemed to know how long whale meat would stay fresh.

From the back of the golf cart came a high-pitched electronic beeping. Kingsbury quickly pulled off the path and parked in a stand of Australian pines. He unzipped his golf bag and removed a cellular telephone.

When he heard who was on the other end, he lowered his voice and turned away. Jake Harp took the hint; he slipped into the trees to get rid of the two Bloody Marys he'd had for breakfast. It was several seconds before he realized he was pissing all over somebody's brand-new Titleist. He carefully wiped it dry with a handkerchief and dropped it in his pocket.

Francis X. Kingsbury was punching a new number into the phone when Jake Harp returned to the golf cart.

"Get me that dildo Chelsea," he was saying. "No . . . who? I don't care—where did you say he is? Twenty minutes, he's not in my office and that's it. And get that fucking Pedro, he's in his car. Keep him on the line till—right—I get back."

He touched a button and the cellular phone made a burp. Kingsbury put it away. He was steaming mad.

Jake Harp said, "More problems?"

"Yeah, a major goddamn problem," said Kingsbury. "Only this one works for me."

"So fire him."

"Oh, I am," Kingsbury said, "and that's just for starters."

14

Molly McNamara came out of the kitchen carrying a silver teapot on a silver tray.

"No thank you," said Agent Billy Hawkins.

"It's herbal," Molly said, pouring a cup. "Now I want you to try this."

Hawkins politely took a drink. It tasted like cider.

"There now," said Molly. "Isn't that good?"

Hiding behind the door of the guest bedroom, Bud Schwartz and Danny Pogue strained to hear what was going on. They couldn't believe she was serving tea to an FBI man.

"I'd like to ask you a few questions," Billy Hawkins was saying.

Molly cocked her head pleasantly. "Of course. Fire away."

"Let's begin with the Mothers of Wilderness. You're the president?"

"And founder, yes. We're just a small group of older folks who are deeply concerned about the future of the environment." She held her teacup steady. "I'm sure you know all this."

Agent Hawkins went on: "What about the Wildlife Rescue Corps? What can you tell me about it?"

Molly McNamara was impressed by the FBI man's grammar; most people would have used "them" instead of "it."

"Just what I've read in the papers," she said, sipping. "That's the organization that is taking credit for freeing the mango voles, is that correct?"

"Right."

"I'm assuming this is what gives you jurisdiction in this matter—the fact that the voles are a federally protected endangered species."

"Right again," said Hawkins. She was a sharp one.

Behind the bedroom door, Bud Schwartz was ready to yank his hair out. The crazy old twat was screwing with the FBI, and enjoying it!

Danny Pogue looked as confused as ever. He leaned close and whispered: "I thought sure he was after you and me."

"Shut up," Bud Schwartz said. He was having a hard enough time hearing the conversation in the living room.

The FBI man was saying: "We have reason to suspect a connection between the Wildlife Rescue Corps and the Mothers of Wilderness—"

"That's outlandish," said Molly McNamara.

Agent Hawkins let the idea hang. He just sat there with his square shoulders and his square haircut, looking impassive and not the least bit accusatory.

Molly asked: "What evidence do you have?"

"No evidence, just indications."

"I see." Her tone was one of pleasant curiosity.

Billy Hawkins opened his briefcase and took out two shiny pieces of paper. Xeroxes. "Last month the Mothers of Wilderness put out a press release. Do you remember?"

"Certainly," said Molly. "I wrote it myself. We were calling for an investigation of zoning irregularities at Falcon Trace. We thought the grand jury should call a few witnesses."

The FBI agent handed her the papers. "That one's a copy of your press release. The other is a note delivered to the Amazing Kingdom of Thrills soon after the theft of the blue-tongued mango voles."

Molly held both documents in her lap. "It looks like they were done on the same typewriter," she remarked.

In the bedroom, Bud Schwartz slumped to his knees when he heard what Molly said. He thought: She's insane. She's crazy as a goddamn bedbug. *We're all going to jail!*

Back in the living room, Molly was saying, "I'm no expert, but the typing looks very similar."

If Agent Billy Hawkins was caught off guard, he masked it well.

"You're right," he said without expression. "Both of these papers were typed on a Smith-Corona model XD 5500 electronic. We don't know yet if they came out of the same machine, but they were definitely done on the same model."

Molly cheerfully took the half-empty teapot back to the kitchen.

Hawkins heard a faucet running, the sound of silverware clanking in the sink. In the bedroom, Danny Pogue put his mouth to Bud Schwartz's ear and said: "What if she shoots him?"

Bud Schwartz hadn't thought of that. Christ, she couldn't be that loony, to kill an FBI man in her own apartment! Unless she planned to pin it on a couple of dirtbag burglars in the bedroom. . . .

When Molly came bustling out again, Billy Hawkins said: "We've sent the originals to Washington. Hopefully they'll be able to say conclusively if it was the same typewriter."

Molly sat down. "It's quite difficult to tell, isn't it? With these new electronic typewriters, I mean. The key strokes are not as distinct. I read that someplace."

The FBI man smiled confidently. "Our lab is very, very good. Probably the best in the world."

Molly McNamara took out a pale blue tissue and began to clean her eyeglasses: neat, circular swipes. "I suppose it's possible," she said, "that somebody in our little group has gotten carried away."

"It's an emotional issue," agreed Billy Hawkins, "this animal-rights thing."

"Still I cannot believe any of the Mothers would commit a crime. I simply cannot believe they would steal those creatures."

"Perhaps they hired somebody to do it."

Hawkins went into the briefcase again and came out with a standard police mug shot. He handed it to Molly and said: "Buddy Michael Schwartz, a convicted felon. His pickup truck was seen leaving the Amazing Kingdom shortly after the theft. Two white males inside."

Behind the bedroom door, Bud Schwartz steadied himself. His gut churned, his throat turned to chalk. Danny Pogue looked frozen and glassy-eyed, like a rabbit trapped in the diamond lane of I-95. "Bud," he said. "Oh shit." Bud Schwartz clapped a hand over his partner's mouth.

They could hear Molly saying, "He looks familiar, but I just can't be sure."

The hair prickled on Bud Schwartz's arms. The old witch was going to drop the dime. Unbelievable.

Agent Hawkins was saying, "Do you know him personally?"

There was a pause that seemed to last five minutes. Molly nudged her eyeglasses up the bridge of her nose. She held the photograph near a lamp, and examined it from several angles.

"No," she said finally. "He looks vaguely familiar, but I really can't place the face."

"Do me a favor. Think about it."

"Certainly," she said. "May I keep the picture?"

"Sure. And think about the Wildlife Rescue Corps, too."

Molly liked the way this fellow conducted an interview. He knew precisely how much to say without giving away the good stuff—and he certainly knew how to listen. He was a pro.

"Talk to your friends," said Billy Hawkins. "See if they have any ideas."

"You're putting me in a difficult position. These are fine people."

"I'm sure they are." The FBI man stood up, straight as a flagpole. He said, "It would be helpful if I could borrow that Smith-Corona—the one that was used for your press announcements. And the ribbon cartridge as well."

Molly said, "Oh dear."

"I can get a warrant, Mrs. McNamara."

"That's not it," she said. "You see, the typewriter's been stolen."

Billy Hawkins didn't say anything.

"Out of my car."

"That's too bad," the agent said.

"The trunk of my car," Molly added. "While I was grocery-shopping."

She walked the FBI man to the front door. "Can I ask you something, Agent Hawkins? Are you fellows investigating the death of the killer whale, as well?"

"Should we?"

"I think so. It looks like a pattern, doesn't it? Terrible things are happening at that park." Molly looked at him over the tops of her glasses. He felt as if he were back in elementary school. She said, "I know the mango voles are important, but if I may make a suggestion?"

"Sure," said Hawkins.

"Your valuable time and talents would be better spent on a thorough investigation of the Falcon Trace resort. It's a cesspool down there, and Mr. Francis X. Kingsbury is the root of the cess. I trust the FBI is still interested in bribery and public corruption."

"We consider it a priority."

"Then you'll keep this in mind." Molly's eyes lost some of their sparkle. "They've up and bulldozed the whole place," she said. "The trees, everything. It's a crime what they did. I drove by it this morning."

For the first time Billy Hawkins heard a trembling in her voice. He handed her a card. "Anything solid, we'll look into it. And thank you very much for the tea."

She held the door open. "You're a very polite young man," she said. "You renew my faith in authority."

"We'll be talking soon," said Agent Hawkins.

As soon as he was gone, Molly McNamara heard a whoop from the bedroom. She found Danny Pogue dancing a one-legged jig, ecstatic that he was not in federal custody. Bud Schwartz sat on the edge of the bed, nervously pounding his fist in a pillow.

Danny Pogue took Molly by the arms and said: "You did good. You stayed cool!"

Bud Schwartz said, "Cool's not the word for it."

Molly handed him the mug shot. "Next time comb your hair," she said. "Now then—let's have a look at those files you boys borrowed from Mr. Kingsbury."

▼ ▼ ▼

Joe Winder took Nina's hand and led her down the trail. "You're gonna love this guy," he said.

"What happened to the movie?"

"Later," Winder said. "There's a ten-o'clock show." He hated going to the movies. Hated driving all the way up to Homestead.

Nina said, "Don't you have a flashlight?"

"We've got a good hour till dusk. Come on."

"It's my night off," she said. "I wanted to go someplace."

Winder pulled her along through the trees. "Just you wait," he said.

They found Skink shirtless, skinning a raccoon at the campsite. He grunted when Joe Winder said hello. Nina wondered if the plastic collar around his neck was from a prison or some other institution. She stepped closer to get a look at the dead raccoon.

"Import got him," Skink said, feeling her stare. "Up on 905 about two hours ago. Little guy's still warm."

Winder cleared a spot for Nina to sit down. "How do you know it was a foreign car?" he asked. He truly was curious.

"Low bumper broke his neck, that's how I know. Usually it's the tires that do the trick. That's because the rental companies prefer mid-sized American models. Fords and Chevys. We get a ton of rentals up and down this stretch."

He stripped the skin off the animal and laid it to one side. To Nina he said: "They call me Skink."

She took a small breath. "I'm Nina. Joe said you were the governor of Florida."

"Long time ago." Skink frowned at Winder. "No need to bring it up."

The man's voice was a deep, gentle rumble. Nina wondered why the guys who phoned the sex line never sounded like that. She shivered and said: "Joe told me you just vanished. Got up and walked away from the job. It was in all the papers."

"I'm sure. Did he also tell you that I knew his daddy?"

"Ancient history," Winder cut in. "Nina, I wanted you to meet this guy because he saved my life the other night."

Skink sliced the hindquarters off the dead raccoon and placed them side by side in a large fry pan. He said to Nina: "Don't believe a word of it, darling. The only reason he wanted you to meet me was so you'd understand."

"Understand what?"

"What's about to happen."

Nina looked uncomfortable. With one hand she began twisting the ends of her hair into tiny braids.

"Don't be nervous," Joe Winder said, touching her knee.

"Well, what's he talking about?"

Skink finished with the raccoon carcass and slopped the innards into a grocery bag, which he buried. After he got the fire going, he wiped his palms on the seat of his new canvas trousers, the ones he'd taken off Spearmint Breath. He watched, satisfied as the gray meat began to sizzle and darken in the fry pan.

"I don't suppose you're hungry," Skink said.

"We've got other plans." Nina was cordial but firm.

Skink foraged through a rubble of old crates and lobster traps, mumbled, stomped into the woods. He came back carrying a dirty blue Igloo cooler. He took out three beers, opened one and gave the other two to Nina and Joe Winder.

Before taking a drink, Nina wiped the top of the can on the sleeve of Winder's shirt. She touched a hand to her neck and said, "So what's with the collar?"

"Telemetry." Skink pointed a finger at the sky. "Every week or so, a plane comes around."

"They think he's a panther," Joe Winder explained. "See, it's a radio collar. He took it off a dead panther."

Skink quickly added: "But I'm not the one who killed it. It was a liquor truck out of Marathon. Didn't even stop."

Nina wasn't plugging in. After a pause she said, "Joe, don't forget about our movie."

Winder nodded. Sometimes he felt they were oceans apart. "The panther's all but extinct," he said. "Maybe two dozen left alive. The Game and Fish Department uses radio collars to keep track of where they are."

Skink drained his beer. "Two nights later, here comes the liquor truck again. Only this time he blows a tire on some barbed wire."

"In the middle of the road?" Nina said.

"Don't ask me how it got there. Anyway, I had a good long talk with the boy."

Winder said, "Jesus, don't tell me."

"Cat's blood was still on the headlights. Fur, too." Skink spat into the fire. "Cracker bastard didn't seem to care."

"You didn't . . ."

"No, nothing permanent. Nothing his insurance wouldn't cover."

In her smoothest voice Nina asked, "Did you eat the panther, too?"

"No, ma'am," said Skink. "I did not."

The big cat was buried a half-mile up the trail, under brilliant bougainvilleas that Skink himself had planted. Joe Winder thought about showing Nina the place, but she didn't act interested. Darkness was settling in, and the mosquitoes had arrived by the billions. Nina slapped furiously at her bare arms and legs, while Joe Winder shook his head to keep the little bloodsuckers out of his ears.

Skink said, "I got some goop if you want it. Great stuff." He held his arms out in the firelight. The left one was engulfed by black mosquitoes; the right one was untouched.

"It's called EDTIAR," Skink said. "Extended Duration Topical Insect/Arthropod Repellent. I'm a field tester for the U.S. Marines; they pay me and everything." Studiously he began counting the bites on his left arm.

Nina, on the shrill edge of misery, whacked a big fat arthropod on Joe Winder's cheek. "We've got to get going," she said.

"They're nasty tonight," Skink said sympathetically. "I just took seventeen hits in thirty seconds."

Winder himself was getting devoured. He stood up, flailing his own torso. The bugs were humming in his eyes, his mouth, his nostrils.

"Joe, what's the point of all this?" Nina asked.

"I'm waiting for him to tell me who killed Will Koocher."

"Oh, for God's sake."

Skink said, "We're in dangerous territory now."

"I don't care," Winder said. "Tell me what happened. It had something to do with the mango voles, I'm sure."

"Yes," said Skink.

Nina announced that she was leaving. "I'm getting eaten alive, and we're going to miss the movie."

"Screw the movie," said Joe Winder, perhaps too curtly.

For Nina was suddenly gone—down the trail, through the woods. Snapping twigs and muffled imprecations divulged her path.

"Call me Mr. Charm," Winder said.

Skink chuckled. "You'd better go. This can wait."

"I want to know more."

"It's the voles, like you said." He reached into his secondhand trousers and took out a bottle so small it couldn't have held more than four ounces. He pressed it into the palm of Joe Winder's right hand.

"Ah, the magic bug goop!"

"No," Skink said. "Now take off, before Snow White gets lost in the big bad forest."

Blindly Winder jogged down the trail after his girlfriend. He held one arm across his face to block the branches from slashing him, and weaved through the low viny trees like a halfback slipping tacklers.

Nina had given up her solo expedition forty yards from Skink's campsite, and that's where Winder found her, leaning against the slick red trunk of a gumbo-limbo.

"Get us out of here," she said, brushing a squadron of plump mosquitoes from her forehead.

Out of breath, Winder gave her a hug. She didn't exactly melt in his arms. "You were doing fine," he said. "You stayed right on the trail."

They were in the car, halfway to Homestead, when she spoke again: "Why can't you leave it alone? The guy's nothing but trouble."

"He's not crazy, Nina."

"Oh right."

"A man was murdered. I can't let it slide."

She picked a buttonwood leaf from her sleeve, rolled down the window and flicked the leaf away. She said, "If he's not crazy, then how come he lives the way he does? How come he wears that electric collar?"

"He says it keeps him on his toes." Joe Winder plugged a Zevon tape in the stereo. "Look, I'm not saying he's normal. I'm just saying he's not crazy."

"Like you would know," Nina said.

15

On Sunday, July 22, Charles Chelsea got up at eight-thirty, showered, shaved, dressed (navy slacks, Cordovan loafers, blue oxford shirt, burgundy necktie), trimmed his nose hairs, splashed on about three gallons of Aramis and drove off to work in his red Mazda Miata, for which he had paid thirty-five hundred dollars over dealer invoice.

Chelsea had two important appointments at the Amazing Kingdom of Thrills. One of them would be routine, and one promised to be unpleasant. He had not slept well, but he didn't feel exceptionally tired. In fact, he felt surprisingly confident, composed, tough; if only he could remain that way until his meeting with Joe Winder.

A crew from Channel 7 was waiting outside the main gate. The reporter was an attractive young Latin woman wearing oversized sunglasses. Chelsea greeted her warmly and told her she was right on time. They all got in a van, which was driven by a man wearing a costume of bright neoprene plumes. The man introduced himself as Baldy the Eagle, and said he was happy to be their host. He began a long spiel about the Amazing Kingdom of Thrills until Charles Chelsea flashed his ID badge, at which point the bird man shrugged and shut up. Chelsea slapped his arm when he tried to bum a Marlboro off the Channel 7 cameraman.

When they arrived at the killer-whale tank, Chelsea stepped from the van and held the door for the reporter, whose first name was Maria. Chelsea led the way inside the marine stadium, where the TV crew unpacked and began to set up the equipment. Chelsea sat next to Maria in the front row, facing the empty blue pool. Above them, men on scaffolds were sandblasting the word "Orky" from the coral-colored wall.

Chelsea said, "I guess the others will be along soon."

Maria removed her sunglasses and brushed her hair. She took out a spiral notebook and flipped to a blank page.

"The other stations," Chelsea said, "they must be running a little late."

Five others had received the same fax as Channel 7 had. Surely more crews would show up—it was Sunday, after all, the slowest news day of the week.

Maria said, "Before we go on the air—"

"You want some background," Chelsea said helpfully. "Well, to be perfectly frank, Orky's death left us with a rather large vacancy. Here we have this beautiful saltwater tank, as you see, and a scenic outdoor stadium. A facility like this is too special to waste. We thought about getting another whale, but Mr. Kingsbury felt it would be inappropriate. He felt Orky was irreplaceable."

Charles Chelsea glanced over Maria's shoulder to see the Minicam pointed at him. Its red light winked innocuously as the tape rolled. The cameraman was on his knees. Squinting through the viewfinder, he signaled for Chelsea to keep talking.

"Are we on?" the PR man said. "What about the mike? I don't have a mike."

The cameraman pointed straight up. Chelsea raised his eyes. A gray boom microphone, the size of a fungo bat, hung over his head. The boom was controlled by a sound man standing to Chelsea's right. The man wore earphones and a Miami Dolphins warm-up jacket.

Maria said, "You mentioned Orky. Could you tell us what your staff has learned about the whale's death? What exactly killed it?"

Chelsea fought to keep his Adam's apple from bobbing spasmodically, as it often did when he lied. "The tests," he said, "are still incomplete."

Maria's warm brown eyes blinked inquisitively. "There's a rumor that the whale died during an encounter with an employee of the Amazing Kingdom."

"Oh, that's a good one." Chelsea laughed stiffly. "Where did you hear that?"

"Is it true?"

The camera's blinking red light no longer seemed harmless. Charles Chelsea said, "I'm not going to dignify such a question by responding."

The reporter said nothing, just let the tape roll. Let him choke on the silence. It worked.

"We did have a death that night," Chelsea admitted, toying with his cuffs. "An employee of the park apparently took his own life. It was very, very tragic—"

"What was the name of this employee?"

Chelsea's tone became cold, reproachful. "It is our strict policy not to discuss such matters publicly. There is an issue of privacy, and respect for the family."

Maria said, "The rumor is—"

"We don't respond to rumors, Ms. Rodríguez." Now Chelsea was leaning forward, lecturing. The boom mike followed him. "Would you like to hear about our newest attraction, or not?"

She smiled like a moray eel. "That's why we're here."

Oh no it isn't, thought Chelsea, trying not to glare, trying not to perspire, trying not to look like the unvarnished shill he was.

"I brought a bathing suit," Maria said, "as you suggested."

"Maybe we should wait for the others."

"I think we're it, Mr. Chelsea. I don't think any of the other stations are coming."

"Fine." He tried not to sound disappointed.

The cameraman stopped taping. Chelsea dabbed his forehead in relief; he needed to collect himself, recover from the ambush. Everybody wants to be Mike Wallace, he thought bitterly. Everybody's a hardass.

Maria picked up a tote bag and asked directions to the lady's room. When she returned, she was wearing a tight melon-colored tonga that required continual adjustment. At the sight of her, Charles Chelsea inadvertently licked the corners of his mouth. It wasn't so bad after all, coming to work on a Sunday.

"Should I get in?" Maria asked.

"Sure." Chelsea signaled across the pool to a young man dressed in khaki shorts. This was one of the trainers.

Maria slipped into the whale pool, dipped her head underwater, and smoothed her hair straight back. The tape was rolling again.

Eyes twinkling, she smiled up at the camera. The guy with the boom mike leaned over the wall of the tank to capture her words.

"Hi, this is Maria Rodríguez. Today we're visiting the Amazing Kingdom of Thrills in North Key Largo. As you can see, it's a gorgeous summer day—"

Chelsea was thinking: Good girl, stick to the fluff.

"—and we're about to meet the newest star of the Kingdom's outdoor marine show. His name is Dickie the Dolphin . . . cut! Hold it, Jimmy."

The cameraman stopped the tape. Bobbing in the whale pool, Maria groped beneath the surface, frowned and spun away. Chelsea could see that she was struggling to realign the bathing suit.

"Damn thing's riding up my crack."

"Take your time," said the cameraman. "We got plenty of light."

Moments later, Maria was ready again; fresh, sleek, languid. She splashed herself lightly in the face so that droplets glistened in her eyelashes; Charles Chelsea was transfixed.

"Hi, this is Maria Rodríguez reporting from the Amazing Kingdom of Thrills in North Key Largo. As you can see, it's a gorgeous summer day in South Florida—perfect for a swim with the newest star of the Amazing Kingdom's marine show. His name is Dickie the Dolphin and, starting tomorrow, you can swim with him, too!"

Chelsea cued the trainer, who pulled the pin on the gate to the whale pool. Pushing a V-shaped wake, the dolphin charged from the holding tank and sounded.

The TV reporter continued: "It's the latest concept in marine theme parks—customer participation. Instead of sitting in the bleachers and watching these remarkable mammals do tricks, you can actually get in the water and play with them. It costs a little more, but—believe me—it's worth it."

A few yards behind her, Dickie the Dolphin rolled, blowing air noisily. Maria kept her poise, glancing over one shoulder with a breezy, affectionate smile. Chelsea was impressed; she had the whole script memorized.

Turning back to the camera, Maria said: "To be in the water with these gentle, intelligent creatures is an experience you'll never forget. Scientists say the dolphin's brain is actually larger than ours, and much of their complex social behavior remains a mystery. . . ."

Dickie the Dolphin surfaced lazily near Maria, who grabbed its dorsal fin with both hands. Chelsea stood up quickly and waved a warning, but it was too late. The dolphin carried the TV reporter across the top of the water; she closed her eyes and squealed with childlike excitement.

"Great fucking video," remarked Jimmy the cameraman, panning expertly with the action.

The boom man said, "She's getting out of range."

Charles Chelsea cupped his hands and shouted. "Let go! No rides allowed!"

Maria couldn't hear a word. She was holding her breath underwater while the dolphin imitated a torpedo. Every few seconds her long brown legs would slice the surface as she was dragged along, like the tail of a kite. Chelsea bit his lip and watched in queasy silence. Finally Maria splashed to the surface—and she was laughing, thank God! She thought it was all in fun, and maybe it was.

The sound man scurried along the rim of the tank and repositioned the boom. Giggling, short of breath, Maria's eyes found the camera. She said, "Folks, this is unbelievable. Bring the family, you're gonna love it!" Dickie the Dolphin appeared at her side, and she stroked its sleek flank. Wondrously, it seemed to nuzzle her bosom with its snout.

"He's so *adorable!*" Maria exclaimed.

From the feeding platform on the side of the tank, the trainer called out, "Hey, be careful!" Then he started peeling off his khakis.

"Such friendly animals," Maria was saying. "Notice how they always look like they're smiling!"

Dickie the Dolphin slapped its tail on the surface and pushed even closer. Maria threw both arms around the slippery mammal, which obligingly rolled on its back.

Chelsea saw the trainer dive in. He saw Maria's expression change from tenderness to awe. Then he saw the dolphin hook her with its flippers and drag her down.

When she broke to the top, Maria's giggle had become a low fearful moan. As the dolphin's dark form appeared beneath her, she seemed to rise from the water. Then, just as slowly, the creature drew her under.

The cameraman muttered that he was running out of tape. A voice behind him said: "You'll miss the best part."

It was Joe Winder. He stood next to Charles Chelsea, who was clutching the rail with knuckles as pink as shrimp. In the water, the trainer was trying without much success to separate the dolphin from the TV reporter.

Chelsea said to Winder: "Maybe it's a new trick—"

"It's no trick. He's trying to boink her."

"That's not funny, Joe."

Winder pointed. "What do you think *that* is? See?"

"I—I don't know."

"It's a dolphin shlong, Charlie. One of Nature's marvels."

Chelsea began to stammer.

"They get in moods," Joe explained. "Same as dogs."

"My God."

"Don't worry, Charlie, it'll pass."

With the trainer's help, Maria Rodríguez finally broke free from Dickie the Dolphin's embrace. Cursing, tugging at her tonga, she paddled furiously toward the ladder on the wall of the tank.

"Faster!" Charles Chelsea hollered. "Here he comes again!"

▼ ▼ ▼

Two hours later, he was still trying to apologize without admitting the truth. "Sometimes they play too rough, that's all."

"Playing?" Maria sniffed sarcastically. "Excuse me, Mr. Chelsea, but I know a dick when I see one." She had changed back to TV clothes, although her hair was still wrapped in a towel. "I ought to sue your ass," she said.

They were sitting in Chelsea's office—the reporter, Charles Chelsea, and Joe Winder. The crew had returned to the truck to put the dish up, just in case.

"Come on," Winder said to Maria, "be a sport."

"What?" She gave him an acid glare. "What did you say?" She whipped the towel off her head and tossed it on the floor.

Very impolite, Winder thought, and unprofessional. "Take it easy," he said. "Nothing unspeakable happened."

Maria pointed a finger in his face and said, "Someone could get killed out there."

Charles Chelsea was miserable. "How can we make it up to you?" he asked Maria Rodríguez. "How about we comp you some passes to the Wild Bill Hiccup show?"

She was gone before he could come up with something better. On her way out, she kicked at the towel.

Joe Winder said, "Don't worry, she won't sue."

"How do you know?"

"It's too embarrassing. Hell, she'll probably destroy the tape on the way back to Miami."

Defensively Chelsea said, "She wasn't supposed to grab the dolphin. No touching is allowed—swimming only."

"This was a terrible idea, Charlie. Who thought of it?"

"Fifty bucks a head. They've got a bunch of these places in the Keys."

Joe Winder asked where Kingsbury had purchased the new dolphin.

"How should I know?" Chelsea snapped. "A dolphin's a dolphin, for Christ's sake. They don't come with a pedigree."

"This one needs a female," Winder said, "before you let tourists in the water."

"Thank you, Doctor Cousteau." The publicity man got up and closed the door. He looked gravely serious when he returned to the desk.

Joe Winder said, "I hope you're not going to make me write a press release about this. I've got more important things to do."

"Me, too." To steel himself, Charles Chelsea tightened his stomach muscles. "Joe, we're going to have to let you go."

"I see."

Chelsea studied his fingernails, trying not to make eye contact with Winder. "It's a combination of things."

"My attitude, I suppose."

"That's a factor, yes. I tried to give some latitude. The hair. The casual clothing."

Winder said, "Anything else?"

"I understand you broke into the vole lab."

"Would you like to hear what I found?"

"Not particularly," Chelsea said.

"A paper written about the blue-tongued mango voles. The one you sent to Will Koocher when you were recruiting him."

Chelsea gave Winder a so-what look. "That it?"

"Funny thing, Charlie. The person who supposedly wrote that paper, this Dr. Sarah Hunt? Rollins College never heard of her." Winder raised his palms in mock puzzlement. "Never on the faculty, never graduated, never even attended—what do you make of that, Charlie?"

"Pedro told me of your ridiculous theory." Chelsea's lips barely moved when he spoke; he looked like a goldfish burping. "Dr. Koocher wasn't murdered, Joe, but in your twisted brain I'm sure you've made some connection between his unfortunate death and this . . . this ty-pographical error."

Winder laughed. "A typo? You're beautiful, Charlie. The paper's a goddamn fake."

Chelsea rolled his eyes. "And I suppose a simpler explanation is impossible—that perhaps the author's name was misspelled by the publisher, or that the university was misidentified. . . ."

"No way."

"You're not a well person," Chelsea said. "And now I learn that you've telephoned Koocher's widow in New York. That's simply inex-cusable." The way he spit out the word was meant to have a lacerating effect.

"What's inexcusable," said Winder, "is the way you lied."

"It was a judgment call." Chelsea's cheek twitched. "We were trying to spare the woman some grief."

"I told her to get a lawyer."

Chelsea's tan seemed to fade.

Joe Winder went on: "The newspapers are bound to find out the truth. 'Man Gobbled by Whale. Modern-Day Jonah Perishes in Freak Theme Park Mishap.' Think about it, Charlie."

"The coroner said he drowned. We've never denied it."

"But they didn't say how he drowned. Or why."

Charles Chelsea began to rock back and forth. "This is all aca-demic, Joey. As of this moment, you no longer work here."

"And here I thought I was your ace in the hole."

Chelsea extended a hand, palm up. "The keys to the Cushman, please."

Winder obliged. He said, "Charlie, even though you're an obsequious dork, I'd like to believe you're not a part of this. I'd like to believe that you're just incredibly dim."

"Go clean out your desk."

"I don't have to. There's nothing in it."

Chelsea looked momentarily confused.

Winder waved his arms. "Desks are places to keep facts, Charlie. Who needs a desk when the words simply fly off the tops of our heads! Hell, I've done my finest work for you while sitting on the toilet."

"If you're trying to insult me, it won't work." Chelsea lowered his eyelids in lizardly disinterest. "We all fudge the truth when it suits our purposes, don't we? Like when you told me you got that scar in a car accident."

So he knew all along, just as Joe Winder had suspected.

"I heard it was a fight in the newsroom," Chelsea said, "a fistfight with one of your editors."

"He had it coming," said Winder. "He screwed up a perfectly good news story."

The story concerned Joe Winder's father bribing a county commissioner in exchange for a favorable vote on a zoning variance. Winder had written the story himself after digging through a stack of his father's canceled checks and finding five made out to the commissioner's favorite bagman.

Though admiring of Winder's resourcefulness, the editor had said it created an ethical dilemma; he decided that someone else would have to write the piece. You're too emotionally involved, the editor had told him.

So Winder had gotten a firm grip on the editor's head and rammed it through the screen of the word processor, cutting himself spectacularly in the struggle that followed.

"I'm sorry, Charlie," he said. "Maybe you shouldn't have hired me."

"The understatement of the year."

"Before I go, may I show you something?" He took out the small bottle that Skink had given him and placed it in the center of Chelsea's desk blotter.

The publicity man examined it and said, "It's food coloring, so what?"

"Look closer."

"Betty Crocker food coloring. What's the point, Joe?"

"And what color?"

"Blue." Chelsea was impatient. "The label says blue."

Winder twisted the cap off the bottle. He said, "I believe this came from the vole lab, too. You might ask Pedro about it."

Baffled, Charles Chelsea watched Joe Winder toss back his head and empty the contents of the bottle into his mouth. He sloshed the liquid from cheek to cheek, then swallowed.

"Ready?" Winder said. He stuck out his tongue, which now was the color of indigo dye.

"That's a very cute trick." Chelsea sounded nervous.

Joe Winder climbed onto the desk on his hands and knees. "The voles were phony, Charlie. Did you know that?" He extended his tongue two inches from Chelsea's nose, then sucked it back in. He said, "There's no such thing as a blue-tongued mango vole. Kingsbury faked the whole deal. Invented an entire species!"

"You're cracking up," Chelsea said thinly.

Winder grabbed him by the collar. "You fucker, did you know all along?"

"Get out, or I'm calling Security."

"That's why Will Koocher was killed. He'd figured out everything. He was going to rat, so to speak, on the upstanding Mr. Kingsbury."

Chelsea's upper lip was a constellation of tiny droplets. He tried to pull away. "Let me go, Joe. If you know what's good for you."

"They painted their tongues, Charlie. Think of it. They took these itty-bitty animals and dyed their tongues blue, all in the name of tourism."

Straining against Winder's grasp, Chelsea said, "You're talking crazy."

Joe Winder licked him across the face.

"Stop it!"

Winder slurped him again. "It's your color, Charlie. Very snappy."

His tongue waggled in mockery; Chelsea eyed the fat blue thing as if it were a poisonous slug.

"You can fire me," Winder announced, "but I won't go away."

He climbed off the desk, careful not to drop the bottle of food coloring. Chelsea swiftly began plucking tissues from a silver box and wiping his face, examining each crumpled remnant for traces of the dye. His fingers were shaking.

"I should have you arrested," he hissed.

"But you won't," Winder said. "Think of the headlines."

He was halfway to the door when Chelsea said, "Wait a minute, Joey. What is it you want?"

Winder kept walking, and began to laugh. He laughed all the way down the hall, a creepy melodic warble that made Charles Chelsea shudder and curse.

16

As a reward for the successful theft of Francis X. Kingsbury's files, Molly McNamara allowed Bud Schwartz and Danny Pogue to keep the rented Cutlass for a few days.

On the evening of July 22, they drove down Old Cutler Road, where many of Miami's wealthiest citizens lived. The homes were large and comfortable-looking, and set back impressively from the tree-shaded road. Danny Pogue couldn't get over the size of the yards, the tall old pines and colorful tropical shrubbery; it was beautiful, yet intimidating.

"They got those Spanish bayonets under the windows," he reported. "God, I hate them things." Wicked needles on the end of every stalk—absolute murder, even with gloves.

Bud Schwartz said, "Don't sweat it, we'll find us a back door."

"For sure they got alarms."

"Yeah."

"And a goddamn dog, too."

"Probably so," said Bud Schwartz, thinking: Already the guy's a nervous wreck.

"You ever done a house like this?"

"Sure." Bud Schwartz was lying. Mansions, that's what these were, just like the ones on "Miami Vice." The bandage on his bad hand was damp with perspiration. Hunched over the steering wheel, he thought: Thank God for the rental—at least we got a car that'll move.

To cut the tension, he said: "Ten bucks it's a Dobie."

"No way," said Danny Pogue. "I say Rottweiler, that's the dog nowadays."

"For the Yuppies, sure, but not this guy. I'm betting on a Dobie."

Danny Pogue fingered a pimple on his neck. "Okay, but give me ten on the side."

"For what?"

"Give me ten on the color." Danny Pogue slugged him softly on the shoulder. "Black or brown?"

Bud Schwartz said, "I'll give you ten if it's brown."

"Deal."

"You're a sucker. Nobody in this neighborhood's got a brown Doberman."

"We'll see," said Danny Pogue. He pointed as they passed a crimson Porsche convertible parked on a cobbler drive. A beautiful dark-haired girl, all of seventeen, was washing the sports car under a quartet of halogen spotlights. The girl wore a dazzling green bikini and round reflector sunglasses. The sun had been down for two hours.

Danny Pogue clapped his hands. "Jesus, you see that?"

"Yeah, hosing down her Targa. And here we are in the middle of a drought." Bud Schwartz braked softly to peer at the name on a cypress mailbox. "Danny, what's that house number? I can't see it from here."

"Four-oh-seven."

"Good. We're almost there."

"I was wondering," said Danny Pogue.

"Yeah, what else is new."

"Do I get twenty bucks if it's a brown Rottweiler?"

"They don't come in brown," said Bud Schwartz. "I thought you knew."

▼ ▼ ▼

It wasn't a Doberman pinscher or a Rottweiler.

"Maybe some type of weasel," whispered Danny Pogue. "Except it's got a collar on it."

They were kneeling in the shadow of a sea-grape tree. "One of them beady-eyed dogs from Asia," said Bud Schwartz, "or maybe it's Africa." Dozing under the electric bug lamp, the animal showed no reaction to the sizzle and zap of dying moths.

Carefully Bud Schwartz inserted four Tylenol No. 3 tablets into a ten-ounce patty of prime ground sirloin. With his good hand he lobbed the meat over the fence. It landed with a wet slap on the patio near the pool. The weasel-dog lifted its head, barked once sharply and got up.

Danny Pogue said, "That's the ugliest goddamn thing I ever saw."

"Like you're Mel Gibson, right?"

"No, but just look."

The dog found the hamburger and gulped it in two bites. When its front legs began to wobble, Danny Pogue said, "Jesus, what'd you use?"

"About a hundred milligrams of codeine."

Soon the animal lay down, snuffling into a stupor. Bud Schwartz hopped the fence and helped his crutchless partner across. The two burglars crab-walked along a low cherry hedge until they reached the house. Through a glass door they saw that all the kitchen lights were on; in fact, lamps glowed in every window. Bud Schwartz heard himself take a short breath; he was acting against every instinct, every fundamental rule of the trade. Never *ever* break into an occupied dwelling—especially an occupied dwelling protected by four thousand dollars' worth of electronic burglar alarm.

Bud Schwartz knew the screens would be wired, so busting the windows was out of the question. He knew he couldn't jimmy the sliding door because that would trip the contact, also setting off the alarm. The best hope was cutting the glass door in such a way that it wouldn't trigger the noise detectors; he could see one of the matchbook-sized boxes mounted on a roof beam in the kitchen. Its tiny blue eye winked insidiously at him.

"What's the plan?" asked Danny Pogue.

Bud Schwartz took the glass cutter out of his pocket and showed it to his partner, who hadn't the faintest idea what it was. Bud Schwartz got to his knees. "I'm going to cut a square," he said, "big enough to crawl through."

"Like hell." Danny Pogue was quite certain they would be arrested any moment.

Bud Schwartz dug the blades of the glass cutter into the door and pressed with the full strength of his good arm. The door began to slide on its rollers. "Damn," said Bud Schwartz. Cold air rushed from the house and put goose bumps on his arms.

Danny Pogue said: "Must not be locked."

The door coasted open. No bells or sirens went off. The only sound came from a television, probably upstairs.

They slipped into the house. Bud Schwartz's sneakers squeaked on the kitchen tile; hopping on one leg, Danny Pogue followed his partner through the living room, which was decorated hideously in black and red. The furniture was leather, the carpeting a deep stringy shag. On a phony brick wall over the fireplace hung a painting that was, by Bud Schwartz's astonished calculation, larger than life-sized. The subject of the painting was a nude blond with a Pepsodent smile and breasts the size of soccer balls. She wore a yellow visored cap, and held a flagstick over her shoulder. A small brass plate announced the title of the work: "My Nineteenth Hole."

It was unspeakably crude, even to two men who had spent most of their adult lives in redneck bars and minimum-security prisons.

Bud Schwartz gazed at the painting and said: "I'll bet it's the wife."

"No way," said Danny Pogue. He couldn't imagine being married to somebody who would do such a thing.

As they moved cautiously through the house, Bud Schwartz couldn't help but notice there wasn't much worth stealing, even if they'd wanted to. Oh, the stuff was expensive enough, but tacky as hell. A Waterford armadillo—how could millionaires have such lousy taste?

The burglars followed the sound of the television down a hallway toward a bedroom. Bud Schwartz had never been so jittery. *What if the asshole has a gun?* This had been Danny Pogue's question, and for once Bud Schwartz couldn't answer. The asshole probably *did* have a gun; it was Miami, after all. Probably something in a semi-automatic, a Mini-14 or a MAC-11. Christ, there's a pleasant thought. Ten, fifteen rounds a second. Hardly time to piss in your pants.

Danny Pogue's whiny breathing seemed to fill the hallway. Bud Schwartz glared, held a finger to his lips. The door to the bedroom was wide open; somebody was switching the channels on the television. Momentously, Bud Schwartz smoothed his hair; Danny Pogue did the same. Bud Schwartz nodded and motioned with an index finger; Danny Pogue gave a constipated nod in return.

When they stepped into the room, they saw the blond woman from the golf painting. She was lying naked on the bed; two peach-colored pillows were tucked under her head, and the remote control was propped on her golden belly. At the sight of the burglars, the woman covered her chest. Excitedly she tried to speak—no sounds emerged, though her jaws moved vigorously, as if she were chewing a wad of bubble gum.

Inanely, Bud Schwartz said, "Don't be afraid."

The woman forced out a low guttural cry that lasted several seconds. She sounded like a wildcat in labor.

"Enough a that," said Danny Pogue tensely.

Suddenly a door opened and a porky man in powder-blue boxer shorts stepped out of the bathroom. He was short and jowly, with skin like yellow lard. Tattooed on his left forearm was a striking tableau: Minnie Mouse performing oral sex on Mickey Mouse. At least that's what it looked like to Danny Pogue and Bud Schwartz, who couldn't help but stare. Mickey was wearing his sorcerer's hat from *Fantasia*, and appeared to be whistling a happy tune.

Danny Pogue said, "That'd make a great T-shirt."

With fierce reddish eyes, the man in the boxer shorts studied the two intruders.

"Honey!" cried the woman on the bed.

The man scowled impatiently. "Well, shit, get it over with. Take, you know, whatever the hell."

Bud Schwartz said, "We didn't mean to scare you, Mr. Kingsbury."

"Don't fucking flatter yourself. And, Penny, watch it with that goddamn thing!"

Still recumbent, the naked Mrs. Kingsbury now was aiming a small chrome-plated pistol at Danny Pogue's midsection.

"I knew it," muttered Bud Schwartz. He hated the thought of getting shot twice in the same week, especially by women. This one must've had it under the damn pillows, or maybe in the sheets.

Danny Pogue's lips were quivering, as if he were about to cry. He held out his arms beseechingly.

Quickly Bud Schwartz said: "We've not here to rob you. We're here to talk business."

Kingsbury hooked his nubby thumbs into the elastic waistband of his underpants. "Make me laugh," he said. "Break into my house like a couple of putzes."

"We're pros," said Bud Schwartz.

Kingsbury cackled, snapping the elastic. "Two hands, babe," he reminded his wife.

Danny Pogue said, "Bud, make her drop it!"

"It's only a .25," said Kingsbury. "She's been out to the range— what?—a half-dozen times. Got the nerves for it, apparently."

Bud Schwartz tried to keep his voice level and calm. He said to Kingsbury: "Your office got hit yesterday, right?"

"As a matter of fact, yeah."

"You're missing some files."

The naked Mrs. Kingsbury said, "Frankie, you didn't tell me." Her arms were impressively steady with the gun.

Kingsbury took his hands out of his underwear and folded them in a superior way across his breasts, which were larger than those of a few women whom Danny Pogue had known.

"Not exactly the Brink's job," Kingsbury remarked.

"Well, we got your damn files," said Bud Schwartz.

"That was you? Bullshit."

"Maybe you need some proof. Maybe you need to see some credit-card slips."

Kingsbury hesitated. "Selling them back, is that the idea?"

Some genius businessman, thought Bud Schwartz. The guy was a bum, a con. You could tell right away.

"Tell your wife to drop the piece."

"Penny, you heard the man."

"And tell her to go lock herself in the john."

"What?"

The wife said, "Frankie, I don't like this." Carefully she placed the gun on the nightstand next to a bottle of Lavoris mouthwash. A tremor of relief passed through Danny Pogue, starting at the shoulders. He hopped across the room and sat down on the corner of the bed.

"It's better if she's in the john," Bud Schwartz said to Francis X. Kingsbury. "Or maybe you don't care."

Kingsbury gnawed his upper lip. He was thinking about the files, and what was in them.

His wife wrapped herself in a sheet. "Frank?"

"Do what he said," Kingsbury told her. "Take a magazine, something. A book if you can find one."

"Fuck you," said Penny Kingsbury. On her way to the bathroom, she waved a copy of GQ in his face.

▼ ▼ ▼

"At Doral is where I met her. Selling golf shoes."

"How nice," said Bud Schwartz.

"Fuzzy Zoeller, Tom Kite, I'm not kidding. Penny's customers." Kingsbury had put on a red bathrobe and turned up the television, in case his wife was at the door trying to eavesdrop. Bud Schwartz lifted the handgun from the nightstand and slipped it into his pocket; the cold weight of the thing in his pants, so close to his privates, made him shudder. God, how he hated guns.

Kingsbury said, "The painting in the big room—you guys get a look at it?"

"Yeah, boy," answered Danny Pogue.

"We did that up on the Biltmore. Number seven or ten, I can't remember. Some par three. Anyway, I had to lease the whole fucking course for a day, that's how long it took. Must've been two hundred guys standing around, staring at her boobs. Penny didn't mind, she's proud of 'em."

"And who wouldn't be," said Bud Schwartz, tight as a knot. "Can we get to it, please? We got plenty to talk about."

Francis X. Kingsbury said, "I'm trying to remember. You got the Ramex Global file. Jersey Premium. What else?"

"You know what else."

Kingsbury nodded. "Start with the American Express. Give me a number."

Bud Schwartz sat down in a high-backed colonial chair. From memory he gave Kingsbury an inventory: "We got a diamond tennis necklace in New York, earrings in Chicago. Yeah, and an emerald stickpin in Nassau of all places, for like three grand." He motioned to Danny Pogue, who hobbled over to Mrs. Kingsbury's dresser and began to look through the boxes.

Dispiritedly, Kingsbury said, "Forget it, you won't find it there."

"So who got it all?"

"Friends. It's not important."

"Not to us, maybe." Bud Schwartz nodded toward the bathroom. "I got a feeling your old lady might be interested."

Kingsbury lowered his voice. "The reason I use the credit card, hell, who carries that much cash?"

"Plus the insurance," said Danny Pogue, pawing through Mrs. Kingsbury's jewelry. "Stuff gets broke or stolen, they replace it, no questions. It's a new thing."

Great, Bud Schwartz thought; now he's doing commercials.

"There's some excellent shit here. Very nice." Danny Pogue held up a diamond solitaire and played it off the light. "I'm guessin' two carats."

"Try one-point-five," said Kingsbury.

"There were some dinners on your card," Bud Schwartz said. "And plane tickets, too. It's handy how they put it all together at the end of the year where you can check it."

Kingsbury asked him how much.

"Five grand," Bud Schwartz said, "and we won't say a word to the wife."

"The file, Jesus, I need it back."

"No problem. Now let's talk about serious money."

Kingsbury frowned. He pulled on the tip of his nose with a thumb and forefinger, as if he were straightening it.

Bud Schwartz said, "The Gotti file, Mr. King."

"Mother of Christ."

" 'Frankie, The Ferret, King.' That's what the indictment said."

"You got me by surprise," Kingsbury said.

Danny Pogue looked up from an opal bracelet he was admiring. "So who's this Gotti dude again? Some kinda gangster is what Bud said."

"How much?" said Kingsbury. He leaned forward and put his hands on his bare knees. "Don't make it, like . . . a game."

Bud Schwartz detected visceral fear in the man's voice; it gave him an unfamiliar feeling of power. On the other side of the bathroom door, Francis Kingsbury's wife shouted something about wanting to get out. Kingsbury ignored her.

"The banks that made the loans on Falcon Trace, do they know who you are?" Bud Schwartz affected a curious tone. "Do they know you're a government witness? A mob guy?"

Kingsbury didn't bother to reply.

"I imagine they gave you shitloads a money," Bud Schwartz went on, "and I imagine they could call it back."

Francis Kingsbury went to the bathroom door and told Penny to shut up and sit her sweet ass on the can. He turned back to the burglars and said: "So what's the number, the grand total? For Gotti, I mean."

Danny Pogue resisted the urge to enter the negotiation; expectantly he looked at his partner. Bud Schwartz smoothed his hair, pursed his mouth. He wanted to hear what kind of bullshit offer Kingsbury would make on his own.

"I'm trying to think what's fair."

"Give me a fucking number," said Kingsbury, "and I'll goddamn tell you if it's fair."

What the hell, thought Bud Schwartz. "Fifty grand," he said calmly. "And we toss in Ramex and the rest for free."

Excitedly Danny Pogue began excavating a new pimple.

Kingsbury eyed the men suspiciously. "Fifty, you said? As in five-oh?"

"Right." Bud Schwartz gave half a grin. "That's fifty to give back the Gotti file . . ."

"And?"

"Two hundred more to forget what was in it."

Kingsbury chuckled bitterly. "So I was wrong," he said. "You're not such a putz."

▼ ▼ ▼

Danny Pogue was so overjoyed that he could barely control himself on the ride back to Molly's condominium. "We're gonna be rich," he said, pounding both hands on the upholstery. "You're a genius, man, that's what you are."

"It went good," Bud Schwartz agreed. Better than he had ever imagined. As he drove, he did the arithmetic in his head. Five thousand for the American Express file, fifty for the Gotti stuff, another two hundred in hush money . . . rich was the word for it. "Early retirement," he said to Danny Pogue. "No more damn b-and-e's."

"You don't think he'll call the cops?"

"That's the last place he'd call. Guy's a scammer, Danny."

They stopped at a U-Tote-Ém and bought two six-packs of Coors and a box of jelly doughnuts. In the parking lot they rolled down the windows and turned up the radio and stuffed themselves in jubilation. It was an hour until curfew; if they weren't back by midnight, Molly had said, she would call the FBI and say her memory had returned.

"I bet she'll cut us some slack," said Danny Pogue, "if we're a little late."

"Maybe." Bud Schwartz opened the door and rolled an empty beer can under the car. He said, "I'm sure gettin' tired of being her pet burglar."

"Well, then, let's go to a tittie bar and celebrate." Danny Pogue said he knew of a place where the girls danced naked on the tables, and let you grab their ankles for five bucks.

Bud Schwartz said not tonight. There would be no celebration until they broke free from the old lady. Tonight he would make a pitch for the rest of the ten grand that she'd promised. Surely they were square by now; Molly had been so thrilled by the contents of the Ramex file that she'd given him a hug. Then she'd gone out and had eight copies made. What more could she want of them?

Back on the road, Bud Schwartz said: "Remember, don't say a damn thing about what we done tonight."

"You told me a hundred times."

"Well, it'll screw up everything. I mean it, don't tell her where we been."

"No reason," said Danny Pogue. "It's got nothin' to do with the butterflies, right?"

"No, it sure does not."

Danny Pogue said he was hungry again, so they stopped to pick up some chicken nuggets. Again they ate in the parking lot, listening to a country station. Bud Schwartz had never before driven an automobile with a working clock, so he was surprised to glance at the dashboard of the Cutlass and find that is was half past twelve, and counting.

"Better roll," Danny Pogue said, "just in case."

"I got a better idea—gimme a quarter." Bud Schwartz got out and walked to a pay telephone under a streetlight. He dialed the number of Molly McNamara's condominium and let it ring five times. He hung up, retrieved the quarter and dialed again. This time he let it ring twice as long.

In the car, speeding down U.S. 1, Danny Pogue said, "I can't believe she'd do it—maybe she went someplace else. Maybe she left us a note."

Bud Schwartz gripped the wheel with both hands; the bullet wound was numb because he had forgotten about it. Escape was on his mind —what if the old bitch had run to the feds? Worse, what if she'd found the Gotti file? What if she'd gone snooping through the bedroom and found it hidden between the mattress and the box spring, which in retrospect was probably not the cleverest place of concealment.

"Shit," he said, thinking of the bleak possibilities.

"Don't jump the gun," said Danny Pogue, for once the optimist.

They made it back to the condo in twenty-two minutes, parked the rental car and went upstairs. The door to Molly's apartment was unlocked. Bud Schwartz knocked twice anyway. "It's just us," he announced lightly, "Butch and Sundance."

When he went in, he saw that the place had been torn apart. "Oh Jesus," he said.

Danny Pogue pushed him with the crutch. "I can't fucking believe it," he said. "Somebody hit the place."

"No," said Bud Schwartz, "it's more than that."

The sofas had been slit, chairs broken, mirrors shattered. A ceramic Siamese cat had been smashed face-first through the big-screen television. While Danny Pogue hopscotched through the rubble, Bud Schwartz went directly to the bedroom, which also had been ransacked and vandalized. He reached under the mattress and found the Kingsbury files exactly where he had left them. Whoever did the place hadn't been looking very hard, if it all.

A hoarse shout came from the kitchen.

Bud Schwartz found Danny Pogue on his knees next to Molly McNamara. She lay on her back, with one leg folded crookedly under the other. Her housecoat, torn and stained with something dark, was bunched around her hips. Her face had been beaten to pulp; beads of blood glistened like holly berries in her snowy hair. Her eyes were closed and her lips were gray, but she was breathing—raspy, irregular gulps.

Danny Pogue took Molly's wrist. "God Almighty," he said, voice quavering. "What—who do we call?"

"Nobody." Bud Schwartz shook his head ruefully. "Don't you understand, we can't call nobody." He bent down and put his bandaged hand on Molly's forehead. "Who the hell would do this to an old lady?"

"I hope she don't die."

"Me, too," said Bud Schwartz. "Honest to God, this ain't right."

17

Joe Winder's trousers were soaked from the thighs down. Nina took a long look and said: "You've been fishing."

"Yes."

"In the middle of the day."

"The fish are all gone," Winder said dismally. "Ever since they bulldozed the place."

Nina sat cross-legged on the floor. She wore blue-jean shorts and a pink cotton halter; the same outfit she'd been wearing the day he'd met her, calling out numbers at the Seminole bingo hall. Joe Winder had gone there to meet an Indian named Sammy Deer, who purportedly was selling an airboat, but Sammy Deer had hopped over to Freeport for the weekend, leaving Joe Winder stuck with three hundred chain-smoking white women in the bingo hall. Halfway out the door, he'd heard Nina's voice ("Q 34; Q, as in 'quicksilver,' 34!"), spun around and went back to see if she looked as lovely as she sounded, and she had. Nina informed him that she was part-timing as a bingo caller until the telephone gig came through, and he confided to her that he was buying an airboat so he could disappear into the Everglades at will. He changed his plans after their first date.

Now, analyzing her body language, Joe Winder knew that he was in danger of losing Nina's affections. A yellow legal pad was propped on her lap. She tapped on a bare knee with her felt-tipped pen, which she held as a drummer would.

"What happened to your big meeting?" she said. "Why aren't you at the Kingdom?"

He pretended not to hear. He said, "They dumped a ton of fill in the cove. The bottom's mucky and full of cut trees." He removed his trousers and arranged them crookedly on a wire hanger. "All against the law, of course. Dumping in a marine sanctuary."

Nina said, "You got canned, is that it?"

"A mutual parting of the ways, and not a particularly amicable one." Joe Winder sat down beside her. He sensed a lecture coming on.

"Put on some pants," she said.

"What's the point?"

Nina asked why his tongue was blue, and he told her the story of the bogus mango voles. She said she didn't believe a word.

"Charlie practically admitted everything."

"I don't really care," Nina said. She stopped drumming on her kneecap and turned away.

"What is it?"

"Look, I can't afford to support you." When she looked back at him, her eyes were moist and angry. "Things were going so well," she said.

Winder was stunned. Was she seriously worried about the money? "Nina, there's a man dead. Don't you understand? I can't work for a murderer."

"Stop it!" She shook the legal pad in front of his nose. "You know what I've been working on? Extra scripts. The other girls like my stuff so much they offered to buy, like, two or three a week. Twenty-five bucks each, it could really add up."

"That's great." He was proud of her, that was the hell of it. She'd never believe that he could be proud of her.

Pen in mouth, Nina said: "I wrote about an out-of-body experience. Like when you're about to die and you can actually see yourself lying there—but then you get saved at the very last minute. Only my script was about making love, about floating out of yourself just as you're about to come. *Suspended in air, I looked down at the bed and saw myself shudder violently, my fingernails raking across your broad tan shoulders.* I gave it to the new girl, Addie, and she tried it Friday night. One guy, she said, he called back eleven times."

"Is that a new record?"

"It just so happens, yes. But the point is, I'm looking at a major opportunity. If I start selling enough scripts, maybe I can get off the phones. Just stay home and write—wouldn't that be better?"

"Sure would." Winder put his arm around her. "You can still do that, honey. It would be great."

"Not with you sitting here every day. Playing your damn Warren Zevon."

"I'll get another job."

"No, Joe, it'll be the same old shit." She pulled away and got up from the floor. "I can't write when my life is in turmoil. I need a stabilizer. Peacefulness. Quiet."

Winder felt wounded. "For God's sake, Nina, I know a little something about writing. This place is plenty quiet."

"There is tension," she said grimly, "and don't deny it."

"Writers thrive on domestic tension. Look at Poe, Hemingway—and Mailer in his younger days, you talk about tense." He hoped Nina would appreciate being included on such an eminent roster, but she didn't. Impatiently he said, "It isn't exactly epic literature, anyway. It's phone porn."

Her expression clouded. "Phone porn? Thanks, Joe."

"Well, Christ, that's what it is."

Coldly she folded her arms and leaned against one of the tall speakers. "It's still writing, and writing is hard work. If I'm going to make a go of it, I need some space. And some security."

"If you're talking about groceries, don't worry. I intend to pull my own weight."

Nina raised her hands in exasperation. "Where can you find another job that pays so much?"

Joe Winder couldn't believe what he was hearing. Why the sudden anxiety? The laying on of guilt? If he'd known he was in for a full-blown argument, he indeed would have put on some pants.

Nina said, "It's not just the money. I need someone reliable, someone who will be here for me."

"Have I ever let you down?"

"No, but you will."

Winder didn't say anything because she was absolutely correct; nothing in his immediate plans would please her.

"I know you," Nina added, in a sad voice. "You aren't going to let go of this thing."

"Probably not."

"Then I think we're definitely heading in different directions. I think you're going to end up in jail, or maybe dead."

"Have some faith," Joe Winder said.

"It's not that easy." Nina stalked to the closet, flung open the door and stared at the clutter. "Where'd you put my suitcase?"

▼ ▼ ▼

In the mid-1970s, Florida elected a crusading young governor named Clinton Tyree, an ex-football star and Vietnam War veteran. At six feet six, he was the tallest chief executive in the history of the state. In all likelihood he was also the most honest. When a ravenous and politically connected land-development company attempted to bribe Clinton Tyree, he tape-recorded their offers, turned the evidence over to the FBI and volunteered to testify at the trial. By taking a public stand against such omnipotent forces, Clinton Tyree became something of a folk hero in the Sunshine State, and beyond. The faint scent of integrity attracted the national media, which roared into Florida and anointed the young governor a star of the new political vanguard.

It was, unfortunately, a vanguard of one. Clinton Tyree spoke with a blistering candor that terrified his fellow politicians. While others reveled in Florida's boom times, Clinton Tyree warned that the state was on the brink of an environmental cataclysm. The Everglades were drying up, the coral reefs were dying, Lake Okeechobee was choking on man-made poisons and the bluegills were loaded with mercury. While other officeholders touted Florida as a tropical dreamland, the governor called it a toxic dump with palm trees. On a popular call-in radio show, he asked visitors to stay away for a couple of years. He spoke not of managing the state's breakneck growth, but of halting it altogether. This, he declared, was the only way to save the place.

The day Clinton Tyree got his picture on the cover of a national newsmagazine, some of the most powerful special interests in Florida —bankers, builders, highway contractors, sugar barons, phosphate-mining executives—congealed in an informal conspiracy to thwart the new governor's reforms by stepping around him, as if he were a small lump of dogshit on an otherwise luxuriant carpet.

Bypassing Clinton Tyree was relatively easy to do; all it took was money. In a matter of months, everyone who could be compromised, intimidated or bought off was. The governor found himself isolated from even his own political party, which had no stake in his radical bluster because it was alienating all the big campaign contributors. Save Florida? Why? And from what? The support that Clinton Tyree enjoyed among voters didn't help him one bit in the back rooms of Tallahassee; every bill he wanted passed got gutted, buried or rebuffed. The fact that he was popular with the media didn't deter his enemies; it merely softened their strategy. Rather than attack the governor's agenda, they did something worse—they ignored it. Only the most gentlemanly words were publicly spoken about young Clint, the handsome war hero, and about his idealism and courage to speak out. Any reporter who came to town could fill two or three notebooks with admiring quotes—so many (and so effusive) that someone new to the state might have assumed that Clinton Tyree had already died, which he had, in a way.

On the morning the Florida Cabinet decided to shut down a coastal wildlife preserve and sell it dirt cheap to a powerful land-sales firm, the lone dissenting vote trudged from the Capitol Building in disgust and vanished from the political landscape in the back of a limousine.

At first authorities presumed that the governor was the victim of a kidnapping or other foul play. A nationwide manhunt was suspended only after a notarized resignation letter was analyzed by the FBI and found to be authentic. It was true; the crazy bastard had up and quit.

Journalists, authors and screenwriters flocked to Florida with hopes of securing exclusive rights to the renegade governor's story, but none could find him. Consequently, nothing was written that even bordered on the truth.

Which was this: Clinton Tyree now went by the name of Skink, and lived in those steamy clawing places where he was least likely to be bothered by human life-forms. For fifteen years the governor had been submerged in an expatriation that was deliberately remote and anonymous, if not entirely tranquil.

▼ ▼ ▼

Joe Winder wanted to talk about what happened in Tallahassee. "I read all the stories," he said. "I went back and looked up the microfiche."

"Then you know all there is to know." Skink was on his haunches, poking the embers with a stick. Winder refused to look at what was frying in the pan.

He said, "All this time and they never found you."

"They quit searching," Skink said. A hot ash caught in a wisp of his beard. He snuffed it with two fingers. "I don't normally eat soft-shell turtle," he allowed.

"Me neither," said Joe Winder.

"The flavor makes up for the texture."

"I bet." Winder knelt on the other side of the fire.

Out of the blue Skink said, "Your old man wasn't a bad guy, but he was in a bad business."

Winder heard himself agree. "He never understood what was so wrong about it. Or why I was so goddamn mad. He died not having a clue."

Skink lifted the turtle by the tail and stuck a fork in it. "Ten more minutes," he said, "at least."

It wasn't easy trying to talk with him this way, but Winder wouldn't give up: "It's been an interesting day. In the space of two hours I lost my job and my girlfriend."

"Christ, you sound like Dobie Gillis."

"The job was shit, I admit. But I was hoping Nina would stay strong. She's one in a million."

"Love," said Skink, "it's just a kiss away."

Dejectedly, Winder thought: I'm wasting my time. The man couldn't care less. "I came to ask about a plan," Winder said. "I've been racking my brain."

"Come on, I want to show you something." Skink rose slowly and stretched, and the blaze-orange rainsuit made a crackling noise. He pulled the shower cap tight on his skull and, in high steps, marched off through the trees. To the west, the sky boiled with fierce purple thunderheads.

"Keep it moving," Skink advised, over his shoulder.

Joe Winder followed him to the same dumpsite where the corpse of Spearmint Breath had been hidden. When they walked past the junker Cadillac, Winder noted that the trunk was open, and empty. He didn't ask about the body. He didn't want to know.

Skink led him through a hazardous obstacle course of discarded household junk—shells of refrigerators, ripped sofas, punctured mattresses, crippled Barcaloungers, rusty barbecue grills, disemboweled air conditioners—until they came to a very old Plymouth station wagon, an immense egg-colored barge with no wheels and no windshield. A yellow beach umbrella sprouted like a giant marigold from the dashboard, and offered minimal protection from blowing rain or the noonday sun. Skink got in the car and ordered Joe Winder to do the same.

The Plymouth was full of books—hundreds of volumes arranged lovingly from the tailgate to the front. With considerable effort, Skink turned completely in the front seat; he propped his rear end on the warped steering wheel. "This is where I come to read," he said. "Believe it or not, the dome light in this heap still works."

Joe Winder ran a finger along the spines of the books, and found himself smiling at the exhilarating variety of writers: Churchill, Hesse, Sandburg, Steinbeck, Camus, Paine, Wilde, Vonnegut, de Tocqueville, Salinger, García Márquez, even Harry Crews.

"I put a new battery in this thing," Skink was saying. "This time of year I've got to run the AC at least two, three hours a day. To stop the damn mildew."

"So there's gas in this car?" Winder asked.

"Sure."

"But no wheels."

Skink shrugged. "Where the hell would I be driving?"

A cool stream of wind rushed through the open windshield, and overhead the yellow beach umbrella began to flap noisily. A fat drop of rain splatted on the hood, followed by another and another.

"Damn," said Skink. He put a shoulder to the door and launched himself out of the station wagon. "Hey, Flack, you coming or not?"

▼ ▼ ▼

The storm came hard and they sat through it, huddled like Sherpas. The campfire washed out, but the soft-shelled turtle was cooked to perfection. Skink chewed intently on its tail and blinked the raindrops from his good eye; the other one fogged up like a broken headlight. Water trickled down his bronze cheeks, drenching his beard. Lightning cracked so close they could smell it—Winder ducked, but Skink showed no reaction, even when thunder rattled the coffeepot.

He adjusted the blaze weather suit to cover the electronic panther collar on his neck. "They say it's waterproof, but I don't know."

Winder could scarcely hear him over the drum of the rain against the trees. Lightning flashed again, and reflexively he shut his eyes.

Skink raised his voice: "You know about that new golf resort?"

"I saw where they're putting it."

"No!" Skink was shouting now. "You know who's behind it? That fucking Kingsbury!"

The wind was getting worse, if that was possible. With his free hand, Skink wrung out the tendrils of his beard. "Goddammit, man, are you listening? It all ties together."

"What—with Koocher's death?"

"Everything—" Skink paused for another white sizzle of lightning. "Every damn thing."

It made sense to Winder. A scandal at the Amazing Kingdom would not only be bad for business, it might jeopardize Francis Kingsbury's plans for developing Falcon Trace. If anyone revealed that he'd lied about the "endangered" voles, the feds might roll in and halt the whole show. The EPA, the Army Corps of Engineers, the Department of Interior—they could jerk Kingsbury around until he died of old age.

"Look at the big picture," Skink said. With a tin fork he cleaned out the insides of the turtle shell. The wind was dying quickly, and the rain was turning soft on the leaves. The clouds broke out west, revealing raspberry patches of summer sunset. The coolness disappeared and the air turned muggy again.

Skink put down the fry pan and wiped his mouth on the sleeve of his rainsuit. "It's beautiful out here," he remarked. "That squall felt damn good."

"It might be too late," Joe Winder said. "Hell, they've started clearing the place."

"I know." The muscles in Skink's neck tightened. "They tore down an eagle nest the other day. Two little ones, dead. That's the kind of bastards we're talking about."

"Did you see—"

"I got there after the fact," Skink said. "Believe me, if I could've stopped them . . ."

"What if we're too late?"

"Are you in or not? That's all I need to know."

"I'm in," said Winder. "Of course I am. I'm just not terribly optimistic."

Skink smiled his matinee smile, the one that had gotten him elected so many years before. "Lower your sights, boy," he said to Joe Winder. "I agree, justice is probably out of the question. But we can damn sure ruin their day."

He reached under the flap of his rainsuit, grunted, fumbled inside his clothing. Finally his hand came out holding a steel-blue semi-automatic pistol.

"Don't worry," he said. "I've got an extra one for you."

▼ ▼ ▼

The woman who called herself Rachel Lark was receiving a vigorous massage when Francis X. Kingsbury phoned. She'd been expecting to hear from him ever since she'd read in the *Washington Post* about the theft of the blue-tongued mango voles in Florida. Her first thought, a natural one, was that Kingsbury would try to talk her into giving some of the money back. Rachel Lark braced for the worst as she sat up, naked, and told the masseur to give her the damn telephone.

On the other end, Kingsbury said: "Is this my favorite redhead?"

"Forget it," said the woman who called herself Rachel Lark, though it was not her true name.

Kingsbury said, "Can you believe it, babe? My luck, the goddamn things get swiped."

"I've already spent the money," Rachel Lark said, "and even if I didn't, a deal's a deal."

Instead of protesting, Kingsbury said, "Same here. I spent mine, too."

"Then it's a social call, is it?"

"Not exactly. Are you alone, babe?"

"Me and a nice young man named Sven."

The image gave Kingsbury a tingle. Rachel was an attractive woman, a bit on the heavy side, but a very hot dresser. They had met years before in the lobby of a prosecutor's office in Camden, where both of them were waiting to cut deals allowing them to avert unpleasant prison terms. Frankie King had chosen to drop the dime on the Zubonis, while the woman who now called herself Rachel Lark (it was Sarah Hunt at that time) was preparing to squeal on an ex-boyfriend who had illegally imported four hundred pounds of elephant ivory. In the lobby that day, the two informants had amiably traded tales about life on the lam. Later they'd exchanged phone numbers and a complete list of aliases, and promised to keep in touch.

Rachel's specialty was wildlife, and Kingsbury phoned her soon after opening the Amazing Kingdom of Thrills. Before then, he had never heard of the Endangered Species Act, never dreamed that an obscure agency of the federal government would casually fork over two hundred thousand dollars in grant money for the purpose of preserving a couple of lousy rodents. Rachel Lark had offered to provide the animals and the documentation, and Kingsbury was so intrigued by the plan—not just the dough, but the radiant publicity for the Amazing Kingdom—that he didn't bother to inquire if the blue-tongued mango voles were real.

The government check had arrived on time, they'd split it fifty-fifty and that was that. Francis Kingsbury paid no further attention to the creatures until customers started noticing that the voles' tongues were no longer very blue. Once children openly began grilling the Amazing Kingdom tour guides about how the animals got their name, Kingsbury ordered Pedro Luz to get some food coloring and touch the damn things up. Unfortunately, Pedro had neither the patience nor the gentle touch required to be an animal handler, and one of the voles—the female—was crushed accidentally during a tongue-painting session. Afraid for his job, Pedro Luz had told no one of the mishap. To replace the deceased vole, he had purchased a dwarf hamster for nine dollars from a pet store in Perrine. After minor modifications, the hamster had fooled both the customers and the male vole, which repeatedly attempted to mount its chubby new companion. Not only had the hamster rejected these advances, it had counterattacked with such ferocity that Pedro Luz had been forced to hire a night security guard to prevent a bloodbath.

Matters were further complicated by the appearance of an ill-mannered pinhead from U.S. Fish and Wildlife, who had barged into the theme park and demanded follow-up data from the "project manager." Of course there was no such person because there was no project to manage; research consisted basically of making sure that the rodents were still breathing every morning before the gates were opened. With the feds suddenly asking questions, Charles Chelsea had quietly put out an all-points bulletin for a legitimate biologist—a recruiting effort that eventually induced Dr. Will Koocher to come to the Amazing Kingdom of Thrills.

Kingsbury decided not to burden Rachel Lark with the details of the doctor's grisly demise; it was irrelevant to the purpose of his call.

"Forget the money," Kingsbury told her.

"I must be hearing things."

"No, I mean it."

"Then what do you want?"

"More voles."

"You're joking."

"My customers, hell, they go nuts for the damn things. Now I got spin-offs, merchandise—a major warehouse situation, if you follow me."

"Sorry," Rachel Lark said, "it was a one-time deal." She'd pulled off the endangered-species racket on two other occasions—once for a small Midwestern zoo, and once for a disreputable reptile farm in South Carolina. Neither deal made as much money as the mango-vole scam, but neither had wound up in the headlines of the *Washington Post*, either.

Kingsbury said, "Look, I know there's no more mango voles—"

"Hey, sport, there never *were* any mango voles."

"So what you're saying, we defrauded the government."

"God, you're quick."

"I'm wondering," said Kingsbury, "those fucking furballs I paid for —what were they? Just out of curiosity."

Rachel Lark said, "Give me some credit, Frankie. They were voles. *Microtus pitymys*. Common pine voles."

"Not endangered?"

"There's billions of the darn things."

It figures, Kingsbury thought. The blue tongues were a neat touch. "So get me some more," he said. "We'll call 'em something else, banana voles or whatever. The name's not important, long as they're cute."

The woman who called herself Rachel Lark said: "Look, I can get you other animals—rare, not endangered—but my advice is to stay away from the feds for a while. You put in for another big grant, it's a swell way to get audited."

Again Kingsbury agreed without objection. "So what else have you got, I mean, in the way of a species?"

"Lizards are your best bet." Rachel Lark stretched on her belly and motioned the masseur, whose real name was Ray, to do her spine.

"Christ on a Harley, who wants goddamn lizards!" Kingsbury cringed at the idea; he had been thinking more along the lines of a panda or a koala bear. "I need something, you know, soft and furry and all that. Something the kiddies'll want to take home."

Rachel Lark explained that the Florida Keys were home to a very limited number of native mammals, and the sudden discovery of a new species (so soon after the mango-vole announcement) would attract more scientific scrutiny than the Amazing Kingdom could withstand.

"You're saying, I take it, forget about pandas."

"Frank, they'd die of heatstroke in about five minutes."

Exasperated, Kingsbury said, "I got problems down here you wouldn't believe." He nearly told her about the blackmailing burglars.

"A new lizard you can get away with," she said, "especially in the tropics."

"Rachel, what'd I just say? Fuck the lizards. I can't market lizards."

Rachel Lark moaned blissfully as the masseur kneaded the muscles of her neck. "My advice," she said into the phone, "is stay away from mammals and birds—it's too risky. Insects are another story. Dozens of species of insects are discovered every year. Grasshoppers, doodle-bugs, you name it."

There was a grumpy pause on the other end. Finally, Francis X. Kingsbury said, "Getting back to the lizards. I mean, for the sake of argument . . ."

"They're very colorful," said the woman who called herself Rachel Lark.

"Ugly is out of the question," Kingsbury stated firmly. "Ugly scares the kiddies."

"Not all reptiles are ugly, Frankie. In fact, some are very beautiful."

"All right," he said. "See what you can do."

The woman who called herself Rachel Lark hung up the phone and closed her eyes. When she awoke, the masseur was gone and the man from Singapore was knocking on the door. In one hand was a small bouquet of yellow roses, and in the other was a tan briefcase holding a large down payment for a shipment of rare albino scorpions. Real ones.

18

On the morning of July 23, a semi-tractor truck leaving North Key Largo lost its brakes on the Card Sound Bridge. The truck plowed through the tollbooth, jackknifed and overturned, blocking both lanes of traffic and effectively severing the northern arm of the island from the Florida mainland. The gelatinous contents of the container were strewn for ninety-five yards along the road, and within minutes the milky-blue sky filled with turkey buzzards—hundreds of them, wheeling counterclockwise lower and lower; only the noisy throng of gawkers kept the hungry scavengers from landing on the crash site. The first policeman to arrive was Highway Patrol Trooper Jim Tile, who nearly flipped his Crown Victoria cruiser when he tried to stop on the freshly slickened pavement. The trooper tugged the truck driver from the wreckage and, while splinting the man's arm, demanded to know what godforsaken cargo he'd been hauling.

"A dead whale," moaned the driver, "and that's all I'm saying."

▼ ▼ ▼

Charles Chelsea was summoned to Francis X. Kingsbury's office at the unholy hour of seven in the morning. Kingsbury looked as if he hadn't slept since Easter. He asked Chelsea how long it would take to get the TV stations out to the Amazing Kingdom of Thrills.

"Two hours," Chelsea said confidently.

"Do it." Kingsbury blew his nose. "On the horn, now."

"What's the occasion, if I might ask."

Kingsbury held up five fingers. "Today's the big day. Our five-millionth visitor. Arrange something, a fucking parade, I don't care."

Charles Chelsea felt his stomach yaw. "Five million visitors," he said. "Sir, I didn't realize we'd reached that milestone."

"We haven't." Kingsbury hacked ferociously into a monogrammed handkerchief. "Damn my hay fever, I think it's the mangroves. Every morning my whole head's fulla snot." He pushed a copy of the *Wall Street Journal* at Chelsea. A column on the front page announced that

Walt Disney World was expanding its empire to build a mammoth retail shopping center, one of the largest in the Southeastern United States.

"See, we can't just sit here," Kingsbury said. "Got to come back strong. Big media counterpunch."

Chelsea skimmed the *Journal* article and laid it on his lap. Tentatively he said, "It's hard to compete with something like this. I mean, it goes so far beyond the realm of a family theme park—"

"Bullshit," said Kingsbury. "The Miami-Lauderdale TV market is —what, three times the size of Orlando. Plus CNN, don't they have a bureau down here?" Kingsbury spun his chair and gazed out the window. "Hell, that new dolphin I bought—can't you work him into the piece? Say he rescued somebody who fell in the tank. A pregnant lady or maybe an orphan. Rescued them from drowning—that's your story! 'Miracle Dolphin Saves Drowning Orphan.' "

"I don't know if that's such a good plan," said Chelsea, though inwardly he had to admit it would have been one helluva headline.

"This celebration, make it for noon," Kingsbury said. "Whoever comes through the turnstiles, strike up the band. But make sure it's a tourist, no goddamn locals. Number five million, okay? In giant letters."

His gut tightening, Chelsea said, "Sir, it might be wiser to go with two million. It's closer to the real number . . . just in case somebody makes an issue of it."

"No, two is—chickenshit, really. Five's better. And the parade, too, I'm serious." Kingsbury stood up. He was dressed for golf. "A parade, that's good video," he said. "Plenty of time to get it for the six-o'clock news. That's our best demographic, am I right? Fucking kids, they don't watch the eleven."

Chelsea nodded. "What do we give the winner? Mr. Five Million, I mean."

"A car, Jesus Christ." Kingsbury looked at him as if he were an idiot. A few years earlier, Disney World had given away an automobile every day for an entire summer. Kingsbury had never gotten over it. "Make it a Corvette," he told Chelsea.

"All right, but you're looking at forty thousand dollars. Maybe more."

Kingsbury extended his lower lip so far that it seemed to touch his nose; for a moment he wore the pensive look of a caged orangutan. "Forty grand," he repeated quietly. "That's brand new, I suppose."

"When you give one away, yes. Ordinarily the cars should be new."

"Unless they're classics." Kingsbury winked. "Make it a classic. Say, a 1964 Ford Falcon. You don't see many of those babies."

"Sure don't."

"A Falcon convertible, geez, we could probably pick one up for twenty-five hundred."

"Probably," agreed Chelsea, not even pretending enthusiasm.

"Well, move on it." Francis X. Kingsbury thumbed him out of the office. "And tell Pedro, get his ass in here."

▼ ▼ ▼

Pedro Luz was in the executive gym, bench-pressing a bottle of stanozolol tablets. He was letting the tiny pink pills drop one by one into his mouth.

A man named Churrito, lounging on a Nautilus, said: "Hiss very bad for liver."

"Very good for muscles," said Pedro Luz, mimicking the accent.

Churrito was his latest hire to the security squad at the Amazing Kingdom of Thrills. He had accompanied Pedro Luz on his mission to Miami, but had declined to participate in the beating. Pedro Luz was still miffed about what had happened—the old lady chomping off the top joint of his right index finger.

"You're useless," he had told Churrito afterward.

"I am a soldier," Churrito had replied. "I dun hit no wooman."

Unlike the other security guards hired by Pedro Luz, Churrito had not been a crooked cop. He was a Nicaraguan *contra* who had moved to Florida when things were bleak, and had not gotten around to moving back. While Churrito was pleased at the prospect of democracy taking seed in his homeland, he suspected that true economic prosperity was many years away. Elections notwithstanding, Churrito's buddies were still stuck in the border hills, frying green bananas and dynamiting the rivers for fish. Meanwhile his uncle, formerly a sergeant in Somoza's National Guard, now lived with a twenty-two-year-old stewardess in a high-rise condo on Key Biscayne. To Churrito, this seemed like a pretty good advertisement for staying right where he was.

Pedro Luz had hired him because he looked mean, and because he'd said he had killed people.

"*Comunistas*," Churrito had specified, that night at the old lady's apartment. "I only kill commoonists. And I dun hit no wooman."

And now here he was, lecturing Pedro Luz about the perils of anabolic steroids.

"Make you face like balloon."

"Shut up," said Pedro Luz. He was wondering if the hospital in Key Largo would sell him extra bags of dextrose water for the IV. Grind up the stanozolols, drop them in the mix and everything would be fine again.

"Make you bulls shrink, too."

"That's enough," Pedro Luz said.

Churrito held up two fingers. "Dis big. Like BBs."

"Quiet," said Pedro Luz, "or I call a friend a mine at INS." He couldn't decide whether to fire the guy or beat him up. He knew which would give more pleasure.

"They got, like, three flights a day to Managua," he said to Churrito. "You getting homesick?"

The Nicaraguan grimaced.

"I didn't think so," said Pedro Luz. "So shut up about my medicines."

Charles Chelsea appeared at the foot of the weight bench. He had never seen Pedro Luz without a shirt, and couldn't conceal his awe at the freakish physique—the hairless bronze trunk of a chest, cantaloupe biceps, veins as thick as a garden hose. Chelsea didn't recognize the other fellow—shorter and sinewy, with skin the color of nutmeg.

"I'm working out," said Pedro Luz.

"Mr. Kingsbury needs to see you."

"Who ees that?" Churrito said.

Pedro Luz sat up. "That be the boss."

"Right away," said Charles Chelsea.

"Can I go?" asked Churrito. He didn't want to miss an opportunity to meet the boss; according to his uncle, that's what success in America was all about. Kissing ass.

"I'm sorry," Chelsea said, "but Mr. Kingsbury wants to see Chief Luz alone."

"Yeah," said Pedro Luz. As he rolled off the bench, he made a point of clipping Churrito with a casual forearm. Churrito didn't move, didn't make a sound. His eyes grew very small and he stared at Pedro Luz until Pedro Luz spun away, pretending to hunt for his sweatshirt.

Churrito pointed at the scarlet blemishes on Pedro Luz's shoulder blades and said: "You all broke out, man."

"Shut up before I yank your nuts off."

Backing away, Charles Chelsea thought: Where do they get these guys?

▼ ▼ ▼

Francis X. Kingsbury offered a Bloody Mary to Pedro Luz, who guzzled it like Gatorade.

"So, Pedro, the job's going all right?"

The security chief was startled at Kingsbury's genial tone. A ration of shit was what he'd expected; the old fart had been livid since the burglary of his private office. The crime had utterly baffled Pedro Luz, who hadn't the first notion of how to solve it. He had hoped that the mission to Eagle Ridge would absolve him.

"I took care of that other problem," he announced to Kingsbury.

"Fine. Excellent." Kingsbury was swiveling back and forth in his chair. He didn't look so good: nervous, ragged, droopy-eyed, his fancy golf shirt all wrinkled. Pedro Luz wondered if the old fart was doing coke. The very idea was downright hilarious.

"She won't bother you no more," he said to Kingsbury.

"You made it look, what—like muggers? Crack fiends?"

"Sure, that's what the cops would think. If she calls them, which I don't think she will. I made it clear what could happen."

"Fine. Excellent." Kingsbury propped his elbows on the desk in a way that offered Pedro Luz an unobstructed view of the lurid mouse tattoo.

"Two things—" Kingsbury paused when he spotted the bandage on Pedro Luz's finger.

"Hangnail," said the security chief.

"Whatever," Kingsbury said. "Two things—some assholes, the guys who stole my files, they're blackmailing me. You know, shaking me down."

Pedro Luz asked how much money he had promised them.

"Never mind," Kingsbury replied. "Five grand so far is what I paid. But the files, see, I can't just blow 'em off. I need the files."

"Who are these men?"

Francis Kingsbury threw up his hands. "That's the thing—just ordinary shitheads. White trash. I can't fucking believe it."

Pedro Luz had never understood the concept of white trash, or how it differed from black trash or Hispanic trash or any other kind of criminal dirtbag. He said, "You want the files but you don't want to pay."

"Exacto!" said Kingsbury. "In fact, the five grand—I wouldn't mind getting it back."

Pedro Luz laughed sharply. Months go by and the job's a snooze— now suddenly all this dirty work. Oh well, Pedro thought, it beats painting rat tongues. He hadn't shed a tear when the mango voles were stolen.

Kingsbury was saying, "The other thing, I fired a guy from Publicity."

"Yeah?" Watching that damn tattoo, it was driving Pedro silly. Minnie on her knees, polishing Mickey's knob—whoever did the drawing was damn good, almost Disney caliber.

"You need to go see this guy I fired," Kingsbury was saying. "Find out some things."

Pedro Luz asked what kind of things.

Kingsbury moved his lips around, like a camel getting ready to spit. Eventually he said, "The problem we had before? This is worse, okay. The guy I mentioned, we're talking major pain in the rectum."

"Okay."

"As long as he worked for us, we had some control. On the outside, hell, he's a major pain. I just got a feeling."

Pedro Luz gave him a thumbs-up. "Don't worry."

"Carefully," Kingsbury added. "Same as before would be excellent. Except no dead whales this time."

God, thought Pedro Luz, what a fuckup *that* was.

"Do I know him?" he asked Kingsbury.

"From Publicity. Joe Winder's his name."

"Oh." Pedro Luz perked up. Winder was the smartass who'd been hassling him about Dr. Koocher. The same guy he'd sent Angel and Big Paulie to teach a lesson, only something went sour and Angel ended up dead and Paulie must've took off. Next thing Pedro knows, here's this smartass Winder snooping around the animal lab in the middle of the night.

Mr. X was right about the guy. Now that he was fired, he might go hog-wild. Start talking crazy shit all over the place.

"You look inspired," Kingsbury said.

Pedro Luz smiled crookedly. "Let's just say I got some ideas."

▼ ▼ ▼

When Molly McNamara opened her eyes, she was surprised to see Bud Schwartz and Danny Pogue at her bedside.

"I thought you boys would be long gone."

"No way," said Danny Pogue. His eyes were large and intent, like a retriever's. His chin was in his hands, and he was sitting very close to the bed. He patted Molly's brow with a damp washcloth.

"Thank you," she said. "I'm very thirsty."

Danny Pogue bolted to the kitchen to get her a glass of ginger ale. Bud Schwartz took a step closer. He said, "What happened? Can you remember anything?"

"My glasses," she said, pointing to the nightstand.

"They got busted," said Bud Schwartz. "I used some Scotch tape on the nose part."

Molly McNamara put them on, and said, "Two men. Only one did the hitting."

"Why? What'd they want—money?"

Molly shook her head slowly. Danny Pogue came back with the ginger ale, and she took two small sips. "Thank you," she said. "No, they didn't want money."

Danny Pogue said, "Who?"

"The men who came. They said it was a warning."

"Oh Christ."

"It's none of your concern," said Molly.

Grimly Bud Schwartz said, "They were after the files."

"No. They never mentioned that."

Bud Schwartz was relieved; he had worried that Francis X. Kingsbury had somehow identified them, connected them to Molly and sent goons to avenge the burglary. It was an irrational fear, he knew, because even the powerful Kingsbury couldn't have done it so quickly after their blackmail visit.

Still, it was discouraging to see how they had battered Molly McNamara. These were extremely bad men, and Bud Schwartz doubted they would have allowed him and Danny Pogue to survive the encounter.

"I think we ought to get out of here," he said to Molly. "Take you back to the big house."

"That's a sensible plan," Molly agreed, "but you boys don't have to stay."

"Like hell," Danny Pogue declared. "Look at you, all busted up. You'll be needing some help."

"You got some bad bruises," agreed Bud Schwartz. "Your right knee's twisted, too, but I don't think it's broke. Plus they knocked out a couple teeth."

Molly ran her tongue around her gums and said, "I was the only one in this building who still had their own."

Danny Pogue paced with a limp. "I wanted to call an ambulance or somebody, only Bud decided we better not."

Molly said that was a smart decision, considering what the three of them had been up to lately. She removed the damp cloth from her forehead and folded it on the nightstand.

Danny Pogue wanted to know all about the attackers—how big they were, what they looked like. "I bet they was niggers," he said.

Molly raised herself off the pillow, cocked her arm and slapped him across the face. Incredulous, Danny Pogue rubbed his cheek.

She said, "Don't you ever again use that word in my presence."

"Christ, I didn't mean nothin.' "

"Well, it just so happens these men were white. White Hispanic males. The one who beat me up was very large and muscular."

"My question," said Bud Schwartz, "is how they slipped past that crack security guard. What's his name, Andrews, the ace with the flashlight."

Molly said: "You won't believe it. The big one had a badge. A police badge, City of Miami."

"Wonderful," Bud Schwartz said.

"I saw it myself," Molly said. "Why do you think I even opened the door? He said they were plainclothes detectives. Once they had me down, I couldn't get to my purse."

Danny Pogue looked at his partner with the usual mix of confusion and concern. Bud Schwartz said, "It sounds like some serious shitkickers. You say they were Cubans?"

"Hispanics," Molly said.

"Did they speak American?" asked Danny Pogue.

"The big one did all the talking, and his English was quite competent. Especially his use of four-letter slang."

Danny Pogue rocked on his good leg, and slammed a fist against the wall. "I'll murder the sumbitch!"

"Sure you will," said his partner. "You're a killer and I'm the next quarterback for the Dolphins."

"I mean it, Bud. Look what he done to her."

"I see, believe me." Bud Schwartz gave Molly McNamara two Percodans and said it would help her sleep. She swallowed the pills in one gulp and thanked the burglars once again. "It's very kind of you to look after me," she said.

"Only till you're feeling better," said Bud Schwartz. "We got some business that requires our full attention."

"Of course, I understand."

"We made five grand tonight!" said Danny Pogue. Quickly he withered under his partner's glare.

"Five thousand is very good," Molly said. "Add the money I still owe you, and that's quite a handsome nest egg." She slid deeper into the sheets, and pulled the blanket to her chin.

"Get some rest," Bud Schwartz said. "We'll take you to the house in the morning."

"Yeah, get some sleep." Danny Pogue gazed at her dolorously. Bud Schwartz wondered if he was about to cry.

"Bud?" Molly spoke in a fog.

"Yeah."

"Did you boys happen to find a piece of finger on the floor?"

"No," said Bud Schwartz. "Why?"

"Would you check in the kitchen, please?"

"No problem." He wondered how the pills could mess her up so quickly. "You mean, like a human finger?"

But Molly's eyes were already closed.

19

Charles Chelsea worked feverishly all morning. By half past eleven the parade was organized. The gateway to the Amazing Kingdom of Thrills was festooned with multicolored streamers and hundreds of Mylar balloons. Cheerleaders practiced cartwheels over the turnstiles while the Tavernier High School band rehearsed the theme from *Exodus*. Several of the most popular animal characters—Robbie Raccoon, Petey Possum and Barney the Bison—were summoned from desultory lunch breaks in The Catacombs to greet and be photographed with the big winner. Above a hastily constructed stage, a billowy hand-painted banner welcomed "OUR FIVE-MILLIONTH SPECIAL GUEST!!!"

And there, parked in the courtyard, was a newly restored 1966 Chevrolet Corvair, one of Detroit's most venerated deathtraps. Charles Chelsea had been unable to locate a mint-condition Falcon, and the vintage Mustangs were beyond Francis Kingsbury's budget. The Corvair was Chelsea's next choice as the giveaway car because it was a genuine curiosity, and because it was cheap. The one purchased by Chelsea had been rear-ended by a dairy tanker in 1972, and the resulting explosion had wiped out a quartet of home-appliance salesmen. The rebuilt Corvair was seven inches shorter from bumper to bumper than the day it had rolled off the assembly line, but Charles Chelsea was certain no one would notice. Two extra coats of cherry paint and the Corvair shouted classic. It was exactly the sort of campy junk-mobile that some dumb Yuppie would love.

The scene was set for the coronation of the alleged five-millionth visitor to the Amazing Kingdom. The only thing missing from the festive tableau, Chelsea noted lugubriously, was customers. The park had opened more than two hours ago, yet not a single carload of tourists had arrived. The trams were empty, the cash registers mute; no one had passed through the ticket gates. Chelsea couldn't understand it—the place had not experienced such a catastrophic attendance drop since salmonella had felled a visiting contingent of Rotarians at Sally's Cimarron Saloon.

Chelsea prayed with all his heart that some tourists would show up before the television vans. He did not know, and could not have envisioned, that an eighteen-wheeler loaded with the decomposing remains of Orky the Whale had flipped on Card Sound Road and paralyzed all traffic heading toward the Amazing Kingdom. The highway patrol diligently had set up a roadblock at the junction near Florida City, where troopers were advising all buses, campers and rental cars filled with Francis X. Kingsbury's customers to turn around and return to Miami. The beleaguered troopers did not consider it their sworn duty to educate the tourists about an alternate route to the Amazing Kingdom—taking Highway 1 south past Jewfish Creek, then backtracking up County Road 905 to the park. The feeling among the troopers (based on years of experience) was that no matter how simple and explicit they made the directions, many of the tourists would manage to get lost, run out of gas and become the victims of some nasty roadside crime. A more sensible option was simply to tell them to go back, there'd been a bad accident.

Consequently Charles Chelsea stood in eery solitude on the makeshift stage, the cheery banner flapping over his head as he stared at the empty parking lot and wondered how in the hell he would break the news to Francis X. Kingsbury. Today there would be no celebration, no parade, no five-millionth visitor. There were no visitors at all.

▼ ▼ ▼

Joe Winder felt like a Jamn redneck—he hadn't been to a firing range in ten or twelve years, and that was to shoot his father's revolver, an old Smith. The gun Skink had given him was a thin foreign-made semi-automatic. It didn't have much weight, but Skink promised it would do the job, whatever job needed doing. Winder had decided to keep it for ornamental purposes. It lay under the front seat as he drove south on County Road 905.

He stopped at a pay phone, dialed the sex-talk number and billed it to his home. Miriam answered and started in with a new routine, something about riding bareback on a pony. When Winder broke in and asked for Nina, Miriam told him she wasn't there.

"Tell her to call me, please."

"Hokay, Joe."

"On second thought, never mind."

"Whatever chew say. You like the horsey business?"

"Yes, Miriam, it's very good."

"Nina wrote it. Want me do the end?"

"No thank you."

"Is hot stuff, Joe. Cheese got some mansionation."

"She sure does."

Joe Winder drove until he reached the Falcon Trace construction site. He parked on the side of the road and watched a pair of mustard-colored bulldozers plow a fresh section of hammock, creating a tangled knoll of uprooted tamarinds, buttonwoods, pigeon plums and rouge-berry. Each day a few more acres were being destroyed in the name of championship golf.

A team of surveyors worked the distant end of the property, near Winder's fishing spot. He assumed they were marking off the lots where the most expensive homes would be built—the more ocean frontage, the higher the price. This was how Francis X. Kingsbury would make his money—the golf course itself was never meant to profit; it was a real-estate tease, plain and simple. The links would be pieced together in the middle of the development on whatever parcels couldn't be peddled as residential waterfront. Soon, Winder knew, they'd start blasting with dynamite to dig fairway lakes in the ancient reef rock.

He saw that both bulldozers had stopped, and that the drivers had gotten down from the cabs to look at something in the trees. Joe Winder stepped out of the car and started running. He remembered what Skink had told him about the baby eagles. He shouted at the men and saw them turn. One folded his arms and slouched against his dozer.

Winder covered the two hundred yards in a minute. When he reached the men, he was panting too hard to speak.

One of them said: "What's your problem?"

Winder flashed his Amazing Kingdom identification badge, which he had purposely neglected to turn in upon termination of employment. The lazy bulldozer driver, the one leaning against his machine, studied the badge and began to laugh. "What the hell is this?"

When Joe Winder caught his breath, he said: "I work for Mr. Kingsbury. He owns this land."

"Ain't the name on the permit. The permit says Ramex Global."

The other driver spoke up: "Anyway, who gives a shit about some goddamn wolves?"

"Yeah," the first driver said. "Bury 'em."

"No," said Joe Winder. They weren't wolves, they were gray foxes —six of them, no larger than kittens. The bulldozers had uprooted the den tree. Half-blind, the little ones were crawling all over each other, squeaking and yapping in toothless panic.

Winder said, "If we leave them alone, the mother will probably come back."

"What is this, 'Wild Kingdom'?"

"At least help me move them out of the way."

"Forget it," the smartass driver said. "I ain't in the mood for rabies. Come on, Bobby, let's roll it."

The men climbed back in the dozers and seized the gear sticks. Instinctively Joe Winder positioned himself between the large machines and the baby foxes. The drivers began to holler and curse. The smartass lowered the blade of his bulldozer and inched forward, pushing a ridge of moist dirt over the tops of Joe Winder's shoes. The driver grinned and whooped at his own cleverness until he noticed the gun pointed up at his head.

He quickly turned off the engine and raised his hands. The other driver did the same. In a scratchy whine he said, "Geez, what's your problem?"

Winder held the semi-automatic steady. He was surprised at how natural it felt. He said, "Is this what it takes to have a civilized conversation with you shitheads?"

Quickly he checked over his shoulder to make sure the kits hadn't crawled from the den. The outlandishness of the situation was apparent, but he'd committed himself to melodrama. With the gun on display, he was already deep into felony territory.

The smartass driver apologized profusely for burying Winder's shoes. "I'll buy you some new ones," he offered.

"Oh, that's not necessary." Winder yearned to shoot the bulldozers but he didn't know where to begin; the heavy steel thoraxes looked impervious to cannon fire.

The lazy driver said: "You want us to get down?"

"Not just yet," said Joe Winder, "I'm thinking."

"Hey, there's no need to shoot. Just tell us what the hell you want."

"I want you to help me fuck up these machines."

▼　▼　▼

It was nine o'clock when the knock came. Joe Winder was sitting in the dark on the floor of the apartment. He had the clip out of the gun, and the bullets out of the clip. A full load, too, sixteen rounds; he had lined up the little rascals side by side on a windowsill, a neat row of identical copper-headed soldiers.

The knocking wouldn't go away. Winder picked up the empty gun.

He went to the door and peeked out of the peephole. He saw an orb of glistening blond; not Nina-style blond, this was lighter. When the woman turned around, Winder flung open the door and pulled her inside.

In the darkness Carrie Lanier took a deep breath and said: "I hope that's you."

"It's me," Joe Winder said.

"Was that a gun I saw?"

"I'm afraid so. My situation has taken a turn for the worse."

Carrie said, "That's why I came."

Winder led her back to the living room, where they sat between two large cardboard boxes. The only light was the amber glow from the stereo receiver; Carrie Lanier could barely hear the music from the speakers.

"Where's your girlfriend?" she asked.

"Moved out."

"I'm sorry." She paused; then, peering at him: "Is that a beret?"

"Panties," Joe Winder said. "Can you believe it—that's all she left me. Cheap ones, too. The mail-order crap she sold over the phone." He pulled the underwear off his head to show her the shoddy stitching.

"You've had a rough time," said Carrie Lanier. "I didn't know she'd moved out."

"Yeah, well, I'm doing just fine. Adjusting beautifully to the single life. Sitting here in a dark apartment with a gun in my lap and underpants on my head."

Carrie squeezed his arm. "Joe, are you on drugs?"

"Nope," he said. "Pretty amazing, isn't it?"

"I think you should come home with me."

"Why?"

"Because bad things will happen if you stay here."

"Ah." Winder scooped the bullets off the windowsill and fed them into the gun clip. "You must be talking about Pedro Luz."

"It's all over the Magic Kingdom," Carrie said, "about the reasons you were fired."

"Mr. X doesn't kill the his former employees, does he?"

She leaned closer. "It's no joke. The word is, you're number one on Pedro's list."

"So that's the word."

"Joe, I get around. Spend the day in a raccoon suit, people forget there's a real person inside. I might as well be invisible—the stuff I pick up, you wouldn't believe."

"The spy wore a tail! And now you hear Pedro's irritated."

"I got it from two of the other guards on lunch break. They were doing blow behind the Magic Mansion."

Winder was struck by how wonderful Carrie looked, her eyes all serious in the amber light. Impulsively he kissed her on the cheek. "Don't worry about me," he said. "You can go home."

"You aren't listening."

"Yes, I—"

"No, you aren't." Her tone was one of motherly disapproval. "I warned you about this before. About sticking your nose where it doesn't belong."

"You did, yes."

"Last time you were lucky. You truly were."

"I suppose so." Joe Winder felt oppressively tired. Suddenly the handgun weighed a ton. He slid it across the carpet so forcefully that it banged into the baseboard of the opposite wall.

Carrie Lanier told him to hurry and pack some clothes.

"I can't leave," he said. "Nina might call."

"Joe, it's not just Pedro you've got to worry about. It's the police."

Winder's chin dropped to his chest. "Already?"

"Mr. X swore out a warrant this afternoon," Carrie said. "I heard it from his secretary."

Francis Kingsbury's secretary was a regular visitor to The Catacombs, where she was conducting an athletic love affair with the actor who portrayed Bartholomew, the most shy and bookish of Uncle Ely's Elves.

Carrie said, "She mentioned something about destruction of private property."

"There was an incident," Joe Winder acknowledged, "but no shots were fired."

Under his supervision, the two bulldozers had torn down the three-dimensional billboard that proclaimed the future home of the Falcon Trace Golf and Country Club. The bulldozers also had demolished the air-conditioned double-wide trailer (complete with beer cooler and billiard table) that served as an on-site office for the construction company. They had even wrecked the Port-O-Lets, trapping one of the foremen with his anniversary issue of *Hustler* magazine.

Afterwards Joe Winder had encouraged the bulldozer operators to remove their clothing, which he'd wadded in the neck of the gas tanks. Then—after borrowing the smartass driver's cigarette lighter—Joe Winder had suggested that the men aim their powerful machines toward the Atlantic Ocean, engage the forward gear and swiftly exit the cabs. Later he had proposed a friendly wager on which of the dozers would blow first.

"They spotted the flames all the way from Homestead Air Base," Carrie Lanier reported. "Channel 7 showed up in a helicopter, so Kingsbury made Chelsea write up a press release."

"A freak construction accident, no doubt."

"Good guess. I've got a Xerox in my purse."

"No thanks." Joe Winder wasn't in the mood for Chelsea's golden lies. He stood up and stretched; joints and sockets popped in protest. Lights began to flash blue, green and red on the bare wall, and Winder assumed it was fatigue playing tricks with his vision.

He squinted strenuously, and the lights disappeared. When he opened his eyes, the lights were still strobing. "Shit, here we go." Winder went to the window and peeked through the curtain.

"How many?" Carrie asked.

"Two cops, one car."

"Is there another way out?"

"Sure," he said.

They heard the tired footsteps on the front walk, the deep murmur of conversation, the crinkle of paper. In the crack beneath the door they saw the yellow flicker of flashlight as the policemen examined the warrant one more time, probably double-checking the address.

Winder picked up the semi-automatic and arranged it in his waistband. Carrie Lanier followed him to the kitchen, where they slipped out the back door just as the cops got serious with their knocking. Once outside, in the pale blue moonlight, she deftly grabbed the gun from Joe Winder's trousers and put it in her handbag.

"In case you go stupid on me," she whispered.

"No chance of that," he said. "None at all."

20

A thin coil of copper dangled by a string from Carrie Lanier's rearview mirror. Joe Winder asked if it was some type of hieroglyphic emblem.

"It's an IUD," said Carrie, without taking her eyes off the road. "A reminder of my ex-husband."

"I like it." Winder tried to beef up the compliment. "It's better than fuzzy dice."

"He wanted to have babies," Carrie explained, shooting into the left lane and passing a cement truck. "A baby boy and a baby girl. House with a white picket fence and big backyard. Snapper riding mower. Golden retriever named Champ. He had it all planned."

Joe Winder said, "Sounds pretty good, except for the golden. Give me a Lab any day."

"Well, he wanted to get me pregnant," Carrie went on. "Every night, it was like a big routine. So I'd say sure, Roddy, whatever you want, let's make a baby. I never told him about wearing the loop. And every month he'd want to know. 'Did we do it, sweetie? Is there a zygote?' And I'd say 'Sorry, honey, guess we'd better try harder.'"

"Roddy was his name? That's a bad sign right there."

"He was a screamer, all right."

"What happened?" Winder asked. "Is he still around?"

"No, he's not." Carrie hit the intersection at Highway 1 without touching the brakes, and merged neatly into the northbound traffic. She said, "Roddy's up at Eglin doing a little time."

"Which means he's either a drug dealer or a crooked lawyer."

"Both," she said. "Last month he sent a Polaroid of him with a tennis trophy. He said he can't wait to get out and start trying for a family again."

"The boy's not well."

"It's all Oedipal, that's my theory." Carrie nodded at the IUD and said, "I keep it there to remind myself that you can't be too careful when it comes to men. Here's Roddy with his Stanford diploma and his fancy European car and his heavy downtown law firm, everything in the whole world going for him. Turns out he's nothing but a dipshit, and a dumb dipshit to boot."

Winder said she'd been smart to take precautions.

"Yeah, well, I had my career to consider." Carrie turned a corner into a trailer park, and coasted the car to the end of a narrow gravel lane. "Home sweet home," she said. "Be sure to lock your door. This is not a wonderful neighborhood."

Joe Winder said, "Why are you doing this for me?"

"I'm not sure. I'm really not." She tossed him the keys and asked him to get the raccoon costume from the trunk of the car.

▼ ▼ ▼

Bud Schwartz and Danny Pogue helped Molly McNamara up the steps of the old house in South Miami. They eased her into the rocker in the living room, and opened the front windows to air the place out. Bud Schwartz's hand still throbbed from the gunshot wound, but his fingers seemed to be functioning.

Danny Pogue said, "Ain't it good to be home?"

"Indeed it is," said Molly. "Could you boys fix me some tea?"

Bud Schwartz looked hard at his partner. "I'll do it," said Danny Pogue. "It don't bother me." Cheerfully he hobbled toward the kitchen.

"He's not a bad young man," Molly McNamara said. "Neither of you are."

"Model citizens," said Bud Schwartz. "That's us."

He lowered himself into a walnut captain's chair but stood again quickly, as if the seat were hot. He'd forgotten about the damn thing in his pocket until it touched him in the right testicle. Irritably he removed it from his pants and placed it on an end table. He had wrapped it in a blue lace doily.

He said, "Can we do something with this, please?"

"There's a Mason jar in the cupboard over the stove," Molly said, "and some pickle juice in the refrigerator."

"You're kidding."

"This is important, Bud. It's evidence."

In the hall he passed Danny Pogue carrying a teapot on a silver tray. "You believe this shit?" Bud Schwartz said. He held up the doily.

"What now?"

"She wants me to pickle the goddamn thing!"

Danny Pogue made a squeamish face. "What for?" When he returned to the living room, Molly was rocking tranquilly in the chair. He poured the tea and said, "You must be feeling better."

"Better than I look." She drank carefully, watching Danny Pogue over the rim of the cup. In a tender voice she said: "You don't know what this means to me, the fact that you stayed to help."

"It wasn't just me. It was Bud, too."

"He's not a bad person," Molly McNamara allowed. "I suspect he's a man of principle, deep down."

Danny Pogue had never thought of his partner as a man of principle, but maybe Molly had spotted something. While Bud was an incorrigible thief, he played by a strict set of rules. No guns, no violence, no hard drugs—Danny Pogue supposed that these could be called principles. He hoped that Molly recognized that he, too, had his limits—moral borders he would not cross. Later on, when she was asleep, he would make a list.

He said, "So what are you gonna do now? Stay at it?"

"To tell the truth, I'm not certain." She put down the teacup and dabbed her swollen lips with a napkin. "I've had some experts go over Kingsbury's files. Lawyers, accountants, people sympathetic to the cause. They made up a cash-flow chart, ran the numbers up and down and sideways. They say it's all very interesting, these foreign companies, but it would probably take months for the IRS and Customs to sort it out; another year for an indictment. We simply don't have that kind of time."

"Shoot," said Danny Pogue. He hadn't said "shoot" since the third grade, but he'd been trying to clean up his language in Molly's presence.

"I'm a little discouraged," she went on. "I guess I'd gotten my hopes up prematurely."

Danny Pogue felt so lousy that he almost told her about the other files, about the blackmail scam that he and Bud Schwartz were running on the great Francis X. Kingsbury.

He said, "There's nothing we can do? Just let him go ahead and murder off them butterflies and snails?" Molly had given him a magazine clipping about the rare tropical snails of Key Largo.

She said, "I didn't say we're giving up—"

"Because we should talk to Bud. He'll think a something."

"Every day we lose precious time," Molly said. "Every day they're that much closer to pouring the concrete."

Danny Pogue nodded. "Let's talk to Bud. Bud's sharp as a tack about stuff like this—"

Molly stopped rocking and raised a hand. "I heard something, didn't you?"

From the kitchen came muffled percussions of a struggle—men grunting, something heavy hitting a wall, a jar breaking.

Danny Pogue was shaking when he stood up. The bum foot made him think twice about running.

"Hand me the purse," Molly said. "I'll need my gun."

But Danny Pogue was frozen to the pine floor. His eyelids fluttered and his arms stiffened at his side. All he could think was: *Somebody's killing Bud!*

"Danny, did you hear me? Get me my purse!"

A block of orange appeared in the hallway. It was a tall man in a bright rainsuit and a moldy-looking shower cap. He had a damp silvery beard and black wraparound sunglasses and something red fastened to his neck. The man carried Bud Schwartz in a casual way, one arm around the midsection. Bud Schwartz was limp, gasping, flushed in the face.

Danny Pogue's tongue was as dry as plaster when the stranger stepped out of the shadow.

"Oh, it's you," Molly McNamara said. "Now be careful, don't hurt that young man."

The stranger dropped Bud Schwartz butt-first on the pine and said, "I caught him putting somebody's fingertip in a Mason jar."

"I'm the one who told him to," said Molly. "Now, Governor, you just settle down."

"What happened to you?" the stranger demanded. "Who did this to you, Miss McNamara?"

He took off the sunglasses and glared accusingly at Danny Pogue, who emitted a pitiful hissing noise as he shook his head. Bud Schwartz, struggling to his feet, said: "It wasn't us, it was some damn Cuban."

"Tell me a name," said the stranger.

"I don't know," said Molly McNamara, "but I got a good bite out of him."

"The finger," Bud Schwartz explained, still gathering his breath.

The stranger knelt beside the rocking chair and gently examined the raw-looking cuts and bruises on Molly's face. "This is . . . intolerable." He was whispering to himself and no one else. "This is barbarism."

Molly touched the visitor's arm and said, "I'll be all right. Really."

Bud Schwartz and Danny Pogue had seen men like this only in prison, and not many. Wild was the only way to describe the face . . . wild and driven and fearless, but not necessarily insane. It would be foolish, perhaps even fatal, to assume the guy was spaced.

He turned to Bud Schwartz and said, "How about giving me that Cuban's nub."

"I dropped it on the floor." Bud Schwartz thought: Christ, he's *not* going to make me go pick it up, is he?

Danny Pogue said, "No sweat, I'll find it."

"No," said the man in the orange rainsuit. "I'll grab it on the way out." He squeezed Molly's hands and stood up. "Will you be all right?"

"Yes, they're taking good care of me."

The stranger nodded at Bud Schwartz, who couldn't help but notice that one of the man's eyes was slipping out of the socket. The man calmly reinserted it.

"I didn't mean to hurt you," he said to Bud Schwartz. "Well, actually, I *did* mean to hurt you."

Molly explained: "He didn't know you fellows were my guests, that's all."

"I'll be in touch," said the stranger. He kissed Molly on the cheek and said he would check on her in a day or two. Then he was gone.

Bud Schwartz waited until he heard the door slam. Then he said: "What the hell was that?"

"A friend," Molly replied. They had known each other a long time. She had worked as a volunteer in his gubernatorial campaign, whipping up both the senior-citizen vote and the environmental coalitions. Later, when he quit office and vanished, Molly was one of the few who knew what happened, and one of the few who understood. Over the years he had kept in touch in his own peculiar way—sometimes a spectral glimpse, sometimes a sensational entrance; jarring cameos that were as hair-raising as they were poignant.

"Guy's big," said Danny Pogue. "Geez, he looks like—did he do time? What's his story?"

"We don't want to know," Bud Schwartz said. "Am I right?"

"You're absolutely right," said Molly McNamara.

▼ ▼ ▼

Shortly before midnight on July 23, Jim Tile received a radio call that an unknown individual was shooting at automobiles on Card Sound Road. The trooper told the dispatcher he was en route, and that he'd notify the Monroe County Sheriff's Office if he needed backups—which he knew he wouldn't.

The cars were lined up on the shoulder of the road a half-mile east of the big bridge. Jim Tile took inventory from the stickers on the bumpers: two Alamos, a Hertz, a National and an Avis. The rental firms had started putting bumper plates on all their automobiles, which served not only as advertisement but as a warning to local drivers that a disoriented tourist was nearby. On this night, though, the bright stickers had betrayed their unsuspecting drivers. Each of the vehicles bore a single .45-caliber bullet hole in the left-front fender panel.

Jim Tile knew exactly what had happened. He took brief statements from the motorists, who seemed agitated by the suggestion that anyone would fire at them simply because they were tourists. Jim Tile assured them that this sort of thing didn't happen every day. Then he called Homestead for tow trucks to get the three rental cars whose engine blocks had been mortally wounded by the sniper in the mangroves.

One of the drivers, a French-Canadian textile executive, used a cellular phone to call the Alamo desk at Miami International Airport and explain the situation. Soon new cars were on the way.

It took Jim Tile several hours to clear the scene. A pair of Monroe

County deputies stopped by and helped search for shell casings until the mosquitoes drove them away. After the officers had fled, and after the tourists had motored north in a wary caravan of Thunderbirds, Skylarks and Zephyrs, Jim Tile got in his patrol car and mashed on the horn with both fists. Then he rolled up the windows, turned up the air conditioner and waited for his sad old friend to come out of the swamp.

▼ ▼ ▼

"I'm sorry." Skink offered the trooper a stick of EDTIAR insect repellent.

"You promised to behave," said Jim Tile. "Now you've put me in a tough position."

"Had to blow off some steam," Skink said. "Anyway, I didn't hurt anybody." He took off his sunglasses and tinkered unabashedly with the fake eyeball. "Haven't you ever had days like this? Days where you just had to go out and shoot the shit out of something, didn't matter what?"

Jim Tile sighed. "Rental cars?"

"Why the hell not."

The tension dissolved into weary silence. The men had talked of such things before. When Clinton Tyree was the governor of Florida, Jim Tile had been his chief bodyguard—an unusually prestigious assignment for a black state trooper. After Clinton Tyree resigned, Jim Tile immediately lost his job on the elite security detail. The new governor, it was explained, felt more comfortable around peckerwoods. By the end of that fateful week, Jim Tile had found himself back on road patrol, Harney County, night shifts.

Over the years he had stayed close to Clinton Tyree, partly out of friendship, partly out of admiration and partly out of certitude that the man would need police assistance now and then, which he had. Whenever Skink got restless and moved his hermitage to deeper wilderness, Jim Tile would quietly put in for a transfer and move, too. This meant more rural two-lanes, more night duty and more ignorant mean-eyed crackers—but the trooper knew that his friend would have done the same for him, had fortunes been reversed. Besides, Jim Tile was confident of his own abilities and believed that one day he'd be in charge of the entire highway patrol—dishing out a few special night shifts himself.

Usually Skink kept to himself, except for the occasional public sighting when he dashed out of the pines to retrieve a fresh opossum or squirrel off the road. Once in a while, though, something triggered him in a tumultuous way and the results were highly visible. Standing on the crowded Fort Lauderdale beach, he'd once put four rounds into the belly of an inbound Eastern 727. Another time he'd crashed the Miss Florida pageant and tearfully heaved a dead baby manatee on stage to dramatize the results of waterfront development. It was fortunate, in such instances, that no one had recognized the hoary cyclopic madman as Clinton Tyree; it was even more fortunate that Jim Tile had been around to help the ex-governor slip away safely and collect what was left of his senses.

Now, sitting in the trooper's patrol car, Skink polished his glass eye with a bandanna and apologized for causing his friend so much inconvenience. "If you've got to arrest me," he said, "I'll understand."

"Wouldn't do a damn bit of good," said Jim Tile. "But I tell you what—I'd appreciate if you'd let me know what's going on down here."

"The usual," Skink said. "The bad guys are kicking our collective ass."

"We got a dead body off the bridge, a guy named Angel Gaviria. You know about that, right?" The trooper didn't wait for an answer. "The coroner is saying suicide or accident, but I was there and I don't think it's either one. The deceased was a well-known scumbucket and they don't usually have the decency to kill themselves. Usually someone else does the honor."

"Jim, we live in troubled times."

"The other day I pull over a blue Ford sedan doing eighty-six down the bridge. Turns out to be a Feeb."

"FBI?" Skink perked up. "All the way down here?"

"Hawkins was his name. He badges me, we get to chatting. Turns out he's working a case at the Amazing Kingdom. Something to do with militant bunny huggers and missing blue-tongued rats." Jim Tile gave a lazy laugh. "Now this is the FBI, interviewing elves and cowboys and fairy princesses. I don't suppose you can fill me in."

Skink was pleased that the feds had taken notice of events in North Key Largo. He said, "All I know is bits and pieces."

"Speaking of which, what can you tell me about killer whales? This morning a semi rolls over and I got stinking gobs of dead whale all over my nice clean blacktop. I'm talking tonnage."

Skink said, "That would explain the buzzard shit on this state vehicle." Secretly he wished he would have been there to witness the spectacle.

"You think it's funny?"

"I think," said Skink, "you should prepare for the worst."

Jim Tile took off his Stetson and lowered his face in front of the dashboard vents; the cool air felt good on his cheeks. A gumdrop-shaped sports car blew by doing ninety-plus, and the trooper barely glanced up. He radioed the dispatcher in Miami and announced he was going off duty. "I'm tired," he said to Skink.

"Me, too. You haven't seen anybody from Game and Fish, have you?"

"The panther patrol? No, I haven't." Jim Tile sat up. "I haven't seen the plane in at least a month."

Skink said, "Must've broken down. Else they're working the Foka-hatchee."

"Listen," the trooper said, "I won't ask about the dead guy on the bridge, and I won't ask about the whale—"

"I had nothing whatsoever to do with the whale."

"Fair enough," said Jim Tile, "but what about torching those bull-dozers up on 905? Were you in on that?"

Skink looked at him blankly. The trooper described what had happened that very afternoon at the Falcon Trace construction project. "They're looking for a guy who used to work at the Kingdom. They say he's gone nuts. They say he's got a gun."

"Is that right?" Skink tugged pensively at his beard.

"Do you know this person?"

"Possibly."

"Then could you *possibly* get him a message to stop this shit before it gets out of hand?"

"It's already out of hand," Skink said. "The sons-of-bitches are beating up little old ladies."

"Damn." The trooper stared out the window of the car. A trio of mosquitoes bounced off the glass and circled his head. Skink reached over and snatched the insects out of the air. Then he opened the window and let them buzz away into the thick fragrant night.

Jim Tile said, "I'm worried about you."

Skink grinned. "That's a good one."

"Maybe I should haul you in after all."

"Wouldn't stick. No one saw me do it, and no one found the gun. Hell, they wouldn't even hold me overnight."

"Yeah, they would," Jim Tile said, "on my word."

Skink's smile went away.

The trooper said, "The charge wouldn't stick, that's true. But I could take you out of circulation for a month or two. Let the situation simmer down."

"Why?" Skink demanded. "You know I'm right. You know what I'm doing is right."

"Not shooting rental cars."

"A lapse of judgment," Skink admitted. "I said I was sorry, for God's sake."

Jim Tile put a hand on his friend's shoulder. "I know you think it's the right thing, and the cause is good. But I'm afraid you're gonna lose."

"Maybe not," Skink said. "I think the Mojo's rising."

The trooper always got lost when Skink started quoting old rock-and-roll songs; someday he was going to sit Skink's shiny ass down and make him listen to Aretha. Put some soul in his system. Jim Tile said, "I've got a life, too. Can't spend the rest of it looking out for you."

Skink sagged against the car door. "Jim, they're paving the god-damn island."

"Not the whole thing—"

"But this is how it begins," Skink said. "Jesus Christ, you ought to know. This is how it begins!"

There was no point in pushing it. The state had bought up nearly all North Key Largo for preservation; the Amazing Kingdom and the Falcon Trace property were essentially all that remained in private hands. Still, Skink was not celebrating.

Jim Tile said, "This guy you recruited—"

"I didn't recruit him."

"Whatever. He's in it, that's the main thing."

"Apparently so," Skink said. "Apparently he's serious."

"So locking you up won't do any good, will it? Not with him still out there." The trooper put on his hat and adjusted it out of habit. In the darkness of the car, Skink couldn't read the expression on his friend's face. Jim Tile said, "Promise me one thing, all right? Talk some sense to the boy. He's new at it, Governor, and he could get hurt. That stunt with the bulldozers, it's not cool."

"I know," said Skink, "but it's got a certain flair."

"Listen to me," Jim Tile said sternly. "Already he's got some serious people after his ass, you understand? There's things I can help with, and things I can't."

Skink nodded. "I'll talk to him, I promise. And thanks."

Then he was gone. Jim Tile reached across to shut the door and his arm instantly was enveloped by an influx of mosquitoes. Frenzied humming filled the car.

He stomped the accelerator and the big Crown Victoria sprayed a fusillade of gravel into the mangroves. Westbound at a hundred fifteen miles an hour, the trooper rolled down the windows to let the wind suck the bugs from the car.

"Two of them." His words were swallowed in the roar of the open night. "Now I got two of the crazy bastards."

21

Carrie Lanier's place was furnished as exquisitely as any mobile home. It had a microwave, an electric can opener, a stove, a nineteen-inch color TV, two paddle fans and a Naugahyde convertible sofa where Joe Winder slept. But there was no music, so on his third day as a fugitive Winder borrowed Carrie's car and went back to the apartment to retrieve his stereo system and rock tapes. He was not totally surprised to find that his place had been broken, entered and ransacked; judging by the viciousness of the search, Pedro Luz was the likely intruder. The inventory of losses included the portable television, three champagne glasses, a tape recorder, the plumbing fixtures, the mattress, a small Matisse print and the toaster. One of Nina's pink bras, which she had forgotten, had been desecrated ominously with cigarette burns, and hung from a Tiffany lamp. Also, the freshwater aquarium had been shattered, and the twin Siamese fighting fish had been killed. It appeared to Joe Winder that their heads were pinched off.

The stereo tuner and tape deck escaped harm, though the turntable was in pieces. A pair of hedge clippers protruded from one of the speakers; the other, fortunately, was undamaged.

"It's better than nothing," Joe Winder said when he got back to the trailer. "Low fidelity is better than no fidelity."

While he reassembled the components, Carrie Lanier explored the box of cassettes. Every now and then she would smile or go "Hmmm" in an amused tone.

Finally Winder looked up from the nest of colored wires and said, "You don't like my music?"

"I like it just fine," she said. "I'm learning a lot about you. We've got The Kinks. Seeger live at Cobo Hall. Mick and the boys."

"Living in the past, I know."

"Oh, baloney." She began to stack the tapes alphabetically on a shelf made from raw plywood and cinder blocks.

"Do you have a typewriter?" he asked.

"In the closet," Carrie said. "Are you going to start writing again?"

"I wouldn't call it writing."

She got out the typewriter, an old Olivetti manual, and made a place for it on the dinette. "This is a good idea," she said to Joe Winder. "You'll feel much better. No more shooting at heavy machinery."

He reminded her that he hadn't actually pulled the trigger on the bulldozers. Then he said, "I stopped writing a long time ago. Stopped being a journalist, anyway."

"But you didn't burn out, you sold out."

"Thanks," Winder said, "for the reminder."

It was his fault for staggering down memory lane in the first place. Two nights earlier, Carrie had quizzed him about the newspaper business, wanted to know what kind of stories he'd written. So he'd told her about the ones that had stuck with him. The murder trial of a thirteen-year-old boy who'd shot his little sister because she had borrowed his Aerosmith album without asking. The marijuana-smuggling ring led by a fugitive former justice of the Florida Supreme Court. The bribery scandal in which dim-witted Dade County building inspectors were caught soliciting Lotto tickets as payoffs. The construction of a $47 million superhighway by a Mafia contractor whose formula for high-grade asphalt included human body parts.

Joe Winder did not mention the story that had ended his career. He offered nothing about his father. When Carrie Lanier had asked why he'd left the newspaper for public relations, he simply said, "Because of the money." She had seemed only mildly interested in his short time as a Disney World flack, but was impressed by the reckless sexual behavior that had gotten him fired. She said it was a healthy sign that he had not become a corporate drone, that the spark of rebellion still glowed in his soul.

"Maybe in my pants," Winder said, "not in my soul."

Carrie repeated what she had told him the first night: "You could always go back to being a reporter."

"No, I'm afraid not."

"So what is it you want to type—love letters? Maybe a confession?" Mischievously she tapped the keys of the Olivetti, two at a time, as if she were playing "Chopsticks."

The trailer was getting smaller and smaller. Joe Winder felt the heat lick at his eardrums. He said, "There's a reason you've hidden that gun."

"Because it's not your style." Carrie slapped the carriage and made the typewriter ring. "God gave you a talent for expression, a gift with the language."

Winder moaned desolately. "Have you ever read a single word I've written?"

"No," she admitted.

"So my alleged talent for expression, this gift—"

"I'm giving you the benefit of the doubt," she said. "The fact is, I don't trust you with a firearm. Now come help me open the wine."

▼ ▼ ▼

Every evening at nine sharp, visitors to the Amazing Kingdom of Thrills gathered on both sides of Kingsbury Lane, the park's main thoroughfare, to buy overpriced junk food and await the rollicking pageant that was the climax of the day's festivities. All the characters in the Kingdom were expected to participate, from the gunslingers to the porpoise trainers to the elves. Sometimes a real marching band would accompany the procession, but in the slow months of summer the music was usually canned, piped in through the garbage chutes. Ten brightly colored floats comprised the heart of the parade, although mechanical problems frequently reduced the number of entries by half. These were organized in a story line based loosely on the settlement of Florida, going back to the days of the Spaniards. The plundering, genocide, defoliation and gang rape that typified the peninsula's past had been toned down for the sake of Francis X. Kingsbury's younger, more impressionable customers; also, it would have been difficult to find a musical score suitable to accompany a mass disemboweling of French Hugenots.

For the feel-good purposes of the Amazing Kingdom's nightly pageant, the sordid history of Florida was compressed into a series of amiable and bloodless encounters. Floats celebrated such fabricated milestones as the first beachfront Thanksgiving, when friendly settlers and gentle Tequesta Indians shared wild turkey and fresh coconut milk under the palms. It was a testament to Charles Chelsea's imagination (and mortal fear of Kingsbury) that even the most shameful episodes were reinterpreted with a positive commercial spin. A float titled "Migrants on a Mission" depicted a dozen cheery, healthful farm workers singing Jamaican folk songs and swinging their machetes in a precisely choreographed break-dance through the cane fields. Tourists loved it. So did the Okeechobee Sugar Federation, which had bankrolled the production in order to improve its image.

One of the highlights of the pageant was the arrival of "the legendary Seminole maiden" known as Princess Golden Sun. No such woman and no such lore ever existed; Charles Chelsea had invented her basically as an excuse to show tits and ass, and pass it off as ethnic culture. Traditional Seminole garb was deemed too dowdy for the parade, so Princess Golden Sun appeared in a micro-bikini made of simulated deerskin. The authentic Green Corn Dance, a sacred Seminole rite, was politely discarded as too solemn and repetitious; instead Golden Sun danced the *lambada*, a pelvic-intensive Latin step. Surrounded by ersatz Indian warriors wearing bright Brazilian slingshots, the princess proclaimed in song and mime her passionate love for the famous Seminole chieftain Osceola. At the news of his death, she broke into tears and vowed to haunt the Everglades forever in search of his spirit. The peak of the drama, and the parade, was the moment when Golden Sun mounted a wild panther (in this case, a heavily drugged African lioness) and disappeared from sight in a rising fog of dry ice.

It was the role most coveted among the female actors employed at the Amazing Kingdom, and for six months it had belonged to Annette Fury, a dancer of mountainous dimensions whose previous job was as a waitress at a topless doughnut shop in Fort Lauderdale. A competent singer, Miss Fury had done so well with the role of Princess Golden Sun that the newspaper in Key Largo had done a nice write-up, including a photograph of Miss Fury straddling the bleary-eyed cat. The reporter had been careful to explain that the spavined animal was not actually a Florida panther, since real panthers were all but extinct. Given Princess Golden Sun's appearance, it was doubtful that a single reader even noticed the lion in the picture. Miss Fury's pose—head flung back, eyes closed, tongue between the teeth—was suggestive enough to provoke indignant outcries from a fundamentalist church in Big Pine Key, as well as the entire Seminole Nation, or what was left of it. At the first whiff of controversy, Charles Chelsea swiftly purchased the negatives from the newspaper and converted the most provocative one to a color postcard, which went on sale for $1.95 in all gift shops in the Amazing Kingdom of Thrills. As far as Chelsea was concerned, a star had been born.

On the night of July 25, however, Annette Fury's stint as Princess Golden Sun ended abruptly in a scandal that defied even Chelsea's talents for cosmetic counter-publicity. Shortly before the pageant, the dancer had ingested what were probably the last three Quaalude tablets in the entire continental United States. She had scrounged the dusty pills from the stale linty recesses of her purse, and washed them down with a warm bottle of Squirt. They had kicked in just as the float made the wide horseshoe turn onto Kingsbury Lane. By the time it rolled past the Cimarron Saloon, Annette Fury was bottomless, having surrendered her deerskin costume to a retired postal worker who had brought his wife and family all the way from Providence, Rhode Island. By the time the float reached the Wet Willy, the stone-faced Indian entourage of Princess Golden Sun had been augmented by nine rowdy Florida State fraternity men, who were taking turns balancing the drowsy young maiden on their noses, or so it must have appeared to the children in the audience. Afterwards, several parents threatened to file criminal obscenity charges against the park. They were appeased by a prompt written apology signed by Francis X. Kingsbury, and a gift of laminated lifetime passes to the Amazing Kingdom. Reluctantly, Charles Chelsea advised the Talent Manager to inform Annette Fury that her services were no longer required. The following day, Carrie Lanier was told that the role of Princess Golden Sun was hers if she wanted it. This was after they'd asked for her measurements.

So tonight she'd splurged on a bottle of Mondavi.

"To the late Robbie Raccoon," Carrie said, raising her glass.

"No one did him better," said Joe Winder.

He put on a tape of Dire Straits and they both agreed that it sounded pretty darn good, even with only one speaker. The wine was tolerable, as well.

Carrie said, "I told them I want a new costume."

"Something in beads and grass would be authentic."

"Also, no lip-synching," she said. "I don't care if the music's canned, but I want to do my own singing."

"What about the lion?" Joe Winder asked.

"They swear she's harmless."

"Tranked out of her mind is more like it. I'd be concerned, if I were you."

"If she didn't maul Annette, I can't imagine why she'd go after me."

A police siren penetrated the aluminum husk of the trailer; Joe Winder could hear it even over the guitar music and the tubercular groan of the ancient air conditioner. Parting the drapes, he watched one Metro squad car, and then another, enter the trailer park at high speed. Throwing dust, they sped past the turnoff to Carrie's place.

"Another domestic," Winder surmised.

"We average about four a week." Carrie refilled the wineglasses. "People who take love too damn seriously."

"Which reminds me." He opened his wallet and removed twelve dollars and placed it on a wicker table. "I was a very bad boy. I called her three times."

"You shmuck."

The Nina Situation. Every time he picked up the phone, it added four bucks to Carrie Lanier's bill. Worse, Nina pretended not to recognize his voice—stuck to the script to the bitter end, no matter how much he pleaded for her to shut up and listen.

"It is pathetic," Winder conceded.

"No other word for it."

"Haven't you ever been like this?" Obsessed is what he meant.

"Nope." Carrie shrugged. "I've got to be honest."

"So what's the matter with me?"

"You're just having a bad week."

She went to the bedroom and changed to a lavender nightshirt that came down to the knees—actually, a good four inches above the knees. Her hair was pulled back in a loose, sandy-colored ponytail.

Winder said, "You look sixteen years old." Only about three dozen other guys must have told her the same thing. His heart was pounding a little harder than he expected. "Tomorrow I'll get a motel room," he said.

"No, you're staying here."

"I appreciate it but—"

"Please," Carrie said. "Please stay."

"I've got serious plans. You won't approve."

"How do you know? Besides, I'm a little nervous about this new job. It's nice to have someone here at the end of the day, someone to talk with."

Gazing at her, Winder thought: God, don't do this to me. Don't make me say it.

But he did: "You just want to keep an eye on me. You're afraid I'll screw everything up."

"You're off to a pretty good start."

"It's only fair to warn you: I'm going after Kingsbury."

"That's what I figured, Joe. Call it a wild hunch." She took his hand and led him toward the bedroom.

I'm not ready for this, Winder thought. Sweat broke out in a linear pattern on the nape of his neck. He felt as if he were back in high school, the day the prettiest cheerleader winked at him in biology class; at the time, he'd been examining frog sperm under a microscope, and the wink from Pamela Shaugnessy had fractured his concentration. It had taken a month or two for Joe Winder to recover, and by then Pamela was knocked up by the co-captain of the junior wrestling squad. The teacher said that's what she got for not paying attention in class.

The sheets in Carrie Lanier's bedroom were rose, the blanket was plum. A novel by Anne Tyler was open on the bedstand, next to a bottle of nose drops.

A fuzzy stuffed animal sat propped on the pillow: shoe-button eyes, round ears and short whiskers. Protruding slightly from its upturned, bucktoothed mouth was a patch of turquoise cotton that could only be a tongue.

"Violet the Vole," Carrie explained. "Note the sexy eyelashes."

"For Christ's sake," Joe Winder said.

"The Vance model comes with a tiny cigar."

"How much?" Winder asked.

"Eighteen ninety-five, plus tax. Mr. X ordered a shipment of three thousand." Carrie stroked his arm. "Come on, I feel like cuddling."

Wordlessly, Winder moved the toy mango vole off the bed. The tag said it was manufactured in the People's Republic of China. What must they think of us on the assembly line? Winder wondered. Stuffed rats with cigars!

Carrie Lanier said, "I've got the jitters about singing in the parade. I don't look much like a Seminole."

Winder assured her she would do just fine. "Listen, I need to ask a favor. If you say no, I'll understand."

"Shoot."

"I need you to steal something for me," he said.

"Sure."

"Just like that?"

Carrie said, "I trust you. I want to help."

"Do you see the possibilities?"

"Surprise me." she said.

"Don't worry, it won't be dangerous. A very modest effort, as larcenies go."

"Sure. First thing tomorrow."

"Why are you doing this?" he asked.

"Because it's a fraud, the whole damn place. But mainly because an innocent man is dead. I liked Will Koocher." She paused. "I like his wife, too."

She didn't have to add the last part, but Winder was glad she did. He said, "You might lose your job."

Carrie smiled. "There's always dinner theater."

It seemed a good time to break the ice, so he tried—a brotherly peck on the cheek.

"Joe," she murmured, "you kiss like a parakeet."

"I'm slightly nervous myself."

Slowly she levered him to the bed, pinning his arms. "Why," she said, giggling, "why are you so nervous, little boy?"

"I really don't know." Her breasts pressed against his ribs, a truly wonderful sensation. Winder decided he could spend the remainder of his life in that position.

Carrie said, "Lesson Number One: How to smooch an Indian maiden."

"Go ahead," said Winder. "I'm all lips."

"Now do as I say."

"Anything," he agreed. "Anything at all."

As they kissed, an unrelated thought sprouted like a mushroom in the only dim crevice of Joe Winder's brain that was not fogged with lust.

The thought was: If I play this right, we won't need the gun after all.

22

Pedro Luz was in Francis Kingsbury's den when the blackmailers called. He listened to Kingsbury's half of the conversation, a series of impatient grunts, and said to Churrito, "Looks like we're in business."

Kingsbury put down the phone and said, "All set. Monkey Mountain at four sharp. In front of the baboons."

Monkey Mountain was a small animal park off Krome Avenue, a cut-rate imitation of the venerable Monkey Jungle. To Pedro Luz, it didn't sound like an ideal place to kill a couple of burglars.

With a snort, Kingsbury said, "These assholes, who knows where they get these cute ideas. Watching television, maybe."

"What is this monkey place?" Churrito asked.

"For Christ's sake, like the name says, it's basically monkeys. Two thousand of the damn things running all over creation." Kingsbury disliked monkeys and had summarily vetoed plans for a Primate Pavilion at the Amazing Kingdom of Thrills. He felt that apes had limited commercial appeal; Disney had steered clear of them, too, for what that was worth.

"For one thing, they bite. And, two, they shit like a sewer pipe." Kingsbury put the issue to rest. "If they're so damn smart, how come they don't hold it. Like people."

"They tasty good," Churrito remarked, licking his lips. "Squirrel monkey is best, where I come from."

Pedro Luz sucked noisily on the open end of the IV tube. He had purchased a dozen clear bags of five-percent dextrose solution from a wholesale medical shop in Perrine. The steroid pills he pulverized with the butt of his Colt, and funneled the powder into the bags. No one at the gym had ever heard of getting stoked by this method; Pedro Luz boasted that it was all his idea, he'd never even checked with a doctor. The only part that bothered him was using the needle—a problematic endeavor, since anabolic steroids were usually injected into muscle, not veins. Whenever Pedro Luz was having second thoughts, he'd yank out the tube and insert it directly in his mouth.

Sitting in Kingsbury's house, it gave him great comfort to feel again these magnificent potent chemicals flooding his system. With nourishment came strength, and with strength came confidence. Pedro Luz was afraid of nothing. He felt like stepping in front of a speeding bus, just to prove it.

Churrito pointed at the intravenous rig and said: "Even monkeys aren't that stupid."

"Put a lid on it," Pedro growled. He thought: No wonder these dorks lost the war.

"Stuff make you bulls shrink up. Dick get leetle tiny." Churrito seemed unconcerned by the volcanic mood changes that swept over Pedro Luz every few hours. To Francis Kingsbury he said, "Should see the zits on his cholders."

"Some other time," Kingsbury said. "You guys, now, don't get into it. There's work to do—I want these assholes off my back, these fucking burglars, and I want the files. So don't start up with each other, I mean, save your energy for the job."

Pedro Luz said, "Don't worry."

The phone rang and Kingsbury snatched it. The call obviously was long-distance because Kingsbury began to shout. Something about a truck accident ruining an important shipment of fish. The caller kept cutting in on Kingsbury, and Kingsbury kept making half-assed excuses, meaning some serious money already had changed hands.

When Kingsbury hung up, he said, "That was Hong Kong. Some cat-food outfit, I set up this deal and it didn't work out. What the hell, they'll get their dough back."

"My uncle had a fish market," remarked Pedro Luz. "It's a very hard business."

Without warning Mrs. Kingsbury came into the room. She wore terry-cloth tennis shorts and the top half of a lime-colored bikini. She nodded at Churrito, who emitted a low tomcat rumble. Pedro Luz glowered at him.

She said, "Frankie, I need some money for my lessons."

Under his breath, Churrito said, "I give her some lessons. Chew bet I will."

Kingsbury said, "I just gave you—was it yesterday?—like two hundred bucks."

"That was yesterday." Mrs. Kingsbury's eyes shifted to Pedro Luz, and the bottle of fluid on the hanger. "What's the matter with him?" she asked.

"One of them crash diets," said her husband.

Churrito said, "Yeah, make your muscles get big and your dick shrivel up like a noodle."

Pedro Luz reddened. "It's vitamins, that's all." He gnawed anxiously on the end of the tube, as if it were a piece of beef jerky.

"What kind of vitamins?" asked Kingsbury's wife.

"For men," said Pedro Luz. "Men-only vitamins."

As always, it was a test to be in the same room with Mrs. Kingsbury and her phenomenal breasts. Pedro Luz had given up sex three years earlier in the misinformed belief that ejaculation was a waste of precious hormones. Somehow, Pedro Luz had acquired the false notion that semen was one-hundred-percent pure testosterone, and consequently he was distraught when a popular weightlifter magazine reported that the average sexually active male would squirt approximately 19.6 gallons in a lifetime. For a fitness fiend such as Pedro Luz, the jism statistic was a shocker. To expend a single pearly drop of masculine fuel on a recreational pleasure was frivolous and harmful and plainly against God's plan; how could it do anything but weaken the body?

As it happened, Pedro Luz's fruit-and-steroid diet had taken the edge off his sex drive anyway. Abstinence had not proved to be difficult, except when Mrs. Kingsbury was around.

"I don't like needles," she announced. "I don't like the way they prick."

Again Churrito began to growl lasciviously. Pedro Luz said, "After a while, you don't even notice." He showed Mrs. Kingsbury how the IV rig moved on wheels.

"Like a shopping cart," she said gaily. Her husband handed her a hundred-dollar bill and she waved goodbye.

"There she goes," Kingsbury said. "Pedro, did you show your little buddy the golf painting? The one we did at Biltmore?"

"I saw," Churrito said. "In the living room."

"Those are the real McCoys," said Kingsbury.

Churrito looked perplexed. "McCoys?"

"Her tits, I mean. How you say, *hoot-aires?*" Kingsbury cackled. "Now, about this afternoon, these assholes—I'm not interested in details. Not at all interested."

That was fine with Pedro Luz. He'd skipped the details the last time, too, when they had roughed up the old lady at the condo. Although Churrito had nagged him to lighten up, the beating had been therapeutic for Pedro, a venting of toxic brain fumes. Like the rush he got while pinching the heads off Joe Winder's goldfish.

"I doubt this monkey place will be crowded," Kingsbury was saying, "except for the baboons."

"We'll be careful," Pedro Luz assured him.

"You get caught, no offense, but I don't know you. Never seen you bastards before in my life."

"We won't get caught."

Kingsbury snapped his fingers. "The files, I'll give you a list. Don't do anything till you get my files back. After that, it's your call."

Pedro Luz looked at his wristwatch and said it was time to go. The wheels on the IV rig twittered as it followed him to the door.

"I wanted to ask," Churrito said, "is it okay I look at the pitcher again? The one with your wife and those real McCoys."

"Be my guest," said Kingsbury, beaming. "That's what it's there for."

▼ ▼ ▼

One problem, Bud Schwartz realized, was that he and his partner had never done a blackmail before. In fact, he wasn't sure if it was blackmail or extortion, technically speaking.

"Call it a trade," said Danny Pogue.

Bud Schwartz smiled. Not bad, he thought. A trade it is.

They were waiting in the rented Cutlass in the parking lot of Monkey Mountain. Mrs. Kingsbury's chrome-plated pistol lay on the seat between them. Neither of them wanted to handle it.

"Christ, I hate guns," said Bud Schwartz.

"How's your hand?"

"Getting there. How's your foot?"

"Pretty good." Danny Pogue opened a bag of Burger King and the oily smell of hot fries filled the car. Bud Schwartz rolled down the window and was counter-assailed by the overpowering odor of monkeys.

Chewing, Danny Pogue said, "I can't get over that guy in the house, Molly's friend. Just come right in."

"Bigfoot," said Bud Schwartz, "without the manners."

"I just hope he don't come back."

"You and me both."

Bud Schwartz was watching out for Saabs. Over the phone Kingsbury had told him he'd be driving a navy Saab with tinted windows; so far, no sign of the car.

He asked his partner: "You ever done a Saab?"

"No, they all got alarms," said Danny Pogue. "Like radar is what I heard. Just look at 'em funny, and they go off. Same with the Porsches, I fucking whisper just walkin' by the damn things."

At two minutes after four, Bud Schwartz said it was time to get ready. Gingerly he put the gun in his pocket. "Leave the files under the seat," he said. "We'll make the trade after we got the money."

At the ticket window they got a map of Monkey Mountain. It wasn't exactly a sprawling layout.

"Hey, they even got a gorilla," said Danny Pogue, "name of Brutus. From the picture it looks like an African silverback."

"Fascinating," Bud Schwartz said. He'd had about enough of animal lore. Lately Danny Pogue had been spending too many hours watching wildlife documentaries on the Discovery Channel. It was all he talked about, he and Molly, and it was driving Bud Schwartz up the wall. One night, instead of the Cubs game, he had to sit through ninety minutes of goddamn hummingbirds. To Bud Schwartz they resembled moths with beaks; he got dizzy watching the damn things, even the slow-motion parts. Danny Pogue, on the other hand, had been enthralled. The fact that hummingbirds also inhabited North Key Largo heightened his sense of mission against Francis X. Kingsbury.

As they set out for the Baboon Tree, Danny Pogue said, "Why'd you pick this place, Bud?"

" 'Cause it's out in public. That's how you do these things, extortions."

"Are you sure?"

The visitor paths through Monkey Mountain were enclosed by chicken wire, giving the effect that it was the humans who were encaged while the wild beasts roamed free. Bud Schwartz was uncomfortable with this arrangement. Above his head, screeching monkeys loped along the mesh, begging for peanuts and crackers that Bud Schwartz had neglected to purchase at the concession stand. The impatient animals—howlers, gibbons, rhesus and spider monkeys—got angrier by the second. They bared yellow teeth and spit maliciously and shook the chicken wire. When Danny Pogue reached up to give one of them a shiny dime, it defecated in his hair.

"You happy now?" said Bud Schwartz.

"Damn, I can't believe it." Danny Pogue stopped to stick his head under a water fountain. "Don't they ever feed these goddamn things?" he said.

Above them, the gang of furry, shrieking, incontinent beggars had swollen to three dozen. Bud Schwartz and Danny Pogue shielded their heads and jogged the rest of the way to the Baboon Tree, an ancient ficus in the hub of a small plaza. Bud Schwartz was relieved to escape the yammering din and the rain of monkey feces. With a sigh he sat next to a Japanese family on a concrete bench. A moat of filmy brown water separated them from the bustling baboon colony in the big tree.

Danny Pogue said: "Know why they don't let the other monkeys together with the baboons?"

"Why not?"

"Because the baboons'd eat 'em."

"What a loss that would be."

"Let's go see Brutus."

"Danny, we're here on business. Now shut the fuck up, if you don't mind."

The Japanese husband apparently understood at least one word of English, because he gave Bud Schwartz a sharp look. The Japanese wife, who hadn't heard the profane remark, signaled that she would like a photograph of the whole family in front of the moat. Bud Schwartz motioned that his partner would do the honors; Danny Pogue had stolen many Nikons, but he'd never gotten a chance to use one. He arranged the Japanese in a neat row according to height, and snapped several pictures. In the back round were many wild-eyed baboons, including a young male gleefully abusing itself.

Bud Schwartz was glad the children weren't watching. After the Japanese had moved on, Danny Pogue said: "That was two hundred bucks right there, a Nikon with autofocus. I got a guy in Carol City fences nothing but cameras."

"I told you," said Bud Schwartz, "we're through with that. We got a new career." He didn't sound as confident as he would've liked. Where the hell was Kingsbury?

Danny Pogue joined him on the concrete bench. "So how much is he gonna bring?"

"Fifty is what I told him." Bud Schwartz couldn't get the tremor out of his voice. "Fifty thousand, if he ever shows up."

▼ ▼ ▼

In the parking lot, Pedro Luz and Churrito got into a heated discussion about bringing the IV rack. Churrito prevailed on the grounds that it would attract too much attention.

The first thing they noticed about Monkey Mountain was the stink, which Churrito likened to that of a mass grave. Next came the insistent clamor of the creatures themselves, clinging to the chickenwire and extending miniature brown hands in hopes of food. Churrito lit up a Marlboro and handed it to a rhesus, who took a sniff and hurled it back at him. Pedro Luz didn't think it was the least bit funny; he was sinking into one of his spells—every heartbeat sent cymbals crashing against his brainpan. An act of irrational violence was needed to calm the mood. It was fortunate, then, that the monkeys were safely on the other side of the chicken wire. Every time one appeared on the mesh over his head, Pedro Luz would jump up and smash at it savagely with his knuckles. This exercise was repeated every few seconds, all the way to the Baboon Tree.

The burglars—and it *had* to be them, greasy-looking rednecks—were sitting on a bench. Nobody else was around.

Pedro Luz whispered to Churrito: "Remember to get their car keys. They left the damn files in the car."

"What if they dint?"

"They did. Now be quiet."

Danny Pogue wasn't paying attention. He was talking about a TV program that showed a male baboon killing a zebra, that's how strong they were. A monkey that could kill something as big as a horse! Bud Schwartz was tuned out entirely; he was sizing up the two new men. The tall one, God Almighty, he was trouble. Built like a grizzly but that wasn't the worst of it; the worst was the eyes. Bud Schwartz could spot a doper two miles away; this guy was buzzing like a yellow jacket. The other one was no prize, dull-eyed and cold, but at least he was of normal dimensions. What caught Bud Schwartz's eye was the Cordovan briefcase that the smaller man was carrying.

"Get ready," he said to Danny Pogue.

"But that ain't Kingsbury."

"You don't miss a trick."

"Bud, I don't like this."

"Really? I'm having the time of my life." Bud Schwartz stood up and approached the two strangers. "Where's the old man?"

"Where's the files?" asked Pedro Luz.

"Where's the money?"

Churrito held up the briefcase. It was plainly stuffed with something, possibly fifty thousand in cash.

"Now," said Pedro Luz, "where's the damn files?"

"We give 'em to the old man and nobody else."

Pedro Luz checked over both shoulders to make sure there were no tourists around. In the same motion his right hand casually fished into the waistband of his trousers for the Colt. Before he could get to it, something dug into his right ear. It was another gun. *A burglar with a gun!* Pedro Luz was consumed with fury.

Bud Schwartz said, "Don't move." The words fluttered out. Danny Pogue gaped painfully.

Churrito laughed. "Good work," he said to Pedro Luz. "Excellent."

"I'm gonna be straight about this," said Bud Schwartz, "I don't know shit about guns."

The veins in Pedro Luz's neck throbbed like a tangle of snakes. He was seething, percolating in hormones, waiting for the moment. The gun barrel cut into his earlobe but he didn't feel a thing. Trying not to snarl, he said, "Don't push it, *chico.*"

"I ain't kidding," Bud Schwartz said in a voice so high he didn't recognize it as his own. "You even fart, I may blow your brains out. Explain that to your friend."

Churrito seemed indifferent to the idea. He shrugged and handed the briefcase to Danny Pogue.

"Open it," Bud Schwartz told him.

Again Pedro Luz asked, "Where are the files?" He anticipated that the burglars would soon be unable to answer the question, since he intended to kill them. And possibly Churrito while he was in the mood.

Even the baboons sensed trouble, for they had fallen silent in the boughs of the ficus. Danny Pogue opened the Cordovan briefcase and showed Bud Schwartz what was inside: sanitary napkins.

"Too bad," said Bud Schwartz. And it was too bad. He had no clue what to do next. Danny Pogue took one of the maxi-pads out of the briefcase and examined it, as if searching for insight.

Pedro Luz's steroid-marinated glands were starting to cook. Infused with the strength of a thousand warriors, he announced that he wouldn't let a mere bullet spoil Mr. Kingsbury's plan. He told Bud Schwartz to go ahead and fire, and went so far as to reach up and seize the burglar's arm.

As they struggled, Pedro Luz said, "Shoot me, you pussy! Shoot me now!"

Out of the corner of his eye, Bud Schwartz spotted Danny Pogue running away in the general direction of the gorilla compound—moving impressively for someone fresh off crutches.

Just as Pedro Luz was preparing to snap Bud Schwartz's arm like a matchstick, Mrs. Kingsbury's chrome-plated pistol shook loose from the burglar's fingers and flew over the moat. The gun landed in a pile of dead leaves at the foot of the ficus tree, where it was retrieved by a laconic baboon with vermilion buttocks. Bud Schwartz wasn't paying attention, what with Pedro Luz hurling him to the ground and kneeling on his neck and trying to twist his head off. Meanwhile the other man was going through Bud Schwartz's trousers in search of the car keys.

When Bud Schwartz tried to shout for help, Pedro Luz slapped a large moist hand over his mouth. It was then that Bud Schwartz spotted the bandaged nub of the right index finger, and assimilated in his dying deoxygenated consciousness the probability that this was the same goon who had brutalized Molly McNamara. The burglar decided, in the hastening gray twilight behind his eyeballs, that the indignity of being found mugged and dead in a monkey park might be mitigated by a final courageous deed, such as disfiguring a murderous steroid freak—which Bud Schwartz attempted to do by sucking Pedro Luz's hand into his jaws and chomping down with heedless ferocity.

The wailing of Pedro Luz brought the baboon colony to life, and a hellish chorus enveloped the three men as they fought on the ground. A gunshot was heard, and the monkeys scattered adroitly to the highest branches of the graceful old tree.

Pedro Luz rolled off Bud Schwartz and groped with his bloody paw for the Colt. It was still in his waistband. Only two things prevented him from shooting the burglar: the sight of fifty chattering children skipping toward him down the monkey trail, and the sight of Churrito lying dead with a grape-sized purple hole beneath his left eye.

Pedro Luz pushed himself to his feet, stepped over the body and ran. Bud Schwartz did the same—much more slowly and in the opposite direction—but not before pausing to contemplate the visage of the dead Nicaraguan. Judging by the ironic expression on Churrito's face, he knew exactly what had happened to him.

Now the killer was halfway up the ficus tree, barking and slobbering and shaking the branches. Mrs. Kingsbury's gun glinted harmlessly in the brackish shallows, where the startled baboon had dropped it.

The oxygen returning to Bud Schwartz's head brought a chilling notion that maybe the monkey had been aiming the damn thing. Maybe he'd even done it before. Stranger things had occurred in Miami.

Bud Schwartz lifted the keys to the Cutlass from the dead man's hand and jogged away just as Miss Juanita Pedrosa's kindergarten class marched into the plaza.

23

Francis X. Kingsbury was on the thirteenth green at the Ocean Reef Club when Charles Chelsea caught up with him and related the problem.

"Holy piss," said Kingsbury as Jake Harp was about to putt. "If it's not one thing, it's—hell, you deal with it, Charlie. Isn't that what I pay you for, to deal with this shit?"

Jake Harp pushed the putt to the right. He looked up stonily and said, "Thank you both very much."

"Sorry," Chelsea said. "We've got a little emergency here."

Kingsbury said, "If you're gonna be a crybaby, Jake, then do it over. Take another putt. And you, Charlie, what emergency? This is nothing, a goddamn prank."

Charles Chelsea suggested that it was considerably more serious than a prank. "Every television station in South Florida received a copy, Mr. Kingsbury. Plus the *Herald* and the *New York Times*. We'll be getting calls all day, I expect."

He followed Kingsbury and Jake Harp to the fourteenth tee. "The reason I say it's serious, we've got less than a week until the Summerfest Jubilee." It was set for August 6, the day Kingsbury had rescheduled the arrival of the phony five-millionth visitor to the Amazing Kingdom of Thrills. The postponement caused by the truck accident had been a blessing in one way—it had given Charles Chelsea time to scout for a flashy new giveaway car. The "classic" Corvair had been junked in favor of a jet-black 300-Z, which had been purchased at bargain prices from the estate of a murdered amphetamine dealer. Chelsea was further buoyed by the news that NBC weatherman Willard Scott had tentatively agreed to do a live broadcast from the Kingdom on Jubilee morning, as long as Risk Management cleared it with the network.

Overall, the publicity chief had been feeling fairly positive about

Summerfest until some worm from the *Herald* called up to bust his hump about the press release.

What press release? Chelsea had asked.

The one about hepatitis, said the guy from the newspaper. The hepatitis epidemic among Uncle Ely's Elves.

In his smoothest, most controlled tone, Chelsea had asked the newspaper guy to please fax him a copy. The sight of it creeping off the machine had sent a prickle down the ridge of his spine.

As Jake Harp prepared to tee off, Chelsea showed the press release to Francis X. Kingsbury and said, "It's ours."

"What the hell you—I don't get it. Ours?"

"Meaning it's the real thing. The stationery is authentic."

Kingsbury frowned at the letterhead. "Jesus Christ, then we got some kinda mole. That what you're saying? Somebody on the inside trying to screw with our plans?"

"Not necessarily," Chelsea said.

Jake Harp hooked his drive into a fairway bunker. He said, "Don't you boys know when to shut up."

This time Charles Chelsea didn't bother to apologize. He itched to remind Jake Harp that dead silence hadn't helped him one bit in the '78 Masters, when he'd four-putted the third hole at Augusta and let Nicklaus, Floyd, everybody and their mothers blow right past him.

Kingsbury said, "Probably it's some bastard from Disney. A ringer, hell, I should've known. Somebody they sent just to screw me up for the summer."

"It's nobody on the inside," said Chelsea. "It wasn't done on one of our typewriters."

"Who then? I mean, why in the name of fuck?"

Jack Harp marveled at the inventive construction of Kingsbury's profanity. He imagined how fine it would feel to take a two-iron and pulverize the man's skull into melon rind. Instead he said, "You're up, Frank."

Charles Chelsea stood back while Kingsbury took a practice swing. It was not a thing of beauty. From the safety of the cart path, Chelsea said, "I think it's Joe Winder. The fellow we fired last week. The one we've had some trouble with."

"What makes you so sure—wait, Christ, didn't he used to work for The Rat?"

"Yes, briefly. Anyway, there's some stationery missing from Publicity. I thought you ought to know."

"How much?"

"Two full boxes," Chelsea replied. Enough to do one fake press release every day for about three years. Or one hundred a day until the Summerfest Jubilee.

Kingsbury knocked his drive down the left side of the fairway and grunted in approval. He plopped his butt in the golf cart and said to Chelsea: "Let me see it one more time."

Chelsea gave him the paper and climbed on the back of the cart, wedging himself between the two golf bags. He wondered if this was how the Secret Service rode when the President was playing.

Pointing over Kingsbury's shoulder, Chelsea said, "It's definitely Winder's style. I recognize some of the dry touches."

The press release said:

> Medical authorities at the Amazing Kingdom of Thrills announced today that the outbreak of viral hepatitis that struck the popular theme park this week is "practically under control."
>
> Visitors to the Amazing Kingdom are no longer in immediate danger of infection, according to specialists who flew in from the National Centers for Disease Control in Atlanta. So far, five cases of hepatitis have been positively diagnosed. All the victims were actors who portray Uncle Ely's Elves, a troupe of mischievous trolls who frolic and dance in daily performances throughout the park.
>
> Experts say there is no reason to suspect that the highly contagious disease is being transmitted in the food and beverages being served at the Amazing Kingdom. A more likely source is the vending machine located in a dressing room often used by Uncle Ely's Elves and several other performers.
>
> Charles Chelsea, vice president in charge of publicity, said: "We know that the candy machine down there hadn't been serviced for about seven months. There are serious questions regarding the freshness and edibility of some of the chocolate products, as well as the breath mints. All items have been removed from the machine and are presently being tested for contamination."
>
> Although no cases of hepatitis have been reported among visitors to the Amazing Kingdom, Monroe County health officials advise testing for anyone who has had recent contact with any of Uncle Ely's Elves —or food products handled by the elves. This advi-

sory applies to all persons who might have posed for photographs or danced with one of the little people during the Nightly Pageant of Tropics.

Moe Strickland, the veteran character actor who popularized the role of Uncle Ely, said the stricken performers are resting quietly at Baptist Hospital in Miami, and are expected to recover. He added, "I'm worried about what the kids will think when they don't see us around the park for a few weeks. I guess we'll have to tell them that Uncle Ely took the elves on a summer vacation to Ireland, or wherever it is that elves go."

Chelsea said there are no plans to close the Amazing Kingdom to the public. "This was a freakish incident, and we are confident that the worst is over," he said. "From now on, we get back to the business of having fun."

Beginning tonight, the Amazing Kingdom of Thrills will present a multi-media tribute to Vance and Violet, the last surviving blue-tongued mango voles. The gentle animals were stolen from the park ten days ago in a daring daylight robbery, and later died tragically.

The show will be presented at 8 p.m. in the Rare Animal Pavilion, and will feature color slides, videotapes, rare outdoor film footage and a Claymation exhibit. Admission is $4 for adults, $2.50 for children.

Kingsbury reread the press release as they jolted down the cart path with Jake Harp at the wheel. When they stopped next to his golf ball, Kingsbury shoved the paper back at Chelsea. "It sounds awfully damn . . . what's the word?"

"Authentic, sir. This is what we're up against."

"I mean, hell, it sure puts me off the candy machines."

"It's fooling the reporters, too," Chelsea said.

"You say this maniac's got—what, two goddamn boxes?"

"That's what's missing."

Jake Harp said, "If you're not going to play that lie, pick the damn thing up."

Kingsbury paid no attention. "I guess we'll need—obviously, what am I saying!—get a new letterhead for Publicity."

"I ordered it this morning," Chelsea reported. "I'm afraid it won't be ready for two weeks."

"Don't tell me—God, two weeks. So what do we do if your theory's right? If it's Winder, I mean." Kingsbury took his stance and rifled a six-iron dead into the heart of a tea-colored pond.

"See what happens when you run your mouth," said Jake Harp.

"The options are limited," Chelsea told Kingsbury. "Do we come right out and admit it's a fake? A disgruntled former employee, blah, blah, blah. Or do we roll with it? Take the hit and hope it's over."

"Is that your advice? Roll with it?"

"For now, yes."

"Me, too," Francis Kingsbury said. "Besides, Pedro's on the case." A brand-new golf ball appeared in Kingsbury's right hand, and he dropped it with a flourish on the fairway. This time he nailed the six-iron to the center of the green, fifteen feet from the flag.

Jake Harp blinked sullenly and said nothing.

▼ ▼ ▼

A duel.

That's how Charles Chelsea saw it. The ultimate test of skills. He warmed up the word processor and began to write:

> The outbreak of viral hepatitis among performers at the Amazing Kingdom of Thrills was not as serious as first believed, according to a respected epidemiologist who visited the popular tourist attraction Friday.
>
> The disease was confined to only four persons, none of whom became seriously ill, according to Dr. Neil Shulman, an international expert on liver pathology.
>
> "Visitors to the Amazing Kingdom are in absolutely no danger," Dr. Shulman declared. "There's no evidence that the disease originated here. The food and beverages I've sampled are perfectly safe—and tasty, too!"
>
> Initially it was believed that five persons were infected with hepatitis. Later, however, it was determined that one of the ill employees was actually suffering from gallstones, a common and nontransmittable disorder.
>
> The four men who were diagnosed with hepatitis all began showing symptoms on Wednesday morning. Contrary to earlier reports, however, the victims did not contract the virus from contaminated candy pur-

chased at a vending machine in the Amazing Kingdom. It is now believed that the men—all of whom portray members of Uncle Ely's Elves—became infected during a recent promotional trip to the Caribbean aboard a Nassau-based cruise ship.

Moe Strickland, the crusty character actor who immortalized the character of Uncle Ely, recalled how some of his troupe had complained of "funky-tasting lobster" during the four-day excursion. Viral hepatitis has an incubation period of 15 to 45 days.

Those who were stricken spent only one night in the hospital, and are now resting comfortably at home. Although their conditions are good, they will not return to work until doctors are sure that they are not contagious.

Dr. Shulman, who has written extensively for national medical journals, said he is certain that the disease has been contained, and that no other employees or visitors to the Amazing Kingdom are in jeopardy. "It's as safe as can be," he said. "In fact, I'm staying over the weekend myself so I can ride the new porpoise!"

Skimming the text, Charles Chelsea changed the word "outbreak" to "incidence." Then, with uncharacteristic fire, he punched the Send button.

To an invisible enemy he snarled, "All right, Joey. It's go time."

The queasy feeling that always accompanied the prospect of bad publicity had given way to a fresh sense of challenge; Chelsea felt he'd been training his whole professional life for such a test. He was up against an opponent who was talented, ruthless and quite possibly insane.

As much as Chelsea feared and distrusted Winder, he respected his creative skills: the vocabulary, so rich in adjectives; the glib turn of an alliterative phrase—and, of course, the speed. Joe Winder was the fastest writer that Chelsea had ever seen.

Now it was just the two of them: Winder, holed up God knows where, hammering out inflammatory libels as fast as his fingers could fly. And on the other end, Chelsea himself, waiting to catch these malicious grenades and smother them. The alternative—meaning, to tell the truth—was unthinkable. To admit a hoaxster was loose, forging demented fantasies on Amazing Kingdom letterhead . . . what a story *that* would make. In their excitement the media would come all over themselves. Even worse, each publicity announcement from the theme park would be scrutinized severely by reporters and editors, whose careers are seldom enhanced by getting duped into print. One thing that Charles Chelsea (or any PR flack) didn't need was a more toxic level of skepticism and suspicion among the journalists he was supposed to manipulate.

So telling the truth about Joe Winder was out of the question. Whatever revolting fable Winder concocted next, Chelsea would be ready to extinguish it with press releases that were both calm and plausible. One pack of lies softening another.

It was going to be one roaring hell of a battle.

As the Publicity Department's fax machines were launching Chelsea's counterattack against the hepatitis scare, Moe Strickland arrived to bitch about sick pay and what the almighty Screen Actors Guild would say.

He lit up a cigar and said, "The union would go nuts."

"We don't recognize the union," Chelsea said coolly. "I really don't understand your objections, Moe. Most people would kill for two weeks off."

Moe Strickland protested with a wet cough. "You're docking us sick days, that's the objection. Because we're not really sick."

"That's something to be taken up with Personnel. It's simply not my bailiwick." Charles Chelsea waved his hands to clear the rancid smoke. The office was starting to smell like dead mice.

"I don't see why they can't just give us two weeks paid," said Moe Strickland, "and leave us our sick days. Whatever happened, it's sure not our fault."

"No, it's not," Chelsea agreed. "Listen to me, Moe. Uncle Ely and the Elves are on vacation, all right? They went to Ireland. That's the official story."

"For Christ's sake—Ireland? Does Ely sound like an Irish name?" Moe Strickland sneered in contempt.

"I'm not here to argue," Chelsea said. "But I do wish to caution you against speaking to the media. All interview requests are to be routed through me, understand?"

"You mean like the newspapers."

"Newspapers, television, anybody asking questions about a cruise. You tell them to call me. And make sure the elves do the same."

"What, now you don't trust us?"

"No interviews, Moe. The order comes straight from Mr. X."

"Figures," said Moe Strickland. "What's the name of that disease? Tell me again."

"Viral hepatitis."

"Sounds terrible."

"It's a nasty one," Chelsea conceded.

"Who in hell would make up a story like that?" The actor smacked on the soggy stump of cigar. "What kind of sick bastard would say such a thing?"

Chelsea did not reply. He was watching a string of brown drool make its way down Moe Strickland's snowy beard.

"I feel like suing the sonofabitch," Moe Strickland remarked.

Chelsea said, "Don't take it personally. It's got nothing to do with you."

"I never had hepatitis. Is it some kind of dick disease? Because if it is, we're definitely suing the bastard. The boys're as clean as a whistle down there and they can sure prove it."

"Moe," said Chelsea, "please settle down."

"Does this mean we can't march in the Jubilee?"

"Not as Uncle Ely and the Elves. We'll get you some other costumes—gunslingers, how about that?"

"Oh great, midget gunslingers. No thanks." On his way out the door, Moe Strickland spit something heavy into Charles Chelsea's wastebasket.

▼ ▼ ▼

That night, Channel 7 devoted forty seconds to the hepatitis scare, closing the piece with a sound-bite from Charles Chelsea, cool in a crisp blue oxford shirt and tortoiseshell eyeglasses. The glasses were a new touch.

Not bad, thought Joe Winder, if you like the George Will look.

He was watching the news with a notebook on his lap. He called toward the kitchen: "He got the number of victims down from five to four. Plus he's planted the idea that the disease was picked up in the Caribbean, not at the Amazing Kingdom. Pretty damn slick on short notice!"

Carrie Lanier was fixing popcorn. "So they're toughing it out," she said.

"Looks that way."

She came out and placed the bowl on the sofa between them. "They've got to be worried."

"I hope so." Joe Winder thanked her again for stealing the letterhead paper from the stockroom in the Publicity Department. "And for renting the fax," he added. "I'll pay you back."

"Not necessary, sir. Hey, I heard somebody shot up some rental cars on Card Sound Road."

"Yeah, it was on the news."

"Did they catch the guy?"

"No," he said, "and they won't." He wondered if Skink's sniper attack was the beginning of a major offensive.

Carrie pointed at the television. "Hey, look, it's Monkey Mountain!"

A blue body bag was being carried out of the amusement park. A florid middle-aged schoolteacher, a Miss Pedrosa, was being interviewed about what happened. She said her students thought the man was merely sleeping, not dead. The news reporter said the victim was believed to be a recent immigrant, a Latin male in his mid-thirties. A police detective at the scene of the shooting said it appeared to be a suicide. The detective's voice was nearly drowned out by the jabbering of angry baboons in a tree behind him.

Carrie said, "Well, Mr. X ought to be happy. Finally someplace else is getting bad press."

"Strange place for a suicide," observed Joe Winder.

Carrie Lanier stuffed a handful of popcorn into his mouth. "They gave me my new costume today. You're gonna die."

"Let's see."

It was a white fishnet tank suit. Carrie put it on and struck a Madonna pose. "Isn't it awful?" she said.

Joe Winder said she looked irresistibly slutty. "The Indians aren't going to like it, though."

"I've got a headband, too. And a black wig."

"The Seminoles didn't wear fishnets; they used them on bass. By the way, are those your nipples?"

"Who else's would they be?"

"What I mean is, isn't there supposed to be something underneath?"

"A tan body stocking," Carrie said. "I must've forgot to put it on."

Winder told her not to bother. Exuberantly she positioned herself on his lap and fastened her bare legs around his waist. "Before we make love," Carrie said, "you've got to hear the song."

It was a bastardized version of the famous production number in *Evita*. They both burst out laughing when she did the refrain. "I can't believe it," Joe Winder said.

Carrie kept singing, "Don't Cry for Me, Osceola!" Winder buried his face in her breasts. Unconsciously he began nibbling through the fishnet suit.

"Now stop." Carrie clutched the back of his head. "I've forgotten the rest of the words."

Still gnawing, Winder said, "I feel like a shark."

"You do indeed." She pulled him even closer. "I know a little boy who forgot to shave this morning, didn't he?"

"I was busy writing." A muffled voice rising out of her cleavage.

Carrie smiled. "I know you were writing, and I'm proud of you. What's the big news at the Kingdom tomorrow—typhoid? Trichinosis?"

He lifted his head. "No more diseases. From now on, it's the heavy artillery."

She kissed him on the nose. "You're a very sick man. Why do I like you so much?"

"Because I'm full of surprises."

"Oh, like this?" Carrie grabbed him and gave a little tug. "Is this for me?"

"If you're not careful."

"Hold still," she told him.

"Aren't you going to take off that outfit?"

"What for? Look at all these convenient holes. We've just got to get you lined up."

"It's a good thing," Joe Winder said, "it doesn't have gills."

He held his breath as Carrie Lanier worked on the delicate alignment. Then she adjusted the Naugahyde sofa cushion behind his head, and braced her hands on the windowsill. The lights from the highway skipped in her eyes, until she closed them. Slowly she started rocking and said, "Tonight we're shooting for four big ones."

"Excuse me?"

"I told you, Joe, I'm a very goal-oriented person."

"I think I'm tangled."

"You're doing fine," she said.

He was still hanging on, minutes later, when Carrie stopped moving.

"What is it?"

"Joe, did you go back to the apartment tonight?" She was whispering.

"Just for a minute. I needed some clothes."

"Oh boy."

"What's the matter?"

Carrie said, "Somebody's watching us. Somebody followed you here." She lowered herself until she was flat against him, so she couldn't be seen from the window. "It's a man," she said. "He's just standing out there."

"What's he look like?"

"Very large."

"Guess I'd better do something."

"Such as?"

"I'm not exactly sure," Joe Winder said. "I need to refocus here."

"In other words, you want me to climb off."

"Well, I think the mood has been broken."

"The thing is—"

"I know. We'll need a scissors." His fingers, his chin, everything was tangled in the netting.

Outside the trailer, something moved. A shadow flickering across the windowpane. Footsteps crunching on the gravel. Then a hand on the doorknob, testing the lock.

Carrie's muscles tightened. She put her lips to his ear. "Joe, are we going to die like this?"

"There are worse ways," he said.

And then the door buckled.

24

Skink said he was sorry, and turned away. Joe Winder and Carrie Lanier scrambled to disengage, tearing the fishnet suit to strings.

"I heard noises," said Skink. "Thought there might be trouble."

The adrenaline ebbed in a cold tingle from Winder's veins. Breathlessly he said, "How'd you know I was here?"

"Followed you from the apartment."

"In what—the bookmobile?"

"I've got friends," Skink said.

While Joe Winder fastened his trousers, Carrie Lanier dived into a University of Miami football jersey. Skink turned to face them, and Carrie gamely shook his hand. She said, "I didn't catch your name."

"Jim Morrison," said Skink. "*The* Jim Morrison."

"No, he's not," Winder said irritably.

Carrie smiled. "Nice to meet you, Mr. Morrison." Winder considered her cordiality amazing in view of Skink's menacing appearance.

Skink said, "I suppose he told you all about me."

"No," Carrie replied. "He didn't say a word."

Skink seemed impressed by Joe Winder's discretion. To Carrie he said: "Feel free to stare."

"I am staring, Mr. Morrison. Is that a snake you're eating?"

"A mud snake, yes. Medium-rare." He took a crackling bite and moved through the trailer, turning off the television and all the lights. "A precaution," he explained, peeking out a window.

In the darkness Carrie found Joe Winder's hand and squeezed it. Winder said, "This is the man who saved my life a couple weeks ago—the night I got beaten up, and you gave me a lift."

"I live in the hammocks," Skink interjected. "The heavy rains have brought out the snakes."

Winder wondered when he would get to the point.

Carrie said, "Can I ask about the red collar? Is it some sort of neck brace?"

"No, it isn't." Skink crouched on his haunches in front of them, beneath the open window. The highway lights twinkled in his sunglasses.

"Events are moving haphazardly," he said, gnawing a piece of the cooked reptile. "There needs to be a meeting. A confluence, if you will."

"Of whom?" Winder asked.

"There are others," Skink said. "They don't know about you, and you don't know about them." He paused, cocking an ear toward the ceiling. "Hear that? It's the plane. They've been tracking me all damn day."

Carrie gave Joe Winder a puzzled look. He said, "The rangers from Game and Fish—it's a long story."

"Government," Skink said. "A belated pang of conscience, at taxpayer expense. But Nature won't be fooled, the damage is already done."

Sensing trouble, Winder lurched in to change the subject. "So who are these mysterious others?"

"Remember that afternoon at the Amazing Kingdom, when a stranger gave you something?"

"Yeah, some old lady at the Rare Animal Pavilion. She handed me a note and then I got my lights punched out."

Skink said, "That was me who slugged you."

"What an odd relationship," Carrie remarked.

"My specialty," Joe Winder said. Then to Skink: "Can I ask why you knocked the door down tonight? Your timing stinks, by the way."

Skink was at the window again, lurking on the edge of the shadow. "Do you know anyone who drives a blue Saab?"

"No—"

"Because he was waiting at your apartment this morning. Big Cuban meathead who works at the park. He saw you arrive." Skink dropped down again. He said to Winder, "You were driving the young lady's car, right?"

"She loaned it to me. So what?"

"So it's got a parking sticker on the rear bumper."

"Oh shit, you're right." Joe Winder had completely forgotten; employees of the Amazing Kingdom were issued Petey Possum parking permits. Each decal bore an identification number. It was a simple matter to trace the car to Carrie Lanier.

"I need to go to fugitive school," Winder said. "This was really stupid."

Carrie asked Skink about the man in the blue Saab. "Did he follow Joe, too? Is he out there now?"

"He was diverted," Skink said, "but I'm sure he'll be here eventually. That's why we're leaving."

"No," Winder said, "I can't."

Skink asked Carrie Lanier for a paper napkin. Carefully he wrapped the uneaten segment of mud snake and placed it in a pocket of his blaze rainsuit.

He said, "There'll be trouble if we stay."

"I can't go," Winder insisted. "Look, the fax lines are already set up. Everything's in place right here."

"So you've got something more in mind?"

"You know I do. In fact, you've given me a splendid inspiration."

"All right, we'll wait until daybreak. Can you type in the dark?"

"It's been a while, but sure." Back in the glory days, Winder had once written forty inches in the blackness of a Gulfport motel bathroom—a Royal manual typewriter balanced on his lap. This was during Hurricane Frederic.

Skink said, "Get busy, genius. I'll watch the window."

"What can I do to help?" Carrie asked.

"Put on some Stones," said Skink.

"And some panties," Winder whispered.

She told him to hush and quit acting like an old prude.

▼ ▼ ▼

While the tow truck hooked up the Saab, Pedro Luz forced himself to reflect on events.

There he was, waiting for Winder to come out of the apartment when here comes this big spade highway patrolman knocking on the window of the car.

"Hey, there," he says from behind those damn reflector shades.

"Hey," says Pedro Luz, giving him the slight macho nod that says, I'm one of you, brother.

But the spade doesn't go for it. Asks for Pedro's driver's license and also for the registration of the Saab. Looks over the papers and says, "So who's Ramex Global?"

"Oh, you know," Pedro says, flashing his old Miami PD badge.

Trooper goes "Hmmm." Just plain "Hmmm." And then the fucker jots down the badge number, like he's going to check it out!

Pedro resists the urge to reach under the seat for his gun. Instead he says, "Man, you're burning me. I'm sitting on a dude out here."

"Yeah? What's his name?"

Pedro Luz says, "Smith. José Smith." It's the best he can do on short notice, with his brain twitching all crazy inside his skull. "Man, you and that marked unit are burning me bad."

Trooper doesn't act too damn concerned. "So you're a police officer, is that right?"

"Hell," Pedro says, "you saw the badge."

"Yes, I sure did. You're a long way from the city."

"Hey, *chico*, we're in a war, remember."

"Narcotics?" The trooper sounds positively intrigued. "This man Smith, he's some big-time dope smuggler, eh?"

"Was," Pedro says. "He sees your car sitting out here, he's back in wholesale footwear."

"Hmmm," the spade trooper says again. Meanwhile Pedro's fantasizing about grabbing him around the middle and squeezing his guts out both ends, like a very large tube of licorice toothpaste.

"Don't tell me you're gonna run my tag," Pedro says.

"Nah." But the trooper's still leaning his thick black arms against the door of the Saab, his face not a foot from Pedro's, so that Pedro can see himself twice in the mirrored sunglasses. Now the trooper says: "What happened to your finger?"

"Cat bite."

"Looks like it took the whole top joint."

"That's right," says Pedro, aching all over, wishing he'd brought his intravenous bag of Winstrol-V. Talking high-octane. Same stuff they use on horses. One thousand dollars a vial, and worth every penny.

Trooper says, "Must've been some cat to give you a bite like that."

"Yeah, I ought to put the damn thing to sleep."

"Sounds like a smart idea," says the trooper, "before he bites you someplace else."

And then the sonofabitch touches the brim of his Stetson and says so long. Like John Fucking Wayne.

And here comes Winder, cruising out of the apartment with an armful of clothes. Gets in the car—not his car, somebody else's; somebody with an employee sticker from the Kingdom—and drives off with the radio blasting.

Pedro Luz lays back cool and sly, maybe half a mile, waiting until the cocky bastard reaches that long empty stretch on Card Sound Road, south of the Carysfort Marina. That's where Pedro aims to make the big move.

Until the Saab dies. Grinds to a miserable wheezing halt. A *Saab!*

Pedro Luz is so pissed he yanks the steering wheel off its column and heaves it into a tamarind tree. Only afterwards does it dawn on him that Mr. X isn't going to appreciate having a $35,000 automobile and no way to steer it.

An hour later, here comes Pascual's Wrecker Service. Guy lifts the hood, can't find a thing. Slides underneath, zero. Then he says maybe Pedro ran out of gas, and Pedro says don't be an asshole. Guy pulls off the gas cap, closes one eye and looks inside, like he can actually *see* something.

Then he sniffs real hard, rubs his nose, sniffs again. Then he starts laughing like a fruit.

"Your friends fucked you up real good," he says.

"What are you talking about?"

"Come here and take a whiff."

"No, thanks," Pedro says.

Guy hoots. "Now I seen everything."

Pedro's trying to figure out when it happened. Figures somebody snuck up and did it while he was talking to that hardass trooper. Which means the trooper was in on it.

"Did a number on your engine," says the tow-truck man, chuckling way too much.

Pedro Luz grabs him by the arm until his fingers lock on bone. He says, "So tell me. What exactly's in the gas tank?"

"Jack Daniels," the guy says. "I know that smell anywhere."

So now Pedro's watching him put the hook to Mr. Kingsbury's Saab and wondering what else could go wrong. Thinking about the monkeys and shithead burglars and what happened to Churrito. Thinking about the black state trooper busting his balls for no reason, and how somebody managed to pour booze in the tank without Pedro even knowing it.

Pedro thinks he'd better shoot some horse juice in his arms as soon as possible, and get tight on Joe Winder's ass.

In one of his pockets he finds the scrap of paper where he wrote the decal number off the car Winder was driving. It's not much, but it's the only thing he's got to show for a long sorry morning.

So Pedro tells the tow-truck guy he's going to ride in the busted Saab on the way to the shop. Use Kingsbury's car phone to make a few calls.

Guy says no way, it's against company policy. Gotta sit up front in the truck.

Which is not what Pedro wants to hear after such a shitty day. So he tackles the guy and yanks his arms out of the sockets one at a time, pop-pop. Leaves him thrashing in the grass by the side of the road.

Jumps in the tow truck and heads for the Amazing Kingdom of Thrills.

▼ ▼ ▼

The Mothers of Wilderness listened solemnly as Molly McNamara recounted the brutal assault. They were gathered in the Florida room of Molly's old house, where a potluck supper had been arranged on a calico tablecloth. Normally a hungry bunch, the Mothers scarcely touched the food; a huge bacon–cheese ball lay undisturbed on a sterling platter—a sure sign that the group was distracted.

And no wonder: Molly's story was appalling. No one dreamed that the battle against Falcon Trace would ever come to violence. That Molly had been attacked by thugs in her own apartment was horrifying; equally unsettling was her lurid description of the finger-biting episode. In disbelief, several of the older members fiddled frenetically with the controls to their hearing aids.

"Obviously we've struck a nerve with Kingsbury," Molly was saying. "Finally he considers us a serious threat."

One of the Mothers asked why Molly had not called the police.

"Because I couldn't prove he was behind it," she replied. "They'd think I was daffy."

The members seemed unsatisfied by this explanation. They clucked and whispered among themselves until Molly cut in and asked for order. The lawyer, Spacci, stood up and said it was a mistake not to notify the authorities.

"You're talking about a felony," he said. "Aggravated assault, possibly even attempted murder."

One of the Mothers piped up: "It's not worth dying for, Molly. They're already clearing the land."

Molly's gray eyes flashed angrily. "It is not too late!" She wheeled on Spacci. "Did you file in federal court?"

"These things take time."

"Can you get an injunction?"

"No," said the lawyer. "You mean, to stop construction? No, I can't."

Molly drummed her fingers on the portable podium. Spacci was preparing to sit down when she jolted him back to attention: "Give us a report on the blind trust."

"Yes, well, I talked to a fellow over in Dallas. He tells me the paperwork comes back to a company called Ramex Global, which is really Francis Kingsbury—"

"We *know*."

"—but the bulk of the money isn't his. It's from some S & L types. Former S & L types, I should say. Apparently they were in a hurry to invest."

"I'll bet," said one of the Mothers in the front row.

"They moved the funds through Nassau," Spacci said. "Not very original, but effective."

Molly folded her arms. "Perfect," she said. "Falcon Trace is being built with stolen savings accounts. And you people are ready to give up!"

"Our options," the lawyer noted, "are extremely limited."

"No, they're not. We're going to kill this project."

A worried murmuring swept through the Mothers. "How?" one asked. "How can we stop it now?"

"Sabotage," Molly McNamara answered. "Don't you people have any imagination?"

Immediately Spacci began waving his arms and whining about the ramifications of criminal misconduct.

Molly said: "If it makes you feel better, Mr. Spacci, get yourself a plate of the chicken Stroganoff and go out on the patio. And take your precious ethics with you."

Once the lawyer was gone, Molly asked if anyone else was having doubts about the Falcon Trace campaign. One board member, a devout Quaker, fluttered his hand and said yes, he was afraid of more bloodshed. Then he made a motion (quickly seconded) that the Mothers telephone the police to report the two men who had attacked Molly.

"We don't need the police," she said. "In fact, I've already retained the services of two experienced security men." With both hands she motioned to the back of the room, where Bud Schwartz and Danny Pogue stood near an open door. Danny Pogue flushed at the introduction and puffed his chest, trying to look like a tough customer. Bud

Schwartz focused sullenly on an invisible tarantula, dangling directly over Molly McNamara's hair.

Eventually the Mothers of Wilderness quit staring at the burglars-turned-bodyguards, and Molly resumed her pep talk. Danny Pogue picked up a spoon and sidled over to the cheese ball. Bud Schwartz slipped out the door.

▼ ▼ ▼

In a butcher shop near Howard Beach, Queens, a man known as The Salamander picked up the telephone and said: "Talk."

"Jimmy gave me the number. Jimmy Noodles."

"I'm listening," said The Salamander, whose real name was Salvatore Delicato.

"I got Jimmy's number from Gino Ricci's brother."

The Salamander said, "Fine. Didn't I already say I was listening? So talk."

"In case you wanna check it out—I'm calling from Florida. I did time with Gino's brother."

"How thrilling for you. Now I'm hangin' up, asshole."

"Wait," said the voice. "You been lookin' for a certain rat. I know where he is. The man who did the Zubonis."

The Salamander slammed down his cleaver. "Gimme a number I can call you back," he said. "Don't say another word, just tell me a number."

The caller from Florida repeated it twice. Sal Delicato used a finger to write the numerals in pig blood on a butcher block. Then he untied his apron, washed his hands, combed his hair, snatched a roll of quarters from the cash register and walked three blocks to a pay phone.

"All right, smart guy," he said when the man answered in Florida. "First off, I don't know any Zuboni brothers."

"I never said they was brothers."

"You didn't?" Shit, thought The Salamander, I gotta pay closer attention. "Look, never mind. Just hurry up and tell me what's so important."

"There's this creep in the Witness Relocation Program, you know who I'm talking about. He testified against the Zuboni brothers, the ones you never heard of. Anyway, they gave this creep a new name, new Social Security, the whole nine yards. He's doing real nice for himself. In fact, he's worth a couple million bucks is what I hear."

Sal Delicato said, "You're a dreamer."

"Well, maybe I got the wrong man. Maybe I got some bad information. I was under the impression you people were looking for Frankie King, am I wrong?"

"I don't know no Frankie King."

"Fine. Nice talkin' with you—"

"Hold on," said The Salamander. "I probably know somebody who might be interested. What'd you say your name was?"

"Schwartz. Buddy Schwartz. I was with Gino's brother at Lake Butler, Florida. You can check it out."

"I will."

"In the meantime, you oughta talk to Mr. Gotti."

"I don't know no Gotti," said The Salamander. "I definitely don't know no fucking Gotti."

"Whatever."

Over the phone Bud Schwartz heard the din of automobile horns and hydraulic bus brakes and jackhammers and police sirens. He felt glad he was in Miami instead of on a street corner in Queens. At the other end, Sal Delicato cleared his throat with a series of porcine grunts. "You said they gave him a new name, right? This Frankie King."

"Yep," said Bud Schwartz.

"Well, what name does he got at the moment?"

"See, this is what I wanna talk about."

"Sounds like you're playin' games, huh?"

Bud Schwartz said, "No, sir. This ain't no game."

"All right, all right. Tell you what to do: First off, you might already got some problems. The phone lines to my shop aren't so clean, understand?"

Bud Schwartz said, "I'll be gone from here in a few days."

"Be that as it may," said The Salamander, "next time you call me at the shop, do it from a pay booth—they got pay booths in Florida, right? And don't say shit, either. Just say you want five dozen lamb chops, all right? That's how I know it's you—five dozen lamb chops."

"No problem," said Bud Schwartz.

"Thirdly, it don't matter what phones we're on, don't ever mention that fucking name."

"Frankie King?"

"No, the other one. The one starts with 'G.'"

"The one you never heard of?"

"Right," said Salvatore (The Salamander) Delicato. "That's the one."

▼ ▼ ▼

Later, drinking a beer on the porch, Danny Pogue said, "I can't believe you done that."

"Why not?" said Bud Schwartz. "The asshole double-crossed us. Tried to rip us off."

"Plus what he done to Molly."

"Yeah, there's that."

Danny Pogue said, "Do you think they'll kill him?"

"Something like that. Maybe worse."

"Jesus, Bud, I wouldn't know how to call up the Mafia, my life depended on it. The Mafia!"

"It wasn't easy finding the right people. They're not in the Yellow Pages, that's for sure."

Danny Pogue laughed uproariously, exposing cheese-spackled teeth. "You're a piece a work," he said.

"Yeah, well." Bud Schwartz had surprised himself with the phone call. He had remained cool and composed even with a surly mob heavyweight on the other end of the line. Bud Schwartz felt he had braved a higher and more serious realm of criminality; what's more, he had single-handedly set in motion a major event.

Danny Pogue said, "How much'll they give us for turning the bastard in?"

"Don't know," said Bud Schwartz. "The man's checking it out."

Danny Pogue drained his beer and stared at his dirty tennis shoes. In a small voice he said, "Bud, I'm really sorry I ran away at the monkey place."

"Yeah, what a surprise. You taking off and leaving me alone to get my brains knocked out. Imagine that."

"I got scared is all."

"Obviously." What the hell could he expect? Like all thieves, Danny Pogue was low on valor and high on self-preservation.

He said, "It's okay if you killed that guy. I mean, it was definitely self-defense. No jury in the world would send you up on that one."

Great, Bud Schwartz thought, now he's Perry Mason. "Danny, I'm gonna tell you one more time: it wasn't me, it was a damn baboon."

Here was something Danny Pogue admired about his partner; most dirtbags would have lied about what happened so they could take credit for the shooting. Not Bud—even if a monkey was involved. That was Danny Pogue's idea of class.

"I got a feeling they meant to kill us," Bud Schwartz said. He had replayed the scene a hundred times in his head, and it always added up to a murderous rip-off. It made him furious to think that Francis Kingsbury would try it . . . so furious that he'd tracked down his old cellmate Mario, who steered him to Jimmy Noodles, who gave him the number of the butcher shop in Queens.

Nothing but revenge was on Bud Schwartz's mind. "I want them to know," he said to Danny Pogue, "that they can't screw with us just 'cause we're burglars."

The screen door squeaked open and Molly McNamara joined the men on the porch. Her eyes looked puffy and tired. She asked Danny Pogue to fix her a glass of lemonade, and he dashed to the kitchen. She adjusted her new dentures and said, "The meeting went poorly. There's not much support for my ideas."

One hand moved to her chest, and she took a raspy, labored breath.

Bud Schwartz said, "You ain't feeling so good, huh?"

"Not tonight, no." She placed a tiny pill under her tongue and closed her eyes. A flash of distant lightning announced a thunderstorm sweeping in from the Everglades. Bud Schwartz spotted a mosquito on Molly's cheek, and he brushed it away.

She blinked her eyes and said, "You boys have been up to something, I can tell."

"It's going to be a surprise."

"I'm too old for surprises," said Molly.

"This one you'll like."

"Be careful, please." She leaned forward and dropped her voice. "For Danny's sake, be careful. He's not as sharp as you are."

Bud Schwartz said, "We look out for each other." Unless there's trouble, then the little dork runs for the hills.

"There's a reason I can't spill everything," Bud Schwartz said to Molly, "but don't you worry." She was in a mood, all right. He'd never seen her so worn out and gloomy.

Danny Pogue returned with a pitcher of lemonade. Molly thanked him and held her glass with both hands as she drank. "I'm afraid we won't be able to count on the Mothers of Wilderness," she said. "I sensed an alarming lack of resolve in the meeting tonight."

"You mean, they wimped out."

"Oh, they offered to picket Falcon Trace. And sign a petition, of course. They're very big on petitions." Molly sighed and tilted her head. The oncoming thunder made the pine planks rumble beneath their feet.

"Maybe it's me. Maybe I'm just a batty old woman."

Danny Pogue said, "No, you're not!"

Yes, she is, thought Bud Schwartz. But that was all right. She was entitled.

Molly gripped the arms of the chair and pulled herself up. "We'll probably get a visitor soon," she said. "The tall fellow with the collar on his neck."

"Swell," Bud Schwartz muttered. His ribs still throbbed from last time.

"He's not to be feared," Molly McNamara said. "We should hear what he has to say."

This ought to be good, thought Bud Schwartz. This ought to be priceless.

25

Early on the morning of July 29, a Sunday, the fax machine in the wire room of the *Miami Herald* received the following transmission:

REPTILE SCARE CLOSES THEME PARK; HIGH WATER BLAMED

The Amazing Kingdom of Thrills will be closed Sunday, July 29, due to an infestation of poisonous snakes caused by heavy summer rains and flooding. Cottonmouth moccasins numbering "in the low hundreds" swarmed the popular South Florida theme park over the weekend, according to Charles Chelsea, vice president of publicity.

Several workers and visitors were bitten Saturday, but no deaths were reported. "Our medical-emergency personnel responded to the crisis with heroic efficiency," Chelsea stated.

Reptile experts say snakes become more active in times of heavy rainfall, and travel great distances to seek higher ground. Even the so-called water moccasin, which thrives in canals and brackish lagoons, becomes uncommonly restless and aggressive during flood-type conditions.

The cottonmouth is a pit viper known for its large curved fangs and whitish mouth. While extremely painful, the bite of the snake is seldom fatal if medical treatment is administered quickly. However, permanent damage to muscle and soft tissue often occurs.

The moccasin is prevalent throughout South Florida, although it is rare to find more than two or three snakes together at a time. Cluster migrations are a rarity in nature. "They appeared to be hunting for toads," Chelsea explained.

Officials ordered the theme park to be closed temporarily while teams of armed hunters captured and removed the wild reptiles, some of which were nearly six feet in length.

Chelsea said that the Amazing Kingdom will reopen Tuesday morning with a full schedule of events. He added: "While we are confident that the grounds will be perfectly safe and secure, we are also suggesting, as a precaution, that our visitors wear heavy rubber boots. These will be available in all sizes, for a nominal rental fee."

▼ ▼ ▼

Reporters began calling before eight o'clock. Charles Chelsea was summoned from home; he arrived bleary-eyed and tieless. Clutching a Styrofoam cup of black coffee, he hunched over the desk to examine Joe Winder's newest atrocity.

"Wicked bastard," he said after reading the last line.

A secretary told him about the TV helicopters. "We've counted five so far," she reported. "They're trying to get an aerial shot of the snakes."

"The snakes!" Chelsea laughed dismally.

To ignite his competitive spirit, the secretary said, "I can't believe they'd fall for a dumb story like this."

"Are you kidding?" Chelsea buried his hands in his hair. "Snakes are dynamite copy. Anything with a snake, the media eats it up." A law of journalism of which Joe Winder, the ruthless sonofabitch, was well aware.

Chelsea sucked down the dregs of the coffee and picked up the phone. Francis X. Kingsbury answered on the seventeenth ring.

"I've got some extremely bad news," Chelsea said.

"Horseshit, Charlie, if you get my drift." It sounded as if Kingsbury's hay fever was acting up. "Calling me at home, Christ, what's your job description anyway—*professional pussy?* Is that what I hired you for?"

"No, sir." The publicity man gritted his teeth and told Kingsbury what had happened. There was a long unpleasant silence, followed by the sound of a toilet being flushed.

"I'm in the can," Kingsbury said. "That's what you get for calling me at home."

"Sir, did you hear what I said? About the snake story that Winder put out?"

"Yes, hell, I'm not deaf. Hold on." Chelsea heard the toilet flush again. Grimly he motioned for his secretary to get him another cup of coffee.

On the other end, Kingsbury said, "All right, so on this snake thing, what do you think?"

"Close the park for a day."

"Don't be an idiot."

"There's no choice, Mr. Kingsbury. Even if we came clean and admitted the press release was fake, nobody's going to believe it. They'll think we're covering up." That was the insidious genius of Joe Winder's strategy.

Kingsbury said: "Close the goddamn park, are you kidding? What about business?"

"Business is shot," Chelsea replied. "Nobody but reptile freaks would show up today. We're better off closing the Kingdom and taking our lumps."

"Un-fucking-real, this is."

"I forgot to mention, we'll also need to purchase some boots. Several hundred pairs." Chelsea's fingers began to cramp on the telephone receiver. He said, "Don't worry, I'll put something out on the wires right away."

"Everything's under control, blah, blah, blah."

"Right," said Chelsea. Now he could hear the water running in Francis Kingsbury's sink.

"I bruffing my teef," Kingsbury gargled.

Chelsea waited for the sound of spitting. Then he said, "I'll call a press conference for noon. We'll get somebody, some scientist, to say the snakes are almost gone. Then we'll reopen tomorrow."

Kingsbury said, "Four hundred grand is what this fucking clown is costing me, you realize? A whole day's receipts."

"Sir, it could get worse."

"Don't say that, Charlie."

In a monotone Chelsea read the phony press release to Francis Kingsbury, who said: "Christ Almighty, they get six feet long! These poison cottonheads do?"

"I don't know. I don't know how big they get." Chelsea wanted to tell Kingsbury that it really didn't matter if the imaginary snakes were two feet or twenty feet, the effect on tourists was the same.

Over the buzz of his electric razor, Kingsbury shouted, "What does he want—this prick Winder—what's he after?"

"Nothing we can give him," Chelsea said.

"It's got to stop or he'll kill our business."

"Yes, I know."

"And I'll tell you what else," Francis Kingsbury said. "I'm very disappointed in that fucking Pedro."

▼ ▼ ▼

Molly McNamara was writing a letter to her daughter in Minneapolis when Danny Pogue rushed into the den. Excitedly he said: "I just saw on the news about all them snakes!" His Adam's apple juked up and down.

"Yes," Molly said, "it's very odd."

"Maybe you could get your people together. The Mothers of Wilderness. Maybe go down to Key Largo and demonstrate."

"Against what?"

"Well, it said on the news they're killing 'em all. The snakes, I mean. That don't seem right—it ain't their fault about the high water." Danny Pogue was rigid with indignation, and Molly hated to dampen the fervor.

Gently she said, "I don't know that they're actually killing the snakes. The radio said something about capture teams."

"No, unh-uh, I just saw on the TV. A man from the Amazing Kingdom said they were killing the ones they couldn't catch. Especially the preggy ones." He meant "pregnant." "It's that Kingsbury asshole, pardon my French."

Molly McNamara capped her fountain pen and turned the chair toward Danny Pogue. She told him she understood how he felt. "But we've got to choose our battles carefully," she said, "if we hope to get the public on our side."

"So?"

"So there's not much sympathy for poisonous snakes."

Danny Pogue looked discouraged. Molly said, "I'm sorry, Danny, but it's true. Nobody's going to care if they use flamethrowers, as long as they get rid of the cottonmouths."

"But it ain't right."

Molly patted his knee. "There's plenty of snakes out there. Not like the mango voles, where there were only two left in the entire world."

With those words she could have hammered an icepick into Danny Pogue's heart. Morosely he bowed his head. As his environmental consciousness had been awakened, the vole theft had begun to weigh like a bleak ballast on his soul; he'd come to feel personally responsible for the extinction of the voles, and had inwardly promised to avenge his crime.

He said to Molly: "What's that word you used before—'*atome*'?"

"Atone, Danny. A-t-o-n-e. It means making amends."

"Yeah, well, that's me."

Molly smiled and removed her reading glasses. "Don't worry, we've all made mistakes in our lives. We've all committed errors of judgment."

"Like when you shot me and Bud. Before you got to know us better."

"No, Danny, that wasn't a mistake. I'd do the same thing all over again, if it became necessary."

"You would?"

"Oh, now, don't take it the wrong way. Come here." Molly reached out and took him by the shoulders. Firmly she pulled his greasy head to her breast. The heavy jasmine scent brought the tickle of a sneeze to Danny Pogue's nostrils.

Molly gave him a hug and said, "Both you boys mean so much to me." Danny Pogue might have been moved to tears, except for the familiar bluish glint of the pistol tucked in the folds of Molly's house-dress.

He said, "You want some tea?"

"That would be lovely."

▼ ▼ ▼

As soon as Carrie Lanier left for work, Skink curled up in the shower, turned on the cold water and went to sleep.

Joe Winder kept writing for thirty minutes, until his will dissolved and he could no longer concentrate. He dialed Miriam's house and asked for Nina.

"It's six-dirty inna morning," Miriam complained.

"I know what time it is. May I speak to her, please?"

"What if chee no here?"

"Miriam, I swear to God—"

"All rye, Joe. Chew wait."

When Nina came on the line, she sounded wide awake. "This is very rude of you," she said crossly, "waking Miriam."

"What about you?"

"I was writing."

"Me, too," Joe Winder said. "You were working on your phone fantasies?"

"My stories, yes."

"That's the main reason for the call. I had an idea for you."

Nina said, "I've got some good news, Joe. I'm getting syndicated."

"Hey, that's great." Syndicated? What the hell was she talking about. Ann Landers was *syndicated*. Ellen Goodman was syndicated. Not women who write about bondage on Olympic diving boards.

"There's a company called Hot Talk," Nina said. "They own, like, two hundred of these adult phone services. They're going to buy my scripts and market them all over. Chicago, Denver, even Los Angeles."

"That's really something."

"Yeah, in a few months I'll be able to get off the phones and write full-time. It's like a dream come true."

She asked about Joe's idea for a fantasy and he described it. "Not bad," Nina admitted. "It just might work."

"Oh, it'll work," Winder said, but Nina didn't take the bait. She expressed no curiosity. "Remember," he added, "it has to be a fishnet suit with absolutely nothing underneath."

"Joe, please. I understand the principle."

He was hoping she would ask how he was doing, what he'd been up to, and so on. Instead she told him she'd better go because she didn't want to keep Miriam awake.

Winder fought for more time. "Basically, I called to see how you're doing. I admit it."

"Well, I'm doing fine."

"Things might get crazy in the next week or so. I didn't want you to worry."

"I'll try not to." Her tone was disconcertingly sincere. Winder waited for a follow-up question, but none came.

He blurted: "Are you seeing anybody?"

"Not exactly."

"Oh?"

"What I mean is, there's a man."

"Oh, ho!" A hot stab in the sternum.

"But we're not exactly seeing each other," Nina said. "He calls up and we talk."

"He calls on the 976 number? You mean he's a customer?"

"It's not like the others. We talk about deep things, personal things —I can't describe it, you wouldn't understand."

"And you've never actually met him?"

"Not face-to-face, no. But you can tell a lot from the way a person talks. I think he must be very special."

"What if he's a hunchback? What if he's got pubic lice?" Joe Winder was reeling. "Nina, don't you see how sick this is? You're falling in love with a stranger's voice!"

"He's very sensual, Joe. I can tell."

"For God's sake, the man's calling on the come line. What does that tell you?"

"I don't want to get into it," Nina said. "You asked if I was interested in anyone, and I told you.. I should've known you'd react this way."

"Just tell me, is he paying for the telephone calls?"

"We've agreed to split the cost."

"Sweet Jesus."

"And we're meeting for dinner Tuesday up in the Gables."

"Wonderful," said Joe Winder. "What color trench coat did he say he'd be wearing?"

"I hate you," Nina remarked.

They hung up on each other at precisely the same instant.

▼ ▼ ▼

Pedro Luz slithered beneath Carrie's mobile home. Lying on his back in the cool dirt, he listened to the shower running and laughed giddily. He placed both hands on a wooden floor beam and pushed with all his strength; he was certain that he felt the double-wide rise above him, if only a few millimeters. With a bullish snort, he tried again. To bench-press a mobile home! Pedro Luz grimaced in ecstasy.

He was proud of himself for tracing the car, even if the detective work entailed only the pushing of three lousy buttons on a computer. He was equally proud of himself for locating the address in the dark and remaining invisible to the occupants of the trailer. At dawn he had watched the woman drive off to work, leaving him alone with that crazy doomed bastard, Joe Winder.

Pedro Luz had spent a long time fueling himself for the task. He had strung the intravenous rigs in the storage room of the Security

Department at the Amazing Kingdom of Thrills. There, stretched on a cot, he had dripped large quantities of horse steroids into both arms. Afterwards, Pedro Luz had guzzled nine Heinekens and studied himself naked in a full-length mirror.

The mirror examination had become a ritual to make sure that his penis and testicles were not shrinking, as Churrito had warned they would. Pedro Luz had become worried when his security-guard uniform had gotten baggy in the crotch, so every night he took a measuring tape and checked his equipment. Then he would leaf through some pornographic magazines to make sure he could still get a hard-on; on some evenings, when he was particularly anxious, he would even measure the angle of his erection.

On the night he went after Joe Winder, the angle was exactly zero degrees. Pedro Luz blamed it on the beer.

▼ ▼ ▼

Inside the trailer, Winder finished typing another counterfeit press release, which said:

> The widow of a young scientist killed at the Amazing Kingdom of Thrills has been offered a settlement of $2.8 million, officials of the popular amusement park have announced.
>
> The payment would be made in a single installment to Deborah Koocher, age 31, of New York. Her husband, Dr. William Bennett Koocher, was a noted wildlife biologist who helped supervise the Endangered Species Program at the Amazing Kingdom. Dr. Koocher died two weeks ago in a tragic drowning at the park's outdoor whale tank. That incident is still under investigation.
>
> Charles Chelsea, vice president of publicity, said the cash offer to Mrs. Koocher "demonstrates our sense of loss and sorrow over the untimely death of her husband."
>
> Added Chelsea: "Will was instrumental in our rare-animal programs, and his heroic efforts to save the blue-tongued mango vol won international acclaim."
>
> In a statement released Sunday morning, Francis X. Kingsbury, founder and chairman of the Amazing Kingdom, said that Dr. Koocher's death "was a tragedy for all of us at the park. We had come to love and

admire Will, who was as much a part of our family as Robbie Raccoon or Petey Possum."

The $2.8 million settlement offer is "a gesture not only of compassion, but fairness," Mr. Kingsbury added. "If Dr. Koocher's family isn't satisfied, we would certainly consider increasing the payment."

Joe Winder reread the announcement, inserted the word "completely" before "satisfied," and fed the paper into the fax machine. He considered phoning Nina again, but decided it was no use; the woman was groping recklessly for male companionship. What else could explain her irrational attraction to a disembodied masculine voice?

Besides, Joe had Carrie now—or she had him. The dynamics of the relationship had yet to be calibrated.

Winder was in the mood for acoustic guitar, so he put on some Neil Young and fixed himself four eggs, scrambled, and two English muffins with tangerine marmalade. Glancing out the kitchen window, he noticed a tow truck parked crookedly on the shoulder of the dirt lane. He didn't see a driver.

The shower had been running for some time. Winder cracked the door and saw Skink curled in a fetal snooze, cold water slapping on the blaze weather suit. Winder decided not to wake him.

Suddenly he heard a pop like a car backfiring, and a hole the size of a nickel appeared in the tile six inches above Skink's face. Then came another bang, another hole.

Joe Winder yelled and dived out of the doorway.

▼ ▼ ▼

In a way, Carrie Lanier was glad that the Amazing Kingdom was closed. It meant an extra day to work on her singing, which was still rusty, and to design a new costume for Princess Golden Sun.

Driving back toward the mainland, she couldn't wait to tell Joe about all the TV trucks and helicopters at the park's main gate. A reporter from Channel 10 had approached the car and thrust a microphone in her face and asked if she had seen any snakes. Quickly Carrie had improvised a story about a teeming herd—she wasn't sure it was the right term—slithering across County Road 905 near Carysfort. The fellow from Channel 10 had marshaled his camera crew and sprinted off toward the van.

Carrie was impressed by the immediate and dramatic effect of Joe Winder's hoax: everyone was wearing sturdy rubber hip boots.

On the way home, she practiced another song from the show:

You took our whole Indian nation,
Stuck us on this reservation.
Took away our way of life,
The garfish gig and the gator knife.
Seminole people! Seminole tribe!

It was a variation of a song called "Indian Reservation," which was recorded by Paul Revere and the Raiders, a band not generally remembered for its biting social commentary. Carrie Lanier thought the new lyrics were insipid, but she liked the simple tune and tom-tom rhythms. She was singing the third verse when she turned into the trailer park and spotted a bloated bodybuilder firing a pistol into the side of her double-wide.

Without hesitating, without even honking the horn, Carrie Lanier took aim.

Pedro Luz was so thoroughly engrossed in assassinating Joe Winder in the shower that he didn't hear the 1979 Buick Electra until it mowed a row of garbage cans ten feet behind him. Pedro Luz started to run but tripped over a garden hose and pitched forward, arms outstretched; it seemed as if he were tumbling in slow motion. When he stopped, the Buick was parked squarely on his left foot.

He lay there for a full minute, bracing for agony that never came. Each of the twenty-six bones in Pedro Luz's foot had been pulverized, yet the only sensation was a mildly annoying throb. Four thousand pounds of ugly Detroit steel on his toes and not even a twinge of pain. Incredible, Pedro thought; the ultimate result of supreme physical conditioning! Or possibly the drugs.

Apparently the driver had abandoned the Buick with the engine running. Steroids and all, Pedro Luz could not budge the sedan by himself. Meanwhile, the gunfire and crash had awakened other denizens of the trailer park; bulldogs yapped, doors slammed, babies wailed, a rooster cackled. Probably somebody had phoned the police.

Pedro Luz probed at the bloody burrito that was now his left foot, protruding beneath a Goodyear whitewall, and made a fateful decision.

What the hell, he mused. Long as I'm feeling no pain.

▼ ▼ ▼

Dr. Richard Rafferty's assistant called him at home to say there was an emergency, he'd better come right away. When he arrived at the office, the doctor sourly observed a tow truck parked in the handicapped zone. Inside the examining room, a husky one-eyed man with a radio collar lay prone on the steel table.

Dr. Rafferty said: "Is this some kind of joke?"

The couple who had brought the injured man said he had been shot at least twice.

"Then he's got a big problem," said Dr. Rafferty, "because I'm a veterinarian."

The couple seemed to know this already. "He won't go to a regular doctor," Joe Winder explained.

Carrie Lanier added, "We took him to the hospital but he refused to get out of the truck."

Dr. Rafferty's assistant pulled him aside. "I believe I saw a gun," he whispered.

Skink opened his good eye and turned toward the vet. "Richard, you remember me?"

"I'm not sure."

"The night that panther got nailed by the liquor truck."

Dr. Rafferty leaned closer and studied the face. "Lord, yes," he said. "I do remember." It was the same fellow who'd charged into the office with a hundred-pound wildcat in his bare arms. The doctor remembered how the dying panther had clawed bloody striations on the man's neck and shoulders.

Skink said, "You did a fine job, even though we lost the animal."

"We gave it our best."

"How about another try?"

"Look, I don't work on humans."

"I won't tell a soul," Skink said.

"Please," Joe Winder cut in, "you're the only one he'll trust."

Skink's chest heaved, and he let out a groan.

"He's lost some blood," Carrie said.

Dr. Rafferty slipped out of his jacket and told the assistant to prepare a surgical tray. "Oh, we've got plenty of blood," the doctor said, "but unless you're a schnauzer, it won't do you much good."

"Whatever," Skink mumbled, drifting light-headedly. "If you can't fix me up, then put me to sleep. Like you would any old sick dog."

26

Charles Chelsea decided that "dapper" was too strong a word for Francis X. Kingsbury's appearance; "presentable" was more like it.

Kingsbury wore a gray silk necktie, and a long-sleeved shirt to conceal the lewd mouse tattoo. The reason for the sartorial extravagance was an invitation to address the Tri-County Chamber of Commerce luncheon; Kingsbury intended to use the occasion to unveil a model of the Falcon Trace Golf and Country Club Resort Community.

Impatiently he pointed at Charles Chelsea's belly and said: "So? The damn snake situation—let's hear it."

"The worst is over," said Chelsea, with genuine confidence. He had countered Joe Winder's moccasin attack with a publicity blurb announcing that most of the reptiles had turned out to be harmless banded water snakes that only *looked* like deadly cottonmouths. For reinforcement Chelsea had released videotape of a staged capture, peppered with reassuring comments from a local zoologist.

"By the end of the week, we can send back all those boots," Chelsea said in conclusion.

"All right, that's fine." Kingsbury swiveled toward the window, then back again. Restlessly he kneaded the folds of his neck. "Item Number Two," he said. "This shit with the doctor's widow, is that cleared up yet?"

Here Chelsea faltered, for Joe Winder had stymied him with the Koocher gambit. The publicity man was at a loss for remedies. There was no clever or graceful way to recant a $2.8 million settlement offer for a wrongful death.

Anxiety manifested itself in a clammy deluge from Chelsea's armpits. "Sir, this one's a stumper," he said.

"I don't want to hear it!" Kingsbury clasped his hands in a manner suggesting that he was trying to control a homicidal rage. "What was it, two-point-eight? There's no fucking way—what, do I look like Onassis?"

Chelsea's jaws ached from nervous clenching. He pushed onward:

"To rescind the offer could have very grave consequences, publicity-wise. The fallout could be ugly."

"Grave consequences? I'll give you grave, Charlie. Two million simoleons outta my goddamn pocket, how's that for grave?"

"Perhaps you should talk to the insurance company."

"Ha!" Kingsbury tossed back his head and snorted insanely. "They just jack the rates, those assholes, every time some putz from Boise stubs his little toe. No way, Charlie, am I talking to those damn insurance people."

In recent years the insurance company had tripled its liability premium for the Amazing Kingdom of Thrills. This was due to the unusually high incidence of accidents and injuries on the main attractions; the Wet Willy water slide alone had generated seventeen lawsuits, and out-of-court settlements totaling nearly three-quarters of a million dollars. Even more costly was the freakish malfunction of a mechanical bull at the Wild Bill Hiccup Corral—an elderly British tourist had been hospitalized with a 90-degree crimp in his plastic penile implant. The jury's seven-figure verdict had surprised no one.

There was no point rehashing these sad episodes with Francis Kingsbury, for it would only appear that Charles Chelsea was trying to defend the insurance company.

"I think you should be aware," he said, "Mrs. Koocher has retained an attorney."

"Good for her," Kingsbury rumbled. "Let her explain to a judge what the hell her old man was doing, swimming with a damn killer whale in the middle of the night."

Chelsea was now on the precipice of anger himself. "If we drag this out, the *Herald* and the TV will be all over us. Do we really want a pack of reporters investigating the doctor's death?"

Kingsbury squinted suspiciously. "What are you getting at?"

"I'm simply advising you to take time and think about this. Let me stall the media."

The swiveling started again, back and forth, Kingsbury fidgeting like a hyperactive child. "Two-point-eight-million dollars! Where the hell did that crazy number come from? I guess he couldn't of made it a hundred grand, something do-able."

"Winder? No, sir, he tends to think big."

"He's trying to put me out of business, isn't he?" Francis Kingsbury stopped spinning the chair. He planted his elbows on the desk and dug his polished fingernails into his jowls. "The fucker, this is my theory, the fucker's trying to put me under."

"You might be right," Chelsea admitted.

"What's his—you hired him, Charlie—what's his angle?"

"I couldn't begin to tell you. For now, my advice is to get the insurance company in touch with Mrs. Koocher's lawyer. Before it blows up even worse."

Kingsbury gave an anguished moan. "Worse? How is that possible?"

"Anything's possible." Chelsea was alarmed by the weariness in his own voice. He wondered if the tempest of bad news would ever abate.

The phone buzzed and Kingsbury plucked it off the hook. He listened, grunted affirmatively and hung up. "Pedro's on his way in," he said. "And it better be good news or I'm gonna can his fat ass."

Pedro Luz did not look like a cheery bundle of good tidings. The wheelchair was one clue. The missing foot was another.

Kingsbury sighed. "Christ, now what?" He saw a whopper of a worker's comp claim coming down the pike.

"An accident," Pedro Luz said, wheeling to a stop in front of Kingsbury's desk. "Hey, it's not so bad."

Chelsea noticed that the security man's face was swollen and mottled like a rotten melon, and that his massive arms had exploded in fresh acne sores.

Kingsbury drummed on a marble paperweight. "So? Let's hear it."

Pedro Luz said, "I shot the bastard."

"Yeah?"

"You better believe it."

Charles Chelsea deftly excused himself; talk of felonies made him uncomfortable. He closed the door softly and nearly sprinted down the hall. He was thinking: Thank God it's finally over. No more dueling flacks.

Kingsbury grilled Pedro Luz on the details of the Joe Winder murder, but the security man edited selectively.

"He was in the shower. I fired eleven times, so I know damn well I hit him. Besides, I heard the shouts."

Kingsbury asked, "How do you know he's dead?"

"There was lots of blood," said Pedro Luz. "And like I told you, I fired almost a dozen goddamn rounds. Later I set the place on fire."

"Yeah?" Kingsbury had seen footage of a trailer blaze on Channel 4; there had been no mention of bodies.

Pedro Luz said, "It went up like a damn torch. One of them cheap mobile homes."

"You're sure the bastard was inside?"

"Far as I know. And the bitch, too."

Francis Kingsbury said, "Which bitch? You're losing me here."

"The dumb bitch he was staying with. The one who ran me over."

Pedro Luz gestured at the bandaged stump on the end of his leg. "That's what she did to me."

The puffy slits made it difficult to read the expression in Pedro Luz's eyes. Kingsbury said, "She hit you with a car?"

"More than that, she ran me down. Parked right on top of me."

"On your foot? Jesus Christ." Kingsbury winced sympathetically.

Pedro Luz said: "Good thing I'm in shape." Self-consciously he folded his bulging arms and spread his hands in a way that covered the pimples.

Kingsbury said, "So what happened?"

"What do you mean? I told you what happened."

"No, I mean with the car on your foot. How'd you get free?"

"Oh, I chewed it off," said Pedro Luz, "right below the ankle."

Kingsbury stared at the stump. He couldn't think of anything to say.

"Animals do it all the time," Pedro Luz explained, "when they get caught in traps."

Francis Kingsbury nodded unconsciously. His eyes roamed the office, searching for a convenient place to throw up.

"The hard part wasn't the pain. The hard part was the reach." Pedro Luz bent down to demonstrate.

"Oh Lord," Kingsbury muttered.

"Like I said, it's a good thing I'm in shape."

▼ ▼ ▼

At the campsite, Joe Winder told Molly McNamara it was nice to see her again. Molly congratulated Joe for blowing up Kingsbury's bulldozers. Skink thanked Molly for the bottle of Jack Daniels, and briefly related how it had been utilized. Carrie Lanier was introduced to the burglars, whom she instantly recognized as the scruffy vole robbers. Bud Schwartz and Danny Pogue were stunned to learn that Robbie Raccoon was a woman, and apologized for knocking Carrie down during the heist.

The heat was throbbing and the hammock steamed. No breeze stirred off the water. A high brown haze of African dust muted the hues of the broad summer sky. Skink handed out cold sodas and tended the fire; he wore cutoff jeans, the panther collar and a thick white vest of tape and bandages.

"You were lucky," Molly told him.

"Guy was aiming high," Skink said. "He assumed I'd be standing up."

As most people do in the shower, thought Joe Winder. "He also assumed that you were me," he said.

"Maybe so." Skink smeared a stick of EDTIAR bug repellent on both arms. Then he sat down under a buttonwood tree to count the mosquitoes biting his legs.

Carrie Lanier told the others about the breakneck ride to the veterinarian. "Dr. Rafferty did a great job. We're lucky he knew somebody over at the Red Cross."

Between insect frenzies, Danny Pogue struggled to follow the conversation. "You got shot?" he said to Skink. "So did me and Bud!"

Sharply, Molly cut in: "It wasn't the same."

"Like hell," mumbled Bud Schwartz miserably. The humidity made him dizzy, and his arms bled from scratching the bugs. In addition, he wasn't thrilled about the lunch menu, which included fox, opossum and rabbit—Skink's road-kill bounty from the night before.

Joe Winder was in a lousy mood, too. The sight of Carrie's burned-out trailer haunted him. The fax machine, the Amazing Kingdom stationery, his stereo—all lost. Neil Young, melting in the flames. Helpless, helpless, helpless, helpless.

Skink said, "It's time to get organized. Those damn John Deeres are back." He looked at Winder. "Now they've got cops on the site."

"What can we blow up next?" Molly asked.

Skink shook his head. "Let's try to be more imaginative."

"All the building permits are in Kingsbury's name," Winder noted. "If he goes down, the project goes under."

Carrie wondered what Joe meant by "goes down."

"You mean, if he dies?"

"Or gets bankrupt," Winder said.

"Or lost," added Skink, glancing up from his mosquito census.

Danny Pogue elbowed Bud Schwartz, who kept his silence. He had spoken again to the butcher in Queens, who had relayed an offer from unnamed friends of the Zubonis: fifty thousand for the whereabouts of Frankie King. Naturally Bud Schwartz had agreed to the deal; now, sitting in the wilderness among these idealistic crusaders, he felt slightly guilty. Maybe he should've ratted on Kingsbury for free.

"Mr. X had a terrible run of luck the last few days," Carrie was saying, "thanks to Joe."

Skink got up to check the campfire. He said, "It's time for a full-court press."

"Each day is precious," agreed Molly McNamara. She dabbed her forehead with a linen handkerchief. "I think we should move against Mr. Kingsbury as soon as possible."

Bud Schwartz crumpled a soda can. "Why don't we hold off a week or so?"

"No." Skink offered him a shank of opossum on a long-handled fork. He said, "Every hour that passes, we lose more of the island."

"Kingsbury's got worse problems than all of us put together," said Bud Schwartz. "If we can just lay back a few days."

Joe Winder urged him to elaborate.

"Tell him, Bud, go on!" Danny Pogue was nearly bursting.

"I wisht I could."

Skink fingered the silvery tendrils of his beard. Towering over the burglar, he said, "Son, I'm not fond of surprises."

"This is serious shit." Bud Schwartz was pleading. "You gotta understand—heavy people from up North."

Wiping the condensation from her eyeglasses, Molly said, "Bud, what on earth are you talking about?"

Winder leaned toward Carrie and whispered: "This is getting interesting."

"No damn surprises," Skink repeated balefully. "We act in confluence, you understand?"

Reluctantly Bud Schwartz took a bite of fried opossum. He scowled as the warm juices dripped down his chin.

"Is that blood?" asked Danny Pogue.

Skink nodded and said, "Nature's gravy."

Suddenly he turned his face to the sky, peered toward the lemon sun and cursed vehemently. Then he was gone, running barefoot into the bright tangles of the hammock.

The others looked at one another in utter puzzlement.

Joe Winder was the first to stand. "When in Rome," he said, reaching for Carrie's hand.

▼ ▼ ▼

Humanity's encroachment had obliterated the Florida panther so thoroughly that numerals were assigned to each of the few surviving specimens. In a desperate attempt to save the species, the Game and Fresh Water Commission had embarked on a program of monitoring the far-roaming panthers and tracking their movements by radio telemetry. Over a period of years most of the cats were treed, tranquilized and fitted with durable plastic collars that emitted a regular electronic signal on a frequency of 150 megahertz. The signals could be followed by rangers on the ground or, when the animal was deep in the swamps, by air. Using this system, biologists were able to map the territories traveled by individual cats, chart their mating habits and even locate new litters of kittens. Because the battery-operated collars were activated by motion, it was also possible for rangers to know when a numbered panther was sick or even dead; if a radio collar was inert for more than a few hours, it automatically began sending a distress signal.

No such alarm was transmitted if an animal became abnormally active, but the rangers were expected to notice any strange behavior and react accordingly. For instance, a panther that was spending too much time near populated areas was usually captured and relocated for its own safety; the cats had a long and dismal record of careless prowling along busy highways.

Sergeant Mark Dyerson had retrieved too many dead panthers that had been struck by trucks and automobiles. Recently the ranger had become certain that if something wasn't done soon, Panther 17 would end up the same way. The Game and Fish files indicated that the animal was a seven-year-old male whose original range stretched from Homestead south to Everglades National Park, and west all the way to Card Sound. Because this area was crisscrossed by high-speed roads, the rangers paid special attention to the travels of Number 17.

For months the cat had seemed content to hunker in the deep upland hammocks of North Key Largo, which made sense, considering the dicey crossing to the mainland. But Sergeant Dyerson had grown concerned when, two weeks earlier, radio readings on Number 17 began to show extraordinary, almost unbelievable movement. Intermittent flyovers had pinpointed the cat variously at Florida City, North Key Largo, Homestead, Naranja and South Miami—although Sergeant Dyerson believed the latter coordinates were a mistake, probably a malfunction of the radio tracking unit. South Miami was simply an impossible destination; not only was it well out of the panther's range, but the animal would have had to travel at a speed of sixty-five miles an hour to be there when the telemetry said it was. Unlike the cheetah, panthers prefer loping to racing. The only way Number 17 could go that far, Sergeant Dyerson joked to his pilot, is if it took a bus.

Even omitting South Miami from the readings, the cat's travels were inexplicably erratic. The rangers were concerned at the frequency with which Number 17 crossed Card Sound between Key Largo and the mainland. The only two possible routes—by water or the long bridge—were each fraught with hazards. It was Sergeant Dyerson's hope that Number 17 chose to swim the bay rather than risk the run over the steep concrete span, where the animal stood an excellent chance of getting creamed by a speeding car.

On July 29, the ranger took up the twin Piper to search for the wandering panther. The homing signal didn't come to life until the plane passed low over a trailer park on the outskirts of Homestead. It was not a safe place for humans, much less wild animals, and the panther's presence worried Sergeant Dyerson. Though the tawny cats were seldom visible from the Piper, the ranger half-expected to see Number 17 limping down the center lane of U.S. Highway 1.

Later that afternoon, Sergeant Dyerson went up again; this time he marked the strongest signal in thick cover near Steamboat Creek, on North Key Largo. The ranger couldn't believe it—twenty-nine miles in one day! This cat was either manic, or chained to the bumper of a Greyhound.

When Sergeant Dyerson landed in Naples, he asked an electrician to double-check the antenna and receiver of the telemetry unit. Every component tested perfectly.

That night, the ranger phoned his supervisor in Tallahassee and reviewed the recent radio data on Number 17. The supervisor agreed that he'd never heard of a panther moving such a great distance, so fast.

"Send me a capture team as soon as possible," Sergeant Dyerson said. "I'm gonna dart this sonofabitch and find out what's what."

▼ ▼ ▼

The twin Piper made three dives over the campsite. Joe Winder and Carrie Lanier watched from the bank of Steamboat Creek.

"Game and Fish," Winder said, "just what we need."

"What do we do?" Carrie asked.

"Follow the water."

They didn't get far. A tall uniformed man materialized at the edge of the tree line. He carried an odd small-bore rifle that looked like a toy. When he motioned to Joe and Carrie, they obediently followed him through the hammock out to the road. Molly McNamara and the two burglars already had been rounded up; another ranger, with a clipboard, was questioning them. There was no sign of Skink.

Sergeant Mark Dyerson introduced himself and asked to see some identification. Joe Winder and Carrie Lanier showed him their driver's licenses. The ranger was copying down their names when a gaunt old cracker, pulled by three lean hounds, came out of the woods.

"Any luck?" Sergeant Dyerson asked.

"Nope," said the tracker. "And I lost me a dog."

"Maybe the panther got him."

"They ain't no panther out there."

"Hell, Jackson, the radio don't lie." The ranger turned back to Joe Winder and Carrie Lanier. "And I suppose you're bird-watchers, too. Just like Mrs. McNamara and her friends."

Beautiful, thought Winder. We're bird-watchers now.

Playing along, Carrie informed the ranger they were following a pair of nesting kestrels.

"No kidding?" Sergeant Dyerson said. "I've never met a birder who didn't carry binoculars—and here I get five of 'em, all at one time."

"We're thinking of forming a club," said Carrie. Joe Winder bit his lip and looked away. Molly's Cadillac took off, eastbound—a crown of white hair behind the wheel, the burglars slouched in the back seat.

"I'll give you this much," the ranger said, "you sure don't look like poachers." A Florida Highway Patrol car pulled up and parked beside Sergeant Dyerson's Jeep. A muscular black trooper got out and tipped his Stetson at the ranger.

"Whatcha know?" the trooper said affably.

"Tracking a panther. These folks got in the way."

"A panther? You *got* to be kidding." The trooper's laughter boomed. "I've been driving this stretch for three years and never saw a bobcat, much less a panther."

"They're very secretive," Sergeant Dyerson said. "You wouldn't necessarily spot them." He wasn't in the mood for a nature lesson. He turned to the old tracker and told him to run the frigging dogs one more time.

"Ain't no point."

"Humor me," said Sergeant Dyerson. "Come on, let's go find your other hound."

Once the wildlife officers were gone, the trooper's easygoing smiled dissolved. "You folks need a lift."

"No, thanks," Joe Winder said.

"It wasn't a question, friend." The trooper opened the back door of the cruiser, and motioned them inside.

27

The trooper took them to lunch at the Ocean Reef Club. The clientele seemed ruffled by the sight of a tall black man with a sidearm.

"You're making the folks nervous," Joe Winder observed.

"Must be the uniform."

Carrie popped a shrimp into her mouth. "Are we under arrest?"

"I'd be doing all three of us a favor," Jim Tile said, "but no, unfortunately, you're not under arrest."

Winder was working on a grouper sandwich. Jim Tile had ordered the fried dolphin and conch fritters. The dining room was populated by rich Republican golfers with florid cheeks and candy-colored Izod shirts. The men shot anxious squinty-eyed glances toward the black trooper's table.

Jim Tile motioned for iced tea. "I can't imagine why I've never gotten a membership application. Maybe it got lost in the mail."

"What's the point of all this?" Winder asked.

"To have a friendly chat."

"About what?"

Jim Tile shrugged. "Flaming bulldozers. Dead whales. One-eyed woodsmen. You pick the subject."

"So we've got a mutual friend."

"Yes, we do." The trooper was enjoying the fish platter immensely; despite the stares, he seemed in no hurry to finish. He said, "The plane scared him off, right?"

"It doesn't make sense," Winder said. "They're not after him, they're after a cat. Why does he run?"

Jim Tile put down the fork and wiped his mouth. "My own opinion —he feels a duty to hide because that's what the panther would've done. He wears that damn collar like a sacred obligation."

"To the extreme."

"Yeah," the trooper said. "I don't expect they'll find that missing dog. You understand?"

Carrie said, "He's a very interesting person."

"A man to be admired but not imitated." Jim Tile paused. "I say that with no disrespect."

Winder chose not to acknowledge the warning. "Where do you think he went?" he asked the trooper.

"I'm not sure, but it's a matter of concern."

The manager of the restaurant appeared at the table. He was a slender young man with bleached hair and pointy shoulders and brand-new teeth. In a chilly tone he asked Jim Tile if he were a member of the club, and the trooper said no, not yet. The manager started to say something else but changed his mind. Jim Tile requested a membership application, and the manager said he'd be back in a jiffy.

"That's the last we'll see of him," the trooper predicted.

Joe Winder wanted to learn more about Skink. He decided it was safe to tell Jim Tile what the group had been doing in the hammock before the airplane came: "We were hatching quite a plot."

"I figured as much," the trooper said. "You know much about rock and roll?"

Carrie pointed at Winder and said, "Hard core."

"Good," said Jim Tile. "Maybe you can tell me what's a Mojo? The other day he was talking about a Mojo flying."

"*Rising*," Winder said. "Mojo rising. It's a line from The Doors—I believe it's got phallic connotations."

"No," Carrie jumped in. "I think it's about drugs."

The trooper looked exasperated. "White people's music, I swear to God. Sinatra's all right, but you can keep the rest of it."

"Shall we discuss rap?" Joe Winder said sharply. "Shall we examine the lyrical genius of, say, 2 Live Crew?" He could be very defensive when it came to rock. Carrie reached under the table and pinched his thigh. She told him to lighten up.

"Rikers Island," Jim Tile said. "Is there a song about Rikers Island?"

Winder couldn't think of one. "You sure it's not Thunder Island?"

"No." Jim Tile shook his head firmly. "Our friend said he'd be leaving Florida one day. Go up to Rikers Island and see to some business."

"But that's a prison," Carrie said.

"Yeah. A prison in New York City."

Joe Winder remembered something Skink had told him the first day at the campsite. If it was a clue, it foreshadowed a crime of undiluted madness.

Winder said, "Rikers is where they keep that idiot who shot John Lennon." He cocked an eyebrow at Jim Tile. "You *do* know who John Lennon was?"

"Yes, I do." The trooper's shoulders sagged. "This could be trouble," he added emptily.

"Our mutual friend never got over it," Winder said. "The other night, he asked me about the Dakota."

"Wait a minute." Carrie Lanier made a time-out signal with her hands. "You guys aren't serious."

Gloomily Jim Tile stirred the ice in his tea. "The man gets his mind set on things. And these days, I've been noticing he doesn't handle stress all that well."

Joe Winder said, "Christ, it was only an airplane. It's gone now, he'll calm down."

"Let's hope." The trooper called for the check.

Carrie looked sadly at Winder. "And here I thought *you* were bonkers," she said.

▼ ▼ ▼

Agent Billy Hawkins told Molly McNamara that the house was simply beautiful. Old-time Florida, you don't see pine floors like this anymore. Dade County pine.

Molly said, "I've got carpenter ants in the attic. All this wet weather's got 'em riled."

"You'd better get that seen to, and soon. They can be murder on the beams."

"Yes, I know. How about some more lemonade?"

"No, thank you," said Agent Hawkins. "We really need to talk about this telephone call."

Molly began to rock slowly. "I'm completely stumped. As I told you before, I don't know a living soul in Queens."

Hawkins held a notebook on his lap, a blue Flair pen in his right hand. He said, "Salvatore Delicato is an associate of the John Gotti crime family."

"Goodness!" Molly exclaimed.

"Prior arrests for racketeering, extortion and income-tax evasion. The phone call to his number was made from here. It lasted less than a minute."

"There must be some mistake. Did you check with Southern Bell?"

"Miss McNamara," Hawkins said, "can we please cut the crap."

Molly's grandmotherly expression turned glacial. "Watch your language, young man."

Flushing slightly, the agent continued: "Have you ever met a Jimmy Nardoni, otherwise known as Jimmy Noodles? Or a man named Gino Ricci, otherwise known as Gino The Blade?"

"Such colorful names," Molly remarked. "No, I've never heard of them. Do you have my telephone bugged, Agent Hawkins?"

He resisted the impulse to tell her that Sal Delicato's telephone was tapped by a squadron of eavesdroppers—not only the FBI, but the New York State Police, the U.S. Drug Enforcement Administration, the Tri-State Task Force on Organized Crime and the Bureau of Alcohol, Tobacco and Firearms. The New York Telephone box on the utility pole behind The Salamander's butcher shop sprouted so many extra wires, it looked like a pigeon's nest.

"Let me give you a scenario," Agent Hawkins said to Molly. "A man used your phone to call Sal Delicato for the purpose of revealing the whereabouts of a federally protected witness now living in Monroe County, Florida."

"That's outlandish," Molly said. "Who is this federal witness?"

"I imagine you already know." Hawkins jotted something in the notebook. "The man who made the phone call, we believe, was Buddy Michael Schwartz. I showed you his photograph the last time we visited. You said he looked familiar."

"I vaguely remember."

"He has other names," Hawkins said. "As I told you before, Schwartz is wanted in connection with the animal theft from the Amazing Kingdom."

"Wanted?"

"For questioning," the agent said. "Anyway, we believe the events are connected." The ominous wiretap conversation had elevated the vole investigation from zero-priority to high-priority. Billy Hawkins had been yanked off a bank-robbery case and ordered to find out why anyone would be setting up Francis X. Kingsbury, aka Frankie King. The Justice Department had pretty much forgotten about Frankie The Ferret until the phone call to Sal Delicato. The renewed interest in Washington was not a concern for Frankie's well-being so much as fear of a potential publicity nightmare; the murder of a protected government informant would not enhance the reputation of the Witness Relocation Program. It could, in fact, have a profoundly discouraging effect on other snitches. Agent Hawkins was told to track down Buddy Michael Schwartz and then call for backup.

Molly McNamara said, "You think this man might have broken into my house to use the phone!"

"Not exactly," Hawkins said.

She peered at him skeptically. "How do you know it was he on the line? Did you use one of those voice-analyzing machines?"

The FBI man chuckled. "No, we didn't need a machine. The caller identified himself."

"By name?" The blockhead! Molly thought.

"No, not by name. He told Mr. Delicato that he was an acquaintance of Gino Ricci's brother. It just so happens that Buddy Michael Schwartz served time with Mario Ricci at the Lake Butler Correctional Institute."

Molly McNamara said, "Could be a coincidence."

"They shared a cell. Buddy and Gino's brother."

"But still—"

"Would you have a problem," the agent said, "if I asked you to come downtown and take a polygraph examination?"

Molly stopped rocking and fixed him with an indignant glare. "Are you saying you don't believe me?"

"Call it a hunch."

"Agent Hawkins, I'm offended."

"And I'm tired of this baloney." He closed the notebook and capped the pen. "Where is he?"

"I don't know what you're talking about."

Hawkins stood up, pocketed his notebook, straightened his tie. "Let's go for a ride," he said. "Come on."

"No!"

"Don't make it worse for yourself."

"You're not paying attention," Molly said. "I thought G-men were trained to be observant."

Billy Hawkins laughed. "G-men? I haven't heard that one in a long—"

It was then he noticed the pistol. The old lady held it impassively, with both hands. She was pointing it directly at his crotch.

"This is amazing," said the agent. "The stuff of legends." Wait till the tough guys at Quantico hear about it.

Molly asked Billy Hawkins to raise his hands.

"No, ma'am."

"And why not?"

"Because you're going to give me the gun now."

"No," said Molly, "I'm going to shoot you."

"Lady, gimme the goddamn gun!"

Calmly she shot him in the thigh, two and one-quarter inches below the left hip. The FBI man went down with a howl, clawing at the burning hole in his pants.

"I told you to watch your language," Molly said.

The pop of the pistol brought Danny Pogue and Buddy Schwartz scrambling down the stairs. From a living-room window they cautiously surveyed the scene on the porch: Molly rocking placidly, a man in a gray suit thrashing on the floor.

Danny Pogue cried, "She done it again!"

"Christ on a bike," said Bud Schwartz, "it's that dick from the FBI."

The burglars cracked the door and peeked out. Molly assured them the situation was under control.

"Flesh wound," she reported. "Keep an eye on this fellow while I get some ice and bandages." She confiscated Billy Hawkins's Smith & Wesson and gave it to Bud Schwartz, who took it squeamishly, like a dog turd, in his hands.

"It works best when you aim it," Molly chided.

Danny Pogue reached for the barrel. "I'll do it!"

"Like hell," said Bud Schwartz, spinning away. He sat in the rocker and braced the pistol on his knee. The air smelled pungently of gunpowder; it brought back the memory of Monkey Mountain and the trigger-happy baboon.

Watching the gray-suited man squirm in pain, Bud Schwartz fought the urge to get up and run. What was the old bat thinking this time? Nothing good could come of shooting an FBI man. Surely she understood the consequences.

Danny Pogue opened the front door for Molly, who disappeared into the house with a pleasant wave. Danny Pogue sat down, straddling an iron patio chair. "Take it easy," he told the agent. "You ain't hurt so bad."

Billy Hawkins grunted up at him: "What's your name?"

"Marcus Welby," Bud Schwartz cut in. "Don't he look like a doctor?"

"I know who you are," the agent said. It felt as if a giant wasp were boring into his thigh. Billy Hawkins unbuckled his trousers and grimaced at the sight of his Jockey shorts soaked crimson.

"You assholes are going to jail," he said, pinching the pale flesh around the bullet wound.

"We're just burglars," said Danny Pogue.

"Not anymore." Hawkins attempted to rise to his feet, but Bud Schwartz wiggled the gun and told him to stay where he was. The agent's forehead was sprinkled with sweat, and his lips were gray. "Hey, Bud," he said, "I've seen your jacket, and this isn't your style. Assault on a federal officer, man, you're looking at Atlanta."

Bud Schwartz was deeply depressed to hear the FBI man call him by name. "You don't know shit about me," he snapped.

"Suppose you tell me what the hell's going on out here. What's your beef with Frankie King?"

Bud Schwartz said, "I don't know who you're talkin' about."

Miraculously, Danny Pogue caught on before saying something

disastrous. He flashed a checkerboard grin and said, "Yeah, who's Frankie King? We never heard a no Frankie King."

"Bullshit," Agent Billy Hawkins growled. "Go ahead and play it stupid. You're all going to prison, anyhow. You and that crazy old lady."

"If it makes you feel any better," said Danny Pogue, "she shot us, too."

▼ ▼ ▼

The campsite was . . . gone.

"I'm not surprised," Joe Winder said. He took Carrie's hand and kept walking. A light rain was falling, and the woods smelled cool.

Carrie asked, "What do we do if he's really gone?"

"I don't know."

Ten minutes later she asked if they were lost.

"I got turned around," Winder admitted. "It can't be too far."

"Joe, where are we going?"

The rain came down harder, and the sky blackened. From the west came a roll of thunder that shook the leaves. The birds fell silent; then the wind began to race across the island, and Joe Winder could taste the storm. He dropped Carrie's hand and started to jog, slapping out a trail with his arms. He called over his shoulder, urging Carrie to keep up.

It took fifteen more minutes to find the junkyard where the ancient Plymouth station wagon sat on rusty bumpers. The yellow beach umbrella—still stuck in the dashboard—fluttered furiously in the gale.

Joe Winder pulled Carrie inside the car, and hugged her so tightly she let out a cry. "My arms are tingling," she said. "The little hairs on my arms."

He covered her ears. "Hold on, it's lightning."

It struck with a white flash and a deafening rip. Twenty yards away, a dead mahogany tree split up the middle and dropped a huge leafless branch. "God," Carrie whispered. "That was close."

Raindrops hammered on the roof. Joe Winder turned around in the seat and looked in the back of the car. "They're gone," he said.

"What, Joe?"

"The books. This is where he kept all his books."

She turned to see. Except for several dead roaches and a yellowed copy of the *New Republic*, the station wagon had been cleaned out.

Winder was vexed. "I don't know how he did it. You should've seen —there were hundreds in here. Steinbeck, Hemingway. Jesus, Carrie, he had García Márquez in Spanish. First editions! Some of the greatest books ever written."

"Then he's actually gone."

"It would appear to be so."

"Think we should call somebody?"

"What?"

"Somebody up in New York," Carrie said, "at the prison. I mean, just in case."

"Let me think about this."

"I can't believe he'd try it."

The thunderstorm moved quickly over the island and out to sea. Soon the lightning stopped and the downpour softened to a drizzle. Carrie said, "The breeze felt nice, didn't it?"

Joe Winder wasn't listening. He was trying to decide if they should keep looking or not. Without Skink, new choices lay ahead: bold and serious decisions. Winder suddenly felt responsible for the entire operation.

Carrie turned to kiss him and her knee hit the glove compartment, which popped open. Curiously she poked through the contents—a flashlight, a tire gauge, three D-sized batteries and what appeared to be the dried tail of a squirrel.

And one brown envelope with Joe Winder's name printed in small block letters.

He tore it open. Reading the note, he broke into a broad smile. "Short and to the point," he said.

Carrie read it:

> Dear Joe,
> You make one hell of an oracle.
> Don't worry about me, just keep up the fight.
> We all shine on!

Carrie folded the note and returned it to the envelope. "I assume this means something."

"Like the moon and the stars and the sun," Joe Winder said. He felt truly inspired.

28

The Amazing Kingdom of Thrills reopened with only a minimal drop in attendance, thanks to a three-for-one ticket promotion that included a free ride on Dickie the Dolphin, whose amorous behavior was now inhibited by four trainers armed with electric stun guns. Francis X. Kingsbury was delighted by the crowds, and emboldened by the fact that many customers actually complained about the absence of wild snakes. Kingsbury regarded it as proof that closing the Amazing Kingdom had been unnecessary, a costly overestimation of the average tourist's brainpower. Obviously the yahoos were more curious than afraid of lethal reptiles. A thrill is a thrill, Kingsbury said.

The two persons forced to sit through this speech were Pedro Luz and Special Agent Ron Donner of the U.S. Marshal Service. Agent Donner had come to notify Francis X. Kingsbury of a possible threat against his life.

"Ho! From who?"

"Elements of organized crime," the marshal said.

"Well, fuck 'em."

"Excuse me?"

"This is just, I mean really, the word is horseshit!" Kingsbury flapped his arms like a tangerine-colored buzzard. He was dressed for serious golf; even his cleats were orange.

Agent Donner said: "We think it would be wise if you left town for a few weeks."

"Oh, you do? Leave town, like hell I will."

Pedro Luz spun his wheelchair slightly toward the marshal. "Organized crime," he said. "You mean the Mafia?"

"We're taking it very seriously," said Agent Donner, thinking: Who's the freak with the IV bag?

With the proud sweep of a hand, Francis Kingsbury introduced his chief of Security. "He handles everything for the park and so on. Personal affairs, as well. You can say anything in front of him, understand? He's thoroughly reliable."

Pedro Luz casually adjusted the drip valve on the intravenous tube.

The marshal asked, "What happened to your foot?"

"Never mind!" blurted Kingsbury.

"Car accident," Pedro Luz volunteered affably. "I had to chew the damn thing off." He pointed with a swathed, foreshortened index finger. "Right there above the anklebone, see?"

"Tough luck," said Agent Donner, thinking: Psycho City.

"It's what animals do," Pedro Luz added, "when they get caught in traps."

Kingsbury clapped his hands nervously. "Hey, hey! Can we get back to the issue, please, this Godfather thing. For the record, I'm not going anyplace."

The marshal said, "We can have you safely in Bozeman, Montana, by tomorrow afternoon."

"What, do I look like fucking Grizzly Adams? Listen to me—*Montana*, don't even joke about something like that."

Pedro Luz said, "Why would the Mafia want to kill Mr. Kingsbury? I don't exactly make the connection." Then his chin dropped, and he appeared to drift off.

Agent Donner said, "I wish you'd consider the offer."

"Two words." Kingsbury held up two fingers as if playing charades. "Summerfest Jubilee. One of our biggest days, receipt-wise, of the whole damn year. Parades, clowns, prizes. We're giving away . . . I forget, some kinda car."

"And I suppose you need to be here."

"Yeah, damn right. It's my park and my show. And know what else? You can't make me go anywhere. I kept my end of the deal. I'm free and clear of you people."

"You're still on probation," said the marshal. "But you're right, we can't force you to go anyplace. This visit is a courtesy—"

"And I appreciate the information. I just don't happen to believe it." But a part of Francis Kingsbury did believe it. What if the men who stole his files had given up on the idea of blackmail? What if the damn burglars had somehow made touch with the Gotti organization? It strained Kingsbury's imagination because they'd seemed like such jittery putzes that night at the house. Yet perhaps he'd misjudged them.

"Where'd you get the tip?" he demanded.

Agent Donner was briefly distracted by the cartoon depiction of rodent fellatio that adorned Kingsbury's forearm. Eventually the marshal looked up and said, "It surfaced during another investigation. I can't go into details."

"But, really, you guys think it's on the level? You think some guineas are coming after me?" Kingsbury struggled to maintain an air of amused skepticism.

Soberly the marshal said, "The FBI is checking it out."

"Well, regardless, I'm not going to Montana. Just thinking about it hurts my mucous membranes—I got the world's worst hay fever."

"So your mind is made up."

"Yep," said Kingsbury. "I'm staying put."

"Then let us provide you with protection here at the park. A couple of men, at least."

"Thanks, but no thanks. I got Pedro."

At the mention of his name, Pedro Luz's swollen eyelids parted. He reached up and squeezed the IV bag. Then he tugged the tube out of the needle in his arm, and fitted the end into the corner of his mouth. The sound of energetic sucking filled Francis Kingsbury's office.

Agent Donner was dumbfounded. In a brittle voice he assured Kingsbury that the marshals would be extremely discreet, and would in no way interfere with the Summerfest Jubilee events. Kingsbury, in a tone approaching politeness, declined the offer of bodyguards. The last thing he needed was federal dicks nosing around the Amazing Kingdom.

"Besides, like I mentioned, there's Pedro. He's as tough as they come."

"All right," said Agent Donner, casting his eyes once again on the distended, scarified, cataleptic, polyp-headed mass that was Pedro Luz.

Kingsbury said, "I know what you're thinking but, hell, he's worth ten of yours. Twenty of yours! Any sonofabitch that would bite off his own damn leg—you tell me, is that tough or what?"

The marshal rose stiffly to leave. "Tough isn't the word for it," he said.

▼ ▼ ▼

The trailer fire had left Carrie Lanier with only three possessions: her Buick Electra, the gun she had taken from Joe Winder and the newly retired raccoon suit. The costume and the gun had been stowed in the trunk of the car. Everything else had been destroyed in the blaze.

Molly McNamara offered her a bedroom on the second floor of the old house. "I'd loan you the condo but the cleaners are in this week," Molly said. "It's hard to rent out a place with bloodstains in the carpet."

"What about Joe?" Carrie said, "I'd like him to stay with me."

Molly clucked. "Young lady, I really can't approve. Two unmarried people—"

"But under the circumstances," Carrie persisted, "with all that's happened."

"Oh . . . I suppose it's all right." Molly had a sparkle in her eyes. "I was teasing, darling. Besides, you act as if you're in love."

Carrie said it was a long shot. "We're both very goal-oriented, and very stubborn. I'm not sure we're heading in the same direction." She paused and looked away. "He doesn't seem to fit anywhere."

"You wouldn't want him if he did," Molly said. "The world is full of nice boring young men. The crazy ones are hard to find and harder to keep, but it's worth it."

"Your husband was like that?"

"Yes. My lovers, too."

"But crazy isn't the word for it, is it?"

Molly smiled pensively. "You're a smart cookie."

"Did you know that Joe's father built Seashell Estates?"

"Oh dear," Molly said. A dreadful project: six thousand units on eight hundred acres, plus a golf course. Wiped out an egret rookery. A mangrove estuary. And too late it was discovered that the fairways were leaching fertilizer and pesticides directly into the waters of Biscayne Bay.

Molly McNamara said, "Those were the bad old days."

"Joe's still upset."

"But it certainly wasn't his fault. He must've been barely a teenager when Seashell was developed."

"He's got a thing about his father," Carrie said.

"Is that what this is all about?"

"He hears bulldozers in his sleep."

Molly said, "It's not as strange as you might imagine. The question is, can you take it? Is this the kind of fellow you want?"

"That's a tough one," Carrie said. "He could easily get himself killed this week."

"Take the blue bedroom at the end of the hall."

"Thank you, Miss McNamara."

"Just one favor," Molly said. "The headboard—it's an antique. I found it at a shop in Williamsburg."

"We'll be careful," Carrie promised.

▼ ▼ ▼

That night they made love on the bare pine floor. Drenched in sweat, they slid like ice cubes across the slick varnished planks. Eventually they wound up wedged headfirst in a corner, where Carrie fell asleep with Joe Winder's earlobe clenched tenderly in her teeth. He was starting to doze himself when he heard Molly's voice in the adjoining bedroom. She was talking sternly to a man who didn't sound like either Skink or the two redneck burglars.

When Winder heard the other door close, he delicately extricated himself from Carrie's bite and lifted her to the bed. Then he wrapped himself in an old quilt and crept into the hall to see who was in the next room.

The last person he expected to find was Agent Billy Hawkins of the Federal Bureau of Investigation. Trussed to a straight-backed chair, Hawkins wore someone else's boxer shorts and black nylon socks. A bandage was wadded around one bare thigh, and two strips of hurricane tape crisscrossed his mouth. He reeked of antiseptic.

Joe Winder slipped into the room and twisted the lock behind him. Gingerly he peeled the heavy tape from the agent's face.

"Fancy meeting you here."

"Nice getup," Bill Hawkins remarked. "Would you please untie me?"

"First tell me what happened."

"What does it look like? The old bird shot me."

"Any particular reason?"

"Just get me loose, goddammit."

Winder said, "Not until I hear the story."

Reluctantly, Hawkins told him about Bud Schwartz and the long-distance phone call to Queens and the possible exposure of a federally protected witness.

"Who's the flip?"

"I can't tell you *that*."

Joe Winder pressed the hurricane tape over Hawkins's lips—then fiercely yanked it away. Hawkins yelped. Tears of pain sprang to his eyes. In colorful expletives he offered the opinion that Winder had gone insane.

The excruciating procedure was repeated on one of Billy Hawkins's bare nipples and nearly uprooted a cluster of curly black hairs. "I can do this all night," Winder said. "I'm way past the point of caring."

The agent took a long bitter moment to compose himself. "You could go to prison," he mumbled.

"For assaulting you with adhesive tape? I don't think so." Winder placed one gummy strip along the line of soft hair that trailed south-ward from Billy Hawkins's navel. The agent gaped helplessly as Winder jerked hard; the tape came off with a sibilant rip.

"You—you're a goddamn lunatic!"

"But I'm your only hope. Who's going to believe you were shot and abducted by an elderly widow? And if they should believe it, what would that do to your career?" Joe Winder spread the quilt on the floor and sat cross-legged in front of the hog-tied agent.

"Blaine, Washington," Winder said. "Isn't that the FBI's equivalent of Siberia?"

Hawkins conceded the point silently. The political cost of prosecuting a grandmother and a pair of candyass burglars would be high. The Bureau was hypersensitive to incidents incongruous with the lantern-jawed crime-buster image promoted by J. Edgar Hoover; for an FBI agent to be overpowered by a dottering senior citizen was a disgrace. An immediate transfer to some godforsaken cowtown would be a certainty.

"So what can you do?" Hawkins asked Winder sourly.

"Maybe nothing. Maybe save your skin. Did Molly make you call the office?"

The agent nodded. "At gunpoint. I told them I was taking a couple of sick days."

"They ask about this Mafia thing?"

"I told them it wasn't panning out. Looked like a bullshit shakedown." Hawkins sounded embarrassed. "That's what she made me say. Threatened to shoot me again if I didn't go along with the routine—and it didn't sound like a bluff."

"You did the right thing," Joe Winder said. "No sense chancing it." He stood up and rewrapped himself in the quilt. "You'll have to stay like this a while," he told the agent. "It's the only way."

"I don't get it. What's your connection to these crackpots?"

"Long story."

"Winder, don't be a jackass. This isn't a game." Hawkins spoke sternly for a man in his ridiculous predicament. "Somebody could get killed. That's not what you want, is it?"

"Depends. Tell me the name of this precious witness."

"Frankie King."

Joe Winder shrugged. "Never heard of him."

"Moved down from New York after he snitched on some of Gotti's crowd. This was a few years back."

"Swift move. What's he calling himself these days?"

"That I can't possibly tell you."

"Then you're on your own, Billy. Think about it. Your word against Grandma Moses. Picture the headlines: 'Sharpshooter Widow Gunned Me Down, Nude G-Man Claims.'"

Hawkins sagged dispiritedly. He said, "The flip's name is Francis Kingsbury. You happy now?"

"Kingsbury?" Joe Winder raised his eyes to the heavens and crackled raucously. "The Mafia is coming down here to whack Mr. X!"

"Hey," Billy Hawkins said, "it's not funny."

But it was very funny to Joe Winder. "Francis X. Kingsbury. Millionaire theme-park developer and real-estate mogul, darling of the Chamber of Commerce, 1988 Rotarian Citizen of the Year. And you're telling me he's really a two-bit jizzbag on the run from the mob?"

Ecstatically, Joe Winder hopped from foot to foot, spinning in a circle and twirling Molly's quilt like a calico cape.

"Oh, Billy boy," he sang, "isn't this a great country!"

▼ ▼ ▼

They were thirty minutes late to the airport because Danny Pogue insisted on watching the end of a *National Geographic* television documentary about rhinoceros poachers in Africa.

In the car he couldn't stop talking about the program. "The only reason they kill 'em, see, what they're after is the horns. Just the horns!" He put his fist on his nose to simulate a rhinoceros snout. "In some places they use 'em for sex potions."

"Get off it," said Bud Schwartz.

"No shit. They grind the horns into powder and put it in their tea."

"Does it work?"

"I don't know," Danny Pogue said. "The TV didn't say."

"Like, it gives you a super big boner or what?"

"I don't know, Bud, the TV didn't say. They just talked about how much the powder goes for in Hong Kong, stuff like that. Thousands of bucks."

Bud Schwartz said, "You ask me, they left out the most important part of the show. Does it work or not?"

He drove into one of the airport garages and snatched a ticket from the machine. He parked on Level M, as always. "M" for Mother; it was the only way Bud Schwartz could remember how to find his car. He was annoyed that his partner wasn't sharing in the excitement of the moment: they were about to be rich.

"After today, you can retire," Bud Schwartz said. "No more b-and-e's. Man, we should throw us a party tonight."

Danny Pogue said, "I ain't in the mood."

They stepped onto the moving sidewalk and rode in silence to the Delta Airlines concourse. The plane had arrived on time, so the visitor already was waiting outside the gate. As promised, he was carrying a blue umbrella; otherwise Bud Schwartz would never have known that he was the hit man. He stood barely five feet tall and weighed at least two hundred pounds. He had thinning brown hair, small black eyes and skin that was the color of day-old lard. Under a herringbone sport coat he wore a striped polyester shirt, open at the neck, with a braided gold chain. The hit man seemed fond of gold; a bracelet rattled on his wrist when he shook Bud Schwartz's hand.

"Hello," said the burglar.

"You call me Lou." The hit man spoke in a granite baritone that didn't match the soft roly-polyness of his figure.

"Hi, Lou," said Danny Pogue. "I'm Bud's partner."

"How nice for you. Where's the car?" He pointed to a Macy's shopping bag near his feet. "That's yours. Now, where's the car?"

On the drive south, Danny Pogue peeked in the Macy's bag and saw that it was full of cash. Lou was up in the front seat next to Bud Schwartz.

"I wanna do this tomorrow," he was saying. "I gotta get home for my wife's birthday. She's forty." Then he farted loudly and pretended not to hear it.

"Forty? No kidding?" said Bud Schwartz. He had been expecting something quite different in the way of a mob assassin. Perhaps it wasn't fair, but Bud Schwartz was disappointed in Lou's appearance. For Francis Kingsbury's killer, he had envisioned someone taut, snake-eyed and menacing—not fat, balding and flatulent.

Just goes to show, thought Bud Schwartz, these days everything's hype. Even the damn Mafia.

From the back seat, Danny Pogue asked: "How're you gonna do it? What kinda gun?"

Lou puffed out his cheeks and said, "Brand X. The fuck do you care, what kinda gun?"

"Danny," Bud Schwartz said, "let's stay out of the man's private business, okay?"

"I didn't mean nothin'."

"You usually don't."

The man named Lou said, "This the neighborhood?"

"We're almost there," said Bud Schwartz.

"I can't get over all these trees," Lou said. "Parts a Jersey look like this. My wife's mother lives in Jersey, a terrific old lady. Seventy-seven years old, she bowls twice a week! In a league!"

Bud Schwartz smiled weakly. Perfect. A hit man who loves his mother-in-law. What next—he collects for the United Way?

The burglar said to Lou: "Maybe it's better if you rent a car. For tomorrow, I mean."

"Sure. Usually I do my own driving."

Danny Pogue tapped his partner on the shoulder and said, "Slow down, Bud, It's up here on the right."

Kingsbury's estate was bathed in pale orange lights. Gray sedans with green bubble lights were parked to block both ends of the driveway. Three men sat in each sedan; two more, in security-guard uniforms, were posted at the front door. It was, essentially, the complete private security force of the Amazing Kingdom of Thrills—except for Pedro Luz, who was inside the house, his wheelchair parked vigilantly at Francis Kingsbury's bedroom door.

Bud Schwartz drove by slowly. "Look at this shit," he muttered. Once they had passed the house, he put some muscle into the accelerator.

"An army," Lou said, "that's what it was."

Danny Pogue sank low in the back seat. With both hands he clutched the Macy's bag to his chest. "Let's just go," he said. "Bud, let's just haul ass."

29

On the morning of August 2, Jake Harp crawled into the back of a white limousine and rode in a dismal gin-soaked stupor to the construction site on North Key Largo. There he was met by Charles Chelsea, Francis X. Kingsbury and a phalanx of armed security men whose crisp blue uniforms failed to mitigate their shifty felonious smirks. The entourage moved briskly across a recently bulldozed plateau, barren except for a bright green hillock that was cordoned with rope and ringed by reporters, photographers and television cameramen. Kingsbury took Jake Harp by the elbow and, ascending the grassy knob, waved mechanically; it reminded Charles Chelsea of the rigidly determined way that Richard Nixon had saluted before boarding the presidential chopper for the final time. Except that, compared to Francis Kingsbury, Nixon was about as tense as Pee Wee Herman.

Jake Harp heard himself pleading for coffee, please God, even decaf, but Kingsbury seemed not to hear him. Jake Harp blinked amphibiously and struggled to focus on the scene. It was early. He was outdoors. The sun was intensely bright. The Atlantic Ocean murmured at his back. And somebody had dressed him: Izod shirt, Sansibelt slacks, tasseled Footjoy golf shoes. What could this be! Then he heard the scratchy click of a portable microphone and the oily voice of Charles Chelsea.

"Welcome, everybody. We're standing on what will soon be the first tee of the Falcon Trace Championship Golf Course. As you can see, we've got a little work ahead of us. . . ."

Laughter. These numbnuts are laughing, thought Jake Harp. He squinted at the white upturned faces and recognized one or two as sportswriters.

More from Chelsea: ". . . and we thought it would be fun to inaugurate the construction of this magnificent golfing layout with a hitting clinic."

Jake Harp's stomach clenched as somebody folded a three-wood into his fingers. The golf pro stared in disgust: a graphite head. They expect me to hit with metal!

Charles Chelsea's well-tanned paw settled amiably on Jake Harp's shoulder; the stench of Old Spice was overpowering.

"This familiar fellow needs no introduction," Chelsea was saying. "He's graciously agreed to christen the new course by hitting a few balls into the ocean—since we don't actually have a fairway yet."

Laughter again. Mysterious, inexplicable laughter. Jake Harp swayed, bracing himself with the three-wood. What had he been drinking last night? Vodka sours? Tanqueray martinis? Possibly both. He remembered dancing with a banker's wife. He remembered telling her how he'd triple-bogeyed the Road Hole and missed the cut at the British Open; missed the damn cut, all because some fat Scotsman booted the ball. . . .

Jake Harp also remembered the banker's wife whispering something about a blowjob—but did it happen? He hoped so, but he truly couldn't recall. One thing was certain: today he was physically incapable of swinging a golf club; it was simply out of the question. He wondered how he would break the news to Francis Kingsbury, who was bowing to the photographers in acknowledgment of Charles Chelsea's effusive introduction.

"Frank," said Jake Harp. "Where am I?"

With a frozen smile, Kingsbury remarked that Jake Harp looked about as healthy as dog barf.

"A bad night," the golfer rasped. "I'd like to go home and lie down."

Then came an acrid gust of cologne as Chelsea leaned in: "Hit a few, Jake, okay? No interviews, just a photo op."

"But I can't use a fucking graphite wood. This is Jap voodoo, Frank, I need my MacGregors."

Francis Kingsbury gripped Jake Harp by the shoulders and turned him toward the ocean. "And would you please, for Christ's sake, try not to miss the goddamn ball?"

Chelsea cautioned Kingsbury to keep his voice down. The sportswriters were picking up on the fact that Jake Harp was seriously under the weather.

"Coffee's on the way," Chelsea chirped lightly.

"You want me to hit it in the ocean?" Jake Harp said. "This is nuts."

One of the news photographers shouted for the security officers to get out of the way, they were blocking the picture. Kingsbury commanded the troops of Pedro Luz to move to one side; Pedro Luz himself was not present, having refused with vague mutterings to exit the storage room and join the phony golf clinic at Falcon Trace. His men, however, embraced with gusto and amusement the task of guarding Francis X. Kingsbury from assailants unknown.

Having cleared the security force to make an opening for Jake Harp, Kingsbury ordered the golfer to swing away.

"I can't, Frank."

"What?"

"I'm hung over. I can't lift the bloody club."

"Assume the position, Jake. You're starting to piss me off."

Tottering slightly, Jake Harp slowly arranged himself in the familiar stance that *Golf Digest* once hailed as "part Hogan, part Nicklaus, part Baryshnikov"—chin down, feet apart, shoulders square, left arm straight, hands interlocked loosely on the shaft of the club.

"There," Jake Harp said gamely.

Charles Chelsea cleared his throat. Francis Kingsbury said, "A golf ball would help, Jake."

"Oh Jesus, you're right."

"You got everything but a goddamn ball."

Under his breath, Jake Harp said, "Frank, would you do me a favor? Tee it up?"

"What?"

"I can't bend down. I'm too hung over, Frank. If I try to bend, I'll fall on my face. I swear to God."

Francis Kingsbury dug in his pocket and pulled out a scuffed Maxfli and a plastic tee that was shaped like a naked woman. "You're quite an athlete, Jake. A regular Jim Fucking Thorpe."

Gratefully Jake Harp watched Kingsbury drop to one knee and plant the tee. Then suddenly the sun exploded, and a molten splinter tore a hole in the golfer's belly, spinning him like a tenpin and knocking him flat. A darkening puddle formed as he lay there and floundered, gulping for breath through a mouthful of fresh Bermuda sod. Jake

Harp was not too hung over to realize he could be dying, and it bitterly occurred to him that he would rather leave his mortal guts on the fairways of Augusta or Muirfield or Pebble Beach.

Anywhere but here.

▼ ▼ ▼

Bud Schwartz and Danny Pogue had driven up to Kendall to break into a house. The house belonged to FBI Agent Billy Hawkins, who was still tied up as Molly McNamara's prisoner.

"Think he's got a dog?" said Danny Pogue.

Bud Schwartz said probably not. "Guys like that, they think dogs are for pussies. It's a cop mentality."

But Bud Schwartz was wrong. Bill Hawkins owned a German shepherd. The burglars could see the animal prowling the fence in the backyard.

"Guess we gotta do the front-door routine," said Bud Schwartz. What a way to end a career: breaking into an FBI man's house in broad daylight. "I thought we retired," Bud Schwartz complained. "All that dough we got, tell me what's the point if we're still pullin' these jobs."

Danny Pogue said, "Just this one more. And besides, what if Lou takes the money back?"

"No way."

"If he can't get to the guy, yeah, he might. Already he thinks we tipped Kingsbury off, on account of all those rent-a-cops."

Bud Schwartz said he wasn't worried about Lou going back on the deal. "These people are pros, Danny. Now gimme the scroogie." They were poised at Billy Hawkins's front door. Danny Pogue checked the street for cars or pedestrians; then he handed Bud Schwartz a nine-inch screwdriver.

Skeptically Danny Pogue said, "Guy's gotta have a deadbolt. Anybody works for the FBI, probably he's got an alarm, too. Maybe even lasers."

But there was no alarm system. Bud Schwartz pried the doorjamb easily. He put his shoulder to the wood and pushed it open. "You believe that?" he said to his partner. "See what I mean about cop mentality. They think they're immune."

"Yeah," said Danny Pogue. "Immune." Later he'd ask Molly McNamara what it meant.

They closed the door and entered the empty house. Bud Schwartz would never have guessed that a federal agent lived there. It was a typical suburban Miami home: three bedrooms, two baths, nothing special. Once they got used to the idea, the burglars moved through the rooms with casual confidence—wife at work, kids at school, no sweat.

"Too bad we're not stealin' anything," Bud Schwartz mused.

"Want to?" said his partner. "Just for old times' sake."

"What's the point?"

"I saw one of the kids has a CD player."

"Wow," said Bud Schwartz acidly. "What's that, like, thirty bucks. Maybe forty?"

"No, man, it's a Sony."

"Forget it. Now gimme the papers."

In captivity Billy Hawkins had agreed to notify his family that he was out of town on a top-secret assignment. However, the agent had displayed a growing reluctance to call the FBI office and lie about being sick. To motivate him, Molly McNamara had composed a series of cryptic notes and murky correspondence suggesting that Hawkins was not the most loyal of government servants. Prominently included in the odd jottings were the telephone numbers of the Soviet Embassy and the Cuban Special Interest Section in Washington, D.C. For good measure, Molly had included a bank slip showing a suspicious $25,000 deposit to Agent Billy Hawkin's personal savings account—a deposit that Molly herself had made at the South Miami branch of Unity National Savings & Loan. The purpose of these maneuvers was to create a shady portfolio that, despite its sloppiness, Billy Hawkins would not wish to try to explain to his colleagues at the FBI.

Who would definitely come to the house in search of clues, if Agent Hawkins failed to check in.

Molly McNamara had entrusted the bank receipt, phone numbers and other manufactured evidence to Bud Schwartz and Danny Pogue, whose mission was to conceal the material in a semi-obvious location in Billy Hawkins's bedroom.

Bud Schwartz chose the second drawer of the nightstand. He placed the envelope under two unopened boxes of condoms. "Raspberry-colored," he marveled. "FBI man uses raspberry rubbers!" Another stereotype shattered.

Danny Pogue was admiring a twelve-inch portable television as if it were a rare artifact. "Jesus, Bud, you won't believe this."

"Don't tell me it's a black-and-white."

"Yep. You know the last time I saw one?"

"Little Havana," said Bud Schwartz, "that duplex off Twelfth Avenue. I remember."

"Remember what we got for it."

"Yeah. Thirteen goddamn dollars." The fence was a man named Fat Jack on Seventy-ninth Street, near the Boulevard. Bud Schwartz couldn't stand Fat Jack not only because he was cheap but because he smelled like dirty socks. One day Bud Schwartz had boosted a case of Ban Extra Dry Roll-on Deodorant sticks from the back of a Publix truck, and given it to Fat Jack as a hint. Fat Jack had handed him eight bucks and said that nobody should ever use roll-ons because they cause cancer of the armpits.

"I don't get it," said Danny Pogue. "I thought the FBI paid big bucks—what's a baby Magnavox go for, two hundred retail? You'd think he could spring for color."

"Who knows, maybe he spends it all on clothes. Come on, let's take off." Bud Schwartz wanted to be long gone before the mailman arrived and noticed what had happened to the front door.

Danny Pogue turned on the portable TV and said, "That's not a bad picture." The noon news was just starting.

"I said let's go, Danny."

"Wait, look at this!"

A video clip showed a heavyset man in golf shoes being hoisted on a stretcher. The man's shirt was drenched in blood, but his eyelids were half open. A plastic oxygen mask covered the man's face and nose, but the jaw moved as if he were trying to speak. The newscaster reported that the shooting had taken place at a new resort development called Falcon Trace, near Key Largo.

"Lou! He did it!" exclaimed Danny Pogue. "You were right."

"Only trouble is, that ain't Mr. Kingsbury."

"You sure?"

Bud Schwartz sat down in front of the television. The anchorman had tossed the sniper story to a sportscaster, who was somberly recounting the stellar career of Jake Harp. The golfer's photograph, taken in happier times, popped up on a wide green mat behind the sports desk.

Danny Pogue said, "Who the hell's that?"

"Not Kingsbury," grunted Bud Schwartz. The mishap confirmed his worst doubts about Lou's qualifications as a hit man. It was unbelievable. The asshole had managed to shoot the wrong guy.

"Know what?" said Danny Pogue. "There's a Jake Harp Cadillac in Boca Raton where I swiped a bunch of tape decks once. Is that the same guy? This golfer?"

Bud Schwartz said, "I got no earthly idea." What was all this crap the TV guy was yakking about—career earnings, number of Top Ten finishes, average strokes per round, percentage of greens hit in regulation. To Bud Schwartz, golf was as foreign as polo. Except you didn't see so many fat guys playing polo.

"The main thing is, did they catch the shooter?"

"Nuh-huh." Danny Pogue had his nose to the tube. "They said he got away in a boat. No arrests, no motives is what they said."

Bud Schwartz was trying to picture Lou from Queens at the helm of a speedboat, racing for the ocean's horizon.

"He's gonna be pissed," Danny Pogue said.

"Yeah, well, I don't guess his boss up North is gonna be too damn thrilled, either. Whackin' the wrong man."

"He ain't dead yet. Serious but stable is what they said."

Bud Schwartz said it didn't really matter. "Point is, it's still a fuckup. A major *major* fuckup."

The Mafia had gunned down a life member of the Professional Golfers Association.

▼ ▼ ▼

Pedro Luz finally emerged from the storage room, where he had been measuring his penis. He rolled the wheelchair out to Kingsbury Lane for the morning rehearsal of the Summerfest Jubilee, a greatly embellished version of the nightly musical pageant. Pedro Luz needed something to lift his spirits. His leg had begun to throb in an excruciating way; no combination of steroids and analgesics put a dent in the pain. To add psychic misery to the physical, Pedro Luz had now documented the fact that his sexual wand was indeed shrinking as a result of prolonged steroid abuse. At first, Pedro Luz had assured himself that it was only an optical illusion; the more swollen his face and limbs became, the smaller everything else appeared to be. But weeks of meticulous calibrations had produced conclusive evidence: His wee-wee had withered from 10.4 centimeters to 7.9 centimeters in its flaccid state. Worse, it seemed to Pedro Luz (although there was no painless way to measure) that his testicles had also become smaller—not yet as tiny as BBs, as Churrito had predicted, but more like gumballs.

These matters weighed heavily on his mind as Pedro Luz sat in the broiling sun and watched the floats rumble by. He was hoping that the sight of Annette Fury's regal bosom would buoy his mood, and was disappointed to see that she had been replaced as Princess Golden Sun. The new actress looked familiar, but Pedro Luz couldn't place the face. She was a very pretty girl, but the black wig needed some work, as did the costume—buckskin culottes and a fringed halter top. Her singing was quite lovely, much better than Annette's, but Pedro Luz would've preferred larger breasts. The lioness that shared the Seminole float was in no condition to rehearse; panting miserably in the humidity, the animal sprawled half-conscious on one side, thus thwarting the cat-straddling exit that culminated the princess's dramatic performance.

As the parade disbanded, Pedro Luz eased the wheelchair off the curb and approached the Seminole float. The pretty young singer was not to be seen; there was only the driver of the float and Dr. Kukor, the park veterinarian, who had climbed aboard to revive the heatstruck lioness. Dr. Kukor was plainly flabbergasted by the sight of Pedro Luz.

"I lost my foot in an accident," the security chief explained.

Dr. Kukor hadn't noticed the missing foot. It was the condition of Pedro Luz's face, so grossly inflated, that had generated the horror. The man looked like a blowfish: puffed cheeks, bulging lips, teeny eyes wedged deep under a pimpled, protuberant brow.

To Pedro Luz, Dr. Kukor directed the most inane inquiry of a long and distinguished career: "Are you all right?"

"Just fine. Where's the young lady?"

Dr. Kukor pointed, and Pedro Luz spun the wheelchair to see: Princess Golden Sun stood behind him. She was zipping a black Miami Heat warm-up jacket over the halter.

Pedro Luz introduced himself and said, "I've seen you before, right?"

"It's possible," said Carrie Lanier, who recognized him instantly as the goon who shot up her double-wide, the creep she'd run over with the car. She noticed the bandaged trunk of his leg, and felt a pang of guilt. It passed quickly.

"You sing pretty nice," Pedro Luz said, "but you could use a couple three inches up top. If you get my meaning."

"Thanks for the advice."

"I know a doctor who specializes in that sort of thing. Maybe I could get you a discount."

"Actually," said Carrie, patting her chest, "I kind of like the little fellas just the way they are."

"Suit yourself." Pedro Luz scratched brutally at a raw patch on his scalp. "I'm trying to figure where I saw you before. Take off the wig for a second, okay?"

Carrie Lanier pressed her hands to her eyes and began to cry—plaintive, racking sobs that attracted the concern of tourists and the other pageant performers.

Pedro Luz said, "Hey, what's the matter?"

"It's not a wig!" Carrier cried. "It's my real hair." She turned and scampered down a stairwell into The Catacombs.

"Geez, I'm sorry," said Pedro Luz, to no one. Flustered, he rolled full tilt toward the security office. Speeding downhill past the Wet Willy, he chafed his knuckles trying to brake the wheelchair. When he reached the chilled privacy of the storage room, he slammed the door and drove the bolt. In the blackness Pedro Luz probed for the string that turned on the ceiling's bare bulb; he found it and jerked hard.

The white light revealed a shocking scene. Someone had entered Pedro's sanctuary and destroyed the delicate web of sustenance. Sewing shears had snipped the intravenous tubes into worthless inch-long segments, which littered the floor like plastic rice. The same person had sliced open every one of Pedro's unused IV bags; the wheelchair rested, literally, in a pond of liquid dextrose.

But by far the worst thing to greet Pedro Luz was the desolate sight of brown pill bottles, perhaps a half-dozen, open and empty on the floor. Whoever he was, the sonofabitch had flushed Pedro's anabolic steroids down the john. The ceramic pestle with which he had so lovingly powdered his Winstrols lay shattered beneath the toilet tank.

And, on the wall, a message in coral lipstick. Pedro Luz groaned and backed the wheelchair so he could read it easier. A wild rage heaved through his chest and he began to snatch items from the storage shelves and hurl them against the cinder block: nightsticks, gas masks, flashlights, handcuffs, cans of Mace, pistol grips, boxes of bullets.

Only when there was nothing left to throw did Pedro Luz stop to read the words on the wall again. Written in a loopy flamboyant script, the message said:

> Good morning, Dipshit!
> Just wanted you to know I'm not dead.
> Have a nice day, and don't forget your Wheaties!

It was signed, "Yours truly, J. Winder."

Pedro Luz emitted a feral cry and aimed himself toward the executive gym, where he spent the next two hours alone on the bench press, purging the demons and praying for his testicles to grow back.

30

Somehow Charles Chelsea summoned the creative energy necessary for fabrication:

Golf legend Jake Harp was accidentally shot Thursday during groundbreaking ceremonies for the new Falcon Trace Golf and Country Club Resort on North Key Largo.

The incident occurred as Mr. Harp was preparing to hit a ball off what will be the first tee of the 6,970-yard championship golf course, which Mr. Harp designed himself. The golfer apparently was struck by a stray bullet from an unidentified boater, who may have been shooting at nearby sea gulls.

Mr. Harp was listed in serious but stable condition after undergoing surgery at South Miami Hospital.

"This is a tragedy for the entire golfing world, professionals and amateurs alike," said Francis X. Kingsbury, the developer of Falcon Trace, and a close personal friend of Mr. Harp.

"We're all praying for Jake to pull through," added Kingsbury, who is also the founder and chairman of the Amazing Kingdom of Thrills, the popular family theme park adjacent to the sprawling Falcon Trace project.

By mid-afternoon Thursday, police had not yet arrested any suspects in the shooting. Charles Chelsea, vice president of publicity for Falcon Trace Ltd., disputed accounts by some reporters on the scene who claimed that Mr. Harp was the victim of a deliberate sniper attack.

"There's no reason to believe that this terrible event was anything but a freak accident," Chelsea said.

Kingsbury approved the press release with a disgusted flick of his hand. He drained a third martini and asked Chelsea if he had ever before witnessed a man being shot.

"Not that I can recall, sir."

"Close up, I mean," Kingsbury said. "Dead bodies are one thing— car wrecks, heart attacks—I'm not counting those. What I mean is, *bang!*"

Chelsea said, "It happened so damn fast."

"Well, you know who they were aiming at? *Moi*, that's who. How about that!" Kingsbury pursed his lips and drummed his knuckles.

"You?" Chelsea said. "Who would try to kill you?" He instantly thought of Joe Winder.

But Kingsbury smiled drunkenly and began to hum the theme from *The Godfather*.

Chelsea said, "There's something you're not telling me."

"Of course there's something I'm not telling you. There's tons of shit I'm not telling you. What, I look like a total moron?"

Watching Francis Kingsbury pour another martini, Chelsea felt like seizing the bottle and guzzling himself into a Tanqueray coma. The time had come to look for another job; the fun had leaked out of this one. A malevolent force, unseen and uncontrollable, had perverted Chelsea's role from cheery town crier to conniving propagandist. Reflecting on the past weeks, he realized he should've quit on the day the blue-tongued voles were stolen, the day innocence was lost.

We are all no longer children, Chelsea thought sadly. We are potential co-defendants.

"No offense," Kingsbury was saying, "but you're just a flack. I only tell you what I've absolutely got to tell you. Which is precious damned little."

"That's the way it should be," Chelsea said lifelessly.

"Right! Loose dicks sink ships. Or whatever." Kingsbury slurped at the gin like a thirsty mutt. "Anyhow, don't worry about me. I'm taking —well, let's just say, the necessary precautions. You can be goddamn sure."

"That's wise of you."

"Meanwhile, sharpen your pencil. I ordered us more animals." Kingsbury wistfully studied his drink. "Who's the guy in the Bible, the one with the ark. Was it Moses?"

"Noah," Chelsea said. Boy, was the old man smashed.

"Yeah, Noah, that's who I feel like. Me and these fucking critters. Anyhow, we're back in the endangered-species business, saving the animals. There oughta be some publicity when they get here. You see to it."

The woman named Rachel Lark had phoned all the way from New Zealand. She said she'd done her best on such short notice, and said Kingsbury would be pleased when he saw the new attractions for the Rare Animal Pavilion. I hope so, he'd told her, because we could damn sure use some good news.

Fearing the worst, Charles Chelsea said, "What kind of animals are we talking about?"

"Cute is what I ordered. Thirty-seven hundred dollars' worth of cute." Kingsbury snorted. "Could be anything. The point is, we've got to rebound, Charlie. We got a fucking void to fill."

"Right."

"Speaking of which, we also need another golfer. In case Jake croaks, God forbid."

Chelsea recoiled at the cold-bloodedness of the assignment. "It won't look good, sir, not with what happened this morning. It's best if we stick by Jake."

"Sympathy's all fine and dandy, Charlie, but we got more than golf at stake here. We got waterfront to sell. We got patio homes. We got club memberships. Can Jake Harp—don't get me wrong—but in his present situation can Jake do promotional appearances? TV commercials? Celebrity programs? We don't even know if Jake can still breathe, much less swing a fucking five-iron."

For once Francis Kingsbury expressed himself in nearly cogent syntax. It must be excellent gin, Chelsea thought.

"I want you to call Nicklaus," Kingsbury went on. "Tell him money is no problem."

"Jack Nicklaus," the publicity man repeated numbly.

"No, *Irving* Nicklaus. Who the hell do you think! And if you can't get the Bear, try Palmer. And if you can't get Arnie, you try Trevino. And if you can't get the Mex, try the Shark. And so on. The bigger the better, but make it quick."

Knowing it would do no good, Chelsea reminded Kingsbury that he had tried to recruit the top golfing names when he was first planning Falcon Trace, and that they'd all said no. Only Jake Harp had the stomach to work for him.

"I don't care what they said before," Kingsbury growled, "you call 'em again. Money is no problem, all right?"

"Again, I'd just like to caution you about how this might appear to people—"

"I need a hotshot golfer, Charlie. The hell do you guys call it—a media personality?" Kingsbury raised one plump fist and let it fall heavily on the desk. "I can't sell a golf resort when my star golfer's on a goddamn respirator. Don't you understand? Don't you know a goddamn thing about Florida real estate?"

▼ ▼ ▼

They rode to the airport in edgy silence. Danny Pogue was waiting for Lou to say something. Like it was all *their* fault. Like the people in Queens wanted their money back.

Earlier Bud Schwartz had pulled his partner aside and said, look, they want the dough, we give it back. This is the mob, he said, and we're not playing games with the mob. But it's damned important, Bud Schwartz had said, that Lou and his Mafia people know that we didn't tip off Kingsbury. How the hell he found out about the hit, it don't matter. It wasn't us and we gotta make that clear, okay? Danny Pogue agreed wholeheartedly. Like Bud Schwartz, he didn't want to go through the rest of life having somebody else start his car every morning. Or peeking around corners, watching out for inconspicuous fat guys like Lou.

So when they got to the Delta Airlines terminal, Danny Pogue shook Lou's hand and said he was very sorry about what had happened. "Honest to God, we didn't tell nobody."

"That's the truth," said Bud Schwartz.

Lou shrugged. "Probably a wire. Don't sweat it."

"Thanks," said Danny Pogue, flushed with relief. He pumped Lou's pudgy arm vigorously. "Thanks for—well, just thanks is all."

Lou nodded. His nose and cheeks were splashed pink with raw sunburn. He wore the same herringbone coat and striped shirt that he had when he'd gotten off the airplane. There was still no sign of the gun, but the burglars knew he was carrying it somewhere on his corpulent profile.

Lou said, "Since I know you're dyin' to ask, what happened was this: the asshole bent over. Don't ask me why, but he bent over just as I pulled the trigger."

"Bud thought you probably got the two guys mixed up—"

"I didn't get nobody mixed up." Lou's upper lip curled when he directed this bulletin toward Bud Schwartz. "The guy leaned over is all. Otherwise he'd be dead right now, trust me."

Despite his doubts about Lou's marksmanship, Bud Schwartz didn't want him to leave Miami with hard feelings. He didn't want any hit man, even a clumsy one, to be sore at him.

"Could've happened to anybody," Bud Schwartz said supportively. "Sounds like one hell of a tough shot from the water, anyway."

A voice on the intercom announced that the Delta flight to LaGuardia was boarding at Gate 7. Lou said, "The guy that got hit, I heard he's hanging on."

"Yeah, some golfer named Harp," said Danny Pogue. "Serious but stable."

"Maybe he'll make it," Lou said. "That would be good."

Bud Schwartz asked what would happen when Lou returned to Queens.

"Have a sitdown with my people. Find out what they want to do next. Then I got this big birthday party for my wife's fortieth. I bought her one a them electric woks—she really likes Jap food, don't ask me why."

Danny Pogue said, "Are you in big trouble?"

Lou's chest bounced when he laughed. "With my wife or the boys? Ask me which is worse."

He picked up his carry-on and the blue umbrella, and waddled for the gate.

Bud Schwartz waved. "Sorry it got so screwed up."

"What the hell," said Lou, still laughing. "I got me a nice boat ride outta the deal."

▼ ▼ ▼

Joe Winder and Carrie Lanier met Trooper Jim Tile at the Snapper Creek Plaza on the Turnpike extension. They took a booth at the Roy Rogers and ordered burgers and shakes. Winder found the atmosphere more pleasant than it had been at Ocean Reef. Carrie asked Jim Tile if he had phoned Rikers Island.

"Yeah, I called," the trooper said. "They thought it was crazy, but they said they'd watch for anything out of the ordinary."

"Out of the ordinary hardly begins to describe him."

"New Yorkers," said Jim Tile, "think they've cornered the market on psychopaths. They don't know Florida."

Joe Winder said, "I don't think he's going to Rikers Island. I think he's still here."

"I heard about Harp," said Jim Tile, "and my opinion is no, it wasn't the governor. I'll put money on it."

"How can you be so sure?" asked Carrie.

"Because (a) it's not his style, and (b) he wouldn't have missed."

Winder said, "Mr. X was the target."

"Had to be," agreed Jim Tile. "Who'd waste a perfectly good bullet on a golfer?"

Carrie speculated that it could have been a disgruntled fan. Joe Winder threw an arm around her and gave her a hug. He'd been in a good mood since trashing Pedro Luz's steroid den.

The trooper was saying Skink might've headed upstate. "This morning somebody shot up a Greyhound on the interstate outside Orlando. Sixty-seven Junior Realtors on their way to Epcot."

Panic at Disney World! Winder thought. Kingsbury will come in his pants.

"Nobody was hurt," Jim Tile said, "which leads me to believe it was you-know-who." He pried the plastic cap off his milkshake and spooned out the ice cream. "Eight rounds into a speeding bus and nobody even gets nicked. That's one hell of a decent shot."

Carrie said, "I'm assuming they didn't catch the culprit."

"Vanished without a trace," said the trooper. "If it's him, they'll never even find a footprint. He knows that area of the state very well."

Winder said it was a long way to go for a man with two fresh gunshot wounds.

Jim Tile shrugged. "I called Game and Fish. The panther plane hasn't picked up the radio signal for days."

"So he's really gone," Carrie said.

"Or hiding in a bomb shelter."

"Joe thinks we should go ahead and make a move. He's got a plan all worked out."

Jim Tile raised a hand. "Don't tell me, please. I don't want to hear it."

"Fair enough," Winder said, "but I've got to ask a small favor."

"The answer is no."

"But it's nothing illegal."

The trooper used the corner of a paper napkin to polish the lenses of his sunglasses. "This falls into the general category of pressing your luck. Just because the governor gets away, don't think it's easy. Or even right."

"Please," said Carrie, "just listen."

"What is it you want me to do?"

"Your job," Joe Winder replied. "That's all."

▼ ▼ ▼

Later, in the rental boat, Joe Winder said he almost felt sorry for Charles Chelsea. "Getting your sports celebrity shot with the press watching, that's tough."

Carrie Lanier agreed that Chelsea was earning his salary. She was at the helm of the outboard, expertly steering a course toward the ocean shore of North Key Largo. A young man named Oscar sat shirtless on the bow, dangling his brown legs and drinking a root beer.

Carrie told Joe he had some strange friends.

"Oscar thinks he owes me a favor, that's all. Years ago I left his name out of a newspaper article and it wound up saving his life."

Carrie looked doubtful, but said nothing. Her hair was tied back in a ponytail. She wore amber sunglasses with green Day-Glo frames and a silver one-piece bathing suit. Oscar didn't stare, not even once. His mind was on business, and the soccer game he was missing on television. Most Thursdays he was on his way to Belize, only this morning there'd been a minor problem with Customs, and the flight was canceled. When Joe Winder called him at the warehouse, Oscar felt honorbound to lend a hand.

"He thinks I cut him a break," Winder whispered to Carrie, "but the fact is, I *did* use his name in the story. It just got edited out for lack of space."

"What was the article about?"

"Gunrunning."

From the bow, Oscar turned and signaled that they were close enough now. Kneeling on the deck, he opened a canvas duffel and began to arrange odd steel parts on a chamois cloth. The first piece that Carrie saw was a long gray tube.

"Oscar's from Colombia," Joe Winder explained. "His brother's in the M-19. They're leftist rebels."

"Thank you, Professor Kissinger." Carrie smeared the bridge of her nose with mauve-colored zinc oxide. It was clear from her attitude that she had reservations about this phase of the plan.

She said, "What makes you think Kingsbury needs another warning? I mean, he's got the mob after him, Joe. Why should he care about a couple of John Deeres?"

"He's a developer. He'll care." Winder leaned back and squinted at the sun. "Keep the pressure on, that's the key."

Carrie admired the swiftness with which Oscar went about his task. She said to Winder: "Tell me again what they call that."

"An RPG. Rocket-propelled grenade."

"And you're positive no one's going to get hurt?"

"It's lunch hour, Carrie. You heard the whistle." He took out a pair of waterproof Zeiss binoculars and scanned the shoreline until he found the stand of pigeon plums that Molly McNamara had told him about. The dreaded bulldozers had multiplied from two to five; they were parked in a semicircle, poised for the mission against the plum trees.

"Everybody's on their break," Winder reported. "Even the deputies." At the other end of the boat, Oscar assembled the grenade launcher in well-practiced silence.

Carrie cut the twin Evinrudes and let the currents nudge the boat over the grassy shallows. She took the field glasses and tried to spot the bird nest that Molly had mentioned. She couldn't see anything, the hardwoods were so dense.

"I'm not sure I understand the significance of this gesture," she said. "Mockingbirds aren't exactly endangered."

"These ones are." Winder peeled off his T-shirt and tied it around his forehead like a bandanna. The air stuck to his chest like a hot rag; the temperature on the water was ninety-four degrees, and no breeze. "You don't approve," he said to Carrie. "I can tell."

"What bothers me is the lack of imagination, Joe. You could be blowing up bulldozers the rest of your life."

The words stung, but she was right. Clever this was not, merely loud. "I'm sorry," he said, "but there wasn't time to come up with something more creative. The old lady said they were taking out the plum trees this afternoon, and it looks like she was right."

Oscar gave the okay sign from the bow. The boat had drifted close enough so they could hear the voices and lunchtime banter of the Falcon Trace construction crew.

"Which dozer you want?" Oscar inquired, raising the weapon to his shoulder.

"Take your pick."

"Joe, wait!" Carrie handed him the binoculars. "Over there, check it out."

Winder beamed when he spotted it. "Looks like they're pouring the slab for the clubhouse."

"That's a large cement mixer," Carrie noted.

"Sure is. A *very* large cement mixer." Joe Winder snapped his fingers and motioned to Oscar. Spying the new target, the young Colombian smiled broadly and readjusted his aim.

In a low voice Carrie said, "I take it he's done this sort of thing before."

"I believe so, yes."

Oscar grunted something in Spanish, then pulled the trigger. The RPG took out the cement truck quite nicely. An orange gout of flame shot forty feet into the sky, and warm gray gobs of cement rained down on the construction workers as they sprinted for their cars.

"See," Carrie said. "A little variety's always nice."

Joe Winder savored the smoky scent of chaos and wondered what his father would have thought.

We all shine on.

▼ ▼ ▼

That night Carrie banished him from the bedroom while she practiced her songs for the Jubilee. At first he listened in dreamy amazement at the door; her voice was crystalline, delicate, soothing. After a while Bud Schwartz and Danny Pogue joined him in the hallway, and Carrie's singing seemed to soften their rough convict features. Danny Pogue lowered his eyes and began to hum along; Bud Schwartz lay on the wooden floor with hands behind his head and gazed at the high pine beams. Molly McNamara even unlocked the door to the adjoining bedroom so that Agent Billy Hawkins, gagged but alert, could enjoy the beautiful musical interlude.

Eventually Joe Winder excused himself and slipped downstairs to make a call. He went through three telephone temptresses before they switched him to Nina's line.

"I'm glad it's you," she said. "There's something you've got to hear."

"I'm honestly not in the mood—"

"This is different, Joe. It took three nights to write."

What could he possibly say? "Go ahead, Nina."

"Ready?" She was so excited. He heard the rustle of paper. Then she took a breath and began to read:

> "Your hands find me in the night, burrow for my warmth.
> Lift me, turn me, move me apart.
> The language of blind insistence,
> You speak with a slow tongue on my belly,
> An eyelash fluttering against my nipple.
> This is the moment of raw cries and murmurs when
> Nothing matters in the vacuum of passion
> But passion itself."

He wasn't sure if she had finished. It sounded like a big ending, but he wasn't sure.

"Nina?"

"What do you think?"

"It's . . . vivid."

"Poetry. A brand-new concept in phone sex."

"Interesting." God, she's making a career of this.

"Did it arouse you?"

"Definitely," he said. "My loins surge in wild tumescence inside my jeans."

"Stop it, Joe!"

"I'm sorry. Really it's quite good." And maybe it was. He knew next to nothing about poetry.

"I wanted to try something different," Nina said, "something literate. A few of the girls complained—Miriam, of course. She's more comfortable with the old sucky-fucky."

"Well," Winder said, "it's all in the reading."

"My editor wants to see more."

"You have an editor?"

"For the syndication deal, Joe. What'd you think of the last part? *Nothing matters in the vacuum of passion but passion itself.*"

He said, " 'Abyss' is better than 'vacuum.' "

"The abyss of passion! You're right, Joe, that's much better."

"It's a long way from dry-humping on the Amtrak."

Nina laughed. He had almost forgotten how wonderful it sounded.

"So how was your hot date with The Voice?"

"It was very enjoyable. He's an exceptional man."

"What does he do?"

Without skipping a beat: "He markets General Motors products."

"Cars? He sells cars! That *is* exceptional."

Nina said, "I don't want to talk about this."

"Buicks? Pontiacs? Oldsmobiles? Or perhaps all three?"

"He is a surprisingly cultured man," Nina said. "An educated man. And it's Chevrolets, for your information. The light-truck division."

"Boy." Winder felt exhausted. First the poetry, now this. "Nina, I've got to ask. Does the face match the voice?"

"There's nothing wrong with the way he looks."

"Say no more."

"You can be such a prick," she observed.

"You're right. I'm sorry—again."

"He wants to marry me."

"Showing excellent taste," Winder said. "He'd be nuts if he didn't."

There was a brief pause, then Nina asked: "Are you the one who shot the golfer?"

"Nope. But I don't blame you for wondering."

"Please don't kill anybody, Joe. I know how strongly you feel about these issues, but please don't murder anyone."

"I'll try not to."

"Better sign off," she said. "I'm tying up the phone."

"Hey, I'm a paying customer."

"You really liked the poem?"

"It was terrific, Nina. I'm very proud."

He could tell she was pleased. "Any more suggestions?" she said.

"Well, the line about the nipple."

"Yes. *An eyelash fluttering against my nipple.*"

"The imagery is nice," Winder said, "but it makes it sound like you've got just one. Nipple, I mean."

"Hmm," said Nina. "That's a good point."

"Otherwise it's great."

"Thanks, Joe," she said. "Thanks for everything."

31

Joe Winder held Carrie in his arms and wondered why the women he loved were always a step or two ahead of him.

"So what are you planning?" he asked.

She stirred but didn't answer. Her cheek felt silky and warm against his chest. When would he ever learn to shut up and enjoy the moment?

"Carrie, I know you're not asleep."

Her eyes opened. Even in the darkness he could feel the liquid stare. "You're the only man I've ever been with," she said, "who insists on talking afterward."

"You inspire me, that's all."

"Aren't you exhausted?" She raised her head. "Was I hallucinating, or did we just fuck our brains out?"

Winder said, "I'm nervous as hell. I've been rehearsing it all in my head."

She told him to stop worrying and go to sleep. "What's the worst thing that could happen?"

"Jail is a distinct possibility. Death is another."

Carrie turned on her belly and slid between his legs. Then she propped her elbows on his rib cage, and rested her chin on her hands.

"What are you smiling at?" Winder said.

"It's all going to work out. I've got faith in you."

"But you're planning something, just the same."

"Joe, it might be my only chance."

"At what?"

"Singing. I mean really singing. Am I hurting you?"

"Oh, no, you're light as a feather."

"You asshole," she giggled, and began to tickle him ferociously. Winder locked his legs around her thighs and flipped her over in the sheets.

They were kissing when he felt compelled to pull back and say, "I'm sorry I dragged you into this mess."

"What mess? And, besides, you're doing the honest thing. Even if it's slightly mad."

"You're speaking of the major felonies?"

"Of course," Carrie said. "But your motives are absolutely pure and unassailable. I'll be cheering for you, Joe."

"Clinical insanity isn't out of the question," he said. "Just thinking about Kingsbury and that damn golf course, I get noises inside my skull."

"What kind of noises?"

"Hydraulic-type noises. Like the crusher on a garbage truck."

Carrie looked concerned, and he couldn't blame her. "It goes back to my old man," he said.

"Don't think about it so much, Joe."

"I'd feel better if the governor were here. Just knowing I wasn't the only lunatic—"

"I had a dream about him," she said quietly. "I dreamed he broke into prison and killed that guy—what's his name?"

"Mark Chapman," said Winder. "Mark David Chapman."

She heard sadness in the reply, sadness because she didn't remember the details. "Joe, I was only fourteen when it happened."

"You're right."

"Besides, I've always been lousy with names. Oswald, Sirhan, Hinkley—it's easy to lose track of these idiots."

"Sure is," Winder agreed.

Carrie tenderly laced her hands on the back of his neck. "Everything's going to be fine. And no, you're not crazy. A little zealous is all."

"It's not a bad plan," he said.

"Joe, it's a terrific plan."

"And if all goes well, you'll still have your job."

"No, I don't think so. I'm not much of a Seminole go-go dancer."

Now it was his turn to smile. "I take it there may be some last-minute changes in the musical program."

"Quite possibly," Carrie said.

He kissed her softly on the forehead. "I'll be cheering for you, too."

"I know you will, Joe."

▼ ▼ ▼

As far as Bud Schwartz was concerned, he'd rather be in jail than in a hospital. Practically everyone he ever knew who died—his mother, his brother, his uncles, his first probation officer—had died in hospital beds. In fact, Bud Schwartz couldn't think of a single person who'd come out of a hospital in better shape than when they'd gone in.

"What about babies?" Danny Pogue said.

"Babies don't count."

"What about your boy? Mike, Jr., wasn't he borned in a hospital?"

"Matter of fact, no. It was the back of a Bronco. And his name is *Bud*, Jr., like I told you." Bud Schwartz rolled down the window and tried to spit the toothpick from the corner of his mouth. It landed on his arm. "A hospital's the last place for a sick person to go," he said.

"You think she'll die there?"

"No. I don't wanna set foot in the place is all."

"Jesus, you're a cold shit."

Bud Schwartz was startled by his partner's anger. Out of pure guilt he relented and agreed to go, but only for a few minutes. Danny Pogue seemed satisfied. "Let's get some roses on the way."

"Fine. A lovely gesture."

"Hey, it'll mean a lot to her."

"Danny, this is the same woman who shot us. And you're talking flowers."

Molly McNamara had driven herself to Baptist Hospital after experiencing mild chest pains. She had a private room with a gorgeous view of a parking deck.

When he saw her shriveled in the bed, Danny Pogue gulped desperately to suppress the tears. Bud Schwartz also was jarred by the sight—she looked strikingly pallid and frail. And small. He'd never thought of Molly McNamara as a small woman, but that's how she appeared in the hospital: small and caved-in. Maybe because all that glorious white hair was stuffed under a paper cap.

"The flowers are splendid," she said, lifting the thin plastic tube that fed extra oxygen to her nostrils.

Danny Pogue positioned the vase on the bedstand, next to the telephone. "American Beauty roses," he said.

"So I see."

The burglars stood on opposite sides of the bed. Molly reached out and held their hands.

She said, "A touch of angina, that's all. I'll be as good as new in a few days."

Danny Pogue wondered if angina was contagious; it sounded faintly sexual. "The house is fine," he said. "The disposal jammed this morning, but I fixed it myself."

"A spatula got stuck," Bud Schwartz added. "Don't ask how."

Molly said, "How is Agent Hawkins?"

"Same as ever."

"Are you feeding him?"

"Three times a day, just like you told us."

"Are his spirits improved?"

"Hard to tell," Bud Schwartz said. "He don't talk much with all that tape on his face."

"I heard about the golfer being shot," said Molly. "Mr. Kingsbury's had quite a run of bad luck, wouldn't you say?" She asked the question with a trace of a smile. Danny Pogue glanced down at his shoes.

To change the subject, Bud Schwartz asked if there was a cafeteria in the hospital. "I could sure use a Coke."

"Make that two," said Danny Pogue. "And a lemonade for Molly."

"Yes, that would hit the spot. Or maybe a ginger ale, something carbonated." She patted Danny Pogue's hand. Again he looked as if he were about to weep.

In the elevator Bud Schwartz couldn't shake the vision of the old woman sunken in bed. It was all Kingsbury's fault—Molly hadn't felt right since those bastards beat her up at the condo. That one of them had been gunned down later by a baboon was only a partial consolation; the other goon, the one with nine fingertips, was still loose. Joe Winder had said don't worry, they'll all pay—but what did Winder know about the law of the street? He was a writer, for Chrissakes. A goddamn dreamer. Bud Schwartz had agreed to help but he couldn't pretend to share Winder's optimism. As a lifelong criminal, he knew for a fact that the bad guys seldom get what they deserve. More often they just plain get away, even assholes who beat up old ladies.

Bud Schwartz was so preoccupied that he got off on the wrong floor and found himself standing amidst throngs of cooing relatives at the window of the nursery. He couldn't believe the number of newborn babies—it baffled him, left him muttering while others clucked and pointed and sighed. In a world turning to shit, why were so many people still having children? Maybe it was a fad, like CB radios and

Cabbage Patch dolls. Or maybe these men and women didn't understand the full implications of reproduction.

More victims, thought Bud Schwartz, the last damn thing we need. He gazed at the rows of sleeping infants, crinkly and squinty-eyed and blissfully innocent, and silently foretold their future. They would grow up to have automobiles and houses and apartments that would all, eventually, be burglarized by lowlifes such as himself.

When Bud Schwartz returned to Molly McNamara's room, he sensed he was interrupting something private. Danny Pogue, who had been talking in a low voice, became silent at the sight of his partner.

Molly thanked Bud Schwartz for the cup of ginger ale. "Danny's got something to tell you," she said.

"Yeah?"

"I must admit," Molly said, "he left me speechless."

"So let's hear it already."

Danny Pogue lifted his chin and thrust out his bony chest. "I decided to give my share of the money to Molly."

"Not to me personally," she interjected. "To the Mothers of Wilderness."

"And the Wildlife Rescue Corps!"

"Unofficially, yes," she said.

"The mob money," Danny Pogue explained.

Bud Schwartz didn't know whether to laugh or scream. "Twenty-five grand? You're just givin' it away?"

Molly beamed. "Isn't that a magnificent gesture?"

"Oh, magnificent," said Bud Schwartz. Magnificently stupid.

Danny Pogue picked up on his partner's sarcasm and tried to mount a defense. He said, "It's just somethin' I wanted to do, okay?"

"Fine by me."

Molly said, "It automatically makes him a Golden Lifetime Charter Member!"

"It also automatically makes him broke."

"Come on," Danny Pogue said, "it's for a good cause."

Bud Schwartz's eyes narrowed. "Don't even think about asking."

"Danny, he's right," said Molly. "It's not fair to pressure a friend."

Warily Bud Schwartz scanned Molly's bed sheets for any lumps that might reveal the outline of a pistol. He said, "Look, I wanna go straight. That money's my future."

Danny Pogue rolled his eyes and snorted. "Cut the bull— I mean, don't kid yourself. All we're ever gonna be is thieves."

"Now there's a happy thought. That's what I mean about you and your fucking attitude."

To Danny Pogue's relief, Molly barely flinched at the profane adjective. She said, "Bud, I respect your ambitions. I really do."

But Danny Pogue wasn't finished whining. "Man, at least can't you spare *something*?"

For several moments the only sound was the muted whistle of Molly's oxygen machine. Finally she said, in a voice creaky with fatigue, "Even a small donation would be appreciated."

Bud Schwartz ground his molars. "How does a grand sound? Is that all right?" Christ, he must be insane. One thousand dollars to a bunch of blue-haired bunny huggers!

Molly McNamara smiled kindly. Danny Pogue exuberantly chucked him on the shoulder.

Bud Schwartz said, "Why don't I feel wonderful about this?"

"You will," Molly replied, "someday."

▼ ▼ ▼

Among the men hired by Pedro Luz as security officers was Diamond J. Love, Diamond being his given name and the "J" standing for Jesus. As was true with most of the guards at the Amazing Kingdom of Thrills, Diamond J. Love's personal history was investigated with only enough diligence to determine the absence of outstanding felony warrants. It was a foregone conclusion that Diamond J. Love's career in law enforcement had been derailed by unpleasant circumstances; there was no other logical reason for applying as a private security guard at a theme park.

Initially, Diamond J. Love was apprehensive about his employment chances at the Amazing Kingdom. He knew that Disney World and other family resorts were scrupulous about hiring clean-cut, enthusiastic, All-American types; Diamond J. Love was worried because in all ways he defied the image, but he need not have worried. Nobody from the Amazing Kingdom bothered to check with previous employers, such as the New York City Police Department, to inquire about allegations of bribery, moral turpitude, substance abuse, witness tampering and the unnecessary use of deadly force, to wit, the pistol-whipping of a young man suspected of shoplifting a bag of cheese-flavored Doritos.

Diamond J. Love was elated to be hired for the security force at the Amazing Kingdom, and pleased to find himself surrounded with colleagues of similarly checkered backgrounds. On slow days, when they weren't breaking into the RVs of tourists, they'd sit around and swap stories about the old police days—tales of stacking the civil-service boards to beat a brutality rap; perjuring themselves silly before grand juries; rounding up hookers on phony vice sweeps just to cop a free hummer; switching kilos of baking soda for cocaine in the evidence rooms. Diamond J. Love enjoyed these bull sessions, and he enjoyed his job. For the most part.

The only area of concern was the boss himself, a monster steroid freak whose combustible mood swings had prompted several of his own officers to leave their holsters permanently unsnapped, just in case. Some days Pedro Luz was reasonable and coherent, other days he was a drooling psycho. The news that he had chewed off his own foot only heightened the anxiety level on the security squad; even the potheads were getting jumpy.

Which is why Diamond J. Love did not wish to be late for work on this very important morning, and why he reacted with exceptionally scathing impudence to the mild-mannered inquiry of a black state trooper who had pulled over his car on County Road 905.

"May I see your driver's license, please?"

"Get serious, Uncle Ben."

From there it went downhill. The trooper was singularly unimpressed by Diamond J. Love's expired NYPD police badge; nor was he particularly understanding on the issue of Diamond J. Love's outdated New York driver's license. Or the fact that, according to some computer, the serial numbers on Diamond J. Love's Camaro matched precisely those of a Camaro stolen eight months earlier in New Smyrna Beach.

"That's bullshit," suggested Diamond J. Love.

"Please get out of the car," the trooper said.

At which point Diamond J. Love attempted to speed away, and instead felt himself dragged by the collar through the window and deposited face-first on the macadam. Upon regaining consciousness, Diamond J. Love discovered Plasticuffs cinched painfully to his wrists and ankles. He further was surprised to see that he shared his predicament with several other security guards, who had apparently encountered the highway patrol on the pre-dawn journey to the Amazing Kingdom of Thrills. There sat Ossie Cano, former Seattle robbery detective-turned-fence; William Z. Ames, former Orlando patrolman-turned-pornographer; Neal "Bart" Bartkowski, former sergeant with the Atlanta police, currently appealing a federal conviction for tax evasion.

"The hell's going on here?" demanded Diamond J. Love.

"Roadblock," Cano replied.

"A one-man roadblock?"

"I heard him radio for backup."

"But still," said Diamond J. Love. "One guy?"

By sunrise there were nine of them handcuffed or otherwise detained, a row of sullen penguins lined up along County Road 905. Basically it was the Amazing Kingdom's entire security force, except for Pedro Luz and one other guard, who had spent the night at the amusement park.

Trooper Jim Tile was impressed by the accuracy of Joe Winder's intelligence, particularly the make and license numbers of the guards' personal cars—information pilfered by Carrie Lanier from the files of the Personnel Department. Jim Tile was also impressed that not a single one of the guards had a clean record; to a man there arose problems with driver's licenses, expired registration stickers, doctored title certificates or unpaid traffic tickets. Each of the nine attempted to slide out of the road check by flashing outdated police ID—"badging," in cop vernacular. Two of the nine had offered Jim Tile a whispered inducement of either cash or narcotics; three others had sealed their fate by making racial remarks. All had been disarmed and handcuffed so swiftly, and with such force, that physical resistance had been impossible.

When the van from the Monroe County Sheriff's Office arrived, the deputy's eyes swept from Jim Tile to the cursing horde of prisoners and back again.

The deputy said, "Jimmy, you do this all by yourself?"

"One at a time," the trooper answered. "A road check, that's all."

"I know some of these boys."

"Figured you might."

"We lookin' at anything serious?"

"We're considering it."

From the end of the line came an outcry from Diamond J. Love: "Dwight, you gonna let this nigger get away with it?"

Jim Tile gave no indication of hearing the remark. The deputy named Dwight did, however. "Damndest thing," he said in a hearty voice. "The air-conditioning broke down in the paddy wagon. Just now happened."

The trooper said, "What a shame."

"Gonna be a long trip back to the substation."

"Probably gets hot as hell inside that van."

"Like an oven," Dwight agreed with a wink.

"Fuck you!" shouted Diamond J. Love. "Fuck the both of you."

▼ ▼ ▼

The phone bleeped in Charles Chelsea's apartment at seven-fifteen. It might as well have been a bomb.

"That fucking Pedro, I can't find him!" Who else but Francis X. Kingsbury.

"Have you tried the gym?" Chelsea said foggily.

"I tried everywhere, hell, you name it. And there's no guards! I waited and waited, finally said fuck it and drove myself to work." He was on the speaker phone, hollering as he stormed around the office.

"The security men never showed up?"

"Wake up, dicklick! I'm alone, *comprende?* No Pedro, no guards, *nada.*"

Dicklick? Charles Chelsea sat up in bed and shook his head like a spaniel. Do I really deserve to be called a dicklick? Is that what I get for all my loyalty?

Kingsbury continued to fulminate: "So where in the name of Christ Almighty is everybody? Today of all days—is there something you're not telling me, Charlie?"

"I haven't heard a thing, sir. Let me check into it."

"You do that!" And he was gone.

Chelsea dragged himself to the kitchen and fine-tuned the coffee-maker. In less than two hours, some lucky customer would breach the turnstiles at the Amazing Kingdom of Thrills and be proclaimed the Five-Millionth Visitor. Officially, at least. Chelsea was fairly certain that at least one enterprising journalist would take the time to add up the park's true attendance figures and expose the promotion for the hoax that it was. The scene was set for a historic publicity disaster; already the national newsmagazines and out-of-state papers were snooping around, waiting for poor Jake Harp to expire. In recent days Chelsea's office had been deluged with applications for media credentials from publications that previously had displayed no interest in covering the Amazing Kingdom's Summerfest Jubilee. Chelsea wasn't naive enough to believe that the New York *Daily News* was seriously interested in a feature profile of the engineer who'd designed the Wet Willy water slide; no, their presence was explained by pure rampant bloodlust. The kidnapped mango voles, the dead scientist, the dead Orky, the nearly dead Jake Harp, flaming bulldozers, phony snake invasions, exploding cement trucks—an irresistible convergence of violence, mayhem and mortality!

Charles Chelsea understood that the dispatches soon to be filed from the Amazing Kingdom of Thrills wouldn't be bright or warm or fluffy. They would be dark and ominous and chilling. They would describe a screaming rupture of the civil order, a culture in terminal moral hemorrhage.

And this would almost certainly have a negative effect on tourism.

Oh well, Chelsea thought, I gave it my best.

He foraged in the refrigerator, unearthed a stale bagel and began gnawing dauntlessly. Hearing a knock at the door, he assumed that the pathologically impatient Kingsbury had sent a car for him.

"Just a second!" Chelsea called, and went to put on a robe.

When he opened the door, he faced the immutable, bewhiskered grin of Robbie Raccoon.

Who was holding, in his three-fingered polyester paw, a gun.

Which was pointed at Charles Chelsea's throat.

"What's this?" croaked the publicity man.

"Show time," said Joe Winder.

32

The raccoon suit was musty and stifling, but it smelled reassuringly of Carrie's hair and perfume. Even the lint seemed familiar. Through slits in the cheeks Joe Winder was able to see the procession: Bud Schwartz, Danny Pogue and the captive Charles Chelsea, entering the gates of the Amazing Kingdom of Thrills.

To affect Robbie Raccoon's most recognizable mannerisms, Winder took floppy exaggerated steps (the way Carrie had showed him) and jauntily twirled the bushy tail. In spite of the serious circumstances, he felt a bolt of childlike excitement as the amusement park prepared to open for the Summerfest Jubilee. Outside, the trams were delivering waves of eager tourists—the children stampeding rabidly toward the locked turnstiles; the women bravely toting infants and designer baby bags; the men with shoulder-mounted Camcorders aimed at anything that moved. Fruity-colored balloons decorated every lamppost, every shrubbery, every concession; Broadway show tunes blasted through tinny public-address speakers. Mimes and jugglers and musicians rehearsed on street corners while desultory maintenance crews collected cigarette butts, Popsicle sticks and gum wrappers off the pavement. A cowboy from the Wild Bill Hiccup show tested his six-shooter by firing blanks at Petey Possum's straggly bottom.

"Show business," said Joe Winder, "is my life." The words echoed inside the plaster animal head.

If the costume had a serious flaw (besides the nonfunctioning air conditioner), it was a crucial lack of peripheral vision. The slits, located several inches below Robbie Raccoon's large plastic eyes, were much too narrow. Had the openings been wider, Winder would have spotted the fleshy pale hand in time to evade it.

It was the hand of famed TV weatherman Willard Scott, and it dragged Joe Winder in front of a camera belonging to the National Broadcasting Company. Danny Pogue, Bud Schwartz and Charles Chelsea stopped in their tracks: Robbie Raccoon was on the "Today Show." *Live.* Willard flung one meaty arm around Winder's shoulders, and the other around a grandmother from Hialeah who said she was 107 years old. The old woman was telling a story about riding Henry Flagler's railroad all the way to Key West.

"A hunnert and seven!" marveled Danny Pogue.

Charles Chelsea shifted uneasily. Bud Schwartz shot him a look. "What, she's lying?"

Morosely the publicity man confessed. "She's a complete fake. A ringer. I arranged the whole thing." The burglars stared as if he were speaking another language. Chelsea lowered his voice: "I *had* to do it. Willard wanted somebody over a hundred years old, they told me he might not come, otherwise. But I couldn't find anyone over a hundred —ninety-one was the best I could do, and the poor guy was completely spaced. Thought he was Rommel."

Danny Pogue whispered, "So who's she?"

"A local actress," Chelsea said. "Age thirty-eight. The makeup is remarkable."

"Christ, this is what you do for a living?" Bud Schwartz turned to his partner. "And I thought *we* were scumballs."

To the actress, Willard Scott was saying: "You're here to win that 300-Z, aren't you, sweetheart? In a few minutes the park opens and the first lucky customer through the gate will be Visitor Number Five Million. They'll get the new sports car and all kinds of great prizes!"

"I'm so excited!" the actress proclaimed.

"You run along now, but be careful getting in line. The folks are getting pretty worked up out there. Good luck, sweetheart!" Then Willard Scott gave the bogus 107-year-old grandmother a slurpy smooch on the ear. As he released his grip on the woman, he tightened his hug on Joe Winder.

And an awakening nation heard the famous weatherman say: "This ring-tailed rascal is one of the most popular characters here at the Amazing Kingdom of Thrills. Go ahead, tell us your name."

And in a high squeaky voice, Joe Winder gamely replied: "Hi, Willard! My name is Robbie Raccoon."

"You're certainly a big fella, Robbie. Judging by the size of that tummy, I'd say you've been snooping through a few garbage cans!"

To which Robbie Raccoon responded: "Look who's talking, lard-ass."

Briefly the smile disappeared from Willard's face, and his eyes searched desperately off-camera for the director. A few feet away, Charles Chelsea tasted bile creeping up his throat. The burglars seemed pleased to be standing so close to a genuine TV star.

A young woman wearing earphones and a jogging suit held up a cue card, and valiantly the weatherman attempted to polish off the segment: "Well, spirits are obviously running high for the big Summerfest Jubilee, so pack up the family and come down to"—here Willard paused to find his place on the card—"Key Largo, Florida, and enjoy the fun! You can swim with a real dolphin, or go sliding headfirst down the Wet Willy or bust some broncos with Wild Bill Hiccup. And you kids can get your picture taken with all your favorite animal characters, even Robbie Raccoon."

Obligingly Joe Winder cocked his head and twirled his tail. Willard appeared to regain his jolly demeanor. He prodded at something concealed under one of the fuzzy raccoon arms. "It looks like our ole pal Robbie's got a surprise for Uncle Willard, am I right?"

From Winder came a strained chirp: " 'Fraid not, Mr. Scott."

"Aw, come on. Whatcha got in that paw?"

"*Nothing.*"

"Let's see it, you little scamp. Is it candy? A toy? Whatcha got there?"

And seventeen million Americans heard Robbie Raccoon say: "That would be a gun, Willard."

Chelsea's ankles got rubbery and he began to sway. The burglars each grabbed an elbow.

"My, oh, my," Willard Scott said with a nervous chuckle. "It even *looks* like a real gun."

"Doesn't it, though," said the giant raccoon.

Please, thought Bud Schwartz, not on national TV. Not with little kids watching.

But before anything terrible could happen, Willard Scott adroitly steered the conversation from firearms to a tropical depression brewing in the eastern Caribbean. Joe Winder was able to slip away when the weatherman launched into a laxative commercial.

On the path to the Cimarron Saloon, Charles Chelsea and the

burglars heard howling behind them; a rollicking if muffled cry that emanated from deep inside the globular raccoon head.

"Aaaahhh-ooooooooooo," Joe Winder sang. "We're the werewolves of Florida! Aaaahhh-ooooooooooo!"

▼ ▼ ▼

The smoke from Moe Strickland's cigar hung like a purple shroud in The Catacombs. Uncle Ely's Elves had voted unanimously to boycott the Jubilee, and Uncle Ely would honor their decision.

"The cowboy getups look stupid," he agreed.

The actor who played the elf Jeremiah, and sometimes Dumpling, lit a joint to counteract the stogie fumes. He declared, "We're not clowns, we're actors. So fuck Kingsbury."

"That's right," said another elf. "Fuck Mr. X."

Morale in the troupe had been frightfully low since the newspapers had picked up the phony story about a hepatitis outbreak. Several of the actor-elves had advocated changing the name of the act to escape the stigma. Others wanted to hire a Miami attorney and file a lawsuit.

Moe Strickland said, "I heard they're auditioning up at Six Flags."

"Fuck Six Flags," said Jeremiah-Dumpling elf. "Probably another damn midget routine."

"Our options are somewhat limited," Moe Strickland said, trying to put it as delicately as possible.

"So fuck our options."

The mood began to simmer after they'd passed the joint around about four times. Moe Strickland eventually stubbed out the cigar and began to enjoy himself. On the street above, a high-school marching band practiced the theme from 2001: A Space Odyssey. Filtered through six feet of stone, it didn't sound half bad.

One of the actor-elves said, "Did I mention there's a guy living in our dumpster?"

"You're kidding," said Moe Strickland.

"No, Uncle Ely, it's true. We met him yesterday."

"In the dumpster?"

"He fixed it up nice like you wouldn't believe. We gave him a beer."

Moe Strickland wondered how a homeless person could've found a way into The Catacombs, or why he'd want to stay where it was so musty and humid and bleak.

"A nice guy," said the actor-elf. "A real gentleman."

"We played poker," added Jeremiah-Dumpling. "Cleaned his fucking clock."

"But he was a sport about it. A gentleman, like I said."

Again Moe Strickland raised the subject of Six Flags. "Atlanta's a great town," he said. "Lots of pretty women."

"We'll need some new songs."

"That's okay," said Moe Strickland. "Some new songs would be good. We'll have the whole bus ride to work on the arrangements. Luther can bring his guitar."

"Why not?" said Jeremiah-Dumpling. "Fuck Kingsbury anyhow."

"That's the spirit," Moe Strickland said.

From the end of the tunnel came the sound of boots on brick. A man bellowed furiously.

"Damn," said one of the actor-elves. He dropped the nub of the joint and ground it to ash under a long, curly-toed, foam-rubber foot.

The boots and the bellowing belonged to a jittery Spence Mooher, who was Pedro Luz's right-hand man. Mooher was agitated because none of the other security guards had shown up for work on this, the busiest day of the summer. Mooher had been up all night patrolling the Amazing Kingdom, and now it looked as if he'd be up all day.

"I smell weed," he said to Moe Strickland.

In this field Mooher could honestly boast of expertise; he had served six years with the U.S. Drug Enforcement Administration until he was involuntarily relieved of duty. There had been vague accusations of unprofessional conduct in Puerto Rico—something about a missing flash roll, twenty or thirty thousand dollars. As Spence Mooher was quick to point out, no charges were ever filed.

He shared his new boss's affinity for anabolic steroids, but he strongly disapproved of recreational drugs. Steroids hardened the body, but pot and cocaine softened the mind.

"Who's got the weed?" he demanded of Uncle Ely's Elves.

"Lighten up, Spence," sighed Moe Strickland.

"Why aren't you shitheads up top in rehearsal? Everybody's supposed to be there."

"Because we're boycotting," said Jeremiah-Dumpling. "We're not going to be in the damn show."

Mooher's mouth twisted. "Yes, you are," he said. "This is the Summerfest Jubilee!"

"I don't care if it's the second coming of Christ," said Jeremiah-Dumpling. "We're not performing."

Moe Strickland added, "It's a labor action, Spence. Nothing you can do."

"No?" With one hand Mooher grabbed the veteran character actor by the throat and slammed him against a row of tall lockers. The actor-elves could only cry out helplessly as the muscular security officer banged Uncle Ely's head again and again, until blood began to trickle from his ears. The racket of bone against metal was harrowing, and amplified in the bare tunnel.

Finally Spence Mooher stopped. He held Moe Strickland at arm's length, three feet off the ground; the actor kicked spasmodically.

"Have you reconsidered?" Mooher asked. Moe Strickland's eyelids drooped, but he managed a nod.

A deep voice down the passageway said, "Let him go."

Spence Mooher released Uncle Ely and wheeled to face . . . a bum. An extremely tall bum, but a bum nonetheless. It took the security guard a few moments to make a complete appraisal: the damp silver beard, braided on one cheek only; the flowered plastic rain hat pulled taut over the scalp; the broad tan chest wrapped in heavy copper-stained bandages; a red plastic collar around the neck; one dead eye steamed with condensation, the other alive and dark with anger; the mouthful of shiny white teeth.

Here, thought Spence Mooher, was a bum to be reckoned with. He came to this conclusion approximately one second too late, for the man had already seized Mooher's testicles and twisted with such force-fulness that all strength emptied from Mooher's powerful limbs; quivering, he felt a rush of heat down his legs as he soiled himself. When he tried to talk, a weak croaking noise came out of his mouth.

"Time to go night-night," said the bum, twisting harder. Spence Mooher fell down unconscious.

With a slapping of many oversized feet, the actor-elves scurried toward the slack figure of Moe Strickland, who was awake but in considerable pain. Jeremiah-Dumpling lifted Moe's bloody head and said, "This is the guy we told you about. The one in the dumpster."

Skink bent down and said, "Pleased to meet you, Uncle Ely. I think your buddies better get you to the vet."

▼ ▼ ▼

Charles Chelsea tested the door to Francis X. Kingsbury's office and found it locked. He tapped lightly but received no reply.

"I know he's in there," Chelsea said.

Danny Pogue said, "Allow us." He produced a small screwdriver and easily popped the doorjamb.

"Like ridin' a bicycle," said Bud Schwartz.

From inside the raccoon costume came a hollow command. The others stood back while Joe Winder opened the door. Upon viewing the scene, he clapped his paws and said: "Perfect."

Francis X. Kingsbury was energetically fondling himself in front of a television set. On the screen, a dark young man in a torn soccer jersey was copulating with a wild-haired brunette woman, who was moaning encouragement in Spanish. Other video cassettes were fanned out like a poker hand on the desk.

Kingsbury halted mid-pump and wheeled to confront the intruders. The boxer shorts around his ankles greatly diminished his ability to menace. Today's hairpiece was a silver Kenny Rogers model.

"Get out," Kingsbury snarled. He fumbled for the remote control and turned off the VCR. He seemed unaware that the Amazing Kingdom's stalwart mascot, Robbie Raccoon, was pointing a loaded semi-automatic at him. Joe Winder tucked the gun under one arm while he unzipped his head and removed it.

"So you're alive," Kingsbury hissed. "I had a feeling, goddammit."

Bud Schwartz laughed and pointed at Kingsbury, who shielded his receding genitals. The burglar said, "The asshole's wearing golf shoes!"

"For traction," Joe Winder theorized.

Charles Chelsea looked disgusted. Danny Pogue tossed a package on the desk. "Here," he said to Kingsbury, "even though you tried to kill us."

"What's this?"

"The files we swiped. Ramex, Gotti, it's all there."

Kingsbury was confused. Why would they return the files now? Bud Schwartz read his expression and said, "You were right. It was out of our league."

Which was baloney. The true reason for returning the files was to ensure that no one would come searching for them later. Like the police or the FBI.

"I suppose you want, what, a great big thank-you or some such goddamn thing." Francis X. Kingsbury tugged the boxer shorts high on his gelatinous waist. The indignity of the moment finally had sunk in. "Get out or I'm calling Security!"

"You've got no Security," Winder informed him.

"Charlie?"

"I'm afraid that's right, sir. I'll explain later."

Bud Schwartz said to his partner, "This is pathetic. Let's go."

"Wait." Danny Pogue stepped up to Kingsbury and said: "Beating up an old lady, what's the matter with you?"

"What the hell do you care." By now Kingsbury had more or less focused on Joe Winder's gun, so he spoke to Danny Pogue without looking at him. "That fucking Pedro, he gets carried away. Not a damn thing I can do."

"She's a sick old woman, for Chrissake."

"What's your point, Jethro?"

"My point is this," said Danny Pogue, and ferociously punched Francis Kingsbury on the chin. Kingsbury's golf cleats snagged on the carpet as he toppled.

Surveying the messy scene, Charles Chelsea felt refreshingly detached. He truly didn't care anymore. Outside, a roar of thousands swept the Amazing Kingdom, followed by gay cheers and applause. Chelsea went to the window and parted the blinds. "What do you know," he said. "Our five-millionth customer just walked through the gate."

With gray hands Kingsbury clutched the corner of the desk and pulled himself to his feet. In this fashion he was also able to depress a concealed alarm button that rang in the Security Office.

Bud Schwartz said, "We'll be saying good-bye now."

"You're welcome to stay," offered Joe Winder.

"No thanks." Danny Pogue examined his knuckles for bruises and abrasions. He said, "Molly's having surgery this afternoon. We promised to be at the hospital."

"I understand," Winder said. "You guys want to take anything?" He motioned with his gun paw around the lavish office. "The VCR? Some tapes? How about a cellular phone for the car?"

"The phone might be good," said Danny Pogue. "What'd you think, Bud? You could call your little boy from the road, wouldn't that be cool?"

"Let's roll," Bud Schwartz said.

Later they were driving on Card Sound Road, halfway back to the mainland, when Bud Schwartz motioned with a thumb and said: "Right about here's where it all started, Danny. Me throwin' that damn rat in the convertible."

"It was a vole," said Danny Pogue. "A blue-tongued mango vole. *Microtus mango*. That's the Latin name."

Bud Schwartz laughed. "Whatever you say." There was no denying he was impressed. How many burglars knew Latin?

A few more miles down the road, Danny Pogue again brought up the topic of portable phones. "If we had us one right now, we could call the hospital and see how she's doin'."

"You know the problem with cellulars," said Bud Schwartz.

"The reception?"

"Besides the reception," Bud Schwartz said. "The problem with cellulars is, people always steal the damn things."

"Yeah," said his partner. "I hadn't thought about that."

▼ ▼ ▼

The emergency buzzer awakens Pedro Luz in the storage room. He sits up and blinks. Blinks at the bare light bulb. Blinks at the pitted walls. Blinks at the empty intravenous bags on the hangers. He thinks, What the hell was it this time? Stanozolol, yeah. He'd pilfered a half-dozen tabs from Spence Mooher's locker. Ground them up with the toe of a boot, stirred it in the bag with the dextrose.

Feeling good. Feeling just fine. The beer sure helped.

Then comes Kingsbury's alarm and it sounds like a dental drill. Better get up now. Better get moving.

Pedro Luz pulls the tubes from his arms and tries to stand. Whoa, hoss! He forgot all about his foot, the fact that it was missing.

He grabs a wooden crutch and steadies himself. Facing the mirror, Pedro notices he's buck naked from the waist down. The image shocks him; his legs are as thick as oaks, but his penis is no larger than a peanut. Hastily he scrambles into the trousers of his guard uniform, the gun belt, one sock, one shoe.

Time to go to work. It's the Summerfest Jubilee and Mr. Kingsbury's in some kind of trouble.

And the damn door won't open.

Pedro can't fucking believe it. Okay, now somebody's either locked the damn thing from the outside, which don't make sense, or maybe welded it shut, which is even crazier. Pedro lowers one shoulder and hits the door like a tackle dummy. *Nada.* Now he's getting pissed. Through the steel he yells for Cano or Spence or Diamond J. Love, and gets no answer. "Where the hell *is* everybody?" hollers Pedro Luz.

Next logical step is using his skull as a battering ram. Wedging the crutch against the baseboard, he uses it to vault himself headfirst at the door. Amazing thing is, it don't hurt after a while. Tense the neck muscles just before impact and it acts like a spring. Boom, boom, boom. Boing, boing, boing.

No more door! Flattened.

What a fine feeling, to be free again.

The Security Office is empty, which is a mystery. Pedro checks the time cards and sees that none of the other guards have clocked in; something's going on here. Outside, the morning sun burns through a milky August haze, and the park is crawling with customers. There's a middle-aged lady at the security window complaining how somebody swiped her pocketbook off the tram. Behind her is some guy from

Wisconsin, red hair and freckles, says he locked his keys in the rental car. And behind him is some bony old man with a shnoz that could cut glass. Claims one of the animals is walking around the park with a gun. Which one? Pedro asks. The possum? The raccoon? We got bunches of animals, says Pedro Luz. And the old guy scratches his big nose and says he don't know the difference from animals. Was Wally Wolverine for all he knows, but it damn sure was a gun in its paw. Sure, says Pedro, whatever you say. Here's a form to fill out. I'll be back in a few minutes.

Between the whiny tourists and all that banging with his head, Pedro's finally waking up. On the floor near the broken door he spots something shiny, and checks it out: a new Master padlock, still fastened to the broken hasp.

Pedro never would've imagined it was the lovely Princess Golden Sun who'd locked him in the storage room with his drugs and beer. He figured it was Spence Mooher or one of the other security guards, playing a joke.

He could deal with those jerk-offs later. Now it was time to haul ass over to Mr. Kingsbury's office and see what was wrong. For a moment Pedro Luz thought he heard the alarm go off again, but then he realized no, it was just the regular buzzing in his eardrums. Only it seemed to be getting louder.

33

"First things first," Joe Winder said. "Who killed Will Koocher?"

Francis X. Kingsbury was rolling a shiny new Titleist from hand to hand across the top of his desk. The brassy strains of a marching band rose from the street below; the Summerfest Jubilee was in full swing.

"This Koocher," Kingsbury said, "he was threatening to go public about the voles. Pangs of conscience, whatever. So what I did, I told that fucking Pedro to go talk sense with the boy. See, it would've been a disaster—and Charlie'll back me up on this—a goddamn mess if it came out the voles were fake. Especially after the stupid things got stolen—talk about embarrassing."

Winder said, "So the answer to the question is Pedro. That's who committed the murder."

Kingsbury smothered his nose with a handkerchief and snuffled like a boar. "Damn hay fever!" The handkerchief puckered with each breath. "Far as I'm concerned, Koocher drowned in the Orky tank. Plain and simple. Case closed."

"But everyone knew the truth."

"No!" Chelsea protested. "I swear to God, Joey."

"Tell me about the blue-tongued mango voles," said Joe Winder. "Whose clever idea was that?"

From behind the veil of the soggy hanky, Kingsbury said: "I figured wouldn't it be fantastic if the Amazing Kingdom had an animal we could save. Like Disney tried to do with the dusky sparrow, only I was thinking in terms of a panda bear. People, I've seen this, they go fucking nuts for pandas. Only come to find out it's too hot down here, they'd probably croak in the sun.

"So I call this connection I got, this old friend, and I ask her what's endangered in Florida and she says all the good ones are taken—the panthers and manatees and so forth. She says it'd be better to come up with an animal nobody else had or even knew about. She says we might even get a government grant, which it turns out we did. Two hundred grand!"

Chelsea tried to act appalled; he even made a sound like a gasp. Impatiently, Winder said, "Charlie, this might come as a shock, but I don't care how much you knew and how much you didn't. For the purposes of settling this matter, you've become superfluous. Now show Mr. Kingsbury what we've prepared."

From an inside pocket Chelsea withdrew a folded sheet of Amazing Kingdom stationery. He handed it across the desk to Francis X. Kingsbury, who set aside both the handkerchief and the golf ball in order to read.

"It's a press release," Chelsea said.

"I see what it is. Horseshit is what it is." Kingsbury scanned it several times, including once from the bottom up. His mouth moved in twitchy circles, like a mule chewing a carrot.

"You ought to consider it," Winder advised him, "if you want to stay out of jail."

"Oh, so now it's blackmail?"

"No, sir, it's the cold fucking hand of fate."

Nervously Kingsbury fingered the bridge of his nose. "The hell is your angle, son?"

"You arranged an elaborate scientific fraud for the purposes of profit. An ingenious fraud, to be sure, but a felony nonetheless. Two hundred thousand is just about enough to interest the U.S. Attorney's Office."

Kingsbury shrugged in mockery. "Is that, what, like the end of the world?"

"I forgot," Winder said, "you're an expert on indictments. Aren't you, Frankie?"

Kingsbury turned color.

"Frankie King," said Winder. "That's your real name, in case you don't remember."

Kingsbury shrank into the chair. Winder turned to Charles Chelsea and said, "I think somebody's finally in the mood to talk."

"Can I leave?"

"Certainly, Charlie. And thanks for a terrific job on the publicity release."

"Yeah, right."

"I mean it," Winder said. "It's seamless."

Chelsea eyed him warily. "You're just being sarcastic."

"No, it was perfect. You've got a definite flair."

"Thanks, Joe. And I mean it, too."

▼ ▼ ▼

The rescue of Francis Kingsbury was further delayed when a disturbance broke out near the front gate of the Amazing Kingdom; a tense and potentially violent dispute over the distribution of prizes, specifically a Nissan 300-Z.

The security-guard uniform is what gave Pedro Luz away. As he crutched toward Kingsbury's office, he was spotted and intercepted by a flying wedge of disgruntled customers. Something about the Summerfest contest being rigged. Pedro Luz insisted he didn't know about any damn contest, but the customers were loud and insistent. They led the security man back to the stage, where a short plump tourist named Rossiter had just been presented the keys to the sleek new sports car. Draped around Mr. Rossiter's neck was a shiny streamer that said: "OUR FIVE-MILLIONTH SPECIAL GUEST!" In response to questions from a tuxedoed emcee, Mr. Rossiter said he was visiting the Amazing Kingdom with his wife and mother-in-law. He said it was only his second trip to Florida.

Mr. Rossiter gave the car keys to his wife, who squeezed her torso into the driver's seat and happily posed for pictures. Several persons in the crowd began to hiss and boo. Somebody threw a cup of frozen yogurt, which splattered against one of the car's wire wheels.

This was too much for Pedro Luz's jangled, hormone-flooded sensory receptors. He grabbed the microphone from the emcee and said, "Next person that throws food, I break their fucking spine."

Instantly a lull came over the mob. Pedro Luz said, "Now somebody explain what's going on."

At first no one spoke up, but there was a good bit of whispering about the bloody purple knots on the security chief's forehead. Finally a man in the crowd pointed at the Rossiters and shouted, "They cheated, that's what!"

Another male voice: "He cut in line!"

Pedro Luz said, "Jesus, I can't believe you people." He turned to the Rossiters. "Is it true? Did you cut in line?"

"No, Officer," Mr. Rossiter answered. "We got here first, fair and square."

Mrs. Rossiter popped her head from the car and said, "They're just a bunch of sore losers." Mrs. Rossiter's mother, a stubby woman wearing sandals and a Petey Possum T-shirt, said she'd never seen such rude people in all her life.

Pedro Luz didn't know what to do next; for one pleasantly deranged moment, he considered throwing the Rossiters off the stage and claiming the 300-Z for himself. *Daring* anyone to try to take it away from him. Then Charles Chelsea materialized and Pedro Luz gratefully surrendered the microphone. His ears buzzed and his head clanged and all he really wanted to do was limp to the gymnasium and pump some iron.

"Ladies and gentlemen," Chelsea intoned, "please settle down." He looked smooth and confident in a crisp blue oxford shirt and a wine-colored tie. He looked as if he could talk his way out of practically anything.

"I've reviewed the tapes from our security cameras," Chelsea told the crowd, "and whether or you like it or not, Mr. Rossiter and his family were clearly the first ones through the turnstiles this morning—"

"But he threatened me!" yelled a teenager in the crowd. "I was here first but he said he'd kill me!"

A middle-aged woman in a straw Orky hat hollered: "Me, too! And I was ahead of that kid—"

The crowd surged toward the stage until Pedro Luz drew his revolver and aimed it toward the sky. Seeing the gun, the tourists grew quiet and rippled back a few steps.

"Thank you," Chelsea said to Pedro Luz.

"I got an emergency."

"You can go now. I'll be fine."

"You need a gun?"

"No," said Chelsea, "but thanks just the same."

▼　▼　▼

"You got something against fun."

Francis Kingsbury made it an indictment. "What, you got something against little children? Little cutey pies having a good time?"

Joe Winder said: "You can keep the park, Frankie. The park is already built. It's the golf resort that's eighty-sixed, as of today."

"Oh, ho," said Kingsbury. "So you got something against golf?"

"That's the deal. Take it or leave it."

"You think you can scare me? Hell, I got gangsters shooting at me. Professionals." Kingsbury cut loose an enormous sneeze, and promptly plugged his nostrils with the handkerchief.

Winder said, "I was hoping to appeal to the pragmatic side of your nature."

"Listen, I know how to handle this situation from up North. The way to handle it is, I cut the wop bastards in. The Zubonis, I'm talking about. I cut 'em in on Falcon Trace, you'd be surprised how fast they let bygones be bygones. You watch what good friends we are once I start using Zuboni roofers, Zuboni drywall, Zuboni plumbing." Kingsbury looked positively triumphant. "Blackmail, my ass. The fuck are you going to blackmail me with now?"

"I believe you misunderstood the offer," Joe Winder said. "I'm not planning to go to the mob. I'm planning to go to the media."

Defiantly Kingsbury snatched the hanky from his nose. "Jesus, you're pissing me off." He picked up the phone and commanded the operator to connect him with Security. Joe Winder took two steps toward the desk, raised his paw and shot the telephone console to pieces.

Impressed, Kingsbury probed at the tangle of wires and broken plastic. "Goddamn lunatic," he said.

Winder sat down and tucked the gun into the furry folds of the costume. "Think in terms of headlines," he said. "Imagine what'll happen when the newspapers find out the Amazing Kingdom of Thrills is run by a Mafia snitch. You'll be famous, Frankie. Wouldn't you love to be interviewed by Connie Chung?"

"Let me just say, fuck you."

Winder frowned. "Don't make me shoot up more office equipment. Stop and consider the facts. You obtained the bank notes and financing for Falcon Trace under false pretenses; to wit, using a false name and phony credit references. Ditto on your construction permits. Ditto on your performance bond. Once the money boys find out who you really are, once they read about it on the front page of the *Wall Street Journal*, not only is Falcon Trace dead, you can look forward to spending the rest of your natural life at the courthouse, getting your fat ass sued off. Everybody'll want a piece, Frankie. We're talking cluster-fuck."

He now had Francis X. Kingsbury's undivided attention. "And last but not least," Winder said, "is the criminal situation. If I'm not mistaken, you're still on probation."

"Yeah, so?"

"So the terms of probation strictly prohibit consorting with known felons and other unsavory dirtbags. However, a review of your Security Department indicates you're not only consorting with known criminals, you've surrounded yourself with them."

"This isn't Orlando," Kingsbury said. "Down here it's not so easy to get good help. If I was as strict as Disney, I'd have nobody working for me. What, maybe altar boys? Mormons and Brownie Scouts? This is Miami, for Chrissakes, I got a serious recruiting problem here."

"Nonetheless," Joe Winder said, "you've gone out of your way to dredge up extremely primitive life-forms."

"What's wrong with giving a guy a second chance?" Kingsbury paused for a second, then said, "I'm the first to admit, hell, Pedro was a bad choice. I didn't know about the damn drugs." Speaking of Pedro, he thought, where the hell is he?

"What's done is done," Winder said. He fanned himself with his spare paw; it was wretchedly hot inside the costume. "Frankie, this is a matter for you and the probation bureau. Between us boys, I wouldn't be surprised if they packed you off to Eglin for six or eight months. You do play tennis, don't you?"

The haughtiness ebbed from Kingsbury's face. Pensively he traced a pudgy finger along the lines of his infamous rodent tattoo. "Winder, what exactly is your problem?"

"The problem is you're mutilating a fine chunk of island so a bunch of rich people have a warm place to park their butts in the winter. You couldn't have picked a worse location, Frankie, the last green patch of the Keys. You're bulldozing next door to a national wildlife refuge. And offshore, in that magnificent ocean, is the only living coral reef in North America. I believe that's where you intended to flush your toilets—"

"No!" Kingsbury snapped. "We'll have deep-well sewage injection. High-tech facilities—no runoff, no outfall."

"Imagine," Winder mused, "the shit of millionaires dappling our azure waters."

Kingsbury reddened and clenched his fists. "If I go along with this deal, what, it's some major victory for the environment? You think the ghost of Henry Fucking Thoreau is gonna pin a medal or some such goddamn thing on your chest?"

Joe Winder smiled at the thought. "I've got no illusions," he said. "One less golf course is one less golf course. I'll settle for that."

"The lots, Jesus, they're worth millions. That's what this goddamn piece of paper'll cost me."

"I'll settle for that, too."

Kingsbury was still stymied. He glared furiously at Charles Chelsea's final publicity release.

"You'll never understand," Winder said, "because you weren't born here. Compared to where you came from, this is always going to look like paradise. Hell, you could wipe out every last bird and butterfly, and it's still better than Toledo in the dead of winter."

With a dark chuckle, Kingsbury said, "No kidding."

"Don't read too much into this operation, Frankie. I'm just sick of asshole carpetbaggers coming down here and fucking up the place. Nothing personal."

It came out of the blue, Kingsbury saying, "There was a guy named Jack Winder. Big-time land developer, this goes back a few years, before I was selling waterfront. Winder Planned Communities was the company."

"My father."

"What?" said Kingsbury. "Quit whispering."

"Jack Winder was my father."

"Then what the hell are you doing? Biting the hand is what I'd call it. Dishonoring the family name."

"Depends on your point of view."

Kingsbury sneered. "I hear this line of bullshit all the time: 'We got our slice of sunshine, fine, now it's time to close the borders.' Selfish is what you are."

"Maybe so," Winder said. "I'd like to fish that shoreline again, that's for sure. I'd like to see some tarpon out there next spring."

Dramatically, Francis Kingsbury straightened in the chair. He began talking with his eyes and hands, unmistakably a sales pitch: "People come to the Amazing Kingdom, they might like to play some golf. Mommy takes the kids to the theme park, Daddy hits the fairways. So what?"

Winder said nothing. Kingsbury began to knead his jowls in exasperation. "What the hell's so wrong with that picture? Eighteen lousy holes, I just don't see the crime. It's what Disney did. It's what everybody does with prime acreage. This is Florida, for Chrissakes."

"Not the way it ought to be, Frankie."

"Then you're living in what they call a dreamworld. This ain't Oz, son, and there's no fairy wizard to make things right again. Down here the brick road's not yellow, it's green. Plain and simple. Case closed."

But Joe Winder wasn't changing his mind. "I hope the papers get your name right," he said.

Bleakly Kingsbury thought of front-page headlines and multi-million-dollar lawsuits and minimum-security prisons with no driving range. "All right," he said to Winder, "let's talk."

"You've got my offer. Read the press release, it's all tied up with a pretty ribbon. You shut down Falcon Trace for the noblest of reasons and you're a hero, Frankie. Isn't that what you want?"

"I'd rather have my oceanfront lots."

Then the door flew open and there, bug-eyed and seething, was Pedro Luz. He aimed a large blue handgun at Joe Winder and grunted something unintelligible.

"Nice of you to put in an appearance," Kingsbury remarked. His eyes flooded with a mixture of rage and relief. "This asshole, get him out of my sight! For good this time."

"Drop the gun," Pedro Luz told Winder. "And put on your goddamn head."

Winder did as he was told. Zipping himself in, he felt cumbersome and helpless and feverishly short of breath.

Kingsbury said, "He doesn't leave the park alive, you understand?"

"No problem," said Pedro Luz.

"*No problem,*" mimicked Kingsbury. "No problem, my ass. This is Mr. Crackerjack Bodyguard, right? Mr. Lightning Response Time."

For a moment Pedro Luz felt an overwhelming urge to turn the pistol on Francis X. Kingsbury; something told him it would be every bit as satisfying as shooting Joe Winder. Maybe another time, he decided. After payday.

A muted voice inside the raccoon head said: "This is a big mistake, Frankie."

Kingsbury laughed mordantly and blew his nose. "Pedro, it's your last fucking chance. I hope you still got enough brain cells to do this one simple chore."

"No problem." With the crutch he roughly shoved Joe Winder toward the door.

"Hey, Pedro."

"What, Mr. Kingsbury?"

"That's a six-hundred-dollar animal costume. Try not to mess it up."

34

Carrie Lanier was practicing a song at the mirror as she dressed for the pageant. The door opened behind her, and she saw a flash of orange.

"Hey! We thought you were headed for New York."

"I seriously considered it." Skink shut the door with his foot.

"Your friend Officer Tile mentioned Orlando. Somebody shot up a tour bus, he figured it might be you."

"Another pale imitation, that's all. Where's your boyfriend?"

Carrie described Winder's plan to confront Francis Kingsbury. "Joe's got all the bases covered."

Skink shook his head. "It'll never work."

"Where have you been, anyway?"

"Down here in the underground, away from all radio beams. I needed a break from that damn plane."

Carrie moved closer to the mirror and began to put on her makeup. "What's with the gas cans?" she asked.

Skink carried one in each hand. "Let's pretend you didn't see these," he said. "I just want to make sure you've got a way out of the park."

"When?"

"Whenever."

"What about Joe?"

"I expect he's in some trouble," Skink said. "I've got a chore to do, then I'll check around."

"Don't worry, Pedro's locked in the storage room."

"How? With what?"

When Carrie told him, Skink frowned. "I guess I'd better get going."

She said, "Can you zip me up? There's a little hook at the top."

Skink set down the gas cans and fastened the back of her gown. He wondered what had happened to the Indian theme.

"When do you go on?" he asked.

"Half an hour."

"The dress is lovely," he said, stepping back. "Half an hour it is."

"Thanks. Wish me luck."

"You'll do fine."

Carrie turned from the mirror. "Should I wait for Joe?"

"Of course," said Skink, "but not too long."

▼   ▼   ▼

When they got to the security office, Pedro Luz ordered Joe Winder to remove the racoon costume and hang it neatly in the uniform closet. Then Pedro Luz dragged Winder into the storage room, clubbed him to the floor and beat him seven or eight times with the crutch—Joe Winder lost count. Every time Pedro Luz struck a blow, he emitted a queer high-pitched peep that sounded like a baby sparrow. When he finally stopped to rest, he was panting heavily and his face shone with damp splotches. Spying from a fetal position on the floor, Joe Winder watched Pedro Luz swallow two handfuls of small orange tablets. Winder assumed these were not muscle relaxants.

"I can kill you with my bare hands," Pedro Luz said informatively.

Winder sat up, hugging his own chest to prevent pieces of broken ribs from snapping off like dead twigs. He couldn't figure out why Pedro Luz kept a full-length mirror in the storage room.

"It's raining outside," Pedro Luz said.

"That's what we're waiting for?"

"Yeah. Soon as it stops, I'll take you out and kill you."

Pedro Luz stripped off his shirt and began to work out with a pair of heavy dumbbells; he couldn't take his eyes off his own glorious biceps. The syncopation of Pedro's breathing and pumping put Joe Winder to sleep. When he awoke much later, still on the floor, he saw that Pedro Luz had put on a fresh uniform. The security man rose unsteadily and reached for the crutch; his hands trembled and his eyelids were mottled and puffy.

"The parade starts soon," he said. "Everyone in the park goes to watch—that's when you're gonna break into the ticket office to rip off the cashboxes."

"And you're going to catch me in the act, and shoot me."

"Yeah," Pedro Luz wheezed, "in the back."

"Pretty sloppy. The cops'll have plenty of questions."

"I'm still thinking it through." His head lolled and he shut his eyes. Joe Winder sprang for the door and regretted it instantly. Pedro Luz was on him like a mad bear; he grabbed Winder at the base of the neck and hurled him backward into the stock shelves.

"And that was one-handed," Pedro Luz bragged. "How much do you weigh?"

Winder answered, with a groan, "One seventy-five."

The security man beamed. "Light as a feather. No problem."

"I'd like to speak with your boss one more time."

"No way." Pedro Luz hoisted Winder from a tangle of intravenous tubes and set him down in a bare corner. He said, "Remember, I still got that gun you were carrying—I figure that's my throwdown. The story is, I had to shoot you because of the gun."

Winder nodded. "I'm assuming there'll be no witnesses."

"Course not. They'll all be at the parade."

"What about the rain, Pedro? What if the parade's washed out?"

"It's August, asshole. The rain don't last long." Pedro Luz hammered the heel of his hand against the side of his skull, as if trying to knock a wasp out of his ear. "God, it's loud in here."

"I don't mean to nag," Joe Winder said, "but you ought to lay off the steroids."

"Don't start with me!" Pedro Luz cracked the door and poked his head out. "See, it's stopped already. Just a drizzle." He gripped Joe Winder by the shoulder. "Let's go, smartass."

But Winder could barely walk for the pain. Outside, under a low muddy sky, the tourists rushed excitedly toward Kingsbury Lane, where a band had begun to play. Pedro Luz marched Winder against the flow of yammering, gummy-faced children and their anxious, umbrella-wielding parents. The ticket office was on the other side of the park, a long hike, and Joe Winder had planned to use the time to devise a plan for escape. Instead his thoughts meandered inanely; he noticed, for example, what a high percentage of the Amazing Kingdom's tourists were clinically overweight. Was this a valid cross-section of American society? Or did fat people travel to Florida more frequently than thin people? Three times Winder slowed to ponder the riddle, and three times Pedro Luz thwacked the back of his legs with the dreaded crutch. No one stopped to interfere; most likely they assumed that Winder was a purse snatcher or some other troublemaker being rousted by Security.

Eventually the crowds thinned and the light rain stopped. The two men were alone, crossing the walkway that spanned the dolphin tank. The swim-along attraction had closed early because the trainers were needed at the parade, in case the lion got testy. Joe Winder heard a burst of applause across the amusement park—fireworks blossoming over Kingsbury Lane. The pageant had begun!

Winder thought of Carrie Lanier, and hoped she had the good sense not to come looking for him. He felt Pedro Luz's crutch jab him between the shoulder blades. "Hold it," the security man commanded.

A hoary figure appeared at the end of the walkway ahead of them. It was a tall man carrying two red containers.

"Now what?" said Pedro Luz.

Joe Winder's heart sank. Skink didn't see them. He went down two flights of stairs and stacked the gas cans on the back of a Cushman motor cart. He ran back up the steps, disappeared through an unmarked door near the Rare Animal Pavilion and quickly emerged with two more cans of gasoline.

"The Catacombs," Pedro Luz said, mainly to himself.

Joe Winder heard him unsnap the holster. He turned and told Pedro Luz not to do anything crazy.

"Shut up, smartass."

As they watched Skink load the second pair of cans onto the Cushman, Winder realized his own mistake: he had tried too hard to be reasonable and civilized and possibly even clever. Such efforts were wasted on men such as Francis X. Kingsbury. Skink had the right idea.

Pedro Luz aimed his .45 and shouted, "Freeze right there!" Skink stopped at the top of the steps. Pedro Luz ordered him to raise his hands, but Skink acted as if he didn't hear.

"Don't I know you?" Skink said, coming closer.

Pedro Luz found it difficult to look directly at the bearded stranger because one of the man's eyeballs seemed dislodged from the socket. As Skink approached, he gave no indication of recognizing Joe Winder.

"Hello, gentlemen," he said. Casually he bent to examine the taped stump of Pedro Luz's leg. "Son, you're dropping more parts than a Ford Pinto."

Flustered, Pedro Luz fell back on standard hardass-cop colloquy: "Lemme see some ID."

Skink reached into the blaze-orange weather suit and came out with a small kitchen jar. He handed it to the security man and said, "I believe this belongs to you."

Pedro Luz felt his stomach quake. At the bottom of the jar, drifting in pickle juice, was the tip of his right index finger. It looked like a cube of pink tofu.

"The old woman bit it off," Skink reminded him, "while you were beating her up."

Beautiful, Joe Winder thought. We're both going to die long horrible deaths.

Hoarsely, Pedro Luz said, "Who the hell are you?"

Skink gestured at the soiled bandages around his chest. "I'm the one you shot at the trailer!"

All three of them jumped as a Roman candle exploded high over Kingsbury Lane. A band was playing the theme from *2001: A Space Odyssey*. It sounded dreadful.

In the tank below, Dickie the Dolphin rolled twice and shot a light spray of water from his blowhole. A few drops sprinkled the barrel of Pedro Luz's gun, and he wiped it nervously on the front of his trousers. The circuits of his brain were becoming badly overloaded; assimilating new information had become a struggle—the drugs, the finger in the jar, the one-eyed stoner with the gas cans, the fireworks, the god-awful music. It was time to kill these sorry bastards and go to the gym.

"Who first?" he asked. "Who wants it first?"

Joe Winder saw no evidence of urgency in Skink's demeanor, so he took it upon himself to ram an elbow into the soft declivity beneath Pedro Luz's breastbone. Winder was stunned to see the bodybuilder go down, and idiotically he leapt upon him to finish the job. Winder's punching ability was hampered by the searing pain in his rib cage, and though Pedro Luz was gagging and drooling and gulping to catch his wind, it was a relatively simple exercise to lock his arms around all hundred and seventy-five pounds of Joe Winder and squeeze the breath out of him. The last thing Winder heard, before blacking out, was a splash in the tank below.

He hoped like hell it was the pistol.

▼ ▼ ▼

Marine biologists debate the relative intelligence of the Atlantic bottle-nosed dolphin, but it is generally accepted that the graceful mammal is extremely smart; that it is able to communicate using sophisticated underwater sonics; that it sometimes appears capable of emotions, including grief and joy. Noting that the dolphin's brain is proportionally larger and more fully developed than that of human beings, some experts contend that the animals are operating in a superior cognitive realm that we simply cannot comprehend.

A more skeptical view (and one endorsed by Joe Winder) is that dolphins probably aren't quite as smart as tourist lore suggests. Otherwise why would they allow themselves to be so easily captured, subjugated, trained and put on public display? It seemed to Winder that somersaulting through hula hoops in exchange for a handful of sardines was not proof of high intellect. Given fins and some Milk-Bones, your average French poodle could master the same feat.

It is certainly true, however, that captive dolphins exhibit distinct and complex personalities. Some are gregarious and easily tamed, while others are aloof and belligerent; some are happy to perform stunts for cheering tourists, while others get ulcers. Because each dolphin is so sensitive and unique, curators must be extremely careful when selecting the animals for commercial aquarium shows.

When it came to jumping hula hoops, Dickie the Dolphin was competent if unspectacular. The same could be said for his tail-walking, his backward flips and his mastery of the beach ball. While most spectators thought he was a lovable ham, experienced dolphin trainers could see he was just going through the motions. Ever since replacing the deceased Orky as the Amazing Kingdom's aquatic star, Dickie had approached each performance with the same sullen indifference. He took a similar attitude into the swim-along sessions, where he habitually kept a large distance between himself and whatever loud pale humanoid had been suckered into entering the tank.

The exception, of course, was when Dickie the Dolphin got into one of his "moods." Then he would frolic and nuzzle and rub eagerly against the swimmer, who inevitably mistook these gestures for honest affection. Dolphin researchers have documented numerous sexual advances upon human beings of both genders, but they cannot agree on the animal's intention in these circumstances. If dolphins truly are second to people on the intelligence scale, then they most certainly would not mistake a bikini-clad legal secretary for a member of their own species. Which raises a more intriguing hypothesis: that captive male dolphins attempt these outrageous liaisons out of mischief, or perhaps even revenge. The truth is locked deep inside the dolphin's large and complicated cerebrum, but the phenomenon has been widely reported.

On the evening of August 6, Dickie the Dolphin was in a state of high agitation as he circled the darkened whale tank at the Amazing Kingdom of Thrills. Perhaps it was the percussion of the nearby fireworks that disrupted the powerful creature's peace, or perhaps it was the effect of a long and lonely confinement. Although the trained seals and pelicans could be entertaining, Dickie the Dolphin probably would have preferred the companionship of a female partner. And he would have had one if Francis X. Kingsbury had not been so cheap. In any event, the solitary dolphin was keeping a sharp and wily eye on the commotion taking place along the walkway above.

At the first splash, Dickie swiftly sounded, tracking a small steel object to the bottom of his tank. He never considered retrieving the item, as there would be no reward for his effort—the buckets of cut fish had been hauled away hours ago. So the dolphin disregarded Pedro Luz's gun, glided slowly to the surface and waited.

The second splash was different.

▼ ▼ ▼

Pedro Luz was astonished by the strength of the one-eyed man. He took a punch as well as anyone that Pedro Luz had ever assaulted, plus he was quick. Every time Pedro Luz swung and missed, the bearded stranger hit him two or three times in the gut. It was starting to hurt immensely.

Having lost his own gun, Pedro Luz tried to retrieve the spare—Joe Winder's gun—from the pocket of his trousers. Every attempt brought a new flurry of punches from the one-eyed hobo, so Pedro Luz abandoned the plan. With a bellowing lunge, he was able to get a grip on the stranger's collar—an animal collar!—and pull him close. Pedro Luz preferred squeezing to boxing, and was confident he could end the fight (and the big freak's life) with a vigorous hug. That's when somebody grabbed Pedro Luz's hair from behind, and yanked his head back so fiercely that a popping noise came from his neck. Next thing he knew, his pants were off and he was thrashing in the warm water. Above him stood Joe Winder and the stranger, peering over the rail.

Swimming is an exercise that depends more on style than muscle, and Pedro Luz was plainly a terrible swimmer. The throbbing of his truncated leg added pain to ineptitude as he paddled the tank haplessly in search of a ladder. When the massive dolphin rolled beside him in the dark, Pedro Luz cursed and splashed his arms angrily. He was not the least bit afraid of a stupid fish; perhaps he was deceived by the dolphin's friendly smile, or misled by childhood memories of the hokey "Flipper" television series. In any event, Pedro Luz struck out at the creature with the misguided assumption that he could actually hurt it, and that it was too tame and good-natured to retaliate. Pedro's drug-inflamed brain failed to register the fact that Dickie the Dolphin was a more attuned physiological specimen than Pedro Luz himself, and about five hundred pounds larger. When the animal nudged him playfully with its snout, Pedro Luz balled his fists and slugged its silky gray flank.

"Be careful," Joe Winder advised from the walkway, but Pedro Luz paid no attention. The damn fish would not go away! Using its pectoral flippers almost as arms, it held Pedro Luz in a grasp that was gentle yet firm.

Spitting curses, he kicked the dolphin savagely and pushed away.

Stroking clumsily for the wall of the tank, he saw the long sleek form rise beneath him. A fin found Pedro Luz's armpit and spun him roughly. He came up choking, but again the creature tugged him down. Once more Pedro Luz fought his way to the top, and this time Dickie the Dolphin began to nip mischievously—tiny needle-like teeth raking Pedro's neck, his shoulders, his bare thighs. Then the dolphin rolled languidly on its side and gave a soft inquisitive whistle, the same sound Flipper used to make at the end of the TV show when he waved at the camera. Pedro Luz tried not to be afraid, but he couldn't understand what this dolphin was trying to say, or do. The salt water stung his eyes and his throat, and the stump of his leg felt as if it were on fire.

Again Pedro Luz felt cool fins slide under his arms as the dolphin gradually steered him toward the deepest part of the tank. The security man tried to break free, but it did no good. Something else propelled him now—a formidable protuberance that left no doubt as to Dickie the Dolphin's true purpose.

Pedro Luz was awestruck and mortified. The long pale thing loomed from the gray water and touched him—hooking, in fact, around his buttocks. The amphibious prodding brought an unfamiliar plea to Pedro Luz's lips: "Help!"

Watching events unfold in the tank below, Skink agreed it was an extraordinary scene.

"I told you," said Joe Winder. "It's one of Nature's marvels."

Pedro Luz began to whimper. No regimen of weight training and pharmaceutical enhancement could have prepared him, or any mortal man, for an all-out sexual attack by a healthy bottle-nosed dolphin. Pedro Luz had never felt so helpless, exhausted and inadequate; desperately he punched at the prodigious inquiring tuber, only to be rebuked by a well-placed slap from Dickie's sinewy fluke.

Leaning over the rail, Joe Winder offered more advice: "Just roll with it. Don't fight him."

But the futility of resistance was already clear to Pedro Luz, who found himself—for the first time in his adult life—completely out of strength. As he was pulled underwater for the final time, terror gave way to abject humiliation: he was being fucked to death by a damn fish.

35

Nina asked where he was calling from.

"Charlie's office," Winder said. "Here's what I'm going to do: I'll leave the phone off the hook all night. That way you can work on your poetry and still make money."

"Joe, that'll cost him a fortune. It's four bucks a minute."

"I know the rates, Nina. Don't worry about it."

"You ready for the latest?"

"Just one verse. Time's running out."

"Here goes," she said, and began to recite:

> "You flooded me with passions
> Hard and lingering.
> You took me down again
> Pumping breathless, biting blind.
> Hot in your bloodrush, I dreamed of more."

"Wow," Winder said. Obviously things were going gangbusters between Nina and the light-truck salesman.

"You really like it? Or are you patronizing me again?"

"Nina, you're breaking new ground."

"Guess what the moron at the phone syndicate wants. Limericks! Sex limericks, like they publish in *Playboy*. That's his idea of erotic poetry!"

"Stick to your guns," Winder said.

"You bet I will."

"The reason I called was to say good-bye."

"So tonight's the night," she said. "Will I be seeing you on the news?"

"I hope not." He thought: What the hell. "I met a woman," he said.

"I'm very happy for you."

"Aw, Nina, don't say that."

"I *am*. I think it's great."

"Christ Almighty, aren't you the least bit jealous?"

"Not really."

God, she was a pisser. "Then lie to me," Winder said. "Have mercy on my lunatic soul and lie to me. Tell me you're mad with jealousy."

"You win, Joe. You saw through my act."

"Was that a giggle I heard?"

"No!" Nina said. The giggle burst into a full-blown laugh. "I'm dying here. I might just leap off the building, I'm so damn jealous. Who is she? Who is this tramp?"

Now Winder started laughing, too. "I'd better go," he said, "before I say something sensible."

"Call me, Joe. Whatever happens, I'd love to get a phone call."

"I know the number by heart," he said. "Me and every pervert on the Gold Coast."

"You go to hell," Nina teased. "And be careful, dammit."

He said good-bye and placed the receiver on Charles Chelsea's desk.

▼ ▼ ▼

Skink mulched a cotton candy and said, "These are excellent seats."

"They ought to be." Joe Winder assumed Francis X. Kingsbury would arrive at any moment; it was his private viewing box, after all— leather swivel chairs, air-conditioning, video monitors, a wet bar. Thirty rows up, overlooking the parade route.

"What will you do when he gets here?" Skink asked.

"I haven't decided. Maybe he'd like to go swimming with Pedro's new friend."

The grandstand was packed, and Kingsbury Lane was lined five deep with eager spectators. As the history of Florida unfolded in song and skit, Joe Winder imagined that the Stations of the Cross could be similarly adapted and set to music, if the audience would only forgive a few minor revisions. Every float in the Summerfest pageant was greeted with the blind and witless glee displayed by people who have spent way too much money and are determined to have fun. They cheered at the sight of a bootless Ponce de León, an underaged maiden on each arm, wading bawdily into the Fountain of Youth; they roared as the pirate Black Caesar chased a concubine up the mizzenmast while his men plundered a captured galleon; they gasped as the Killer Hurricane of 1926 tore the roof off a settler's cabin and the smock off his brave young wife.

Skink said, "I never realized cleavage played such an important role in Florida history." Joe Winder told him to just wait for the break-dancing migrants.

▼ ▼ ▼

Carrie Lanier gave a cassette of the new music to the driver, and took her place on the last float. The Talent Manager showed up and demanded to know why she wasn't wearing the Indian costume.

"That wasn't an Indian costume," Carrie said, "unless the Seminoles had streetwalkers."

The Talent Manager, a middle-aged woman with sweeping peroxide hair and ropes of gold jewelry, informed Carrie that a long gown was unsuitable for the Jubilee parade.

"It's ideal for what I'm singing," Carrie replied.

"And what would that be?"

"That would be none of your business." She adjusted the microphone, which was clipped into the neck of her dress.

The Talent Manager became angry. "Paul Revere and the Raiders isn't good enough for you?"

"Go away," said Carrie.

"And where's our lion?"

"The lion is taking the night off."

"No, missy," the Talent lady said, shaking a finger. "Thousands of people out there are waiting to see Princess Golden Sun ride a wild lion through the Everglades."

"The lion has a furball. Now get lost."

"At least put on the wig," the Talent lady pleaded. "There's no such thing as a blond Seminole. For the sake of authenticity, put on the damn wig!"

"Toodle-loo," said Carrie. And the float began to roll.

▼ ▼ ▼

At first, Sergeant Mark Dyerson thought the telemetry was on the fritz again. How could the panther get back on the island? No signal had been received for days, then suddenly there it was, beep-beep-beep. Number 17. The sneaky bastard was at it again!

Sergeant Dyerson asked the pilot to keep circling beneath the clouds until he got a more precise fix on the transmitter. The greenish darkness of the hammocks and the ocean suddenly was splayed by a vast sparkling corridor of lights—the Amazing Kingdom of Thrills. The plane banked high over a confetti of humanity.

"Damn," said the ranger. Sharply he tapped the top of the radio receiver. "This can't be right. Fly me over again."

But the telemetry signals were identical on the second pass, and the third and the fourth. Sergeant Dyerson peered out the window of the Piper and thought, He's down there. He's inside the goddamn park!

The ranger told the pilot to call Naples. "I need some backup," he said, "and I need the guy with the dogs."

"Should I say which cat we're after?"

"No, don't," Sergeant Dyerson said. The top brass of the Game and Fish Department was tired of hearing about Number 17. "Tell them we've got a panther in trouble," said Sergeant Dyerson, "that's all you need to say."

The pilot reached for the radio. "What the hell's it doing in the middle of an amusement park?"

"Going crazy," said the ranger. "That's all I can figure."

▼ ▼ ▼

The break-dancing migrant workers were a sensation with the crowd. Skink covered his face during most of the performance; it was one of the most tasteless spectacles he had ever seen. He asked Joe Winder if he wished to help with the gasoline.

"No, I'm waiting for Kingsbury."

"What for?"

"To resolve our differences as gentlemen. And possibly pound him into dog chow."

"Forget Kingsbury," Skink advised. "There's your girl."

Carrie's float appeared at the end of the promenade; a spotlight found her in a black sequined evening gown, posed among ersatz palms and synthetic cypress. She was perfectly dazzling, although the crowd reacted with confused and hesitant applause—they'd been expecting a scantily clad Indian princess astride a snarling wildcat.

Joe Winder tried to wave, but it hurt too much to raise his arms. Carrie didn't see him. She folded her hands across her midriff and began to sing:

> *"Vissi d'arte, vissi d'amore*
> *Non feci mai male ad animal viva!*
> *Con man furtiva*
> *Quante miserie conobbi, aiutai. . . ."*

Winder was dazed, and he was not alone; a restless murmuring swept through the stands and rippled along the promenade.

"Magnificent!" Skink said. His good eye ablaze, he clutched Winder's shoulder: "Isn't she something!"

"What is that? What's she singing?"

Skink shook him with fierce exuberance. "My God, man, it's Puccini. It's *Tosca!*"

"I see." It was a new wrinkle: opera.

And Carrie sang beautifully; what her voice lacked in strength it made up in a flawless liquid clarity. The aria washed sorrowfully across the Amazing Kingdom and, like a chilly rain, changed the mood of the evening.

Skink put his mouth to Winder's ear and whispered: "This takes place in the second act, where Tosca has just seen her lover tortured by the ruthless police chief and sentenced to death by a firing squad. In her failed effort to save him, Tosca herself becomes a murderess. Her song is a lamentation on life's tragic ironies."

"I'd never have guessed," Winder said.

As the float passed the Magic Mansion, Carrie sang:

> *Nell'ora del dolore*
> *Perchè, perchè, Signore,*
> *Perchè me ne rimuneri così?*

Skink closed his eyes and swayed. "Ah, why, dear Lord," he said. "Ah, why do you reward your servant so?"

Winder said the audience seemed fidgety and disturbed.

"Disturbed?" Skink was indignant. "They ought to be distraught. Mournful. They ought to be *weeping.*"

"They're only tourists," Joe Winder said. "They've been waiting all afternoon to see a lion."

"Cretins."

"Oh, she knew," Winder said fondly. "She knew they wouldn't like it one bit."

Skink grinned. "Bless her heart." He began to applaud rambunctiously, "Bravo! Bravo!" His clapping and shouting caught the attention of spectators in the lower rows, who looked up toward the VIP box with curious annoyance. Carrie spotted both of them in Kingsbury's booth, and waved anxiously. Then she gathered herself and, with a deep breath, began the first verse again.

"What a trouper." Joe Winder was very proud.

Skink straightened his rain cap and said, "Go get her."

"Now?"

"Right now. It's time." Skink reached out to shake Winder's hand. "You've got about an hour," he said.

Winder told him to be careful. "There's lots of kids out there."

"Don't you worry."

"What about Kingsbury?"

Skink said, "Without the park, he's finished."

"I intended to make him famous. You should've heard my plan."

"Some other time," Skink said. "Now go. And tell her how great she was. Tell her it was absolutely wonderful. Giacomo would've been proud."

"*Arrivederci!*" said Joe Winder.

▼ ▼ ▼

From his third-floor office above Sally's Cimarron Saloon, Francis X. Kingsbury heard the parade go by. Only Princess Golden Sun's dolorous aria brought him to the window, where he parted the blinds to see what in the name of Jesus H. Christ had gone wrong. The disposition of the crowd had changed from festive to impatient. Unfuckingbelievable, thought Kingsbury. It's death, this music. And what's with the evening gown, the Kitty Carlisle number. Where's the buckskin bikini? Where's the tits and ass? The tourists looked ready to bolt.

Carrie hit the final note and held it—held it forever, it seemed to Kingsbury. The girl had great pipes, he had to admit, but it wasn't the time or place for Italian caterwauling. And God, this song, when would it end?

As the float trundled by, Kingsbury was surprised to see that Princess Golden Sun wasn't singing anymore; in fact, she was drinking from a can of root beer. Yet her final melancholy note still hung in the air!

Or was it something else now?

The fire alarm, for instance.

Kingsbury thought: Please, don't let it be. He tried to call Security but no one answered—that fucking Pedro, he should've been back from his errand hours ago.

Outside, the alarm had tripped a prerecorded message on the public-address system, urging everyone to depart the Amazing Kingdom in a calm and orderly fashion. When Kingsbury peeked out the window again, he saw customers streaming like ants for the exits; the performers and concessionaires ran, as well. Baldy the Eagle ripped off his wings and sprinted from the park at Olympic speed; the animal trainers fled together in a hijacked Cushman, but not before springing the hinge on the lion's cage and shooing the wobbly, tranquilized beast toward the woods.

Kingsbury ran, too. He ran in search of Pedro Luz, the only man who knew how to turn off the fire alarm. Golf spikes clacking on the concrete, Kingsbury jogged from the security office to King Arthur's Food Court to The Catacombs, where he found Spence Mooher limping in mopey addled circles, like a dog who'd been grazed by a speeding bus.

But there was no trace of Pedro, and despair clawed at Kingsbury's gut. People now were pouring out of the park, and taking their money with them. Even if they had wished to stop and purchase one last overpriced souvenir, no one was available to sell it to them.

Chickenshits! Kingsbury raged inwardly. All this panic, and no fire. *Can't you idiots see it's a false alarm?*

Then came the screams.

Kingsbury's throat tightened. He ducked into a photo kiosk and removed the laminated ID card from his belt. Why risk it if the crowd turned surly?

The screaming continued. In a prickly sweat, Kingsbury tracked the disturbance to the whale tank, where something had caught the attention of several families on their way out of the park. They lined the walkway, and excitedly pointed to the water. Assuming the pose of a fellow tourist, Kingsbury nonchalantly joined the others on the rail. He overheard one man tell his wife that there wasn't enough light to use the video camera; she encouraged him to try anyway. A young girl cried and clutched at her mother's leg; her older brother told her to shut up, it's just a plastic dummy.

It wasn't a dummy. It was the partially clothed body of Pedro Luz, facedown in the Orky tank. His muscular buttocks mooned the masses, and indeed it was this sight—not the fact he was dead—that had shocked customers into shrieking.

Francis X. Kingsbury glared spitefully at the corpse. Pedro's bobbing bare ass seemed to mock him—a hairy faceless smile, taunting as it floated by. So this is how it goes, thought Kingsbury. Give a man a second chance, this is how he pays you back.

Suddenly, and without warning, Dickie the Dolphin rocketed twenty feet out of the water and performed a perfect triple-reverse somersault.

The tourists, out of pure dumb reflex, broke into applause.

▼ ▼ ▼

The Amazing Kingdom of Thrills emptied in forty minutes. Two hook-and-ladder rigs arrived from Homestead, followed by a small

pumper truck from the main fire station in lower Key Largo. The fire
fighters unrolled the hoses and wandered around the park, but found
no sign of a fire. They were preparing to leave when three green Jeeps
with flashing lights raced into the empty parking lot. The fire fighters
weren't sure what to make of the Game and Fish officers; an amusement park seemed an unlikely hideout for gator poachers. Sergeant
Mark Dyerson flagged down one of the departing fire trucks and asked
the captain if it was safe to take dogs into the area. The captain said
sure, be my guest. Almost immediately the hounds struck a scent, and
the old tracker turned them loose. The wildlife officers loaded up the
dart guns and followed.

Francis Kingsbury happened to be staring out the window when he
spotted the lion loping erratically down Kingsbury Lane; a pack of dogs
trailed closely, snapping at its tail. The doped-up cat attempted to
climb one of the phony palm trees, but fell when its claws pulled loose
from the Styrofoam bark. Swatting at the hounds, the cat rose and
continued its disoriented escape.

Lunacy, thought Kingsbury.

Someone knocked twice on the office door and came in—a short
round man with thin brown hair and small black eyes. A hideous
polyester-blend shirt identified him as a valued customer. Pinned
diagonally across the man's chest was a wrinkled streamer that said
"OUR FIVE-MILLIONTH SPECIAL GUEST!" In the crook of each arm sat a
stuffed toy animal with reddish fur, pipestem whiskers and a merry
torquoise tongue.

Vance and Violet Vole.

"For my nieces," the man explained. "I got so much free stuff I can
hardly fit it in the car."

Kingsbury smiled stiffly. "The big winner, right? That's you."

"Yeah, my wife can't fuckin' believe it."

"Didn't you hear it, the fire alarm? Everybody else, I mean, off they
went."

"But I didn't see no fire," the man said. "No smoke, neither." He
arranged the stuffed animals side by side on Kingsbury's sofa.

The guy's a total yutz, Kingsbury thought. Does he want my autograph or what? Maybe a snapshot with the big cheese.

"What's that you got there?" the man asked. "By the way, the
name's Rossiter." He nodded toward a plaid travel bag that lay open
on Kingsbury's desk. The bag was full of cash, mostly twenties and
fifties.

The man said, "Looks like I wasn't the only one had a lucky day."

Kingsbury snapped the bag closed. "I'm very busy, Mr. Rossiter.

What's the problem—something with the new car, right? The color doesn't match your wife's eyes or whatever."

"No, the car's great. I got no complaints about the car."

"Then what?" Kingsbury said. "The parade, I bet. That last song, I swear to Christ, I don't know where that shit came from—"

"You kiddin' me? It was beautiful. It was Puccini."

Kingsbury threw up his hands. "Whatever. Not to be rude, but what the fuck do you want?"

The man said, "I got a confession to make. I cheated a little this morning." He shrugged sheepishly. "I cut in line so we could be the first ones through the gate. That's how I won the car."

It figures, thought Kingsbury. Your basic South Florida clientele.

The man said, "I felt kinda lousy, but what the hell. Opportunity knocks, right? I mean, since I had to be here anyway—"

"Mr. Rossiter, do I look like a priest? All this stuff, I don't need to hear it—"

"Hey, call me Lou," the man said, "and I'll call you Frankie." From his Sansibelt slacks he withdrew a .38-caliber pistol with a silencer.

Francis Kingsbury's cheeks went from pink to gray. "Don't tell me," he said.

"Yeah," said Lou, "can you believe it?"

36

Francis X. Kingsbury asked the hit man not to shoot.

"Save your breath," said Lou.

"But, look, a fantastic new world I built here. A place for little tykes, you saw for yourself—roller coasters and clowns and talking animals. Petey Possum and so forth. I did all this myself."

"What a guy," said Lou.

Kingsbury was unaccustomed to such bald sarcasm. "Maybe I make a little dough off the operation, so what? Look at all the fucking happiness I bring people!"

"I enjoyed myself," Lou admitted. "My wife, she's crazy about the Twirling Teacups. She and her mother both. I almost spit up on the damn thing, to be honest, but my wife's got one a them cast-iron stomachs."

Kingsbury brightened. "The Twirling Teacups, I designed those myself. The entire ride from scratch."

"No shit?"

The hit man seemed to soften, and Kingsbury sensed an opening. "Look, I got an idea about paying back the Zubonis. It's a big construction deal, we're talking millions. They'd be nuts to pass it up—can you make a phone call? Tell 'em it's once in a lifetime."

Lou said, "Naw, I don't think so."

"Florida waterfront—that's all you gotta say. Florida fucking waterfront, and they'll be on the next plane from Newark, I promise."

"You're a good salesman," said the hit man, "but I got a contract."

Kingsbury nudged the plaid travel bag across the desk. "My old lady, she wanted me to go on a trip—Europe, the whole nine yards. I was thinking why not, just for a couple months. She's never been there."

Lou nodded. "Now's a good time to go. The crowds aren't so bad."

"Anyhow, I emptied the cash registers after the parade." Kingsbury patted the travel bag. "This is just from ticket sales, not concessions, and still you're talking three hundred and forty thousand. Cash-ola."

"Yeah? That's some vacation, three hundred forty grand."

"And it's all yours if you forget about the contract."

"Hell," said Lou, "it's mine if I don't."

Outside there was a bang, followed by a hot crackling roar. When Kingsbury spun his chair toward the window, his face was bathed in flickering yellow light.

"Lord," he said.

The Wet Willy was on fire—hundreds of feet of billowed latex, squirming and thrashing like an eel on a griddle. White sparks and flaming bits of rubber hissed into the tropical sky, and came down as incendiary rain upon the Amazing Kingdom of Thrills. Smaller fires began to break out everywhere.

Francis Kingsbury shivered under his hairpiece.

Lou went to the window and watched the Wet Willy burn. "You know what it looks like?"

"Yes," Kingsbury said.

"A giant Trojan."

"I know."

"It ain't up to code, that's for sure. You must've greased some county inspectors."

"Another good guess," Kingsbury said. Why did the alarm cut off? he wondered. Where did all the firemen go?

Lou farted placidly as he walked back to the desk. "Well, I better get a move on."

Kingsbury tried to hand him the telephone. "Please," he begged, "call the Zuboni brothers."

"A deal's a deal," Lou said, checking the fit of the silencer.

"But you saw for yourself!" Kingsbury cried. "Another five years, goddamn, I'll be bigger than Disney."

Lou looked doubtful. "I wasn't gonna say anything, but what the hell. The car and the prizes are great, don't get me wrong, but the park's got a long ways to go."

Petulantly, Kingsbury said, "Fine, let's hear it."

"It's the bathrooms," said Lou. "The fuckin' Port Authority's got cleaner bathrooms."

"Is that so?"

"Yeah, and it wouldn't hurt to keep an extra roll a toilet paper in the stalls."

"Is that it? That's your big gripe?"

Lou said, "People notice them things, they really do." Then he stepped toward Francis X. Kingsbury and raised the pistol.

▼ ▼ ▼

Joe Winder led her through the dense hammock, all the way to the ocean's edge. It took nearly an hour because Carrie wore high heels. The gown kept snagging on branches, and the insects were murder.

"I'm down two pints," she said, scratching at her ankles.

"Take off the shoes. Hurry." He held her hand and waded into the water.

"Joe!" The gown rose up around her hips; the sequins sparkled like tiny minnows.

"How deep are we going?" she asked.

At first the turtle grass tickled her toes, then it began to sting. Winder kept walking until the water was up to his chest.

"See? No more bugs."

"You're full of tricks," Carrie said, clinging to his arm. From the flats it was possible to see the entire curving shore of the island, including the naked gash made by the bulldozers at Falcon Trace. She asked if the trees would ever come back.

"Someday," Joe Winder said, "if the bastards leave it alone."

Stretching toward the horizon was a ribbon of lights from the cars sitting bumper-to-bumper on County Road 905—the exodus of tourists from the Amazing Kingdom. Winder wondered if Skink had waited long enough to make his big move.

He listened for the distant sound of sirens as he moved through the shallows, following the shoreline south. The warm hug of the tide soothed the pain in his chest. He pointed at a pair of spotted leopard rays, pushing twin wakes.

"What else do you see?" Carrie said.

"Turtles. Jellyfish. A pretty girl with no shoes." He kissed her on the neck.

"How far can we go like this?" she asked.

"Big Pine, Little Torch, all the way to Key West if you want."

She laughed. "Joe, that's a hundred miles." She kicked playfully into the deeper water. "It feels so good."

"You sang beautifully tonight. Watch out for the coral."

When Carrie stood up, the water came to her chin. Blowing bubbles, she said, "I didn't know you liked opera."

"I hate opera," Winder said, "but you made it wonderful."

She splashed after him, but he swam away.

They didn't leave the ocean until the road was clear and the island was dark. They agreed it would be best to get out of Monroe County for a while, so they took Card Sound Road toward the mainland. The pavement felt cool under their feet. They wanted to hold hands, but it hampered their ability to defend themselves against the swarming mosquitoes. Every few minutes Winder would stop walking and check the sky for a change in the light. One time he was sure he heard a helicopter.

Carrie said, "What's your feeling about all this?"

"Meaning Kingsbury and the whole mess."

"Exactly."

"There's thousands more where he came from."

"Oh, brother," Carrie said. "I was hoping you'd gotten it all out of your system."

"Never," said Winder, "but I'm open to suggestions."

"All right, here's one: Orlando."

"God help us."

"Now wait a second, Joe. They're shooting commercials at those new studios up there. I've got my first audition lined up for next week."

"What kind of commercial?"

"The point is, it's national exposure."

"Promise me something," Winder said. "Promise it's not one of those personal-hygiene products."

"Fabric softener. The script's not bad, all things considered."

"And will there be singing?"

"No singing," Carrie said, picking up the pace. "They've got newspapers in Orlando, don't they?"

"Oh no, you don't."

"It'd be good for you, Joe. Write about the important things, whatever pisses you off. Just write *something*. Otherwise you'll make me crazy, and I'll wind up killing you in your sleep."

The Card Sound Bridge rose steeply ahead. A handful of crabbers and snapper fishermen sleepily tended slack lines. Joe and Carrie took the sidewalk. For some reason she stopped and gave him a long kiss.

Halfway up the rise, she tugged on his hand and told him to turn around.

There it was: the eastern sky aglow, fat clouds roiling unnaturally under a pulsing halo of wild pink and orange. Baleful columns of tarry smoke rose from the Amazing Kingdom of Thrills.

Joe Winder whistled in amazement. "There's arson," he said, "and then there's arson."

▼ ▼ ▼

Bud Schwartz and Danny Pogue were surprised to find Molly McNamara wide awake, propped up with a stack of thin hospital pillows. She was brushing her snowy hair and reading the *New Republic* when the burglars arrived.

"Pacemaker," Molly reported. "A routine procedure."

"You look so good," said Danny Pogue. "Bud, don't she look good?"

"Hush now," Molly said. "Sit down here, the news is coming on. There's a story you'll both find interesting." Without being asked, Danny Pogue switched the television to Channel 10, Molly's favorite.

Bud Schwartz marveled at the old woman in bed. Days earlier, she had seemed so weak and withered and close to death. Now the gray eyes were as sharp as a hawk's, her cheeks shone, and her voice rang strong with maternal authority.

She said, "Danny, did you get the bullets?"

"Yes, ma'am." He handed Molly the yellow box.

"These are .22-longs," she said. "I needed shorts. That's what the gun takes."

Danny Pogue looked lamely toward his partner. Bud Schwartz said, "Look, we just asked for .22s. The guy didn't say nothin' about long or short."

"It's all right," Molly McNamara said. "I'll pick up a box at the range next week."

"We don't know diddly about guns," Danny Pogue reiterated. "Neither of us do."

"I know, and I think it's precious." Molly put on her rose-framed glasses and instructed Bud Schwartz to adjust the volume on the television. A nurse came in to check the dressing on Molly's stitches, but Molly shooed her away. She pointed at the TV and said, "Look here, boys."

The news opened with videotape of a colossal raging fire. The scene had been recorded at a great distance, and from a helicopter. When the TV reporter announced what was burning, the burglars simultaneously looked at one another and mouthed the same profane exclamation.

"Yes," Molly McNamara said rapturously. "Yes, indeed."

Danny Pogue felt mixed emotions as he watched the Amazing Kingdom burn. He recalled the gaiety of the promenade, the friendliness of the animal characters, the circus colors and brassy music, the wondrous sensation of being inundated with fun. Then he thought of Francis X. Kingsbury killing off the butterflies and crocodiles, and the conflagration seemed more like justice than tragedy.

Bud Schwartz was equally impressed by the destruction of the theme park—not as a moral lesson, but as a feat of brazen criminality. The torch artist had been swift and thorough; the place was engulfed in roaring, implacable flames, and there was no saving it. The man on TV said he had never witnessed such a fierce, fast-moving blaze. Bud Schwartz felt relieved and lucky and wise.

"And you wanted to stay," he said to Danny Pogue. "You wanted to ride the Jungle Jerry again."

Danny Pogue nodded solemnly and slid the chair close to the television. "We could be dead," he murmured.

"Fried," said his partner. "Fried clams."

"Hush now," Molly said. "There's no call for melodrama."

She announced that she wasn't going to ask why they'd gone to the Amazing Kingdom that night. "I don't like to pry," she said. "You're grown men, you've got your own lives."

Danny Pogue said, "It wasn't us who torched the place."

Molly McNamara smiled as if she already knew. "How's your foot, Danny?"

"It don't hardly hurt at all."

Then to Bud Schwartz: "And your hand? Is it better?"

"Gettin' there," he said, flexing the fingers.

Molly removed her glasses and rested her head against the pillows. "Nature is a wonder," she said. "Such power to renew, or to destroy. It's an awesome paradox."

"A what?" said Danny Pogue.

Molly told them to think of the fire as a natural purge, a cyclical scouring of the land. Bud Schwartz could hardly keep a straight face. He jerked his chin toward the flickering images on television, and said, "So maybe it's spontaneous combustion, huh? Maybe a bolt a lightning?"

"Anything's possible," Molly said with a twinkle. She asked Danny Pogue to switch to the Discovery Channel, which just happened to be showing a documentary about endangered Florida manatees. A mating scene was in progress as Danny Pogue adjusted the color tint.

Not tonight, thought Bud Schwartz, and got up to excuse himself.

Molly said, "There's a Dodgers game on ESPN. You can watch across the hall in Mr. McMillan's room—he is in what they call a nonresponsive state, so he probably won't mind."

"Swell," Bud Schwartz muttered. "Maybe we'll go halfsies on a keg."

Danny Pogue heard none of this; he was already glued to the tube. Bud Schwartz pointed at his partner and grinned. "Look what you done to him."

Molly McNamara winked. "Go on now," she said. "I think Ojeda's pitching."

▼ ▼ ▼

Trooper Jim Tile braked sharply when he saw the three green Jeeps. The wildlife officers had parked in a precise triangle at the intersection of Card Sound Road and County 905.

"We'll be out of the way in a minute," said Sergeant Mark Dyerson.

The rangers had gathered between the trucks in the center of the makeshift triangle. Jim Tile joined them. He noticed dogs pacing in the back of one of the Jeeps.

"Look at this," Sergeant Dyerson said.

In the middle of the road, illuminated by headlights, was a battered red collar. Jim Tile crouched to get a closer look.

"Our transmitter," the ranger explained. Imprinted on the plastic was the name "Telonics MOD-500."

"What happened?" Jim Tile asked.

"The cat tore it off. Somehow."

"That's one tough animal."

"It's a first," Sergeant Dyerson said. "We've never had one that could bust the lock on the buckle."

Another officer asked, "What now?" It was the wretched plea of a man being devoured by insects.

"If the cat wants out this bad," said Sergeant Dyerson, "I figure we'll let him be."

From the south came the oscillating whine of a fire truck. Sergeant Dyerson retrieved the broken panther collar and told his men to move the Jeeps off the road. Minutes later, a hook-and-ladder rig barreled past.

Jim Tile mentioned that the theme park was on fire.

"It's breaking my heart," Sergeant Dyerson said. He handed the trooper a card. "Keep an eye out. My home number is on the back."

Jim Tile said, "All my life, I've never seen a panther."

"You probably never will," said the ranger, "and that's the crime of it." He tossed the radio collar in the back of the truck and slid behind the wheel.

"Not all the news is bad," he said. "Number Nine's got a litter of kittens over in the Fokahatchee."

"Yeah?" Jim Tile admired the wildlife officer's outlook and dedication. He was sorry his old friend had caused the man so much trouble and confusion. He said, "So this is all you do—track these animals?"

"It's all I do," Sergeant Dyerson said.

To Jim Tile it sounded like a fine job, and an honorable one. He liked the notion of spending all day in the deep outdoors, away from the homicidal masses. He wondered how difficult it would be to transfer from the highway patrol to the Game and Fish.

"Don't you worry about this cat," he told Sergeant Dyerson.

"I worry about all of them."

"This one'll be all right," the trooper said. "You've got my word."

▼ ▼ ▼

As soon as he spotted the police car, Joe told Carrie to hike up her gown and run. She followed him down the slope of the bridge and into a mangrove creek. Breathlessly they clung to the slippery roots; only their heads stayed dry.

"Don't move," Joe Winder said.

"There's a june bug in your ear."

"Yes, I'm aware of that." He quietly dunked his face, and the beetle was swept away by the milky-blue current.

She said, "May I raise the subject of snakes?"

"We're fine." He wrapped his free arm around her waist, to hold her steady against the tide. "You're certainly being a good sport about all this," he said.

"Will you think about Orlando?"

"Sure." It was the least he could do.

The metronomic blink of the blue lights grew stronger, and soon tires crunched the loose gravel on the road; the siren died with a tremulous moan.

Winder chinned up on a mangrove root for a better view. He saw a highway patrol cruiser idling at an angle on the side of the road. The headlights dimmed, and the trooper honked three times. They heard a deep voice, and Winder recognized it: Jim Tile.

"We lucked out," he said to Carrie. "Come on, that's our ride." They climbed from the creek and sloshed out of the mangroves. Before reaching the road, they heard another man's voice and the slam of a door.

Then the patrol car started to roll.

Joe Winder sprinted ahead, waving both arms and shouting for the trooper to stop. Jim Tile calmly swerved around him and, by way of a farewell, flicked his brights as he drove past.

Winder clutched his aching rib cage and cursed spiritedly at the speeding police car. Carrie joined him on the centerline, and together they watched the flashing blue lights disappear over the crest of the Card Sound Bridge.

"Everyone's a comedian," Joe Winder said.

"Didn't you see who was in the back seat?"

"I didn't see a damn thing."

Carrie laughed. "Look what he threw out the window." She held up a gooey stick of insect repellent. The top-secret military formula.

"Do me first," she said. "Every square inch."

Epilogue

A team of police divers recovered the body of PEDRO LUZ from the whale tank at the Amazing Kingdom of Thrills. The Monroe County medical examiner ruled drowning as the official cause of death, although the autopsy revealed "minor bite marks, contusions and chafing of a sexual nature."

▼

JAKE HARP recovered from his gunshot wound and rejoined the professional golfing circuit, although he never regained championship form. His next best finish was a tie for 37th place at the Buick Open, and subsequently he set a modern PGA record by missing the cut in twenty-two consecutive tournaments. Eventually he retired to the Seniors' Tour, where he collapsed and died of a cerebral hemorrhage on the first hole of a sudden-death play-off with Billy Casper.

▼

With his payoff money from the mob, BUD SCHWARTZ started a private security company that specializes in high-tech burglar-alarm systems for the home, car and office. Bearing a letter of recommendation from Molly McNamara, DANNY POGUE moved to Tanzania, where he is training to be a game warden at the Serengeti National Park.

▼

After Francis X. Kingsbury's murder, AGENT BILLY HAWKINS was docked a week's pay, and given a written reprimand for taking an unauthorized leave of absence. A month later he was transferred to the FBI office in Sioux Falls, South Dakota. He endured one winter before resigning from the Bureau and returning to Florida as an executive consultant to Schwartz International Security Services Ltd.

▼

NINA WHITMAN quit the phone-sex syndicate after three of her poems were published in the New Yorker. A later collection of prose and short fiction was praised by Erica Jong as a "fresh and vigorous reassessment of the female sexual dynamic." Shortly after receiving the first royalty statement from her publisher, Nina gave up poetry and moved to Westwood, California, where she now writes motion-picture screenplays. Her husband owns the second-largest Chevrolet dealership in Los Angeles County.

▼

The estate of FRANCIS X. KINGSBURY, aka FRANKIE KING, was sued by the Walt Disney Corporation for copyright infringement on the characters of Mickey and Minnie Mouse. The lawsuit was prompted by accounts of a pornographic tattoo on the decedent's left forearm, as described by newspaper reporters attending the open-casket funeral. After deliberating only thirty-one minutes (and reviewing a coroner's photograph of the disputed etching), an Orlando jury awarded the Disney company $1.2 million in actual and punitive damages. PENNY KINGSBURY is appealing the decision.

▼

CHARLES CHELSEA accepted a job as executive vice president of public relations for Monkey Mountain. Four months later, disaster struck when a coked-up podiatrist from Ann Arbor, Michigan, jumped a fence and attempted to leg-wrestle a male chacma baboon. The podiatrist was swiftly killed and dismembered, and the animal park was forced to close. Chelsea retired from the public-relations business, and is now said to be working on a novel with Gothic themes.

▼

At his own request, TROOPER JIM TILE was reassigned to Liberty County in the Florida Panhandle. With only 5.1 persons per square mile, it is the least densely populated region of the state.

▼

DICKIE THE DOLPHIN survived the fire that destroyed the Amazing Kingdom of Thrills, and was temporarily relocated to a holding pen at an oceanfront hotel near Marathon. Seven months later, a bankruptcy judge approved the sale of the frisky mammal to a marine attraction in Hilton Head, South Carolina. No swimming is allowed in Dickie's new tank.

▼

After the Amazing Kingdom closed, UNCLE ELY'S ELVES never worked together again. Veteran character actor MOE STRICKLAND branched into drama, taking minor roles in television soap operas before miraculously landing the part of Big Daddy in a Scranton dinner-theater production of *Cat on a Hot Tin Roof*. A free-lance critic for the *Philadelphia Inquirer* described Strickland's performance as "gutsy and brooding."

▼

Several weeks after fire swept through Francis X. Kingsbury's theme park, a piano-sized crate from Auckland, New Zealand, was discovered outside the padlocked gate. No one was certain how long the crate had been there, but it was empty by the time a security guard found it; whatever was inside had clawed its way out. Soon residents of the nearby Ocean Reef Club began reporting the disappearance of pet cats and small dogs at a rate of two per week—a mystery that remains unsolved. Meanwhile, Kingsbury's estate received a handwritten invoice from a person calling herself RACHEL LARK. The bill, excluding shipping, amounted to $3,755 for "miscellaneous wildlife."

▼

The widow of DR. WILL KOOCHER hired a Miami lawyer and filed a wrongful-death action against the Amazing Kingdom of Thrills, Ramex Global Trust, N.A. and Bermuda Intercontinental Services, Inc. The insurance companies hastily settled the lawsuit out of court for approximately $2.8 million. The gutted ruins of the Amazing Kingdom were razed, and the land was replanted with native trees, including buttonwoods, pigeon plums, torchwoods, brittle palms, tamarinds, gumbo-limbos and mangroves. This restoration was accomplished in spite of rigid opposition from the Monroe County Commission, which had hoped to use the property as a public dump.

▼

The surviving owners of the FALCON TRACE golf resort sold all construction permits and building rights to a consortium of Japanese investors who had never set foot in South Florida. However, the project stalled once again when environmentalists surveying the Key Largo site reported the presence of at least two blue-tongued mango voles, previously thought to be extinct. According to an unsigned press release faxed to all major newspapers and wire services, the tiny mammals were spotted at Falcon Trace during a nature hike by MOLLY MCNAMARA and the Mothers of Wilderness, who immediately reported the sighting to the U.S. Department of Interior.

▼

Eventually the Falcon Trace and Amazing Kingdom properties were purchased from bankruptcy by the state of Florida, and became part of a preserve on NORTH KEY LARGO. In the spring of 1991, a *National Geographic* photographer set out to capture on film the last surviving pair of blue-tongued mango voles. After two months in the woods, the photographer contracted mosquito-borne encephalitis and was airlifted to Jackson Memorial Hospital, where he spent three weeks on clear fluids. He never got a glimpse of the shy and nocturnal creatures, although he returned to New York with a cellophane packet of suspect rodent droppings and a pledge to keep searching.

Clare Francis
Special limited edition
Night Sky/Red Crystal £4.99
Two bestsellers for the price of one!

Two nailbiting dramas from master thriller writer Clare Francis that
have topped the bestseller lists all over the world.

Night Sky – an epic born out of the chaos of World War Two. As the
Allies fight to protect a devastating scientific discovery from the
Nazis, two men and a woman become caught in a deadly web of
betrayal and love . . .

Red Crystal – a tough and daring adventure set among the student
riots of the 1960s. Secretly funded by Moscow, the Crystal Faction
come to England to wage war. At their heart is beautiful Gabriele. An
agent of death for whom killing has become a compulsion . . .

'Thoroughly professional adventure' *Sunday Times*

'Sexy . . . fast-paced . . . thrilling' *Daily Express*

All Pan Books are available at your local bookshop or newsagent, or can be ordered direct from the publisher. Indicate the number of copies required and fill in the form below.

Send to: Pan C. S. Dept
              Macmillan Distribution Ltd
              Houndmills Basingstoke RG21 2XS

or phone: 0256 29242, quoting title, author and Credit Card number.

Please enclose a remittance* to the value of the cover price plus £1.00 for the first book plus 50p per copy for each additional book ordered.

*Payment may be made in sterling by UK personal cheque, postal order, sterling draft or international money order, made payable to Pan Books Ltd.

Alternatively by Barclaycard/Access/Amex/Diners

Card No.

Expiry Date

_____

Signature

Applicable only in the UK and BFPO addresses.

While every effort is made to keep prices low, it is sometimes necessary to increase prices at short notice. Pan Books reserve the right to show on covers and charge new retail prices which may differ from those advertised in the text or elsewhere.

NAME AND ADDRESS IN BLOCK LETTERS PLEASE

. . . .

Name _____

Address _____

_____

_____

_____

6/92